PRAISE FOR M. L. BUCHMAN

Top 10 Romance of 2012, 2015, and 2016.

— BOOKLIST: THE NIGHT IS MINE, HOT POINT, HEART STRIKE

One of our favorite authors.

— RT BOOK REVIEWS

Buchman has catapulted his way to the top tier of my favorite authors.

— FRESH FICTION

A favorite author of mine. I'll read anything that carries his name, no questions asked. Meet your new favorite author!

— THE SASSY BOOKSTER, FLASH OF FIRE

M.L. Buchman is guaranteed to get me lost in a good story.

— THE READING CAFE, WAY OF THE WARRIOR: NSDQ

I love Buchman's writing. His vivid descriptions bring everything to life in an unforgettable way.

— PURE JONEL, HOT POINT

THE COMPLETE WHERE DREAMS - VOL 1 OF 2

A SEATTLE ROMANCE

M. L. BUCHMAN

Buchman Bookworks

Receive a free Starter Library and discover more by this author at: www.mlbuchman.com

Cover images:

Sailboat and Seattle Space Needle © mwp1969

Wine Bottle - red © Tristan3d

Lighthouse © the author

CONTENTS

Other works by M. L. Buchman:

To my Lady Fair:
My thanks for the calendar,
And the journeys we shared
to explore the settings of this tale.
And to my sister:
A tintypist.
Who taught me the love of photography
in the darkroom we shared as teens.

WHERE DREAMS ARE BORN

A BEGINNING

*R*ussell *locked his studio's* door behind the last of the staff, leaned his back against it, and turned off his camera.

He knew it was good. The images were there; he'd really captured them.

But something was missing.

The groove ran so clean when he slid into it. First his Manhattan high-ceilinged loft would fade into the background, then the strobe lights, reflector umbrellas, and blue and green backdrops all became texture and tone.

Image, camera, and man then became one and they were all that mattered—a single flow of light, beginning before time was counted, and ending its journey in the printed image. One ray of primordial light traveling forever to glisten off the BMW roadster still parked in one corner of the rough-planked wood floor worn smooth by generations of use. Another ray lost in the dark blackness of the finest leather bucket seats. A hundred more picking out the supermodel's perfect hand dangling a single shining and golden key—the image shot just slow enough that the key blurred as it spun, but the logo remained clear.

He couldn't quite put his finger on it...

It would be another great ad by Russell Morgan, Inc. The client would be knocked dead—the ad leaving all others standing still as it roared down the passing lane. This one might get him another Clio, or even a second Mobius.

But...

There wasn't usually a "but."

And there definitely wasn't supposed to be one.

The groove had definitely been there, but he hadn't been in it.

That was the problem. It had slid along, sweeping his staff into their own orchestrated perfection, but he'd remained untouched. That ideal, seamless flow hadn't included him at all.

"Be honest, boyo, that session sucked," he told the empty studio. Everything had come together so perfectly for yet another ad for yet another high-end glossy. *Man, the Magazine* would launch spectacularly in a few weeks, a high-profile mid-December launch, and it would include a never before seen twelve-page spread by the great Russell Morgan. The rag would probably never pay off the lavish launch party of hope, ice sculptures, and chilled magnums of champagne before disappearing like a thousand before it.

He stowed the last camera he'd been using with the others piled by his computer. At the breaker box he shut off the umbrellas, spots, scoops, and washes. The studio shifted from a stark landscape in hard-edged relief to a nest of curious shadows and rounded forms. The tang of hot metal and deodorant were the only lasting result of the day's efforts.

"Morose tonight, aren't we?" he asked his reflection in the darkened window, stories above the streetlights of West 10th. His reflection was wise enough to not answer back. There was never a "down" after a shoot; there was always an "up."

Not tonight.

He'd kept everyone late—even though it was Thanksgiving eve—hoping for that smooth slide of image-camera-man. It was only when he saw the power of the images he captured that he knew he wasn't a part of the chain anymore and decided he'd paid enough triple-time expenses.

The next to last two-page spread was the killer—shot with the door open against a background as black as the sports car's finish. The model's single perfect leg wrapped in thigh-high red-leather boots was all that was visible in the driver's seat. The sensual juxtaposition of woman and sleek machine served as an irresistible focus. It was an ad designed to wrap every person with even a hint of a Y-chromosome around its little finger. And those with only X-chromosomes would simply want to be her. He'd shot a perfect combo of sexuality for the guys and power for the women.

Even the final one-page image, a close-up of driver's seat from exactly the same angle, revealing not the model but instead a single rose of precisely the same hue as the leather boot, hadn't moved him despite its perfection.

Without him noticing, Russell had become no more than the observer, merely a technician behind the camera. Now that he faced it, months, maybe even a year had passed since he'd been yanked all the way into the light-image-camera-man slipstream. Tonight was a wakeup call and he didn't like it one bit. Wakeup calls were supposed to happen to others, not him. But tonight he could no longer ignore it, he hadn't even trailed in the churned-up wake.

"You're just a creative cog in the advertising machine." Ouch! That one stung, but it didn't turn aside the relentless steamroller of his thoughts speeding down some empty, godforsaken autobahn.

His career was roaring ahead, his business' growth running fast and smooth, but, now that he considered it, he really couldn't bring himself to care.

His life looked perfect, but—"Don't think it!"—his autobahn mind finished despite the command, *it wasn't.*

Russell left his silent reflection to its own thoughts and went through the back door that led to his apartment—closing it tightly on the perfect BMW, the perfect rose, and somewhere, lost among a hundred other props from dozens of other shoots, the long pair of perfect red-leather Chanel boots that had been wrapped around the most expensive legs in Manhattan. He didn't care if he never walked back through that door again. He'd been doing his art by rote; how pathetic was that?

And just to rub salt in the wound, he shot *commercial* art.

He'd never had the patience to do art for art's sake. Delayed gratification was his idea of no fun at all. He left the apartment dark with only the city's soft glow through the blind-covered windows revealing the vaguest outlines of the framed art on the wall. Even that almost overwhelmed him tonight.

He didn't want to see the huge prints by the *art* artists: autographed Goldsworthy, Liebowitz, and Joseph Francis' photomosaics for the moderns. A hundred and fifty rare, even one-of-a-kind prints adorned his walls—all the way back through Bourke-White to Russell's prize, an original Daguerre. The Museum of Modern Art kept begging to borrow his collection for a show...and at the moment he was half tempted to dump the whole lot in their Dumpster if they didn't want it.

Crossing the one-room loft apartment—as spacious as the studio —he bypassed the circle of avant-garde chairs that were almost as uncomfortable as they looked and avoided the lush black-leather wrap-around sectional sofa of such ludicrous scale that it could be a playpen for two or host a party for twenty. He cracked the fridge in the stainless-steel-and-black corner kitchen searching for something other than his usual beer.

A bottle of Krug.

Maybe he was just being grouchy after a long day's work.

Juice.

No. He'd run his enthusiasm into the ground but good.

Milk even.

Would he miss the camera if he never picked it up again?

No reaction.

Nothing.

Not even a twinge.

That was an emptiness he did not want to face. Especially not alone, in his apartment, in the middle of the world's most vibrant city.

Russell turned away, and just as the door swung closed, the last sliver of light—the relentless chilly blue-white of the refrigerator bulb—shone across his bed. A quick grab snagged the edge of the door and left the narrow beam illuminating a long pale form on his black bedspread.

The Chanel boots weren't in the studio after all. They were still wrapped around those three thousand dollar-an-hour legs: the only clothing on a perfect body, five foot-eleven of intensely toned female anatomy, right down to her exquisitely stair-mastered behind. Her long, white-blond hair lay as a perfect Godiva over her tanned bosom—except for the too-exact symmetry, even the closest inspection didn't reveal the work done there. She lay with one leg raised just ever so slightly to hide what was meant to be revealed later.

Melanie.

By the steady rise and fall of her flat stomach, he knew she'd fallen asleep while waiting for him to finish in the studio.

How long had they been an item? Two months? Three?

She'd made him feel alive...at least when he was actually with her. Melanie was the supermodel in his bed or on his arm at yet another SoHo gallery opening. Together they journeyed to sharp parties and trendy three-star restaurants where she dazzled and wooed yet another gathering of New York's finest with her ever so soft, so sensual, and so studied French accent. Together they were wired into the heart of the in-crowd.

But that wasn't him, was it? It didn't sound like the Russell he once knew.

Perhaps "they" were about how *he* looked on *her* arm?

Did she know tomorrow was the annual Thanksgiving ordeal at his parents? The grand holiday gathering that he'd rather die than attend? Any number of eligible woman would be floating about his parents' house out in Greenwich; anyone able to finagle an invitation would attend in hopes of snaring one of *People Magazine's* "100 Most Eligible." They all wanted to land the heir to a billion or some such; though he was wealthy enough on his own, by his own sweat, to draw anyone's attention. He ranked number twenty-four on the list this year—up from forty-seven the year before despite Tom Cruise being available yet again.

But not Melanie. He knew that it wasn't the money that drew her. Yes, she wanted him. But even more, she wanted the life that came with him—wrapped in the man-package. She wanted The Life. The one that *People Magazine* readers dreamed about between glossy pages.

His fingertips were growing cold where they held the refrigerator door cracked open.

If he woke her they'd have a great time heating up the sheets. Or a great party to go to. Or…

Did he want "Or"? What more did he want from her?

The supermodel in his bed. Companionship. An energy, a vivacity, a thirst he feared that he lacked. Yes.

But where was that smooth synchronicity hiding, like the light-image-camera-man of photography that he'd lost? Where lurked that perfect flow from one person to another? Did she feel it? Could he ever feel it?

"More?" he whispered into the darkness to test the sound.

The refrigerator door slid shut—escaping from his numbed fingers —which plunged the apartment back into darkness, taking Melanie along with it.

His breath echoed in the vast darkness. Proof that he was alive, if nothing more.

It was time to close the studio—time to be done with Russell Incorporated.

Then what?

Maybe Angelo would know what to do. He always claimed that he did. Maybe this time Russell would actually listen to his almost-brother, though he knew from the experience of being himself for the last thirty years that was unlikely.

Seattle.

No! He'd have to go to Seattle, of all ridiculous places, to find his best friend. There was a possible upside to such a trip—maybe there'd be a flight out before tomorrow's mess at his parents'. He slapped his pocket, but once again he'd set his phone down in some unknown corner of the studio and it would take forever to find. He really needed two—one chained down so that he could always find it to call the other.

Russell considered the darkness. He could guarantee that Seattle wouldn't be a big hit with Melanie.

Now if he only knew whether that was a good thing or bad.

WEST POINT LIGHTHOUSE

*D*iscovery Park, Seattle
First lit: 1881
Automated: 1985
47.6617 -122.43499

CHIEF BOATSWAIN'S MATE CHRISTIAN FRITZ served as the lighthouse keeper for many years in the early 1900s. One of the reasons he chose the West Point lighthouse posting was that the terrain from the keeper's cottage to the lighthouse was relatively level. This allowed his blind wife to freely stroll the station's grounds accompanied by her guide dog, a boxer named Cookie.

In 1985, it was the last lighthouse in Washington State to be automated despite its close proximity to Seattle.

JANUARY 1

"*If you were still* alive, you'd pay for this one, Daddy." The moment the words escaped her lips, Cassidy Knowles slapped a hand over her mouth to negate them, but it was too late.

The sharp wind took her words and threw them back into the pines, guilt and all. It might have stopped her, if it didn't make this the hundredth time she'd cursed him this morning.

She leaned in and forged her way downhill until the muddy path broke free from the mossy smell of the forest. Her Stuart Weitzman boots were long since soaked through, and now her feet were freezing. In a last gasp effort before the chill trees would let her go, a root snagged two-inch heels again and tried to flip her into the mud.

Free at last, Cassidy stared at the lighthouse. It perched upon a point of rock: tall and white, with its red roof as straight and snug as a prim bonnet. A narrow trail traced along the top of the breakwater leading to the lighthouse. The parking lot, much to her chagrin, was empty; six, beautiful, empty spaces.

"Sorry, ma'am," park rangers were always polite when telling you what you couldn't do. "The parking lot by the light is for physically-challenged visitors only. You'll have to park here. It *is* just a short walk to the lighthouse."

The fact that she was dressed for an afternoon lunch at Pike Place Market safe in Seattle's downtown rather than a blustery mile-long trek on the first day of the year didn't faze the ranger in the slightest.

Cassidy should have gone home, would have if it hadn't been for the letter stuffed deep in her pocket. So, instead of a tasty treat in a cozy deli, she'd buttoned the top button of her suede Bernardo jacket and headed out onto the trail. At least the promised rain had yet to arrive, so the jacket was only cold, not wet.

Finally free of the trees, a new problem arose. Beyond the lighthouse ranged a vast expanse of Puget Sound and it was being whipped into a frenzy like someone desperate to make a towering meringue rather than a smooth zabaglione custard. Whitecaps tore off the tops of waves, dark clouds scudded low over the water, and the far shore might as well have been the North Pole rather than Bainbridge Island for how inviting it looked. The towering heights of the Olympic Mountains scraped at the clouds with glacier-clad peaks.

Her jacket's stylish cut had never been intended to fight off these bajillion mile-an-hour gusts that snapped it painfully against her hips. Her black leggings ranged about five layers short of tolerable and a far, far cry from warm.

Approaching the lighthouse across the exposed—and utterly vacant—parking lot, any part of her that had been merely numb slipped right over to quick frozen. Leaning into the wind to stay upright, tears streaming from her eyes, she could think of a thing or two to tell her father despite his recent demise and her general feelings about the usefulness of upbraiding a dead man.

"What a stupid present!" Her shout was torn word-by-word, syllable-by-syllable and sent flying back toward her nice warm car and the ever-so-polite park ranger.

A calendar. Her dad had given her a stupid calendar of stupid lighthouses and a stupid letter to open at each stupid one. He'd been very insistent, made her promise. One she couldn't ignore. A deathbed promise.

Cassidy leaned grimly forward to walk through the onslaught only to have the wind abruptly cease. She staggered, nearly planting her face on the pavement before another gust rescued her but sent her crabbing sideways. With resolute force, she planted one foot in front of the other until she'd crossed the open pavement. There weren't any handicapped people crazy enough to come here New Year's morning. No people at all for that matter.

The empty lot and the lighthouse were separated by a short path along the top of a rocky breakwater. Boulders the size of her car had been piled up to resist the pounding of the sea. The top had been made into a solid path, so her footing was sure even if the wind continued to buffet her wildly.

The building's wall was concrete, worn smooth by a thousand storms and a hundred coats of brilliant white paint. With the wind practically pinning her to the outside of the building, she peeked into one of the windows. Her hair blew about so that it beat on her eyes and mouth trying to simultaneously blind and choke her. With one hand, she smashed the unruly mass mostly to one side. With the other she shaded the dusty window.

The cobwebbed glass revealed an equally unkempt interior: no lightkeeper sitting in his rocking chair before a merry fire with his smoking pipe and a lighthouse cat curled in his lap. There was some sort of a rusty engine not attached to anything. A bucket of old tools. A couple of paint cans.

A high wave crashed into the rocks with a thundering shudder that ran up through the heels of her boots and whipped a chill spray into the wind. Salt water on suede—Daddy now owed her a new coat as well.

Cassidy edged along the foundation until she found a calmer spot, a little windshadow behind the lighthouse where the wind chill ranked merely miserable rather than horrific on the suck-o-meter. Squatting down behind one of the breakwater's boulders helped a tiny bit more. She peeled off her thin leather gloves and blew against her fingertips to warm them enough so that they'd work. Once she'd regained some modicum of feeling, she pulled out the letter.

She couldn't feel his actual writing, though she ran her fingertips over it again and again. His Christmas present: a five-dollar calendar of Washington lighthouses from the hospital gift store and a dozen thin envelopes wrapped in an old x-ray folder with no ribbon, no paper.

In the end he'd foiled her final Christmas hunt. It had been her great yearly quest—the ultimate grail of childhood—finding the key present before Christmas morning. There was no present he could hide that she couldn't find. Not the Cabbage Patch Kid when she was six; the one she'd had to hold with her arm in a cast after falling off the kitchen stool she'd dragged into her father's closet to aid the search. Not the used VW Rabbit he'd hidden out in the wine shed thinking that she never went there anymore. And she didn't, except for some reason that day before her eighteenth Christmas.

A part of her wanted to crumple the letter up and throw it into the sea. It was too soon. She didn't want to face the pain again.

Too soon.

She looked out at the crashing waves. With a sudden howl of wind, a slash of spray roared by mere feet from her face, barely averted by the staunch tower of the lighthouse. Clearly someone wasn't happy about her desire to avoid the task at hand.

The rest of her body did what it supposed to do. The dutiful daughter opened the envelope and pinned the letter against her thigh so that she could read the slashing scrawl that was her father's. Even as weak with sickness as he must have been, it looked scribed in stone. His bold-stroke writing gave the words a force and strength just as his deep voice had once sounded strong enough to keep the world at bay for a little girl.

Dearest Ice Sweet,

He'd always called her that. Icewine. The grapes for icewine were traditionally harvested on her birthday, December twenty-first. "The sweetest wine of all, my little ice sweet girl." By the age of five she knew about the sugar content of icewine, Riesling, Chardonnay, and a dozen others. By eight she could identify scores of vintages just by the scent of the cork and hundreds by their logos though she'd yet to taste more than thimblefuls of watered wine at any one time.

Cassidy stared at the waves digging angrily at the rocks not far below her feet. The wind dragged tears from her eyes even as she struggled to blink them dry. She hadn't cried in a long time and she was damned if she was going to start now simply because she was cold and there was a hole in her heart.

Just seven days. She'd looked away for a one moment seven days ago—and he was gone. Christmas morning. He'd hung on long enough to tell her of his last present, hidden in plain sight in the used x-ray folder on the bedside table. A long list of crossed-out names had shuttled films back and forth across Northwest Hospital.

I bought this calendar the day you moved back to Seattle. Marked in all the "dates." Now I know that I won't get to go with you. I'm sorry to leave you so young.

"I'm twenty-nine, Daddy." But it felt young. Her birthday gone unremarked because he'd never woken that day so close to his last.

The hole in her heart was so broad that it would never be filled. He'd only been gone a week. Cremated, waked, and ashes spread on his beloved vineyard by the permission of the new owners. They'd owned his vineyard for five years, but still, they were the new ones. It wasn't right—them living in the place where her father belonged. She could picture him so easily striding among the vines, rubbing the soil in his palm, showing his only child the wonders of the changing seasons, the lifecycle of a grapevine, and the nurturing of honeybees.

For our first "date" I will just tell you how proud I am of you. My daughter took a vintner's education and turned herself into the best food-and-wine columnist ever.

He always believed in her. Always rooted for her. Her number one fan had always cheered her on. He'd been the same way with her boyfriends: welcoming them when they arrived, consoling her when they were gone, and offering no harsh judgment—not even about the boys she should have avoided like a bottle of rotgut Thunderbird.

The wind rattled the paper, drawing her attention back to the letter.

You are so like me. You figure out what feels right and you just go do it; damn the consequences. I could never fault you for leaving. I always did what I wanted, too. Saw it and went right for it, no discussion needed, always wearing perfect blinders that blocked out everything else. You got that from me. You come by your whimsical stubbornness honestly, Ice Sweet.

But he was wrong, she wasn't stubborn. It had taken years of careful planning for her to reach this far. Even her move to Seattle to be with him had been calculated, though she never told him about that. She shifted on the hard rock that was in imminent danger of freezing her butt.

Her father kept apologizing for all the wrong things. Seattle had ended up being a great career move, or was finally becoming one as she'd hoped. In New York, she worked as one of a thousand food and wine reviewers. Okay one in fifty—maybe even one in twenty-five, she was damn good—but there were only three women at that level. The other twenty-two were members of longstanding in the old boys' club.

"We're looking for someone with a more refined palate." Read that as someone who was "male."

She'd let go of her sublet in Manhattan when she'd found out her father was sick. Bought a condo in Seattle to be near, but not too near him on Bainbridge Island. Helped him move into the elder-care by Northgate when he couldn't care for himself any longer and from there to Northwest Hospital where she'd lived out his last two weeks in the chair by his bed.

The Village Voice dropped her the day she left Manhattan. That had hurt as they'd run her first-ever review, a short piece on Jim and Charlie's Punk and Wine Bistro. Jim and Charlie's was still there, partly thanks to that review that was still framed and hung in the center of bar's mirror.

But in Seattle she was rapidly rising to the very upper crust of the apple pie. Her reviews ran in every local paper. The *San Francisco Chronicle* had picked her up for their Travel section the next week making it difficult to stay grumpy about the loss of *The Voice.* Then AAA took her national with a regular column for their magazines. From there, it hadn't been a big step to national syndication. Six more months in New York and she'd have still been grinding her way up from the twentieth spot to the nineteenth. She was going to bypass the lot of them by skipping right past the "required" and sitting at the head table herself.

Her father's cancer had brought at least that much good.

Now if only it hadn't taken him with it.

And she wasn't whimsical no matter what he thought. Her dad had always described her mother as the organized one. And Cassidy had done her best to be just like her. You didn't become a top columnist by following the wind all willy-nilly.

If she didn't hurry, she was going to freeze in place. She chafed at her legs with one hand and then the other, but it didn't help. She was cold past any cure less than a piping hot bath. She peeked ahead in the letter, just two and a bit more pages. She turned to the second sheet, barely managing not to lose the first to the wind.

I started the vineyard after my tour in Vietnam. Got signed off the base and walked out of San Francisco right across the Golden Gate. No home, no job, and no one to go back to. I headed up into the hills; didn't even know why or where I was. I walked and hitched 'til dark, slept, woke with the light, and kept moving.

One morning, I woke up in a field close to a rotting, wooden fencepost, looking at the saddest little vineyard you could imagine. Poor vines dying of thirst. I found an old bucket and started watering them from a nearby stream. An old man came out to lean on the fence. Watched me quite a while, a couple hours maybe. I didn't care about him. Those vines were the first thing I'd cared about in a long, long time.

"You want 'em?" the old guy asked. "Five hundred bucks and they're yours."

I don't even remember how it happened. One minute my final pay was in my pocket, then in his. Later on, other vets drifted in. I charged them fifty bucks to join. Five of us worked the land and recovered those vines. That was the start of the thirty acres of Knowles Valley Vineyard.

She'd never heard how his first vineyard started. Didn't even really know where it was, somewhere in the hills of northern California. Though he might have ambled all the way to Oregon for how much she knew.

Walk the year with me. Let's take our time. My past is mine, but your future is not. That's only up to you. That I leave you to walk alone, though I'll warn you that it's a rough trail often over rocky soil. But keep your head high and you'll go far.

Whatever happens, know that I love you. I'm so proud of you.

Love you Ice Sweet,

Vic

Vic. He always signed his letters "Vic." Never what she'd always called him. "Daddy."

I could never fault you for leaving.

Yet between the lines that's just what he did. Nothing on the backs of any of the pages. She worked to refold the pages in the wind. The damp chill was now worse inside than outside her skin. The weather was a nasty, temperamental thing, clawing to reach her; this pain she felt right down to deep inside.

"No, you're imagining things, Cass. You think too much. Get your head out of your own butt." And she mostly did. One of the many gifts Vic Knowles had given her, the ability to be clear about her own actions and reactions.

He'd financed her dream of getting away from the rain capital of the Pacific Northwest. He'd paid for her college in full and cooking school after that. It was only while cleaning up his papers this last week that she saw how close it had come to breaking him. He'd just made it a natural assumption that she'd go to college and he'd pay. Just like her mom who had a degree in economics from Vassar. He'd always talked about how smart Cassidy's mother was.

"Just look in the mirror, Ice Sweet, and you'll see she was the most beautiful woman you can imagine. I miss her every day."

She tried to see, but all she ever saw was herself. She did better without the mirror. Even now, looking north along the steep, conifer-clad shore and over the heavy waves she could imagine her father happy. A woman with soft brown hair who did and didn't look like Cassidy at his side.

He hadn't gone to college himself, not even high school. His past was little more than a few facts she'd winnowed over the years. His own dad had left before he could remember. He'd dropped out of third grade to help his mother run the grocery store. They were desperately poor when she died. Then he'd gone to Vietnam at eighteen as the only way to make a living wage. And walked to a vineyard. But he gave Cassidy that gift of education as if it was no hardship to him.

Did he now begrudge her that past? The future he never had.

No. That didn't make any sense. He hadn't thought about the money, he'd invested in his dreams for her. She was just going nuts from missing him so much and angry at him for being dead.

"Useful, Cass, real useful."

To prove her sanity, she forced the rumpled letter back into the envelope, as neatly as possible in the midst of the maelstrom, and she forced that back into her leather pack.

Her father, the self-educated man, also the most well-read man she'd ever met. But she'd learned early on to do her math and science homework before he came home from the fields. His frustration at being unable to help her there had always been a strain.

Cassidy's mother was a single solitary memory. It had been a night as foul-tempered as this day. Mama had been standing in the open doorway of the house, leaving to answer a call to the hospital. Odd, Daddy had never mentioned her nursing school days, but talking about her had always hurt him, so Cassidy had learned not to ask.

The wind at the door had blown her mother's long hair across her face as she leaned on Daddy's arm. That was Cassidy's only memory of Adrianne Knowles, a woman with no face. Then Bea Clark had rushed in from next door to sit with her.

She and Daddy did talk about the many books though. He had sharpened her mind as they puzzled them out together. Ayn Rand piled next to Shakespeare, Heinlein beside Hugo, and Dickens leaning against a biography of Jimi Hendrix. Their house was always awash in books. And the massive collection of wine books, thumbed again and again by both of them, the only books to have a proper bookcase, had sat in the place of honor in the living room. Everything else jumbled into stacked wooden crates, mounded on tops of dressers, and enough on the dining table to make it a battle to find room for their two plates.

The chill spray of a particularly large wave spattered her with a few drops, and the next with a few more. The tide must be coming in.

She scrambled from her hiding place and rose back into the wind which threatened to topple her off the breakwater and down into the roaring waves. She forged her way back to the parking lot. The wind tore at her backpack and thumped it against her spine. The camera. Right.

She squatted to get out of the wind and pulled out her trusty point-and-shoot. The wind nearly blinded her when she turned back into it. Her hair swirled about her head, completely in the way.

A sailboat. Two lunatics in a sailboat were off the point of land. A cobalt-blue hull climbed out of one wave, pointing its bow to the sky, and then plunged down and buried its nose in the front of the next wave before rising again in a great arc of spray and green water. Huge, maroon sails snapped in the wind, loud enough to sound like a gunshot above the roaring surf.

Whoever the captain was, he and his buddy were crazy. They must both be male because no woman in her right mind would ever go out into a storm like this. But if they wanted to sail right into her picture, she wasn't going to complain; it was a beautiful boat. At the perfect moment she snapped the photo then turned for the woods and the long trail home.

***

"Hey Angelo. Take the helm." Russell had to shout to be heard above the sharp crack of the dark-red mainsail.

"Got it, Captain." His friend grinned at him as he grabbed the tiller and they slid across the waves off the West Point lighthouse.

Russell let out a whoop as they rode high over a crest, paused, and went briefly weightless before they plunged into the next trough. The *Lady Amalthea* had been built for weather like this. At first Russell had been afraid of such heavy weather. His parents' boat, *Julia*—a twenty-eight footer they kept at the summer place on Fire Island—would have had a very tough time in this sea. At fifty feet long, the *Lady* just ate it up; she practically flew over the wavetops.

He ducked below and grabbed his camera.

Belowdecks would definitely need some work. Okay, a lot of work. The only decent thing in the old gal was the forward stateroom. Russell could hardly wait. The marine surveyor had pronounced both the hull and mast sound and that was all he cared about. The interior just needed to be torn out and redone. He'd have to figure out a better system for diesel than that old beer keg strapped to the engine room wall. Get her plumbed for fresh water and wired with more than an old car battery charger. But she really had potential. Most importantly, the *Lady* sailed like there was no tomorrow.

He scrambled back on deck and started snapping pictures. Angelo posed in his foul weather gear, the yellow slicks and orange float jacket making him look as much like a clown as a sailor. He made some foolish faces to go with it and Russell captured them for posterity. He'd send the most ridiculous one to Angelo's mother, Maria, just to shame him on his next visit home.

Then he aimed at the lighthouse and snapped off a couple dozen images. He didn't even bother to check the LCD, they'd be good. The lighthouse perched on the rocky edge of Discovery Park was too photogenic a place for bad pictures. He bracketed the exposure and focus just to be sure. It was perfect. Steep, wooded cliff rising up behind the pristine white and red of the squat lighthouse. He'd crop the image to avoid the sprawl of the treatment plant just around the rocks to the north.

He tried to get the rhythm of the lighthouse's flash: alternating white and red every ten seconds. He got them both then stowed the camera away.

"Ready about?" Angelo called from above.

Russell scrambled back on deck, checked the lines, and preset the port jib sheet next to the winch. The line felt oversized but solid in his hand, the rope was a half-inch thick just to handle the sail, the same size as the anchor line on his parents' *Julia.*

"Ready."

"Helm's a lee!" Angelo threw over the tiller and the *Lady* lifted up her bow and spun like a dancer.

Russell waited until the very last second before releasing the starboard line and heaving in on the port one. Moments later the line snapped taught and would have flipped him overboard if he hadn't let go, a rope burn creased his palms with searing heat.

Angelo was laughing his head off. "And you, Mister Great Sailor, are going to solo around the world?"

"Shaddup, Angelo. It was your idea."

"I gave you a hundred ideas on Thanksgiving Day, I figured you wouldn't listen to any of them like usual, especially not this one. What about being a scuba instructor off Fiji with all of the cute tourists?"

The boat slammed over another wave like she was skating on glass.

"Nah! Not for me. Don't like getting my hair wet."

He saw Angelo twitch the tiller, but he didn't move fast enough. A wave plowed into his face, freezing rivulets of seawater running right past the tight collar of his float jacket and down his back underneath.

He lost the line for the jib sheet again and the line whipped away. The jib sail luffing with sharp slaps and cracks.

He sputtered and spat as Angelo pointed the boat's bow back into the wind.

Russell retrieved the sheet and hauled it back in, and leery of Angelo, passed it several times around the winch as he did so. Russell grabbed the winch handle and ratcheted in the last few feet of line.

"She's bigger than Dad's *Julia*."

"Duh! That jib, the sail that's so much smarter than you, has more area than both of hers."

True. He'd bought a big boat. But she flew so sweet that he knew he'd made the right choice. And only a nut would try crossing an ocean in a twenty-eight footer. He'd looked at a sixty-five footer, but it was more boat than he wanted to wrestle with. That really would need two people and heaven knows you couldn't count on two.

Melanie had been some serious kind of pissed. And that was before he'd decided to stay in Seattle past a few days to visit Angelo. Now she wasn't even speaking to him; at least he didn't think she was. He'd dropped his phone overboard and hadn't gotten around to replacing it yet.

Russell looked back at the lighthouse.

"You know they wanted to automate her in 1979. The lighthouse keeper begged them to let him keep running it, at least until her hundredth birthday. On her centenary in 1981, the keeper climbed up to the outside of the light and sprayed a bottle of champagne over her. Legend has it he also danced a hornpipe up there."

"A good choice for the January lighthouse." Angelo pointed ahead. "Where are we going?"

Russell ducked low to peek under the sail. The western shore of the Sound was a half-dozen miles off. Some rain was moving in, but they were dressed for that. It was too perfect a day to turn back for the marina yet. He waved ahead.

"Thatta way. The isle of Tortuga."

"Aye, *Mon Capitaine*." They both laughed. Nothing like a good pirate movie quote when you were off sailing. The crazed French accent made as much sense from his short, Italian friend as it had from a tall, English Basil Rathbone.

Russell let the main out a bit to get better air flow across the upper third of the sail and then headed forward to inspect the boat under way. The tail end of the jib halyard had slipped free and was snaked all over the deck. He checked aloft. The halyard ran clean up to the top of the mast, over a pulley at the top and down to the top of the jib sail. Damn that was a tall mast. Sixty-five feet from water to masthead, sixty from where he stood on the cabin roof. He looped the line into a neat hank and hung it back over the cleat. The lines would have to be routed back to the cockpit so that he could single-hand her in rougher weather. That meant longer lines. He glanced aloft again.

"Well, I'm gonna have to climb you someday. Just like a six-story walkup back in Manhattan, so I should be okay." He didn't feel so certain as he watched it whipping back and forth across the sky each time she leapt over the next wave.

He made an inventory as he walked forward. New hatches, these were old and leaking despite their layers of duct tape. Most of the rope rigging would have to go. Some of the wire too.

His heel found another of the squishy spots in the decking. He'd have to rip off the bubbled fiberglass covering from the whole deck and deal with any rot under there. And the bowsprit definitely needed safety lines—the sprit stuck six feet over the emptiness of heaving waves. That would take some thinking.

A thirty-five pound anchor rested in the split and worn mahogany of a deck chock. The *Julia's* anchor weighed fifteen. When he'd unearthed the *Lady's* sixty-pound storm anchor under the forward bunk with another twenty-five pounds of chain, he felt a little humbled.

Leaning against the taut jib sail for support, he edged out onto the slender bowsprit. He grabbed hold of the wire forestay that rose from the tip of the sprit and soared to the top of the mainmast—fine for Puget Sound, not up for an ocean crossing. He added, "make it a double stay," to his mental list.

Then he got his face into the air ahead of the sail. The wind roared in his ears. The bow sliced the waves below his feet laying twin white curls of water to either side. The air was so fresh and so clean it was impossible that it was the same stuff that he'd breathed every day in New York. Here it was in his face, in his hair—in his soul.

It was the most alive he'd ever felt and he never wanted it to end.

***

BEFORE CASSIDY HAD FELT EVEN a little normal after yesterday's outing, it had required a very long, very hot bath and most of an afternoon curled up in front of the gas fire. The drenching rain had caught her halfway back to the car. Her suede jacket was a ruin and her leggings had defended her for thirty seconds, at most.

This, at least, she knew how to solve. REI may have expanded into a national brand, but their flagship store was just a few blocks from the *Seattle Times* where Jack was an editor. She should have set up a lunch date, they hadn't seen each other in a week, but she couldn't find the energy. Not the best of signs, but she'd think about that later.

The underground parking garage was a collection of small, ratty cars that should never have seen the light of day and a fleet of Toyota and Honda hybrids. She parked her dad's five-year-old Jetta and glanced around for the inevitable parking level reminders. "Evergreen." She wasn't on level "2," she was parked on a tree. And there was no sign of an elevator anywhere.

The small exit sign indicated that the garage was in no way connected to the store.

She went back outside and clambered up the walkways and bridges over an artificial waterfall that was actually quite impressive. It roared and splashed, even had spray. She could smell the damp mist on the morning air as she hiked up concrete stairs spiraling through the trees.

The elevator, when she finally found it, was outdoors as well and wholly unused. Apparently everyone who came here was so damn outdoorsy that they took the stairs up above the waterfall. She stabbed the button for the top level. Rapped it twice more for good measure.

The glass elevator stopped on a wide concrete veranda that afforded a view out over downtown Seattle and the older buildings of the Denny Regrade. It was a magnificent view of the city. Though Puget Sound would soon be gone as Seattle continued its growth, Queen Anne Hill would be visible for decades to come.

A latte vendor tended his outdoor stall and a crowd clustered about pretending it wasn't thirty-six degrees and drizzling on the second of January. They were clearly all certifiable. Being born and raised locally had not provided her with the die-hard, outdoorsman independent spirit that was still *de rigueur* in Seattle.

She raced through the foyer doors. A greeter smiled and asked if she needed any help. Cassidy assured her she was okay. It was warm inside and buying clothes was one thing she could handle.

A shout drew her attention upward. A twisted rock some forty feet high soared upward at the end of the lobby. A woman was falling— Cassidy let out a scream to match the climber's just as a safety rope jerked tight and the climber swung brutally against the stone.

Then Cassidy heard the woman's laughter over the pounding of her own heart.

A man clung to another face. "Quit goofing around, Teri. You fall on El Capitan and we're going to let you go."

"Gimme a break, Tom. I slipped is all."

Cassidy hurried through the main door, resisting the hesitancy about grabbing the nasty ice axes that served as door handles.

Maybe she did need help, like help packing a moving van and getting back to New York. Or at least with the vast arrays of equipment that spread before her in every direction. To her left was a rack of backpacks big enough for her to climb into, each with a thousand straps. To her right were more sleeping bags than she'd seen since her one Girl Scouts' camp-out.

"Keep moving, Cass." Books, energy bars, silvery packets marked "stroganoff" and another "ice cream." Even as she watched, someone selected a half dozen packets and put them into a basket. She moved on and entered a world of kayaks, with nothing but canoes and bicycles beyond. To her right, skis and snowboards. A bit farther, boots.

Boots!

She needed boots, good start. She'd work from the bottom up. A plan of attack, excellent. It still took her some exploring to discover these were all ski boots and that walking boots were up on the massive mezzanine level.

Once there, she moved across the plank flooring and entered the racks of boots, but it didn't smell like it should. There was no canvas and fine leather of Nordstrom or Saks nor the mellower tang of Gucci, not even the smooth sweetness of Armani. There was a heaviness like saddles that had hung too long in a tack room. Manly boots doing manly things.

Reaching the end of the boot aisle, she faced the wall of individual boots waiting for their mates. There wasn't a single manufacturer she recognized. Neither Anne Klein nor Kenneth Cole walked here. These all had tough, outdoorsy names: Vasque, Montrail, Ugg. Even the women's boots were from these companies marinated in testosterone.

"Can I help you?" Cassidy turned, and an incredibly fit girl who looked no more than nineteen confronted her in a little green vest and a white turtleneck. This time she'd take the assistance.

"I need some new boots." Her three-hundred dollar Weitzman's had dissolved on the trail back to the car. She'd lost a heel when it got stuck between two rocks. As she prowled about the park in the driving rain seeking the right parking lot among the forest, the leather had actually separated from the sole. She'd done the last hundred yards with the broken boot in her hand, her sock-covered foot squishing with freezing mud, and the other leg two inches longer at the heel. It was amazing she hadn't gotten frostbite or something.

"Do you know what kind you want?"

Again she faced the wall. They all looked the same, with brown tops and black rubber soles. But she knew how to handle that as well.

"The best."

"What kind of hiking are you doing?"

"That matters?"

The girl was really polite. Not at a Nordstrom personal shopper level, but she managed to hide any disdain she was feeling from her perfect, teenage face.

"Oh, yes." She pointed at the one pair with a four-hundred dollar price tag. "We just sold eight pairs of those to a women's team who are taking on the seven summits challenge."

"The seven summits?" Cassidy had entered not only another world, but they spoke a different language here.

"Kilimanjaro, Denali, Elbrus, Aconcagua, Carstenz Pyramid, and Everest. I'm forgetting one. Hold on. Don't tell me."

As if Cassidy might have a clue what she was talking about.

Her blue eyes searched about. "Oh, and Vinson. I always forget Vinson."

"Vinson?" Kilimanjaro, Denali, and Everest were the only ones she'd ever heard of but she finally got the idea. The highest peaks on each continent. And a team of women were going to climb them in those boots. The ones perched smugly right there on the wall glaring down at her for daring to enter their presence.

"Antarctica. Nearly five thousand meters. I like to read about it, but I'd never be crazy enough to try it." The girl was terribly cheerful, which would be irritating if it weren't so genuine.

"I, uh, won't be climbing Vinson."

The girl laughed, "Everest either?"

"Nope." She joined in the laugh and it felt good.

"Heavy backpack?" The girl inspected her from the black leather jacket down to her Josef Seibel heeled, leather loafers, but was nice enough to keep her thoughts to herself as Cassidy was demoted another level.

"Nope."

"Walks around Greenlake?"

"A bit tougher than that." Slogging uphill through the mud and the moss, definitely a bit tougher than the three-mile, paved jogging path.

"Light hiking, but the best?"

"Yes, that sounds good."

The girl reached out and unerringly grabbed a boot that looked just like all the others. She excitedly launched into a long description, but after Cassidy heard the word "waterproof," she tuned out the rest. That would teach the sticky mud to mess with a veteran shopper.

Most of the other items fell to similar tactics. She became better at it as item after item filled her basket. On the second floor "light hiking" linked with "cold weather" had gotten her a lecture about skipping polar fleece and going with the traditional layering of silk socks under wool. Including "year round" had added long underwear of Merino wool. "All weather" had added waterproof yet breathable pants from some company named by aliens, Arc'Teryx. Or maybe they were a dinosaur. But the price was the highest, over two hundred dollars, so they must be the best.

She threw in a black PolarTec fleece jacket with no one's help at all. But the waterproof jackets were impossible. Even asking for help didn't clarify the mess. The selection was larger than Saks designer racks and apparently each jacket had a different feature that made it particularly wonderful. She finally walked away when she learned that they all stopped at the waist.

Cassidy wanted something longer and warmer. Thankfully she knew right where to get that. Michael Kors had a beautiful, knee-length, down-filled coat in this year's line. He didn't make it in black, but there was a brilliant red one that would look great. That would make it easier to tolerate the massive damage she was doing to her shopping budget with clothing she'd wear only twelve times in her life. Eleven, she'd already been to the January lighthouse.

The basket was getting heavy. This was nuts. There was over a thousand dollars in there. Of course her agent had just e-mailed her about the *London Times* picking up her column in their Travel section with a query about a wine-only column in the Sunday edition; she was going international. Cassidy would justify this splurge as a proper celebration.

Back on the ground floor, she passed close to a counter covered in a nest of electronics. She was nearly attacked by an overeager boy who looked so healthy he'd probably climbed Vinson before his fifteenth birthday. With his eyes closed. Backwards.

"I see you're going out in the weather," she followed his glance to her basket. On the top were the red fleece watchcap that she'd chosen because it would match the Kors coat and the heavy gloves that she'd reluctantly chosen over the nice pair of sheepskin ones. "All weather" and "waterproof" had combined for the win there.

"Yes, I am."

"Going off the beaten path at all?"

The two hours she'd spent slogging through the muddy forest of Discovery Park answered that clearly for her.

At her nod, the boy nearly exploded with joy.

"You've just gotta have one of these!" He waved something at her too quickly to focus on.

"What is it?" As soon as he stopped waving it about she saw the price tag of three hundred dollars and prepared to walk away.

"GPSs." At her blank expression, he launched ahead. "Global Positioning System. These toys tell you exactly where you are. See?" He punched a couple buttons and a pair of numbers appeared. Numbers a lot like the ones she'd been unable to decipher on the outside of her dad's lighthouse envelopes.

"Then you can key in your destination, latitude, then longitude. We're west so we're minus."

So that was what the numbers on the envelope were, latitude and longitude. She felt foolish for not figuring that out, not that there was any reason she should have. She'd never seen coordinates in decimal form before. This whole REI experience been an adventure like Hansel and Gretel, always searching behind herself to see just where she'd dropped all of those IQ points she'd had before she walked through the doors. But hey, now she knew where Mount Vinson was. Or was it Vinson Mountain? Massif? She looked behind her, but didn't see anything on the floor.

He continued stabbing at the keys like a pro then turned it to her. "And there you go."

The tiny screen connected a green dot to a red one by a thin wandering line of red.

"The nearest Starbucks coffee. That's your route. How you get there."

She inspected it more carefully and could see that the line followed the streets of a tiny map. He tapped it and it zoomed in. A bright arrow pointed toward the front door.

"Do you have one of those that would show," she clamped down on her tongue for a moment, "parks and other such places?"

He waved it at her again. "This is it. Look. I've loaded in Washington State detail and the National Parks and the Blue chart. This is really cool. Look." More button pushing and he turned it back to her.

It showed a map in tan and white with tiny numbers on the white.

At her blank look, he rambled on. "Blue chart. Water. The blue stuff. It has all the coastline info."

"Like lighthouses?" It slipped out before she could stop it.

"You bet!"

She'd clearly been labeled as a tourist.

"Did you know we have one right here in Seattle city limits? Here it is over in Discovery Park. Shows the water depth." He aimed a ragged fingernail—probably broken while wrestling a grizzly bear for food—at one set of numbers. "There's the lighthouse and how often her light flashes. Then you just toggle it like this and, bang, there's the park and most of the trails. The maps are pretty good even down at that level. Hit this button and you get the topo overlay so you can see which trails go up and which ones down. It's just the best."

That last did it for her.

CASSIDY DIDN'T glance toward the last covered bottle of wine. She always preferred to let a wine speak for itself. She had little respect for judges who looked ahead, setting their expectations before they had discovered what was really in the wine.

But this was different.

This was a blind-tasting challenge. Ten bottles of wine lined up on an immaculate white tablecloth. An okay ambience with a modern motif, the restaurant had been around six months or so.

They should have decanted the wines into identical carafes for a truly blind tasting, but at least the foil had been stripped away and the brown paper presentation was always more popular with the crowd.

The final wine's color was splendid. A ruby red so opaque it was almost black. The initial nose was a bit closed, but the wine had been properly served at sixty degrees, nicely below room temperature. Another point to the event's sponsor. A quick swirl revealed abundant tears running down the inside of the glass. And the wine opened a bit. She swirled again. Dark fruit. Brown spice. Tarragon. Even… No, she wasn't going to jump to conclusions. A bad habit on one hand. And on the other, she had an audience.

The restaurant owner had done a nice job of marketing his "Ten on January Tenth" challenge, pulling more than just the usual crowd of oenophiles out of the woodwork. He'd promised some fine wines in the collection, both U.S. and European. The nice spread of free appetizers hadn't hurt either, though they needed to be farther from the tasting table. Twice she'd had to cross to the far side of the dining room to make sure the scent was the wine and not his Italian herbs. The second time the owner noticed, and in moments the waiters had shifted the more aromatic foods to the farther end of the buffet. Good service.

The sip and quick intake of breath over the wine as it still swam on her tongue gave the expected results. Lemony, and a confirmation of the anise on the nose rode into the finish. She spit into the bucket and nosed the wine again.

There was something more. She didn't have it yet.

Another swirl and sip. More air. Another spit. Exactly the same dark richness.

Ah, there it was: not something there, but something missing. Almost no tannins at all. A wine this dark, yet so clean; it definitely wasn't mainstream. It was a true challenge wine to set apart the real tasters.

She opened her eyes and realized that the restaurant was

completely silent. Every face was turned in her direction, even the early diners had stopped eating to watch her. Mr. Terence, that obnoxious cookbook chef who coyly avoided any request for his first name—it probably said "Mister" on his birth certificate—had peeked at the wine label and then crumpled his bit of notepaper. The restaurant owner had noticed and was scowling. There was someone who had just lost his next invitation here.

Cassidy didn't need to look.

It took her several moments to come back to the wine, the taste still rolling across her tongue. To come back and realize that she really had done something; she had moved out of the crowd of being but one of many in the New York tastings. Here, in Seattle, the many were waiting to hear her verdict. Hers.

The temptation to dismiss the phenomenon as a big frog in a small pond was there. But Josh was here from *Gourmet Week* as well, which had made her nervous through the first four wines. He'd actually trained under Parker. He too wore a look of anticipation. He held up a piece of notepaper, carefully folded to show he was ready, and nodded for her to go ahead. Well, there was no avoiding it, and she didn't need to on this one.

"Italian. Apulia." Some of the diners' faces blanked. "That's the region. The boot-heel of Italy."

Josh was grinning when she turned to face Mister Terence who was making a show of hiding the bottle.

"Taurino from the Negroamaro grape. The Notarpanaro Salento Rosso. Either the '97 or the '01, but I'd bet on the former."

Terence's face fell and Josh flipped open his slip of paper and turned it for her to see. He'd written just a number on it, "97." The restaurant owner clapped his hands together and laughed, his teeth bright in his dark, Italian face.

"An exquisite final choice, Mr. Parrano. It truly completes the other wines. Even a rearrangement of your last name. A nice touch."

He bowed deeply before taking her shoulders and kissing each cheek.

"Angelo." He had one of those Italian accents that was designed to make a woman melt and it wasn't hard to give in to it. "Please call me, Angelo, Ms. Knowles. Always Angelo."

"Cassidy then." She let herself melt a bit farther, her wine columnist attitude slipping off a little more.

He took her hand and raised it. "Ten wines and not a miss." Josh had missed one, but a totally understandable mixup unless you'd specifically studied the Loire Valley Vouvrays. He'd gotten the region and grape, but not the winery. Mister Terence had missed the Vouvray placing it as an Oregon Pinot of all silliness, the Taurino, and three others, two of them quite obvious mistakes. Two of the three amateurs had bested his score though they both missed the Vouvray, a tricky wine because of its gentle voice, and the Taurino.

"A meal on the house. No, you don't get to order, I will make the menu specially for you."

Everyone applauded as he conducted her to a table set for two. Angelo looked around and waved for Josh to take the other seat; Josh might be happily married but he was an old friend and a lively dinner companion. Angelo left Terence out in the cold with the three amateurs to browse the free appetizer table.

"If you give me the meal, I can't write it up. Conflict of interest."

"Some other time, you come back and I charge you double. Not tonight." He lowered his voice. "I've been waiting for an excuse to chase that hoity-toity Mr. Terence out of here, but you have taken care of that for me. He won't dare show his face for quite a while to come. For this I am eternally grateful. And you are eternally welcome in my restaurant."

She nodded, not minding being used to that end in the least, and then glanced at Josh. "Perhaps I could make one request about the menu."

She raised an eyebrow and Josh laughed, then flipped open his slip of paper again. Angelo tried to look angry but he couldn't hold it for more than a moment. He stepped back to the tasting table and, securing the Taurino from Terence with a slight tug, he placed it at their table.

"The meal shall match this perfectly."

"Damn, you're good!" Russell took another piece of garlic bread and mashed it around in the red sauce to soak up as much as he could.

Angelo's kitchen was now in full swing. Dinner was happening with a crash of pans and calls back and forth across the cook line. Russell had grabbed some pasta and retreated to the sidelines to watch the mayhem. The kitchen ran with a smooth perfection that should happen only in movies.

"You should see what I sent out on the floor tonight. Exquisite. The Cingale with Truffle Sauce." Angelo kissed his fingertips and threw the kiss to the kitchen's ceiling. "Outdid myself even if I'm the one who says so."

He slapped Russell on top of the head. "That's grilled boar meat to you, you peasant."

"I know what *cingale* is," he cuffed Angelo back somewhat harder. "And your food is always awesome, buddy." Russell kissed his own fingers and then made a show of licking them clean of the garlic butter.

"Yeah, you need to clean up. You're messing up my kitchen, man. Just by breathing." Angelo peeked into an oven and closed it again. He returned to slicing chives at an impossible rate for some garnish.

Russell looked down to inspect himself. His jeans were smeared with white fiberglass resin from the seals on the new decking. It had hardened into crackling streaks that wouldn't let go of the cloth even when he picked at them. His shirt was clean, just a couple tears from where he'd caught it on the old decking he'd been tearing off the boat. Maybe he was a bit disreputable for the stainless-steel-and-white-tile kitchen.

Just because Angelo was right, Russell wasn't about to admit it.

"Wait until I start the woodwork. Then I can offer you a healthy dose of sawdust on your tile floor to make it look properly lived in. You could eat off the damn thing now."

"Thanks, but no thanks. I think a health inspector would rather see a rat in my kitchen than you." Angelo danced around a half-dozen desserts with a squirt bottle adding little swirls of reduced pomegranate sauce even as the waiters put them on their trays. A moment later his *sous chef* dumped a steaming cauldron of homemade pasta into a colander. Angelo attacked it with quick tongs and a bit of oil before plating it next to an Eggplant Parmigiana that still bubbled from the oven.

Russell licked another dribble of butter off the back of his hand.

He smelled her before he saw her. Like warm wood and something else he couldn't identify but could never forget.

He turned to look and wasn't disappointed. Trim and chic in a black pantsuit over a black turtleneck. The cut was perfect for her figure which was pleasantly womanly in its curves. It suited her five foot ten very nicely, making her look even taller and more slender than she was. He checked her shoes, okay, five foot eight without the heels, which fit her even better. Her face was so subtly made up it looked as if she wore no makeup at all. Her russet hair pulled back into a tight chignon from which not a single strand strayed. The shape of jawline to neck, of ear to cheek, was like a flash from the past.

For the first time in the month and a half since he'd closed the studio, he wished for lights and a camera. But she was everything he was leaving behind. Everything that had been wrong with his former life. He could imagine Melanie on his boat much easier than this one, even Melanie let her hair down on occasion—she actually made a trademark of just that.

Where Melanie's voice was affected French, to cover her New York accent, this woman's voice was throaty and warm as she did the "thank you so much" thing with Angelo. She glanced at him twice with intensely hazel eyes that were deeper than the ocean. A glance he could easily read. "What is this slob doing dirtying up Angelo's pristine kitchen?"

Then she was gone and Angelo just stood there beaming.

"Hey, Buddy-boy." Russell poked his fork into his pasta. He had to do it a couple times before he finally landed some. "She's got you bad."

"Oh yeah." Angelo sounded a little dreamy. "You weren't here. She's just the nation's hottest food-and-wine columnist. It took me six months to tempt her here." He shook himself and then punched Russell's arm hard.

"And she loves my food and my restaurant!"

"Hey! Ow already!" He knocked Angelo's hat to the floor just as Angelo kicked Russell's stool over backward. He landed hard against the refrigerator. Once he had his balance, he prepared to lunge forward.

Angelo moved faster and aimed his weapon at Russell's chest.

"More garlic bread?"

Russell kicked the stool back into place and took another steaming slice from the wicker basket. He easily matched his friend's grin.

"THE WHAT OF JANUARY?"

"Just grab a bottle, cheese and crackers if you have 'em and come along."

Russell dug around in the cooler, found a couple of beers. The cardboard box that was his pantry had some Ritz crackers, his absolute weakness. He slapped the package against his thigh to dislodge the worst of the wood dust from the box.

He closed up his sailboat and followed Dave down onto the floating slipway. They turned toward the far end of 'D' dock. The thousand masts of Shilshole Marina cluttered the night sky. To the east, brightly lit houses looked down on them from atop the high cliff. To the west, Puget Sound stretched to the moonlit peaks of the Olympics. It was clear and cold enough to freeze a sailboat's tail, or at least his own.

"The what of January?" He repeated, his breath puffing a white cloud into the night air. He had to trot down the dock to catch up with Dave even though the man had to be in his fifties.

"The ides."

"I thought only March had ides. The day Brutus stabbed his buddy Caesar in the behind."

"The ides. The fifteenth of March, May, July, and October, I think.

The thirteenth of all the others. And today's the thirteenth. Sounds like a good reason for a party."

Russell didn't need any more prompting than that.

"Lead on, Brutus. Just be careful of any desire to do some stabbing." They arrived at Dave and Betsy's forty-four foot catamaran. Russell had been sorely tempted to buy one of these; they were fast, spacious, and stable as could be. Unless you got flipped. In something nasty, like a hurricane, a monohull would roll under and usually self-right, sometimes without its mast, but at least it would right. A catamaran was more stable upside down than rightside up. A little too wild for him. It would also be a hell of a lot of boat to single-hand in a storm.

He'd befriended Dave just to get a look inside and they'd spent hours talking about ocean crossings and ports of call. Russell had helped a buddy do the New York-Bahamas run on his friend's J/boat, but that was a long step from crossing one of the oceans. Dave and Betsy had taken the *Lark* on a four-year tour that included both capes, Good Hope and Horn and all of the seven seas.

"Ponds," Betsy had corrected him. "Not seas. We talk about crossing the ponds, not so scary that way."

Still scared him either way.

He clambered aboard and joined the crowd of 'D' dock liveaboards. Teri and Tom were curled up on one of the settees, a bottle of cheap white wine in front of them. He'd been here barely two weeks and he already knew of their reputation. It had been hard to miss actually.

They had terrible fights when running in the local races, and screamingly good, or at least loud sex when at dock. Few secrets could be kept through a few millimeters of fiberglass hull. Even his *Lady's* double-plank oak hull wasn't going to muffle all that much if he ever had a flesh-and-blood lady aboard. Most sailors were discreet, Teri obviously didn't care or didn't think to. He eyed the incredibly tight sweater on the shapely dishwater blond. Or maybe she liked bragging.

Russell slid in next to Perry. The old man had a bottle of decent whiskey capped beside him, a small tumbler in his massive fist. He rarely spoke, but Betsy had told Russell that the old-timer had been born on a tugboat off Vashon Island. Had worked boats, mostly log tugs and fishing tenders, for the eighty years since. He lived on a 1904 Arrow tug, one of only four built that year, that he was restoring it a little way down the dock.

Dave and Betsy had made their money then moved to the boat and the seas. He drank Heineken and she had a glass of red wine in a short, wide glass that wouldn't tip easily at sea.

Others he didn't know drifted in behind him, each arriving with a cold blast of the chill January air and a muttered curse from those closest to the hatch. As the crowd grew, he refused to be nudged from the small table with Perry and Dave. Soon, people were perched on counters or squatting by the windows.

"What do you do to keep yourself busy?" Dave grabbed a couple of his Ritz crackers.

"Other than my boat, you mean?"

"Other than your boat."

"I take pictures. Used to." Russell thought of the images of Angelo and the lighthouse still in his camera. "Still do."

"Any good?"

Dave had asked the question, but it was Perry who inspected him with blue eyes shaded by a black Greek sailor's hat, the rest of his face mostly lost in a white beard and mustache that would have put Santa Claus to shame.

"Used to make a pretty decent living at it."

Perry nodded and sipped his whiskey.

"Good," Dave agreed. "Need something to give purpose to your wanderings. Betsy there is a marine botanist. Must've logged five thousand samples over the last decade. She has this little rig that lets her grab water at surface, then one, two, five, and ten meters all at once. Keeps her moving ahead. She catalogs the whole mess and ships the data to the Scripps Institute. They love her for it, though I'd hate to be staff grad student when she sends in a case. Me, I'm a writer. Spent thirty years doing technical writing. Now I'm doing the travel narrative thing and might do a fiction book set in the seaports of the world. What are you gonna do?"

"You mean about 'moving ahead'?" Russell munched on a couple of crackers and opened another bottle of beer. "Hadn't really thought about it."

Hadn't thought at all really. Back at Thanksgiving—when he'd made a joke to match every one of Angelo's ideas about what to do with his life—Angelo had finally pulled a next-year's calendar off the wall and heaved it at him.

"Here, you big idiot. Buy a sailboat. Sail to each one on the calendar. By the end of the year you'll be good enough to sail outta my life and let me get some peace." It had taken him only two days to find the *Lady* and he'd bought her before her hull was even wet after the boat appraiser was done with it.

Angelo had laughed when Russell told him of his purchase. "Getting pretty sick of you moping on my couch, when can you move?" Three weeks of slavery, but he'd got her watertight and moved aboard just yesterday afternoon.

Hadn't thought about what it meant to be a liveaboard; he simply did it.

He glanced about the crowded cabin. Liveaboards came in two main varieties: couples and single men. Not a single woman in the whole crowd. Teri had gathered a small court, all of whom she flirted with shamelessly. Tom was approaching meltdown, even though she was snuggled back against him while she flirted with the others.

"We know what those two will be doing."

Perry and Dave glanced over and answered in unison. "Fighting." Perry's first word of the evening.

"Can't imagine them making it out of the Sound, never mind anywhere further."

"She's a handful, that one." Dave took another cracker. "They've been married and living on that thirty-two footer for two years now. Trying to pay off the boat so they can go offshore. Don't think they're any closer to it than when they started."

Russell would rather go solo any day of the week. Then he looked at Betsy. She and a couple he didn't know were lounging together against the galley counters sharing gentle conversation and easy laughs. Both women were healthy and attractive. Any lack in the raw sexual appeal that Teri radiated was more than balanced by… What was the word to describe the tableau of friends? Comfortable. They were comfortable together, with those around them, with this setting, this boat.

It just took the right kind of woman. Maybe he'd find one. If not, he'd go and trust to his journey. He'd know the right one when she showed up.

Funny to have a boat now. As a kid he'd always dreamed of sailing around the world. The streetlights that had shown up through his Upper West Side Manhattan bedroom windows had painted a map of shadow and light that he had peopled with pirates and discovery.

In all his boyhood dreams, he'd never pictured a woman on the boat. Of course he hadn't hit puberty then either. At first, he'd imagined he and his grandfather sailing together. After he'd died, Russell had always pictured himself solo without really thinking about it. Once puberty hit, he'd thought about women and not sailboats. He hadn't remembered the boats until Angelo heaved the calendar at his head. He tried to mentally place Melanie aboard, but it wouldn't stick. And that was far more likely than Angelo's wine lady. There was a laugh.

Solo. Why had he always pictured himself sailing solo?

"Careful what you wish for, buddy, you're gonna get it," he muttered under his breath.

Maybe he could wish for this. A couple dozen people all crowded together. Nothing more important to do than spend some time with each other. Thank god no one sidling up to discuss the next shoot, no one after his parents' money. He definitely wouldn't miss someone barfing while they held themselves upright with a palm in the middle of one of his ten-thousand dollar photographs.

He'd given his whole damn art-photo collection to MoMA on permanent loan. Pete, the head of the art handling team who'd come to cart it off, had practically cried on his shoulder. His diminutive wife actually had—oddly enough at a tiny tintype self-portrait by a young Bourke-White.

Russell was already closer to Dave and Perry than he'd been to most of the people at the final studio party. The people here from Perry to Dave and even Teri were more real than any of his former... associates—except perhaps Melanie.

He looked back at Perry and Dave with a shrug, "I'm just gonna sail."

Dave looked a bit unsure but didn't say anything.

Perry poured another short whiskey and rolled the glass back and forth between his callused palms. The surface rippled with golden light in the heavy cut glass.

"Pictures."

He and Dave faced the old salt who continued to study his glass.

"Pictures? I dunno. Boats and port towns?" Russell offered. A real yawn once spoken aloud.

"Quiet streets and pretty women?" Dave added. That was a little better.

Perry slid back into his silence, but Russell would swear there was a smile going on somewhere behind that bushy mustache.

"What?"

The old man just shook his head and sipped his whiskey. With a wink, he took a couple of Russell's Ritz crackers.

RUSSELL WOKE when his boat shifted. Someone was aboard—without knocking on the hull first. Someone was breaking the first rule of boat etiquette.

Teri. Crap. Teri was coming on board. She'd been eyeing him toward the end of the party last night. Did she have a late night welcome ritual for any new single man on the dock? Certain parts of his body were indicating they wouldn't complain about that sort of welcome. But no way.

He scrabbled about for his pants, knocked his head sharply on a deck support he'd been meaning to wrap in foam rubber. He was going to give himself a permanent crease in his skull pretty soon.

"Don't be dumb, Russ. It's just been too long since you've had sex." Not since Melanie had jumped him Thanksgiving morning before he'd had a chance to tell that he was leaving for Seattle in a few hours.

She hadn't stayed after the studio closing party that he'd flown back for a week later and he couldn't blame her. Others had offered to stay, but he wasn't that crass. Or, now that he thought about it, that interested. It hadn't been a cheerful bash though it had all of the catering and blues band trappings of a good go.

The bright flashes before his eyes eased and he struggled into his pants as the boat rocked again. Then there was a step thudding back down onto the dock. He tried to think if there was anything to steal up on deck.

The forward porthole showed no one; no one crossing past the bow toward land. Who'd be up in the middle of the night prowling around the marina? He'd better stop them before they hit a boat that had something to lose.

He ran down the short companionway, the wood shavings and sawdust were prickly against his bare feet, and threw open the rear hatch. The cold hit his bare chest like a slap. He looked along the dock and could just make out a broad figure in a dark coat with white hair.

"Perry?" he half-whispered sending a puff of steamy breath out into night.

The old man waved a hand over his head, but didn't turn around. He continued toward his battered old tug.

That's when Russell heard it, the faintest sound at his feet.

He looked down.

Perry had left a cardboard box.

Russell shivered as the chill air wrapped around his body.

The box moved. There was something inside.

And then the box mewed.

ALKI LIGHTHOUSE

*A*lki Point, West Seattle
First lit: 1868
Automated: 1970
47.5762 -122.4206

ALKI, the Washington State motto, means "by-and-by" in Chinook, a local Native American language. In 1851 the first white settlers in the area landed at the present day location of the lighthouse. They named the settlement New York-Alki.

A few years later a young entrepreneur named Doc Maynard was made unwelcome there and moved on to found another settlement a few miles from the inhospitable point. It is one of the ironies of his life that in his last years, a near destitute Maynard lived very close to the lighthouse where New York-Alki had long since succumbed to Doc's city, which he'd named Seattle.

FEBRUARY 1

assidy parked the car and pounded a fist against the steering wheel. The horn blared and she'd have jumped out of the seat if it hadn't been for the seat belt.

Once again she glanced at the GPS. The "current position" and "destination" coordinates were superimposed. The coordinates matched the numbers on the envelope sitting beside the stick shift. She looked out her windshield. No question, that was it. The Alki Point lighthouse stood barely a dozen yards off the main beach road. She'd even found a parking spot right in front of the gate. Over two thousand dollars of hiking clothes and hour upon hour learning how to use the GPS in case she ever got lost again.

And there was the lighthouse in plain view down a little garden path.

She tossed her stupid alien-manufactured rain pants over the stupid GPS and climbed out of the car. Maybe if she left it unlocked, someone would steal all of the crap and she could pretend this was just a bad dream. Deep breath, Cass. Take a deep breath. She pressed the button and the car sealed everything safely inside with a contented chirp.

She pushed on the gate and the lock rattled, but it didn't open. A bronze plaque was bolted onto the fence.

"Winter hours: Sat-Sun 12-3. Mon-Fri closed."

Today was Saturday, the first of February. But it was nine in the morning which meant three hours to wait.

She kicked the gate.

Hard.

Well, that was one advantage to her new light-hiking, all-weather, waterproof boots by Vasque, which sounded like a plaque rinse more than a boot. They gave her the ability to kick a solid iron gate and not break her foot.

She couldn't even get a decent snapshot from the road, too many trees had grown up in the gardens. The expensive houses were packed side-by-side and she couldn't see any passage through.

She returned to the driver's seat and glared out at the neighborhood. Pounding her feet on the floormat made her feel a little better. She started the car and popped the clutch badly enough to stall the engine.

"Okay, Cassidy, you can do this. You know how to drive a goddamn car." She hadn't needed one in New York, so it had been something of an adventure to drive one when she returned to Seattle. She'd learned on a stick, but after a decade in the city, it hadn't come back as quickly as she'd expected.

She was glad she hadn't invited Jack James along; she was in no mood for a date. At least not if she wanted it to go well. And Jack's everlasting calm would just irritate her more. He never engaged his emotions in anything. Not in anything at all, now that she thought about it.

Once again: start the engine, in gear, ease out the clutch. She rolled out of the parking spot and down the street looking for a place to turn around. Fifty feet farther on, a little sign was posted on a rusted fence.

Two words.

"Beach Access."

"Yes!" Lighthouses were on beaches.

She checked the rearview mirror. Someone was pulling into her spot.

"That was mine, mister."

The next one she could find was halfway around the bay over a quarter-mile away according to her smug GPS. She considered taking the instrument with her to throw in the ocean but resisted the urge.

The wind was at her back as she walked back to the little flight of gritty concrete steps down to the sand and rock beach. There was no park ranger to refuse her a parking pass, she'd have an easy walk along the water's edge on a bright blue winter's day.

At the bottom of the steps she turned right along the sandy verge and was confronted by a much bigger sign.

"Residents only beyond this point."

Well, her car was parked in the neighborhood, sort of, so she was resident here at the moment. Besides, she formed the argument in her head, the sign was faded and was badly broken in one corner. "Broken sign, rule no longer valid."

Finally she rationalized that no one would be out on a day like this to give a damn anyway. It was blowing stiffly, though not like last month and the air was definitely cold enough to snow. Thankfully the sky was sparkling blue, not a white, puffy cloud in sight—very little danger of a soaking rain today.

She strode past the sign warm in her red watchcap, her knee-length Michael Kors parka, and her Vasque hiking boots that could definitely climb this beach, which was much less steep than any of those seven peaks.

The view was once again spectacular. The bay curved away to the left, the tall hills of West Seattle towered behind, dotted with beautiful houses and massive pine trees. In front of her, almost too vivid to be real, floated Vashon and Maury Island. Beyond them, soaring up into the sky were the Olympic Mountains; the Brothers peaks postured— each striving to raise his rugged, white-capped shoulders higher than the other.

The sand disappeared and she was forced to clamber over huge rocks that had been piled up in front of the houses as a breakwater. In addition to the breakwater each house had a massive seawall of concrete. She could see over the top of one to the array of kayaks and children's toys in the narrow back yard. The next house had a crane with a dock actually dangling from the end of it. It must be able to swing out and drop into the water on calmer, warmer days.

The third house had a tall tree that blocked her view of the house and looked as if it blocked the owner's view of the Sound. Well, that certainly made no sense. This view was so valuable the land here was probably sold by the square foot.

Then there was the lighthouse. The same angle as it appeared on the calendar. Maybe the photographer had come on a day when the front entrance was closed as well. A small yard of perfect grass surrounded the old keeper's house, set back among the gardens.

The lighthouse itself was perched on the edge of the massive boulders, just feet above the sea. All around its base were small white stones, as if the building were afloat in its own little white sea of foam. The Alki light lacked the rigid stoutness of the West Point lighthouse. Rather than squat and powerful, its red-capped light soared three stories into the blue sky. The white paint shone so brilliantly in the sunlight that it was painful to look at. Maybe she should have bought a pair of those polarized, glacier-expedition sun goggles.

She tugged out her camera and snapped a couple of photos. Only after the last shot did she notice that a sailboat had sailed right into the picture on the far side of the lighthouse. Cobalt blue hull, red sails. If there hadn't been a photo of the first lighthouse with that same boat framed on her condo wall, she'd think she was losing her mind.

She took another picture just so that she could prove later that it was real. Maybe this was a trademark in Seattle and lots of sailboats looked like that. Though she couldn't imagine why. It was as if the last month hadn't really happened. Or was happening again.

Sitting down on a moderately flat rock, she watched the waves for a while, without the slashing spray this time. She tugged the Michael Kors jacket over her knees and almost down to her ankles. The watch cap pulled down over her ears kept her head reasonably warm.

"Becoming quite the adventuress, aren't we, Cass?" She felt

strangely light, as if the breeze that was making her nose and cheeks sting with the cold could lift her up and she'd just fly away. Unfettered. Bound to no one.

Except a couple kajillion readers. That slammed her back to earth and she could feel the cold rock against her butt despite the jacket, her leggings, and the woolen underwear that she just might start wearing year round it was so warm.

She pulled off her heavy gloves and dug out her father's letter. Nothing new on the outside of the envelope. Just a destination point for this month's crazy journey.

Dearest Ice Sweet,

His voice sounded in her head. He wrote the same way he spoke. Warm, friendly, his letters were always an intimate conversation.

We made it to the second lighthouse. Alki, by-and-by. That's what it means. Maybe you remember that from school; it is the state motto after all. I always sat on the south side of the ferry just to watch for this lighthouse.

"I remember, Daddy." He must have pointed it out to her a thousand times, on every single trip to Seattle, both directions. He'd said it so many times that it had lost all meaning, just words that were a part of the day like, "Good morning." or "How was school?" Ignored, forgotten.

Suddenly she was a child in the big ferry boat once again, hundreds of people milling about, trying to find a way to be comfortable on the hard plastic seats for the half-hour crossing. Children racing up and down the aisles waving their Gameboys or Walkmans. Tourists snapping photos through the salt-stained glass that would never come out the way they pictured them; the journey a blur of half-forgotten images of a place they'd never been and could barely remember.

Things really do happen by-and-by, especially the good things. We were working the vineyard. A couple of the guys had drifted off, and one had slashed his leg so badly with a rototiller that he'd gone into the VA hospital after coming out of the war unharmed. Strange, I can't remember his name. Don't even know what happened to him.

We made some of the worst wine you can imagine those first years. But we got better, figured it out the hard way. It was still a brutal amount of work, but it was drinkable by the time your mother first came by.

She was a tourist, vacationing in California after getting out of school. Came to the coast to check out Berkeley for graduate work. She and a carload of girlfriends were doing the vineyard circuit. I opened a bottle of our Merlot for them to taste. Our very best. Hadn't meant to do that, but your mother always had the ability to turn me into a bumbling fool, right from the first time I saw her. She came back the next weekend with one friend, the week after alone. Soon she was helping in the fields. The rest, as they say, is history.

"Pretty slick, Daddy. Hitting on a college girl on vacation." She remembered the story. Daddy always told it exactly the same way, as if the tracks of it had been burned forever upon his heart. Unchanging, unchangeable over the years.

This lighthouse always made me think about the strange course my life has taken. The wanderings that took me to a place I'd never been or imagined going. That gave me a family, a wife and daughter, and a place to be in the world. Looking back, everything happened as if there were some great master plan. From the past looking forward, it was the most haphazard series of choices and chance.

Remember, Cass, pursue your dreams, but don't expect them to follow that straight and narrow path that you see so clearly in your head.

Life happens in its own fashion. At its own pace. I learned not to second-guess it. All that is good in my life came to me "by-and-by."

Vic

"Ha!" There was another memory she'd lost track of. That's what he'd said every single time he saw the lighthouse. "It'll come to me by-and-by." She glanced back over her shoulder.

The lighthouse stood there looking down at her.

"By-and-by, huh?"

It didn't answer.

"Good thing I didn't wait for by-and-by, Daddy. I'd never have gotten here."

Or would she? Mama went to Vassar in economics. Cassidy attended her mother's alma mater and got her degree in marketing, most of it done as an independent study.

While other students were partying, she was taking courses at the CIA. The Culinary Institute of America was less than a dozen miles up the road after all and it was too good a chance to pass up. No big surprise, what with being her father's daughter, that she had an exceptionally well-trained palate. By the time she'd graduated from high school at sixteen, she'd read a hundred books about wine. She'd graduated from both Vassar and the CIA at twenty. Columbia School of Journalism had occurred by chance as much as conscious choice. The class assignment to write a review of the Punk and Wine Bistro had led to her first sale and she'd never looked back.

Daddy was wrong, it certainly hadn't been by chance. She'd planned and she'd worked so hard and given up so much. She was out here alone wasn't she?

"Given up a hell of a lot, Daddy." She brushed at a tear raised by the cold wind.

Her fingers were frozen, even colder than her cheeks. Blowing into her curled hands warmed them little. She pulled the gloves back on, forming fists with her hands, leaving the chilly fingers of the gloves empty.

The lighthouse stood high above. The sailboat was disappearing southward, continuing its own chilly journey. A container ship sliced northward, but there were few other craft on so bitter a day.

She'd planned...to get as far away from Seattle and Bainbridge Island as she could. Marketing had started out as a degree in business. A thousand times she'd pictured herself smashing through the glass ceiling at some huge corporation. Of being like Carly Fiorina, then a top AT&T exec. She'd gone on to be president of Hewlett-Packard.

Cassidy had written her a piece of teen fan mail, the only she'd ever written, but no answer came. One thing Cassidy knew, though, a woman could do anything.

"If Carly can do it, so can I."

"Absolutely!" Her father would agree. "Anything but food or wine. The reviewers are such an old boys' club." His voice was a whisper in her memory, as warm as the wind was cold. He'd warned her of that so many times that she'd taken on the challenge.

"But I found a way through. You know, Daddy, I did an end run on them."

"Right," she waved her arms about to make her point and then waved them some more to get a decent blood flow. "I ignored that old boys' club completely and forged my own path to the tables." She'd cut quite a swath; and stepped on a number of toes, but success forgave many sins.

"I knew what I was doing." Even as she said it, the words went sour. Her path that had been so clear, was only so in retrospect. Maybe that part of Daddy's letter was true.

"But I'm in control now. The rest of your letter is just plain silly. I know where I'm going." And she did. A year maybe two more on the west coast, a couple in Europe, and she'd swing back into New York at the very top. Let the *New York Times* beg her to come aboard. They were the only major metro newspaper that didn't syndicate her column. Well, other than the *Washington Post,* but that was such an inside-the-Beltway paper that it didn't bother her nearly as much.

"I know what I'm doing. My path is clear, Daddy."

The roar of the wind and the crash of the waves against the beach were her only answers.

"Crystal clear." Again the sour taste. Her path wasn't that clear. What was clear was that she was losing her mind.

She was sitting on the windiest point of Seattle in a below-freezing day on the first of February. Sitting here with icicles where most people had fingers, holding a conversation with her dead father about career choices he'd be the first to argue were hers to make.

That was a laugh. Actually, it was. It bubbled up from somewhere deep inside her. It started small and it built and built until it burst forth and she could barely catch her breath.

"Totally and completely nutso!" she shouted at the wind and her words drifted away, wrapping around the lighthouse on their way landward.

"It will all make sense by-and-by, my ice sweet girl."

She spun around, but there was no one near. No one but memory to whisper to her with her father's voice.

ANGELO LAY back on one of the cockpit benches of the sailboat, his back against the cabin wall. His hood was raised against the wind. He clutched a silver travel mug in his gloved hands.

Russell imagined that someday he'd be able to feel his cheeks again, but not anytime soon—damn but it was cold.

"Hey Angelo." His friend had been quiet for the whole trip.

"What?" A one-word answer. His friend was Italian and never gave one-word answers.

"It's Saturday. How can you afford to be out here with me? Thought you did a Saturday lunch. Not that I don't appreciate it and all." He pointed the boat up a few points tighter to the wind. Even with the reef in the main and the small jib up forward, she still skidded over the wave tops at better than seven knots.

"We do a lunch." Angelo's voice was so quiet Russell could barely make out his answer over the wind.

"Well?"

"Well, what?" It wasn't like him to be obtuse. Angelo took a long pull of his coffee, so long he seemed to be avoiding the answer.

"Well?"

"No traffic, my man. Saturday lunch is so slow, the *sous chef* can handle it. With one arm behind his back." More coffee. "And his head in a sack."

"But you're the best cook there is, Angelo."

"Don't let my mother hear you say that."

He still had his sense of humor, that at least was a good sign. Russell kept them headed down the Sound, maybe they'd circle Vashon Island.

"What about your wonderful wine reviewer? Didn't she make it all better?"

Angelo shook his head. "A nice article about the tasting, business picked up a little, but people don't come to restaurants to drink hundred-dollar bottles of wine. They come for food. I still haven't really paid off the tasting and that was three weeks ago."

"How much did you spend?"

"Publicity, a couple of ads in the right places, I picked up the hotel for the guy from *Gourmet Week*, all the appetizers. The wines alone cost a grand. Wholesale."

"Shit!" Russell eased out the sails a bit so that he could pay less attention to the boat and more to his friend.

"How close are you to failing?"

Angelo shrugged and he didn't look up.

"Look. You need money, it's not an issue. You know that."

Angelo nodded. He'd never taken money from the Morgans, except for the college expenses Russell's dad had insisted on giving him. Not even pocket change from the Morgan millions.

"What's your hook?"

Angelo squinted up at him. "My hook?"

"Sure, every ad has a hook. Every business has one too. My hook as an ad photographer was, 'Highest quality, spare no expenses.' And I didn't. If I needed an elephant in the distant background, I hired the elephant, handlers, and whatever. My clients paid, man did they pay. And they got the best damn quality that could be achieved in return. What do you have?"

Angelo looked puzzled for a moment, shifted on the cockpit seat.

"Authentic Italian cooking."

"Tony's fast pizza claims that in every mall store."

Angelo's glare was intense enough that Russell decided to back off rather than push harder. He really didn't want to go for a swim in February. They'd reached the north tip of Vashon Island and he decided to take the western side. The wind was just right to take the narrower Colvos Passage south and then they'd have room to tack back and forth coming up the wider East Passage into the wind. It would be his longest sail yet, and it might give them some time to work something out.

"Other than your mother, you're the best damn cook. Right?"

"Damn straight." Angelo was still pissed about the mall store crack.

"And still you aren't a big success."

The pissed look eased back toward sad, such an unusual expression on his friend's face that it took Russell several moments to identify it.

"So we need to come up with a hook. Something to get you noticed—other than a thousand dollars of wine."

"Damn good Italian food should be enough."

"That's better."

"What is?"

"Damn Good Italian Food. It's a good pitch."

"My mother would slap us both and wash out our mouths with soap." But there was a shadow of a smile. Better.

"Your mother gonna slap you even worse if you give up."

Angelo nodded and for the first time on the trip, took some interest in the sailboat. He pulled a winch handle out of the pocket mounted inside the cockpit and cranked a couple of turns on the jib sheet. A little too far, but Russell decided that the better part of valor was to keep his mouth shut. Sailing with the wind was warmer and quieter, but also less demanding. If Angelo was still sulking when they rounded the south end of Vashon, his mother wasn't the only one who'd be slapping him.

"What part of Italy do you know better than any other?"

Angelo shrugged, "You know that. Liguria. Mama's from Liguria; Pop was from Tuscany. Mama and I went back every year. You came with me for the whole summer after senior year in high school. Why you ask such a *stupido* question?"

"I knew the answer. Wanted to make sure you did, dummy."

Angelo's glare finally had a bit of energy behind it.

"How much of your menu is Ligurian, even northern Italian?"

Angelo gazed off the side of the boat at the big ferry passing off the stern.

"Maybe half. Maybe less. Sicilian is a big draw. So is the far north, up in the Piedmont."

"So you've got to stock ingredients for everywhere from Sicily to Venice to Milan. And all those fancy wines you served to the Madonna wine lady?" About the right image with her perfect coif and perfect poise.

He blinked this time. "Why…uh…none. Only two were even Italian."

"*Mi amico.* I, the great Russell Morgan, have found your problem and your answer. The best damn Ligurian food in the Western Hemisphere. Okay, the title sucks. No one knows nothing from Liguria anyway. Best Damn Tuscan Food in the West. Still sucks. We'll work on that. First thing, you sell off or drink any wine not from northern Italy. Eat the out of region ingredients on your days off."

He pinched Angelo's cheek and pulled on it like a matron auntie.

"Then I make-a you an ad spread," he blew a kiss in the air off his fingertips, "that will-a make you mama proud."

"You? I thought you were done with that, man."

Russell had thought he was as well, but Angelo needed help. His kind of help.

"That's okay, I'm gonna make you pay, brother. Through the nose."

Angelo lost some of his happiness. "You know I don't have that kind of money."

"No. But you make the best damn pasta sauce on the planet."

Angelo perked up. "I do, don't I."

His punch thudded into Russell's shoulder hard enough to hurt. He'd let his friend get away with that…for now.

"YOU LEFT NEW YORK FOR THIS?" Melanie stood on the pitching dock barely wide enough to walk on and clutched tightly onto Russell's arm for stability.

"Yep! Isn't she beautiful?" Melanie was used to being called beautiful, and had made a career of it. But if it meant that she was similar to this boat, a shudder rippled up her spine, she'd give it up.

The boat, which was moving with a life of its own that had nothing to do with the dock, lay spread out before her. In the late afternoon light she could see the blue paint on the side was peeling. The white masts were doing the same. There was a great expanse of red material wrapped about the horizontal piece—the boom, Russell called it. It looked like a virulent growth that one should spray immediately with Lysol. A lot of it. Before burning it in the bathtub. The floor was all torn up, great strips of gray and black canvas had been peeled up to reveal rough wood that looked even worse.

"Want to come aboard?"

"No!" But Russell was already stepping up onto the boat and her tight grip on his arm dragged her along. The boat was so small that it rolled back and forth just from their weight. The only boat she'd ever been on was the New York Circle Line, a massive ferry filled with thousands of tourists. And that had been for a fashion shoot, so she hadn't paid much attention to anything but the photographer. That had been her second spread and first cover for *Elle*. Even for that she might not have climbed aboard this boat.

"See, over here I've been replacing the deck."

Deck, not floor. She repeated the word a couple of times to remind herself.

He had ducked under the virulent boom thing and was pointing at a place she couldn't see along the cabin. She took a breath and leaned over to see. If felt as if she was going to be flung headfirst into the inky depths between Russell's boat and the ragged old powerboat parked next door.

The deck looked better on this side. More like the parquet of her kitchen floor though not nearly as pretty.

"It's so," narrow, she wanted to shout. The water was right there.

"Nice." She checked Russell's face and he beamed like a newborn's father. The right answer. Perhaps it was okay to relax a little.

"Down below is still a mess." She hadn't really thought about the inside of the boat. The cabin was barely as tall as her knees. There was a tiny door that might do for the White Rabbit, but she was no Alice in Wonderland to go crawling on her hands and knees, especially not in her cashmere coat.

He opened the door and then slid a part of the roof back. A little ladder went much farther down than she thought. Down far enough to stand in. Down until, she glanced over the side and then back down the ladder, until she'd be standing underwater to her knees.

"Make sure to hold on as you come down." Russell clambered down into the cabin like he was born to it, facing forward as he dropped down the ladder holding onto nothing at all. She knew from experience that men lived in a world of their own. Russell had always been a cut above: more civilized, more polite, and usually more thoughtful.

At the moment, she could kill him.

But if she wanted him, she was going to have to do this patronizingly thoughtless male test. One of thousands they threw at women, but at least with Russell it didn't have a backing of cruelty behind it, just his own version of naïveté. And she did want him. Why else had she cancelled two shoots on short notice when he'd called with a Valentine's Day invitation to come to Seattle? Even at her level, those cancellations would have ripples across her career for months to come.

"Get a grip, girl." She took hold of either side of the doorway, thankful for her leather gloves. Though they didn't stop the cold, at least she didn't have to risk a splinter. There was no way to descend the ladder as Russell had. She turned and went down it backwards. Even one at a time, the steps were steep and difficult. The boat kept shifting, little jerks in unexpected directions. This is how clumsy people must feel. She hated it. Hated it so much she wanted to cry. She clamped down on that hard, careful not to bite her lip.

The floor was a surprise when she ran out of steps. Then she turned. There was just enough room to stand upright, but her instincts wanted to hunch down like a troll.

The ceiling was high in the middle, but sloped down to either side. The floor was a narrow strip running all the way to the front. The walls sloped outward from the floor. Seating was perched part way up the wall, making more use of the wider space. God, it was even smaller than her father's trailer—may the old bastard rot in hell.

"I'm going to put the galley here," he pointed to a couple cardboard boxes of groceries, an ice chest and a small camping stove.

"Pilot's berth there." A bed no bigger than a coffin, across the narrow walkway from the galley. How could you even climb into the thing? The deck was just two or three feet above the narrow bench.

"A settee that can be a dining table or collapse into a comfortable double bed right here across from this little woodstove." He continued forward oblivious of the fact that all this meant nothing to her. Whatever he was calling a settee was now a card table and two folding chairs. And how that became a bed for two was beyond her and a place she'd certainly never be found.

A section of the flooring was pulled up and she half expected to see the ocean beneath it. Instead, about six inches down, was concrete and, she swallowed hard, a wash of blackish water running back and forth with each motion of the boat.

A loud buzz below her right foot made her jump. There were splashing noises and slowly the skin of water disappeared. The buzzing stopped with a sigh and a gurgle.

"That's just the bilge pump."

The smell of fresh-cut wood and paint added to the queasiness in her stomach. The bilge pump, she did her best to catalog all of the strange words he kept using. Booms and tillers and hulls. Even something called a fang or a vang that he wanted to replace for reasons she'd never understand.

Again she focused on the curve of the hull. It had looked wider from outside. She peeked out one of the round windows and could just see the water. The floor was deeper than she'd thought, she was in the ocean up to her waist.

The "head" was next on the tour.

She blinked twice but it didn't go away. A porcelain toilet. With handles and levers that would make a dentist chair look safe. Sitting right there in the open on the floor. It was a good thing that he'd promised her a hotel room or she'd be on the red-eye back to New York.

He waved at a blank section of hull, "Books, maybe a bench seat that could double as a bunk. Don't really know yet."

The last of the tour was the forward stateroom. A fancy name for a double bed jammed into the pointy end of the boat. He was dreaming if he thought they were going to make love there. The place wasn't as cold as a meat locker, by maybe five degrees but not by ten. She hadn't roughed it since she and her mother had escaped the trailer park and she wasn't about to start again now.

Tools were piled everywhere. Cans of paint and who knew what. They smelled—it all smelled—nasty.

He was waiting for her to join him at the far end.

Deep breath. Deep breath.

He was so damn handsome. And he'd never looked better. Standing with his legs spread like a sea pirate standing on his treasure. The work on the boat had flattened his stomach even more and his arms had a power that was stronger, safer than she'd imagined possible when they'd hugged at the airport.

Keeping her attention on his eyes, and where the hole in the floor was, she headed in his direction. When the boat shifted, she reached up and a small rail was in just the right place to grab. She could do this.

She was halfway there when something shot between her legs. She gasped and hung on to the too thin rail with both hands.

Russell casually reached down with one hand and scooped up...a kitten. A black kitten with shaggy hair and outrageously long whiskers.

"This is Nutcase. She has absolutely no fear. She sticks her little nose in the strangest of places. One day she fiberglassed her tail and it took me an hour to trim it off because she wouldn't hold still." It climbed up his chest to perch on his shoulder.

"You can see where it hasn't grown back yet." He pulled the long tail from around his throat and one side was indeed shaved.

A cat.

When she was just starting out, her career was almost aborted by a cat. Right before a shoot when she was ten, she'd tried to pet the photographer's cat. It had swiped her with its claws and left a long red scratch down the side of her finger. They had to get another hand model.

Her mother had been furious.

Melanie didn't sleep for four days as she watched it to make sure it healed. Skipped school and rubbed in salves and moisturizers to make sure there was no unsightly puckering. Finally wept herself to sleep with relief when she could no longer find exactly where it had been. She turned down every shoot with a cat since then.

There was no way she was going to pet Russell's cat.

"She's really quite sweet. She likes being scritched under the chin like this." He demonstrated and Nutcase purred loudly.

How badly did she want this? How badly did she want him? She'd never told him the cat story. Never told anyone that she could still feel the outline of her mother's slap on her face that had shone as livid a red as the cat's mark for days—the mark that still burned though her mother was long dead.

"She won't hurt you."

How many tests did she have to pass? Clearly there would always be another. But she hadn't reached her limit yet. She'd manage this one.

Melanie extended her finger until the cat had to lean forward to sniff the black leather. After a careful inspection, its pink and black nose wiggling like a tiny bumblebee, another of her fears, the cat leaned even farther out and rubbed its chin along her finger. Russell was right. She was gentle.

But there was no way she was taking off her gloves.

"No, it cannot be." Jo Thompson insisted in her best lawyer voice.

Before Cassidy could add her own protest, Perrin continued on, excitement rippling off her in high-energy waves.

"Uh-huh! Way! Could I make something like this up? Well, I could, I guess, if I wanted to but I'm not." Perrin spoke loudly enough that half-a-dozen heads turned in their direction despite the noise level in Cutters.

The lounge was hopping and it was barely six o'clock. Another hour and it would really be rolling. The décor was simple and modern in a plush-chairs-around-knee-high-glass-tables motif. The air smelled of exquisite seafood being served in the restaurant beyond the tinted glass wall. The wrap-around windows revealed the tail end of an awesome winter sunset over Puget Sound.

Cassidy had learned from long practice that it wasn't worth the effort to quiet her friend. Perrin didn't mind being shushed, but ten seconds later she'd be bound to forget and her volume would climb once again.

Everything about Perrin Williams was loud. She'd dyed her hair half chrome-blue and half the black of India ink. And not side-to-side or front-to-back, but in diagonal stripes three inches wide spiraling down from the high part. The stripes followed the line of the sloping haircut that started well down her bare left shoulder and rose shorter and shorter to the line of her jaw on the right. The clothes following the line of the hair from bare shoulder to a high collar on the other side. It was quite striking once you got past the strangeness of it.

Cassidy hoped that maybe it was wig, but it was always hard to tell with Perrin because she did her fashion statements so perfectly.

Her clothes matched the shocking blue and her accessories the black. Fashion was her life, her shop was as much gallery as boutique, but there was a streak in her that had never left sixteen behind. She giggled merrily at the effect of her news.

"Pamela and Janice? But I thought they each had long-term boyfriends."

Perrin nodded and took a gulp of her Cosmo.

"I kinda set them up, though I didn't know at the time I was setting them up, I just kinda did it. Separately I sold them those cute blouses. The ones that were mirror images of each other. You know the ones. Anyway, I showed them to you the last time you were in the shop. The green velour with blue silk sleeves and the other blue velour with the green silk sleeves. Isn't there a song about that somewhere?"

Jo nodded and Cassidy followed suit even though she didn't remember the blouses or the song. They'd both learned long ago to never stop Perrin in the middle of a story or she'd sidetrack and you'd never get the ending.

"Well, two best friends dating two guys who were also best friends. You know, the mirror twins on a double date. Totally cute and sure to make the guys' eyes pop. That's what I thought. How was I supposed to know they'd decide they were a set and they'd take a trip down the other side of the street? They came in a couple days later to buy the matching pantsuits."

Cassidy could remember those. Everything switched, which side of the jacket buttoned over, which lapel had been cut on a different slant, which breast had the pocket kerchief, opposite swirls of the slanted pinstripe. She could picture Pamela and Janice, the Swedish-pale and the Jamaican-dark, both very tall, both very curved, an unlikely pair. They probably looked amazing together.

Jo was laughing and Cassidy joined in just a moment late, a moment off beat, but neither of the others noticed. No one else in the lounge noticed—neither the fashionable women nor any of the busi-ness-suited men. Thankfully most of her little social ineptitudes were invisible; she'd gotten good enough to hide them even from her closest friends.

"How about you, Jo? What adventures in the wondrous world of law? Huh? Huh? Come on, something juicy," Perrin begged like a puppy dog eager for a new toy. "Don't let Perrin be the only one with good gossip. I hate that I always have the best gossip."

She cocked her head sideways and her hair swirled back and forth in a hypnotic spiral.

"No, actually, I don't mind. I kinda like knowing more than everyone about everything. So give me some juicy law stuff to add to my collection."

Jo brushed back the long, black hair that her half Alaskan-native heritage had made as naturally dark as Perrin's dyed locks. That half-heritage had also granted her a scholarship from the state. Law under-grad followed by corporate law grad.

Her heritage had also given her a broad face that always looked as if it had a nice tan, and round brown eyes that welcomed you in. She brushed some imaginary dust off the navy blue pantsuit that made her look terribly professional and immensely sexy at the same time. There wasn't a male judge who didn't smile when she entered their court-room; nor an opposition lawyer who didn't groan.

"I made partner, does that count?"

Perrin screamed loudly enough to turn every head in the place and then raised her Cosmo in a toast. Cassidy's Merlot and Jo's Irish Coffee followed.

"That's great! Why didn't you tell us sooner?" Cassidy sipped her wine, they really needed a better house red than Ste. Michelle. Nice enough at the price, but limited. Overly fruity.

She flagged a passing pretty-boy waiter, "Could we have three flutes and a bottle of Moet and Chandon? The Brut Imperial '99 if you have it."

He scribbled a note and left without saying a word. Clearly he had no idea what it was.

"Ooo, Cassie's ordering. This should be good." Perrin knocked back her Cosmo and then rubbed her hands together in excitement.

Jo set aside her Irish Coffee and nibbled on one of the crackers. Being Cassidy's roommate in college for four years had taught her about clearing her palate. Perrin had been the wild girl across the hall who had taken Jo and Cassidy under her wing to make sure they didn't stay too focused through all those years together. They hadn't.

"I found out just a few hours ago."

"Tell us. Tell us." Perrin's hair swung about as she bounced in her seat.

The bottle arrived and he presented the label. She nodded, exactly right.

The sommelier was going to be pissed when he found out that a hundred-dollar bottle of champagne—at retail—had been opened from his collection without his being present. Opened as casually as a ten-dollar Cook's.

He uncorked it well, with a restrained pop beneath his cupped hand. He just dropped the cork on the table and she picked it up for a sniff. Warm and bright with just the hint of wood she remembered. Never much in a champagne cork, but she liked them for that.

Three baseless flutes that looked like picked flowers were resting at a tilt in a tall, curved vase. Before she could stop him, he began pouring. The flutes were colored, making it impossible to see the wine's hue. Then she noticed Jo and Perrin's reactions to the glasses. They were oo'ing and ah'ing about how much they looked like flowers.

She let it go.

Perrin laughed after she sipped, "It tickles."

Jo took her taste and blinked as if she'd just woken up.

"Cassidy, that's wonderful. Thank you."

She took a sip herself. The wine effervesced strongly, releasing its flavors. Pear and citrus. Balanced. She couldn't detect any real shift. She swallowed…almond. She waited for the hint of toast, but the aroma of garlic bread and steamed clam appetizers arriving at their table made her miss it.

"You earned it. So, how did it happen?"

"You are aware that I recently beat that Class Action suit against the Alaskan fisheries? The partners called me in, all three of them so serious." Jo drew her face down into a frown. " 'Well, Ms. Thompson. We, with our most recent victory in Alaska, are now the most sought after corporate law firm in the Pacific Northwest. So, we're going to have to make a change.' He pulled a blank piece of letterhead out of his portfolio and pushed it across the table toward me."

Jo brushed her hair back over her shoulders.

"First of all it was not their win, it was mine. And second, if they thought I was going to write my own letter of resignation, they could go…"

"Fuck themselves!" Perrin filled in. Gave her a thumbs up. "You go, girl!"

Jo tipped her flute in Perrin's direction, "Exactly my thoughts, though I was preparing to express them differently. Then I looked at the letterhead. You look at something like that a hundred times a day and it just disappears. But there was a change. It didn't take me long to discover the alteration. My name had been added to the letterhead."

"Cool!"

"To our Jo." Cassidy raised her glass and clicked it with the other two. They all knocked it back and she refilled their flutes. Leave it to Jo to make partner two years ahead of any normal schedule.

"It gets better."

"Better?" The second flute had lost a bit of the effervescence but none of the brightness. This time she caught the toast in the smooth finish.

"By the time I left the boardroom, my name was gold-leafed onto a corner-office door and everything moved in for me. When I left this afternoon, parked right where my old Toyota should be, sat one of those new BMW roadsters I've been lusting after. The one I showed you in that ad. Right down to the red rose on the front seat."

Cassidy remembered the ad, it wasn't one that you could miss. Something about it leapt out and grabbed you by the…well, clearly she'd had too much to drink already.

"I get first ride," Perrin giggled and topped off all of their glasses. "Let's get smashed tonight. Tomorrow you can take me for a drive."

"I'll take seconds…I guess." Long time since she'd done that. Funny thing about being back with them. It was almost like being in college. Perrin always so loud and wild, attracting all the worst boyfriends of course. Which were the ones Perrin always fell for: wild flings, roaring breakups, and a heart that was permanently broken…until the next one. She remained that way still.

But Perrin also attracted the best, yet she never kept those. Cassidy had learned to wait for the ones who recovered quickly from Perrin's dazzle. Some of them had been quite interesting and she'd never have had a chance at them if they hadn't flocked first to her friend's light.

Jo dated the same guy for all four years of college. Where Perrin was long and elegant, Jo was voluptuous and sure of herself in a way that an unsure, sixteen-year-old freshman Cassidy had done her best to copy. Jo so quiet and studious, college valedictorian, *summa cum laude*. Cassidy had always been second, finishing as the salutatorian.

Cassidy had some good boyfriends, but none who were four years steady nor even near worth that. She'd forgotten all that, right until this moment.

She'd had enough seconds to last her a lifetime. That was one of the few good things about having left New York. There, she'd been relegated to the second tier of reviewers as well. She was so done with that, too.

She'd been casually watching the people parade through the door when one caught her full attention. A tall blond of such perfection that she looked right out of a magazine. The noise in the bar dropped by a third as every man, as if on some hidden cue, turned to watch her walk down the side of the lounge toward the restaurant.

Had her companion been any less striking, he would have been invisible in her presence. He wasn't all that handsome. Okay, she had to admit to herself, not as handsome as Jack James for example, but he made up for it in a breadth of shoulder, a confidence of motion, and an easy smile making him impossible to ignore.

Cassidy recognized him from somewhere. A *nouveau riche* software guy on the news or some such.

Perrin stuck her pinkies in her mouth and let out a wolf whistle. The bar broke into self-conscious laughter. The girl smiled and moved past the tinted glass partition. The man faced their table directly for a moment.

A jolt of recognition pounded against her champagne-befuddled memory.

Where had she seen him?

Recently.

Close, very close.

It was the eyes; she remembered his nice eyes. Okay, screw that. She remembered his unbelievably amazing eyes.

Jo tapped her on the shoulder. "Cassidy. Earth to Cassidy."

"Um, yeah?" He was gone and she sipped her champagne but didn't notice anything except that it was wet in her suddenly dry throat.

" 'Yeah,' she says. Good. Articulate." Jo waved her flute toward the entrance. "Didn't know you had a penchant for women."

"I don't. What woman?"

"Miss Playboy centerfold. Miss Cover of *Vogue, Elle,* and practically every other magazine out there."

"Oh."

"Oh?"

"I was noticing her companion."

Perrin craned her neck around but they were out of sight. "Boy or girl?"

"Boy. Man." Definitely man.

Perrin looked again. "I missed him. I don't usually miss the guys."

"Then why did you whistle?"

"Every guy here wanted to whistle at the girl but was too inhibited. So I did it for them. It's just the kinda helpful person I am."

RUSSELL HAD ORDERED dinner and the first hors d'oeuvre had arrived, seared bay scallops with a brandy glaze, before he noticed that Melanie was unusually quiet. When had she changed? She'd been a little tentative on his boat, but she'd opened up to Nutcase. Silly pest did have its uses.

When they'd arrived at the restaurant, she gone quiet. He hadn't planned to make quite such an entrance.

"You okay, Melanie? You want to get somewhere else where they don't whistle at you?"

She sipped her diet Coke and shrugged. "I get that everywhere."

"Huh. Guess you would."

"Though that's the first time it was by a woman punker."

"Punker?" Russell hadn't noticed a punker.

"Sitting at that table, three dykes all together, all so buddy-buddy."

All he'd noticed was that wine reviewer Angelo was so hyped up on. Now that Melanie mentioned it, there were two other women at the table. He could see them as clearly as a photograph in his mind's-eye. Not punk and he doubted the dyke remark. They weren't dressed for each other, they were dressed to be looked at: all three very high-end, very city. Her companions were really attractive, but neither matched the russet-haired reviewer once again in her tight black turtleneck and designer jacket. The woman had a clear sense of what looked good on her.

He brought his attention back to Melanie.

"Well, I guess I'm just not used to it is all."

"That's because you're where you don't belong. Back in our crowd they know me. They knew you. Beauty isn't as big a deal there as it is out here in the sticks. Don't you miss it?"

He dipped another scallop in the mango-pineapple sauce and popped it into his mouth. Other than Angelo's, this was rapidly becoming one of his favorite places to eat. He didn't usually face the Friday night crowd; late Wednesday lunches were more his speed. Sometimes there were less than a dozen diners and those were business people. He always brought a good book, but spent most of the time watching the amazing view, the ever-busy Seattle waterfront bustling with ferries and freighters and sailboats, and the shifting light on the permanent snowfields atop the Olympic Mountains. All that was lost now in the winter evening's darkness.

"No. I'm sorry, Melanie. I really don't miss the life. I miss you." Far more than he'd expected. Flying her out for Valentine's Day was about more than the great sex they'd have tonight at the Sorrento. It was more than that. But he hadn't given much thought to what more.

"I don't miss the city or the studio at all." That last was a surprise. He stabbed the last scallop while he thought about it. He really didn't miss it.

The waiter showed up and slid a petite filet mignon in front of Melanie and a platter with a matching filet and a large Australian lobster tail before him. He put his nose down to the plate and inhaled the heady mix of beef and seafood. The almond-flecked butter tickled his nose and the dollop of horseradish nearly made him sneeze it was so fresh.

"And I certainly don't miss the food." He cut into the steak. "You'll see, Melanie. I've got Dave and Betsy all lined up to take us out on a daysail tomorrow afternoon. Their boat is in a lot better shape than mine. You'll like it. Tomorrow night we'll dine at the top of the Space Needle and have a nightcap at the Alexis, very old world, very traditional. Sunday I've got a pilot to fly us around Rainier and St. Helens. They're amazing from the air. I'm thinking of taking lessons."

He'd intended to let the itinerary be a surprise as they went, but she looked so down that he'd spilled the beans. She seemed to perk up a bit and take a bite of her steak.

Wait until she saw the city from the rooftop, outdoor hot tub perched outside the penthouse at the Sorrento with its awesome night view of the city.

BY THE TIME they'd finished dissecting Jo's promotion, the lawsuit that had done it for her, and who she was going to tackle next, they'd worked their way through most of the bottle of champagne, the clams, a Dungeness Crab Seafood Cocktail, some Coconut Tiger Prawns, and a mountainous pile of onion rings that none of their waistlines would appreciate in the morning.

Cassidy decided to just splurge and took a big piece of the focaccia bread and dipped it in the olive oil and garlic.

"What 'bout you, Cassidy? Tell us the wonders of your week." Jo's voice had slipped out of power lawyer, back into Vassar casual. It took a lot of wine to do that.

"Yeah, what 'bout you? Something more exciting than the man with two first names, puh-lease. He is just such a total drip." Perrin mocked Jo's slip but everyone was too tipsy to care.

Jack James, the man with two first names. He was handsome, polite, sometimes lover, and a useless jerk.

"Seconds."

"What's that?"

"Sick of 'em."

"She's shhick of 'em." Perrin was now mocking her.

Her mind wasn't connecting the bits and pieces together. But somewhere or other the thought did have sense of purpose even if she was too drunk to see it.

"No more sad second-raters for this girl."

Jo grew quiet. One very drunken night in their dorm room, Cassidy had confessed to how much she hated being second to both of them. Perrin with all her flash and confidence, Jo with her perfect grades and steady boyfriend.

"No more thankless thirds either, huh?" Perrin purred pleasantly.

Cassidy started to giggle at the alliteration in her head. Perrin purring pleasantly through a pursed pucker.

"Thankfully through with the, uh, thoughtless thirds," Cassidy acknowledged.

Jo cracked a smile but suppressed it quickly, but not before Cassidy caught her.

"And those sad, sad sloppy seconds." Perrin started nodding, then kept doing so as if she'd forgotten she'd started. Her hair swooshed back and forth in a mesmerizing pattern of diagonal stripes.

It sounded even worse put that way. Cassidy glanced at Jo, but she shook her head ever so slightly. She'd never told her about Cassidy's complaints, Perrin was just on a roll.

"And those fucking fourths. Even I don't want those," Perrin continued.

"I'm done with them all," Cassidy declared. "I'm better than that."

Perrin jutted out her chin, "Damn straight, girlfriend. So what now? Fancy frolicsome firsts?"

"Damn straight!" she shot back. "Nothing but the best for Cassidy Knowles from now on."

Jo raised her flute, and Perrin her third Cosmo.

"To Cassidy's fun firsts."

"To Cassidy." Jo nodded to her so she'd know that Jo had meant to end it there.

Perrin slowly scanned about the room, then abruptly turned and leaned in so close that Cassidy could smell the Triple Sec, lime, and cranberry on her breath.

"So, what's the news? What are we drinking to again?" Her eyes were squinted as she tried to remember.

"No sad seconds," Jo reminded her quietly.

"That's not news. That's just about fucking time. I want the news."

Cassidy considered as well as the champagne would allow her. News. News. News. There must be something. She still hadn't told them about the lighthouses. But she didn't want to, not yet anyway. It was still too close to losing her father.

What was the topic?

No settling any more—that was it.

"I broke it off with Mr. Jack James."

"Thank God above and Satan below," Perrin clapped her hands together and looked to the ceiling. "He was such a waste of your time."

Jo was waiting. Waiting and watching.

"When?" Jo's soft question barely penetrated Cassidy's whirling thoughts.

It took her three tries to finally slip her flute back into the vase. It kept moving around the table.

"Um," she laughed and it partly came out as a sob. She covered her face with her hands for a moment feeling the burning flush on her cheeks. A quick wipe at her eyes and she sat up straight, slapped her hands down on her thighs.

"About a dozen seconds ago." That laughing sob came out again. She tried to refill the flute and her hands were so unsteady she ended up pouring the champagne into the vase instead. She set the bottle down hard enough that for a moment she was afraid she'd broken the glass table.

Jo handed her own flute over and Cassidy knocked it back. The bubbles burning the back of her throat.

"Why now?"

"What's today?" She waved her hand at them, at the restaurant.

"The fourteenth," Jo blinked hard to focus on her watch. "Still."

"Valentine's Day," Perrin offered.

"Right. And where is the man with two first names? Where is Jack James?"

"Where?" Perrin asked caught up in the question.

"I don't know. But he certainly isn't here. Probably doesn't know what day it is. Handsome, pleasant, and totally lost in his own world."

"Bor-ring!" Perrin declared around a hiccup. She tucked the long side of her hair behind one ear. She took one of Cassidy's hands and held it tightly. In that instant, the flashy designer was gone and one of her best friends sat beside her.

"Cass. He was never even a flatu-, 'scuse me, flatulent fifth. You are so much better than hi-im." That hiccup launched her hair from behind her ear and over half her face again.

Cassidy nodded. She knew she was better. She just didn't feel that way whenever she was with him. She always felt…grateful. Whether it was his doing or hers, it didn't matter; it was too sad for words.

Tears started to flow and she couldn't stop them. It wasn't sadness, not for casting off the man with two first names. A bit of it was for thinking so little of herself in the first place. A big chunk of it was plain and simple relief.

"I am so done with sec-onds." Now she had the hiccups.

Perrin answered with a another hic-nod-hair swirl.

Jo burst out laughing. A rare event in itself.

And totally infectious.

They leaned together as the tears, laughter, and hiccups flowed between them.

"SEE." Melanie waved a negligent flick of her fingers toward the lounge as they left the restaurant.

Russell glanced over the heads of the dozens of little groups in the lounge. One of the top "meat markets" in town. The best place to meet the other fast-rising singles of Seattle's finest, Cutters' bar, if he'd cared for such things. Once he had, which was weird.

Then he spotted them and his mind froze the scenario. The perfect image. The image that passed by when the camera had missed the moment. The image that could never be recreated no matter what was done in the studio.

Angelo's wine reviewer, still perfectly put together, not a hair astray, dressed all in black as before, laughing or maybe crying on her friend's bare shoulder. Blue and black, matching and contrasting. The third, serious, reserved, her clothes as light as her hair dark. A single arm extended forward and hand resting palm-down between the shoulder blades of her grieving friend.

Three women. They were so close. Clearly they knew each other the way new friends couldn't and the way lovers rarely did.

"Traveled Road...partway." That's what he'd call the shot if he had it. Or perhaps that carefully reserved and rarely bequeathed "Untitled" for when no mere title could possibly add more.

It was easy to picture them together in a couple of decades: hair gray, surface beauty faded, and all three still close. Still radiant.

LIME KILN LIGHTHOUSE

San Juan Island
First lit: 1914
Automated: 1962
48.5159 -123.1524

The last major lighthouse established in Washington State, it faces Canada and still watches over the entrance to Haro Strait. It was also the last to receive electricity, not until after WWII.

It is one of the best known lighthouses in the state, known far and wide as a whale observatory. Pods of orcas and gray whales frequently pass close in front of the lighthouse's craggy doorstep.

MARCH 1

"*It sounds like someone* is screaming and laughing at the same time."

The technician, who wore his own set of headphones, nodded. "J-pod. That's their dialect, Ms. Knowles."

"Cassidy. What's J-pod and they have dialects?" The two of them sat shoulder-to-shoulder in the first floor of the Lime Kiln lighthouse. Through the narrow window she could see the Georgia Straits. No whales anywhere in sight.

"The J-pod is one of our local groups of orcas. They wander up and down Puget Sound nattering away like a bunch of old-timers. And then," he paused as a particularly quick set of chirps rattled through her headphones.

"There, hear that? That's a group of youngsters. Sound like they're maybe a mile offshore. The main pod is two or three miles out."

"This is incredible." She was listening to passing whales swimming somewhere out of sight below the surface.

Jeff was typing madly on his laptop.

"What are you doing there?"

"Just recording the time of passage and how many voices I hear, fourteen so far."

She inspected him more carefully. Mid-twenties, nice face, at least what she could see above the heavy beard, with his brown hair back in a ponytail. He sat in front of a console with switches and plug-ins, though clearly most of it occurred in the laptop where wiggling lines mimicked the sound in a series of waves too fast to follow.

"We can only hear about a third of what they say. Most of the rest is ultrasonic to our hearing."

"Ultrasonic, like the planes?" Whale-sized sonic booms?

"That's supersonic. 'Ultra' means too high for us to hear. We had to develop special microphones to hear their full vocal range. See, our hearing stops here," he pointed at a line near the lower part of the wiggles on the screen. Even as he did so, one of the lines shot well above his finger and she didn't hear a thing on the headphones except a creepy sensation of fingernails running up her spine.

"What are they saying?"

He turned to face her, his neutral brown eyes wrinkled with a bit of a smile.

"Not a clue, yet. We think a lot of the high stuff is echo-location so they can find food and one another. Same things bats do. But what they chat about all day is a complete mystery. Their vocabulary is huge whatever it is. Not just squeaks and squawks. There are patterns, thousands of them as far as we can tell. Perhaps a fully evolved and complex language."

Jeff's specialty was as narrow as hers, and as highly trained: nuance, common themes, major notes, and minor notes. Hers were color and smell and taste, and his was sound, but they had far more in common that she'd have guessed.

They sat in companionable silence as the whales sang to each other. She tried to pick them apart. Did one always have a deep, dropping pattern? Heee-whaaa. What would it be like to learn more about another species? To study something with such passion?

Well, she *had* actually; since birth she'd been exposed to the details of wine and food.

Of course her passion didn't require sitting in a concrete lighthouse with peeling white paint.

Maybe Jeff's passion wasn't so charming once she thought about it. The concrete room certainly wasn't very warm despite the heater under the desk. She couldn't smell the ocean just a dozen feet away. Instead it smelled of mold and decaying paint. It smelled of heated metal and sounded of the squeaky fan that was barely keeping her legs above freezing.

Out the slender window, an impossible vision appeared; not a whale breeching nor a row of tall fins skimming the water.

It was a blue sailboat with maroon sails. The same number of sails as the two pictures on her wall. One big one in front of the mast and reaching all the way to the deck. The other one, from the mast back until it reached past where the captain stood in the back. It hung so low that it looked as if it might hit him when it swung.

"Thanks, Jeff." She dropped the headphones and rushed out as he stammered a call after her. She ran over the rocks, digging for her camera in her leather backpack. She managed the picture barely in time before he sailed out of the frame with the lighthouse.

She took another photo just of the boat in case the first one didn't come out.

He must have the same calendar, because this was past coincidence. They'd met three months in a row. Too bad there was no way to signal him. It would be a good laugh to meet in a bar somewhere, maybe see if he had a set of letters too.

No, that would be too weird. Two lost people having their lives shaped by a calendar. She raised a hand in salute, but he was facing away, looking forward. He'd have no possible way of knowing why she was waving. It wasn't as if she wore a huge red sail.

This is what her father had told her. In his letter he'd confirmed that she wasn't unique. She tucked a hand into the pocket of her Kors coat and held the letter as she moved back to the cliff edge beside the lighthouse and looked out at the shining water. In the distance, Vancouver Island lay across the horizon, where she could see some tiny shapes at the limit of visibility, the buildings of the city of Victoria.

Farther south, the Olympic Mountains were still white. She could smell the snow and the sea salt. She could imagine the light, cold breeze starting as a whisper on the distant polar seas, a wave splash pushing the air ahead. The small swirl building along the Aleutians and sweeping down the coast. Threading among the Canadian Gulf Islands on its way to here, the wind's first contact with the continental U.S. And she was the first to breathe it, to take in the salt spray thrown into the air three thousand miles away.

I had no direction. I was out of the Vietnam War, out of the army, and unexpectedly still alive.

Cassidy could hear her dad's voice from the letter, soft and warm on the cold breeze. Not rough with throat cancer. She heard his voice from when she was a teenager, a sound she could wrap safely around herself when she grew scared. She didn't turn to him, didn't want to break the illusion.

Your mama never made it to grad school, I always felt bad about that. After a month we were living together. After six months she'd turned our vineyard into a business, not a big one, but a business. It was the real birth of the Napa Valley and there we were on the ground floor.

"Napa Valley? I certainly didn't grow up in the Napa Valley."

The big surprise came along, you. So we had a wedding in the fields right before the harvest.

September wedding in the vineyards, it must have been beautiful. He'd never told her they'd gotten married because Mama was pregnant. She'd always assumed it was the other way round. Not that it bothered her much.

Not much of a reception. I spent our wedding night out in the fields watching for an early frost. A real freak cold snap slid down from Canada and we weren't big enough to survive the loss of even a single crop. We dodged that one, but then we were into the harvest. Never did have a honeymoon. Too much work to do.

But it didn't matter. Your mama and I were just plain right for each other. From that very first moment when she'd tumbled out of that VW van. Her hair the same dark red as grape leaves in autumn.

You'll find the right man, Ice Sweet.

That was a laugh. She was thirty now and the "right man" was a myth. She did require at least "compatible" though, and Jack James hadn't even been that.

I know you don't believe me, but you will. Until then, don't worry if it doesn't make sense. My life never did.

Love you, Ice Sweet.

"Love you, Daddy."

––––––––

"Damn you, Angelo."

His friend didn't answer. Probably because he wasn't there, but that was a lousy excuse.

"Too busy redesigning your damn restaurant to take four days off to go sailing." Russell grabbed for the jib sheet as he came about, but missed it. And he hadn't tied a knot in the bitter end. The line shot out of the cockpit, nearly snagged Nutcase as it whipped past the cat, making her jump straight up like a furry fireworks, ran out the pulley block, and was over the side trailing in the water.

He brought the boat up into the wind, forcing the sail back over the boat. Then he sprinted forward, snagged the line dripping with freezing water, and ran back for the cockpit letting the rope slip through his fingers. He added a cold rope burn to his list of complaints against Angelo.

The boat fell off the wind again before he could run the line through the block. He whipped a couple turns around the winch and let it draw all wrong while he got control of the tiller again.

The line burned in his sore hand as he got the boat moving again. Once he had some speed up, he brought her into the wind again to take the pressure off the line. This time he got it through the block and around the winch. With the tiller between his knees, he tied a quick figure-eight knot in the end of the line so it couldn't go overboard again. He wouldn't make that mistake again.

He was almost back to the lighthouse by the time he had it under control.

He'd gone out twice now with Angelo along just for the ride while he practiced single-handing the big boat. Angelo had kept up a running commentary that amused himself no end as Russell scrambled about the boat. But he'd done it.

Then he'd set off alone for the Lime Kiln lighthouse on San Juan Island. On the first morning out, he'd thought it was fun plunging through the steep wake of a big tanker. The *Lady* had driven her bow deep into the third wave and water had come running down the deck and sluiced out the scuppers he'd only cut-in a week before. So sweet.

It wasn't until he'd anchored and tried to bunk down last night that he'd discovered his mistake. He hadn't latched the forehatch. The hinged wood must have floated up when the wave came aboard and a two-foot square chunk of wave had poured into the center of the stateroom bed. Everything was sopping. He'd now spent two very uncomfortable nights trying to sleep on the main cabin floor underneath a spare sail. One foot kept slipping through the missing floorboard and thudding down onto the concrete bilge.

Nutcase had curled up on his chest and been perfectly content to snore her way through the night with occasional flails of her tail across his nose during particularly good dreams.

She also hadn't minded Russell's mistake of anchoring that first night right next to a bell buoy. Each tiny swell that ran under the boat made every line slap against the mast with a sharp clack. And then it would reach the buoy and a piercing ring would echo through the boat. Nutcase had snored on.

It was a good thing Melanie wasn't along, roughing it on the floor wouldn't have made her happy.

As a matter of fact, he wasn't sure what would. She'd liked the penthouse well enough, and the sex had been pretty spectacular. She'd appeared to enjoy the sail with Dave and Betsy, even the scenic plane flight. The pilot had let him take the controls for a few minutes, he definitely had to learn to fly someday. Such a feeling of freedom. It didn't have the peace of sailing before the world's winds, but it was a close second.

Russell managed to jibe the boat without losing any lines overboard and ran out from shore a ways before turning back to find a good angle for his photo of the lighthouse.

All through Valentine's Day weekend he'd thought everything was great...right until he'd found Melanie on their last morning together. She was sitting on the shower's floor crying. He'd almost closed the door quietly and let her be, but there was too much between them for that.

Instead, he climbed in beside her and sat down with his back on the opposite wall. She tried to push him out, but he wasn't going to leave that easily. She kept her arms wrapped tightly over her breasts. He reached out to stroke her wet hair, but she slapped his hand aside.

"You don't get it, do you?" Her voice was sharp with accusation.

Despite the steam and pounding hot water, he could see the running tears and snot. He tried to think of what he'd missed. They'd had fine meals, tickets to the ballet, and a some good fun.

"You really don't," she was shaking her head. She looked up into the pounding spray for a moment as if seeking god. One of those perfect hands reached out and she stroked her thumb down his cheek. He turned his head to place a kiss in her palm, but she pulled back before he could.

She sat up straighter.

"You really don't. Oh, Russell." Her soft accent gone, replaced by the flat slap of New York. She wiped at her eyes, her gray eyes filled with infinite sadness.

"I'm sorry for me, but I'm more sorry for you." She rose from the floor, rinsed her face for a moment under the hot spray and stepped from the shower. He'd watched her through the glass door. Sat under the spray while she dried off that gorgeous body. Applied moisturizers. Baby powder. Added makeup. Dried her hair in a roar of blow dryer that didn't penetrate the shower's patter but sent forth long billows of blond.

Even now, two weeks later, he could feel the power of her parting kiss at the airport. She pressed her body to his so that every curve fit —her hold so tight it almost knocked the breath from his body.

Then she was gone, a head of blond sunlight sailing through the crowds at security. Never once turning to see if he was still watching.

He blinked and turned the boat sharply. If he didn't pay more attention, he'd play moth to the lighthouse and ram himself right up on her rocks. Once he had his heading settled, he grabbed his camera and snapped a few quick shots off the stern.

A loud splash sounded beside the boat, and he spun about looking for Nutcase. The cat stood with its nose pressed against the safety netting he'd added to the lifelines, staring down into the water off the starboard side. As he leaned over to follow her gaze, a massive wall of black-and-white whale shot out of the water then splashed down beside him. He shouted in surprise as the orca crashed back into the water less than twenty feet away.

A wave of spray showered onto the boat. Nutcase howled and scrambled below, her coat dripping with seawater.

Russell caught half a dozen photos of the orca before it sounded and disappeared.

Damn!

Angelo was going to be so jealous.

Excellent!

RUSSELL SHOOK any errant sawdust off the paper towel and wrapped it around his sandwich. He grabbed a beer from the cooler and a box of crackers. He set his lunch on the table he'd just finished making. Once more he lifted the top to admire the chart drawer built right into the tabletop. Room for four around the settee or drop the table down level with the benches and it could sleep two. Especially if they were feeling cuddly.

He pulled out his laptop and set it beside his dinner just as Nutcase crawled out from behind a pile of books. He plugged in a mouse and booted the machine while she ambled over to check out his roast beef sandwich. When he flapped a hand at her, she just moved to the other side of his beer and plopped her butt down on the table. Then she started on the impossible task of bringing order to her fur.

Russell took a bite of the sandwich and shoved a Springsteen CD into the car stereo mounted in its little cubby. He flicked a switch to turn off the speakers in the cockpit so that he didn't disturb anyone else in the marina.

Once the laptop was up, he wiped the mustard from his fingers, and plugged in the chip from his camera. It started transferring the pictures automatically. Almost three hundred. Shit! He hadn't done this in a while.

While the copy bar chugged along, he started sorting them out. Lighthouses. Boat remodel. Nutcase. Angelo. More Nutcase. Melanie. Flying. Melanie.

Then one stopped him. It was a shot of just Melanie's face—her watching him as she lounged in the rooftop hot tub with the steam rising into the chill Valentine's Night. A vase of a dozen long-stem roses floated nearly rim deep beside her. A glass of wine perched on the edge of the tub behind her. But it was her eyes he couldn't get away from.

She was right.

There was something he didn't get.

The computer dinged that it was done and he went back to his filing. The last was a series of shots he'd taken of Angelo cooking, plating, greeting customers, visiting tables. And close-ups of many of his dishes.

That's when the idea caught up with him. He did a quick Internet search—there it was. The Bite of Seattle. Twenty-five years old, now one of the major trademark festivals of the city. A Seattle institution. It was perfect.

He popped up his layout software and began tinkering. The first ad came together so fast it worried him a bit, but the first draft was good. It had sharpness. It had edge. He'd have to run the comps past Angelo, but it was the right answer. Seattle, Tuscany, great food, all in one pitch. *Angelo's —a bite of Tuscany.*

No, not homey enough. Angelo's remodel had turned his Pike Place Market address from the American cliché of a modern Italian restaurant into a cozy Tuscan family room.

When Russell was there the worries of the world felt far away. It was safe…comfortable. He tried to picture a lady just beside him. He'd be content. As if sitting with his feet stretched toward—

Angelo's Tuscan Hearth.

Bloody perfect! Damn he was good.

He e-mailed it off to a print shop to run a full-size for Angelo.

Another bite of his sandwich and he cranked up the Bruce a bit before turning back to sorting the images, an action almost automatic with the years of practice. Contact sheets were a thing of the past, which he didn't miss at all, but he did miss the darkroom work. Now it was all load 'em up and crank 'em out.

Nutcase's folder grew faster than he expected. The kitten afraid to leave its box that first night. The kitten discovering that there were things worse than crawling into the bilge, like being washed with soap afterward to remove the muck. Sleeping on the boom was her latest trick. Russell had almost catapulted her overboard when he came about one day. Now he knew to check the boom and Nutcase had learned to dive for the deck when he shouted, "Helms a-lee!"

Nutcase was about halfway through her preening. He reached over and mussed her fur as thoroughly as he could until the cat batted at his hand, rolled over on her back and started to wrestle.

He recovered his hand with only a few scratches and knocked back the rest of his beer.

He created subfolders for each lighthouse. There. That was the shot he'd print out to give to Angelo's mom. Lighthouse blurry with its distance off the stern. Angelo sitting with the tiller in one hand and a stainless-steel travel mug of cocoa in the other. Rain hood blown back off his dark, curly hair, a smile of sheer bliss on his Mediterranean-dark face.

Russell started marking the best images for printing. He'd ship them to Arnie in New York. No one else could do what she did with digital-to-paper; the woman was a magician.

West Point lighthouse was easy. His favorite shot of the Alki light had a red blemish in one corner. It distracted the eye from the lighthouse and ruined the balance of steadfast lighthouse and transitory, upscale homes clustered about it.

Maybe he should check his camera.

The next image had the same red mark. But it wasn't in the same spot in the frame. He flipped through half a dozen before he found one where the mark was a different shape.

He zoomed in. The mark wasn't a blemish, it was a person. They wore a bright red coat, but he didn't have enough resolution. The blemish might have brown hair, or maybe red, or maybe neither. A head made up of three pixels wasn't enough information for any detail.

"Well, man or woman, you're messing up my picture."

Nutcase stuck her nose around the corner of the screen to peer at it intently. As Russell pulled the mouse to select the more recent Lime Kiln lighthouse photos, she pounced on the mouse's wire. He almost picked up the camera, but he already must have a dozen shots of her doing just this.

He opened everything in the Lime Kiln folder. Not many shots of the lighthouse, about as many as of the whale. There were far more of the dumb cat.

He reached for his beer, but his hand never made it there.

"Red coat."

Nutcase ignored him, watching the mouse intently and waiting for movement.

Again no close-ups, though better than Alki, brown hair, rich russet-brown and long. This was not a guy and a guy wouldn't wear a calf-length red coat.

The hair.

Long enough to reach well past her shoulders if it weren't being blown about. He zoomed in, but her face was just a tiny cluster of tan pixels in a sea of russet.

Lime Kiln in March and Alki lighthouse in February.

He pulled the mouse back from Nutcase's grasp and pulled up the West Point photos from January.

No red coat. No one at the lighthouse. That would be too much of a coincidence. He pulled up the spoiled images from the trashcan.

Nothing.

Nothing.

Nothing.

Then the one where he'd misjudged a wave and snapped more of the north shore than he intended. He'd discarded the shot because mostly he'd caught the wastewater treatment plant.

Huddled among the lee-side rocks there was a banner of dusky red hair caught in the wind. She wore a tan coat and black pants, but it was definitely the same hair. And she was very slender.

Someone had the same calendar he did. He double-checked the file dates; the first of every month which proved he wasn't losing what little remained of his mind.

He pulled Angelo's calendar off the bulkhead and flipped to April. Slip Point lay out on the Olympic Peninsula, and most of the way down the straits of San Juan de Fuca. Treacherous water there, but it would be good practice, especially if he was going to go deep sea by year end.

He buzzed through the calendar and looked at the last lighthouse. He dug around until he found a pen and put a note on December first.

Wow! He was really going to do this. He was going to unplug from society and sail into the dream that his thirteen-year-old brain had painted across a New York City bedroom ceiling. Russell reached for the beer, but it was empty.

He'd go to each lighthouse first—by then both he and the boat would be ready. It was taking longer than he'd expected. But there was no real hurry anyway and he wanted to be around until Angelo was really up and rolling. Then who knew where his next port of call would be.

He checked the December note once more before he closed the calendar.

"Leave."

"I'M TELLING YOU, Angelo. It sucks out there."

"What does?"

"This." Russell turned around his bottle of Birra Morena aiming the label in Angelo's direction. The beautiful Italian girl on the label was impossibly beautiful: black hair, blue eyes, perfect skin.

"*Vecchio mio.* You are so sad. You know this. That's my sister."

"You don't have a sister." Russell considered heaving some of the tiramisu at Angelo, but his kitchen staff was mostly done with cleaning up for the night, so he ate it instead.

"You worry too much. She is a pretty Italian and probably a very nice girl. Nice like your Melanie and almost as pretty."

Melanie. Shit! He still couldn't figure out how he'd screwed that up. He dug at the edge of the label with the rough edge of his thumbnail.

Angelo stopped clowning and pulled up a stool next to his.

"Russell, my old friend. What's up? This is me, Angelo. Every time I mention her since you bring her here two weeks ago, you clam up like an oyster. Come on, buddy. Give."

"I don't think she had much fun here."

"Duh!" Angelo took a sip of Russell's beer and set it on the stainless-steel prep table.

"What do you mean?" Russell grabbed his bottle back and took a deep pull that did nothing to slake his thirst.

"Please tell me that you didn't show her the boat?"

Of course he had. Why wouldn't he? He shrugged and finished the bottle.

"Shit, man! You've never been dumb about a girl before. Think, *amico*. Think about Melanie."

Every time he did that he saw her eyes watching him from across the hot tub. Eyes filled not with lust, nor was it playfulness, though that was there...

"That boat is what you want. What do you think she wants?"

He planted the bottle back on the table with a crash and started to get off his stool. Angelo grabbed his arm and jerked him back down to his seat before he could turn away.

He pushed his face so close to his that Russell wanted to pound a fist into it.

"I know what she wants. Even if you're too damn dumb."

He let fly and caught Angelo on the point of his jaw. Angelo flew backwards off his stool and crashed against a rack of storage shelves.

Seconds later a dozen hands had grabbed him and shoved him down on the wet, tile floor. He tried to fight back but they had him pinned until all he could do was scream out his frustration.

They let go of him so abruptly that he didn't move for a moment. He regained his feet to face Angelo who was rubbing his chin. A circle of dishwashers and cooks stood to either side of him; all ready to tackle the bull who'd wandered into their fucking china shop.

"Good thing you're half drunk or that wussy-ass excuse for a punch might have hurt."

"Shit!" The heat roared to his face. He hadn't taken a real stab at Angelo since junior high.

"Great! Just fucking great!" He sat back down on his stool. "Now I'm damn dumb and a wussy-ass."

Angelo moved forward and clapped him hard on his shoulder. One by one the cooks and dishwashers faded back to their cleanup tasks.

"You are always both of those. In spades."

"Fuck you."

"Man, it just makes you sick that I'm smarter than you, and better looking too. We Italians, no one as good as us."

"Yeah? Well, it's your chin that's hurting, not mine."

Angelo opened a fresh pair of beers and sat back down across from him.

"Okay. I'll give you that much credit. Now, you gonna shut up and you gonna listen to your best buddy Angelo."

Russell sipped his beer and nodded. He could still feel the heat on his cheeks.

"How do ya feel about Melanie?"

"She's a lot of fun. We're good together."

His friend waited but Russell couldn't think of what else to say.

Angelo slapped his forehead with his palm. *"Figlio di puttana."*

"Calling me a son of a bitch really isn't helping my mood. Remember who taught me to cuss in Italian." He aimed a finger at his friend's white-smocked chest.

"And don't think Mama didn't give me hell for that when you paraded it all through the house." Angelo pushed off his stool, walked to the far end of the kitchen and back.

"Okay, Russell. We a-gonna talk 'bout sometin' else. Hokay?"

"Hokay, if you lose the crappy fake accent."

"Hokay. I'm making a meal. I think about how I want the diner to enjoy it. Do I start with a light pesto pasta, go to a lemon chicken, and a plate of Santa Lucia cookies with decaf coffee? Or do I start with the same pasta, but with veal meatballs. Then I follow with Rabbit alla Campagnola, a tiramisu, and an aged port. Light and fluffy. Serious and solid. You with me?"

"I have no idea where you're going with this, but I'm not dumb."

Angelo slapped him upside the head. "You're an idiot. Now shut up and listen to Angelo, your only friend in the world."

"Hokay. But I might have to pay you back for that."

Angelo rubbed a hand across his jaw and Russell shut up.

"Now. I tell you about another meal. Then you tell me 'light and fluffy' or 'serious and solid.' Deal?"

"Deal." One of the burlier cooks swung by and stared at Russell to make sure he wasn't getting out of line.

"My boyfriend invites me across the country for a holiday. Not any holiday. Valentine's Day. You probably greeted her with roses."

"A dozen reds. Prickly bastards."

"Shut up. I didn't give you permission to talk."

Russell closed his mouth.

"Takes me to nice restaurants. Has enough damn brains to bring me to the best restaurant in town where his best friend cooks like he never cooked before."

"It was good."

"It was a fuck of a lot better than good. Then a nice hotel."

"The Sorrento. Penthouse."

"Damn nice hotel. More roses?"

"More roses. Champagne. Strawberries."

"Shut up."

Russell shut up.

"Now, my boyfriend does all that for me, what am I thinking?"

"I don't want a boyfriend."

"Shit, Russell. I'm trying to help you out here." For a moment he thought Angelo might return the favor by massaging Russell's chin with a fist.

"Okay. Okay." So, if he were Melanie, he'd be wearing a little— *Yeah. Shaddup, Russell.* If he were Melanie, who had just received first class tickets, roses, scenic flights, penthouse suite...

"Oh shit!"

Angelo raised his hands to the sky. "There but by the grace of god go I."

"I proposed to her."

"But you didn't."

He closed his eyes. But he hadn't.

He'd wanted her to come out Seattle and have a good time. To see that there was life beyond the city and maybe she'd want to go sailing with him. They'd have a hell of a lot of fun.

But they wouldn't.

He would have the fun and she'd be miserable every single day.

He could see her eyes. Finally understood how she'd looked at him in the shower.

He lay his head down on the cool stainless steel of the counter. It burned against his flushed face.

Russell also finally understood the expression in the photograph as she soaked in the hot tub.

Angelo rested his hand on Russell's shoulder for a moment before going to finish closing his restaurant.

Of course he hadn't recognized it.

He'd never photographed love before.

———

THERE WAS no way to apologize. No way to say how sorry he was. He considered flying back to the city, but to what end? He didn't want New York any more than Melanie wanted a sailboat. He wrote her a long letter, doing his damnedest to explain what had happened and how much of an idiot he'd been. Then threw himself into fixing the boat.

He skipped the Ides of March party. Stabbing his lover in the back was a moment he'd rather not remember. It was three weeks since he'd punched Angelo and he was still trying to finish the head. He lay on his right side next to the toilet trying to cut the fiberglass cloth to wrap properly around the base for the shower floor. Nutcase was perched on his left shoulder watching everything he did, insisting on sniffing each tool he picked up to certify it as inedible.

The boat shifted as someone came aboard, but he sure wasn't crawling out from under when he was this close to done.

Nutcase launched toward the entry leaving permanent claw marks burning on his upper arm. Her bright meow signaled that she knew whoever it was.

"Come on in," he shouted loud enough to be heard which made his ears ring in the enclosed space.

"Thanks."

"Angelo." Russell swung upright and banged his head sharply on the counter for the small sink he'd installed. Which he shouldn't have done until he'd finished the floor.

"Crap." He crawled out into the companionway.

"You avoiding me, buddy?" Angelo looked some kind of pissed.

"No." He rubbed where he'd banged his head. "Avoiding myself more like."

Angelo mellowed instantly. "Well, I'd avoid you too if I had the choice."

"Shithead."

"Back at you."

Angelo tossed a couple of white, folded-paper containers on the table. "You eat anything better than crap since I last saw you?"

"No, mother." Then he smelled the food as Angelo started popping lids. He snagged a couple of Cokes and some forks.

He took a forkful of Egg Foo Yung right out of the box. Pork. It burned the roof of his mouth and tasted wonderful.

Angelo pointed at the various containers. "Shrimp Chow Mien, Twice-Cooked Beef with Snow Peas, Fried Rice, and I sat on the fortune cookies. Sorry about that."

Russell stabbed a shrimp for the cat. "Forgiven."

Nutcase took her piece of shrimp and they ate in silence for a bit, at least until the worst of his hunger was gone.

"So, what are you gonna do?"

"You won't leave it alone."

"I'm Italian. Sue me."

Russell shrugged. "Can't do squat. I've thought about it a lot, but I'm so done with New York and all that. If I never go there again, it won't break my heart. And Melanie sure isn't one to go cruising."

"And…" Angelo waved his fork over the chow mien for him to continue.

"You shit. You are Italian." He took a deep breath and felt about half as strong when he let it out. "And whatever I feel for her, which is a lot, it isn't what she feels for me. So, I'm a total heel, like she wasn't good enough for me or something, which isn't true. It's just not there. And she doesn't deserve that, whether she wants it or not."

Angelo offered another shrimp to Nutcase who took it with all the daintiness of a six-inch-tall savannah lion.

"You ain't so dumb after all, buddy."

"Worse," Russell rubbed his hand over his face. "But I'll get over it."

"And who should come to your rescue, once again I might add, but the wonderful, magnificent, handsome Angelo."

"And world class shithead."

Angelo aimed a forkful of snow peas at him. "Keep that up and I won't be helping you."

"Helping me how?"

"Tuesday, April fourth, six days from now, you are having dinner at my place at seven o'clock. And you are going to be on your very best behavior."

"This is my best behavior." He brushed all of Nutcase's fur backwards to prove his point, not that you could really tell the difference on the little fluff ball. She batted at him but was assuaged with a scrap of beef.

"Christ Almighty you really are sad. You screw this up and I really will stop talking to you. Just be there. And dress in clean clothes."

"Why, what's up?" Russell dug the last piece of Egg Foo Yung out of the container and ate it with relish. But didn't have time to swallow it.

"You have a blind date."

Russell choked on his last bite and it was several minutes before he could stop gagging and coughing.

SLIP POINT LIGHTHOUSE

Clallam Bay
 First lit: 1905
Automated: 1977
48.2645 -124.251

Clallam Bay is a small fishing village located halfway between the Cape Flattery and the Ediz Hook lighthouses. Named for a distinctive landslip on the face of the point's rocky bluff, the U.S. Congress appropriated $12,500 dollars in 1900 to build the lighthouse, fog signal, and the keeper's dwelling.

The dwelling was well back from the point. A long, elevated catwalk of wood plank was installed along the face of the cliff permitting the keeper to walk just above the waves' fury.

APRIL 1

"*I've been robbed!*" **Russell** pushed the tiller over and shouted, "Helm's a-lee!" even though Nutcase was sensibly down below already, out of the heavy winds that were buffeting the boat. He'd rigged for rough weather before leaving Port Townsend this morning, reefing down the main to about half its normal size and trading out the big jib for the working foresail.

For what must be the tenth time, he cruised along the sun-bright shore as near as he dared. There were rocks close in and the seas were vicious but he held his course. The *Lady* repeatedly dug her bow into the waves and threw great sheets of water skyward as she rose free. The sharp cliffs of Slip Point plunged down into the mad surf that threw itself against the rocks with the anger of a pissed-off rodeo bull.

He checked the chart again, but there was no question about this being Clallam Bay. The chart didn't report a lighthouse, a fact he'd overlooked on his way here. Instead, it had a marker for a bell buoy named "G" and sure enough, there it was. He'd sailed right up to the thing to check the designation, having to cover his ears against the frantic clang as it pitched in the waves. It had almost whacked the boat in a surprise bob and weave.

But the calendar's picture of a long, narrow catwalk snaking along

103

the dramatic cliffs was nowhere to be seen. The lighthouse, a distant, narrow, white tower in the photo, should be right at the end of the point. Right...he scanned the shore carefully as the bow plunged and the stern lifted him high in the air...there.

The angry waves pulled back for a moment and the gray regularity of concrete foundations showed wetly for a second against the dark slickness of the rock. Somewhere between the photograph for the calendar and now, the lighthouse had been taken down and the walkway ripped from the cliffside without any hint of where it had been. He continued northwest, scanning the cliffs for any sign of the catwalk.

The shore altered abruptly from sheer, soaring crags to the narrow flatlands of the bay. A large, white house stood there; it must have been the keeper's house—it had the trademark whitewashed look with red roof.

His breath caught.

He was in the right place.

At the right time.

Standing just back from where beach met cliff and wave, was a woman in a red coat. He'd put his longest zoom on his camera just for this moment and snapped a quick succession of a dozen or so frames. Then another wave caught the *Lady* and threw his bow to one side. He came about unexpectedly, the main boom nearly cracking him on the skull as it slammed from one side of the boat to the other. The camera would have gone overboard if he hadn't wrapped the strap around his forearm. He plunged it back into its case that was strapped by the tiller, slapped down the waterproof cover, and scrambled to bring the storm sail about.

Even with so little sail, he rocketed most of the way to the next point on the far side of Clallam Bay before he had her fully under control. He brought her about and shot back down the wind.

"Please be there. Please be there."

With the wind and the waves behind him, the *Lady* surged along incredibly quickly. The knotmeter's needle pegged against the stop several times, which was probably eleven knots, well above the theoretical limits of her hull. Rather than her normal top speed of nine miles an hour, he was crossing thirteen.

Full keel boats weren't designed to surf, but that's what she was doing. A wave would lift her stern and she'd fly down the face, the wave moving fast enough that they stayed together in long bursts of exhilarating speed. That was immediately followed by terrifying plunges as she dug her bowsprit and her bow completely into the next wave face. But then she'd soar clear, shedding green water off either side—ready to surf once more.

"I love this boat!" His shout blew ahead, flying past the masts and the bow, reaching ahead and clearing the way.

The ride was less rough going with the wind, so he pulled out the camera early. It took a moment to spot her, she was trudging back toward the parking lot which boasted only three cars. He snapped photos of her and the vehicles. One more pass and he'd get a picture of the lot with one car missing, then he'd know what she drove. Not that it would mean anything. But he'd know.

The wind whipped her hair. It caught at her bulky coat and pushed at her, but she moved with strength and grace.

Then she was gone. He flew downwind looking for her to no avail; she'd stepped behind the white keeper's house with its red roof and simply disappeared.

Coming about—into the teeth of the wind—he fought his way back to Slip Point. Maybe he could slip in close enough and get her attention. Then he could wave her toward the town and the small bay itself. There was a fisherman's marina marked on the chart at the west end of the bay. Unless they'd taken that down too.

They could meet in town. There was bound to be a small café, if he could figure out how to bring the boat in by himself in such weather.

But she was gone.

Two more passes and still no sign of her.

And three vehicles were still there.

CASSIDY PEELED off her gloves and wrapped her hands around a cup of hot cocoa. The receptionist at the Coast Guard station looked very sharp in her pressed white uniform. Though her face said she was maybe twenty, she had enough stripes on her sleeve that Cassidy felt a little inferior being served by her. However, the woman appeared glad for the company on a windy day, enjoying the chance to serve cocoa to a windblown tourist.

Cassidy was warm, except perhaps her cheeks and nose. She'd stood out in the howling wind and, oddly enough, not hated it. She was becoming quite the outdoorsy type, something she'd done her best to leave on Bainbridge Island along with her youth.

She'd stood out there for an hour, thrilled by the power of it all, and then, right on cue, her sailboat had appeared. Only one person aboard this time, thrashing about in the waves. She didn't know what sort of a death-wish sailor would be out in such weather, but it would make a great photograph on her wall of the boat's bow lifted out of the water and pointed toward the sky. The red bottom of the blue boat had been sticking quite far out of the waves with spray showering in every direction and catching the sunlight like a thousand dazzling diamonds.

Her GPS device had shown her that there was no longer a lighthouse, but she'd come anyway because it didn't feel right to open her father's letter while sitting in a Seattle condo. But no matter how she'd turned, the high wind had threatened to shred the paper. This office would have to be close enough. After all, the lighthouse keepers had lived here for almost a hundred years before the Coast Guard moved in its offices.

Yeoman First Class Natalie was on the phone and seemed quite involved.

Cassidy pulled the letter out of her coat pocket. It was much the worse for wear, beaten by the wind into a thousand wrinkles. She tried to imagine what was inside, what had her father thought to say to his thirty-year-old daughter as he lay there dying.

In the last letter, he'd been working the vines and met her mother. It had also included his dumb suggestion that she'd find the right man.

Well, it had taken her a week to call Jack James. She might not have if Jo and Perrin hadn't pushed her. They met for drinks at the Metropolitan Grill in the center of downtown. He had his ridiculous martini "stirred, not shaken." His idea of high humor; it was the opposite of James Bond. He had no idea how true that was. She'd ordered a glass of Sauvignon Blanc without even noticing the vintner. One sip told her it was a Washington white, and not one of the good ones. She'd pushed it aside.

Then she'd told the man with two first names that she was breaking it off. It was her, not him, she just wasn't meant to be in a relationship. He hadn't argued. He hadn't asked for a second chance, not even if there was another man.

"We had a good run, didn't we, Cassidy?" He was about as deep as a puddle; one that had dried up three days before.

Yeoman Natalie excused herself, "I need to get at some of the files in back. Do you need anything?"

"I'm fine, thanks." And she was. She didn't miss Jack James, not even in that moment when he kissed her cheek and they went in separate directions on the sidewalk. She'd gone around a corner and spied on him; he never looked back.

The paper crackled as she opened the letter.

Dearest Ice Sweet,
    We lied to you.

Yeah, about being legitimate. But they'd married right away, and stayed together until the day Mama died. She'd forgiven them before she'd even finished the last letter. So why was the back of her neck prickling?

Your birth wasn't easy. It wasn't idyllic. Your mother went to the doctor one day, I was too busy in the fields to go with her. She came back in the doctor's car. Enforced bedrest. She was allowed to get up only twice a day. I had to hire Dale's wife to feed her and take care of the house. She lay there for two-and-a-half months to make sure you came out okay.

And colicky. Did you know they still don't know what causes that? I just asked the nurse.

In that moment she was back in the hospital room. Her father lying there, tubes running in and out of him, discussing his colicky daughter with some nurse she'd probably never met. She was far colder than she'd been minutes before standing out in the chill wind.

Twelve weeks to the day you howled like there was a knife in you. I'd walk you for hours up and down the vineyards at night just to give your mama some rest. You'd howl like there was no tomorrow. And then week thirteen you just stopped. Like hiccups suddenly gone.

How could he hide that from her? She'd always believed they had the Hallmark family. The happy child, the close couple. That's what her father always told her. That was the dream she wrapped around herself at night.

Don't get me wrong. We couldn't have loved you more. But as one part of my life made more sense, the other parts made less. The winery was growing well, but getting water for the vines was becoming harder and harder. New regulations forbade pumping from the river. I was about to dig a second well, the first wasn't nearly enough, when one of the big boys in the area drove through a new regulation, no drilling new wells unless you had a creek on your land. I didn't. Close, but not on.

The vineyard wasn't lost all at once, rather a piece at a time. I and many others lost water rights due to that one man's maneuvers. I lost hired hands to some millionaire who outbid me for my best people. Soon even my mid-level people were going.

What I learned, was that when one part of your life closes, another one opens. Your mother, our Adrianne, was the only sanity in my life at that time. When you find that person, hold on for all you're worth. And if they have half a brain, they will do their damnedest to hold onto you.

You're great, Ice Sweet, and don't forget that.

Ever!

Vic

"Are you okay?"

Cassidy nodded and wiped at her stinging eyes. Then she took a sip of the still warm cocoa to assure Yeoman Natalie that she was fine.

Just fine.

"YOU'VE GOT to get me out of this, Angelo." Russell wrapped both hands around his beer bottle.

"What are you talking about?"

"This blind date. I'm not coming." He scratched a fingernail on a small drip of paint that had fallen onto the settee table and hardened. It broke free and flew across the table landing on the piece of Brie in Angelo's hand. He debated mentioning it, but decided against it when he saw the look on his friend's face.

"But you are."

"But I'm not."

"Why the hell not? You fall in love in the last six days? You going back to Melanie if she's foolish enough to take you?"

Russell hands ached with how hard they were clenched.

"No." Not really. He glanced over at the laptop tucked safely on the shelf above the table.

"Can you give me a good reason?"

He wanted to, but he didn't have one. Well, he did have one, but it was too ridiculous to call good.

He shook his head.

Angelo pegged the piece of Brie at his face. He ducked, but not enough. It hit him in the forehead. Against all chance, the paint chip dropped into his beer bottle. He pushed it aside.

"This is important, man. Not just for you. It is important to me. I need someone who can be a half-human dinner companion. I promised to introduce her to someone who was decent."

"Find someone else."

"By tomorrow night? What the hell, Russell? This isn't like you. She beautiful. Funny. What more do you want? It was your idea anyway."

"My idea?"

"Look, Russell, if I explained it, where would be the surprise. It's a blind date. That means you go in blind. Unfair to give you an advantage. She doesn't know you either."

"You're not going to back off of this one, are you?"

"Not without a good reason." Angelo cut himself another piece of Brie, completely free of paint chips, and chomped down on it as if he were trying to hack through a tough steak rather than a soft cheese.

"Okay. There is someone."

"Since when did that stop you from having dinner with another woman? Dinner, man. That's all. I'd bet that not even you could get a kiss on the first date from this one, even if you tried."

"Frigid?"

"Lady. Real one. Outside your realm of experience. Don't change the subject. What's your lover's name?"

Russell grabbed his beer and slugged back a big swallow. The paint chip slid down his throat before he could stop it.

He slammed the bottle back on the table. He hit it hard enough that it foamed out over his hand and dripped all over the cheese and the table. He mopped at it with a rag that he'd been using that morning to clean up the new tank under the pilot berth. It still smelled of the sharp tang of diesel. Long streaks of muddy black appeared across the white rind of the cheese. He threw the cloth over the whole mess and took another pull on his beer which was now much flatter than it had been.

"Name?"

"Go to hell, Angelo."

His friend narrowed his eyes for a long moment and then he burst out laughing.

"You don't know her name. Oh, this is too rich. What's she like?"

"She likes the outdoors. Long dark hair."

"Wow. Great description, man. Thanks. I can really picture her now. Clear as mud."

"Asshole."

Angelo just grinned.

Nutcase appeared from somewhere and started sniffing at the mess on the table.

Angelo grabbed the cloth with the cheese in it and mopped up the worst of the beer puddle.

Russell ducked again, but Angelo turned and dropped it into the garbage bag full of sawdust that was drooping in the companionway. Nutcase dropped down to floor, inspected the bag carefully and then wandered back to whatever she'd been doing before.

"Tell me more."

Russell couldn't relax his fists even when he tried.

"You can't?" Angelo was getting far too much fun at Russell's expense.

Russell grabbed the laptop and dropped it onto the table with a crash. He turned it so that they could both see it.

"West Point lighthouse." He pointed her out squatting among the rocks.

"February at Alki." He pulled up the next picture. "March at Lime Kiln. Didn't even know she was in these photos until I looked at them a few weeks ago."

"She's following the same calendar I gave you."

"Duh. Figured that one out on my own, Sherlock. So, for April, I took my big telephoto with me. But the weather was really lousy. I could barely control the boat, much less make it ashore to meet her." He toggled to the last spread of photos. Six of them. Long zoom close-ups. Snapped in rapid-fire succession when the stern of the *Lady* had ridden high up in the air to give him a clear view.

Heavy hiking boots. Slender legs. Body form hidden by the trade-mark bulky red parka. A flag of chestnut hair streaming in the wind just begging to have fingers run through it. Coat zipped up far enough to hide the neck. Nice chin, slender without being angular. And where her face should be, two delicate hands holding a small point-and-shoot camera—aimed right at him. Almost clear enough to read the stupid brand name.

"Nice. When's the wedding?"

"Give me a goddamn break."

Angelo waved a hand at the screen. "She's not real. She a phantom who appears only on the first of each month."

"You couldn't prove otherwise by me, but she feels real. More real than…" He should never have opened his mouth.

Angelo rested a strong hand on Russell's forearm.

"Melanie was real. Is real. She just isn't headed in the same direction you are. And the girl on this screen probably has a voice like a harpy and a husband and seven kids at home. I'm offering you dinner with a flesh-and-blood lady. Nice one. Single too, though you try to touch her and I'll kill you, right at the table, and serve you your own guts over a nice bed of pasta. Eating dinner and making nice conversation isn't cheating on some lighthouse babe that you've never met."

Russell nodded, as much to stop Angelo's pestering him as anything else. He glanced sideways at the screen, studying how her hair appeared to move in the wind in the series of frozen moments of the photograph.

Angelo had missed two details. She was alone in every photo.

And the hands that held the little camera had no rings on them.

"HOW DO I DO THIS?" Cassidy knew she was losing it. Could feel her voice rising and tight. She perched on the impossibly uncomfortable green leather and stainless-steel bar stool in Perrin's Gallery.

The whole shop was done in retro-1950s diner. Instead of tables in the booths, there were mannequins wearing the latest designs. Instead of those music players, there were racks of clothes and accessories that would go with what the seated mannequins were wearing. Instead of a front counter, there were racks of other clothes. Instead of a diner cashier with gum and candy and pies of towering meringue in a display case, the glass cases held handbags, gloves, belts. Through the swinging doors there was no cook line. Rather there was a haven of shoes, boots, coats, and from the ceiling hung an unbelievable selection of umbrellas guaranteed to stand out in any crowd.

"When was the last time you had a blind date?" Jo had her lawyer voice on, the one designed to lull the obstinate into a sense of security, the upset into a pool of calm. Cassidy felt it working on her, and fought it.

"I dunno. Freshman year. And that was plenty."

Jo glanced over at Perrin who shrugged. "How was I supposed to know Richie would take acid to get up his nerve?"

Apparently he'd been telling Perrin that he was really interested in her red-haired friend. Cassidy'd finally agreed to meet him. There'd been something strange about his eyes, a glassiness she hadn't understood at the time. As a naïve, sixteen-year old freshman from an island in the Pacific Northwest, she'd been totally flattered that an upperclassman had even noticed her. They'd had a nice meal at The Atrium, her favorite campus hangout. He was bright, interesting, and definitely enamored. But the way he kept staring at her was somewhere on the line between incredibly flattering and a totally creepy.

She'd finally had to ask.

"How do I look to you?" She'd put a great deal of effort into selecting nice colors that blended well together and shapes that showed off her figure. Perrin had even done her hair and nails for her.

Richie Packer had gazed at her for a moment long enough to warm her cheeks before replying, "The body of a goddess. A neck like a great snake. Your face would scare the hounds of Hell with its slavering jaw, massive fangs. No nose. Eyes of ice and hair of a mighty, writhing inferno."

He'd tried to apologize for weeks afterward, swearing he'd never take drugs again, especially not hallucinogens. She told him it was okay, she'd sworn off ever being in his presence again.

She'd also sworn off blind dates, so how had Angelo talked her into this one? With a promise of great food and a charming man. She'd had enough of charming with Jack James. What she needed was someone with some heart and a little connection to his own emotions.

"You need more confidence. Think of it like your wine-tasting. I've seen you do that with style and panache." Perrin tossed back her head making her lime-green perm swirl about her head like a whirlpool. Impossibly ugly, except on Perrin it was so cute that it made every man under forty turn and go silent whenever she entered a room. Okay, every man of any age who still had a pulse.

"I'm not going to a man-tasting. I'm going on a blind date and I don't know what to do. You're my friends, you're supposed to be helping me."

"Send Jo. She'll wow him."

Cassidy buried her face in her hands. "I can't. I promised Angelo I'd review his restaurant this time. He's probably been preparing for a week."

"I thought they weren't supposed to do that."

"They aren't. They all do. But they've learned that I'm not above begging tastes from nearby tables. So if I get an exceptional meal, so does everyone around me."

"There," Perrin aimed the one finger not covered by her elbow-long, green gloves. "That's the attitude. Remember that feeling, right there. Use that and you'll be invulnerable. And the man will melt and die at your feet unless he's a complete jerk."

"Clothes, Perrin." Jo spoke quietly. "She needs power-dating clothes."

"Black." Cassidy called out as Perrin started wandering around about the shop. "And no dresses."

Perrin held out a black top that had cleavage down to the navel and a swirly, pleated mini-skirt.

"So not."

Perrin laughed.

By the fifth rejection Perrin had stopped laughing.

"You're tricky." She inspected Cassidy carefully. Turned back to her racks and then once more to face Cassidy. She disappeared through the swinging stainless-steel doors into the back room.

Jo met Cassidy's gaze and arched an eyebrow on her rounded face.

Neither of them were willing to guess what Perrin would come up with next.

She reappeared with something definitely not black. "Put this on."

Cassidy rubbed her fingers over the lush, red and orange fabric. "Cashmere. I love cashmere."

"Don't we all, honey. Now put it on."

Cassidy headed for the dressing room, but Perrin called her back.

"Nope. You look incredible in that black turtleneck, just pull this on over it."

She unzipped the front of the sweater and slipped it on. She zipped it partway up and moved to the triple mirror. The waist and the ends of the arms were such a dark red that they were as black as her pants. The sweater lightened upward from red, to dusky orange, and finally a dark gold the color of the inside of a pot of honey as it reached her neckline and the open zipper.

Perrin moved up behind her and looked at her in the mirror over her shoulder. She reached around and tugged the zipper a bit lower.

"I feel more naked than just the turtleneck." The fading colors and low zipper gave her a plunging cleavage, without any exposed skin.

"It works. You're fully covered, and he'll be spending the whole time trying not to look at your breasts. It's perfect. And I'll bet you another bottle of that amazing champagne we had that he won't be able to look away. Besides, you have the nicest set of the three of us; it's time you flaunted them a bit."

"I do?" She looked down, but they were just your average breasts in your average bra wrapped in a black silk turtleneck and cashmere.

"Mine are too flat, and Jo's are a bit too much, though they suit her. Yours, with your figure, they're just great. He'll die. Trust me."

She glanced at Jo over her shoulder. Again the raised eyebrow, with a tilt of the head that indicated there was probably truth there.

Cassidy looked at herself again in the mirror. She did look good.

"On a much later date, the one you want to have sex after," Perrin pulled the zipper up halfway to her throat, "and lose the black turtleneck. He'll remember the undressed look of the first date and spend the whole second date dreaming of pulling that zipper back down."

"How did you learn this stuff?" The instant the words were out of her mouth Cassidy wanted to bite her tongue and kick herself. She met Perrin's eyes in the mirror, suddenly wide and vulnerable like a little girl. She turned and wrapped her arms around Perrin's stiff body.

"Screw them. Screw them both. They can't touch you anymore. Ever." She could feel her friend nod at last and Cassidy held her more tightly until she felt her relax a bit.

They stood back from each other but Cassidy held onto Perrin's thin arms. She felt the anger that came over her whenever she thought about her friend's parents.

"I love you just as you are, Perrin. I think you're incredible. I'm so glad you're in my life."

"Really?" She wiped at her eyes.

"Really. This sweater is perfect. I couldn't get through this without you."

Perrin finally nodded again.

Cassidy kissed her on the cheek and then clapped her hands together.

"What's next?"

"Come-fuck-me boots." Perrin laughed even though tears still trickled down her face.

"Not what I was quite after."

Jo came over, "Kick-ass boots, then."

"Kick-ass boots. Perfect."

They headed for the back room, arm in arm.

She started whistling the tune.

Jo started singing the words.

Perrin laughed and joined in though her voice was still tight. "We're off to see the wizard. The wonderful Wizard—"

Cassidy stumbled to a halt after they pushed through the swinging doors. There it was.

She slipped her arms free from her friends and pulled the knee-length coat off the mannequin holding a hamburger spatula like a submachine gun.

The same length as the Michael Kors parka. The same red, but that's where the similarities stopped. The soft, red leather had been finely tailored. She slipped it on, did up the three giant black buttons and tied the black belt of the same leather once over. Sixties retro gone high end. The broad lapels made her feel part secret agent and part superwoman.

When she turned, Perrin was nodding and the unflappable Jo made a show of dropping her jaw before starting to applaud.

"You look fantastic!"

"And," Perrin pointed, "It matches the sweater and accents her hair. You, my friend, are incandescent hot."

***

"Thanks for cleaning up."

"Is this good enough for your majesty?" Russell tugged once more to settle the corduroy blazer over his sport shirt. He'd even unearthed a tie with sailboats on it, but decided to go with the open neck instead. There had to be some limit.

"You look more than half human. Maybe even three-quarters. Now be nice and have fun."

"Yeah, right." He hadn't been this nervous about a date since sixth grade. Of course, it was strange having your first ever blind date in your early thirties.

"So, Angelo, how is this my idea?"

His friend just grinned at him. "Notice the wine labels at dinner."

"I don't need wine, I need a really big scotch."

"Yeah, well forget it. I'm making you a great meal and I want you to be able to taste it."

For the next couple minutes Angelo rattled off facts about the wines he was planning to serve. Would she be tall and fair, maybe remind him too much of Melanie? Short, dark, and beautiful like his mother? Dumpy and dull like he feared no matter how much Angelo claimed otherwise?

"Got it?"

"Huh? Not a word."

Angelo punched his arm hard enough to get his attention.

"Look. The last wine. The dessert wine. Cinque Terre Sciacchetrà. It's a white: amber and flowery. Look for orange, grapefruit, and lemon tones with a dry finish. A lot of alcohol in this one. Can you remember that much?"

"Sure. Why?" He punched Angelo back just for the hell of it.

"It's your idea. Local. Local. Local. It's not just Tuscan, it's Ligurian, from my family's home town. If you want to leave a good impression on her, knowing that much at the end may help."

"Okay."

"Get out there."

"Is it time already?" Suddenly he wanted to head for the back door and the nearest bar for that good scotch. Hell, he'd take a bad scotch right about now.

"Go." Angelo pointed. "Did you bring something for her?"

"I was supposed to bring something?" He started patting his pockets as his friend sighed. "Jewelry, clothes, what?"

Angelo went over to a huge vase of red roses, pulled one out and brought it back.

"If the girl those are for accepts her boyfriend's proposal tonight, she'll never notice that she's one shy of her two dozen roses."

Russell eyed it carefully. "I didn't do so well with the red roses with Melanie."

Angelo stuffed it in his hand and pushed him out through the swinging doors. The other patrons turned to stare as the restaurant's chef shoved Russell toward a table set for two and pushed him into one of the chairs.

He pulled the rose from Russell's hand and laid it across the opposite place. He leaned down to whisper.

"Stop being such a goddamn wimp."

He left before Russell could hit him again.

Russell missed her entrance.

He'd sipped his water, played with his fork…and started thinking about the layout of the galley. He shook out the swan or whatever the napkin was supposed to be and refolded it into the same general shape of the space he had to work with. A couple of sugar cubes became a row of cupboards. The salt shaker where the sink would go. Pepper mill for the fridge. The knife defined the edge of the counter. More sugar cube storage below.

Stove. He smacked his forehead. He'd forgotten the stove. Had to be in line with the keel so that it could swing when he was on a tack. He might be heeled over ten or fifteen degrees for weeks at a time. Gimbaled stove would have to go where the pepper-mill fridge was. The fridge traded places with the salt shaker. Stove to the right or left? He plucked a petal off the rose and moved it to one side then the other of the sugar cubes.

"Some boys never outgrow their toys."

He glanced up at the woman standing before him. His eyes made it halfway back to his napkin-galley before they were drawn back.

Red coat. She wore a knee-length red coat. He opened his mouth, but closed it again as disappointment rocked him back in his seat.

This was no parka and she wasn't his Lady of the Lighthouses ready for heavy weather. Instead, she'd been wrapped in red leather so tailored to the body beneath that it belonged in his studio, not out on the street.

After a moment she raised her chin and took off the coat. Only then did he realize he should have offered to take it. He started to rise, but she waved him back to his seat. Not a good start.

A waiter took the coat and he could tell that the coat hadn't lied about what was beneath.

Black leather boots with two-inch heels clung tightly up to her knees, ending just where the swirling black skirt began. Her trim waist tapered up into a sweater that started dark and ended with the colors of autumn. The black turtleneck was surprisingly sexy. The sweater brought out the reds in her brown hair, wound back into one of those painfully tight coifs and…

"I've seen you." Somewhere. He'd find it in a moment.

"And I you," she slid into her chair with a grace that was as unconscious as a model's was practiced.

"Where's your girlfriend?"

"My what?" Russell could feel his throat closing.

"The tall blond with legs to her ears. As I recall, you were all over each other. I find it surprising that you are on a blind date after having her on your arm."

"Valentine's Day." That was it. "The woman crying in the bar."

As soon as he saw her reaction he knew it was a mistake. Her face closed. The teasing smile that had been intriguing a moment before was erased as if it'd never been.

"Sorry. Perhaps not your best moment."

"Perhaps not." She kept her gaze down as she fooled around with the rose with elegant fingers. A woman's hand, not with the daintiness of a girl's nor the sensual slenderness of Melanie's. They were a woman's hands.

"But you were beautiful in that moment." Christ. Good one, Russ. Don't know when to leave bad enough alone.

Her hands froze, but she didn't look up.

"I'm a photographer. I would have killed to have a camera to capture you."

"I'd have killed you if you had." She almost raised her gaze.

"The three of you. Like you'd been together forever. I could see you fifty years from now, the same three women. Beautiful. Close."

Under guise of rubbing his chin, he put his hand over his mouth to keep it shut before he shoved his foot in any deeper.

"Since college. Beautiful?" She lifted the rose and smelled it, looking directly at him for the first time. The clothing had shifted the hue of her hazel eyes until they were some combination of summer green and the rich gold that every autumn leaf longed to be. The rose accented the color in her cheeks as she brushed it back and forth below her nose. No detectable makeup.

"Yes," his throat was dry. "Yes, beautiful."

"Perrin maybe. The tall thin one, wild hair."

Russell shook his head barely remembering her companions as little more than positions in a composition. A waiter passed by and in his wake, he caught his date's scent. Warm, unperfumed, and heavenly.

"No. You."

She blushed and looked down again.

"I'm a...Russell. Russell Morgan."

She extended a hand. "Cassidy Knowles. Nice to meet you, a-Russell."

"Real nice." Her grip was firm and warm.

"Charm isn't one of my specialties." She released his hand.

He wished she hadn't. It had felt good, that womanly hand against his rough palm and fingers.

He was trying to think up a good one-liner riposte when the waiter arrived.

"Hallo, I am Giorgio. Mister Angelo has asked me to tell you that he will be choosing your dinner once again."

"Once again?" Russell aimed his question at his date who nodded so sweetly it was hard to argue.

Giorgio waited a moment, but when she didn't speak he continued.

"He has asked me to let you know this. But, also he has said, knowing your preference for a fair sample, he only will serve selections that have been ordered already this night. *Perfetto?*"

"Yes, perfect."

The waiter whisked away.

"Hey, I wanted to see a menu." He and Angelo had spent long enough redesigning the damn thing. Local cuisine, an elegant montage of Tuscany and Liguria. He'd even managed to work his sailboat into the dessert page. It was one of the best pieces he'd done in a long time—had some of the old Russell Morgan flare to it. It had been nice to know he still had it. But, as the waiter was gone and no menu was forthcoming, he turned his attention back to his date.

She'd gone quiet again. He wanted to see that smile some more. It was a hell of a good smile, even if it had been directed at the waiter.

"What's with this 'once again' stuff?"

She opened her mouth, but he cut her off.

"Wine taster. Right. I forgot."

"Did we meet before?"

He thought about the first time, as she'd thanked Angelo for a fabulous meal. He'd been, what, eating spaghetti while covered in boat dust and dirt. No. Fiberglass resin. She'd have discounted him as useless, beneath notice, no more than a blemish on Angelo's pristine kitchen. Best not to remind her.

The sommelier showed up and started chatting wines with her in a way that totally eluded him.

Listen to her, Russell; New York was all over her. Her clothes were so perfect and she probably had her hair done weekly. Her brisk way of addressing the wine steward had used short, clipped, quick words. He wouldn't have noticed if Dave and Betsy hadn't teased him about his own New York way of speaking. She was everything he didn't want. One hundred percent not his lady in the red coat. Crap! She and Melanie could be best friends.

Even her boots were a joke. Who spent four or five hundred dollars on boots except at a fashion shoot? God, his final shoot. Before the red, mid-thigh Chanel's, he'd photographed Melanie in exactly those boots. Though he'd never photographed anything like that sweater. It dipped and swelled in a splendidly provocative—

The sommelier was gone…and he was staring at her breasts. He'd stopped doing that in high school as soon as he learned what a turn-off it was. The great paradox of women: he got to see a lot more breasts unclothed as soon as he stopped staring at them clothed.

He checked her eyes. Oddly, there wasn't anger, but laughter crinkling the edges.

"What?"

She shook her head, but the smile didn't go away.

"THE PENNE AGLI SCAMPI, Angelo. Simply exquisite." Cassidy leaned toward Angelo and rested her chin on her palm, elbow on the table. "But wasn't that a Piedmont white rather than a Tuscan?"

Russell couldn't look away from her. She was so unaware of every motion. There was no posing. Her emotions weren't carefully considered and exhibited for the benefit of the camera or the moment. She had a natural honesty that had him mesmerized.

Angelo pulled up a chair and joined them. "I cannot fool you, Miss Knowles. I thought the Tuscan wines a little too fruity for something as delicate as the scampi. I decided that as long as the wine was Italian, I'd let it wander a little farther afield than the cuisine."

"Absolutely right. Now the heaviness of the San Rocco Barolo was the perfect choice for the Tagliata, I've never had such tender beef. What was the spicing?" She'd described the flavors for him. He could taste the sage and rosemary after she'd told him. But the juniper berry, he had no idea. He'd say she was making it up, but throughout the meal she'd kept a running commentary on flavors for each new dish and wine. When she'd asked about the other flavor in the beef, he had no idea what she'd been talking about.

"Oh no, Miss Knowles. You do not get my mother's secrets so easily."

Secret recipe. Right. He'd seen that. Time to pay back Angelo for setting him up with this New York woman, the one who snagged his attention like a harpoon.

"Anchovy paste instead of salt."

Angelo looked put out as Cassidy inspected him, then he shrugged. "Sometimes it is the simple techniques that are the best."

"I've watched him rub it in."

"Watched him…" She ran the words over her tongue, the same way she rolled the wine there.

Russell really needed to learn when to shut up.

"Watched him…while you ate pasta."

"What was that?" Angelo didn't catch it, but Russell bowed his head in acknowledgement. She had an eye for detail and had finally picked him out of the mess he'd been when she was here for the wine tasting three months ago. She could probably be a decent photographer with a bit of training.

"You aren't a…" She caught her upper lip between her teeth, but he could read it on her face.

"Contractor…or a homeless person eating on Angelo's charity?"

She tilted her head to one side for a moment, made him want to run a finger down the length of neck exposed from ear to turtleneck collar. She arched her eyebrows and shrugged a yes.

He laughed, "Depends on who you ask." Melanie would say he was homeless. So would his parents and any of his New York friends for that matter. And beyond them all, this woman across the table would declare him such. No way would she be happy with the wind blowing through her hair. She might shatter if you took her anywhere rougher than the Cutters' lounge or Angelo's. She had every mark of coming from money and no trace of ever touching the great outdoors.

The shift was clear on her face. Her thoughts, so carefully guarded on her tongue, were easy to see. The slow sifting of information until she moved the smooth photographer to the possibly homeless smartass until she had melded the two into a perfect blend.

Angelo cleared his throat and returned his chair to the next table.

"For dessert I will be giving you Sfogliatina alla Angelo's, a puff pastry filled with a fig and cream custard. And," he bowed to Cassidy, "I hope you will approve of the wine choice."

Angelo managed to kick him under the table without Cassidy noticing before heading back to the kitchen.

It hurt.

"You like him." She aimed those hazel eyes at him.

He had to look down to think up a reply and still couldn't.

"He's a great cook."

"The best."

"How long have you two been at this?"

Russell shrugged, "I can barely heat a can of soup." For years he and Angelo had cooked together. He was a fair cook, but Angelo was in a whole other class.

"You know that wasn't what I meant."

"How long have you been with those two girlfriends of yours I saw at Cutters?" Real nice. Right back where you started the meal, Brutus. Time to stab her with it again. Dufus.

"College. Freshman year. First day." She brought that nice chin up a bit higher. She was a proud woman, who was sure enough of herself to let him know he was being a jerk.

"Right, sorry, you told me that already. Add another decade or so, that's me and Angelo. Practically from the same womb. His mom… was a friend of the family. Very close." She had been his parents' cook.

He'd learned to protect his name, to not mention that he was a part of the Morgans who ran the shipping empire. Women always got weird when they found out you had that kind of money. Melanie had been different. Maybe it influenced her in the beginning, hell, he knew it had. And he'd let it to get her in bed. But by the end it hadn't been about the money. He simply hadn't had the brains to notice the change in her feelings, because he was happy enjoying the fruits of the former not even being aware of the latter.

The dessert arrived. He jabbed at the pastry and a small geyser of cream shot out the end and smeared across the tablecloth. Before he could reach for a napkin, a small flock of waiters appeared. Without appearing to hurry, they lifted each item and replaced the tablecloth in about ten seconds flat.

"Happens all the time, sir," the waiter hurried off with his soiled cloth. It was all a fucking façade—from glossy ads to glossy women. What would his date do if faced with something that wasn't perfectly prepared? If the world weren't perfectly arranged for every step she'd taken since birth?

"So, Cassidy, what is it you want to do? Spend the rest of your life being a critic?"

"I don't know." She dragged her voice out, slowing the reply. She could obviously feel his change of attitude and she wasn't going to answer, at least not completely.

"Hadn't really thought about the long term," she continued with caution. "I wanted to get out of New York, expand my horizons."

"Have they been expanded?"

"I think so. My syndication has grown. I'm not Robert Palmer or even close to what Craig Claiborne was, but I'm becoming known."

"And is that what you want?"

She poked at her dessert. "As I said, I hadn't really thought about long term." He could read the lie on her face. She had every minute of her perfect little life mapped out.

He could hear the note in her voice. The clipped tone that a date always used when they wanted a subject change. Well, screw that.

"Always the critic. Always a step back. A step away. You know all of these wines, but do you really know the true heart of any of them?" He'd met more real people in three months at the marina than he had in twenty-five years in the city. 'Oh, you're one of those Morgans.' And the whole fake-friendly façade would appear. Out here, no one knew but Angelo. And, now that he thought about it, Russell suspected that most of his new friends probably wouldn't have cared.

Again that stillness dropped over her. During the meal he'd learned that's when her emotions were working the hardest and was the only time they were hidden. She could be polite and funny, even, he had to admit, interesting. But whenever he'd asked a loaded question, she'd shut down and turned into zombie girl. She picked up her wine glass and eyed it carefully. Her expression unreadable, as if he suddenly didn't exist.

He needed to shut up. That's what he needed to do. He knocked back a glass of the dessert wine. It was so sweet he almost choked.

"Christ, I need a beer."

She was sipping the wine. Holding the glass just below her nose as she sucked in her breath. Her lips pursed as if ready for a kiss.

What would she look like spread out on a bed, hair undone, clothes askew or missing? All missing except for that sweater.

He really did need a beer if that's what he was thinking. If he was going to go there, he might as well go back to New York and beg Melanie's forgiveness. Melanie at least knew what she was, knew what she wanted from life. And he'd been involved in it, had helped it along now and then even before they became an item.

This woman was so proud of her perfect acuity and ever so careful with her clothes. Clearly so full of herself for her achievements on something as futile as which damn wine was which.

"A lot of citrus," she spoke to herself rather than to him. "Flowers." She held the glass over the white tablecloth and looked down at it again.

"Amber. Not just gold. Amber." Her tone shifted from interest to puzzlement.

"I thought you knew everything."

"There are thousands of wines from nearly as many wineries." Her voice was almost as chilly as the wine. "I can tell you it's Italian, but I can't place it. Perhaps Tuscan. Or close by."

"Notice the lemon? The dry finish?" Why was he being such a jerk? She hadn't earned this but he couldn't help himself. He'd done it to Melanie without knowing, now he was fully aware he was doing it, but that didn't stop the next words.

"Did you miss the high alcohol perhaps?" He couldn't stop, even though he was being an asshole. He'd made Melanie think he loved her and then tossed her aside, practically called her whore with how he'd lavished gifts on her and then used her for sex.

"Obvious marks of a Cinque Terre Sciacchetra." He felt like the old monk with the whip scourging his own back until it bled. He had to strike out. Rake his claws against the pain within.

"Not Tuscan. Ligurian. Very traditional. Very authentic." He was a fucking mess. He knocked back the rest of the oversweet wine.

Staggering to his feet, he turned to see the look of horror on Angelo's face as he stood looking out from the swinging door to the kitchen.

Turned back to the woman frozen with the wine glass an inch from her pursed lips.

"Hope you enjoyed the damn meal. Don't bother to give me your number, you wouldn't want me to call anyway." He slapped a couple of hundred dollar bills on the table to pay for the meal and walked out before he could throw himself on his butter knife in atonement.

127

"The" Ristorante Italiano:

  Angelo's Tuscan Hearth

  There are moments in our lives that stand out. Moments when mother and daughter recognize the woman in each other. When the son finally throws the ball the father can catch. Those moments when a thousand different little things come together into a single event of perfection. When the symphony of musicians truly masters the composition and the composer's intent is revealed, when the dancer disappears into the ballet.

  "Angelo's Tuscan Hearth" Italian restaurant has brought such finesse to the apparently simple task of a meal. Seattle has long been synonymous with salmon and other Northwest seafood. No longer. Now there is a restaurant that harkens us back to the Old World, when chefs were vied for by kings and cardinals alike. Their master is tucked away in Seattle's Pike Place Market on Post Alley.

CASSIDY DESCRIBED the meal easily and quickly. Reliving each taste as it had occurred. Making sidebars for tasting notes on the wines as she went. It was all part of her style, the "friendly, close, personal touch" that many column reviewers had so praised and more than a few had tried to copy. She explained the meal in simple terms that let the owner of an untrained palate imagine they were indeed a master of spice and flavor, of ambience and composition.

  However, one must be careful to choose one's dinner companions as carefully as one's meal or you'll end up with a jerk like Russell Morgan.

She glared at the screen—that wasn't what she'd intended to write at all.

A couple of keystrokes deleted the sentence.

  A fine meal can be destroyed as easily by...

Delete.

Then she was stuck.

The ending wouldn't come. She scrolled back up and read down the page again hoping that when she hit her stopping point, the flow of words would carry her to the end.

Nope.

She looked out the window of her twentieth floor condo at Queen Anne hill, the top of a partially submerged mountain rising hundreds of feet right out of Elliot Bay. Seattle's finest homes perched along its cliff edges. She could also see northern Puget Sound; rough water beneath a glittering sun and clouds zipping by as if they wanted to be anywhere but here. And straight ahead lay Bainbridge Island—no longer her home.

Her column was due by midnight. Seven hours to go and she could find no inspiration in her mind, on the screen, or out the window.

Her hand was halfway to the bookcase before she stopped it. She didn't want to pull out her old columns. They'd just make her feel even less competent at the moment if that was possible. All those fun, enjoyable meals. Meals where a rude-beyond-belief blind date hadn't slapped at her so hard she could still feel the sting across her face.

The door buzzer jolted her out of the chair as if she'd been electro-cuted. The only friends with the passcode to the street door were Jo and Perrin. She really didn't want to face either of them. Through the front door peephole she could see it was worse, it was both of them—Perrin with a happy smile and waving a bottle of wine.

She did her best to put on a cheerful expression before she let them in.

"Ooo, sad face," Perrin threw her arms around Cassidy's shoulders. "Didn't go well last night. In that case we come with consolation rather than cheers."

"Hi, Jo." Her hug was less fierce, but lasted a moment longer. The consolation of a good friend who understood.

"Well, come on. Give us the worst of it. Mr. Ugly, huh? Boy, doesn't that just suck the big one. Why do we say 'boy'? If I said, 'Girl, doesn't that just suck the big one' it wouldn't work as well at all." Perrin shed her yellow, woolen coat onto the hall chair.

Her outfit was '20s flapper, bright yellow with tassels. It looked perfect on her long, slender form. She didn't remove the beaded hat that was nearly a skull cap and hid all but a few wisps of the bright green hair, that still managed to look cute. Even her perfume was a light lemony scent smelling like a blossoming tree rather than furniture polish. For a moment, Cassidy wished that she had a flat, lean figure like Perrin so she could wear such an outfit and look even half as beautiful.

"Remember that fashion model the last time we were at Cutters?"

Jo fetched a corkscrew and glasses from the small kitchen and continued into the living room. Perrin dug around for cheese in the fridge as Cassidy pulled out a selection of crackers and spread them around the edges of a cutting board. Jo sat down on one of the stools on the far side of the maple butcher block counter that separated the rooms, and opened the wine.

Cassidy poured the Lindemans Shiraz. A bit tannic, but one of the most drinkable wines at the price. Fresh, a bit spicy. No real demands on the palate. Exactly what she needed right now.

"The one dressed like a centerfold?" Jo twirled her glass without really looking at it.

"That's the one."

"She was your date?" Perrin slapped her palm against her forehead. "Wow, Cassie, didn't know you were walking both sides. If I'd only known, we could have had a whole different kind of fun in school. You remember Patty Jones? Ooo-wow did she have the hots for you."

"Perrin!" Jo rolled her eyes.

"What?" Cassidy did her best not to laugh. "No. She wasn't my date. And Patty Jones wasn't my type either. Patty? Really? Anyway, remember the guy who was with her?"

Perrin shook her head. Jo thought a moment and shrugged.

"I don't know how you missed him. He was incredible in a broad-shouldered, rough-and-rugged sort of way. Not so much handsome as solid, able to take the weight of the world on his shoulders and amble along as easy as sunshine. And eyes, ocean-deep eyes."

"Damn!" Perrin stamped her stocking-clad foot on the oak parquet and her tassels shimmered about her hemline. "I knew I should have gone and sat in the corner last night. Jo, next time Cassidy goes on a date with him, you and I are going double to spy."

Cassidy cut Jo off before she could reply. "There won't be another. Not with this guy. Not ever."

"Ouch! That bad? Let's go to the living room and you can tell us all. I want every sordid detail. I love the sordid details and it's always me who ends up providing them. Much less fun for poor Perrin. Old Miss Boring Lawyer over there hasn't been laid in over a year or else she's hiding someone in her closet when she could be sharing all the good bits with poor Perrin."

Actually, Cassidy knew Jo had been on a few first dates since she'd finished the lawsuit that had consumed two years of her life. But none of them had led anywhere.

They took the wine and cheese into the living room and settled, she and Jo on the heavily-pillowed couch, Perrin sitting in the matching, oversized chair. The warmth of the decorative swirls in the dark brown cloth and the nearly-black wood of the overstuffed arms made her bright yellow attire stand out even more. Cassidy had always thought of them as hobbit couches, but Perrin was no hobbit. Perhaps a slender, shining elf come to visit Cassidy's cozy cave on the twentieth floor.

"Hey, those are new. They're so cute. Like a set or something."

Jo turned to see where Perrin was pointing over their heads.

Cassidy's four lighthouse and sailboat pictures. The boat's red-and-blue colors strong against the egg-cream walls.

"Where did you get those?"

"I took them." The second she spoke she wished she'd said they were from a flea market.

"You did? They're great. Who's on the sailboat? Some hunky guy I hope. Most sailboat guys are hunky. Egos the size of the Space Needle, but hunky."

"I, um, don't know. He just shows up."

Jo stood up to look at the pictures more closely. "But they were taken at different locations."

She sighed. Leave it to the lawyer to catch the details. Cassidy pointed to the calendar hanging where next month's photo would go. Moving the calendar slowly across the wall made it more of a journey.

"My theory is that we're both following the same calendar. The first of each month, he's there."

"Following the same calendar? Is that like having the same period?" Perrin was giggling at her own joke. She really did look like a twenty-year old flapper talking about something terribly improper.

"Yeah. Sort of. I guess. Not really."

"Why are *you* there?" Jo took down the calendar and flipped through it for a moment as she settled back onto the couch. Then Jo focused on her.

Cassidy couldn't look away from Jo's dark eyes. Even the first day of school she hadn't managed the slightest evasion once Jo focused that lawyer-to-be gaze on her.

"Look at the first day of each month." Jo and Perrin did.

" 'Date with Ice Sweet'?" Perrin glared at her in mock anger. "Are you seeing some hottie and not telling us? I tell you, between you and Jo you always were a quiet pair. It's a good thing I found you two or both would've graduated after four years without anyone knowing you were there. And you'd probably both still be virgins. Even today. You are both—"

"Dad's nickname for me," Cassidy cut her off. "Icewine, the sweetest and rarest wine."

"So, you're going even though he isn't around anymore? That is sweet." Perrin curled back into her chair and tucked her legs under her. "That's really sweet. You and your dad are real close. I always envied that you are still. Um, now that he's gone."

She grimaced. "That came out all wrong as usual, but you know what I mean."

"Yeah, thanks, Perrin. He left letters too." She opened the drawer under the coffee table and pulled out the slim stack of envelopes. "They aren't long, he wrote them in those last weeks when he was barely alive. One for each lighthouse."

"Why didn't you tell us? We'd have gone with you. Three women voyaging to the wilds of the Pacific Northwest. We'd be like the three

Musketeers when they traveled with Lewis and Clark on the voyage of discovery."

"Perhaps, Perrin, she wanted to do it on her own."

"Jo's right. Though your adventuring sounds like fun, I want it to be just Dad and me. His first letter said that he wanted to go to these places with me, bring us closer together. He's telling me stuff about the past I didn't know."

Perrin waved her glass of wine at the photos, came dangerously close to spilling the red shiraz on the white carpet. "So, there's this sailor guy in each photo. Maybe you should forget Mr. Wrong and track down Mr. Hunky Sailor. It's easy to test if he has a sailor's ego. Poke it with a pin and if he explodes, you know it's huge."

Cassidy turned to look at the photos over her shoulder. West Point, Alki, Lime Kiln, Slip Point. There was a continuity to their relationship, even if whoever he was had no way of knowing about it. She'd never been out on a sailboat, only her dad's fishing skiff. What would it be like to go where the wind wanted to take you? To have so little control? Your life changing from one moment to the next due to the slightest whim of the winds?

She shook her head. "No, I'll do as I've always done and leave the wild ones to their own devices."

"Wimp!" Perrin waved her glass at her in a mock toast.

"Sensible," Jo nodded her approval before turning to Perrin. "Have you had so much luck with the wild ones?"

Perrin grimaced. "Not much. Hell of a lot of fun while the ride is on its way up. A mess when it comes crashing back down on me. You remember Jeffie, he was so cute and I was so gone on him. Do you think I'm the reason he went to India to follow that Swami somebody?"

"And now who is it this month?" She always had the best stories.

"No one worth even telling about. But," Perrin pointed a long finger at her. "You never told us about Mr. Wrong. Illegal change of subject. Five yard penalty."

Cassidy grimaced, the last sip of wine distinctly sour.

"Did the sweater work? Did he," Perrin leaned in and dropped her voice to a throaty whisper, "ravish you with his eyes?"

"Yeah. The sweater was perfect, just like you said. I guess I owe you some champagne. He was pretty decent about it once he realized what he was doing, but that sweater certainly gave him trouble more than once."

"Kept him off balance, I bet."

"Yeah. Right until the end when he hit me."

"Hit you?" Jo and Perrin both jerked forward.

She raised her hands. "No, not that. Just metaphorically. A punch right to my gut." She hunched forward and rubbed her face with her hands.

"It wasn't good." Her gut twisted once again, just as it had last night. Just as it had when she'd been trying to finish the article. The date had been going so well. A bit awkward now and then, but a nice change from the boring sameness of Jack James. She'd discussed the tastes of the food and wine to cover the silences. He'd really liked her, or so she'd thought. And she'd definitely started to think he had possibility.

"Turns out he's from New York. For ten years we'd lived in the same city, me down by Greenwich, him on the Upper West Side. We saw some of the same plays, ate in a lot of the same restaurants." They'd both been gentle with each other as they recalled the day the world changed when the Twin Towers fell, but folks outside of New York would never really understand what that day had been like. Even Perrin and Jo had only been able to give sympathy, rather than true understanding, when she'd finally been able to get a call out that she was okay.

"It was all going so well. Then over dessert he attacked my career. When I couldn't figure out the last wine, one I'd never had before, he practically threw it in my face. Tossed money on the table and stormed out."

"He threw money on the table?" Jo asked quietly and Perrin covered her mouth, her eyes wide.

She could only nod.

"Asshole." Jo rarely swore. "What did you do?" She rubbed a soothing hand up Cassidy's back.

She had to gulp for air in her aching lungs. By force of will alone she sat up straight, but couldn't shake off how used she'd felt.

"I paid for the meal in full. Told the owner to return the money to the bastard, or give it to the poor. Then I left. Thank god for that power coat. Perrin, you're the best. It was the only thing that held me together until I got home." And then she'd wept in the shower until she'd nearly drowned. Wept like she hadn't in years. Wept for her loneliness and the gap left in her life by her father's death. Her gut was still sore from the purge.

Perrin moved to the couch and her two best friends hugged her from either side.

"He doesn't deserve you. You are so much better than him."

She wrapped her hands around her friends' arms.

"I am, aren't I?"

"You is," Perrin whispered in one ear. She could feel Jo's nod.

She was. Way better.

"You don't need him. Who cares what a jerk thinks anyway. If he doesn't like our Cassidy, we won't like him either, will we, Jo? Not ever. No matter how nice the restaurant was. Never. Never. Never."

"Ha!" She sat upright and nearly clipped Perrin's chin with her shoulder.

"What?"

"You're brilliant, Perrin. I know exactly how to finish my review of Angelo's."

"I am? How?"

Jo squinted her eyes for a moment and then smiled a smile that would look good on an angel. A wicked angel. "Oh yes, Cassidy. National. Oh my, yes."

Perrin finally got it and jumped to her feet. She clapped her hands and started to dance, her tassels swirling about her thighs and shimmering about her hips.

In moments the three of them were dancing together in the middle of the living room.

RUSSELL SWUNG THE SLEDGEHAMMER AGAIN. The plywood cracked. Again and again he pounded against the counter the previous owner had installed as a galley. He'd used so much glue and near enough a thousand screws that a sledge was the only way to take it out.

He slammed it again and the right side finally broke free.

Demolition. It felt good. Exactly what he needed.

The left side was finally looser. His muscles burned as he drove the hammer repeatedly against the stubborn plywood.

Without warning the whole counter broke free and fell. Twisted as it bounced off the curve of the hull.

He jumped back, slammed his head on an open porthole, his legs were stopped by the pilot berth and the counter clipped his shins so sharply that he collapsed onto the bunk. He tried to kick the counter free, but it was wedged into place and had him pinned.

"Shit!" He managed to grab the edge of it and lift it just enough to pull his legs free. He dropped the counter to the companionway floor with a bang.

He pulled up his pantlegs, doing his best not to hiss at the pain. Blood. On both shins. He touched the back of his head where he'd clipped the porthole. No blood at least, but a painful bump was already rising.

"Double shit!"

He lay down on the pilot berth and held his breath until the searing pain subsided a little. Then he pounded his heels against the boards that would be covered with cushions at some later date. He was ten years old and pounding out his frustration in his final-ever temper tantrum. Everything had gone wrong.

"Triple shit!" He'd really liked the lady despite herself and despite her New York past and her fancy ways. Cassidy was the most attractive woman he'd met since…since he didn't know when. It wasn't that she was beautiful, though she certainly was. She was also intelligent, funny, and fantastic to look at. He could close his eyes and see her—every shape of her face fit together into a unified whole. Not the studied and genetic elegance of Melanie, but what beauty really was about.

And her body was womanly rather than model gaunt. That sweater had almost killed him. Every few minutes his attention was dragged down from her face by that deepening fade of russet toward black and the hidden promise of the black turtleneck beneath. He'd give a pretty penny to know why she smiled rather than snarled each time he couldn't stop his eyes from drifting. She certainly wasn't a tramp. Angelo had been right about that, a real lady.

Nutcase crawled out of wherever she'd been hiding from all his pounding. Seeing him lying on his back, she leapt onto his chest, settled herself in a little ball, and, now in her favorite position, set into purring like a pint-sized buzzsaw.

"But it isn't just her beauty that makes her attractive," he explained to the cat as his shins finally downgraded from excruciating to merely annoying. "See, there's a difference between pretty and attractive that a lot of guys don't understand." Of course, neither had he until he'd started the inevitable comparison of Melanie and Cassidy Knowles.

The cat buzzed a little louder. She loved when he talked and she was curled on his chest.

"Beauty is like stop-you-in-the-street 'Wow!' Attractive, that's something different." He slid a finger along Nutcase's jaw and she closed her eyes with pleasure.

"It's when everything combines in a certain way. She doesn't have to be a knockout; though she is. But you add that on top of funny, a real brain, and all that other stuff and you get a killer combination."

Killer.

He pounded the back of his head against the boards, right where he'd hit his head, and he briefly saw stars again.

And then you blow it by going out of your way to insult her.

He reached back to rub his aching head and his fingers caught in papers. The mail. He'd stopped by the post office box and grabbed it on his way home from the hardware store and then tossed it on the bench so he could try out his new sledge.

Bill. Bill. Junk mail. Victoria's Secret catalog, toss that aside for later. Nah, chuck it. Just more vapid fantasy women. He gave it a quick flip before tossing it aside.

Melanie. She got the center spread, good for her. Damn, she looked really fine with that long body and the red teddy. Shit! If she looked this good on the page, she must have been incredible in real life. And those eyes. He'd never captured that emotion on her. If he had, he would have used her face in some of the ads. But he'd never seen in the camera that wealth of calmness with the alluring dash of pity. Mere mortals couldn't know the joy of wearing scarlet teddies for your man.

But he had seen it on her face once, though not on the camera. It was how she'd looked at him at the airport before turning away and leaving him behind. Calm and pity.

He chucked the catalog toward the garbage bag and missed. It flopped over the open floorboard exposing the bilge where it teetered for a long moment. The corner drooped. It disappeared below with a sodden splat. Crap. He really needed to fix that missing board in the floor.

The last envelope had Angelo's writing on it. His friend hadn't come by in a week and Russell couldn't face going to see him.

Mail, though. That was a bad sign. Angelo had occasionally sent postcards when they'd lived on opposite coasts. Neither of them was much at writing. He tore off the end.

Nutcase appeared to have slipped into another of her mid-afternoon naps.

A newspaper clipping and two, hundred-dollar bills wrapped in a sheet of white paper. One word across the paper.

"Jerk!"

Two hundred dollars. They were for...what? Then he remembered. He'd tossed them on the table, as if paying for...

"Idiot!" He jerked up to a sitting position and banged his head on the low overhead above the pilot berth. He fell back prone as Nutcase growled and dug her claws into his chest at the unannounced change of position. His t-shirt was no defense against her talons. He extracted her claws and tossed her onto the table. He sat up more carefully this time.

Idiot! He'd treated her like…like a babe from 1-900-Dial-a-Babe. "Nice dinner conversation, honey. Here's a couple of bills for your time." Damn! He'd meant to pay for the meal he'd ruined. Well, here it was back in his face once again. He jammed the bills in the pocket of his jeans.

He unfolded the clipping.

A Restaurant for Romance
    by Cassidy Knowles

Oh god! Angelo was going to bloody murder him. He'd forgotten that she'd been there to review the restaurant—the good and the bad. Her article would play from New York to San Francisco. She couldn't break the restaurant, but she could certainly ding it. Ding it bad. He hadn't told her, but he used to follow her columns when he was looking for the hot new restaurant to charm someone into his bed. Usually worked too. The lady had taste and people listened.

He scanned the article.

A good review. Thank god!

No, a great review. It sounded so good, he wouldn't have credited it except that he'd shared the meal with her. The Baby Scallop Kebob had been incredible. He could feel his mouth water again as he read about it. It had also been the high point of the meal right before he…

The chef made exquisite choices. Even the dessert wine, previously unknown to this reviewer, so complemented the fig-custard, puff pastry that this diner was transported back to the chef's home town of Monterosso. The narrow beaches, the high cliffs, the home cooking, and the strong wines of the Ligurian region of Italy.

A little side column described the wine exactly as he'd tasted it. Only he hadn't. He'd been far too grouchy to notice even half that. But she made him think that he had. She was really good at this.

A fine meal can be destroyed as easily by poor company as a poor chef.

Ouch! Okay, here it comes. Here's where she slaughters Angelo's. And it was all his fault. Angelo was never going to forgive him. The thin paper was crumpling in his hands.

Whether making a marriage proposal, as was done and joyously accepted by a bride-to-be, or looking to celebrate fifty glorious years together, there can be no better place than Angelo's Tuscan Hearth. Bring the person you love to this restaurant and you'll never be forgotten for it. Ever.

There it was. Published. Syndicated into over two hundred markets.

Cassidy Knowles was going to forgive him...never!

CAPE FLATTERY LIGHTHOUSE

Cape Flattery, Makah Bay
        First lit: 1857
Automated: 1977
48.3717 -124.7366

Cape Flattery was so named by Captain Cook in 1778 when he arrived at the Northwesternmost point of what would eventually become Washington State. "In this very latitude geographers have placed the pretended Strait of Juan de Fuca. Nothing of that kind presented itself to our view." And so he dubbed the cape a "flatterer."

Cook erred. The nearby Strait of San Juan de Fuca leads to the massive Puget Sound which hosts such cities as Seattle, Tacoma, and Vancouver, British Columbia.

The lighthouse was built with the light tower itself incorporated into the building so that the keepers did not have to risk the hostile natives to maintain the light. The natives were hostile because they had been decimated a few years before by a smallpox epidemic brought in by the light's construction workers.

MAY 1

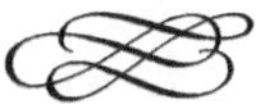

ccording to the GPS, Cassidy was about halfway to the viewpoint for the offshore Tatoosh Island lighthouse. It was such a beautiful day she was practically dancing along the three-quarter-mile long trail. Spring was finally here; the winter rains had eased off and the sun shimmered down from a crystalline sky. These were the moments she was glad she'd returned to the Pacific Northwest. The buds were opening in the vineyards she'd driven past, the flowers edging forth and filling the air with their sweet scent—battling the cherry trees for her nose's attention.

The trail was a bit rough, but just fine in her hiking boots. Actually, according to the GPS, they were overkill, but she wanted to get some use from them. They made her feel solid, standing square upon the earth.

"Is that what men feel like when they do that thumbs-hooked-in-their-pockets thing?" A passing bumblebee was too busy about her task to answer.

The trail had started in a huge empty parking lot. If that lot were filled in the summer, the trail would be nuts. This weekday mid-morning was a far better time to be here. The dirt path descended down through trees, twisting down to simple, split log foot-bridges over muddy passages.

Despite the groomed trail, it was as wild a place as she'd ever been. Twenty or so miles from the nearest town, at the end of the road, at the end of the country for that matter. She was presently the north-westernmost person in the continental U.S. Possibly by that entire twenty miles.

It reminded her of growing up in the country and how much she'd enjoyed it as a child and not enjoyed it as a teen. When had that change taken place? She shrugged. No reason to care today. Today the world consisted of little Cassidy Knowles, a mucky trail, and a new lighthouse.

She followed a side branch to a small viewing platform. A stout rail was all that separated her from an impossibly long drop. The water lay a hundred or more feet below. Sheer islands thrust upward from the ocean into the air, their heads covered in tall caps of fir trees looking like a teen's moussed 'do while the Pacific Ocean rolled and splashed unheeded about their rocky bases.

If she raised her arms, she could fly. If she were to sing, her voice could be heard around the world.

Cassidy returned to the trail and headed for the next lookout, taking the exhilarating floatiness down the trail with her.

"Hey! Wait!"

She looked back to see who was calling. Her foot came down hard on a rock, the shock jarred her whole body.

Russell Morgan. She turned away before he could recognize her, but there was nowhere to go. No escape along the open trail.

She could hear his feet pounding as he ran up the trail.

"Hey! You in the red coat. Wait!"

Resigned, she stopped and turned.

Russell stumbled to a halt, a fancy camera banging against his hip. "I've been looking for… Oh, it's you."

He had the decency to blush bright red at her continued silence.

"Sorry, that came out wrong. Let me start again. Hi, Cassidy. I didn't expect to see you here." He looked down the length of her body as if he were inspecting a mannequin.

Glancing down she saw her red leather coat, it was too warm for the parka. Black leggings and her new, barely dirty, hiking boots. They now appeared as ungainly clown feet at the end of overly skinny, pogo-stick legs. Ridiculous with the high-fashion coat, but she liked the way the soft leather felt no matter how inappropriate it was for the setting.

His gaze returned to her face. "Your hair."

She reached up to check it, but it was still up in the clip that should keep it out of her face even in the wind that every lighthouse apparently cultivated.

"What?"

"It, uh," he shook himself as if coming awake from a dream, "looks nice."

"Thanks." If he thought a lame compliment was going to begin to make up for...

"I'm really sorry for some of the things I said the other night."

"You mean a month ago?"

His expression blanked for a moment.

"A month ago? Really?"

Just how dense was he?

"Twenty-six days." *Ugh, really really lame, Cassidy Knowles.* She sounded like a pining female who counted the days, hours, minutes, and seconds. It was easy. Today was May first and their date, if one could call it that, had been on April fourth. Thirty days hath September, April, June, and...

He flashed one of his killer smiles and she did her best to resist its power. It was a really good smile.

"That makes this a mighty belated apology, doesn't it? Perhaps if I got down on my knees?"

"How about a kow-tow?"

With the light breeze ruffling his brown hair, a worn denim jacket that outlined his wonderful upper body, he dropped to his knees and pounded his forehead three times against a patch of sand.

"Please forgive me, O Great Goddess of the Wines."

He rocked back on his heels and grinned up at her. "Better?"

"That's not fair."

"What?" He stood once again and she noticed that her eyes were about level with his chin. His shoulder was just the right height to lay her head on if they were slow dancing. Stupid image. She definitely didn't want to be around Russell Morgan for a moment longer than she had to—absolutely not long enough for a dance. Her brain had clearly taken a holiday.

"Jerks aren't supposed to make me smile. Especially ones I'm mad at."

"Cheating, huh?" He hooked his thumbs into his jeans pockets as if he were Harrison Ford and he'd just defeated the entire German Army on his own.

"Definitely."

"Well, can I walk with you a bit, if I promise to be less jerky?"

"Is that possible?"

He shrugged eloquently, "I can try, but no guarantees."

It would be tempting to blast him with some witty remark and walk away, but she could never think of them when she most needed them.

"Okay," as if she had a lot of choice in the matter, there was only the one trail and not another soul to be seen.

He bowed slightly and indicated she should walk ahead. They moved toward the point in silence until one of them had to speak or she'd go stark raving mad.

"Do you—"

"Isn't it—"

"You first."

"No, you."

He looked grumpy, but she waited him out.

"Do you come out here often?"

She shook her head. "My first time."

"Me, too. Do you, ah, go to many lighthouses?"

Her foot caught on a rock and she stumbled forward. He reached out a hand to steady her, but she didn't take it.

"Seemed like a nice day for a drive. I wasn't really going for the lighthouse. I thought the northwest point of the U.S. might be amusing." She was babbling like an idiot. But she'd be damned before she'd tell him that she'd been collecting lighthouses for the last five months.

"What about Alaska?"

"Continental U.S." You jerk.

"That always bothered me. 'Continental U.S.' Like Alaska is on some other continent."

"Contiguous U.S. Does that make you happier?"

"Immensely." He started whistling as if he hadn't a care in the world.

"Is this your first time?"

She glanced over in time to see a wolfish grin cross his face for a moment. That definitely hadn't come out right, but she was not going to blush. Her cheeks didn't appear to be paying attention to her orders and were heating up abruptly.

"I meant—"

"Yes and no," he saved her with a casual drawl that might still have a bit of the grinning male ego. "First time here."

She focused on the trail ahead and continued placing one foot in front of the other.

"How about you? Are you a lighthouse virgin?" He said it with every sexual insinuation possible dripping from his tongue. She'd obviously given him too much credit. What were they, in high school?

"Jesus. Do you go out of your way to be insulting?"

He stopped his damn whistling. Actually, he was no longer beside her and she had to backtrack to where he halted.

"No." He shook his head, his voice as soft as the breeze wending its way through the green moss. "No. I'd have to say that you bring out the worst in me."

"I'm honored."

He bit his upper lip and inspected the sky for a moment.

"Can we try this again?"

"You already started twice."

"Third time's the charm?"

If he'd made it a statement, she'd have left him and to hell with the ferry ride, the three-hour drive, and the stupid lighthouse. But he looked pitiable. How a handsome, broad-shouldered man over six feet tall could look so lost was a wonder. Did he know that she had a weak spot for lost souls?

She looped her hand through the crook of his arm and tugged him along the trail. Once they were walking together, he unwound a bit. De-stiffened enough to bend his legs in some semblance of normalcy.

"Hi, I'm Cassidy Knowles. Yes, I'm a lighthouse virgin. This is my first one." She'd be nice to him for Angelo's sake, but that didn't mean she was about to let him one single inch into her life.

"Russell Morgan, pleased to— I really was pleased to meet you. You seemed like a nice lady at dinner, no matter how I mangled it."

"I have rarely been attacked quite so thoroughly."

"Well, you didn't deserve it."

She'd thought a lot about what he'd said. Hard not to.

"I'm less sure of that now than I was then."

Where the trail narrowed, he walked awkwardly with one foot in the mud so that she could stay well on the trail. It did make her think a little better of him.

"You made your feelings for me quite clear in your review."

She had, hadn't she. "I was…"

"Irritated? Hurt?"

"Really, really pissed," but was becoming less so with each step they took together. How was he doing that to her?

"Ah, well. I'd wager that isn't something your average date achieves quite so thoroughly."

"No, Mr. Morgan. You're a first. Though there was this one guy." She told him the story about Richie who had hallucinated her as hell-spawn.

He told a story about a horrid double-date he'd had with Angelo when they were in high school. Twins that Angelo could keep straight just fine, but not him. Kept trying to kiss the wrong one.

He was actually charming when he wasn't in a vicious back-biting mood. Cassidy could feel the muscles under her hand. His strong bicep flexing easily as they moved over the last of the rocks, an unconscious strength easily shifted to aid her balance. She enjoyed holding the man's arm—of feeling, even for an instant, that they belonged side-by-side. A warmth ran through her that had nothing to do with the May sunshine.

Rounding the last bend in the trail, they came upon a small viewing platform raised a half-dozen steep steps above the rocky clifftop. She waved him forward, though he tried to insist that she proceed first. There was chivalry and there was climbing a half-dozen ladder-steep steps—that would place her behind right in his face.

"Jerks before ladies."

"Even redeemed ones?"

"You aren't redeemed yet, go."

He ascended, like most males, using only every other step. Good butt, she couldn't help noticing. And grinned. Turnabout was sometimes fair play. She followed him up the ladder.

Then she stopped noticing Russell Morgan at all.

The sweep of the Cape Flattery shore spread before them. Three-quarters of the horizon was water. To the right was the Straits of San Juan de Fuca. To the left was the endless expanse of the Pacific Ocean. And straight ahead was a rocky, sprawling island, the last land before Alaska and Japan.

A few hundred yards offshore, Tatoosh Island popped from the water like the bottom of a cooking pot—flat-topped and sheer-sided. The green grass and few firs did little to mitigate the desperate isolation of the lighthouse perched on the edge of the cliff. It was no wonder that a lighthouse keeper and his assistant had attempted a duel to the death over some imagined insult. Both had been saved by another assistant who had removed the lead from the bullets before the three shots were fired.

Its beacon winked at her across the narrow passage. The light called out: seeking aid or was it offering guidance?

Perhaps it was both. She scanned the water, right and left. The only thing that was missing was the sailboat.

RUSSELL HAD FINALLY LEFT to amble along the edges of the high cliff. Even now Cassidy could see him poking along inspecting every nook and cranny of the narrow point, as if he'd lost something. Occasionally he'd snap a picture with that fancy camera of his but even that looked less like inspiration and more like habit. At long last he headed down a side trail that appeared to lead to the bottom of the cliff.

She took the moment alone to pull out her father's letter.

Dearest Ice Sweet,

You can hold onto something so tightly that your nerves go numb and you no longer notice your deathgrip on it. Not until it is too late, or near enough.

Adrianne and I spent three years trying to save the vineyard. We sunk every penny we had into it until every belonging was sold and we'd spent almost every ounce of our life's blood. We often lived on beans and rice to stretch the money. By the time you were two, the last threads were unraveling.

Adrianne was too busy raising you to ever take to the fields again for those grueling sixteen-hour days. When her parents took ill, she went home to Bainbridge Island, Washington to take care of them. I struggled to save that which was past saving. I stayed on. Sheer damn stubbornness, I guess. Or maybe just blinders.

April 7th. That was the day. With the lack of water the last harvest had been miserable. I'd spent the winter trying to work the wine, but without your mother's help and wisdom, it failed miserably. Your mother was gone and I didn't think she'd be coming back. I had to choose between my vineyard or her and you. It was the hardest thing I've ever done. Thank all the gods, I made the right choice. I sold out and I moved to the Kitsap Peninsula and started living over your grandparents' garage.

Beware getting so locked in that you don't see what you most need to look at.

Love you, Ice Sweet.

Vic

He'd lost a vineyard and she'd never known, a Napa Valley vineyard. That would be worth a fortune now and it sounded as if he lost it for pennies. He'd taken a body blow to the heart because of her. Then he not only lost his vineyard, but his parents-in-law and then his wife. No wonder he didn't speak much of his past; the pain ran deep roots into his life.

Russell was heading back toward her.

She crumpled the letter and shoved it into her pocket. A quick wipe at her eyes and her wet fingers cooled in the offshore breeze. She turned her face into that light breeze; she'd blame her eyes on the wind if he said anything.

He stopped and scanned the area once more, not even bothering to glance at her. Mr. Sensitive he wasn't.

She checked the ocean again, especially back down the Straits toward Seattle, but no blue sailboat braved the waters. No boat at all had appeared in the last hour except for a pair of container ships and a tanker that looked big enough to carry all the oil of an entire country. Okay, a small country.

She photographed the lighthouse out on the island, but without her sailboat, it looked empty. Felt pointless. It wouldn't really belong in the series on her wall.

Each step he took closer to her was followed by a quick glance around.

"You look as if you've lost something."

He shrugged.

"Stood up by your blond girlfriend?"

He aimed a scathing glance in her direction.

"Sorry." She bit the edge of her tongue. "Now I'm the one being bitchy. I'm sorry."

His gaze didn't soften, but he did manage a jerky nod of acknowledgement. Tit-for-tat. The lowest form of revenge. She wanted to crawl away and hide until he was gone.

He headed back for the parking lot without offering his arm.

She was a little ashamed that she missed it; not that she actually needed any support along the well-groomed trail. His silence was becoming oppressive. She could just fade back and let him disappear ahead. Maybe she could even pretend she had to go back for something she'd dropped and check one more time for her sailboat. But somehow she knew it wasn't coming.

Besides, that was the chicken's way out.

Russell strode ahead, not fast, but with hard, jarring steps. He had powerful legs and a well-formed butt that his worn jeans outlined nicely.

What was she avoiding so much? She stuffed her hands into her pockets and her father's letter crinkled. That was it. The letter had said the same thing Russell had thrown at her.

What did she want to do? She'd walked her career path head down like some kind of bulldog.

Be the best food critic.

Know all the wines.

Be hurt when you don't know about an obscure wine from a remote Italian village.

She'd dropped nearly four hundred dollars the day after their date ordering every wine she could find from the five villages of Cinque Terre. She'd cataloged over half of them, would never forget them, but most were mediocre wines you'd expect from small village wineries. Only a few surprises in the lot and the sciacchetrà was the best of those.

"You were right."

He stumbled and looked back at her.

"What?"

"I said, you were right."

"No, I screwed up with Melanie."

"I meant about having no long-term plan."

For a moment they blinked at each other, both lost on a straight trail with their two cars in clear sight a hundred yards away.

"Her name is Melanie?"

"I'm sorry I said that about you."

Once again they were at a stop. Both too vulnerable. Both with their hearts out on the trail. She couldn't do it. It was a cliff she just couldn't climb. Not with this man.

"I, uh, are you going to the next lighthouse?"

He looked down and kicked at the dirt. "Next lighthouse?"

"There's one a couple of hours south, called Destruction Island. It's —" She almost said, "not on the calendar," but caught herself.

He didn't look at her, still hadn't since rejoining her at the lookout.

"It's offshore a couple miles. They say it should be visible…on a clear day…like today," she finally ran down to a stop.

He looked about the parking lot. Stared for a long moment at Jo's car. Hers was in the shop and Jo had leant her the BMW roadster.

"Nice wheels."

"Um, thanks." What was it with men and fancy cars? It was too racy for her taste, though Russell's car looked even lower and meaner than Jo's. Porsche maybe? Jo had always been the fan of sports cars, the only weakness she'd admit to.

"I think I'll head home. You?" He didn't meet her gaze but continued to be fascinated by the dirt.

"Don't know really. They say a bull lived there who hated the new fog horn. It kept charging the lighthouse whenever it went off— thought it was a competing bull." Why was she trying to talk him into coming?

He finally looked at her; his narrowed eyes indicated that he was certainly asking himself the same question. After a long moment, during which she forgot to breathe, he shrugged.

"Nah. I'm not really feeling up to it." He turned toward his little black car, but turned back and returned to stand in front of her.

He held out a hand.

She took it out of instinct rather than any desire to share contact with him.

Rather than shaking it, he covered it with his other hand. Big, powerful, warm hands enfolded hers, warming away a chill she hadn't noticed.

His sea-dark eyes looked down at her for a long moment. She

could feel her knees going weak. Was he going to kiss her? What would she do if he did?

"Thanks. It was nice to spend some time with you. Perhaps we can do this again sometime. I mean that. I'm lousy company, but you're nice."

She nodded. He let go and walked back to his car. It started with a dull roar, but he didn't disappear in a flurry of gravel as she'd expected. Instead he waited. Waited while she fished out first her keys, then Jo's, got in and started the engine.

As soon as it came to life, he did roar off, fishtailing so wildly on the gravel parking lot that for a moment she thought he'd crash into the trees. Then he regained control and put his foot down, hard. His engine roared loudly over the quiet purr of the BMW's engine even after he was out of sight.

RUSSELL LET the miles flow through him. He wasn't even really aware of where he was until he pulled into Port Angeles.

"Good job, Russ. Real safe way to drive." Eighty miles had rolled by since he'd left Cassidy in the parking lot without really saying goodbye.

He got off Highway 101 and threaded his way through town until he hit the waterfront in a pot-holed gravel parking lot. He stopped with the car's nose pointed toward the water and Canada. He thumped his forehead against the steering wheel.

"Stood up by Melanie?"

Not even close.

"Right about Cassidy Knowles?"

Not a bit closer. She had more class in her little pinky than he'd had in his whole life. She'd forgiven him slashing at her yet again. Forgiven him being there to meet another woman and being so damn obvious about his disappointment that he totally shut her out.

He flopped back in his seat and looked at his hands. He could still feel the outline of her strong fingers imprinted on both his palms.

Could still see all of the colors of both spring and autumn in her eyes. Had seen those lips, those lips that he longed to kiss since the first moment he saw them pursed above a glass of wine.

And that was a path right down the wrong road. Right back into a woman enveloped in a New York state of mind. She wanted to be Craig Claiborne reborn as a woman.

She was so wrong for him.

So why hadn't he been able to stop thinking about her for the last twenty-six days?

<hr>

"YOU REALLY LOOK LIKE SHIT!" Angelo shouted over the serious cranking of the R&B band in the corner of the bar and everyone else shouting to be heard by their companions.

"Thanks, Buddy. Big help." Russell looked up at the mirror behind the broad, wooden bar. Bottles of liquor were lined up and down the mirror's length. He could see only one eye reflected between the silver spouts of a bottle of Johnny Red and the next of Jack Daniels Black. The dark rings beneath the eye made it look more a ghost's than his own.

"I'm serious, man. You look even worse than the night I told you what you did to Melanie."

"Can't you just drink in silence?"

Angelo licked the salt off the back of his hand, knocked back the Cuervo Reserva shooter, and sucked on a piece of lime.

"Nope, I'm a chatty drunk. You know that."

Which usually made them so compatible. Tonight Russell wanted to just... He stared at the one eye in the mirror. He wanted... He didn't know what. Knocking back his tequila, he reached for a chaser but his beer was gone.

Angelo was leaning back against the bar, checking out the crowd, and taking a slug from Russell's pint. He reached for it just as Angelo looked at him and whispered in a quiet shout.

"Target acquired!"

Russell glanced over his shoulder. Sure enough, a pair of women were sitting alone at a tiny table. Long dark hair, thin but in a Seattle-healthy way rather than a New York-anorexic fashion. She wore a halter top that revealed a nice expanse of shoulder and belly, and enough curve beneath to be very pleasing. Her friend was a perky Japanese with denim shorts cut incredibly short. Her hair barely reached her ears—flat and cute as could be in her clingy tube top. They'd noted Angelo's and his attention and were very carefully not looking in their direction, but it was clear he and Angelo were being assessed in sidelong glances that included nice smiles.

Russell turned back to the bar for another tequila, catching their disappointment as he did so.

"Oh shit," Angelo knocked back the rest of Russell's beer. "It's going to be one of those nights?"

Russell punched Angelo's arm but didn't feel much better for it.

SEVERAL DRINKS LATER, Angelo had battered down Russell's defenses and was now giving him worldly advice. Exactly what he didn't need.

"You can no go sailing away from me, my friend. You are no ready. You boat, she is no ready either." The drunker Angelo got, the thicker his accent grew. Half his mother's Italian, half Brooklyn. It would be about three more drinks until he wouldn't understand a word Angelo said. And that would be just fine with him.

In fact, he couldn't wait.

"Look, *vecchio mio.* Sailing off into the unknown, it is a plan. Maybe good. Maybe bad. But it is only sailing off into the unknown. You gonna take you problems with you. You self, he is gun' be dere."

Russell's one eye in the mirror was blearier, but he could still pick it out among the bottles. He definitely wasn't drunk enough yet.

"Melanie is in the past, man. There isn't shit you can do about that one. You go back, you open the studio, you go down on one knee, but even if she say yes, your heart, she fold up and die. I'm Italian. I know this things."

Down on two knees and bowing his head into the sand at Tatoosh. He hadn't been thinking of Melanie. He was thinking of the way Cassidy Knowles looked, standing tall above him, scowling downward as the smile tugged at the corners of her generous mouth. Again, the line of jaw to neck, of cheek to eye made him want to caress, stroke, feel. The wind picking at her tightly controlled hair, but not breaking it free—not a single strand out of control. She didn't have the New York model look. But it was certainly what New York should want.

"Hey! You no listening to me."

He wasn't. "What?"

"I tell you how to fix your whole life and make a million dollars and you not even listening?"

"I already have a million, it's just my life that's unsalvageable."

"Does that mean I should or shouldn't give you my number?" The long dark one was standing beside him paying her tab.

"Shouldn't."

"Should!" Angelo insisted at the same moment.

"He's really an okay guy when he isn't drunk."

"You know we've been waiting over an hour for you two to come over." She looked him up and down, predator trying to decide if the meat was worth dealing with the brain.

"Lady, if you want my advice—"

"She don't!"

He elbowed Angelo in the sternum, who gasped as he lost his breath.

"If the two of you want to jump someone's bones tonight," Angelo smacked him hard on the back of the head, "you should both take him home." He nodded at Angelo.

"He's a much nicer guy than me."

The woman signed her credit slip, with a nice tip he noted, and studied the pen for a long moment before returning it to the bartender without scrawling a phone number on a napkin. She brushed past him, her perfume like a cat in heat.

"You," she whispered loudly to Angelo, "can smack him again."

Angelo did and the woman was gone.

RUSSELL COULD BREATHE. Okay. That was a good sign.

He could open one eye. It was mostly dark except for streetlights reflecting off the ceiling. He placed his little imaginary sailboat among the shadow-shaped ceiling continents and began wending it around to distant shores, shadows with mysterious ports of call. There'd be tropical dark women, towering men, and exotic foods. Leaving the beams of light rising from the dark streets, he sailed toward the great round continent of the ceiling lamp.

Just as his boat arrived, the light blazed on and drove twin balls of fire down his optic nerves and into his brain. Which then exploded as if the sun had gone nova within the confines of his skull.

He dragged a pillow over his face and cursed roundly. The after-image on his retina included an outline of Angelo.

"I'm gonna kill you, you turkey."

Angelo started throwing some extra sofa cushions on top of him. Each made his body shudder with pain.

"You've got fifteen minutes."

"Until I die? Fine. That'll be fourteen minutes after I've killed you." His pulse was pounding against the inside of his skull—hard enough to crack the fragile bone.

"Oh, you really scare me, big man. All talk. No fight."

Russell sat up, thinking he'd lunge at Angelo. It hurt so much that he let his momentum carry him right over to lie the other way around on the sofa.

"Just leave me in peace to die."

"No, you made me promise."

"Promise what? I was drunk. I release you from whatever foul deed I swore you to achieve."

Angelo left him alone for a moment. He was almost back to sleep when a cold, wet towel was slapped against his face.

He let out a roar as he sat up but Angelo dodged back.

"You're going to die, Angelo."

"Someday, probably not today though. I doubt if a fly would be much scared of you in your present state. Here, drink this." He shoved a glass into Russell's hand.

"What is it?" He still kept his eyes closed against the painful light. He could still see every outline of Angelo's living room from the tan walls and the vast array of family photographs, to the yellow and blue pottery, and the wall of cookbooks. The memory of every object was outlined in shimmering rings on his retina.

"Water. A tall glass of cold water."

He knocked it back and nearly threw up. Three fingers of whiskey bored their way down his throat and spilled into his stomach to lie there and burn.

"Oops. Sorry. Wrong glass. That was the hair of the dog and brother did he ever bite you hard last night. Here's an orange juice and aspirin chaser."

Russell forced open an eye to make sure it wasn't sixteen ounces of vodka or gin. He sipped it carefully to get the aspirin down before setting it aside on the teak coffee table.

He opened the other eye. The room only spun a little. Even in his present state, it was cozy and comfortable.

"So. What was this damn promise you are so set on keeping?"

Angelo lounged back against a doorway, well out of harm's reach.

"We're going shopping."

"Do you have any idea how hard this is to do with a hangover?"

"Easy as fish." Angelo was holding a three-foot long salmon and bending it back and forth.

"How fresh is this one? It feels good." He directed his question to the fishmonger, a huge-armed man in his twenties. Someone Russell wouldn't mess with hungover or in top shape. The man was shoveling bucketfuls of crushed ice and spreading them over his display counter as easily as Russell had tossed back shotglasses of tequila.

Russell had seen this on one of those cute local-interest news clips, but he'd never gotten up at five in the goddamn morning to watch it.

A crowd had gathered to watch, phones and cheap cameras poised to capture the upcoming Pike Place Market ritual.

"I kept it aside for you from last night's flight. Out of the water less than twenty-four hours." The fishmonger slapped the side of the fish like it was an old friend.

Angelo handed it back to him to add to the growing pile.

"And it will be on my dinner table in another twelve."

He tuned them out as the other men, all equally biceped, began chucking more fish from the van. Twenty and thirty-pound salmon arced one after another through the air, so fast there was little room between them. They flew out of the back of the truck, arced high over the sidewalk, just skimming below the open eaves of the market. At the far end they were snatched from the air and dropped onto the ice in neat rows, sorted by type, slid deep into the waiting ice in a single smooth motion. Mesh bags of oysters, clams, squid, and worse followed, rapidly filling the iced tables. A four-foot shark flew by and the small crowd of hearty tourists who had braved the early morning air applauded. The sharp tang of raw fish not yet turning bad filled the air faster than the morning breeze could clear it.

Angelo was in position and took first pick of everything that landed.

Russell had seen enough and then some. If he'd had breakfast, he'd have lost it by now.

Angelo finally rescued him from the post he was slowly sliding down and shoved him farther into the market.

"And I made you promise to abuse me this morning for what reason?" His head felt a little better, but his body felt as if he'd been in a brawl. Several brawls and all on the inside of his skin.

"You insisted that you wanted to change your life. See how the other half lived. Whatever that meant."

"Sounds like a crock to me."

"Me too. But you kept insisting you were a boat without a rudder. By the hundredth repetition I promised just to get you to shut up."

He found a stool to sit on as Angelo attacked the produce stand.

Clearly he was well known here, as once again the proprietor brought out a special stash.

"All organic. All fresh within the last two days." Angelo sorted through the offering quickly and kept most of it. The few items he rejected were placed in the prime display spots of the lesser produce.

The market was starting to buzz. More restaurateurs were showing up and picking things over, but Angelo already had the best of it. The tourists, now that all the fish were thrown and their final flights videoed for the neighbors back in Wichita, had retreated to small cantinas perched on the outer edge of the market. There, they'd gather close around their lattes and cinnamon rolls and stare out at the rising sun lighting up the Seattle waterfront a hundred feet below.

All that were left were people living their lives. Fish and lettuce bought, they visited a butcher next—then the baker across the street who promised fresh bread that evening. Each going about their own life.

Finally done, Angelo led him down the block and they wended their way between the vans and hurrying morning people. Later the slower tourists would re-emerge and clog the market until it was faster to walk in the narrow street.

The funny thing was that among all these sellers and buyers and observers, he couldn't tell who was a mess and who had their life together. They all looked so certain and purposeful in their wandering roles. Russell was half tempted to take a poll.

Was the young woman setting up the ice-cream stand looking tired because of a long night of amazing sex or because her two-year old had a toothache? Did the family in the Greek restaurant that filled the corner of a narrow, brick building always start the day with coffee that was so strong the airborne caffeine was enough to wake him up? Did the young Chinese couple know how odd their Mandarin sounded on American ears, pointing with long fingers at the end of outstretched arms to indicate each topic of interest and being a pedestrian hazard? What had drawn them here from whatever land they lived in, China, Taiwan, or San Francisco?

Angelo dragged him to a small cluster of tables along Post Alley not far from the restaurant. They were the only ones outdoors—the morning was still cool and fresh though the day would be warm. Tourists were perched at tables inside. Early-start businesspeople were streaming by in suits and skirts in a frantic pattern that they probably repeated every day, five days a week.

Some goddess, by the name of Jonas, set a double espresso, a huge cup of steaming, black coffee, and a gigantic muffin in front of him with a swish and a bat of the eyelids. He ignored the flirt and the muffin, scorched his mouth when he chugged the espresso, and felt much better for it.

"Okay."

"He's back, folks," Angelo announced to no one in particular. "The man is back. Consciousness has returned."

"Let's not get carried away."

"No, let's. After you go out of your way to insult a beautiful woman who had the hots for you last night and, by the way, chasing away her terribly cute girlfriend who'd been eyeing me, I say let's go wild."

Russell searched around in his brain. A vague memory of long, dark hair swam through, but he couldn't be sure who or what it was attached to. For some reason, his brain kept connecting it to a smack on the back of his head, but he couldn't imagine making a stranger angry enough that she'd do that. Though lately, maybe he could.

"So," Angelo sipped his café leche, "what is it with you and women now? They used to trail around behind you and melt into fluttery little puddles when you actually noticed one of them. Now, you're toxic."

His blood was toxic. It still hurt each time his heart tried to force some to circulate through his brain. He couldn't seem to get the hang of Seattle women.

"Mr. Morgan," Angelo held up half of his croissant like a microphone, "when did you decide to become a misogynist?" He aimed the pastry at Russell.

"Oh, I've always hated women. That's why they can make me feel like such a shmuck." Russell bit the end off the croissant. The act of chewing stung the side of his face right up into his temple. He sipped some coffee to soften it.

Angelo pulled his shortened breakfast back.

"Is that because you truly are a shmuck and they recognize that?" He took a bite himself and continued around a mouthful. "Honestly, what is it with you lately, buddy?"

"I wish I knew, Angelo. I wish..." He'd been idly watching the world go by on the street at the end of the alley.

People were moseying down the hill on their way to the market. Or hurrying up the steep slope with briefcase in one hand and a triple-shot latte in white, carry-out cups of immense size clutched in the other.

—And there she was!

He'd know her anywhere!

A long red-brown ponytail slapping one side to the other. Tight Lycra that followed every curve of her runner's figure exactly as he'd imagined. Better.

She was glancing over her opposite shoulder, checking to cross the street. He saw nothing of her face, nothing but the swinging ponytail. An armband held a music player and thin wires trailed from arm to ears.

Two strides. Three. Then gone. Past the end of the alley.

He stared for a moment, trying to register her in this reality. She was his lighthouse lady and she was here in Seattle. No one else had hair quite like that. And her body: outdoorsy, athletic, and totally stunning.

"Hey!" Angelo grabbed for his coffee as Russell scrambled from the table and bolted to the end of the alley. He heard Angelo curse loudly but kept going.

No one. Not one sign of her.

He sprinted up the street, so steep they actually built lumps into the sidewalk for traction. He made it to First Avenue and nearly stumbled in front of a Metro bus.

Right. Left. Across the street.

Gone!

Gone as if she'd never existed.

He stood for ten minutes, watching and waiting. Just in case she magically reappeared. She didn't, of course.

Had he fallen for a ghost? Did she exist only in photographs of lighthouses and in Lycra among a crowd of suits?

The first he was aware of Angelo was a smack on the back of his head.

"You!" he turned. Of course. It hadn't been the long, dark, stranger lady he'd insulted last night; it was Angelo who had smacked him.

Angelo pointed at his khakis. A long coffee stain ran down one leg.

"What's wrong?" Russell offered his best smirk. "Pee your pants again? Thought you outgrew that in high school."

"WHAT IS IT WITH MEN?" Cassidy pulled the pin on the weight machine and shoved it back in ten pounds heavier. The weight machines were mostly vacant at the moment. That was one reason she and Jo worked out on Sunday mornings. Perrin, not a morning person at the best of times, wouldn't be awake for hours. The rowing machines were moderately busy, the spinning cycles were the hottest new craze and there was actually a short line of men and women jogging in place waiting their turns.

Jo was huffing and puffing her way through her pecs workout. She did her raise-an-eyebrow thing to show she was listening.

"You'd never guess who's taken to standing outside my condo every morning about the time I get back from my run."

"Bradley, huff, Cooper, puff?"

Cassidy sat on the bench, hooked her ankle behind the padded bar and swung her leg forward. It was heavier, but she didn't feel any strain in the knee, just on every muscle around it. About right.

"Guess again. For real."

"The man, huff, with two first names, puff?"

Cassidy started kicking her leg out.

"I don't think that Jack James even noticed I broke up with him.

Not a single phone call or note since, nothing. No. It's Mr. date-from-hell, Mr. showing-up-at-my-lighthouse-thank-you-very-much, Russell the-jerk Morgan."

Jo let the arm pads slap back against the stops and the weights slammed home with a sharp clang. She leaned her head down between her knees for a moment to catch her breath.

"You must be kidding me?"

"I wish. He was just there one morning when I came running up the hill. Almost ran square into his back. He was like one of those children's crossing guards, manning the corner, checking everyone who went by."

"What did you do? And stop kicking that way. You are going to hurt yourself."

Cassidy dropped the kick bar back under the bench and then her knee started to complain. If she'd hurt herself because of Russell, she'd...she'd...she didn't know, but he'd regret it.

"I turned around faster than Picabo Street doing a gold medal slalom and went in through the garage entrance."

"Maybe it was just a coincidence."

"Every day for a week?" Cassidy grabbed a towel and tossed it at Jo, the sweat was forming below her white Nike headband.

"What are you going to do? I could have a restraining order drawn up for you by nine a.m. tomorrow."

"But he hasn't done anything."

Jo threw the towel back at Cassidy's face.

"That doesn't mean he won't do so in the future." Jo was using her implacable lawyer voice.

Cassidy considered it. But it wasn't scary. It was just...weird. "It's not about me."

"Oh, and how does Detective Knowles know that? Can her fine nose now scent a man's true intentions?"

It wasn't like Jo. She didn't usually resort to sarcasm. Cassidy swung her leg over the bench so that she and Jo were sitting knee-to-knee on the machine's two benches.

"It was like when we were out at the lighthouse. He was looking for something. Someone. He was harmless. He just looked lost...and disappointed." By week's end, he had added sullen to that look.

"I still shiver when I think about the two of you being out there alone together."

Cassidy didn't. She remembered his smile as he knelt before her, stray bits of sand still stuck to his forehead. Holding his arm as they walked out to the point. The absolute safety and peace that had washed through her as his hands wrapped around hers the moment before he drove off like a maniac.

"No. I was fine. It was just weird."

"Hi, Ms. Knowles."

She looked up the dark muscular legs, bright blue gym shorts and matching tank top, and finally the powerful shoulders before she found Angelo's face smiling down at her. A sheen of sweat covered his face and he dabbed at it with the ends of the towel hanging around his neck.

"You know better, it's Cassidy to you."

"Thank you, Cassidy. I didn't want to stop your conversation, but I haven't had a chance to say thanks for that wonderful review you gave me. Bookings are up." He laughed with a flash of white teeth. "That's an understatement. I was going to stop serving lunches, now I'm over half full. Dinners are booked out as often as not. It's wonderful."

"It was my pleasure, Angelo, every mouthful. And I think your success has to do with more than my review. I've seen your new ads, they're great." He'd taken the Tuscan Hearth concept and run it heavily in the tourist magazines. Several clips from her review had appeared in the most recent set.

"I got the best man on it. Russell is a-number-one."

"Russell, as in Russell Morgan?" Why didn't she know this about him? She'd spent a whole meal with the man and a couple hours more in his company out at Cape Flattery. He'd never mentioned a single word about his past, his family, or what he did for a living. That was odd—not a single word.

Angelo's smile froze into a cautious look, then a reluctant nod. Suddenly aware of the dangers of mentioning his name in her presence. He'd couldn't have missed the slash at Russell she'd put in the end of the review.

How could a man with so much skill hide it so damn well? A useless bum, who drove a very fancy sports car and was an advertising wizard.

There was something not right about him.

"He's not the most forthcoming person."

Angelo squinted his eyes for a moment. He opened his mouth to say something, then apparently thought better of it and closed it again.

She rested a hand on his arm. "He's your friend, I understand. Topic closed."

He took a deep breath and covered it with a gentle laugh that spoke volumes about the challenges of being Russell's friend.

That's when she caught Jo's expression. She widened her eyes and nodded ever so slightly toward Angelo.

"Oh, where is my head? Angelo Parrano," she turned to Jo. "I told you about his restaurant. Jo Thompson, best lawyer alive and best friend ever."

Angelo bowed low keeping his hands on either end of his towel.

"You two must come to the restaurant. I will promise more civilized company and as wonderful a meal. I will tr—"

Cassidy held up a hand to cut him off. "No. No treats. We'll bring a third and we'll have a merry time of it."

"Deal!" He stuck out his hand and she shook it. When Jo offered her hand, he bent over it with a bow. He'd have clicked his heels if he hadn't been wearing sneakers. "It shall be an honor. And don't worry about the reservations. Let me know when and there will always be a table for you."

He turned and sauntered toward the locker rooms, his shorts hanging interestingly from his hip bones. He wasn't as broad-shouldered as Russell, nor as tall, but was just as handsome in his own way. He pushed through the door and she turned to meet Jo's eyes.

"I think he likes you."

"No, you."

Cassidy shrugged, "He likes the review I wrote of his restaurant, but it wasn't my hand he bowed over. And he wasn't really looking at me when he promised a table would always be waiting."

Jo actually blushed. A most uncommon occurrence. "He was just being charming." Sliding back on the bench, she continued her pec workout with renewed vigor.

Cassidy cleared her throat significantly, but Jo didn't turn, though it looked as if more color rose in her cheeks. Cassidy hooked her other leg on the kick bar and began her reps. Maybe tomorrow she'd go ask Russell who he was waiting for.

RUSSELL SAT in the cockpit and watched the marina come awake as he ate breakfast. Perry had been first up. Stopped by the boat to give Nutcase a good morning scritch before heading off without a word— though the old man had been smiling at him like a crazy leprechaun. Whatever the joke was, he was keeping it to himself.

He spotted Dave and Betsy farther down the pier, sipping coffee in their own cockpit. They waved him over, but he was too lazily comfortable where he was so he casually waved back. The sun was reaching over the high bluff which made the west end of Ballard one of the best places to live in Seattle. The views from up there were incredible. But the lifestyle down here among the boats was the best.

The sun was splashing down on Shilshole Marina. Hundreds of masts etched their sharp lines against the sky, cutting it up into brilliant blue patches of heavenly steel. The constant companionship of the water's soft lapping against the various hulls lulled him like a cradle.

He crumbled up the last bit of bacon, sprinkled it over the remaining forkful of eggs; it was the first meal on his new stove and he needed to share it with the rest of the crew. At his whistle, Nutcase hustled over from the bow and began wolfing it down. No, that was canine origin. Began, um, saber-toothing it down? Nutcase. The ultimate fluffy, tangle-haired descendant of the saber-tooth tiger. That was a laugh.

Just like posting guard on that stupid street corner for a week. What had he been thinking? There were a million people in Seattle not counting transients, commuters, and tourists. And he was expecting to meet a specific unknown person on a specific street corner.

She hadn't been at the last lighthouse, so why would she be on the same street corner? She could have moved, given up, come at a different time, or gotten married. Or could she have been a mirage as Angelo kept insisting?

Was he now hallucinating the perfect woman? It halfway wouldn't surprise him—and with his rotten imagination she probably had a voice like a troll and would despise him on sight.

It was all so dumb. He couldn't get the lighthouse lady out of his head any more than he could eradicate Cassidy Knowles.

Out at Cape Flattery it had been hard to keep his eyes off her. She looked like every sea captain's wife as she stood and scanned the horizon. Every incredibly beautiful sea captain's wife. Why did she have to be so stiff and stuck up?

For a while he'd worried that by some cosmic joke, she'd been his lighthouse companion. But when they'd reached the parking lot, she drove a very unexpected BMW roadster, more high-end New York nonsense. It was also a car that had not been one of the three he'd photographed in the Slip Point lighthouse parking lot.

He couldn't find the Lady of the Lights and he couldn't not find Cassidy. This was really getting ridiculous.

Nutcase crawled onto his lap to clean herself. This was late May, that meant Perry had given him the kitten five months ago. Almost half a year together. Born Thanksgiving Day according to Perry. The day that had changed his life.

But was it for the better? That was the thing he couldn't be sure of.

He'd barely spoken to his parents since then. He could feel their shame even if they never said it. Every conversation was beyond awkward. He could just imagine the dinner parties. "We had such hopes for the boy." "We had no idea you could do so little with such an expensive education." "We did our best not to spoil him, but what are you going to do. He grew up with money."

He *had* grown up with money—and he'd earned every cent he spent since the day he'd graduated from college. He'd busted his ass every summer of college, too, to pay for his room and board the rest of the year. They'd paid tuition and books, but he hadn't let his parents pay for anything else any more than Angelo had.

He wasn't spoiled, he just wanted what he wanted.

And that was half Cassidy Knowles and half his Lady of the Lights.

Stupid pipe dream.

He settled lower on the bench and pulled his cap down over his eyes. Nutcase curled up on his stomach for a nap.

Maybe while he was sleeping, one would come out of his dreams into reality, and the other one would just go away.

HE WASN'T THERE the next morning, no longer stationed at her street corner. Seattle information didn't have a listing for Russell Morgan. Cassidy didn't want to talk to him on the phone anyway; she wasn't really sure that she wanted to talk to him at all. Definitely not enough to call Angelo for his phone number. It would be unfair to put him in the middle anyway.

There were a lot of Russell Morgans on Google, thirty-five thousand hits. There was an American painter, a 1930s jazz trombonist, a UK drum teacher, a millionaire's son on someone's most-eligible bachelors list, a Santa Barbara algebra teacher, and finally an advertising photographer. Russell Morgan Studios in New York—but the link was broken, the website gone. She tried the phone number and got a Chinese dry cleaners.

She did find some credits to a car ad. When she opened it up, there was Jo's car against a mottled steel background. It looked fast and sexy. It had the inevitable cool dashboard shots and it also had a single red rose across the seat—just like the rose he'd given her at Angelo's, now safely pressed in her favorite North Italian cookbook. Even if it was from a jerk, she couldn't stop herself from keeping it. It had been a long time since anyone had given her a rose.

He also had shots of watches, suits, her own boots on someone's very long legs. Maybe Melanie's. It took her a while to notice the pattern: no faces. An Armani ad with a very sexy woman in a man's suit, with clearly nothing else on, but the hat was pulled low, the model looking down toward her hands ready to pull apart the lapels. All that showed was her neck and a hint of the cascading blond hair behind.

Every ad was a gut punch. Each offered high emotional impact of sexuality, status, comfort, and class. He had an amazing eye, as acute in composition as Perrin's in fashion.

There it was.

Some connection had been working its way through her consciousness, reaching for the light, and it had finally made it to the surface.

She was dialing Angelo before she had a chance to second guess herself. He was surprised, but willing enough once she promised it wasn't to gut Russell and string him out on a line as fish bait. Whatever Angelo might imply, he was a staunch friend.

Russell's phone was at the third ring before she realized what door she was opening. She should hang up, but he answered before she could take action. His deep-voiced hello was even mellower on the phone.

"Hi, Russell?"

"Cassidy? Didn't expect to hear from you."

She didn't either, but here she was. And he'd recognized her voice. That unnerved her so she spoke quickly before she could give up.

"I was wondering if you would meet with me. I have a business proposition for you."

"I'm not in business." His voice was gruff, even harsh.

"I saw Angelo's ads. They were… I saw your old ones, too. Armani, BMW, they were…are breathtaking." She was babbling. What had been such a simple thought a moment before was becoming muddled.

She shut up and tried looking at something that would relax her. Five lighthouse pictures, four with sailboats. She moved to the sliding glass door and out onto the deck. There wasn't a single blue-hulled sailboat in Seattle's harbor.

The silence was getting long. Too long.

"Hello, Russell. Are you still there?"

Another pause, long enough for her to look at the phone's screen, it said it was still connected.

"I'm here." It was quiet.

"Look, I don't know if you need the money, but I've got a friend whose business needs help."

"One of those college friends?"

"Yes. You remembered."

"I'm not an idiot." The words were abrupt, then he burst out with a laugh. "Okay, except around you."

"So, do you want to meet? Are you interested?"

Another of those pauses. She'd give a pretty penny to know what he was thinking.

"You know where the Chittendon Locks are?"

Cassidy parked her Jetta, no sign of his little black sports car. She took her time wandering through the gardens and over to the boat locks.

It was a busy day. A whole flock of boats were jostling for position above and below the locks. This was the connection from Lake Washington and all of its multimillion-dollar homes to the ocean, making it a very busy thoroughfare. There was also a large haven of steel commercial fishing boats from Fisherman's Wharf that added to the mayhem.

Boats jostled about waiting their turns to be raised or lowered from one to the other. Tourists wandered up and down the concrete walls on either side as the Army Corps of Engineers did their best to escort the boats in and tie them up.

Cassidy leaned on one of the steel rails to watch.

An eighty-foot fishing boat dominated the group, but the fisherman made the easiest work of it. Little speed boats got in the way of sailboats. Sailboats bumped against the big cruisers. The big cruisers couldn't muster enough sober hands to catch and throw lines and they drifted about the lock as if bobbing in a giant bathtub.

"Idiots."

Russell leaned against the railing beside her. Even as he said it, one of the big cruisers turned completely sideways, scraping the bow along one concrete wall and the stern across the other and getting stuck that way. The lock attendants started swearing to themselves as they hurried over to help. The guys on the fishing boat, covered in clothes that had seen far more fish guts than laundry soap, were all lined up at their railing to watch the show. Not one of them lifted a finger.

"Shouldn't they be helping?"

"No. They know enough to keep out of the attendants' way. To let them do their job."

She inspected the man beside her. Dark jeans, practically new, a polo shirt that hugged his shape tucked in tightly at the waistband. Was it knowing that he was a New York professional that changed how he looked? She couldn't be sure.

"What?" He caught her inspection.

"You clean up nice."

His smile lit up and she felt a warmth that might have been a February frost just moments before.

"So Angelo keeps telling me."

"You two are close." Not a question. She knew it as fact. "One of those long-term, can-screw-up-and-still-get-help kind of friends. Those are few and far between."

"He's the best. Closer than blood."

"I've got a friend—"

"The lawyer or the clothes designer?"

He was right, he wasn't an idiot. She'd mentioned them once at their dinner nearly two months ago and he had that information right on tap.

"The lawyer doesn't need that kind of help, she's already at the top of her field."

He nodded and stared out at the boats. They'd gotten the front end tied off though the steel railing was pretty chewed up. Now they were trying to lever the stern free.

"Fashion. I know a bit about that."

"Perrin's really brilliant, but she has no direction. She won't accept help from her friends, but she might from you."

He shook his head.

"Why not?" Perrin really was struggling and she and Jo hadn't found a way to help her.

"How is it going to work?" He turned to face her and his dark eyes weren't distant or closed, but looking right at her from an arm's-length away. "I waltz in and announce that you sent me, that's sure not going to go over big. No bigger than you doing it yourself."

She hadn't really thought that part through.

"Perhaps you could 'waltz in' and, hell, I don't know. This is your specialty." She was at a loss. It had sounded good when she thought it up, but he was right, there was no way for it to work.

"You trying to set me up with her?"

"No! I—" She wasn't. Hadn't even thought of that. But what about it? Russell and Perrin, she liked macho and he might be just the stable influence… But Cassidy didn't want to see them together. She didn't know why. Couldn't go there, not with him so close that she could smell the ocean and sky on him. So close she could move against that wonderful chest with just the smallest step forward.

"No." She shook her head to clear it. "No. I wasn't going there."

He kept looking at her for a long moment with an intensity that was almost scary. Maybe Jo was right and she wasn't wholly safe this close to him. But was that his doing or hers? She shook her head and he eased back without moving away.

"Okay," he slouched back against the rail. "As long as we have that clear. I assume you've told her all about me." There was a touch of chagrin in his voice.

He clearly had a very good idea of exactly what she'd said.

"So, she'll know my name. You'll need to introduce me, and I'll need to make her pay."

"But she—"

He held up a hand to stop her.

"It'll be something she can afford. Maybe even barter, though I don't have much need for women's clothes. You can pay my real fees."

Cassidy swallowed hard. She was well off, but how much was a New York professional worth? Especially one of Russell's caliber?

"I don't know if *I* can afford you either."

He shrugged easily, "I'm not sure what it will be, but money has little value to me. Deal?" He smiled for a moment, but didn't do the expected rake of his eyes down her body. So, sex wasn't the deal either. Something else. Something he wouldn't want to do. Certainly not judging a wine contest.

"I think I'd rather pay."

He stayed serious a moment longer then burst out laughing. So hard that she started to smile despite herself. He turned back to watch the boats still chuckling under his breath.

They'd finally straightened out the big cruiser, much the worse for the wear, and were filling in the lock with sailboats.

"You're a tough lady, it's hard to make you squirm. Don't even know why I enjoy doing that to you, but I seem to. Hell, your friend, I'd probably help her out just for the fun of it. But I just thought up something better."

"Better?" her voice cracked, her throat was so dry.

This time he did look her up and down. His grin was wicked.

"You're going to hate it."

NEW DUNGENESS LIGHTHOUSE

*D*ungeness Spit
First lit: 1857
Automated: 1994
48.18174 -123.10962

The New Dungeness lighthouse was one of the first built in Puget Sound. It stands at the very end of a sand spit that sticks five miles out into the treacherous Straits of San Juan de Fuca.

Also known as Shipwreck Spit, the narrow bit of land had a long history as a battleground between the various local tribes. Once established, the light often guided warring tribes to its base for their bloody battles. Though the lightkeepers were never harmed, they were often living in a lighthouse surrounded by corpses.

It was a five-mile walk out Dungeness Spit to the lighthouse. There wasn't much of a view, a chilly fog limited Cassidy's sightlines to a few hundred feet, but there was plenty to see. Thousands of birds joined her for her walk along the nature sanctuary: gulls fishing close ashore, cormorants standing out on logs with their wings spread to dry, and grebes diving deep whenever she drew too close. Even a couple of seals followed her, looking like dogs paddling happily through the waves until the moment they dove in a sinuous roll.

Her favorite were the sandpipers racing up and down the beach following the leading edge of the lazy waves, occasionally pecking at the sand. She couldn't see what they caught, but they intently followed each wave down the long beach, then raced madly back to keep their feet dry. They always made her laugh.

The GPS showed her making steady progress toward the lighthouse despite being in the dense, unrevealing fog. An endless loop of land rolled through the bubble of visibility around her. She moved her feet, but it felt as if she and the fog never moved. The land slid into her fog bubble from some unknowable place ahead and disappeared behind taking its wildlife with it. Her hair was soaked by the cool moisture, she'd let it down to keep her neck warm. If not for the parka and the red watchcap she'd be freezing despite the calendar insisting it was June.

The GPS claimed the lighthouse was only two hundred and fifty-four feet away when the fog ended like a curtain. The sunlight glittered off the white lighthouse so that it shone incandescent against the blue sky. The little outbuildings were clustered about its base including an oversized Cape Cod cottage in the now-predictable U.S. Coast Guard paint job of white with a red roof. The actual lighthouse jumped out of the cottage's midsection like a giant spear shot down from the heavens. The seagulls, who had stayed low and flew little in the fog, were soaring about the sunlit sky.

The old Indian battleground was now a pleasant park surrounded on all sides by the ocean and populated by thousands of birds. A bald eagle swooped low out of the fog, pulled up sharply, and cried in surprise at finding a human in its hunting ground. It passed barely a dozen feet away as she ducked—she'd forgotten how huge they were up close.

Cassidy checked quickly before the fog moved in, no sailboat. At least not yet. She had a feeling it would be back this month, not that she could possibly know. Whether it showed up or not, she was going to enjoy the day.

The volunteer keepers at the lighthouse were thrilled to have a guest, the fog had kept away the usual June crowds. But she'd had a date to keep with her father and, like him, possessed a bit more stubbornness than common sense.

They showed her both upstairs and down of the lighthouse and the cozy buildings. The Coast Guard had stopped staffing it in 1994. A local group had taken over management of the buildings and rented it out to people willing to spend a week at the far end of a five-mile spit of land. It sounded like heaven to her: a stack of books, a few interesting wines, and no city craziness. She could go for runs on the beach. She promised to keep it in mind. Maybe in the winter months when few would venture out here and she'd truly have it to herself.

She turned down the keepers' invitation to join them for lunch. It was awkward, but she'd wanted a little picnic by herself at one of the scattered picnic tables. She set up a meal of a small container of Asian noodle salad, half a roast beef sandwich smeared with fat-free mayonnaise and just a touch of Dijon mustard, a small bottle of Pellegrino Limonata, and a humungous chocolate chip cookie. Perfect.

The air was still cool, especially now that she'd stopped moving and the ocean lay only a few hundred feet away all around her. She kept her parka on, though unzipped, as she ate. Several large ships moved along the Straits, slipping quickly and silently along the sparkling water.

As she nibbled on the cookie, she pulled out her father's letter and spread it before her.

Dearest Ice Sweet,

I'm sure now that I will never walk to any lighthouses with you. I probably won't live to hear your adventure to the first one. For that, I am truly sorry.

Regret is a funny thing. I'm lying here dying and I regret having so few years with your mother. I regret how little you knew her or her parents, truly kind people who welcomed me in when I had nothing. Yet I do not regret selling my vineyard to Mondavi.

Cassidy closed her eyes. Pretty much the most respected vintner of the Napa and Sonoma valleys. She'd walked their vineyards on the wine tours. Admired the rolling hills and drunk in the dry smell of grass and oak. The earth there was so rich and built in layers so deep that even the oldest and hardiest of vines could not plumb their depths.

She'd been allowed to walk more of their fields than the average tourist because of her background. She'd even spent a long leisurely afternoon with their horticulturist.

Oh god. She gazed out at the water but instead saw the rolling Napa hills. She might have walked across her father's own soil, strolled where he had poured so much blood and sweat and dreams— and never known.

My future lay in the rugged soils of the Kitsap Peninsula, tending vines that grew so slowly and a daughter who grew so fast. I missed my chance with the wine, which I don't regret. I am thankful every day that I didn't miss with my daughter. Adrianne taught me what was important, and watching you launch yourself against the world was definitely the best part of that.

I loved you then, Ice Sweet, the best I knew how. So, don't waste your time on regrets, for I take too many to my grave.

Love you,

Vic

She lay her head down on her arms and tried to picture Victor Knowles. Not as the dying man with tubes running into his body and his eyes blurry with morphine. Nor as the bent man, old before his time with hard work.

The father she remembered most clearly was sitting in his armchair, a book in his hand and his half-glasses sliding bit by bit toward the end of his nose, only to be pushed back at the last second before escape. A cup of tea, long since cold with forgetfulness, waiting on the small table at his elbow.

She tried to picture Vic Knowles as the young-old man he'd once been. Young, new to his Napa vineyard, but old from Vietnam. Standing where he belonged among the California hills while filled with the hopes of a new season wrapped up in the vines. The first of June thirty years ago. Then the grapes would be small, tight, and dusty green—an entire cluster would fit easily in his cupped palm. His nerves, shattered from war would now be soothed by the new growth reaching down into the deep earth and seeking upward into the sky.

To lose all that was impossible.

She could hear in his letter the regret that he claimed not to have. It had been one of the greatest losses in his life. Last month he had described the heart-wrenching decision to stay with his failing vines or go and follow his wife to a land of failing soil. It would have been so easy for him to be angry at his wife for forcing the choice upon him. Just as easy as it would be for Cassidy to be angry at herself for bringing hardship to her mother and to the poor man who had given up so much.

But he had chosen a different path.

Cassidy looked at the lighthouse built on the old Indian battle-ground. The temporary keepers had told her of one particularly horrid slaughter where one tribe had slain every member of another. A single pregnant woman had crawled to the keeper's residence riddled with twenty stab wounds. They had saved her from the return of the marauding band.

What had she herself sacrificed?

What had Russell said? She thought back to their one date for the hundredth time.

"Always the critic. Always a step back. A step away. You know all of these wines, but do you really know the true heart of any of them?"

The words were burned into her memory and that couldn't have happened if there wasn't some truth there. Her father had known every square foot of his land, even how the light lay upon it at every time of day. He had cherished the vines as if they were Cassidy's brothers and sisters—a part of the family.

Russell had been right. Damn him! She didn't know the true heart of any one wine. Never mind a whole vineyard.

She raised her head to prop her chin on her forearms and opened her eyes.

And there it was.

Her sailboat!

Sliding up from Puget Sound, her burgundy sails looking like cutouts of magnificent triangles against the crystalline waters and the far off Canadian shore.

Letter shoved into pocket, lunch trash crammed into her daypack —Cassidy sprinted to the far side of the lighthouse, near the fog's edge, to get the boat and lighthouse in the same picture. It took forever to emerge from the other side. She was about to go back, see if she was mistaken, when the boat slid clear of the lighthouse just a few hundred yards out.

A couple of quick shots, then she exchanged the camera for the binoculars she'd purchased for just for this moment. "Compact," "high-power," "light-weight," and "weather-resistant" had combined properly at the REI counter. She quickly slid them free and focused on the sailboat.

The boat's bow slipped through the low waves as if they were clouds and air, like a special effect. It was unreal how smoothly it moved and how tidy it looked.

The rich blue of the hull, the dark red of the sails, and the cheerful yellow and white of the decking and the cabin really were picture perfect. She tracked the view toward the back until she saw the skipper.

One man. Bent down and pulling on a line. Then he stood and faced the shore.

She dropped the binoculars. Only the salesman's insistence that she put the strap over her head every time saved them from the rocks and sand beneath her feet.

Russell Morgan.

He hadn't mentioned he was a sailor. He certainly hadn't mentioned he went to lighthouses regularly.

But where had he been last month at Cape Flattery?

Duh! Beside her. On foot rather than under sail.

And he'd been looking for someone, someone he wouldn't admit to.

She grabbed the binoculars again.

He was reaching down for something. His hand came back into view holding a camera with a long lens, a massive telephoto.

He hadn't seen her yet.

Cassidy didn't think.

She turned and sprinted for the fog with the binoculars clutched in her fist. A wave of birds rose before her in a flurry.

The fog was like a cool slap on her burning cheeks. She didn't stop, but kept up the pace for nearly a mile until the pounding of the pack against her back and the desperate pant of her breathing ground her to a halt.

She dropped onto the sandy beach, shedding the pack and the

parka because she was burning up and covered in sweat despite the chill air. She flopped back on the coat and lay like one dead while her breath and her heart pounded.

Cape Flattery. He could have sailed there as easily as he had to the New Dungeness lighthouse.

But he'd come ashore.

Which meant he'd come ashore looking for someone he'd only seen through his camera lens. And he'd been disappointed when he'd found…*her*, almost as disappointed as she'd been to be chased by *him*.

"Hey you in the red coat!" That's what he'd yelled. He'd seen a woman in a red coat. She looked down at the coat she sat on, a woman in a red parka.

But Cape Flattery had been too warm. She'd worn her red *leather* coat. And he'd thought that she was, well, herself.

Her cheeks warmed abruptly.

She'd lied about not being…herself.

This was beyond weird. Jo was going to laugh her ass off.

And maybe that finally explained his week-long vigil outside of her apartment. He must have seen her going by in her red parka and was looking for her. Looking for her, but thoroughly convinced that whoever he was looking for wasn't the evil, snooty Cassidy Knowles.

A smile started tugging at one corner of her mouth. She fought it back, but the other side soon joined in.

Oh brother, was Mr. Russell Morgan ever in for a shock.

And she couldn't wait to be the one to give it to him.

HAD HE SEEN HER, or not?

For a moment she'd been a spot of red just the other side of the lighthouse.

He'd tied off the jib sheet as quickly as he could and grabbed for his camera. But by the time he had the tiller trapped between his knees and the camera aimed, the red coat was disappearing into the fog bank.

He had snapped an image, but it was inconclusive—no more than a fading blur in the fog.

There one moment and then gone the next.

Twenty minutes. It took twenty minutes to anchor safely behind the spit of land, dowse the sails, lower his dinghy over the side, and get ashore.

He was the only one there. There was no one at the picnic tables and no one wandering around the narrow end of Dungeness Spit.

An elderly man and his wife came out of the house at the base of the lighthouse. For lack of any better options, he wandered over to them doing his best to look casual. But no matter how many times he checked over his shoulder, there was no Lady of the Lights.

"Welcome to New Dungeness lighthouse, young man."

"Hi," he shook their hands. "Did you see a woman in a red coat? A long, red coat?"

They both took a step back. Good one, Russell.

"She's a…friend. A friend I was hoping to meet here."

The man was about to say something when his wife cut him off. "What is your friend's name?"

Shit!

"I don't know that."

The man's face closed and they both backed away a bit farther.

"Has there been…" They weren't going to answer that. "I'm…" Crap!

They must think I'm insane. Wouldn't surprise me one bit!

The man pulled his wife closer and squared his aging shoulders, ready to leap to his wife's defense.

Russell spread his hands to show they were empty.

"I'm really not a nut." The old man wasn't buying it. "There's this lady. She keeps showing up at lighthouses."

By the time he was done with his story, they invited him into the cottage. Betty served him tea from a porcelain teapot decorated with sailboats and sat him down in the decent but utilitarian couch in the whitewashed living room. Barney was retired Navy and they'd been high school sweethearts and still looked to be.

Over a plate of oatmeal cookies, they admitted that a young woman had been there and indeed had worn a long, red coat.

"Quite pretty," had earned Barney a loving scowl from his wife. "Very friendly, though I don't think she gave us her name."

Betty stared down into her tea for a long moment. "She did. But I didn't hear it clearly. It was unusual and she was soft-spoken. Didn't seem polite to ask again."

"Perhaps she signed the guest register." Barney led him over to the leather-bound book laid open on the sloped table just inside the front door. The last entry was three days earlier: Betty and Barney's arrival.

"I'm sorry we're of so little help."

Russell bit his tongue against any sharp reply. "At least now I know she's real. I was starting to doubt that as well."

"But she showed up in your photographs."

He nodded his head. He knew the photos didn't lie, but he'd spent his whole career making them do just that. Some part of him would never trust images, especially not digital ones.

At least his Lady of the Lights was real. Angelo might insist that he was nuts...

But she was real.

PHILLIPE, a darkly handsome Latino who apparently had no last name, met Cassidy at the San Francisco airport in a wine-red Miata with the top down. In moments, they were leaving the city behind and zipping up toward the Sonoma Valley. She had tucked Mondavi's two books as well as the coffee table book about Mondavi by Katz into her carry-on and devoured them on the way down. She'd also brought along Fassbender's definitive book on Cabernet Sauvignons, but her German was quite rusty and it was heavy going.

Mondavi might not be the most expensive in the valley—too many little boutique vineyards existed that made a profession of being outrageously priced—but they were far and away the biggest high-quality vintner. Wines of high quality that sold at affordable prices.

She'd called to find out where her father's old vineyard lay and been quickly passed to one of the assistant vintners who'd promised to give her the personal tour. Now, here she was cruising up the length of the Sonoma Valley in a sports car and chatting about the finest details of their vintner process.

"We're really excited this year. Of course, there was that late cold snap, thirty-four degrees, which scared the daylights out of us. It came in right after the set. But then it warmed up at just the perfect pace. And Daryl, you'll meet her later, she's a magician. She knows what the roots are doing better than the vines do. What she does with water and fertilizers is staggering. She's been fooling with some of the organics and they're really playing out. It's only May, so the grapes are still tiny, but we haven't seen better since the '92 set. Boy, was that a year. As I'm sure you know. First year I worked the fields, I was a cutter then. Worked my way up."

He must have started in the fields when he was ten. Maybe he had, after school, weekends, and summers.

She saw signs for the vineyard off to the left, but he kept driving. At her look he offered her a low shout over the wind noise.

"Thought you might want to see the land first."

All she could do was nod, her throat wasn't trustworthy at the moment. A few minutes later he turned right and roared up into the hills. They left behind the busy valley floor; slipped away from the clusters of boutique towns. The masses of tourists didn't venture up here; they were all too busy traveling the valley hunting for that perfect case of prestigious wine to slumber in their basement so they felt like real wine connoisseurs.

The hills were covered in vines and orchards. Apple trees were used as wind breaks, sun breaks, and bee attractors for pollination— the tiny cubes of honeybee hives dotted the fields. Every now and then a mansion of obscene proportions thrust its head above the vines, but it was the vines that formed the texture of the hills.

Green. Carefully tended hillsides lay awash with verdant green and soil so black it looked painted. Not a stray weed was allowed to take any nourishment away from the all-important grape. Here each plant was nurtured individually, each vine coaxed to its greatest potential.

"You picked the perfect time to come." He whipped the car onto a narrow gravel road and sped north with no concern for his undercarriage. "We're just starting the drop on that field."

"I've never seen a big one." As a girl, she'd helped her dad with "the drop." They went vine by vine, cutting off all but the finest of the bunches so that the plant would pump more juice and flavor into the remaining grapes. At the same time, they trimmed back most of the leaves to let the sun soak into the remaining bunches. But in the Northwest, vines grew slowly and weren't treated with the harshness of the California vines.

Another turn and he skidded to a gravel-spewing halt by a closed gate and leapt from the car. He moved like he drove—fast and with a nervous energy vibrating over his body like a new vine in a cold wind.

He led her through the gate and over the first rise. There he stopped and waved his hand before him.

"I looked it up in the records. Your father's property was bounded by those two fence lines there and that row of pear trees. Twenty-nine point three acres. Four point nine seven tons per acre last year. Total yield last year was a hundred and forty-three tons. All Cab-Sauv. When I started, there was still a five-acre section of Merlot on it from the original owner, but that was finally pulled in '02. You can see the lighter stance of the new vines."

Suddenly he colored.

"Sorry, your dad had a Merlot grape planted that just didn't grow very well here. We nursed it, played with it, and phased it out. We've had great luck with the Cab-Sauv on this slope and finally converted the whole field."

He looked as if he wished to erase those last sentences and finally moved away to check the vines.

Cassidy moved slowly forward among the vines. The view across the valley revealed a massive patchwork of fields. Some fields stretched long and narrow, others square, and everywhere rows of vines traced the topography like a map—every rise and dip revealed.

This field, this one small field, a quarter-mile square, was barely an afterthought in the valley's total production.

She'd had Mondavi Merlot and Cab-Sauv many times with dinners. She'd tasted and spit it out at formal events.

The air was thick with the smell of sap. The drop. The rows between the vines were covered in great mats of green grapes and leaves spread across the dark soil. Tons of grapes, literally. Thousands and thousands of bunches lay scattered to rot and return to the soil. The grapes that remained, they were the ones that held this year's hope. This small bunch kept and not the next—which now lay beneath her feet. On the survivors were banked the fortune of the vineyard.

She stepped out on the soil her mother and father had labored to preserve and expand, had nearly buried their hearts and souls to save. She stood now at the core of their greatest failure.

Cassidy knelt and gathered a handful of the mud-dark earth. The vine's roots could go down thirty feet and still not hit rock. Fertile soil piled so thickly that it might as well go down forever. So different from the Pacific Northwest. Bainbridge Island had offered her father two to three feet of rocky soil to plant his roots. And much of that had been painstakingly cleared and set by hand. Here, nascent weeds were scalped back into the soil by the most modern machinery, not a balky old rototiller that she'd never once successfully started on her own. There they battled blackberry vines that towered above her head after a mere week's inattention. Nothing here but the soil and the grapes.

She'd had Mondavi Merlots several times before they replanted this field in 2002. She'd drunk her father's wine without knowing, or at least a blend of it.

No matter what Mondavi had done to this soil, her father's tears were still here.

TRUE TO HIS WORD, Angelo promised them a table for three at eight o'clock on just a few hours' notice. At six they hit the Virginia Inn for a couple of drinks in the cozy bar. By seven, they'd decided to go raid Perrin's store for dinner attire.

Perrin was into a sixties mode. Her hair streaked, part flapper platinum blond, but with darker lines of oak that made her the very authentic sun-bleached gal. Two months seemed to be the longest she could retain a hair color.

She flaunted a generous tie-dye skirt, that showed every bit of difference from the classic, dyed-in-Kool-Aid versus professionally done with Procion dye on the fine-weave of quality cotton. Her peasant blouse was loose, airy, and kept slipping off one shoulder. The outfit invited you to imagine the slender, vibrant woman within.

Jo refused Perrin's insistence that she go without a bra. Instead, she selected a bright red dress that might have been worn by a flamenco dancer. Her shoulders and dark skin revealed by thin straps, and her legs by the knee-length pleated skirt and a minor bell of red petticoats. Hot was the key word to describe the result.

They fussed over Cassidy until she finally agreed to wear the slinkiest of blue dresses—one shoulder bare and her hair up. She'd had just enough to drink that she agreed to go without a bra when Perrin couldn't find a strapless in her size. The perfect tailoring of the top was all that kept her from being indecent. The long skirt had a slit up to mid-thigh which she would do her best to keep closed. The high heels were ridiculous, but her legs did look great in the mirror.

She wore a gold chain with a tiny sailboat dangling at the end— that she'd spotted in a San Francisco airport shop while waiting for her flight home. She hadn't explained it to her friends yet.

Perrin put one of those leather friendship bracelets around each of their wrists. Jo decided to go without further adornment which was exactly right—her long, black hair pushed back over her shoulders was decoration enough.

Perrin had reached for the perfumes, but she and Jo declined. Perrin went for just a touch of lavender, behind one ear only.

Cassidy spotted a poster on Perrin's wall that had a familiar feel. She went up closer to inspect it. Russell's work; it had to be. "Perrin's Glorious Garb –the home of stand-out style." Perrin in her flapper outfit, sitting on a couch that looked homey and made for two like an invitation.

"He's great, Cassie. And the name he chose is sooo much better than Perrin's Gallery. I can't believe you found him. Or that he's so reasonable. You're the best."

Jo inspected the poster, raised one eyebrow at Cassidy, and didn't say a thing. Well, the smokescreen was aimed at Perrin; she shouldn't have expected it to fool Jo for long.

How had the time gone by so fast? She'd meant to call him the day she'd gotten home from Dungeness Spit lighthouse, but researching the vineyard had gotten in the way. That was part of tonight's celebration—actually walking her father's land.

She'd call Russell tomorrow or the next day, once she caught up on her columns.

By the time they reached Angelo's they were in a very merry mood and men were stopping on the street to watch them walk by arm in arm. Sixties chic, flamenco red, and slinky blue sapphire. Even Jo was laughing and whispering about the one who walked squarely into a newspaper box as they went by.

The sun was near setting when they arrived. Long streaks of gold slid up the street between the buildings and a soft breeze slipped up from the Sound. They might regret not having wraps by the time they were done, but for the moment it was too warm to consider them.

Angelo came out of the kitchen personally to seat them. His exclamations over their attire made them giggle, at least she and Perrin. Jo simply blushed crimson and slipped quickly into an inside chair against a wall. Cassidy sat beside her and Perrin took the other side of the table.

"Josh Harper is coming tonight as well."

"Oh, you must seat him with us, Angelo. Set another place." Cassidy turned to her friends. "He's this great guy from *Gourmet Week*. Good friend, too."

When he arrived, Angelo led him over.

"Cute, too," Perrin whispered to her.

"Married," she whispered back. "Happily," she added before

turning to welcome him. He kissed both her cheeks and smiled all around the table at introductions.

"Angelo. For seating me with three such impossibly lovely ladies, I will promise you gold, dancing women, and great reviews. Whatever you need." They shook hands in a very manly-looking clasp. He took the seat by Perrin just as the bruschetta arrived: fresh mozzarella cheese, perfect little squares of roasted red pepper, and a sprinkling of minced fresh basil on tiny slices of toast smeared with olive oil and rubbed with garlic.

"So, Josh. Cassidy says you're happily married." He nodded as he bit into one of the appetizers. She smiled in her most dangerous and charming way.

She leaned her bare shoulder against his.

"How do you feel about polygamy?"

He practically passed the cheese through his nose.

"As always, Angelo," Cassidy raised her tiny cup of decaf espresso.

He doffed his hat and sipped from his own cup, most certainly the leaded variety. "Yes, I make a mean espresso."

They all laughed knowing she'd meant the meal and that he'd known it as well. The restaurant had quieted and slowly emptied as the hours slid by. Now they were the last table that hadn't been cleaned and prepped for the next day. Of course they also had been the noisiest table the whole night.

Perrin's latest exploits and Cassidy's behind-the-label tales of the Mondavi system had kept the conversation lively—egged on by Jo's wry interjections. Cassidy hadn't yet told them about Russell, not with Josh sitting there and especially not now with Angelo joining them. It would be unfair for him to know before Russell did.

The food and wine had flowed almost as lavishly as the laughter. Perrin had flirted wildly with Josh as well as their waitress—a comely Italian girl who sassed her right back—and Angelo every time he came near. Angelo had flirted with Perrin and taken the opportunity to spread his charm to her and Jo.

Especially to Jo, though she claimed not to notice, or be interested in a scruffy Italian. But the more wine Jo drank, the deeper her blush became each time Angelo served them personally. Now only espresso, tiny wedges of an exquisite, richly chocolate-and-hazelnut *pan forte*, and crumpled napkins remained of the meal. Cassidy could feel the electric current passing from Jo on her left to where Angelo had joined them on her right seated at the end of the table. Everyone was talking to everyone, except the two of them. Perhaps she should take Jo to the bathroom and insist that they switch places when they returned. It was the best plan she—

"Hey Angelo, where are you?" Russell Morgan burst through the kitchen doors, his voice overloud in the empty restaurant. "There you..." He stumbled to a halt as his eyes met hers. He looked ready to beat a hasty retreat even as his eyes slid from her face to inspect her bare shoulders and form-fitting dress.

She couldn't help smiling at him. The man seeking the lady in the red parka. Her. Knowing nothing about her except she wore a red coat and went to lighthouses and that was enough to make him desperate to find her. Her: the lovely princess in the tower. He: Prince Charming, who hadn't a clue how he despised his Princess in real life. Perhaps Prince Uncharming, but Cassidy realized that she liked that honest forthrightness of his more and more with time.

His eyes returned to her face as he moved slowly forward. Once again he was as she'd first met him: jeans covered with streaks of dirt and paint, both knees long gone. A blue t-shirt that showed every muscle from belt to shoulder was torn high on one arm. Even his arms had splotches of blue paint on them—the shade of which she now knew the source. He matched his hull perfectly. His hair was a tumble with flecks of sawdust—if it had been combed, it was with his fingers. Her fingers itched to do the same.

"Won't you join us, Mr. Morgan?"

It was a good thing that Angelo had his back to Russell, because his face was definitely laughing at the refined invitation for his scruffy friend.

"Oh, Mr. Morgan. You have to join us." Perrin leaned right into Josh's lap as she reached out a hand toward him. "I love that poster you made. It so captures what I want to do. I've already had three customers who came in just because they saw it."

"Um, you're welcome."

Angelo glanced in Cassidy's direction and started to scoot his chair her way so he'd be between them. She shook her head infinitesimally and Angelo scooted closer to Josh though he did arch his eyebrows in her direction. She wasn't going to say anything—not a chance. But she didn't want Angelo between them. She was just drunk enough to feel brave.

"Are these your clothes as well?" He nodded toward Jo and Cassidy keeping his attention on Perrin. He grabbed a chair from another table.

When Perrin nodded, he smiled a bit. He still hadn't looked in her direction after his initial inspection and she was starting to feel a bit piqued about it.

"I'd like to get a series of shots with the three of you."

"Us?" Cassidy managed to choke out.

Jo was shaking her head.

"Yes."

There was no way she was getting in front of Mr. Testosterone's camera.

Russell spun the chair backwards and straddled it, his exposed knee ending up so close to her thigh she could feel the heat through her thin dress. She glanced down. The slit of her skirt had opened wide exposing her horribly. She pulled it closed before Russell noticed. Though he couldn't have missed it on his arrival, but she held it closed anyway.

"You are three classic, beautiful archetypes. And there is a synergy between you that would work well on camera. You also have the benefit of being free models, at least I assume so. Budget is important in this case." He finally looked at Cassidy. She was well aware they hadn't worked out a payment yet, but he didn't have to rub it in.

Russell leaned in close and whispered for her ears alone, "Told you that you'd hate it."

He was right; she did. And she was well and truly trapped. She'd definitely rather pay the money.

Perrin was so excited by the prospect that she won Jo over with only a minimum of arm-twisting from Cassidy.

Russell was in a thoroughly cheerful mood about having trapped her, albeit for a good cause. He knocked down a large gulp from a beer bottle still covered in beads of condensation. He must have liberated it on his way through the kitchen.

His motion sent a waft of his smell her direction. Beneath the bright tang of teak wood shavings and the bite of paint, there was a raw scent like the musk of the finest red—whole, complete in itself, strong without being overwhelming.

She opened her eyes and he was inspecting her closely. She didn't remember closing them as she'd reveled in his scent. Reveled? She'd have to be careful. Russell Morgan was trouble and she really didn't need the complication.

His eyes were so close. Blue-grey eyes. Ones that would be very easy to get lost in.

She scrambled around in her brain for some way to break his intent study of her face. For a way to change what was occurring in her own mind.

"Um, been to any lighthouses lately, Mr. Morgan?"

Perrin's laugh climbed quickly up the scale toward a giggle, but a quick glance across the table revealed that the others were still discussing the modeling photoshoot.

"Yes, actually," he studied his beer and picked at the corner of the label. "I sailed to one just a couple of weeks ago."

"Which one?" As if she didn't know.

"New Dungeness lighthouse up in the Straits," his tone said that he had no hint that she'd been there.

"Did you find whoever you were looking for at Cape Flattery?"

He started and his attention shifted from his beer back to her face. His eyes widened like a deer in the headlights.

"You were obviously looking for someone at the cape."

He turned back to his label, though he didn't pick at it any more.

"I, uh... No, I didn't."

Angelo leaned over. "He's been chasing a phantom for six months now."

"Three. I didn't see her in the photos at first. And she's not a phantom."

Angelo shrugged his doubts.

Cassidy took another sip of her espresso. This was simply delicious. He'd taken photos of every lighthouse and she'd been in every photo. Had he taken one of her at Cape Flattery? She couldn't remember, but she hoped so. That way his collection would be complete, even if he didn't know it...yet. She'd replaced her own shot of the lighthouse to include one with him in it. But she hadn't yet figured out how to tell him that he was sitting next to his phantom.

"I believe in phantoms." She'd been chasing one for the last six months as well. The phantom of who her father had really been. The man she'd known and loved but was turning into a stranger in the course of a dozen short notes.

"Oh no," Russell held up a hand as if to fend her off. It was callused with hard work, but didn't look heavy despite its size.

"No discussions of ghosts and visitations. I've been with so many woman who were into—" Angelo elbowed him in the ribs. He glared at Angelo, then his eyes widened and he clamped his mouth shut.

"And how many women have you been with, Mr. Morgan?" She hadn't quite meant to drop her question into the lull in conversation, but suddenly she had everyone's attention. Or rather Russell did.

He glared first at her, then at his beer.

She could feel the heat on her own cheeks. She hadn't meant to trap him or back him into a corner.

The conversation at the rest of the table slowly drifted back to life as he stubbornly refused to look up.

She rested a hand on his forearm. She was transported back to the moment she'd taken his arm at Cape Flattery. The strength and warmth were intense against her palm. Her body was reacting in ways that made her feel flush even where the dress did cover her decently.

"I'm sorry," she kept her voice soft so that no others would hear. She squeezed his arm and was about to remove it when he covered it with his other—cool from the beer bottle but warm from the inside.

His gaze met hers and there was a tinge of sadness in how his eyes closed part way.

"We were clearly never meant to have a conversation together. We're like two porcupines with all of our bristles up and all defenses to the fore."

This was a totally different man. This wasn't the abrupt and rude Mr. Russell Morgan. This wasn't the brash sailor she'd expected, nor the cool professional. Suddenly, the man she'd glimpsed in scattered moments at dinner and at the lighthouse kneeling in the sand was seated beside her and holding her hand. It took her breath away and made the pounding of her heart the only sound she could make.

"To answer your question: too many and never the right one."

Question? What question? Her mind had definitely gone else-where. "How many women?" That was it. "Too many and never the right one." What a fantastic answer. She could feel herself melting.

He patted her hand like an old friend and withdrew his arm from her grasp.

"Sorry, dumb thing to say. I meant nothing about you. I meant..." Russell jerked to his feet like a puppet on strings.

"Sorry to be a damper on your party." He bowed to her, "Ms. Knowles." And he was gone before she could react. Before she could protest.

Jo poked her sharply in the ribs which broke the spell that had bound her in place. She startled to her feet and trotted out through the kitchen as fast as her high heels would let her. The staff was all gone. She pushed open the back door and stepped out onto the street.

A few spaces down the block, a car roared to life with a throaty rumble—his car from the Cape Flattery parking lot. She raised an arm to stop him as he dropped it into gear, but he was faced away from her and roared off into the night.

The chill air sent a shiver over her bare leg and shoulder, and up her spine.

"I didn't take it that way."

RUSSELL STARED at the phone number Angelo had given him. He must be insane. Or really, really, really desperate.

"Yeah, that describes it pretty damn well, doesn't it?"

Nutcase sat on the settee table and watched him pace the length of the boat and back.

He reached out to scratch the cat's head. She shied away in time to avoid being whacked by the phone he'd forgotten he was holding.

"Well, there are two choices. I can either agonize over this for another half hour and then it will be too late to decently call in which case I'll be truly screwed. Or I can stop being such a wimp and dial the damn phone."

Nutcase carefully licked a paw and scraped it across the fur between her ears.

"You're no help at all, are you?"

She licked the other paw and went after a spot beside her nose. Cats had it so easy; all they needed was a sucker like him. He could use a little easy right now.

Well, there was nothing for it.

He punched in the number. When it hit the third ring, he began to hope for voicemail, though he had no idea what he'd say to a machine. He'd think of something. Fourth ring.

"Hi, this is Cassidy." Even as a recording her voice was warm, friendly.

"Hi, this is Russell. Russell Morgan. You may recall the rather unpleasant chap from Angelo's. Could you give me a call at—"

"Don't you want to speak to me in person."

"You… Crap! I thought you were a recording."

"Well, that's a new line."

He sat down on the pilot's berth. Then lay down and put his feet up on the companionway ladder.

"Wasn't meant to be." Could he sound any stupider if he tried? "A line I mean." Indeed, apparently he could. Stupider by the second. "Why did you even answer the phone?"

"You mean other than the fact that I had no idea who was calling?"

"Yes, other than that."

"Because I like you."

"You've got to be kidding me." Great. Now his hearing was failing him.

"Well, you do have a certain knack for uncharming and also jumping to conclusions. And your ability to ask me the question I didn't even know I was avoiding doesn't help matters."

She stopped. In the silence he could imagine her, sitting in some high-rise condo, all perfectly manicured. Terry cloth bathrobe and hair done up in a towering swirl of towel. If she had a cat, it would certainly never be a constant mess like Nutcase. Probably an elegant Siamese with a meow that could shatter glass.

Her voice was soft when she resumed, "Remember what you said about porcupines."

"Yeah."

"Well, I apologize. I too become all bristly when I'm talking to you and I don't know why."

"I do."

"You do?"

Russell slapped his hand against his forehead, "No, I mean that I know why I do around you."

"Willing to share?"

"Not really," which sounded awful. "What the hell. This conversation is already nothing like I'd imagined anyway. You remind me too much of my past and not enough of my future."

"Is your past so vile and your future so clear?"

Nutcase clambered up onto his chest and he mussed her hair with his free hand. The silly thing purred madly.

"No. And…" Well, he had to be honest here, though for the life of him he didn't know why. "Not as much as I'd like. It's more that you are right out of my New York past."

"There's a lot you don't know about me." It was a tease—though he couldn't easily imagine Cassidy Knowles teasing. He'd flirted with hundreds of women, every model who came through the studio and every waitress who'd ever served him for starters. But picturing a taunting tease coming from Cassidy simply didn't fit. Maybe it was a statement of fact.

"A part of me isn't interested in knowing more." Great! Insult her again. "But, uh, that sounded lousy, a part of me does." It did. "Very much." Now that he'd said it, it was true.

Nutcase head-butted his chin hard enough that he bit his tongue.

"What would you like to know?" Her voice was cautious.

"Ever been on a sailboat?"

"No."

"Would you like to? I mean," and then he plunged in, "my parents are coming to town and they'd like you more than they like me and I could really use your help with them. It would pay back anything I do for Perrin a hundred times over; I'll even find a different model if you insist though you'd be great. My parents like Angelo well enough, but they have a, um, different relationship." Angelo might be best friends with their son and they might have helped to raise him and send him to college, but he was still the son of their cook.

Nothing but silence so he kept going.

"And the others in the marina, well, they're just like me. And my parents are, they're, well, you know…" He petered out. That was it. He'd hit a new low in charm. "Look, I understand. Pathetic idea. I'll just crawl back into my hole again. Thanks. Sorry to bother—"

"When?"

The word hung on the wires between them.

"Tuesday?" his voice squeaked. It had never done that before. It sounded terribly desperate.

"Day after tomorrow?"

"Ten a.m. 'D' dock at Shilshole Marina?"

There was a long pause during which he couldn't hear a sound except Nutcase's buzzing as she kneaded his chest with her prickly little claws.

"Sure." The word was so small for something so momentous.

"You're kidding? Really?"

"Trying to talk me back out of it?"

"No. Uh-uh. No way. You're committed now." Russell couldn't believe it.

"I said I would come. Are your parents so scary?"

"Only to me."

Then she laughed. It was the most miraculous sound he'd ever heard. He'd never heard her laugh. It rang from her like a thousand bells on a Christmas tree. He felt as if he'd just lost a hundred pounds, the weight he'd gained the moment his mother had called to announce their pending visit.

"What can I bring?"

"Just yourself. I'll bring lunch fixings. Just dress in layers, it can be warm or cool on the water depending on the wind. You don't mind visiting another lighthouse, do you?"

"Oh, is Tuesday the first? I didn't realize."

"What was that?"

She cleared her throat in one of those delicate, feminine ways that indicated a subject change that could never be turned around.

"Tuesday. Ten a.m. 'D' dock. Shilshole," she repeated dutifully.

"Right."

"See you then."

Then he was listening to a dial tone. But what had he said to make her angry? Only she hadn't been. He'd swear she hung up just a moment before laughing aloud.

She was the damnedest woman he'd ever met.

MUKILTEO LIGHTHOUSE

Mukilteo
First lit: 1907
Automated: 1979
47.94871 -122.30453

Mukilteo, in the local Native American language, means "good place for camping." In 1792 Captain George Vancouver came ashore there and named it Rose Point for all the wild roses that bloomed along the grassy shore.

Later renamed Point Elliot, it became the site of the signing of the Treaty of Point Elliot. This treaty of 1855 ended the Indian wars, established the Tulalip Indian Reservation, and truly opened the area up for significant white settlement.

The picturesque lighthouse has hosted hundreds and hundreds of weddings. Not a single one of the first hundred was rained on.

ussell was ten minutes early when he headed for the security gate at the head of the dock. It wasn't so much that he wanted to be there for Cassidy, it was that he needed a breather from his parents. Breakfast at the Palisades had been very civilized and polite. Perfectly friendly to all appearances, and the waitress in constant attendance with a pitcher of mimosas had certainly helped keep his nerves in line. If he'd had half a brain, he'd have invited Cassidy to breakfast as well. Though that might be too high a price, helping Perrin was being more fun than he'd expected.

Cassidy was already waiting there when he reached the head of the dock. He opened the steel gate and stood back to appreciate her as she came through. Brown Docksiders on her feet that had clearly never seen the outside of a shoebox before today. Blue slacks with a crease up the front that was so perfect they must be as new as her unblemished shoes. Her blouse was a pale-blue, fitted, button-up shirt that looked immensely feminine on her shapely frame. Her smile was radiant and her hair back in a neat ponytail.

And over her arm was a red coat. A huge coat, totally inappropriate for the heat of the day...

A red parka.

"Turn around." It was barely a croak as it escaped his throat.

She obliged, doing a slow three-sixty. The runner's ponytail. The auburn hair the same length as... And then her smile came around again, beyond radiant. Mischievous.

If it hadn't been for the railing behind him, he'd have fallen backward into the ocean.

"You!?" He clenched the steel, real and solid beneath his shaking fingers.

She nodded.

"When? How? It can't be."

She slid a hand through the crook of his arm and guided him down the ramp toward the boats.

"It can be. I figured it out at New Dungeness, saw you through my binoculars." She was just as amiable as if they were old friends chatting on a sunny afternoon about the model sailboats racing on the Conservatory Water in Central Park. As if his brain wasn't misfiring on a grand scale already.

"And then you sprinted off into the fog so fast I thought you were a mirage."

"And then I sprinted off into the fog. I didn't think; I just ran. It was a bit of a shock."

"I'm noticing that myself." It was hard to believe that he was able to form whole words. That they were in sentences made it one of the modern miracles. He should probably send a note to some bishop or cardinal if he ever recovered.

She looked from side to side inspecting the various boats they passed: fishing craft, fifty-foot power boats, and a lot of big sailboats. Most of them were deserted and quiet except for the occasional weekend visit, but 'D' dock had a nice share of liveaboards as well. She was being a little obvious about not looking up at him.

"Why didn't you...? Do you know how long I've been looking for you?"

"You mean other than the week you spent camped out in front of my condo?"

"So, that *was* you. You live near there? Somehow I knew that runner was my Lady of the Lights." He looked down at her, shocked to his core that both women were standing embodied in one right here beside him.

"My friends wanted me to call the cops on you. It was getting a little creepy."

"Sorry, I didn't mean to spook you. I was just trying to find…"

"Someone else."

He sighed. What could he do?

"Yes. Someone else." She was right, there was a lot more to her than he'd first suspected.

"Right after New Dungeness, I, uh, had to go to California, and that trip lasted a bit longer than I anticipated. I was going to tell you at Angelo's, but you left too quickly. As to the rest, let's go meet your parents. I think they'll enjoy the story as well."

He considered throwing himself on the dock to rant until he felt better. Some traitorous part of him wanted to dance a happy jig. Another part was seriously considering tossing her off the dock…now there was a tempting image.

As if she'd been reading his mind, she slipped her hand from his arm and took a couple steps ahead.

Just as it had out at Cape Flattery, and the other night at Angelo's, her touch made him feel calm, strong, and protective. The breaking of that touch left its memory. No one, not even Melanie had ever made him feel this way.

Lady of the Lights. Cassidy Knowles. A prettied-up, city girl. A runner. An outdoors woman. He couldn't reconcile it all in his brain. How much he didn't know about her was mind-boggling.

She stopped unerringly by the bow of his boat. Of course she did. She'd seen it five times over the last six months. Christ, he'd walked to Tatoosh Island with her hand on his arm and refused her invitation to Destruction Island light. The world was whacked.

Cassidy reached out a hand toward the bow of his boat. Nutcase was perched on the very end of the bowsprit that rode just a foot or so from the dock. The cat sniffed her extended hand for a second and then launched herself across the water into Cassidy's arms. Rather than withdrawing as Melanie had or simply dodging the scruffy beast, Cassidy caught her and let her snuggle right into her arms and rub her head under Cassidy's chin.

Well, she'd certainly passed the cat test. His father came down the finger pier between his boat and the next to meet the visitor.

But would she survive the parent test?

RUSSELL AIMED the bow into the wind and set the engine to idle. With the ease of a half year of practice he raised the main and cleated off the sheet. He still hadn't run the jib halyard back to the cockpit and he hurried forward to haul it up before the boat slipped off the wind. The big foresail unfurled with a loud snap.

The breeze was fresh without being strong or cool, a near perfect sailing day.

Tying off the line, he hung the loose tail in a quick coil and trotted back to the cockpit. He killed the engine and kicked the tiller over with his knee.

In one smooth sweep the *Lady* slid from loud vibrations and diesel fumes into the solid, silent pull of the world's winds. She heeled over and surged forward—a tug deep in his gut that made him feel everything would be okay. He'd come a long way from his first scary solo out to the Lime Kiln light and back.

His father watched him closely. He'd always been tall and patrician, and would look completely in place as an English lord advising a Queen. His hair was grayer, the lines deeper, but it was still a commanding face.

Russell's mother was in her usual Liz Taylor mode. Blue jeans that cost more than most evening gowns and a cashmere sweater showed off the success of her personal trainer's perseverance on a body nearing sixty. A silk kerchief of royal blue kept her thick, brown hair under perfect control. Large, round-eyed sunglasses were pushed up on her forehead as she eyed Cassidy—who was the only one at ease on the whole boat. Other than Nutcase.

The fur beast had checked in with him on her way to her perch on the boom. In moments the ball of black fur lay curled up in the foot of the sail atop the boom. Far enough out that nothing lay below except ocean waves. Did she enjoy the danger? Or not see it? They'd tried a kitty life preserver: an unsuccessful and painful experiment. The scratches on his arms had taken a week to heal from that one.

Cassidy sat across from his parents on the low side of the cockpit, a plastic tumbler of iced tea held easily in one hand. A tiny fleck of sunscreen remained on the edge of one ear that he longed to rub in, but he didn't dare. They didn't have that kind of a relationship.

Actually, they didn't have any relationship, other than bumping into and despising each other for six months. Without even knowing they knew each other. But they did—Angelo was gonna shit. And he was also going to kill himself for not taking the day off to join them and watch.

Unless Angelo already knew, but hadn't told him. Maybe he'd begged off so he wouldn't be swimming ashore right about now.

"I didn't know you were a model, though I should have guessed."

At Cassidy's words, he dropped the tiller and had to grab for it again as the boat slewed into the wind. Nutcase popped her head up and stared at him. She slowly resettled as he didn't call "helms a'lee."

"You were a model?" he blurted it out.

His mother blushed a moment.

"Miss Puerto Rico," Cassidy informed him.

His dad nodded in agreement and threw an arm around his wife's shoulders giving her a quick hug. That was news as well. They were always so formal and separate; as cold to each other as they were to him. Maybe cold wasn't quite right. Perhaps always on show was more accurate.

"Yes. I took the prize money and moved to New York. Worked the catalog pages and runways to put myself through NYU. Close your mouth, dear. You look foolish."

He clamped his mouth shut and clipped the end of his tongue.

"You didn't know?" Cassidy gave him a puzzled expression. How was he supposed to know everything about his parents' past? She probably knew every detail about her own from the moment she exited the womb until…now. He didn't even know where her parents were.

He shook his head.

She opened her mouth. This was it. He was about to be torpedoed. He really didn't need a lecture from the person who was supposed to be his buffer.

"So, John," Cassidy turned back to his parents, "how did you two meet?"

Russell had to blink. Not only had she slipped in a perfectly natural subject change, but she hadn't sold his soul either. Someday he'd stop underestimating her.

"The opera," his mother answered. There were times he wondered if his father could even speak. She always ran every social occasion, with immaculate finesse and warmth; one he'd always thought a bit artificial.

The look she turned on her husband was electric. They actually held hands; there was another one Angelo would never believe. Russell certainly didn't.

"Well," his father's voice was gruff from lack of use. "I was at a fundraiser for the Met."

"I was in marketing."

"Damn prettiest thing I'd ever seen came walking up to me at the hors d'oeuvres table."

"I had no idea who he was," his mother said off-handedly. "I'd just finessed a million-dollar donation from a usual hundred-thousander and decided to take the rest of the evening for me."

"Walked right up to me."

"I was headed for the bar."

"Walked right by me."

Their sentences were overlapping, their voices soft. Russell glanced at Cassidy who was enraptured by the story. Her body shifting so easily as the boat slid over the waves it was as if she'd spent her life afloat. The sun discovered the hint of red in her hair and made it warm and alive.

"Then she looked back over her shoulder at me."

She smiled up at him, "You were staring."

"She never got her drink."

"He forgot he was holding a piece of shrimp until I stole it from him."

Cassidy's hand shifted over her heart as if she were about to melt.

He ducked to peek under the sail. They were off Edmonds already, this lighthouse was so close. They'd be there in no time. Another hour to the lighthouse if the wind held off the beam. They might go the whole way up the coast on a single tack, Nutcase would appreciate the long nap without the boom swinging about. And it was far too deep off the lighthouse to throw out an anchor. Lunch aboard would get them most of the way back to dock. He might survive the day yet.

"Did you really?" Cassidy was busy looking amazed. What had he missed?

"What else was I supposed to do with him? He had talked my ear off until the hotel kicked us out into the lobby. It was three in the morning. They'd already cleaned everything in the room except the two chairs we were sitting on."

He looked at his father who noticed his scrutiny. He shrugged and nodded with a silly smile on his face.

They'd slept together on their first date. People didn't...well, he had often enough. But parents didn't...his couldn't...had.

"Where did you find a place?"

It was a friggin' hotel, Cassidy. Lots of beds there. His own mother —the little beauty queen-social climber that she was—had climbed right into his father's lap and his fortune.

His mother reached out and touched Cassidy's hand like a best friend emphasizing a point.

"It's New York. There's always someplace to dance."

Dance?

"We found the seediest little dive," John tapped his feet on the cockpit floor. "Smoking dark jazz."

"We slow danced past sunrise."

He was so glad that Cassidy was doing the speaking. He'd have screwed up the conversation eight different ways already. Maybe he could understand some of his father's silences. Julia Morgan had clearly charmed Cassidy Knowles and he suspected that wasn't as easy as his mother made it look. Maybe his mother really was that charming and it hadn't been the act he'd assumed all these years.

When had he decided that anyway? Anne? No, Kristi. His mother had been ever so kind to a coed named Kristi he was about to break up with later that night. His mother totally screwed that up and he'd been so pissed. He'd been stuck with her for another three months before he figured out how to let her down easy. By then he'd totally missed his chance with... Was he really that shallow?

"That first week we went out dancing every night," Former Miss Puerto Rico leaned up against his father. "John, we need to take that up again when you retire."

"You're retiring?" It blurted out of him and lay there on the deck like a week-old fish.

"I've got some bright young men who are ready to move up. You were never interested in the business and they're ready for me to let it go. Finally I realized, so am I." He shrugged off forty years as if it had been a three-month gig.

"The business?" Cassidy took the conversation back before he could fumble it overboard.

"Morganson Shipping. I made up the name even before Russell came along, but the boy was never interested in the business. Perhaps you've heard of us."

Cassidy laughed, that dancing musical sound of a thousand bells. He couldn't help smiling.

"I've seen enough of your shipping containers on my daily run down along Seattle's waterfront."

"Could have bowled me over too," Julia poked a finger into his father's ribs. "He, the jerk, didn't tell me who he was, at least not until that weekend when he casually invited me over for dinner to meet his parents. Herman and Alicia Morgan. I was so scared I almost fainted."

"You were magnificent and almost as beautiful as you are now.

Simply amazing, Russ. She out-niced even your grandmother and that took some doing in those days."

Russell was glad for the tiller. It was the only reason he didn't collapse entirely. Not only hadn't his mother been a gold-digger as he'd finally decided she was, but they'd just told Cassidy he was worth millions. Actually hundreds of millions. Far above and beyond his own comfortable success.

She hadn't reacted.

At least not yet.

He certainly wasn't looking forward to their next time alone. He could count on one hand with all his fingers folded up the number of women who hadn't gunned for him the moment they found out who he was. Even Melanie had originally been drawn by his fortune and it wasn't until after it was over that he understood that she'd moved beyond that.

Imbecile!

He had liked Cassidy.

Did like her.

———

"Catching up on your reading?"

Cassidy rammed the letter in her pocket and looked up, shielding her eyes against the sun.

Russell stood over her, moving easily with the sway of the deck. He looked like the statue of Rhodes: tall, powerful, and gazing out over the harbor and the world that was his domain. One of the seven wonders of the world.

And he was, in an odd way. Once he'd relaxed a bit, he'd been funny, even charming. But there was none of the false, pickup-line smoothness that she'd heard too many times on too many first dates. Perhaps it was because of their history, it was now too late for that.

"A bit," she kept her hand on the letter—it felt as if it might jump out and bite her if she didn't keep it trapped in her pocket.

Russell glanced back at the cockpit. She did too and saw John with a leisurely hand on the tiller. Julia leaned back against him as the boat slid easily over the sparkling water.

From up here on the foredeck, Cassidy had a splendid view of the way ahead and to the left. The big foresail blocked her view to the right. Whidbey Island towered ahead: rocky cliffs, conifer-covered headlands. There were a few small power boats anchored in a narrow cove and they passed a brightly painted buoy over a dozen feet tall that rang its deep bell with each wave that rolled by.

Russell squatted down.

"I wanted to say, thanks. You're great with them."

He didn't even reach out a hand for balance, as if he'd been born on the boat. She'd felt off balance all day. Ever since she'd woken up with her stomach in a knot of nerves that refused to be explained away.

She nodded her head, it was all she trusted herself to do.

He was so close she could easily reach out. See if his hair was truly as soft as it looked, or touch her fingers to his smile.

"I don't know how you do it. I've never seen them so comfortable." He glanced aft again. "And how did I know so little about my own mother?"

Her hand was still on her father's letter, crumpled in her slacks pocket. He'd found work as a carpenter and a field hand and who knew what all. Odd-job man to all the Kitsap Peninsula and Bainbridge Island as well while his wife tended ailing parents and an unhappy toddler. Rebuilding the well house at a tiny, island winery had led to a job as vintner, horticulturist, and general repairman all rolled into one. When the old owner had died, he'd left the whole winery to her father. He'd given up everything to be with his family, and gotten everything in return, just in a different form.

You never know where opportunity lies, Ice Sweet.
    You never know.

"Your parents are charming. I like them a lot."

"And they like you, which may be a first among the women I've brought home."

She'd never met a man with more skill at saying the wrong thing. At first it had made her angry, now she was finding it rather sweet. He was forthright with no games and no filter. His feelings turned into speech before they turned into thought and were carefully groomed and sanitized. He was a lot like his cat in that way—a sweet mess and a bit scruffy around the edges.

"Is that what I am?"

"What?" he looked worried as he reviewed his last comment in his head.

"Am I a woman you've brought home? Konked with a club and dragged to your boat like some mighty Viking?" If a Viking like this kidnapped her, maybe she'd want to go along with it.

He opened his mouth and then thought better of it and closed it again. He shook his head ruefully.

"Porcupines."

She laughed. He'd really grabbed onto that image. He was so close that she could smell him despite the sailing breeze. His sleeves rolled up to reveal powerful arms—big, safe arms to be wrapped in. Her hand reached out, of its own accord, and rested on his knee.

The muscles were shifting easily beneath the denim, working unconsciously to keep his balance on the rocking boat. His eyes were watching hers and she could feel herself melting. Would he kiss her? She finally knew the answer to her much earlier question: if he tried, she certainly wasn't going to resist.

Her body shifted as the boat thumped off a wave and she leaned a little closer to him. Her hand on his knee steadying him as well. They were so close that her head was spinning...oak—he smelled of oak and mahogany and teak and ocean waves. Of heady reds at their prime and of soft, cool whites sipped late at night in front of a warm fire.

She leaned closer. If he wasn't going to kiss her, she'd kiss him.

" 'I didn't realize Tuesday was the first.' "

His words didn't make sense. This was a moment for—

"You've been to every lighthouse."

"Yes," she had, but what did that have to do with a kiss under the midday sun.

"You have the same calendar."

She nodded her head and leaned forward again.

"You lied."

No she hadn't. "About what?" She didn't ever— "Oh."

"Oh, she says. 'Haven't been to a lighthouse before,' she said." He pushed a strong finger against her shoulder. Hard enough to tip her away.

"You lied."

"No, I evaded." Evaded the most exasperating man on the planet.

"You lied."

If he said it one more time, she was going to smack him.

"Didn't."

"You said, and I quote, 'Yes, I am a lighthouse virgin.' " He looked immensely pleased with himself. She shoved his knee hard enough that he tipped back from his squat and landed on his behind against the lifelines.

"Do you catalog everything everyone says so that you can throw it back in their face? I didn't want you of all people to know about..." There was no way she was going to explain her own father to this irritating man.

He stared off across the water for a moment. Looked up at the sails as if he might find a clue up there. His smile twisted slightly to one side and his eyes twinkled as his gaze returned to her. Deep, ocean-deep eyes.

"Nope. Just you. Just everything you've ever said. I'd bet I could repeat every word."

"There you go, doing it again." Her heart rate had definitely jumped, it was all she could hear.

"The jerk being charming?"

He was so full of himself, and he was absolutely right. It was one of the nicest, back-handed compliments she'd ever had.

"Hey, up there." John shouted to make his voice carry above the wind. "We're almost there."

Russell stood with the grace of the wind and stepped out onto the narrow bowsprit to look beyond the sail. He paused for a long moment and then turned to her with a positively wicked grin.

He offered his hand. His grip was warm and firm as he helped her to her feet, and with the slightest little tug he could pull her into his arms whether she wanted to or not. Instead of having the decency to take advantage of the moment, he turned and placed her hand on the lifeline so that they could head back to the cockpit.

His grin didn't abate in the slightest.

ALL THE WAY back to the cockpit, she could feel Julia's scrutiny. Russell's mother didn't miss a thing and it made Cassidy's cheeks burn. She'd seen how close Cassidy had come to kissing her son. John gave no indication of noticing what he'd interrupted—if indeed he had. Maybe John was where Russell had inherited his obtuse nature.

Cassidy slid shakily into the seat.

Julia glanced at her son.

Russell stood at the tiller with his dad, both of them looking up at the sails and absorbed in some silent guy conversation about wind and canvas.

Julia took her hand and patted it, "Don't worry, dear. The Morgan men aren't the sharpest tacks in the bunch, but they get there eventually."

If her cheeks were heated before, they were on fire now. She turned to look away from her reflection in Julia's sunglasses, vague and pale in the dark glass.

There was the Mukilteo lighthouse. It was close, very close as John had sailed them within a few hundred feet. She could easily see the stepped Fresnel lens through the glass windows and the octagonal banister around the third story walkway.

The sun lit the lighthouse and the keeper's cottages to a near blinding white. A brilliant green-and-white state ferry pulled out from behind it. Even the "lawn" before the beacon was white, the white of crushed seashells in the sun.

Then she noticed the canopy. It was white and light as a feather, set across the front lawn for a party. People were sitting in rows of chairs facing the water. Some at the back and sides stood for a better view: a view of a wedding.

The minister was in black and white. A groom in black, right down to the tails on his tuxedo. The boat slid forward and Cassidy saw the bride in profile. She could have been Jo's twin with her straight dark hair and rounded face—and she was absolutely breathtaking in her gown, a clingy satin with a flowing sheer of chiffon to soften the edges. She wore no veil, rather a ring of white flowers worked into her black hair.

Many of the eyes in the audience were looking at her on the sailboat, following her. Before Cassidy could look away, she came to her senses. They were looking at the beautiful sailboat slipping along behind the bride and groom. Cameras clicked and flashed in a brilliant display that must have surprised the bride and groom, for they turned and so did, finally, the minister.

Cassidy pulled out her camera and shot a photo of sail, water, lighthouse, and wedding.

The minister and couple waved at them. Several of the audience joined in. She waved back and felt silly and touched at the same time.

As they slipped past she caught the wedding and lighthouse in the background and Russell Morgan in the foreground, holding the tiller and looking aloft at the set of his sails. This shot would get a place of honor on her wall.

A wedding day memory. What would hers be like? Would some beautiful sailboat pass by while she looked at the man she loved?

And where the hell was he anyway? She stole a glance at Russell.

No! Not possible.

He was pointing out something to his father.

"Helm's a-lee!" He called.

He swung over the tiller and John started doing something with the ropes.

That's when she spotted Nutcase on the swinging boom.

"The cat!" Her cry simply made Russell grin all the more. He was going to flip the cat over the side out of sheer cussedness. She tried to scramble up—Russell's hand landed on her head and drove her back into her seat. The heavy boom swung by just inches above her.

There was a soft thump as Nutcase jumped onto the cabin roof. The boom swung across, Russell ducking underneath with all the grace of long experience, even slapping the massive thing with his hand as it swung by, a smack of flesh on wood, like a man greeting an old friend.

The cat sat on the cabin roof watching the boom complete its swing. Then it daintily raised one paw to its mouth and tugged on an errant claw, leaning against the new slant of the deck to keep its place.

"You jerk!" She spun to face Russell. The adrenalin was still pounding through her, making her temples hurt. "You could have…"

She didn't know what. But he could have.

"Warned me!"

Russell's smile diminished at that point. It wavered for a moment before fading entirely.

John fussed with the lines and didn't look up. Julia sipped her ice tea. The silence in the cockpit stretched out for an overlong moment before Russell cleared his throat.

"Nutcase knows the drill."

Well she sure as hell didn't; he'd scared the daylights out of her. She faced forward feeling angry and foolish simultaneously. And the damned cat, as if nothing had happened, turned to face the sun.

Seafaring cats. They knew their place in life. They knew when to stand fast and when to jump. Why couldn't her life be that easy?

Everything in her life had made sense—right up until she'd received the phone call that her father was dying. Even after all the caregiving and the funeral was over, order had never fully returned to her life. Her career was on the upswing and she loved living near her friends again for the first time since college. It should have all made sense, but it didn't.

Then her father's letters made it worse.

And now to cap it all off, stupid, stupid Russell Morgan.

"You don't really know anything about anything, do you?" She knew she was being angry and putting words in his mouth that he hadn't meant that way. But they stung. Like stumbling on a hive of bees on her last trip to her father's vineyard when she was twelve.

Fourteen stings.

She never went back to his fields. Her father had protested that they weren't even honey bees, just some nasty ground bees. She'd dug in her pre-teenage heels and had never again enjoyed the outdoors he so loved. She'd forgotten that memory; the moment that had turned her away from the vines. Such a small thing in retrospect and yet it had changed the very course of her life.

She shook herself. How did she get her head into such an awful place? Nutcase curled up for a nap on a coil of rope that looked terribly uncomfortable until she settled herself inside the center. She belonged.

Cassidy had been having fun. Right until…

She'd just been afraid for the cat.

That was all.

But Russell had laughed. No, but he'd certainly smiled. Smiled at a joke that had pumped her so full of anger she could still scream.

She glanced back at him. He was eyeing her with a look of extreme caution. As soon as she turned, he glanced away at the sails.

Damn him! If he were still laughing, it would be easier to remain angry.

She checked the action of the boom, but it appeared to be staying safely to the other side of the boat. She stood and did her best to pretend she was stretching. It placed her closer to Russell than either of his parents. She kept her voice low, hoping the wind would make it so that only Russell would hear her.

"Next time, warn me."

He nodded carefully, even had the decency to mouth, "Sorry."

For good measure she moved forward to scratch the cat, who woke up enough to purr appreciatively before going back to sleep.

THE RATTLE and cough of the engine as it started was a rude interruption to a lazy afternoon spent lolling about before a dying breeze. After the warm sun and the water, Cassidy was ready for a long nap though she never napped and her watch insisted it was barely three o'clock.

Russell and his dad moved around in an easy fashion lowering and bundling sails. They hung rubber bumpers along one side. There was lots and lots of coiling and uncoiling of ropes to no purpose that she could quite understand. Sailboats made fixing her old VW Rabbit in college look easy.

Nutcase complained when shooed from her rope coil and showed her displeasure by going below with a flick of her tail and not a backward glance.

Julia sat beside her while the men fussed about. Despite the kerchief over her hair and her sunglasses and dark skin, the bright sheen of a day in the sun flushed her cheeks.

"I believe that you are the first woman that has ever made Russell behave. I certainly was never able to."

If this was Russell behaving, what was he usually like? She had no interest in being someone else's conscience. Half the time she couldn't stand to be around him.

"He and Angelo would get together and that was it."

The other half of the time she couldn't stop thinking about him.

"They'd get into trouble before they'd even left Maria's kitchen."

"Maria? Who's Maria?"

"Maria Amelia Avico Parrano. Angelo's mother has been John's cook since shortly after I came along. Practically a family member. She and I birthed our boys within weeks of each other. Angelo and Russell learned to cook at her knee. Angelo's a better cook, but not by much."

"He told me he could barely heat soup."

"You never saw two boys with such a passion for fine food. Or who could destroy a kitchen so fast." Julia eyed her speculatively. "It's not like Russell to understate his skills if given the chance. You are a very interesting woman, Cassidy Knowles."

Russell was once again at the tiller, guiding the long boat through the busy traffic streaming in and out of the marina. The Shilshole breakwater was so tall that she could only see the very tops of sailboat masts over it.

He ducked from one side of the boom to the other to keep an eye on the traffic. The clutter of boats might move slower than the commuters on I-5, but they also didn't turn as fast or stop as readily.

Russell was completely, smoothly in control, moving as if there was no hurry in the world. The *Lady* slid through a graceful curve at his slightest command. She'd always thought of him as a bumbler, some people naturally were, but not now. Nor when he'd walked through the restaurant with the blond on his arm. Great! She really did bring out the worst in him. He was only an irritating, irrational idiot in her presence. The worst part was, she was little better around him.

The passengers of every boat that went by, some so close she could smell what they were having for lunch over the diesel exhaust, turned to watch them. At first she thought they were watching the majestic blue hull slide through the water.

Then she noticed that the women's stares weren't directed at the boat in general. Instead, most of them watched the skipper who stood tall at the helm.

Now why did that bother her?

Julia whispered in her ear, "Russell is so damn handsome, isn't he? Even more so than his father, which is not an easy thing to do."

He *was* damn handsome. He also belonged out here. She could imagine him crossing the mighty ocean with the wind tousling his hair, his cat winding about his feet, and his lady at his side.

"Ha!"

"What?" Julia turned to her.

"Nothing." No way she was going to say what was going on in her mind. It was beyond ridiculous.

Julia smiled and patted her arm, as if Cassidy's thoughts had just been published across her forehead like a Times Square reader board.

"He'll get around to it eventually. He already can't live without you, it will just take him a bit longer to realize that."

"But we aren't...don't...haven't..." She sounded like a teenager trying to backpedal.

"Yet I know how it looks when I see it."

"How what looks?" She'd better not be saying what she was saying.

Julia placed a hand on one cheek and kissed her on the other.

"We're going to be great friends, Cassidy Knowles and Julia Morgan. You'll see."

Russell aimed the boat into a narrow waterway in the forest of masts and radar thingies that was so dense it obscured the hillside behind them.

"You want me to *what?*" The cordless phone was slippery in her hands, Cassidy grabbed a Kleenex from her living room couch's end table to wipe off the sudden sweat off her palms. It was just as slippery after she did so.

"C'mon, Cassidy. You already told Mom that you didn't have plans for the 4th of July." Russell's voice was deep and soft on the phone. Not the softness of weakness, but the softness of warm fires on quiet evenings. "You were really great with them, by the way. Thanks. You were definitely the highlight of their trip out. I'd have been dead without you."

"A 4th of July boat party?" This made her far more nervous than meeting his parents. This would be a real date.

"Right! We'll cruise down to the Seattle waterfront before sunset and toss out a hook."

"We'll go fishing?"

There was a long silence.

"Toss out an anchor."

"Oh." They really had a language all their own.

"Angelo says there's great music and amazing fireworks along the beach there."

"There is. Who else will be there?" Far more nervous. Her stomach flip-flopped, unable to believe that she was even considering the idea.

"Just a couple of the other boaters. You're welcome to bring some friends. We'll go with Dave and Betsy, they have a boat that puts mine to shame. I also just ripped out my electrical."

"You need electricity on a sailboat?" She really didn't care. She just needed to buy a minute to think. Did she really want to go out on a *date* with him? "Yes," was the surprising answer. Well, not too surprising if she was going to be truthful about it.

He was saying something about running lights and anchor lights and radios.

Did she want to have that date among other people she didn't know? It would certainly be safer. Chaperoned—not that she needed any chaperones—at least not normally. But around Russell maybe she did. Not in case he did something. More to keep herself from jumping him and really regretting it in the morning.

He was on to metering and instrumentation.

She'd beg off on the decision, call him back tomorrow when she'd had a chance to sleep on it.

"It's interesting the different types of cable and equipment that are required to survive salt air corrosion even if it's inside the cabin. Did you know that stainless steel rots in sea air? It rots fast if it gets salt spray."

Delay was definitely a good idea. Better yet, she'd tell him to expect her if she showed up, and not if she didn't.

"Yes."

"Oh, you knew about stainless? Weird, huh?"

"No, I mean, yes, I'll be there. And no, I thought stainless was, well, stainless." That wasn't what she'd meant to say. All her standoffish thoughts were careening together to make her voice silky in a way that sounded nothing like her and a lot like someone with much more confidence.

"Really?" Russell's voice practically squeaked in surprise.

"I'd love to. See you then."

She pressed the hangup button before her mouth could invite him up to the condo which had a great view of the fireworks.

Still clenching the cordless phone, like the lifeline to a woman lost overboard, she staggered up to the glass door to her balcony. The late evening waterfront was dappled with a thousand lights and beyond the water the Olympic Mountains were etched against the pink sky.

Cassidy leaned her forehead against the sun-warmed glass.

Ferries plied the water. Commercial ships unloaded at the piers. Traffic hustled along the waterfront.

She reared her head back a few inches and thumped it forward against the glass.

And she was totally adrift at sea.

PERRIN HAD ALREADY MADE a date with a banker she'd been seeing for a while and had been really pissed about not going along on the sailboat. "I can't believe this dream guy of yours is that same grouch who sat at dinner for thirty seconds. How can you be dating him? Though he's a hunk, I have to admit that. And makes great ads. You should see what we have picked out for you to model. It's wicked."

"He's not my dream guy," Cassidy had insisted over the phone; Russell was too much of a pain in the behind to be anyone's dream guy. So why had she dreamt of him last night and why was she now climbing aboard Dave and Betsy's boat?

Perrin had sniggered.

"I'm not dating him; besides, he's not always a grouch. And I'm not modeling anything lurid."

"I bet deep down he's mean."

Cassidy's guess was just the opposite, but she'd kept it to herself.

She was beginning to think that Russell was a really decent man, all wrapped up in being a guy.

Jo wasn't a fan of boats, her dad had been a deadbeat Alaskan fisherman and boats always reminded her of the stench of fish and too much beer. But she only made Cassidy beg a little before caving in.

Now it was the afternoon of the Fourth and they cast off from the dock and were underway even before she and Jo had a moment to stow their belongings below. Except, here on the catamaran, it wasn't "below," it was "in the salon." She glanced wistfully at the receding dock out the long, narrow windows.

"This is it, Jo; if we jump now, we might still make it."

Her friend shook her head, "You got me on this ridiculous thing, you don't get off the hook so easily. It doesn't look so bad anyway."

And it didn't. Russell's boat below had been a combination of beautiful mahogany shaped into pleasing curves, items neatly stowed in custom cubby holes, and a complete mayhem of sawdust, tools, and half-ripped out sections.

There had been a hole right in the middle of the floor that opened to concrete a few inches down. Being in a boat on the water and seeing that it was filled with concrete hadn't made her feel all warm and fuzzy. When Russell had answered her question that it wasn't just concrete, but rather about six tons of concrete and iron boiler punchings, whatever they were, she'd considered swimming ashore. Through the hole in the floor, she'd seen a thin film of water washing back and forth over the concrete. It had been mesmerizing and left her feeling a bit ill. She'd spent very little time below during the sail with his parents.

Dave and Betsy's salon was like a warm living room. Everything was neatly stowed. There were a hundred homey touches: a quilt throw on a settee, a small group of pictures along the only bit of open wall, even tiny curtains for each window. Water stains on the table and fraying on two chairs in particular added to the lived-in and cozy feel.

The others were on deck: Russell, the owners, and an old man with more white beard than face. Cassidy glanced at Jo and they both moved farther into the boat. At the end of the salon there was a set of a half-dozen stairs to either side, leading down into each hull of the catamaran.

They tip-toed down the set to the left. A tiny kitchen—a galley—wrapped ingeniously around the steps. Forward lay a small bedroom, barely bigger than the double bed stuffed in it. More quilts and pictures, though definitely a guest room. It even had a tiny bathroom with a toilet and shower tucked behind the door.

At the other end of the hull was a floating office. A laptop sat on a cubbyholed desk. There were several bookshelves, mostly filled with novels, but there were three books, all with similar titles, grouped off to one side. They were by Betsy and Dave Howard.

She slipped the first book free of the elastic bungee cord that ran across the front of the bookshelf and showed the cover to Jo.

"Cruising Over Fifty." Jo read aloud.

Their hosts smiled from the cover, looking much as they did now, wearing a tiny bikini and a Speedo respectively.

"If I look that good at fifty, I've won the lottery and gone to heaven."

Cassidy flipped to the copyright page. Ten years ago.

"They're over sixty now. Damn!" She checked the picture again. Fit without the harsh lines of gym machines and definitely no cosmetic surgery. She slid the book back into place.

They returned to the salon. Jo turned for the cockpit, but Cassidy crossed the salon and descended into the other hull.

A couple of seats were built into the hull at the foot of the steps. To the stern was the master bedroom. A sweater was tossed on the made bed and the pillows still showed the dents of their owners' heads. Cassidy could move in here in a heartbeat. Toward the bow was a small sink and a closed door.

Jo plucked her sleeve. "Enough, Miss Snoopy. There is a line between curious and nosy."

"I'm nosy."

"Right," Jo headed up the short flight of steps and Cassidy turned to follow. Behind the door was the unmistakable pumping sound of a marine toilet being flushed. Clank, gurgle, clank, gurgle. It was the first thing Russell had taught her about his boat, this one sounded exactly the same. Someone else was aboard, maybe old white-beard's wife.

The girl who popped out of the door knocked Cassidy back onto the settee at the base of the stairs. Her bikini revealed far more than it covered. She had blond hair, the casual fitness of being in her early twenties, and the serious curves of someone quite dangerous.

She inspected Cassidy with a quick glance from boat shoes and creased navy pants to her silk blouse. She'd never been assessed and discounted so quickly.

Then the woman's face broke out into such a large smile that Cassidy almost doubted the expression that had been there moments before. Dangerous like a shark this one.

"You must be Cassidy. Hi, I'm Teri." She held out a hand and grabbed Cassidy's with a grip that would have fit better in one of those mano-a-mano guy moments. "Russ said you'd be coming."

"He didn't mention you." Nice, Cass, real nice. But it didn't faze her new acquaintance a moment.

"Yeah. Well, with Tommy gone, I was at sorta loose ends. Kinda invited myself aboard, you know."

"Tommy?"

"My ex. I kicked him overboard. He wanted me to go climb this idiotic rock, and after all this training, he like wouldn't take me with him. I was, you know, really pissed."

"Ex-boyfriend? I'm sorry."

"Ex-husband. Two years, three months or some such. At least that's what he said. Fun, but what a waste. He was so, you know, protective. There are times when a girl needs someone to watch over her, it's kinda charming, but not all the time fer crying out loud." She shrugged in a way designed to lift her generous bosom and make it look as if her breasts were about to spring from their tiny bits of cloth.

Jo stuck her head back down, "You coming? Oh, hello."

Jo got the introduction, without the attacking handshake.

They didn't even have to glance at each other to share the thought. This girl was as wild as Perrin had been in college, with none of the class or intelligence. Teri was a disaster waiting to happen.

Back on deck, the dance began, and Cassidy started to feel far worse than a bit of seasickness. She looked longingly back at the marina, now just a tiny cluster of masts disappearing rapidly behind. This boat was much faster than Russell's and had opened the gap quickly. They'd raised sail while she was below, but the wide catamaran had stayed so level she hadn't noticed when they got underway.

Dave stood at the wheel. Instead of a narrow cockpit where everyone's knees were always bumping together in a friendly little circle, here you could spread out. There were two couch-sized places to sit with a small table bolted to the deck between them. They didn't need the wide-bottomed, heavy mugs to avoid spilling drinks, just a good solid glass.

Russell stood by Dave and chatted about the "set of the sails" and "monohull vs. twin-hull leeway." While Cassidy was congratulating Betsy on her beautiful boat, Teri joined the other sailors. In moments she was cranking a handle on a winch and talking about the "lie of the wind."

Lie indeed. Cassidy couldn't believe she'd swallowed Russell's invitation—hook and all.

Cassidy and Jo joined Betsy and Perry for iced tea. It was bitter on her tongue as she watched Teri bend and flex while she worked with the ropes.

And Russell didn't stop watching Teri for a moment.

CASSIDY MOVED to the bow once they'd anchored, wishing she'd had the foresight to bring a book. It was an idyllic setting. Night was falling and Seattle was a shining backdrop as the last of the daylight was replaced by sparkling office and apartment lights. Myrtle Edwards Park was a throbbing mass of people—half the population of Seattle must be jammed in there to watch the fireworks. A band cranked out some serious dance tunes that made her feet twitch despite how she was feeling.

A hundred or more boats clustered as close to the fireworks barge as the police would allow. There were power yachts that must be over a hundred feet long and three stories tall. In between them ski boats, fishing skiffs, and two-person sailboats scuttled around while a massive three-masted sailboat cruised by in deeper water. She wanted to ask about it, but that would mean facing Russell and the permanent attachment to his hip. Teri had staked her territory and Russell played along as if everything was completely normal.

How had she so misjudged him? Perrin had been right. Jo had simply shaken her head sadly, even before Cassidy could ask the question. It wasn't her imagination. At some point, she'd have to return to the cockpit and watch Teri continue to work at seducing Russell. For all she knew, Russell had been consoling her in the night since her ex had departed. She could easily imagine the woman producing big rolling tears that would drip down onto her heaving bosom, all on cue.

At least she hadn't invited him to the condo. There it was, she looked shoreward, not a dozen blocks away. A dozen blocks to safety and a hundred yards of freezing water she couldn't cross. It might as well be a hundred miles. She was good and surely trapped.

"Pretty boat."

The voice came from a canoe close beside the catamaran. A pair of boys in their teens were looking at the boat the same way Teri was tracking Russell.

"Thanks. Um, but it's not mine."

"Still, it's cool."

"Yeah, cool."

She'd rather be anywhere than here.

"Where are you guys from?"

"Wenatchee, you know, east of the mountains."

She did; it was a huge grape growing area. "Did you paddle the whole way?"

The one in front rolled his eyes, but the one in the stern laughed.

"Nah, just the last little bit. We parked pretty close this morning." He nodded toward the beach.

There was a flash and a thump from the barge. A thin trail of sparks soared upward. She followed it and was rewarded by a huge flash. A moment later the bang arrived so loud and hard she could feel it as much against her chest as her eardrums.

Sometimes the answer was so obvious, it was hard to believe she hadn't had it earlier in the long, weary evening. She looked over her shoulder and saw Jo look her direction. Dave, Betsy, and Perry were chatting quietly. Russell and Teri were nowhere to be seen. They must be down below together, doing *what* she didn't want to know.

Cassidy rocked her head toward the canoe.

Jo glanced over, paused for a moment and nodded. She made a shooing motion with one hand that none of the others noticed.

Cassidy tilted her head in a question.

Jo nodded again. She was sure.

"Hey, guys." They were both still staring upward like frogs dazzled by a flashlight.

"Yeah?"

"I'm not feeling real well. Could you give me a lift to the beach?"

"Now?"

"Uh-huh."

They both shrugged. "Sure, climb on in, lady."

Moments later, as the second warning boomed overhead, she stepped onto terra firma and felt much better.

"Thanks, guys, you're great." She kissed each on the cheek. The one in front groaned, but the one in the stern leaned into the kiss for a moment.

"Any time, lady, any—"

The first big firework cut off his sentence as it soared aloft and burst like a huge chrysanthemum.

She was the only one moving away from the beach as flecks of colored light flew through the sky and lit the upturned faces before her. She didn't turn back to look for the sailboat.

"HI, THIS IS CASSIDY."

"Hi, Cassidy. This is Russell. Look, I feel—"

"I'll be out of town for the next couple weeks, but I will be checking for messages. Thanks."

There was a nasty little beep.

"Shit!"

Nutcase scrambled away from where he'd thumped his hand on the table.

"No, that isn't what I meant. Look, um, could you give me a call?"

Unbelievable! He was so abysmally hopeless.

"No, you won't will you."

He wouldn't either if he was her.

"Look, your friend Jo, she read me the riot act. I had no idea. Every time I tried to get near you, you ran off."

Good trick on a sailboat. He'd stopped chasing as soon as he got the message that she wanted nothing to do with him.

Jo had actually laughed in his face when he'd said that.

"I didn't even notice Teri. She isn't anywhere near your league. She's just a lonely kid."

He was sounding really pathetic. There had to be some way to cancel this message.

"Cassidy, I didn't…" but he had. "I wanted to…shit!…I wanted to spend some time with you when I wasn't being freaked out by my parents. I wanted—"

A beep cut him off.

He heard the click as his cell phone disconnected the dead call.

"MISS KNOWLES."

"Cassidy."

"Cassidy, thanks. You said that there are wines that aren't real types of wine? I don't understand that."

Thirty-five students of the Culinary Institute of America eagerly awaited her answer. She always had a great time at the CIA summer-series classes. About the end of the first week, she couldn't imagine why she didn't move back to New York to live along the Hudson River and teach oenology. Invariably, by the end of the second week, she remembered why she never did. But this was the first week and her session had been booked out within hours of the class announcement. At least a dozen of the staff stood along the back wall to listen in.

She'd once sat in those chairs and listened just as eagerly to Craig Claiborne when he'd deigned to lecture. She was standing where Craig had stood and Palmer and Prudhomme and a host of other greats before her. She was either really good or fooling everyone.

"There are new wines all the time. Traditionally, the types of wine were based on grape and region. Bordeaux still only comes from Bordeaux, France. So, here you are, a new wine producer. You want to make your mark. What do you call your wine?"

"You just make up a name?" He was perhaps twenty years old, way too young. Sitting in the first row. Over the phone the night before, she'd bet Jo fifty cents that he'd chat her up afterward. He was damn cute and he knew it.

"They're called varietals. They have some of this grape, a bit of that. No one knows exactly what, except their vintner of course, and she'll know to the nearest thousand pounds what grapes are used. Nearest hundred if they're really good." Not that she could tell. Damn Russell for being right. She didn't really know what happened behind the scenes. Didn't know the life of any wine at the level a vintner did. She'd spent an entire career in wine always a step back, a step away from the heart of the process. Even worse, away from the process that had been so important to her father.

"So, the vintner declares their wine by the grape, or doesn't. I recently tasted a Sangiovese from a cliffside winery in Cinque Terre. The grape wasn't labeled because Sangiovese is not much help to separate the winery from the herd—it makes up over ten percent of the total Italian grape crop, a quarter of a million acres. Instead the winery labeled it, 'Pizza Wine.' It was simple, clear, and to-the-point marketing."

Cassidy didn't want a "pizza wine" fling anyway, and that's all the cute student would be, but still it was flattering.

"Suddenly we have the 'pizza wine' grape. Or the 'Fume Blanc,' which sounds grander. But in either case it means whatever the vintner wants it to mean. Marketing. The higher end wines are generally true to their grape, Cabernet Sauvignon for example. Note that I said higher end, not necessarily better. Wine is matched to meal, occasion, and palate. A $28,000 magnum of Romanee Conti '85 probably won't be nearly as good a match for pizza as that twelve dollar varietal. But you don't often compare a burgundy *grand cru* with a bit of Sangiovese marketing."

Was that what Russell was doing with his daily phone messages? A bit of cheap marketing. Or had she really misread the situation?

Jo, even patient Jo, was getting tired of her long distance second-guessing.

Russell's first message had been desperate. Then he'd left three more trying to explain he hadn't noticed what Teri was doing before giving it up as a bad cause. She'd thought that was the last of him.

The next day, a new message. One deliberately lighter, much less assertive, but also less unsure. The history of the Mukilteo lighthouse. He'd done some digging. One hundred and fourteen weddings there since it was decommissioned. An admiral who couldn't sleep at night because a fog horn sensor went off whenever the moonlight reflected off the white seawall. He had the wall painted black so he could get his sleep.

The day after that, no call from him. Instead, an invitation from his mom to drop down to New York for the weekend, a quick two-hour train ride.

The day after that, a poem that had nothing to do with wine, boat, or lighthouse, but rather flowers, hummingbirds, and wings beating with love—all read in his wonderful deep voice. Way over the top, but so charming she was still weak in the knees. Or maybe in the head.

She didn't want to call him back and have to tell him to stop. *Admit it Cassidy, you don't want him to stop.*

She didn't notice when, at the end of class, the young questioner did indeed try to engage her attention. She walked away and left him talking to empty air.

Even before she was clear of the building, she'd pulled out her cell phone to see what Russell's message was.

<hr>

"One more chance."

There was a silence on the phone to Cassidy's opening salvo.

"Are you there?"

"Yes, just trying to catch my breath." The sound of reprieve in Russell's voice couldn't have been greater if a firing squad had just been ordered back to barracks.

"Your mom was great by the way. They took me to the Four Seasons and completely spoiled me."

"She's good at that."

"So?" She'd waited until she was home to call. Waited until his messages repeated themselves in her head so much she couldn't sleep. Messages about the success and closing of his business. Of his childhood dreams to go sailing. Of the progress of his cat on her never-ending quest for the perfect nap. All passed on in two-minute clips allowed by her voicemail. At first he'd stumbled, been cut off, beeped out in mid-word. By the end of two weeks of silence on her part, he had the timing down. Each message ended with a hook that made her want to start the next. A winding "tale" as soft and comfortable as his cat's.

"Well," his voice was soft and deep. He had the most amazing phone voice which certainly hadn't hurt his cause.

"There's this lighthouse. You can only get there by boat…"

She glanced at the calendar over her sofa.

"Patos Island."

PATOS ISLAND LIGHTHOUSE

*P*atos Island
First lit: 1893
Automated: 1974
48.789 -122.9715

The Isla de Patos, "Island of Ducks" is 210 acres of trees, rock, and sea caves making it a great favorite of smugglers over the years. In the early 1900s the lighthouse keeper and his family made a once per month trip across twenty-six miles of water to Bellingham, Washington for supplies. His nearest neighbor? The Canadian lighthouse keeper on Saturna Island over five miles in the other direction.

When smallpox struck his family, he flew the lighthouse flag upside down as a distress sign to passing ships. By the time help arrived, three of his thirteen children had died.

*M**t. Baker rose like** a beacon, soaring up into the heat of the summer day. Russell's boat slid up to the public pier in Anacortes. He'd told her it was a two-day trip to sail from Seattle to Patos Island and back. Cassidy had covered most of the distance in the two-hour drive north in order to avoid sleeping aboard. He'd promised she could be as safe as she wanted, which was sweet. But since they'd never been together for more than an hour without ticking each other off, she chose to meet him at the closest port.

His boat looked sharp, graceful, prettier than it had before. He'd finally repainted it. The bowsprit now had copper handrails wrapped around it. The dinghy was upside down on the top of the cabin. Everything looked shipshape, even elegant. His grin of pride was infectious.

The boat slid up to the dock and, with a brief, low rumble from her engine, came to a halt in front of Cassidy. He dropped the lifeline and helped her aboard with an extended hand—warm, strong hand.

He retreated to the cockpit and moments later, the dock was sliding away. She didn't feel the pull of the dock as she had before. This time she was glad to be aboard. Some part of her, a wild part, the one that didn't always want to do precisely the right and cautious thing, had won out, perhaps for the first time in her life. She'd driven here with the windows down, the sunroof open, and the oldies station blasting.

"Here, take the tiller."

She stared at the stick of polished wood, longer than her arm. "I don't know how to steer a boat."

Even as she spoke, he grabbed her daypack and lowered it through the hatch. In moments, she was sitting as she'd seen him sit, the wood smooth and warm beneath her hand.

"Just choose a point and aim for it." He pointed over his shoulder. "Mt. Baker should be fine for the moment."

He moved off and began working with the ropes.

"But I don't know…" He probably couldn't hear her over the dull throb of the engine.

She stared at the mountain. It was a little off to the right, starboard. She pulled the tiller that way…and the mountain got further away. Maybe there was a current pushing them the opposite way. She pulled the tiller harder, right into her lap. The situation just got worse.

"Russell!"

He called over his shoulder, without even turning around to help her.

"It's opposite. Steer left to go right."

"Steer left to go right. What kind of a silly system is that?"

Well, right wasn't helping so she pushed the tiller the wrong way—away from her to port.

The boat swung obligingly until its bowsprit was aimed right at the mountain. And then it kept going past the other side.

She pulled it back into her lap. Russell stumbled toward the right rail, she shoved it to the left.

He didn't say anything, just steadied himself and started untying a rope from around the sail.

Smaller corrections. A little pull, a little push, and she finally had it centered on the mountain. As the boat lifted over the small waves, the bow went to the right and as it settled back into the water it went to left, but it was the best she could do. The average was about right and it wasn't as if there were highway lanes on the water she had to stay in. The only other traffic around were two small sailboats, a water skier, and off in the distance a pair of monstrous oil tankers anchored in the broad bay.

Russell pulled up the sails with an easy hand-over-hand motion. As the great flaps of red mainsail slid upward, she expected that there was more muscle to the process than it appeared. He made it look easy.

He tied off the first one and raised the one up front—the jib.

"Turn off the key."

There was one at the end of the cockpit, right next to some dials and meters. Who knew sailboats had keys? With a click, the rumble ceased and the world was suddenly quiet. Several of the dials flopped over to zero.

"Aim for Lummi," he pointed negligently off the left side. Port side. Four letters in port and left, more letters in starboard and right.

"Which one's Lummi?"

"The third island." He returned to the bow, ending the conversation.

Stupid man. Third island? She didn't see any islands, just a line of green hills. Maybe the third hill was the third island. She pulled the tiller toward her and the bow moved the wrong way. She caught it quickly and pushed it away.

Russell didn't stumble this time. Maybe she was getting smoother control—or he'd prepared himself now that he knew she didn't have a clue.

The boat had been coasting since she'd turned off the motor…then the wind caught the sails. In moments they were sliding ahead. The meter labeled in knots slid upward four, five, six and the boat heeled over.

It took some pressure to keep the tiller straight, but not a lot, just enough to know she was steering the boat. Russell took his time tidying up various ropes along the deck. He even stopped to play with his cat. When they were done, he tossed the cat at the sail; it slid down to the boom and settled quickly for a nap.

Damn them both.

By the time he finally returned to the cockpit, she was getting the hang of steering. It was the most powerful feeling she'd ever had—the great craft answered her whim and the force of the wind drove them forward with a happy splashing of the waves down the side. She didn't really want to give it up, but it was his boat.

Russell slid into the cockpit and sat on the bench seat, but made no move to take the tiller.

"Hi, Cassidy. Thanks for coming." He set his feet on the opposite bench and rested his elbows along the back. "Not much wind in August, but it's nice not to be fighting some gale to get to a lighthouse."

He looked great. Cutoff shorts, still showing some of the stains that matched his boat's deck, revealed muscular legs. His dark t-shirt was a perfect match for his dark eyes. The wind tugged at the curls of hair. Bare feet.

"Pirate."

"What?"

"You look like a pirate. Well, a modern pirate."

"I seem to have misplaced my sword. And you seem to have misplaced your heading."

She was aiming square at the second hill, island. She shoved the tiller over. The sails snapped loudly at the sudden change. He pulled on one of the lines and the boom swung closer over the deck.

There was a loud mew from the top of the boom.

"It's okay, girl. Just a newbie on the crew. We pirates can't be too choosy, just have to scavenge what we can find on the high seas."

A man who talked to his cat in whole sentences.

"I must have a thousand photos of that silly beast. I'm thinking of producing a book of cat photos. You know, the cute point-of-sale things by the cash registers."

"Cats of the world?"

"Cats of the world?" He rolled the sound over his tongue. "That's perfect. A whole series. Cats of the South Seas."

"Caribbean Cats."

"Mediterranean Cats."

"Coy Cats of Cancun."

He grinned at her. For the first time since she'd boarded, he really looked at her. And she totally lost her heading. The sails flapped. Nutcase mewed loudly and thumped down onto the deck. But she couldn't look away.

He'd sent her roses on the last day of her class. Not a little bouquet, he'd sent an armful. Dozens of long reds, yellows, and whites delivered in the middle of class right in front of everyone. She hadn't been able to speak over the applause and good-natured laughter.

He slid a hand over hers on the tiller. With a gentle pressure, he eased them back onto course.

She was trapped, the tiller across her lap and Russell Morgan across the only way out from under.

He didn't lean toward her. Didn't hear her heart crashing away but sending no blood at all to her brain. He merely held her gaze with those eyes.

Once they were back on course, he released his hold on her and sat back.

He stared over the side at the water for a long time before he spoke.

"Do you want me to take you back to the dock?"

She could see that the words cost him deeply. He didn't turn to face her—which was good, because if he had, she'd have been lost. She was pretty lost anyway. His offer was perhaps the nicest compliment she'd ever had—it was also about the sexiest.

Cassidy glanced back and was surprised at how far they'd come. Less than an hour from dock and Anacortes had disappeared behind them.

She'd given little thought to what might happen aboard the boat with Russell and only a cat for a chaperone, beyond choosing to drive to Anacortes rather than sail. However, now that she was here, there was little question of what might well happen if she remained. Even if common sense said run, she couldn't deny how it felt to be sitting so closely beside him.

She managed to shake her head. He didn't see, because he wasn't looking.

"Let's…" her voice was barely a whisper. If they had been traveling by engine instead of wind, he wouldn't have heard her.

But he did and turned.

His eyes weren't begging…not quite.

Unable to speak, she shook her head once more.

They both smiled carefully.

He turned back to watch the water.

"WE'RE NEARLY THERE."

Cassidy didn't awake from her afternoon nap with a start as he'd expected. She woke slowly, like a cat stretching and considering her next action carefully. Perhaps a yawn, perhaps another stretch. She'd slept for several hours in the shade of the cockpit bench. He'd managed not to stare too much. Part of him was amazed that she felt safe enough to sleep in his presence. He'd take that as a plus.

She wandered below and was a while coming back up.

She'd changed into shorts and a halter top that nearly blew his blood pressure. Her light blouse was now open, worn more as a shawl against the sun than a cover. It revealed and hid her figure with every motion and breath of the wind. Her hair, let down from its tight bun, cascaded about her shoulders. Her face still had that sleepy look of freshly wakened and washed with cool water.

"Christ! You are so far beyond Teri's league."

The warm-and-washed look turned icy so fast it knocked the air out of his lungs.

"You're gorgeous!" She was.

The chill frost was replaced by a charming blush.

She was beyond that. Teri was shapely, Melanie was beautiful, but

Cassidy Knowles, while not centerfold beautiful, was incredibly attractive. You couldn't not look at her.

"Uh, thanks."

He shook himself. "Sorry, I, that didn't, but you're…" He slapped a hand over his mouth.

She leaned down and kissed him on the forehead. Her hair slid along either side of his face. He had a view right down her neck and into her halter top. But it was her smell that got him. Warmth, home, and the open ocean with no perfume, not even scented soap. There had never been any woman who smelled like that. Ever.

Taking the seat opposite, she stretched her long legs across to his side. So close, he could reach out and stroke them if he dared. Cassidy had runner's legs, every curve just perfect—unpainted toes. Now why did he find that sexy? He was being ridiculous.

Look up, Russell. Look at the island. Check the chart. Reef along the east point. Shoals in close on the north. You'll rip off your keel if you don't pay more attention.

He swung to the south, into deeper water. Slipping around the western point, they slid around into Active Cove. There were two state-run mooring buoys, both open, which was rare for a Friday in August. He did his best to concentrate only on swinging into the wind. He hooked the buoy on the first try and cleated it off, letting the sails back him away until they were at rest.

He had the sails part way down before he noticed Cassidy was standing across the boom, looking lost.

Without speaking, he showed her how to flake the sail into neat folds atop the boom. When it was lying neatly between the lazy jacks, he snapped the bungee cord in place. The jib was dropped and flaked in record time. Her hands were agile and strong once she knew what to do. They didn't have to talk, it was so easy and so natural.

Don't go there, Russell. She's just this incredibly desirable woman who has agreed to come out sailing with you. And only for the day at that.

The sails were set and the boat was well-tied. They were standing on the foredeck, a space barely three by five feet between the cabin and the forehatch.

For the life of him, he didn't know what to do, didn't know what to say. Should he reach for her or turn away before his pounding blood blew his brainpan into a puddle of mush?

"I loved the roses." Her voice was deep and throaty, hoarse on a lesser woman. Sexy as hell on Cassidy Knowles.

She stepped into his arms and their lips met with an electric shock that nearly knocked his knees out from under him.

They hadn't even looked at the damn lighthouse yet.

"I, UH…"

"Don't!" Cassidy was glaring up at him, just a few inches shorter, just a breath away.

"What?"

"You were going to apologize."

He nodded.

"Well, don't."

"But…"

She held up her hand to silence him, but he ignored her.

"I promised safe passage. I promised that you'd be as safe as you want to be aboard my boat." And now he'd gone and kissed her. Kissed her long and hard with a need that had surprised them both—well, it had shocked the hell out of him anyway. And it had been fantastic.

"I said, 'Safe.'"

"You did."

She raised an eyebrow, a smile tickled the corner of her mouth. That soft, strong mouth. He wanted to kiss her again and feel how it changed as that smile took shape.

"And?"

"I took advantage." Stupid. Stupid. Stupid. Angelo would smack him but good.

"Russell?"

"Yeah?"

"Don't you think I'm old enough to know my own mind?"

"You're old enough to—"

"Careful there, big boy."

He bit his tongue and looked away from that maddening smile. The lighthouse was perched a few hundred yards away, on the northernmost San Juan Island. Next stop was Canada. They were out at the limits.

"Old enough to…make me completely insane."

"Nice save."

"Weak, but best I've got on a moment's notice. Did you really like the roses?"

"It'll do. And I loved the flowers. How did you know where to send them? And two weeks of poetry and stories and sea chanties. Gads!" She rested her hand on her heart. Somehow he had touched her, rather than scaring her off. *Duh, she was here, wasn't she?*

He needed to get some distance or he wouldn't be able to control himself. He let her go and moved to the dinghy and began to untie it from the deck cleats.

"I googled you and your class popped up. I called the dean to find out when your last class was."

"You called the dean?" Cassidy undid the other ends of the lines. She started to untie the rope on the bow of the dinghy until he stopped her.

"We'll need that. Couldn't reach him, so I talked to some chef, Clara somebody." Together they lifted the little boat over the lifelines and dropped it bottom down into the water. He should have cleaned it. There were a thousand paint splotches. Globs of epoxy that probably wouldn't let go without taking some of the boat with them.

"You talked to Master Chef Clara Nichols? I barely got to talk to her."

"Nice lady. She helped me find a good florist, too. They want to talk to you about a Christmas class down at the California center as well."

She stood with her fists on her hips. Her eyes snapped with a fire that came out of nowhere—goddamn he loved when she did that.

Cassidy Knowles was feisty and strongheaded, which suited him right down to his toes. He was torn between throwing her overboard or dragging her down to his bunk below. To buy himself a moment of equilibrium, he pulled the oars out of their cradle and tossed them down into the dinghy instead.

Then he turned to face her and matched her stance, fists on hips.

Finally she blew at her bangs.

He blew at his even though he didn't have any.

"What am I supposed to do with you?"

"Either climb into my bed or my boat."

She didn't laugh in his face, she didn't get angry and slap him either. Both were good signs.

Instead, that smile opened up its thousand-watt brilliance on him and he had to restrain himself to not lean across and taste it.

"There's no bed here," she made a show of looking up and down the rocky beach. "I'll take the boat."

They both knew there was one down below, but he managed to keep his mouth shut. Instead, he nodded and untied the painter, using it to lead the dinghy back toward the break in the lifelines.

"Yes, I'll take the boat," her voice behind him little louder than the lapping of the water on the hull. "For now."

The painter slipped from his fingers and he almost lost the whole mess into the sea.

CASSIDY HAD a terrible time hiding her smile as she lay back in the stern of the tiny rowboat. Russell pulled stoutly on the oars, making the dinghy nearly launch with each stroke. His eagerness to return to the sailboat was showing. She did her best to look Victorian and swooning as the pirate dragged her to his lair.

He showed the effects of their afternoon. His shirt had grass stains, a couple of leaves and a bit of branch perched in his hair—right where she'd tucked them in while he kissed her. And now she knew how wonderfully soft his hair truly was.

They had run about like a couple of teenagers. Grabbing a kiss at the very westernmost tip of the island. Slapping her hand against those cut-off jeans of his and discovering a few things about that butt of his. One, his body was just a firm as it looked. Two, it was good that she was fleet of foot, because he was a very fast runner when motivated.

The dinghy thudded into the side of his boat so hard she almost flew forward into his arms. In seconds the boat was tied off and the oars had been tossed aboard.

He climbed up first and offered her a hand. She stepped straight into his arms and probably bruised her lips they came together so hard. They both leaned into it: tasting, touching, groaning. He dragged her blouse open to attack her throat, her neck, the top of her breasts. Everywhere he went was a new adventure.

He definitely wasn't a useless man who didn't know what he wanted. He clearly wasn't thinking about the latest stock deal or sporting event. Russell was completely here with her, wholly present in her arms, and she sure as hell wasn't going to let go.

He moved down to his knees to nuzzle her exposed belly.

Clawing at his shirt, she dragged it over his head. Ran her hands down that broad, strong back. He smelled of sea salt and man. There was no other word for it.

She pulled at his arms until he rose back to his feet so they could once again feast on each other's mouths. He suddenly bent down and put his shoulder into her waist, lifted her from her feet as if she weighed little more than his cat. She pounded his back, hard enough to make him grunt, not hard enough to make him put her down.

Her ears were buzzing loudly as he turned for the cabin.

No, it wasn't her ears. It was a speedboat filled with teenagers, roaring by less than a dozen feet away. A moment later their wake caught the sailboat.

The deck tilted.

She grabbed for what she could and latched onto the back of his belt and the waistband of his shorts.

He staggered one way. Staggered back.

And then she was flying free—soaring through the air in a moment of weightlessness.

They she hit the ocean with a splash.

The water was freezing. She kicked for the surface and gasped for air. The water was so cold it was hard to think.

More water sprayed in her face.

"Goddamn it, Morgan!"

He'd surfaced next to her. "This water is bloody cold."

"No shit!" She palmed a big spray of seawater into his face. While he spluttered, she looked up at the moored sailboat. Even in the few moments they'd been in the water, the current had drifted them away from it. They both swam, but didn't make any headway at first. She dug in deeper, kicked harder; it was slow work against the ocean current. She was getting colder and weaker with each passing moment.

They finally reached the boat where she grabbed onto the stern of the dinghy but couldn't pull herself up. The deck of the boat was far out of reach; what had been an easy step up from the dinghy was now a vast wall of wood. She lunged, but couldn't get close to the edge of the deck. And the cold was making her joints ache.

Russell dove.

"Don't you leave me!" she shouted down at the water.

Then he shot out of the water, half his body shooting into the air. A thousand drops of water sparkled all over him like a merman emerging from the deep. One hand caught the edge of the deck. Biceps flexed, shoulders rippled, and in moments he was aboard.

A hand reached down from above. She grabbed it.

He heaved, practically pulled her arm out of its socket.

Moments later she was sitting in the cockpit, the remains of her blouse wrapped around her as the shivers began to set in. There remained no sign of the kids in the speedboat, not even a wake.

"Come on. We have to get out of these clothes."

She shuddered. "That was the original idea. Now I'm n-n-not so motivated. How can water be so cold?" Her hands wouldn't stop shaking.

He pulled her to her feet and guided her below. The ladder was a major challenge.

"Puget Sound has a huge tide," Russell finally grabbed her by the waist and simply plucked her off the ladder and set her down inside the cabin. "Fresh seawater from Alaska pumps in here every day. Good thing it's summer; it means that you have a life expectancy of about twelve minutes in this water. In the winter, it's more like four before hypothermia sets in."

"Great!" The cool shade inside the boat only chilled her more deeply.

"Can we sue them or something?"

"They're long gone. The little shits."

He peeled off her blouse, halter top, and bra. She'd never felt so unromantic before in her life. Going to the doctor was more exciting than this. She tried to undo her shorts, but couldn't control her fingers. He undid them and shucked them off her legs.

"You are one big goosebump."

"That's because I'm freezing to death, you big hunk of meat. I don't have all the insulation you do."

He grabbed a blanket and wrapped it around her. He held her close and scrubbed his hands up and down her back to warm her up. His chest was cold and wet, but she leaned into it. She didn't want to admit to being scared, but watching the boat drift away in that moment before they'd started swimming had been terrifying. Her life had suddenly gone out of control as she was ripped from everything safe.

He smelled so good. She hid her face against his chest and luxuriated in the warmth of his scrubbing hands. Her very joints hurt with the cold. Moments ago she'd wanted to throw herself against his body, now she wanted to cower there.

Another shiver shook her so hard she couldn't even hold onto the blanket which slipped off her shoulders.

"You really took a chill. Come on," he dragged her forward.

She managed to step around the missing floorboard despite the silly putty that had replaced her knees. Moments later he had her tucked into the bed. She pulled the covers over her head and gave in to the shakes.

Moments later he slid in beside her and wrapped his arms around her.

It was the safest place she'd ever been.

If only it wasn't so damn cold.

CASSIDY DIDN'T REMEMBER when the shivers stopped. She didn't remember falling asleep. She didn't remember it getting dark.

There was a loud purring in her ear.

She rolled toward it and was rewarded with a faceful of fur. Nutcase's purr rose to an active buzz.

Then she became aware of two things simultaneously.

First, she wasn't the only human in this bed.

Second, she had no clothes on.

She lifted the cover and started to slip out of the bunk. A strong arm came from behind, looped around her waist, and pulled her back. In moments she was spooned back against Russell's chest, his arm a powerful rope around her waist.

Third, she discovered, he wore no clothes either. Despite that, she didn't feel trapped.

"Feeling better?" His voice was thick with sleep.

She nodded. Was this what she really wanted? If she didn't, she'd better move soon. Her body chose for her as she shifted closer against the heat of him. She'd never take being warm for granted again.

His arm slid farther around until it encircled her waist and tucked under her rib cage. Then she felt the growing pressure against her behind. Russell loosened his grip and shifted away.

He really was a gentleman. Well, mostly.

"You had to take off all of your clothes, too?" She wrapped her arm over his and pulled it back around her waist to let him know she was teasing.

"They were wet. It seemed like a good idea at the time." The last was said so close to her ear that his breath tickled.

Again he offered to back off. She wondered what it cost him to lean back so a tiny gap of warm air filled the space where his chest had been.

She rolled in his embrace and pushed on his shoulder until he lay on his back and she straddled him.

"Watch the overhead."

Raising her head slowly, she just brushed the underside of the decking. The boat was rocking gently with the rhythm of the sea. It felt so natural that her body followed it as easily as a leaf finding the breeze.

Russell's hands, those big rough hands she'd admired so often, wrapped ever so gently around her waist practically encircling her.

They slid upward, traced the line of her ribcage. Rather than latching onto the breasts in a typical he-man crush, his callused thumbs traced the sides with the softest of touches. He supported her as she leaned down for a kiss.

His mouth, so eager and forceful before, was a soft welcome. He ran one hand into her hair and the other over her behind.

She rubbed up the length of him and he groaned into her mouth. Lip to lip, chest to chest, every curve of him felt wonderful.

And his shoulders were amazing. She slid her arms beneath them and grasped them from behind. Shoulders big enough to carry the world.

Traveling in the upper tiers of the wine and restaurant circles she'd met her share of rich heirs. But Russell played none of their games—showed none of the ego about the wealth he had. His touch didn't assume or demand, rather it coaxed and asked—a question that her own body was more than happy to reply to in the affirmative. He had a body that had been custom made for her. She worked her way down, planting kisses on his throat and chest.

His hands played with her hair.

His groan returned with a gasp as she slid him between her breasts. He arched against her. With near frantic need, he grabbed at her shoulders and dragged her upward.

When they were once again even, she whispered in his ear, "Do you have…?" Christ she was being forward, wasn't she.

He reached somewhere to the side in the dark of the boat. There was a slight crinkle. It repeated with a little more energy. Then a frantic rattling of foil.

"Shit. My fingers, they aren't…"

She silenced him with a kiss and slid her hand along his arm until she found the condom. She sat back up as she unwrapped it. He was nervous. It was so charming that she'd have made the decision now, if she hadn't already.

He moaned again as she unrolled it slowly over him. The delicious contrast of soft and hard made her fingertips want to explore. He was writhing by the time she braced her hands on his chest and lowered herself over him.

When he was finally inside her, they sighed in unison. And they both laughed as Nutcase abandoned the bed in disgust with a loud thump of paws on the floor.

All of the heady need built over months had mellowed and sweetened with a little aging. He traced his hands down from her face, over her breasts, finally cupping her buttocks hard. He thrust up as she thrust down.

It was too much. Some part of her, some part she didn't know, let forth a throaty growl like a wild woman taking down her kill. Her senses closed in to the rocking of the boat and the perfect rhythm as he filled her deeper and deeper. It was a heady swirl of heat and sea salt. Of wave after wave after wave pounding up through her and making her release over and over and over.

When her body had hit its limit, when she could climb no farther, Russell launched himself upward, thrusting so far inside her they could have been the same body. She could feel each pulse of his release, each separate moment, triggering her own body into one last mind-numbing, soul-crashing wave.

When he finished, she slid down against his chest. His hands, soft as kitten fur, brushed against her face and over her hair. He stroked over the bridge of her nose and traced the arc of her eyebrows.

"Oh. My." His voice husked out about an octave lower than usual. She couldn't agree more.

It was late morning when Russell dragged on shorts and wandered down the companionway. Spotting Cassidy on the port bench of the cockpit made his world shift. It wasn't anything she did. She was simply sitting there, her back to him as she faced the stern. One of his dress shirts riding loose on her shoulders, the sleeves rolled up to her elbows.

He hung back in the shadows and watched her. Her head was tilted down as she read something in her lap and her hair hung like a shawl over her shoulders. She wasn't a stranger out of place. She'd taken to the boat as naturally as if she'd always been there—had always been in his life. Nutcase was curled up by her toes, asleep in the sun. In a single day, Cassidy had already become a fixture in the cat's life.

For the first time, ever, Russell could imagine his sea voyage with two. He could see spending time with this incredible woman, a lot of time. *You can't fall in love with someone overnight.* He could almost feel Angelo smacking him on the back of the head. But it wasn't overnight. He'd never known so much about a woman before bedding her.

Even that was wrong. He hadn't bedded her. They'd made love. Repeatedly. Wonderfully. Deliciously. Until exhaustion had finally dragged them back under.

He stepped onto the companionway ladder, which groaned as always.

Cassidy spun to stare at him.

For a single instant he saw the red-rimmed eyes. The tear-stained cheeks, then she turned away.

He froze on the step. Shit! So that's how the morning-after was going to be. What had he screwed up this time? Angelo could probably tell him, but he was nearly a hundred miles and a two-day sail away.

Russell turned back into the cabin and strode back toward the stateroom. He was there in five steps. No space on a goddamn boat. What was he thinking? Two people couldn't live on something this small, not even for one night. It wasn't humanly possible. He needed to punch something.

Punch it really hard.

And what was he supposed to do with her now? They were hours from the nearest port. More than half a day from her car, even with the motor.

Shit!

Why had he gotten his hopes up? Stupid-ass dream about finding the right woman. Instead, he'd found something new to demolish. And there was no guide on what it was this time, or what it would be next time. He pounded the side of his fist against the butt of the mast where it came through the deck. Hitting it felt good. He raised his fist to hit it again.

A cool hand touched the middle of his back and he froze.

He turned slowly, his fist still above his head.

Cassidy didn't look up at it.

Didn't even look at him.

She leaned against his t-shirt and he heard a gasp for breath.

He lowered his arms slowly. She began to shake. Her arms tucked between them just as when she'd been so cold yesterday. With her head tucked under his chin, he could feel her body shudder.

A tentative hand on her back released some unknown dam. In moments she was sobbing against him, long, racking, gasping sobs.

He pulled her closer.

Now he had even less of a clue what to do than before.

"I'm sorry, Cassidy." It would help if he knew what he was apologizing for. "You tell me what to do and I'll make it better."

She rocked her head back and forth keeping her face planted against his sternum and cried harder. That was a clear no.

"I'll go away, if that's what you need." God, how could he say that? Even as he held her he felt more powerful than ever before in his life, as if he could somehow protect her from the world. Unfortunately, what he needed to protect her from was himself.

He took a deep breath. If that's what she needed…

"You won't even need to see me again." Christ! The words ripped his throat as he offered them up.

One of her hands slid from between them and slid around his neck. She again shook her head and held on tighter.

At a complete loss, he decided to just keep his mouth shut. Powerful was replaced by helpless between one breath and the next and it felt lousy.

If he felt this way about her already…

Just shut up, Russell. Your brain is made of undercooked tapioca. One of Angelo's favorite insults. Small, hard nuggets in a slimy matrix of useless goo.

He managed to settle back on the bed with her sitting in his lap. He kissed the top of her head and stroked her hair.

"It'll be okay. Somehow it'll be okay."

In response she pulled her other hand free and shoved a crumpled piece of paper into his hand. He unfolded it as well as he could with one hand. It was a short letter, covered in a spidery scrawl that might have belonged to a child. Actually, it reminded him of one of the funniest letters he'd ever gotten. Angelo had written to him once as he was going under the drugs to have his impacted wisdom teeth removed. The letter had started clear, concise, a little complaining, mixed with some gossip about a pretty nurse. As the handwriting decayed, so had the train of conscious thought. The end of the letter had been an illegible blur—Angelo's pen had actually dragged all the way across the page in a fading line that they'd never been able to translate.

Cassidy's letter was mostly readable. Someone who called her "Ice Sweet." Not a name he'd use, fire and ice maybe, with a lot more fire than he'd ever met before. Cassidy was a deep banked, hot fire; the kind that would burn forever. He glanced at the bottom. Vic somebody.

Dearest Ice Sweet,

I thought about never telling you this part of our past. About letting the truth die with me. But finally decided that taking it to the grave wasn't fair to you. Maybe the drugs have clouded my judgment and your father is wrong, in which case, I'm sorry.

Her father was dead. Russell flipped the page over, one side only. Cassidy had gone quiet. Her head resting on his shoulder, her hand on his chest, like a little girl going to sleep.

Your birth was harder on your mother than she ever let on. I was preoccupied with the loss of one vineyard, which nearly broke my heart, and the start of the next. The work was just as brutal, and your mother wasn't able to help. Her parents were failing fast, your grandfather had a massive stroke and your grandmother just gave up. She caught pneumonia the day before he died and was gone within the week.

And he'd asked Cassidy to help protect him from his parents. His wealthy, healthy, loving parents. Shit!

You were born by C-section. There was an infection. Then other things went wrong. We thought they were treated, but some damage was done, something not removed entirely or... We never knew. When the ovarian cancer struck, it took her so fast I barely had a chance to say goodbye.

I always told you she was called to the hospital and killed on the way. It was almost that fast, but that wasn't what happened.

She wasn't a nurse, though she nursed my heart after Vietnam, and you and her parents. She was a nurse of the heart, the gentlest soul I've ever known. I didn't know she'd never come home when I took her away that last time. Truth of truths, maybe I didn't ever really say goodbye. I still miss her so much that every day it is a hole in my heart.

I feel as if I really did get a chance to say goodbye to you. I'm so glad you moved back to Seattle to spend my last six months with me. It is the greatest gift you could have ever given me.

Love you, Ice Sweet
Vic

He turned the page over again. Still blank. He folded it carefully and tucked it back into her hand. She clenched it slowly into a fist, the paper's crinkling the only sound other than the gentle slap of waves against the hull.

"When did he die?"

"Christmas Day." Her voice was hoarse, barely a whisper. She found a Kleenex and blew her nose with a very unwomanly honk. She was really a mess.

"I hate crying. I haven't wept like that since, I don't know, ever. Maybe since Mama didn't come home."

"But it's August. How…the letter?" She'd been reading a letter on the bow of the boat when his parents were there. And he'd noticed her reading one out at Cape Flattery while he poked around the rocks looking for his Lady of the Lights.

For Cassidy.

"He gave you the calendar of lighthouses."

She nodded against his chest.

"And…a series of letters."

Again the smooth slickness of her hair rubbing back and forth under his chin.

"He's taking a whole year to say goodbye."

This time she was quiet, though he could feel the gentle warmth of her tears soak once more into his t-shirt.

"He sounds like a wonderful man."

"The best."

It took her a while, but she told him about the letters. About his sunny California vineyard followed by the one in rainy Bainbridge Island. Cassidy told him of her trip there and what it had felt like to stand on the soil that had once been his—knowing the vines were gone, but still able to feel his spirit there in that soil.

"You were right." She was leaning back against the mast now. Her feet propped against his thigh as he lay on the curve of the inside of the hull.

"I was?" Wouldn't that just shock the shit out of Angelo. "About what?"

"About my not really knowing a wine."

"It was a stupid-ass remark made to a woman I didn't even know. I thought you were—"

"What?"

He shook his head. It would make him sound even dumber than he was.

She poked one of her toes into his ribs. He tried to scoot away but there was nowhere to scoot. She started to wiggle them and he had to shove her leg away. She slid the other foot up the leg of his shorts and wiggled them there. He sat bolt upright and cracked his head on the underside of the deck.

Her laugh spilled out between her fingers even as she mumbled an apology and tried to reach for his head to check for bumps.

An attempt to push her away achieved nothing. Once she ascertained there was no bump, she kissed the spot.

"All better," she declared.

He turned his head and kissed her. Time slowed, nearly ground to a halt as his blood hammered in his head. Without even thinking about it, he had one hand on her breast, no bra beneath the light dress shirt. She crawled into his lap and in moments they were sprawled back on the stateroom bed.

She pulled his t-shirt out of his shorts and slid a cool hand across his chest.

"Oh. My."

"You said that before."

He had and it was just as true now. How could anything feel so wonderful?

Then she teased his nipples.

"Give."

"Anything."

"What were you going to say?"

He clamped his mouth shut. She ground her hips against his painfully hard erection.

"Give."

Give? He could barely remember how to breathe.

"Give."

"Okay," he gasped for breath, but there wasn't any air on the boat. "Okay, just stop that for a second so I can uncross my eyes."

She stopped. Mostly. As if the slow motion of her hips in perfect rhythm with the ocean was one bit less distracting.

"Give. You thought I was…"

"A stuck-up, Upper East Side, rich bitch, spoiled brat."

Her smile was beatific. "Not a self-made, Northwest island girl, who busted her ass for every inch she ever gained?"

"Uh. No." He couldn't believe this was the same woman who had frozen him out on that first date.

"Not one of the country's leading wine tasters who studied how to be Upper East Side because she didn't have the lazy-ass, Upper West Side fortune?"

With a quick grab at the back pocket of her shorts, he managed to get the leverage to flip her onto her back.

"I busted my ass too, I've earned every damn cent I've ever spent since junior year of high school." Where did the sudden anger come from? It had soared like a flame inside of him. And now here he was pinning her to his bed, taking advantage of his strength. He shoved away—off the bed and into the main part of the cabin.

She caught up with him after he'd climbed into the cockpit.

The boat was just too damned small.

"Sorry. I was just teasing. I know you earned it. Your dad told me about it when we had dinner in New York. About how proud he was of you for finding your own way."

He stared aft. Looking at the sea, the sky, the island, trying to focus on anything.

"You wouldn't joke about that?" Had he misjudged every single event in his life?

She slid her hands around his waist from behind and rested her head on his shoulder. Together they looked out at the lighthouse.

The day was fading. They'd made love all night, and slept most of the day. The sun was already westering, though the long Northwest evening was far from over.

"We make a pretty sad pair of porcupines." Her voice was kind, her hands strong and gentle.

She pulled one of his hands free from where he'd jammed them into his pockets.

He opened his mouth. To explain. To apologize. To thank her for perhaps being the first woman in his life to not care about his money, or his past, or what he might do in the future. The first to like him as he was: a god-awful mortal mess.

She rested a finger gently across his lips to silence him.

Not releasing his hand, she led him back into the cabin.

IN SOME WAYS it was the trickiest shoot Russell had ever done.

Perrin had loaded most of the contents of her store into his boat and he'd anchored off the Seattle waterfront. By the second or third clothing change, the three women had gotten over the self-consciousness that usually caused amateur shoots to look so stiff and miserable.

They laughed more than any group he'd ever been with. They teased him mercilessly, starting with "hubba-hubba" noises and rapidly degenerating to incredibly raunchy—with Perrin definitely taking the lead there. When, in an unthinking moment, Russell had stripped off his shirt because of the sun's heat, Perrin had started a series of catcalls and whistles that could be heard over most of Elliot Bay.

The technical challenges of lighting, background, and a shooting platform that was in constant motion occupied most of his mind. The sun would be right, but the background wrong. The background and light right, but the proper shooting position was a five yards off the beam. Some of Perrin's more classic designs wanted the older part of Seattle in the background. The more outrageous outfits were accented, more vivid, alive with the mid-town skyscrapers as a setting.

Several times he clambered out onto the boom and swung himself over the side, snapping half-a-dozen images before he swung back inboard. He'd tried standing in the dinghy, but the water was a little too lively for him to keep his balance.

Then Cassidy got him. He was sitting in the dinghy, shooting up at the women on the boat. She was dressed in a skimpy summer beach outfit. His white dress shirt, the one she'd never returned, open and blowing in the gentle breeze. She grabbed one of the shrouds that soared up to hold up the mast. She leaned out over the water and, with a siren-like beauty used to tease sailors onto the rocks of despair, flashed one of her killer smiles.

His heart stumbled. His hands wielded the camera more out of habit than intent. He didn't need the camera, smiling Cassidy was forever burned into his mind. Moments later Perrin and Jo were with her.

The Three Sirens.

The Three Fates.

Three Sisters.

Jo, Perrin, and Cassidy.

Truth, Joy, and Beauty.

At some point they fed him a sandwich which he'd eaten without tasting. He had to change out the memory card in his camera three times.

As the sun set, he began to wish he'd rented the flash umbrellas. The changing light—with just a few elegant accents—would set the stage for Perrin's collection of eveningwear.

"Cassidy. Grab the stormsail," he called down. He'd been banished from below, the women's changing room.

Moments later, she tossed it out of the hatchway.

"You sure you never sailed before?"

All that answered was her bright laugh and it definitely did something racy to his heart. Just in one short month, she'd inhaled the knowledge as if she'd been born to it. They'd anchored in quiet coves up in the Canadian Queen Charlottes, ridden out a forty-knot storm in the Straits when they'd decided to visit Destruction Island lighthouse by sail. And love. Holy Christ they'd made incredible love.

He hung the white stormsail from the main boom and the lifelines, then tied the excess off to the boom.

Jo came up first. A black sheath that followed every curve perfectly. It rode low enough to reveal the bounty of her breasts, but high enough to be pure class. Her long black hair was swept forward over one shoulder. As she turned, she revealed the bit of magic that was Perrin's trademark—every piece had some surprise: often subtle, occasionally blatant.

Jo's dress didn't reveal her whole back as might be expected. Rather, only a small, open area revealed her beautiful olive skin. Exactly the spot a man's hand would rest during an intimate waltz or... He had to smile.

He had Jo swing back as if in the throes of a tango, the reserved woman released by the dress and his request. Her hair swept back along the deck and her body arched in pleasure, passion, and joy. The flash reflected off the sail covered her in a ballroom's soft lighting, etching her against the oranges and golds of the sunset beyond the water and the sharply outlined peaks of the Olympic Mountains.

Perrin slid into the picture, taking the man's position in the dance. A pantsuit, but like none he'd ever seen in a dozen years of New York fashion. The slacks had seams that climbed in an iridescent spectrum from ankle to hip. The triple-layered jacket lapels shifted from traditional black to the shades of the rainbow depending on how she moved. But they weren't heavy, rather they accented the plunging cleavage of the single-buttoned front. The cleavage of a woman wearing nothing but the jacket and pants. A perky hat that might have fit a sixties secret agent if not for the single peacock feather above the right ear. She was at once in control, powerful, and incredibly erotic.

She and Jo danced about the narrow deck, posed at the edge of the dance so that he could capture each alone, and then whirled together in a flurry of laughter and sensuality. And there was never a moment, despite all their fooling around, that there could be a doubt about the orientation of these two women. They were friends dancing together, to make the men wild.

In their various meetings preparing for this shoot, she'd revealed tiny glimpses of how they had saved her from her parents' past. The abuser and the whore who had no compunction about using their own daughter, selling her. How she'd surely have gotten herself killed, or killed herself, many times over if it hadn't been for Cassidy and Jo. Her wild experiments with drugs, alcohol, and men had all been tempered by them. She loved her life and she attributed it entirely to her two best friends.

He'd fallen further in love with Cassidy as he heard of the interventions, sometimes in the middle of Vassar campus. Cassidy had brought Perrin home for every vacation so she'd never be alone where her parents could get at her, or even alone with her own originally self-destructive tendencies.

Then Cassidy came up from below and he forgot about everything. She moved slowly, her dress shimmering in the golden light. No sequins, nor glitter. The threads of the material caught, reflected, and refracted light but appeared as plain and simple as a red evening gown. Not the red of a wild woman, but the dusky red of her chestnut hair. The dress wasn't blatant, it wasn't a slap in the face like Perrin's pantsuit, or a sensual masterpiece like Jo's. It spoke as much of the observer as of the wearer. High-necked, long-sleeved, her cascading hair the only adornment other than a small sailboat on a thin gold neck chain.

It was a look that invited him into the warm circle of the woman within. Almost of its own will, his camera raised to his eye. They moved in slow motion. Step, click, flash. Shift, click, flash. This time Russell and Cassidy were the two dancing.

The images of Cassidy shifted about him. The color rising to her cheeks made her that much more alive. The sparkle in her eyes as she relaxed made her that much more desirable.

He moved about the deck to capture different angles, heights, backgrounds, and still her smile dazzled him.

She bent out of one frame giving him a shot of the top of her head. When she stood straight once more, Nutcase, in all her fuzzy disarray, cuddled against Cassidy's chin. He came in closer. The camera never ceased its whirr-click, flash.

Nutcase looking at Cassidy, Cassidy looking directly at him. Whirr-click, flash. Beauty.

Cassidy looked down at the cat. Whirr-click, flash. The nurturer.

Cassidy and the cat both looking at him. Totally self-contained. Whirr-click, flash.

He stopped. Dropped the camera to his side. How could he not want to be with this woman when she looked at him that way? He wanted her in his life.

A loud pop startled him from his reverie.

Perrin laughed aloud and began pouring champagne into small glass tumblers.

He looked back at Cassidy, but she was facing away. Dropping Nutcase onto the cockpit cushions.

"I thought that last outfit would get you." Perrin pushed a glass into his free hand and extracted the camera from his limp fingers, unwinding the strap from behind his elbow. She slid his camera into its case then dropped onto the bench seat next to Jo. She planted a big, sloppy kiss on her friend's cheek.

His knees finally buckled and he landed on the bench across from them. He'd never worked as hard or enjoyed himself so much. He knocked back the glass of bubbly and it scorched his throat as sharply as scalding coffee.

Cassidy still stood by the tiller. Her floor-length dress made her look like some fantasy being, inviting him to be with her forever.

"God, you are so beautiful."

That smile of hers lit the night more brightly than any flash. She slid down beside him, pulled his arm over her shoulders, cuddled in close against his side. The blood hammered so loudly in his ears he couldn't hear a single word being said though he could see Perrin and Jo laughing at something Cassidy said.

They teased Nutcase and drank champagne. He sat outside. They didn't shut him out and it wasn't that he didn't belong.

No. He sat outside himself, observing and amazed. The shock was that he truly did belong.

ADMIRALTY HEAD LIGHTHOUSE

Whidbey Island
First lit: 1861
Extinguished: 1922
48.15702 -122.67943

High on the towering cliffs of Whidbey Island, this lighthouse didn't survive the transition from sailing ships to those driven by steam. The lighthouse marked the farthest side of a wide channel, and ships powered by steam did not need to cross Puget Sound before turning South for Seattle or north for Vancouver. They simply exited the Straits and turned at the Point Wilson light.

The dormant light served as a medical clinic and barracks for the Fort Casey gun emplacements during WWII. At that time it was painted olive-drab and the light room was removed. The Island County Historical Society eventually repainted it white and red and rebuilt a light room.

SEPTEMBER 1

Dearest Ice Sweet,

It's funny. By the time you're reading this, I'll have been dead for most of a year. Time is a strange thing. Life speeds up and slows down—maddeningly slowly when there is pain and sorrow. And it's a blur through the good times. It should be the other way around.

With your mother gone, I thought my life was over. Knowles Valley Vines was lost, and both parents-in-law and my wife were gone. Yet those years were so busy that they'd be hard to remember if they also hadn't been so full. The daughter I'd left in my wife's care needed a father.

I'd thought about moving, you were young enough, it probably wouldn't have mattered. But where? There had been so much heartbreak in the California soil, that I couldn't drag you or myself back there. I didn't want to work for someone else on "my" land and I had no family on either side, so I stayed where I was as much by default as anything else.

The Bainbridge vineyard needed my attention because the vines were finally producing. I mixed in Northwest flavors: strawberry, blackberry, huckleberry. I did some of the marketing your mother had suggested: Eagle White, Dugout Rose, and Olympics Red were all hers.

They were hectic, wonderful years; watching you grow was an education in itself. Your mother had left behind a huge collection of books. You started devouring them thinking they were mine, but that was your dead mother passing on her greatest joy to you. To us. I read like mad to keep up with you. I'm glad that we were able to share that part of our path.

If I could wish anything, it was that you had stayed in the vineyards with me. I think we could have had such a rich life there. I wanted to leave the vineyards to you, but you had your own plans. I sold them for a lot of money, from struggling my whole life to very comfortable in a single moment—a shock to an old man. Enough to set you up for many years to come, but you know that by now, assuming my medical bills don't wipe it out.

We've walked together a long way, let's not stop just yet.

Love you, Ice Sweet

Vic

Cassidy folded the letter and slipped it back into her pocket and looked out at the water from atop Admiralty Head's high perch.

"A long way, Daddy." This year had been both slow and fast. It had been such a mix that she barely knew what to make of it. The loss of her father, enough money to live off for a decade without any other income, her increasing fame as a columnist, and Russell.

Dear Russell. He sat a dozen yards away facing Puget Sound, carefully not looking in her direction. The water stretched from here to the Port Townsend light ten miles away on the Olympic Peninsula. His unease showed in the way he plucked strands of grass from the high bluff edge, then worried them into thin strips with his fingernails before pitching them off the edge. Did he even notice that the sea breeze up the cliff face was lifting his offerings and dumping them behind him?

"Hey there."

He jerked around at her call. Hustling over he almost sat, then stood again. She patted the grass and he thudded down beside her.

"You okay?" His first thought was always for her and she still wasn't used to it.

"Yeah, no gut wrencher this time. Just about my growing up and how much he enjoyed those years."

He pulled her over and kissed the top of her head. "I'm glad. You didn't need another like the last one. I'm still angry about that. Hell of a bomb to leave in a letter; he took the coward's way out."

That was her Russell. He was all straight-ahead and forthright, as strong and straight as the lighthouse that rose three-stories high behind them. Her father's choice had made perfect sense to her, but she'd never been able to explain it to Russell's satisfaction.

Her father was gentle and considerate. He wouldn't risk their last weeks together with a fight. If he'd blamed her or been angry, he'd have put it in the first letter—not waited until August. She was glad she'd opened the letters one a month. If she'd read some of this right after his death, she'd have been hurt much more. And really pissed.

"I hear that you've got more business." Some things it was simply better not to talk about.

He pulled another grass blade and started his inattentive dissection.

"The head of a small consortium of stores were eating at Angelo's —attracted there by my ads. He told them about Perrin's. Turns out she shops there...because of the ads." He shrugged, those big shoulders rising unevenly then settling only part way back.

"Then why did you say yes?"

Again the shrug. "Well, I'm still a month or so from getting the boat ready. And I want to take another navigation class or two. Gives me something to do."

She nodded, not wanting to push. She had enough worries of her own. But she was worried about that hunch as he sat. And she was worried about him sailing off into the sunset and what that might mean to them, though they'd agreed to not discuss such things.

"I got an interesting phone call this morning."

He half turned his head to show he was listening, but he didn't stop his botanical experiments. The scent of new-mown grass escaped from his little cuttings.

"From Italy."

Another blade went flying only to be grabbed by the breeze up the face of the eighty-foot cliff and tossed behind him. Another tiny offering at the base of the lighthouse.

"Sienna."

"What's there?"

"Montalcino wines."

"And this means?" He still wasn't looking at her.

"The Italians heard I was talking to Mondavi and they want a shot at me." It was kind of nice to be wanted. Even though her mind was made up, at least if she were going to make the change. She'd thought Mondavi's stellar treatment of her in June had been nothing more than them wooing a wine reviewer.

Last week they called with a much more serious offer. They offered to create a new position specifically for her, wine director. She was invited to bring her palate to the vintner's aid, her writing to marketing's aid, and her insights to the winery's aid. A hand in shaping one of the finest wineries in America. They even had invited her down for the harvest as a "get to know each other"—all expenses paid, first class of course.

The wine-column world was great, but it was limited. She saw that now. Russell had been onto it way back at the beginning and her dad agreed with him. Wine reviewers lived on the outside looking in and —now that she was aware of it—she hated that feeling. She wanted to be in the game, affecting decisions, shaping flavors, accentuating the superb, and casting out the ordinary.

"Sienna?" His attention shifted at last to her face.

"I'm not really interested, but they were very persuasive. I'm going to California during the harvest in a couple of weeks, so I'll just fly to Italy from there, maybe catch their harvest time as well."

"Sounds good."

BUT IT WASN'T. Russell couldn't think of a thing to say for the whole drive home. Neither of them was grumpy. Cassidy had tried to start the conversation a couple of times, but it always fizzled out. As much her doing as his. It wasn't a comfortable silence, but it was a companionable one; both lost in their own thoughts.

He'd dropped her at the condo to write her next column.

She might come by the boat later.

They spent most nights together, as often as not on the boat. They both claimed it was to keep Nutcase company, but Russell didn't sleep well in high-rise condos—though being with Cassidy in that big bed or sitting before that amazing view from her balcony had already gone a long way toward changing his mind.

California. Italy. Even if she stayed in Seattle or went back to New York, her life was on the land, attached to root and vine.

His future was on the ocean.

The more he thought about that though, the less comfortable it was. He enjoyed the photography. He'd really liked working with Angelo and Perrin. They'd been fun and made him feel good about himself and about what he could do. The boat would be done soon, as done as wooden sailboats ever were. And he liked knowing the local waters. They too were becoming familiar and comfortable without any sign of growing dull.

The consortium of little stores might be fun. But he hadn't told her about the Seattle City Trade Association that had approached him about a national campaign. He'd turned them down cold despite the vast sums in their advertising budget. He didn't do the ads for Angelo or Perrin for the money. The SCTA was maybe a little more personal than a BMW or a Rolex, but maybe not. Maybe it was the same thing, just wrapped up in the softer, kinder style of the Pacific Northwest.

Was the sailing just another escape? Another way to not have to truly make a decision about his life? But that didn't feel right either. He was far happier on the boat than he'd ever been on dry land.

After dropping off Cassidy, he wandered down the dock, and the moment he stepped aboard he felt...home. He fed Nutcase out in the cockpit, grabbed at a beer, and cracked open a fresh tube of Ritz crackers.

Perry strolled by and Russell called him over. "Got something I've been meaning to give you."

He ducked below and grabbed the small album and another beer.

Perry came aboard and was trying to feed a cracker to Nutcase.

"Don't get her started on my private stash."

"Not interested anyway." He ate the cracker himself and opened the beer with a nod of thanks.

"Finally figured out what you were talking about. Made this for you to say thanks." He handed the album to him. It was a small one, one picture on each facing page, forty photos in all.

Perry opened to the first page. A photo of Nutcase, curled up in her cardboard box, not much bigger than the lens cap he'd tucked beside her for scale.

The next pages were her discovering the boat...and him discovering his companion. He knew the rest by heart as Perry paged through the book.

Nutcase sleeping on the boom, another looking out at the lighthouses. A look of fascination, then of terror at a breaching orca. Arguing with a seagull twice her size at close enough range that Russell hadn't been sure whether or not to run to her aid. But she'd won handily, protecting their boat like a hissing hellcat, the seagull flapping off his bowsprit perch in disgust.

The final picture hadn't been his, but it was arguably the best of the lot. Cassidy had been behind the camera. He'd been asleep on the deck with Nutcase asleep on his chest. The high cliffs and towering Destruction Island lighthouse were visible as a soft background. A blow-up of that one hung in his cabin, right next to the final one of Cassidy and Nutcase from Perrin's photoshoot.

Perry stood and went below without asking permission. It was just the way the old man was. He was harmless, so it was easy to ignore his eccentricities. Maybe he needed to use the head.

He came back on deck and held the closed book with both hands for a moment. Then he returned it to Russell.

"No, it's yours. I made it for you."

The old man shook his head. Took a couple of the Ritz crackers, raised his beer in a salute, and stepped off the boat. When he was even with Russell, standing on the finger pier, he took a long swallow of his beer. His old blue eyes wrinkled in what Russell had learned was a smile.

"The Sailing Cat. First in a series. Big hit." Then he was gone.

RUSSELL PLAYED WITH NUTCASE A LITTLE, finished his beer, and idly flipped through the album in the failing light of the day. Perry was right. New York would eat it up. He'd send it to Arnie and she'd have it sitting next to every bookstore cash register in the country by Christmas.

At the second to last page, there was the photo of Nutcase sleeping on his chest. He could have sworn he'd put that one at the end. He turned to the final page.

There she was. Cassidy, in that incredible evening gown with the boat and the city a soft backdrop, and Nutcase curled up in her arms. The look on her face still blew him away. He thought he'd photographed love before, but it was as if he'd only photographed the word itself and here was the true emotion. There was love, humor, passion, and, something indescribable. Whatever it was, it made him feel incredible that for even that instant of time it had been aimed at him.

Perry had nailed it; her entry into his life was what made the book complete and personal—it told the story. The collection would go ballistic.

Stowing the crackers, he locked the cabin and headed for Cassidy's. He couldn't lose her to some status-seeking California winery. Couldn't lose her to a bunch of high-rolling Italians. Screw their tacit agreement not to discuss the future. There had to be a way to keep her and he was going to do something about it now.

He punched in her keycode at the lobby entry and made it all the way to her door, had even raised his hand to knock, before the absurdity of the situation sunk in.

Since when had he ever said the right thing? He should go consult with Angelo. Or should he? His friend had talked about Jo enough, but hadn't done anything. Granted, his restaurant was taking off. Really taking off. Cassidy had done another write-up and this one had caught the attention of the magazines. Suddenly *Sunset*, *Condé Nast*, and *Cigar* were coming out to write up "Angelo's Tuscan Hearth" above and beyond Cassidy's column. Maybe now wasn't the best time to get advice on how to handle his girlfriend.

Girlfriend.

He'd had lovers, but never a girlfriend—at least not since high school. Natasha Beckworth, senior prom—though she'd been a lover, too. Maybe she'd been more lover and less girlfriend. They'd had great sex, but he couldn't remember a thing about what she did or didn't like.

Cassidy had been the one to teach him the difference between lover and loving someone. He didn't need Angelo's advice; Russell knew what woman he wanted.

He knocked on Cassidy's door.

No answer.

Harder.

Still nothing. But he heard a clink of glass, or something from inside.

Harder still.

Now there was an echoing silence.

Then he heard it. A long, low moan. A moan of someone in pain.

He threw his shoulder into the door—there was a loud crackling of wood.

He hit it again—with all the force of his college linebacker days—and the door blew inward.

She wasn't in the kitchen or the bedroom-office. He raced into the living room and stumbled to a halt.

The table was littered with wine bottles and half-empty wine glasses, but no Cassidy. A bottle of red had fallen to the floor and a long red stain spread across the white rug.

No one was in the bathroom…nor the master bedroom.

He heard the moan again and dashed into the bedroom she'd converted into a wine cellar.

There she sat, still dressed in the jeans and shirt she'd worn to the lighthouse this morning, but they no longer looked so pristine. Red stains were dribbled all down her front. Her legs were splayed before her like a little girl and another twenty or more wine bottles were open around her. Most had a matching glass, some part full—but most stood empty.

She moaned again, struggling to uncork yet another bottle. In no condition to do so, the corkscrew kept slipping from her fingers. The moan was part growl of frustration and part wounded animal.

He squatted down in front of her. Russell considered removing the bottle from her hands, but decided that discretion was the better part of valor as she was wielding the corkscrew as much like a sword as a kitchen tool.

"What are you doing, Cass?"

"I've lost it, Daddy. I've lost it somewhere." She looked about the room for a moment, ceasing her efforts to uncork the bottle. She didn't turn his direction.

"Lost what?"

She bowed her head down over the bottle and stopped struggling with it.

"I can't taste it. I can't. I tried. Just like you taught me. But I can't taste it."

He slid the corkscrew and the bottle with its mangled cork from her fingers and set them carefully aside.

"That must have been a hell of a letter." Her dad was really starting to piss him off. Next one, he wouldn't leave until he was sure she really was fine.

He did his best to lift her clear of the nest of glasses. A couple fell onto the hardwood floor and rolled away as he shifted her into his arms; he'd have to deal with those later. Hopefully none of it would leak down into the ceiling of the nineteenth floor below before he could mop it up.

She kept complaining as he moved her.

"My life is over. Can't taste anyting. All those years. So mussh work. Gone. Wasshted. Down the drain. Corked. Thas it. I'm corked. Just like a bad shwine."

Their first stop was the bathroom floor. She wasn't steady enough to stand while he stripped her. Russell looked at the stains all down her front and decided to settle for expediency. He set her in the tub clothes and all, then cranked up the shower.

"Cassidy Knowles. Corked. Spoiled-ed in the bottle. So sad."

Too drunk to even protest, she sputtered at the water as it ran down her face, but that was all. He did his best to clean her up with a washcloth as the water ran over her. He aimed the spray off her face and trotted back to the other room. Four of the bottles she'd knocked over had corks partly rammed into them, thankfully the bulk of the uncorked horde of bottles had remained upright. The three fallen glasses looked as if they had been mostly empty. Either she'd been pouring less as she went, or drinking more—he'd bet on the latter. He threw a towel on the worst patch and decided he'd come back later.

The glasses in the living room were much fuller. She'd still been just tasting in here. The red in the living room was going to be a different cleanup problem. He righted the bottle and saw that it was a 1969 Mouton Rothschild Bordeaux. That stain on her carpet was worth hundreds of dollars. He let his eye range over the dozens of others open on the table, the coffee table, the side table... Thousands of dollars of wine. Damn! And he thought his studio parties had been extravagant.

A curse sounded from the bathroom and the sound of splashing.

He hustled back to the more immediate problem.

RUSSELL SAT on the balcony off Cassidy's bedroom and watched the stars slowly turn over Puget Sound. Once she'd finished emptying the contents of her stomach into the toilet, he'd showered her as well as he could and managed to get her to spit after he brushed her teeth for her. He'd tucked her into bed after forcing her to drink some water and take a B12 vitamin he found in her medicine cabinet. It was the best hangover cure he had to offer, though she was still going to have a doozy.

The cleanup had taken a while—handwashing thirty-seven glasses. Hard to believe she even had that many or the room to store them in the small kitchen. Dinner for eight and four wines for a meal; maybe not that hard to imagine, but it was still a lot of washing. The red wine stain answered fairly well to the old trick of club soda and salt, but she'd still need a professional carpet cleaner.

Now he sat with a glass of the Bordeaux and some crackers and cheese. It was somewhere before dawn. Stars could still be seen, despite the waterfront lights below and some vague twinkling on the distant shore that was Bainbridge Island. What perversity had led her to get a condo facing what her father had lost?

Well, nothing to do but wait.

Wait for what? He must be more tired than he thought. He rubbed a hand over his face. There'd been something so urgent that he'd rushed over.

The future. Their future. Right.

Well, it was hard to go a whole lot further without knowing what Cassidy was thinking. That in itself was kind of funny. He'd done a lot of growing this last year. His mom had pointed it out when he went back to New York for a visit last week; Julia Morgan approved of Cassidy with all her heart—that much was clear.

Russell had walked out on Melanie with little thought for her and no awareness of her feelings. When their intensity surprised him, he'd gone to the West Coast anyway. Now? Now he was in limbo while Cassidy considered her destiny in California and Italy for Christ's sake.

For the hundredth time he looked at the waterlogged letter on the little wrought iron table. He had found it crammed into her jean's pocket.

If I could wish anything, it was that you had stayed in the vineyards with me. Then I wouldn't have had to sell my life's work to strangers.

"Good thing you're dead, old man. Or we'd be having some words right about now." Hell of a burden for a dead man to place on his living daughter. As if we don't have enough problems making our own decisions.

"Russell?" Cassidy's voice trembled out into the darkness. He hadn't heard her get up, even though he'd left the sliding glass door open for that purpose. The late night lull was past and the first sounds of the waking city had begun: street cleaners, service trucks, the crazy, hyper-driven corporates, restaurant owners. It probably wasn't all that long until Angelo would be awake and down at the market visiting the fish, produce, and meat vendors.

"Right here, Cassie."

She came to him in the faint glow of the city lights. She lowered herself into the chair beside him with a hesitancy of movement that he knew well from past experience. Once she was settled, she took his hand. He held it lightly, knowing that everything must be hurting.

"I feel…"

"Shh. I know."

"I don't remember you coming in."

"Good. Then you won't remember that I splintered the frame of your door as I did so. My shoulder appreciates that you locked only the handle and not the dead bolt."

"You busted down my door?"

"I panicked when you wouldn't answer, but I could hear you groan. Sorry, I'll fix it tomorrow." He looked up at the sky. There was no light yet, but there soon would be. "Later today."

"I don't remember."

"Don't remember my tossing you in the tub? Helping you puke? Brushing your teeth for you?"

"I didn't! Not really?"

"How I had my wanton way with you?"

"While I was drunk?" She sat up at that, though she froze and he felt sorry for what the sudden motion must have done to the inside of her head.

"Well, not the last, but all the other stuff, yes. I did shower you and towel you down. Though it wasn't as much fun as usual."

He reached his hand to stroke her cheek, marveling as he did every time how soft it was and how personal it felt. To be so close to someone he wanted to touch so much ranked beyond marvelous.

"What do you remember?"

"I sat down to write my column. It was going fine. I was working on a little section about the effect of climate between California temperate, Washington temperate, and the new Piedmont vineyards that are opening up in the foothills of the Italian Alps. But I couldn't remember the taste of a Bainbridge Island Pinot Noir. I grew up with that wine, probably the first one I ever tasted."

She was rubbing her forehead as if she could pull the memory out with her fingertips.

"I checked my notes, but I never wrote it down. Who could forget their first wine?"

Russell didn't even remember his last wine the way she did though the dregs were still in the glass. It was far and away the best Bordeaux he'd ever had.

"So I opened a bottle—and I couldn't taste it," her hand started to shake in his hand as the memory returned.

"My palate is gone," her voice grew shaky. "I opened a California Pinot, then a French Chardonnay. Nothing. None of them..." Her voice trailed off on a catch of breath. Her thoughts had finally caught up with her words.

"My palate is gone," her silence was echoing, punctuated by the sound of a Metro bus' diesel roaring far below.

"Kiss me."

"What?"

"Kiss me."

"I'm telling you my life is ruined. That it's over. My gift is gone after twenty painstaking years of study and practice and you want me to kiss you?"

Russell nodded, knowing she could see the outlines of his face in the growing light.

She huffed a few times and finally leaned forward to give him a quick peck on the lips.

"Um, thanks for helping me out."

"You're welcome. Now kiss me."

She practically growled when she did so. She leaned in and really kissed him—kissed him so hard that his body went electric. What had started as an attack quickly turned so sensual that it was hard not to drag her through the doors to the bed waiting only a few feet away.

He broke it off before she did.

"Now. Tell me what you tasted."

"The ocean and the sky. You always taste like that." News to him. He considered a moment and decided he could live with that, especially if Cassidy liked it.

"What else?"

She tipped her head sideways, in the way she always did when analyzing a flavor, whether a wine or a chocolate truffle. It was the moment when she was most quiet and most stunning.

"Plum and eucalyptus. Bitter cherry... You inveterate bastard!" She punched his arm hard enough to hurt. To really hurt.

"Am not," he rubbed at his wound as she shook her hand in pain.

"Are too. You didn't ravage me. You ravaged my 1969 Bordeaux. That was a graduation gift from my dad. I was saving it."

"Yup. You were. For last night."

That dropped her back in her chair. "Last night?"

"Most of it was in your carpet when I arrived. I got out the worst of the stain, so I guess it's in your sink now. I had a half glass while watching over you. I saved the last half glass for you."

Her voice was very small. "I don't think I could drink any wine now if my life depended on it."

"How about kissing me again? To make up for punching my arm so hard."

She leaned over just far enough to kiss him on the arm. "What else did I open?"

"I don't know. I lost track somewhere after thirty bottles."

"Thirty?" Little more than a squeak.

"Kiss me again."

"Why?"

"Because," he rose and helped her to her feet. He swung her up into his arms and headed back into the bedroom.

"I like proving that your palate is still just fine."

POINT ROBINSON LIGHTHOUSE

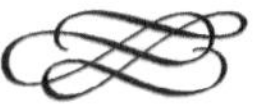

*M*aury Island
First lit: 1887
Automated: 1978
47.3881 -122.3746

The Point Robinson light and foghorn is the principle guiding beacon between Seattle and Tacoma. Fog is an especial problem on this point of Maury Island. In 1897, the sole keeper, who had been asking for an assistant for years, had to run the whistle for 528 straight hours on his own. In those twenty-two long days he shoveled thirty-five tons of coal by hand to power the whistle.

His request for assistance was granted. But it was 1903, six years later, before one was assigned to the light.

OCTOBER 1

"*Y*ou didn't ask her? Mama mia, you're an *idiota!*"

Russell was, but that didn't mean Angelo was going to get away with it. He dug around in the fridge for a couple Cokes.

"And have you called Jo Thompson yet?" He called out the hatchway to Angelo up at the tiller.

"Low blow, my man. Low blow."

"Have you?"

"Shit, no. What's a classy, hot-shot lawyer gonna see in a lousy, Eye-talian servant's son?"

Russell came on deck and shook the bottle hard before handing it to Angelo. Angelo groaned and slipped it into a cup holder unopened.

"She may be a big-time lawyer, but you're a big-time restaurateur."

"Oh, yeah. One whole restaurant. That'll really impress a lady like that."

"Got news for you, buddy boy."

Angelo just glared at him.

"Fisherman's daughter." Russell turned away and peeked under the sail as the light finally dawned over Angelo's face.

"Lighthouse ho."

287

There it was, right on cue. Point Robinson was a windy, god-forsaken spot known for its shrouds of fog and today didn't disappoint. They'd spent much of the morning creeping through fog banks and dead-reckoning from one channel buoy to the next. A little sunlight broke through around the lighthouse itself, enough to make a pretty picture of the light wrapped in a foggy, surreal landscape of mystery.

He pulled out his camera and starting snapping photos for Cassidy. It didn't feel right though. Without her here, the purpose was gone. He wanted to see the lady on the beach in her ridiculous, knee-length parka. Or spend a lazy afternoon teasing the sassy wine-connoisseur lying back in his dinghy. Hell, he'd be glad just watch her as she cranked on a winch or played with the cat. Even Nutcase seemed despondent without her, curled up in the cockpit rather than out on the boom.

"Did you know that some poor chump shoveled thirty-five tons of coal in three weeks to run the fog whistle here." He ran the telephoto out and searched the beach. Not a single woman walked on the beach.

No point in even looking; Cassidy was at thirty-five thousand feet zooming from California to Italy. The wineries were really courting her hard. She'd had a half dozen offers in the last fifteen days, sight unseen. They both knew that she was going to end up in California; the Italy trip was only because she'd committed to go in the initial flush of excitement.

Angelo steered up into the wind a bit making him reset the sails. "Why are you changing the subject?"

"What subject?" Russell didn't want to talk about this with Angelo.

"Why didn't you ask her to marry you?"

He really, really didn't want to talk about this.

CASSIDY HELD the letter in her lap.

She'd promised Russell that she wouldn't read it without him, but it was the first of the month and here it was in her lap. He'd insisted that she wait a week. He would come over after her interviews were done and they'd go and play along the Amalfi coast for a week. He'd bring photos of the lighthouse and be there while she read the letter.

She knew he wanted to protect her from whatever the next letter held. And he'd been kind enough to insist without throwing her last debacle in her face—forty-three bottles, almost six thousand dollars in wine, some of it irreplaceable. Worst of all, it had been days before she could face drinking any wine at all. By the time she could, everything she'd opened that night had gone bad.

No, she was strong enough to do this on her own. She didn't need to depend on Mr. Russell Morgan for strength, no matter how sweet he was about it.

She checked her watch—ten a.m. west coast time. Just about right for Russell to be sailing by the lighthouse.

She tore open the letter. The scrawled hand was weaker and her heart twisted to imagine her father's efforts to scribe even these few words. It was shorter than any prior letter. Even the sentences were shorter. As if he had to rest between each thought.

Dearest Ice Sweet,

There is a truth that I have learned. Be true to your passion. Your mother was true to her great love for family. I loved the vines. Each of us had full, complete lives. We were true to our passion, in whatever form it took.

Your passion isn't the vine, it's the wine. And the writing. Look at why you like it. That is the passion. I thought my passion was Knowles Valley. But it wasn't. It was the vines. I was never happier than when I was walking the rows. California or Bainbridge. For me, it was the vines and you.

Love you Ice Sweet,

Vic

"I know what's important, Daddy. Truly I do." She would listen to what the Italians had to say, but she knew what was important.

RUSSELL TOOK his bottle of Coke and rolled it slowly back and forth between his palms. The cool glass felt good despite the fall day.

"She's over the Atlantic somewhere right now. That's a bit out of reach. I'll ask her when I see her next week."

"You know where you're going yet?"

She was going to meet his plane at Sienna airport with a rental car. They'd poke along the Amalfi coast, or slide over to Monaco and the French Riviera. A whole week, just the two of them and Italy—that's all he cared about.

"I'll know when the time is right. When the mood is right."

Angelo swore loudly, waved for him to take the tiller, and went below. The *Lady* slipped along the shore and Russell fell back to watching the lighthouse slip slowly by. It was a sweet one—all alone at the foot of the hill, guarding the far end of a long, lonely beach road.

Angelo came back on deck after several minutes and shoved a cell phone into his hand.

It was active. He put it to his ear and it was ringing. He looked to his friend, but Angelo just took the tiller and focused on the way ahead.

"Uh, hello?"

"Hi, who is this?"

"You called *me*." The voice was crackly and there was a funny lag.

"Cassidy?"

"How did you call me?"

"I didn't."

"Yes, you did. I was just sitting here and the phone that's mounted on the headrest in front of me rang."

"Uh," Angelo was one sneaky, really good friend. "I miss you. Guess I just wanted to hear your voice. Ange..." Angelo kicked his shin. "Uh, I figured if you could call out from a plane, you could probably call back the other way."

"It's nice to hear your voice, too. I'll be on the ground pretty soon, we're over Sardinia now."

"Cassidy, I was wondering..." He wanted to do this when she was sitting across from him, holding his hand or playing footsie under the tablecloth. Something.

"What?"

"If, ah…"

"You're still coming next week?" The worry in her voice gave him confidence.

"Of course. Can't wait."

"I've picked some great places to go."

"Wonderful." Come on, Russell. Get your shit together. This was probably costing dollars per second. Of course it was Angelo's phone, so why should he care.

"I—"

"We'll be landing shortly," a heavily-accented voice cut across the airwaves. "Please shut down all electronic devices and return your seat backs and tray tables to the upright position."

He could just hear her as they repeated the instructions in Italian. "Thanks for the call. I'll talk to you as soon as I'm settled. Bye."

She was gone before he could respond.

"Wimp."

"We were cut off. They're landing. Thanks, Buddy. Thanks for the try." He went to toss the phone back to Angelo, then noticed it was his, as were any call charges.

He grabbed his soda and twisted the cap. It exploded in his hands spraying foam and sugar all down his shorts and legs, dribbling into his shoes. Nutcase scrambled for cover, splashes of sticky foam all over her coat.

Angelo pulled his own bottle from the cup holder and, with an over-pleased grin, opened it with a small "phsst."

THE PORSCHE ROARED up to the airport terminal. Angelo had promised to treat it nicely while he was gone. Angelo hadn't even bothered to buy a car and Russell sure wasn't going to travel with a bunch of smelly fish in the restaurant van right before climbing on a plane for fifteen hours. Perry was going to take care of his boat and Nutcase. He really had nothing to worry about, so why was he such a nervous wreck?

Angelo whipped up to the curb missing an old lady by inches; probably scared a decade off her life.

Russell started to climb out, but Angelo grabbed his arm.

"You gonna ask her?"

"Yes."

"You promise?"

"I promise."

"Okay, because if you come back from the most romantic country in the world, and you haven't, I'm a-gonna whip your behind."

"You and what army?" Russell went for the sneer, but couldn't find it anywhere handy.

"Me and Cassidy, that's who. You ain't gonna mess with her, are you?"

Russell shook him off, climbed out of the car, and signaled for Angelo to pop the trunk lid. He grabbed the duffle and his camera bag, then slammed the lid back into place.

Angelo pushed up in his seat and looked at him over the windshield.

"And you remember what I told you."

"Cinque Terre. Get idea photos for your next restaurant, 'Angelo's Home Hearth.' It ain't your home, buddy. I keep telling you, 'Umbrian Hearth,' but hey, why listen to me."

"It was home for a thousand years before Mama and Papa came to America."

"They were sixteen and ran away from poverty to the land of opportunity. Even though he didn't live to see you born, your home is Brooklyn, New York, America, the United States of."

"Fine. That'll be my third restaurant. Just get me some good photos. Hokay?"

Russell slung the bags over his shoulder.

Crap! Some romantic getaway. Now he was supposed to work, too.

Angelo dropped the Porsche into gear and would have removed Russell's kneecap if he hadn't dodged quickly. His car and his best friend roared off into the distance.

Crap again!

NOW THIS WAS CLASS. Russell punched the accelerator and the car leapt ahead on the Autostrade.

What woman would have thought to rent a Ferrari Spider rather than a lousy sedan? Cassidy would. He could kiss her, had kissed her. And it had been even more incredible than the first time. She was more confident and more sure of herself than ever before and that was about the sexiest thing he'd ever seen. She'd even rented them a hotel room at the airport so they didn't have to wait more than the time it took to cross the terminal and go up two stories in the elevator. They'd almost done it in the elevator like a couple of teens— might have if there'd been a third floor instead of the second.

She now lay back in her seat, a kerchief over her hair and large Italian sunglasses hiding those luscious hazel eyes. Her hand rested on his thigh as he ripped along, heading north out of Sienna. He was on top of the world, it just couldn't get any better than this.

At Lucca she aimed him south toward Pisa. It was the wrong direction for Cinque Terre but—screw Angelo—Russell just didn't give a damn.

That's when it hit him: he really didn't give a damn. For a month he'd been worrying himself sick about the Seattle City Trade Association contract and then the new offer from the Pioneer Square Association. He just didn't care. That was the old him.

It was Russell Morgan the studio photographer who worried about contracts and sweated over jobs until they were perfect and then some. The new Russell didn't give a damn about Pioneer Square or Seattle City. And he sure as hell didn't need the money, so from now on he'd only do what was fun.

If he took a big contract, it would be the next step on the road to personal oblivion. He knew the old networking routine, had turned it into a highly-profitable, multi-million-dollar business with dozens of employees once already. Hell, he'd had three people whose sole job was to hunt weird props that no one had ever used before: from trained tree frogs to the Smithsonian's collection of every Medal of Honor left at the Wall of the Vietnam Memorial. Then he'd had: office manager, accountant, lighting grip, camera assistant, makeup artist... the list went on and on.

Done and done—never again would he go there. If it wasn't something he could do himself, in his leisure time, then from now on his automatic answer would be "no."

Cassidy pointed for him to exit at Livorno.

He'd had fun doing the ads for Angelo, but that was for his best friend. The ones for Perrin were a blast, but that had far more to do with the three women than the work itself. Perrin had a sharp intelligence hidden behind her frivolous façade. And Jo had a wicked sense of wry humor masked with reserve and sophistication. Cassidy was just plain lovable.

There it was. She was just plain lovable.

He raised her hand from his thigh to his lips and kissed the back of her hand. When he released it to shift, she stroked his cheek just as he had hers. The tingle made him settle deeper into the seat, more aware than ever of the precious cargo he carried.

More directions now, Cassidy led him down smaller streets. Italian drivers really were crazy, but they made some extra space for the slick, black Ferrari. Italians respected sports cars the way the French respected bicycles. He used the extra space to slip through the knotted midday traffic.

She led him past the scenic old city and past rows of businesses. They ran out to the beach, turned left...and there it was.

"Oh. My." He pulled the car to the side of the road and shut off the engine.

"Hey, you're only supposed to say that about me."

He leaned over and kissed her until his lips felt bruised and the catcalls of passing drivers made his ears ring. But he had to look back.

"This is incredible! It must be ten stories high."

"Eleven. The Germans blasted the old lighthouse to smithereens when they were retreating, but the Italians rebuilt it to the original plan using all the original stone they could salvage."

The Livorno lighthouse rose from the edge of the busy shipyard. Cargo ships, loading cranes, and railcars scuttled about its base, but the stepped cylinder soared above them all.

"Boy, these Italians really know how to build a lighthouse."

"Isn't it great? And the best part…"

He turned to her. She'd pushed her sunglasses up on her forehead, just as his mother had worn them. In that moment he could see the woman who would make Julia Morgan a grandmother. Cassidy Knowles-Morgan sitting on their own child's sailboat. She was the woman he wanted in his life more than was possible.

The woman he loved.

He'd never said that before. Not to her and not to himself. Not to anyone, ever. Yes, he'd talk to Angelo about how to propose to Cassidy, but the L-word was completely unexplored territory—that had remained impossibly foreign until he'd arrived in it. Now that he was here, it made perfect sense.

He *loved* Cassidy Knowles.

"The best part," she bubbled on, "is that it was built in 1304, almost two hundred years before Columbus. The oldest we've visited was 1857, Cape Flattery and New Dungeness."

"I'm sorry, Cassidy. I know you're incredible and I love you, but that rates an 'Oh. My.' There's just no way around it."

He watched her closely, it took a moment for it to register. Then he saw it hit, like someone had thumped her in the solar plexus. Her jaw dropped and he heard a gasp. The next moment she swarmed into his lap despite the cramped cockpit and steering wheel. If he thought he'd been soundly kissed ever before, he was happily mistaken.

Being kissed by Cassidy was better than sex with most women.

Finally she whispered in his ear, "I love you, too."

He held her even tighter.

THEY DROVE up to Monterosso along narrow twisty roads that tunneled through mountains, often only a lane wide. In any lesser car than the Ferrari, it would have been a scary ride rather than scenic and fun. They laughed most of the way.

She told him about California and Montalcino. She'd already written a column about the food and wine at each, as well as several more about winemaking to intersperse over the next year.

"I don't give away any company secrets, but it is amazing how similar and how different the processes are. It's like the lighthouses. California is so new and slick. They have their gravity feeds between stainless-steel tanks, and everything is temperature controlled to the degree and staged to the hour—so long in steel then so long in oak. All scientific and you could eat off the floor in any of the mechanical rooms."

"Exactly what I'd want to do."

She thumped his arm playfully and he laughed for the sheer joy of teasing her. He downshifted for another hairpin turn as they climbed then descended then climbed again through the coastal range. The jagged hills broke the vistas into sharp chunks of sky, hill, and tree. Far lower than the mountains of the Cascade Range, but more dramatic in their own way.

"In California they're actually boring caves—carving vast cavities into the mountainsides that don't belong there geologically—just for show. The "caves" come complete with: carpeting, furniture, a wine bar, huge casks that aren't really used. All for show because caves are the 'in' thing now."

To Russell's way of thinking it meant too many New York advertising agencies had opened branches in Napa.

"The Montalcino wineries are done with casks that are older than the vintner's great-grandparents. Wine is processed, tanked, purified through the same steps, but nature has a bigger part in it. The same care, less technologic frenzy. And instead of fabricated caves they have real ones that have been there forever. Some of them date back to the Etruscans—they're the ones who helped the Romans get started."

Her excitement was so high—she was so thrilled by what she'd seen—that he couldn't ask her now. At first he hadn't because he didn't want to spoil her wonderful welcome, then because the drive was so fun. And he was still trying to process that she loved him.

And that he loved her. Had he said it to anyone other than his mother? Ever? And even that had become dutiful, until their last visit. Until he'd realized that she had put up with, for the last fifteen years, his jumping to wrong conclusions about her. And Cassidy had dispelled them all with a few casual questions. Their last visit had been the best ever and it was all Cassidy's doing. How could he spoil this for her?

He'd wait just a little longer.

It was all too perfect to be true. Cassidy had been transported by the magic of her father's letters and the man beside her into a new world, and it was a world of possibilities. She'd aspired to be the next Robert Parker—the first female megastar of the wine-tasting firmament. To become the top of a very small world.

But the vineyards were breathtaking; that's where it all happened. On their third day in Cinque Terre they found the winery in the small village of Corniglia where the Sciacchetrà was made—the wine that had fooled her at their disastrous first date. It was made underneath Carla Parrano's home, a distant cousin of Angelo's. They entered the winery itself through a narrow oak door at street level that had long since grown dark with age and been polished smooth by human hands.

They descended into the mountainside: to an Italian cave turned into a wine cellar over six hundred years before. The air was cool, the floor and walls stone. The casks were packed so tightly together that there was barely room to get around them. And the wine tasted so sweet and light with a gentleness from the vat that didn't, couldn't survive the ten-thousand-mile journey by boat and rail in bottles. This wine wasn't intended for export. To make this wine work, you had to bring the wine tasters to the wine and she could think of a dozen different ways to do that—just a part of her newly expanded view of the big picture.

She led Russell up into the rock-wall terraced vineyards of Cinque Terre. The terraces were barely ten feet wide, each supporting a couple dozen vines in a few feet of soil. For a thousand years, grapes had been cultivated here. Cultivated just this way, in tiny little patches by hard labor. Ingenious, hip-wide monorail cars climbed from one terrace to another transporting the grapes and the more daring tourists.

Russell's camera snapped away, taking pictures of cliff-edge vine-yards, restaurants, and fishing boats dragged up onto the miniature beaches.

In Manarola, the fourth of the five little towns of Cinque Terre, they found a hidden *ristorante*—a true locals' place. They were the only tourists there despite the warm October. Russell's Italian was rusty, but he'd learned it at his cook's knee and it came back quickly. Hers was much worse, just enough of it left from college to make it fun rather than a struggle.

The owner bustled to their table in the middle of the meal and rattled off a flurry of Italian she had no chance of following.

"What did he say?"

"I dropped Angelo's name; they know about him."

"Really? That's great. Local boy made good, huh?"

More Italian rattled back and forth, and then the owner jerked to stare at her, slapped his hands to his heart and ran back into the restaurant.

"What? What did you do to him?"

Russell just shook his head and shrugged. No grin. He didn't appear to know. She looked away and checked again, still no grin. Okay, he was as mystified as she was.

The owner came running back, the waiter and waitress, and a

woman who had to be his wife in tow. He was also waving a worn newspaper over his head.

He thumped it down on table, pointed his finger at an article then brought his fingertips to his lips and tossed the kiss into the air.

They both leaned in. It was titled "Angelo's Tuscan Hearth" and her picture sat at the head of the column. The rest was in Italian, definitely her writing though. Her agent had told her about Italy, she'd just never imagined the translation. It was the second of her three reviews. Down at the bottom, there it was.

She wasn't going to point it out.

She didn't need to.

Russell's groan filled the air much to the consternation of the owner who she quickly reassured. She couldn't quite read the translation, but she didn't need to. She'd written the words herself.

Bring the person you love to this restaurant and you'll never be forgotten for it. Ever.

"In every language," Russell moaned.

"WHY THAT'S TERRIBLY FLATTERING."

Cassidy had been saying that a lot lately. California and Italy were in a bidding war for her expertise. Even hiding away on vacation, news of increased offers trickled her direction. Germany and France had both left lengthy voice messages, or rather a lengthy series of messages in two-minute chunks that Russell was very familiar with.

He leaned against the stone parapet of the microscopic balcony. Barely big enough to stand in, but enough for him to stare down at the tiny harbor. It would be just big enough to tuck the *Lady* in among the fishing boats. Nutcase would love this place.

He could hear Cassidy in the bedroom checking up on the latest flurry of offers. Cassidy Knowles was in play and the games had begun. Salaries, personal villas, cars, and personal assistants were being bandied about in a high stakes poker game that showed no sign of reaching its limit.

Even the Cinque Terre Consortium had anted up, though they'd been outbid before they even made the offer and they knew it. But they'd done it with style, closing the little Manarola restaurant and inviting a couple dozen of the local chefs, vintners, and officials to feast Italian-style around a long table. There'd been far more food and wine than business. Russell had enjoyed the impromptu singing and copious laughter. By the time they were done, he'd been hugged at least twice by every person there.

The Ligurian wine industry here had suffered due to the attraction of the almighty tourist dollar. Vines on cliffs were hard work; turning your five-hundred year old cellar into a quaint restaurant or gift shop was far easier. The five-town Consortium had come up with a solution: they were giving the terraces away before they fell into disrepair and slid into the ocean. To retain ownership, the new owners were required to farm them for at least four years. An ingenious and low price-of-entry way to get new blood into the industry.

Russell could already think of several different campaign ideas. And the Consortium knew that it needed a Cassidy Knowles to make it all happen. Their offer: a small house perched over the beach, with an even smaller budget to fix it up, a survival stipend, and a marketing budget that would barely pay for the rental on the car they'd left parked at Monterosso.

The chances of her throwing it all away to go sailing with him were getting slimmer by the minute. Angelo was right. He should have asked her before she left, before they had a chance to get to her. But then he'd have trapped her and that couldn't be right either.

He could still feel the scars on his back from his own narrow escape from success' taloned claws. There were several major accounts who still called him and the ones who'd spotted his work for Angelo or Perrin were hounding his cell phone with requests for "just one more spread." It was the road to nowhere. It was the road back to a studio, living there because next door would be too far away. Part of the package deal would be a series of lovers who looked like Melanie, or aspired to, but didn't touch his heart.

He'd had enough of too many lovers. He now had a girlfriend, a woman he was in love with. And he wanted more of that. Wouldn't his mother laugh her ass off knowing what he was feeling right about now. Angelo sure would.

Cassidy hung up the phone.

He didn't turn when she ran her hand up his back.

"I'm sorry. It's overwhelming."

He nodded. He knew the temptation was huge. It was "The Life" all over again. Except now it was Cassidy who had set her sights on it, and he wasn't a part of the equation. He didn't want to be a part of *that* Life. He'd been there once and barely survived.

"Hey, lover."

He jolted beneath her touch. That's exactly what he'd called Melanie, the moment before he destroyed her life by asking her to go sailing with him.

He pushed past Cassidy, away from the balcony and into the *pensione.* It was so damn small. He'd been caged. He was Cassidy Knowles' captive lover while she made choices that he could never survive. He groped about the room, found the door, and was out on the streets in moments. He headed up the hill, climbing the cobbled streets, and when they gave out, the terraced fields of vines. It was only when he reached the highest terraces—those which had been abandoned first by the shrinking Cinque Terre wine industry—that he ground to a halt.

Exhausted, he dropped to the earth and rested his head on his arms.

"Shit! Melanie, I'm sorry. You never deserved that." It hurt like hell to be wearing that same burden himself. He didn't want Cassidy's life. No more than she wanted his. And where did that leave them?

Sure, a fish can love a bird, but where would they live? Old joke. Sad joke.

"WHAT THE HELL, RUSSELL?" Her side was killing her, the stitch dug in like a hot knife. All her morning runs through the vast vineyards of

California and Italy hadn't prepared her for the vertical cliffs or the pace that Russell had set up these hills.

He raised his head from his arms and it was the saddest she'd ever seen him.

She dropped to the soil beside him and kneaded her side. She slid an arm around his waist but he shrugged her off.

"What did I do?" Damn it. They were in this incredibly beautiful, romantic wonderland of the Italian coast.

He shook his head, but didn't answer.

"Is it the phone calls? I'll stop those. I won't check another message until we get home."

"Home."

"Well, that's some response. C'mon, Russell. You know I suck at guessing games. Talk to me." Not even a smile.

"Where's home, Cassidy?" His voice was deep and rough. As if he was fighting for every word.

"I don't know. Seattle I guess. Maybe Oakville in Napa soon. How the hell should I know? Where's your home, Russell? On some damn sailboat?"

"Yes," he finally looked at her. "Yes! It's on some damn sailboat. My home has a cat. It has belongings. It is a place where I like myself. It is a place where I'm at my best. How about you, Cassidy? Where are you at your best?"

"In your arms." She'd said it flippantly, but once said, it was true. It was the one place she could be where the world made sense. When the mad jangle in her head went quiet.

"C'mon, Cassie. I'm not talking about sex."

She hadn't been, at least not once she thought about it. But she couldn't answer his scorn—couldn't face his anger.

He closed his eyes. He just sat there with his eyes closed. His arms —those nice, strong, safe arms—crossed over his own knees.

The ocean lay spread out before them. Somewhere over that way lay Sardinia, then France, Spain, the Atlantic, and the entire width of the U.S. So many miles away. But it didn't feel so distant when she sat here with Russell.

She reached for him again, but hesitated with her fingers a scant inch from his shoulder. Finally she withdrew and dropped her hand into her lap.

Everything had been going so perfectly. California had a wonderful offer on the table; they were offering her access to every aspect of the organization. Italy had a nice Old World feel that could be fun, but not as exciting. The U.S. companies, and now there were four of them, exhibited an energy and a vibrancy that egged her on. The French offers were more about status and, she had to admit, a chance to work with *grand crus* was tempting. The Germans were all about money—a lot of money.

"Why can't you just be happy for me?"

He shuddered. He actually shuddered.

"What? Come on, Russell. Talk to me."

"Where is home, Cassidy Knowles?"

HE DIDN'T SPEAK AGAIN EXCEPT to repeat his question. No matter what she did or said.

"Where is home, Cassidy Knowles?"

When the evening settled in with a foggy chill, that raised goosebumps over her whole body, she deserted him and descended back to the hotel. Though she waited all night, there was no sign of Russell.

Some romantic vacation.

She dialed for her messages. Seventeen. She hung up without listening to a one of them.

At dawn there was a knock on the door and she rushed over to open it.

Instead of Russell...instead of throwing their arms around each other and both being sorry...a maid held out a note.

The paper crackled as she opened it. Russell's writing, not her father's. But it was as if they were both speaking from the same page.

Cassidy,

You are really going places. I'm happy for you. Unfortunately, they aren't places I want to go. The car is in your name and the keys are on the bureau. I've taken the 6:30 train to the airport. I've left money and instructions with the front desk to ship my belongings. Just leave them in the room and they'll take care of it. Though if you'd hand carry my camera to Angelo, I'd appreciate it. Don't if it's too weird for you.

Best of luck with your future,

Russell

The first thing she noticed was the clock. 6:45. Gone! He was gone. How could that be? What had she said? She'd gone over it a hundred times in the night. And she still didn't know.

Maybe one of the seventeen phone messages was from him. But she knew none of them would be. He'd spent a cold, lonely night in an abandoned vineyard, come down the hill with the dawn, and left town.

"Where is home, Cassidy Knowles?" As if he were questioning a complete stranger.

Well, to hell with him. She wasn't going to ruin her vacation because of some jerk of a man. Breakfast. That was it. She'd eat breakfast, take a walk, and then she'd feel better. She was just dizzy from the cold and the long night awake in the chair.

She didn't like leaving his camera in the room. She slung it over her shoulder as she went out.

THE CAMERA WAS heavy and dragged at her shoulder. She pulled it into her hand, wrapping the strap as a brace behind her elbow just as he'd taught her.

With the camera in her hand, she started to see pictures to take. A pot with a single red geranium on a narrow set of stone steps, the very stone worn by a thousand years of footsteps. A neon-bright purple door beckoned her to photograph a stone house so old it might have been quarried by Noah's sons. A Dalmatian stuck her nose out between forest-green, wooden shutters to watch her go by. A black and gray dapple cat impossibly asleep on the narrow keel of an up-turned fishing dinghy.

It was different seeing a village through a camera. Each image she took became a memory of its own. A man who would have passed for an aging hippie back home sat in the sun beneath a shingle advertising his surgery. He offered her a nod and a smile before returning to the novel in his lap. A butcher skinning a lamb. A baker totting a huge basket of crusty breads into one restaurant after another, his load lightening with each stop.

Where is home, Cassidy Knowles?

She'd be damned if she knew.

BROWN'S POINT LIGHTHOUSE

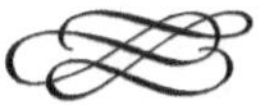

Tacoma

First lit: 1887

Extinguished: 1963

47.3059 -122.444

Oscar Brown was the station's first keeper in the early 1900s. He moved his wife, a horse and a cow, and a piano onto this remote point. He often rowed the three or four miles to Tacoma to attend concerts. An accomplished musician, when the roads finally reached the lighthouse he became a noted piano teacher when he was not tending the light.

The concrete block lighthouse, though less than a hundred yards from the house, was often inaccessible when major storms flooded the swampy ground. Brown would take a rowing dory out through the mud to add oil or trim the wick.

The striking mechanism for the fog bell had to be wound every 45 minutes. Brown slept little during the long spells of dense fog that frequently plague the point. When the mechanism broke, his wife would count out the twenty-second interval between his strikes. Brown had served thirty years before the fog bell was replaced by a powered horn. The bell traveled to a church for some years but has returned to the old lighthouse, with a bowling ball for a clacker.

The keeper's cottage is now the centerpiece of a city park. The dwelling's gardens are filled with rare, heritage plants maintained by the local horticultural society.

NOVEMBER 1

assidy was right back where she'd started.

Alone and huddled behind a lighthouse in a blinding rain and a roaring wind.

Better equipped, Cassidy wasn't likely to freeze to death, but that didn't make her any happier to be here than at West Point lighthouse last January.

Damn you, Russell. Not one message. Not a single note. When she'd handed his duffle and his camera to Angelo it had been so awkward she'd had to run out of the restaurant not knowing if she would speak or cry had she opened her mouth. Russell had ruined everything.

Jo and Perrin had tried to cheer her up. But neither could explain his final question. They agreed that "in your arms" was a good answer. Light and funny, yet romantic and cozy, too. It had the added benefit of being more than a little bit true. Now her condo felt like a foreign land—with Shilshole Marina and Angelo's wholly out of bounds.

Yesterday she'd finally tried to call him, but his phone was disconnected. He hadn't even left a forwarding number. Russell had gone into hiding. Well, good riddance. She didn't want to talk to him anyway—which was a complete and total lie.

309

After tomorrow it wouldn't matter anyway. She'd set aside three days to drive down the coast. Professional movers would empty the condo after she left, and they'd have her house in Napa set up before she got there. A decorator would be there on day four to help her turn it into a home.

So there, Russell Morgan. My home is in the hills above St. Helena, California. In the true heart of American wine country. Is that good enough for you?

She knew it wasn't. Some part of her knew it wasn't, but she was at a loss over why or what to do about it.

Get it done…and get out of the rain before her fingers turned to icicles.

She pulled the last two envelopes from her pocket. She wouldn't be here for December, so she'd brought both. And chosen the closer lighthouse. Besides, she'd visited December's lighthouse at Ediz Hook twice already, on her way to two of the others. She'd even seen it from the water with Russell when they'd sailed out to Destruction Island. There wasn't even a lighthouse anymore, just a flasher atop the Coast Guard station.

Leaving Puget Sound was going to be a major advantage of moving to Mondavi. There was no part of the Sound or Seattle that had escaped Russell's touch—no part of it that could be just hers. Napa would give her a chance to purge her soul of him.

Damn porcupine!

She tore open the first letter and huddled over it to shield it from the rain. The writing was so uneven that she had to construct each word a letter at a time. Her heart clenched with sympathetic pain for the effort he'd taken to write it.

Dearest I. S.,

Too sick to even write her nickname.

I followed my destiny north. I left behind my dreams. I discovered new ones. The most important discovery, the one that made my whole life worthwhile, was the love of my dear Adrianne and for my lovely Cassie. There is ice in your veins, a cold determination to put your head down and battle it out. That you got from me.

From your mother, you got the largest, most loving, sweetest heart there ever was. Listen to that. It is your heart that will make you happy, not your head. And I now know, that is what counts.

You are the Ice and the Sweet,

Vic

"But I followed my heart. I'm following it to the land you loved."

And yet all she felt was misery.

All those years "Ice Sweet" had more meanings, and she hadn't known. Her curse and her legacy had become her nickname, always wanting more and always feeling the pain.

Was there any point in even opening the last letter? She already knew the last words of a dying man.

"You would have loved Knowles Valley." Vic Knowles had spoken his last words to his daughter just minutes before he died. His one great regret and she now had the chance to set it straight. A Knowles would once again walk that land—and she would love it with every *ounce* of willpower in her soul.

She turned the last letter over and over. He'd left off the GPS coordinates. Misspelled the name of the lighthouse. If they'd come this far together, she might as well finish the journey.

Dearest I.S.,

Remember, above all else. Home is neither a place or a state of mind. It is family.

Thank you for being my family. For being my home.

All my love,

Daddy

Daddy.

In the end, he'd finally felt worthy to name his role in her life. And that was his final word, ever. The wonderful father he'd always been.

Always believing in her and—just as strongly—always doubting himself.

Home was family.

No.

It couldn't be.

Had Russell been asking that of her?

Had he proposed and she hadn't even noticed?

The realization burned behind her eyes, in her head and in her heart. Like an oak barrel being charred by fire on the inside; it made the oak accessible to the wine while it also mellowed and aged the wine in the process. The precious oak, used for its own flavor.

But there was a second reason they used oak, for both wine and whiskey. Steel trapped the wine, suffocated it. Even the giants of the ultra-modern Napa Valley spent time in oak. And while there, one or maybe two percent of the alcohol and other aromatics leaked out through the porous wood. They slid from the wine and disappeared. It was a tiny loss, but enough to transform a mediocre wine into a wonder.

Giving up so little gained so much.

Could she let go of that precious percent? And what would it be? Or was it too late? Had she missed her chance, locked up in the steel vat of her own icy stubbornness?

Her father's words were washing off the page of his last ever letter to her. He was gone, taking his past with him. Vic Knowles had left her alone to face her future. Yet another piece for Cassidy to let go of —shed one layer at a time.

She looked at the lighthouse: perched on the rock, a concrete tower surrounded by a barbed wire-topped fence. The old bell was in a small shed at the back of the park. The rowing dory, long gone, replaced with a replica that would never again leave the boat house to be dragged, pushed and prodded, through the mud flats. The remote keeper's dwelling now in the midst of a posh neighborhood, rentable by the day, and tended by the Points Horticultural Society. All of the history had escaped; no sign remained of the remote corner of Puget Sound where the first keeper had managed to land a piano in 1903.

She stood alone.

The only sign of life she could see through the drenching rain was a blue-hulled sailboat with red sails.

She blinked.

But it was still there slicing through the rain.

Russell, coming to their lighthouse.

Coming to her!

She ran from her partial shelter behind the lighthouse and clambered up onto the rocks.

The *Lady* continued straight toward her for a long moment, then it jibbed abruptly, awkwardly, shearing off to the west, away from the lighthouse. No—away from her.

She'd hurt him. Not because she'd meant to, but because she didn't understand.

"Russell," her voice was little more than a croak. She tried again. It was no better.

He was glancing over his shoulder, but he wasn't turning back.

She waved her arms to no effect.

Her coat. She was wearing her red parka, for the first time in six months it was cold and wet enough.

Unable to fight her way out of the zipper with her frozen fingers, she dragged the coat off over her head.

"Russell." She waved it against the wind and rain. "See the coat, damn you. See the coat. Red coat, Russell. Don't leave me behind. Red Coat. Red Coat!" She cried it out into the storm.

The boat continued away from her, until it was barely a shadow in the pounding rain. She was soaked to the bone, but wasn't willing to turn for her car. There was no way she could give up while there was even the slightest hint of a chance. Not even after that.

He *had* to come back.

She waved the coat once more, but knew it was too little too late. The horizon remained empty. Cassidy let the coat slap wetly against her leg and lie on the sea-spattered rocks.

Then off to the north, in a direction she hadn't been watching, the *Lady* once again emerged out of the driving rain.

Cassidy frantically waved the coat again. He was coming back…for her? Please, let him be coming back for her.

The boat pulled close in, a few dozen yards off shore. With one single, emphatic point, Russell indicated the boat launch on the other side of the park.

She ran. She sprinted. She leaned into the rain and flew across the muddy lawn and the rough rocks. She skidded as she leapt onto the wet wood and raced down the dock.

He was there before her. Floating a dozen feet off the end, just a little too far to jump. She considered it anyway, but knew of the bone-aching cold that waited there. The rain pounded off his incandescent yellow slicks like a parade of snare drummers gone mad.

One more time she waved the sopping red coat at him. She didn't know what else to do.

"What?"

She didn't know. How was she supposed to know what to say? She had no idea. His hostility was so open that it pushed her back hard enough to nearly make her stumble and go swimming off the dock's other side. His angry pain lay so sharp and clear, that it made a scar on the face that had once looked at her with such love. It was an ugly scar and she had been the one to put it there.

"Where were you? I tried calling."

"I disconnected the damn thing."

"Why?" As if she didn't know. To avoid her.

"I'm leaving."

"When?" He couldn't. He wouldn't. Not without a goodbye. Not without…

He pointed north. He had the same calendar she did. Ediz Hook lighthouse was the December lighthouse—one of the very last in Puget Sound on the way to the open ocean.

"Now?" She choked out the word.

He nodded without softening. He kept the boat away from the dock with practiced nudges of the controls and the tiller.

She had to think of what to say. Had to get it right. Had to let him know that…

"I'm giving up the angels' share."

"What's that, some special condo deal they offered you on the beach?"

"It's the second reason they use oak barrels in making wine. The first is flavor. The second—the angels' share—is what they call the part that escapes through the porous wood. The extra that is lost, let go of, to make the wine that remains behind even better."

"And what have you let go of?"

How should she know? She didn't have all the answers on tap. She was making this up as she went. She flapped her arms and let them drop to her side. Then wrapped them about herself because she was rapidly turning into a human popsicle. Maybe not sweet, but certainly icy and soaked through to the skin.

"How about this? Crazy idea." And she'd think of it in a second. "Hear me out. Okay?"

"I won't live in Napa."

"I'm not asking you to."

"Or Sienna."

"Will you shut up for a second?"

"Amazing pictures by the way. You have a great eye."

"I have two of them. Now, be quiet."

He bit his upper lip and nodded.

He'd noticed the pictures. She'd loved taking them; loved that connection to place and time. Maybe, just maybe that was a part the answer. Anything was better than the bitter dregs that had chewed up her life these last three weeks.

"You're leaving now because you can't stand to see all of the places we were happy together."

He didn't speak, but she knew now. She knew how to read the pain in his eyes. The wound to his heart shot across his face and he looked away. But he didn't hit the throttle. He didn't leave. Russell simply hung his head against the pain.

She raised her voice, to make sure he could hear her over the rain.

"I have an offer. It's a crazy offer. They don't even know what they need, but I do. I haven't told you about it yet. *They* don't even know about it yet." Neither did she, but an idea, or the idea of an idea was forming. If she could think fast enough, maybe she'd find it.

"I'll make them an offer they can't refuse." Please, Russell, you made the offer once, make it again? Please.

"Who? China? India?"

"I told you to shut up." But the words came gently from her throat. She imagined, hoped that they sounded like the caress they were.

"It's got a lot of great sailing and great people. I know you'll feel connection there. I know it. They need help. They need my help."

He didn't react.

Think, Cassidy. Think harder.

"And, uh, they need an advertising specialist, too. Not some high-end New York studio godlike grunt who doesn't really care. They need someone who is only happy when he connects with his heart. With his really loving heart."

He stopped fussing with the controls. The boat began to twist a bit in the protected waters along the dock. He still looked away, but she could see the shift in his shoulders, in his stance, and read her first signs of hope there. The stark anger was gone. She had a chance. She hopped on one foot and then the other hoping to jog some words loose from her freezing body. Standing out in the November rain just might be colder than falling overboard, but she wasn't about to jump into the water to find out.

The chance that Russell would freeze her out was many times scarier than merely being dragged out to sea.

"It would give me a chance to really be involved in the whole process. Cultivation to viticulture to marketing. Not control, but involved, understanding. Like you said on our first date, I'd get to know the whole story of the wine. And I'll, I'll make it a cooperative of some sort. I'm sure they'll do it. They're really good people. They could be world class with my help. With *our* help"—there it was—"but it only works with the two of us."

He turned to face her.

"They have just a dozen or so wineries but with amazing potential. If they could work together, we could make them into the next great wine region. It's a little place, probably less total acreage than Mondavi, never mind Napa. It's called Puget Sound. Maybe you've heard of it?" Maybe, just maybe you'll remember that you proposed to me among the Italian vineyards and forget that I was too wrapped up in my own world to hear it.

The boat drifted a few feet closer to the dock.

"So I was thinking. We could, um, sail all over the Sound, up the Inside Passage to Alaska on occasion and... Then, you know, we'd..." what Cassidy?

"...together we'd..." What is it you really want? Help me, Daddy.

That was it. He already had.

She stood up straight, moved to the edge of the dock until her toes hung over the ocean, raised her arm, and pointed a finger at his heart now so close as the *Lady* drifted near.

"As long as we're together, that's all that matters."

The stern bumped against the dock, closing the last of the gap between them, her finger actually came to rest against the center of his slicker-covered chest. He looked at her with the eyes she remembered, the ocean-deep eyes that she'd gotten lost in the first time she'd seen them.

This time she knew what to say and how to say it.

"*You* are my home."

END NOTES

My apologies to Brown Point lighthouse for the addition of a dock. The original, much larger dock, installed to service the logging on the hills beyond, was removed in the 1930s.

My joy, to take a year and travel with my wife to the dozen lighthouses pictured on a calendar that she gave me for Christmas. She is my home.

WHERE DREAMS RESIDE

CHAPTER 1

Jo Thompson brushed at her eyes, again. She wasn't the weepy sort. Even a sip of the exceptional champagne that sparkled across her tongue, the taste of spring, only helped a little. She focused on the laughter and bright music of the wedding reception to distract herself.

The setting was so beautiful, a broad white canopy over the vibrant-green lawn. Through its open sides the Mukilteo lighthouse and the large green-and-white Whidbey Island ferry plying the waters of Puget Sound made such an ideal setting. So romantic that even contemplating it choked Jo up all over again. She turned back to the goings-on under the canopy.

Her best friend looked so beautiful and so happy as a bride that it actually made Jo's heart hurt. Cassidy wore a cream-and-ivory lace sheath wedding dress that clung to her shape like a caress. Every time she even breathed, hidden threads of metallic silver glinted and sparkled. On a more provocative woman, or even a lesser one, it would have been indecent. On Cassidy all it did was smolder, which was clearly giving her new husband something to think about.

The first dance hadn't been a tango, but she and Russell had certainly danced it like one, as if they were the only ones present. The reception might be winding down now, but they still moved together, constantly teetering on the edge of a tangle of hot passion.

Jo searched out her other best friend. She was innocently flirting with the father of the groom, who was almost as handsome as his son. And Perrin was doing so despite the wife happily draped on his arm. Julia Morgan took Jo's arrival as an opportunity to get her husband back on the dance floor.

It was clear from their moves that they'd been dancing together for years. Jo had never really learned, but they made it look so intimate and fun that maybe she'd have to find the time. Someday, in her copious spare minutes between lawsuits. Okay, perhaps not. She only really managed to carve out time with Cassidy this week because she was in between cases. A situation that would be ending on Monday morning.

The large tent graced lightly over the lawn, lanterns warmed the scene as the summer evening slowly faded in the background. A live duo were knocking out songs that you couldn't help tapping your foot to. Above them, the Mukilteo lighthouse spun and cast its beam upon the June waters.

"We done good!" Perrin jarred Jo's shoulder with a friendly nudge of her own.

"No, you did. The dress you designed for her is a marvel."

"Does make her look pretty marvelous, not that she doesn't normally. Still wish Russell had let me do something with his outfit." They both looked to where he stood with his best man taking a momentary breather from the dance floor.

Jo arched an eyebrow at her, "Do you think you could make him look even better than that?"

Perrin offered her a bit of a grimace. "Probably not. He's sooo hunky in that tux, but it would have been fun to try."

"He doesn't just look hunky," Cassidy slammed into them from behind and draped her arms over Perrin and Jo's shoulders, the sweet peas laced into her hair scenting the June-summer air with spring. "He is! I can't wait to rip that tux off him." Then she blushed bright red and grinned at the same time.

Jo pulled her in, "You done good, Cassie. Exactly what you're supposed to be doing, and who with."

Cassidy laughed. A laugh she'd lost since they were college roommates over a decade before, but had rediscovered with Russell Morgan.

"When do you fly out?"

Cassidy grabbed a piece of prosciutto-wrapped shrimp from a passing waiter. She tried to eat it, speak, and chortle all at the same time and nearly choked herself.

Jo handed over her glass of champagne from which Cassidy took several swallows and then released a loud hiccup.

"Tomorrow morning."

"Wellll," Perrin drawled out the word. "I'm sure he'll let you finally sleep on the flight, unless you're going for an entry in the mile-high club."

Cassidy's smile and blush definitely grew. "Russell might have mentioned something about that."

"Damn," Perrin stamped her foot. "I am so jealous. I want reports. Perrin wants reports." She began counting on her fingers. "Is married sex better than single sex? Does high altitude make it, well, better somehow? Pluses and minuses of doing it in four-star hotels, Italian villas, and sailboats on the Mediterranean. Take notes. You'll be graded afterward."

"Yes, Perrin. I promise a report. When I get back from three weeks of sailing the Amalfi coast with the man of my dreams, we'll all go out, get drunk, and I'll tell you every little sordid detail about my most private sex life."

"Good." Perrin nodded emphatically. Her hair, presently dyed as black as Jo's, swirled about her thin face. As usual, she'd missed the sarcasm in Cassidy's voice.

Jo also knew from experience that Perrin would indeed be wheedling at least some of the juicier details out of their friend in due time. This allowed Jo to, without parsimony, both share Cassidy's present amusement at Perrin's expense and later enjoy the results of Perrin's somewhat voyeuristic but highly effective curiosity.

Cassidy hugged them both close, "Best friends ever."

"Best friends ever," she and Perrin repeated.

While Perrin was both more tipsy and much more emphatic, Jo could feel the truth of it once more bringing tears to her eyes.

***

"Where's my goddamn camera?"

"Let it go, *mio amico*. You're the best man, Russell. No, wait. You're the groom, I'm the best man, though with how Cassidy is looking in that dress, the groom really oughta be someone handsome and Italian like me." Angelo Parrano slapped Russell on the back hard enough that the groom almost snorted his beer.

"But just look at them." Russell insisted.

There was no question who "them" was.

Angelo took in the scene. Russell had friends from the dock where his sailboat was moored in Seattle at Shilshole Marina. They were mostly dressed for the Northwest in slacks and a clean shirt. They clustered together by the buffet table Angelo had spent most of last night putting together, eating the gourmet food with as much attention as they'd eat a bucket of chicken. He'd bet money they were talking about sailing. It was a topic they never tired of.

A bunch of his and Russell's New York friends had flown out. They were dressed far more fashionably, looking dark, edgy, and wholly out of place at a Northwest wedding reception, outdoors at that, held beside a picturesque lighthouse. Clearly, in their opinions, the wedding of one of America's wealthiest bachelors and an internationally known food-and-wine critic who was starting a cooperative of Pacific Northwest vineyards shouldn't be in a setting more rustic than the ballroom at the Plaza Hotel in Manhattan.

Cassidy's friends were a daunting slice of the restaurant world, chefs and food critics. A dozen or so of the Northwest's top vintners from Cassidy's new Northwest Wines venture were also in attendance. It shouldn't be surprising who Cassidy's friends were. Still, it was his restaurant, Angelo's Tuscan Hearth, where they'd held the rehearsal dinner and it was his buffet they were presently tasting and judging. He looked away because he couldn't stand to watch.

No, there was no question which "them" Russell was referring to or why, as a professional photographer, he was desperate for his camera. The three women laughing together made an amazing picture.

Cassidy was right out of a magazine shoot. As a matter of fact, she soon would be. Angelo knew Russell was planning to use her in that dress for the next ad campaign for Perrin's Glorious Garb. Not just edgy clothes, but now astonishing wedding dresses as well.

Actually he'd be an idiot if he didn't use all three of them in exactly those getups. Perrin had also done one of her fashion-design numbers on herself and Jo Thompson. Courtesy of a dye job, Perrin's hair matched Jo's, a straight fall almost as black as night to the middle of their backs. Their dresses were cut from the same cloth, but that's where the similarity ended.

Perrin's pale skin and blue eyes were offset against the light celery-green fabric by severe lines in the dress' tailoring that accented the slender lines of her body and revealed unexpected flashes of that creamy skin. She looked long and dangerous, like a racing sailboat or a really fine chef's knife.

Jo's darker skin, revealing her part-Alaskan heritage, was kissed by the gentle green curves of her dress. Each swoop and swirl accented her generous figure and the fitness he knew she earned through hard sweat at the gym. A man could become lost while navigating among those curves until there was no hope for his return.

The three women had their foreheads together and their arms around each other's waists.

"Beauty, truth, and joy." Josh Harper observed over Angelo's shoulder even as Perrin burst forth with one of her bubbling laughs. The reviewer from Gourmet Week had come up between Angelo and Russell. He knew Josh from a couple of good reviews of Angelo's Tuscan Hearth and his habit of eating at Angelo's when he was in town, even when he wasn't researching for a review.

"Guess it wasn't hard to tell what was grabbing our attention."

Russell noted. "You're good with words, Josh. Maybe you should write for a living or something."

"Or something." Josh sighed as he watched the three women. "There are moments when being happily married really sucks."

"And moments when it's damn good." Russell took a swallow from his bottle of beer. "So what's your excuse, Angelo?"

He tried to speak, he really did. But Jo Thompson had raised her head and was looking at him from between the other two women. Her dark eyes inspected him as only a top corporate lawyer could, slowly taking him apart like a fine chiffonade, one sliver-thin slice at a time.

Russell's punch on his arm sent him staggering to the side. His wine, thankfully a white Oregon Viognier, spilled down the leg of his gray suit pants, and perfumed him with its warm floral components.

"Shit, Russell!"

"Sorry buddy. I'd feel bad, but I have to go dance with the most beautiful woman here." He finished his beer, handed Angelo the empty before going to fetch his wife. Having his hands full was the only thing that kept him from smacking the groom a good one.

Angelo stood there, empty wine glass in one hand, a drained beer bottle in the other, and a stain down his tuxedo pant that made it look as if he'd just peed himself. Like a lush on display. He shook his leg to try and shake loose the wet pant leg clinging to his skin like cold clam sauce. It didn't work.

Then he looked up and saw that Jo was still watching him. A soft smile, the kind that came the instant before a laugh, lit her face.

Josh clapped Angelo on the shoulder as Russell and Cassidy hit the dance floor, appearing to float several feet above it in their happiness.

"Yep! Happily married has its points." Josh was watching the newly-married couple sizzle across the dance floor.

But Angelo couldn't stop watching Jo Thompson.

"*You've got a special* at table seven," Graziella called out as she breezed through the swinging doors into the kitchen at Angelo's restaurant. She dumped a stack of empty bowls with a clatter in front of Marko the dishwasher.

"What kind of special?" Angelo didn't even bother to look up from the Veal Florentine he was plating. An almost invisible shaving of truffle, followed by a fistful of fresh mozzarella and shove it under the broiler to finish.

"Wants the chef on the floor," she had to shout a little to be heard over the typical kitchen mayhem of orders rattling back and forth and pans clattering against the stove as Manuel, the sous chef caramelized some onions in Marsala wine adding a brightness to the richer tomato overtones that generally permeated the air.

"I'm busy." 'Chef on the floor' was a stupid New York thing anyway, not Seattle. Angelo grabbed the plate as his grillardin slid a medium-rare pan-seared duck breast into a nest of slivered porcini. The dark, fatty duck and the earthy umami of the butter-sautéed mushrooms filled his senses. It was one of his favorite new dishes, because of its richness in all the senses. A sprinkle of bright green chives and deeply yellow lemon zest, as much for the color as the tang. He slid it across to Graziella.

"Told her you were, but she seemed confident you wouldn't mind," She dressed the duck with a side of steamed baby asparagus as he pulled out the veal and then she took both out with her. "She's a looker, if that helps."

Angelo tossed the latest batch of pasta with tongs, and drizzled on cold-pressed olive oil. Now he had to let number seven wait. Because if he didn't, Graziella would assume being pretty was all that was needed to get him out of his kitchen. Definitely, let her wait.

But he couldn't. He'd been side-tracked, knocked out of the groove. The second time his garde manger had a salad ready before Angelo had prepared the plate, he gave it up and called Manuel to take his spot. Manuel might be Mexican rather than Italian, but he could turn out a hundred complex dishes each exactly to Angelo's recipes and repeat it night after night. The perfect sous chef.

Wiping his hands on the towel dangling from his apron's waist-band and checking that there were no flour stains on his charcoal shirt, Angelo pushed through the door into the restaurant. It took a moment for his eyes to adjust from the stark white and steel of his bright kitchen to the soft ambiance of Angelo's Tuscan Hearth.

He and Russell had redesigned the dining area like a traditional Italian kitchen. A large central fireplace. Tables in small clusters scattered about the room. No booths, but comfortable chairs, tasteful paintings and photos of Italy on the walls.

On their last trip, Russell and Cassidy had taken a number of photographs of the old Italian villages that Angelo's mother had left before Angelo's birth. But it lent an authentic feel to the room, photos of home. It was cozy and Angelo forced himself to slow down enough to share a friendly moment or two with some of the diners he recognized as repeats, and a few that he didn't.

"Yes, that's fresh basil," as if he'd use anything else.

"I used the Pacific salmon in this Cioppino, it's a gentler flavor than the Atlantic salmon," and it was more popular here in Seattle even if it was a bit less authentic. It gave patrons a chance to feel slightly superior for living out here on the "wilder" west coast.

"And what can I do…" his words trailed off as he reached table seven.

Jo Thompson sat there wearing a deep yellow blouse the same tone as the wall paint, but richer, more intense. Her black hair was back in a ponytail, leaving her face and neck exposed. Her skin and eyes were lustrous in the restaurant's soft candlelight. Her cleavage, not deeply exposed, was accented by a small dangle of gold in the shape of an orca whale on a hair-thin chain. The subtle adornment made her absolutely stunning.

"Yuri and I were hoping that you could choose dinner for us tonight."

Angelo glanced at Yuri. He was a big man, tall and broad-shouldered. Angelo wasn't that short, but he might not even reach this guy's shoulder. His face was square and rugged in a way that he supposed women would find handsome, but he could never be sure with guys.

His hands were big and rough, a working man's hands. Angelo's animal brain flashed an image of those callused hands groping Jo's beautiful skin and he felt the blood drain out of his soul.

"Of course," his voice nearly broke, it had suddenly gone so dry. "It would be my pleasure Miss Thompson. Do the lady or the gentleman have any preferences?"

The man waved one of those hands dismissively. "Whatever you make will be fine." His voice was deep and smooth, accented lightly with Russian heritage making it even richer.

"Jo says that your taste is impeccable and that's good enough for me." He rested an elbow on the table as he leaned across toward Jo. "Must say that my taste is pretty impeccable too."

Clearly dismissed, Angelo turned for the kitchen. Once back in the world of white and noise, back where the sizzling of the deep fryer battled the dish boy for sonic ambiance, and oregano and garlic scented the air along with the undertones of port reductions, he let his hands fall to his sides.

Cook for them? *Non possibile!* Twice he went to step forward, but he had no idea what to make. So, he'd just make…something.

After his third attempt at a Roasted Artichoke and Venison Carpaccio Bruschetta, he had Marco send out a simple Antipasto-su-baguette. From there it went downhill. Working beside a flustered Angelo, his grillardin slid out of the groove. He ruined the last duck breast, then burned a sirloin so badly that they'd had to open the back doors and turn the fans up to full roar to avoid the charred scent reaching the dining room.

The disaster rippled through the kitchen. The friturier dropped plastic tongs into the deep-fryer, which melted and permanently merged with the fry basket before he was able to recover them. They'd be throwing that basket away. The potager grabbed the salt instead of the sugar and then knocked the last of the asparagus soup across the patissier's station taking out a whole tray of Torte della Nonna.

Angelo considered going to apologize to the patrons at large, but couldn't face Jo's disappointment. Clearly she'd been intending a romantic dinner to show off her savvy in choosing his restaurant. Instead, Angelo took the coward's way out and stayed hidden in the kitchen. Tonight, he knew, he was going to be drinking far too much wine. And with Russell in goddamn Italy, he was going to have to face tomorrow's hangover on his own.

Jo KNEW she'd made a miscalculation the moment she saw Angelo's face. Not only that, but his hands, normally so expressive, had dropped to his sides and hung there. But she didn't know how to take it back. She should have taken Yuri anywhere in Seattle but Angelo's restaurant.

Yuri had called, saying that he'd be in town and he'd love to take her out to dinner. She'd suggested Angelo's Tuscan Hearth without even thinking. The food was exquisite and the atmosphere quiet but cozy. It didn't force absolute isolation like in an American steakhouse with booths so deep and tall that you could be the only couple there.

Nor the merry mayhem of the Moroccan place they gone to for Cassidy's bachelorette party. Jo still wasn't sure quite how Perrin had gotten Cassidy and Jo up with her to join the belly dancer, much to the entertainment of other customers.

Angelo's offered quiet tables, the gentle strains of fine Italian singers sounding from a discrete sound system rather than an uncomfortable trio traveling from table to table. Tasteful. She liked that about his choices, his restaurant was immensely tasteful. It had seemed the perfect place to bring Yuri, especially as fine Italian dining wasn't something easily found in Alaska.

Jo had spent a lot of time with Yuri Andreevich over the last two years working on the Alaskan fisheries lawsuit. He was one of the Russians who had immigrated to the Alaskan coast seeking the rich American life. Unlike most, he had found it. Many of his countrymen had simply traded one fishing boat for another. Yuri had used the lawsuit to leverage himself into position as a "voice of the fishermen" and proven himself to be capable and successful as such. He sounded as if he were the hero of the two-brother boats eking out a family tradition, rather than in the pay of the conglomerates launching hundreds of craft and being sued for price control by the state on behalf of the fishermen.

She hadn't much enjoyed the ethics of the whole thing, but she'd ultimately justified it to herself that the individual fishermen's claims were even more unfair than the conglomerates' practices. And the fees had been astonishing which had paid off her condo and left her little excuse to complain. She'd spent two years ignoring the sharp pinch and it was now past time where she could change anything.

Yuri's big voice was romantic, and his heavily-accented English caused several heads to turn at other tables when he first spoke. It wasn't a booming voice, but it carried, and attracted attention. It had also worked well in interviews and, she had to admit, on the phone with her. Jo liked Yuri, and there had been a connection there. Or at least she'd thought so.

She'd been feeling lonely after the wedding. With Cassidy out of town and Perrin immersed in another of her design frenzies from which she might not emerge for days or weeks, Jo was discovering quite how pitiful her social life had become. She couldn't even throw herself into the next lawsuit, it was only starting to trickle in. Dinner had sounded like a fun and easy answer to an otherwise quiet Thursday evening alone.

But when Angelo saw them, he had looked as if he'd been shot. She'd known he was attracted to her. It was plain to see, but his feelings had left him awkward in her presence. And, she had to admit, it had left her awkward as well. They'd danced together a few times at the wedding last weekend but he'd said little and she'd said less.

If it had been purely physical, that might have been fun as he was very nice to look at. But it wasn't her body that he was always watching, but rather her eyes. Not a good sign. She didn't need any attachments right now. Especially not one that would be complicated by being her best friend's husband's best friend.

Russell was good for Cassidy. If it had been Jo, she would have killed the man inside the first week, but he was good for Cassidy. His carefree attitude forced his wife to loosen up and relax, something she did only a tiny bit better than Jo. Jo had never "gotten the hang" of letting go. Didn't have time for it, truth be told.

Russell's ease, mixed with his ramrod forthrightness, made Cassidy face decisions head-on rather than sliding by them. It did make him the perfect man for her.

Angelo unbalanced Jo and so she determined it was best to simply not consider him at all. But she hadn't meant to wound him by flaunting Yuri in his face. She was always fumbling in Angelo's presence and it was a feeling she wasn't used to. And one that the confident counselor in her didn't like at all.

"This is the Earth calling to the Jo Thompson," Yuri sounded like a Russian flight controller with his gentle destruction of proper English syntax. "Where did you go off flying to just now?"

Jo shook her head.

He was about to press when the appetizer arrived. She took one of the tiny antipasto sandwiches to stall, not one of her usual tactics.

It was good, but nothing exceptional. She'd been here a couple of times with Cassidy and knew this was merely one of Angelo's standard, albeit wonderful, dishes. Clearly not the exceptional food he made for friends.

She had hurt him and he was being petty and spiteful. Yet another reason not to be attracted to him. Spiteful men always became worse with time. She'd focus on Yuri, he was her date after all.

"I was just thinking about the next case I'm taking. It will be bringing me back to Alaska." Now why had she said that? During the fisheries lawsuit, Yuri had been one of their main spokesmen. They had worked long hours together honing both the public talking points and the court messages. Jo had been very careful to make sure the relationship had remained professional. This was the first time they'd seen each other since she'd won that case.

She'd also only recently emerged from a rather intense, even by her standards, lawsuit regarding the crabbing practices along the U.S.-Canadian border, again on behalf of the larger fishing corporations. That particular suit had bankrolled her a very comfortable savings account.

As she'd dressed for dinner, Jo had been uncertain of her own feelings. So, she'd chosen attractive but conservative attire, her yellow St. John blouse buttoned fairly high, with black Donna Karan slacks and sensible heels, that sent a clear message. "I will make myself pretty, but the verdict is still out on whether or not we will be spending the night together."

"Good. Alaska is very good," Yuri sounded very pleased and leaned in a little closer.

No, Alaska really sucked, but she wasn't going to say that aloud.

"You are a woman who it would be a pleasure to see more of, Jo." The momentary dip of his eyes without lingering and his smile might have been charming under different conditions. Had they been sharing sushi at the Old Power House in Kodiak, it probably would have worked.

Sitting in Angelo's, he struck her as not quite coarse. That was the wrong word. Perhaps as a touch crass.

"The case will take me more North Slope than southern coastal," she did her best to backpedal. As if anywhere in Alaska was better than any other. She'd escaped at sixteen—her career constantly forcing her to return was not one of life's little ironies—it was one of life's monster-sized ironies.

"It's about the Arctic's continental shelf rights. Who gets to drill how deep and just where do international waters begin when we're talking about the mineral rights beneath the sea bed where everything converges toward the pole. The state, after losing to me so badly last year, wants me to protect their interests. They've learned that if the corporations don't get what they want, the state won't get their tax revenue."

"That is still good. You will fly through Juneau and I will meet you there. It will be good to see you more often and away from the laws, Jo." And he sounded sincere.

Jo knew what she was looking for in a man. The criteria would change in another three to five years. But for now, she was focused on her career and could afford to dally a bit here and there. When she was ready to settle down more permanently, then she'd pick a quiet, intelligent man. He'd be well-educated and have already passed through whatever crises men passed through. Then she'd think about family.

Each thing in its order. It was a safe maxim, one she'd always liked. There was still plenty of time. She wouldn't "settle" when she was making that final choice, not one little bit.

That's when she knew that Yuri would be sleeping alone tonight. Despite the romance that Cassidy's wedding had briefly awakened in Jo's heart, she wouldn't settle even during the dating phase of her plan, and that's what sleeping with Yuri would be. Not only wasn't he Mister Right for the future, he wasn't even Mister Right for the present.

Thankfully, before she had to respond, the soup arrived. The aroma was rich, the fish broth revealing a depth that even her child-hood-in-Alaska trained senses couldn't fault. It was a cheerful mixture of clams, mussels, and salmon.

Yuri took a spoonful first and nodded his head as if saying, "Good enough."

Jo felt a heat rise. Angelo's cooking deserved more than a "good enough." His ingredients were always the finest. The proteins were always finished impeccably and his seasoning balance was exquisite. He had been written up by so many critics that he was causing some embarrassment to the city's other restaurateurs. For six months his write-ups had commanded as much print and blog presence as all of the others competing for the high-end market combined.

She allowed herself a moment more to appreciate the scents and presentation of the soup. Even the dark blue stoneware bowl, that just happened to match the room's paint accent, against the soft yellow tablecloths promised a depth that a white bowl would not have.

The broth delivered its richness to her tongue as her nose had promised. Living through college with Cassidy, even before she became such a renowned food-and-wine critic, had trained Jo's palate well. She could appreciate the interplay of the basil and oregano and the way they complemented the clam-based broth.

Then it hit her. Square in the center of the tongue, the impossible-to-miss bright sweetness of sugar. It broke the broth. The dusky clam and the subtle salmon were washed beneath it like an ocean wave. Another spoonful from elsewhere in the bowl had the same issue.

It was good. Would have been fine in some spaghetti-house type of restaurant, but it didn't belong in Angelo's.

She barely paid attention once Yuri began creating a fantasy weekend of small fishing cabins along the Sitka shore during a Pacific winter storm. She'd always paid meticulous attention to not revealing her past. As far as anyone other than Cassidy and Perrin knew, Jo Thompson had been born the day she arrived at college.

Yuri would have no way of knowing that she'd dedicated her younger existence to escape exactly such a place that he thought so charming. Since she escaped to college at sixteen after busting her ass to skip two grades, she had never been back. She occasionally met her father in a restaurant in Ketchikan when she was flying through, but she never went back to the hovel filled with too much fish and too much alcohol. At least he'd been a quiet drunk, albeit a morose one.

If Yuri thought he was painting a romantic scenario, he couldn't be more completely wrong. He might have risen to a fishing consultant sought out by corporations and the media as an expert in the field. But at his core, he was still a fisherman who would be happiest out on his boat with the wheel in one hand and a bottle of vodka in the other.

After the soup, a tiny entremets arrived. Angelo had taken to adding little dishes between courses as accent marks, a common enough action in modern French cuisine, but he was perhaps the first to apply it to traditional Italian dining. Definitely the first to do it so successfully. The between-course dishes typically completed the last flavor of the prior course or hinted at the next. Occasionally, they stepped wholly out of the bounds of the meal and were brightly amusing which somehow heightened her awareness of the dishes to either side.

This appeared to fall into the last category. Two delicate shrimp tempura on a single plate, set curve-to-curve so that they nestled together like a yin and yang symbol. They rested upon the sheerest smear of what might be a blackberry sauce set off by the perfectly white plate. The dish might be Japanese in form, but Jo would wager it had some Italian twist to the flavoring.

She took hers, refusing to be embarrassed that Angelo had sent a lover's dish to her table. The first taste pleased her, she'd been right about the blackberry sauce. The second almost made her gag. A sharp bite of plastic rolled along the edge of her tongue and even a swallow of the red wine did nothing to cut the acrid bitterness.

Jo was going to kill him. This wasn't only rude, it was downright nasty.

An exclamation from the next table over drew her attention. A fork clattered down in disgust and a plate was shoved aside, though the others at the table continued to eat. The protesting patron had a different dish from the her own. Something wasn't right.

She looked about the room. Most people were continuing to eat, but here and there, plates were returning to the kitchen, their purported delicacies abandoned.

That just didn't happen here. At Angelo's Tuscan Hearth, people mopped their plates clean with their bread so as not to lose the least drop of sauce. Working here as a dishwasher had to be one of the easiest jobs in the kitchen.

Not tonight.

But if it wasn't personal… Jo began to worry.

Something had definitely gone wrong in the kitchen.

CHAPTER 3

*M*uriel, *Jo's legal assistant* for over five years, carried the towering woven-wicker basket into Jo's office and set it on the corner of her broad oak-wood desk with a thud.

"Shit!"

Muriel stopped and stared at her, "I don't think I've ever heard you curse."

"Sorry. You can just take that right back out." The thing was huge, brimming with flowers and sausages, bags of coffee and wedges of cheese. It was monstrous enough that there could be an entire ham hiding beneath the cheery multicolored cloth. It was late morning, only a little before lunch, and the waft of fresh-baked bread made her stomach growl. That woke up her whole system which then insisted on its desire for a deeply fatty and high-caloric lunch that it certainly was not going to receive, even if it filed a motion for summary judgment in state court.

Jo tried to look back down at the benthic map of the Arctic continental shelf that showed all of the undersea topographic ridges and valleys she'd been studying. The wicker basket's base covered from Ivvavik Park in the Yukon clear over to Prudhoe Bay and well out to sea.

341

"Don't you even want to know who it's from?"

"An arrogant Russian who does not know the meaning of 'just get on the plane and go home'." Suddenly Jo had far more of her assistant's attention than she wanted. Suddenly her personal life was spinning out of her control and she was in over her head as if she were being pulled down a whirlpool. This was a not-familiar and highly-uncomfortable feeling. Normally it remained in the same perfect control as her career and her workout schedule.

"Sorry," Jo rubbed at her eyes. "Bad date last night. What part of 'No!' don't men understand?"

"Oh, they understand it just fine, except for its meaning and how to spell it."

Muriel Mendenbaum, despite her name, was sassy and youthful. Only a year younger, she somehow embodied a vitality that Jo kept committed to her career. The woman was also a gift in Jo's life, they'd been through hell and back over their years together.

Jo wished she was more like Muriel, so confident in all aspects of her life. Muriel talked easily about men and boundaries and good dates and bad. Jo merely felt awkward and so made a point of moving slowly. That had labeled her as overly choosy or, at times, arrogant. Neither was right at all, except perhaps for the choosy part.

She'd hit college at sixteen and been lost in all of the flirting and sexual confidence of the eighteen-year-old's world. She'd found a decent guy and latched onto him for safety. Latched on so hard that she hadn't figured out how to let go of him except by graduating four years later and moving across the country. Richard had been decent, but not exciting, definitely not a keeper. A decade gone and he still e-mailed her occasionally, especially after a bad breakup, which she studiously ignored.

Muriel stood now with her short, dark hair tucked behind her ears, a pink cotton sleeveless blouse with lace shoulders, and a smart black skirt with a flirty hem. She also had her hands fisted on her hips. Jo knew her assistant well enough to know that Muriel would plant herself by Jo's desk until she had the whole story, or at least enough to satisfy.

"Whereas I see you have a date tonight." Jo tried to turn the subject with the compliment to her nice clothes.

Muriel just shook her head no. Not no to the date, but no to Jo's lame evasion.

One of the newbie associates rushed in. She'd hoped for a reprieve, but all he needed was a signature on one of the smaller research matters she'd subbed out to him. He was gone almost before he arrived.

Jo would like to claim she had to get back to work, but Muriel knew Jo's workload better than anyone, frequently even Jo. They both understood that the large map spread across her desk only meant that the first files hadn't started arriving yet. She needed to get the lay of the land, but there was no rush.

Even looking out the corner office windows over Elliot Bay and the Seattle waterfront didn't offer any nice distracting topics. Where was a blizzard when you needed one, who cared if this was June?

"Let me simply say that the meal was not good. Then I almost had to deliver a slap to force him to back off at the front door of my condo."

"Maybe you should have taken him to that place you like so much. The Italian one."

"Yeah, maybe." She wasn't going to mention that she had. The entrée at least had been marvelous, almost as good as the meals she'd had with Cassidy attending. And dessert had finally swept Yuri's attention from her to his food, he couldn't stop saying how deep and rich the chocolate torte was and how the brandy was the perfect match.

Her espresso had been scorched to sludge and the Sweet Ricotta and Meyer Lemon over Amaretti had been so sour she could still feel the dry pucker at the back of her throat. She'd have liked to taste Yuri's dish just to be sure it was okay, but by that time she hadn't wanted the implied intimacy and begged off as being full.

When she didn't eat even a second spoonful of her own dessert, he teased her about it. She'd considered digging out a bit of the amaretti cookie, but they were too soggy to make it worth eating one to shut him up. He'd put the final nail in his own coffin with some remark about her girlish figure. She knew she was a full-figured gal, he didn't need to hammer on the point.

"It was Yuri, from Ketchikan."

"Ooo, good-looking Russian." Muriel almost chortled then caught herself. "But you didn't drag him into your lair."

Jo actually laughed at the image. She'd never "dragged a man into her lair." But the way Muriel said it, perhaps she should try it someday. She made it sound fun.

"No, I didn't. I sent him to his hotel and wished him good travels. He was deeply shocked. Why do men assume that a pleasant meal is always a coquettish invitation to crawl into a woman's bed?"

"Sure, guys are like that. They go from having a sure-thing-with-an-incredibly-hot-and-voluptuous-high-powered-attorney fantasy one moment, to boring-sexless-night-all-alone-and-not-understanding-or-willing-to-admit-why reality the next. For some reason, it's always a shock to their system."

"Anyway," Jo glared at the basket towering above her. "The last thing I want from him is a gift basket."

"Well, how convenient that it isn't from him."

Jo held out her hand and Muriel dropped the card into her palm.

"PPM." Calligraphied on heavy ivory stock. The paper looked like one of those artisanal, handmade cards. "Nothing else?"

Muriel shook her head, though clearly she knew something more, she wasn't going to give it over that easily.

Jo puzzled at the card for a long moment. "I'm assuming that the Presidential Pet Museum is not soliciting my services."

"Nor the Progressive Party of the Maldives," was Muriel's comeback.

Jo wondered if she'd Googled that just to have it ready, or if the woman had already known about it, or made it up. Jo decided it was better not to know. Muriel's smile said she was clearly enjoying her boss' confusion.

But even as Muriel opened her mouth, Jo made the connection. She stood up and looked down into the basket. Whoever had assembled the basket had raided every shop in Pike Place Market. Okay, there were something on the order of two hundred of them, so they'd raided a quarter of the shops, still the bounty was amazing. The cloth covering the gifts wasn't just a remnant of fabric, it was a splendid piece of local weaving. A pound of Market Tea. A salami from the meat merchant, traditional cookies from the Italian grocery. The treats kept going as they probed the contents.

She hoped there wasn't a dead fish somewhere in the depths. She pulled back the corner of the cloth. Actually, there *was* a dead fish, but it was a teriyaki-and-ginger smoked salmon which sounded delicious. Fresh bread from the French baker's stall had been the cause of her stomach's growling.

It was a bounty on a glorious scale. Even splitting it fifty-fifty with Muriel, this was going to last a while. Maybe they should bonus some of it to the junior lawyers she'd be chewing up on the Alaska case to ease their upcoming pain.

"No other note?"

Muriel shook her head. She reached down and pulled out a local artisanal chocolate bar, seventy-percent dark with Bing cherry and marzipan filling.

"It's never too early for chocolate," Jo nodded for her to open it. They broke off squares and tapped them together like champagne flutes. They shared a moment of respectful silence as the flavors bloomed in their mouths.

"Damn!"

Muriel's soft exclamation echoed Jo's feelings exactly.

"Now, what the hell do they want?" Jo noted her own curse and ignored Muriel's pretend shock.

"Maybe the Market's administrators are just being freakishly nice?" Muriel dug around some more and held up a coupon from the Parrot Store for a free parakeet. "After all, you redid their lease agreements for them."

"That was months ago."

They uncovered several more stunning delicacies and a really nice pair of earrings that they joked about arm wrestling for, which Jo resolved by putting them on. But no further information.

When Jo's phone rang, Muriel answered it. After listening for a moment, she handed it across the desk.

Jo MET Renée Linden at the Maximilien French Restaurant for lunch. The Executive Director of the Pike Place Market had deftly avoided Jo's queries on the phone as to the lunch's purpose with a skill that was easy for a trial attorney to appreciate.

They were seated at an immaculate table set on the restaurant's second story, nestled up against the glass that fronted much of this side of the Market. Beyond lay the spread of the Seattle waterfront. From the giant Ferris wheel to the south, past the ferry docks in the foreground, and West Seattle rising like an island in the midst of Puget Sound. Beyond the docks lay the sweeping expanse of Elliot Bay and the majestic Olympic mountains still sporting their glittering white glacial caps despite the June heat. It was one of the finest views in Seattle and Jo let herself be swept up by it.

"I'm so glad you could join me on such short notice."

Maybe Jo shouldn't get swept up too easily. This was Renée Linden across the table.

Jo's Friday lunch plans had transformed and her stomach was going to get what it asked for after all. She'd planned on a cup of soup and a workout at the gym, a rare midday luxury that only happened briefly between cases when her schedule had a little flexibility. Now, she would be power-lunching over a three-course French meal. It was almost as well that her dessert had been awful last night, at least she'd saved those calories. Tonight she'd have that cup of soup and gym workout to balance this splurge.

Renée Linden.

Jo had researched her further in the half hour she'd had between shooing Muriel and much of the contents of the basket out of her office, and this lunch. She'd worked with Renée before and knew what a powerhouse the woman was on the Seattle scene.

What Jo hadn't known was that Renée had been behind the revitalization of Pioneer Square in the '90s. A formerly dangerous district, that lay in the original heart of old-town Seattle, had been turned into a tourist Mecca of edgy theaters, fine galleries, exceptional dining, and bars that featured hot bands instead of Saturday night brawls. She'd also been on the board for the creation of Westlake Center, which drew tourists and shoppers into the heart of the business district.

A key player, and donor, to both the new Symphony Hall and the complete renovation to the Marion Oliver McCaw Opera Hall only a few years later. The list kept going until Jo had closed the bio abruptly and turned to stare blankly at the Arctic map until it was time for the meeting. Jo still couldn't puzzle out the meeting's purpose.

They split an order of Escargots à la Bourguignonne over a glass of Vouvray from Château Moncontour and Renée remained elusive. The woman spoke only on light topics.

Jo followed right along with the informal prelude. This was a business lunch and that was at the center of Jo's skill set, barely a step down from the courtroom.

Renée told of coming to Seattle after re-meeting her husband, now the President of Boeing's business jet division, at a tenth-year college reunion at Oberlin.

"I never would have dated the man in college. He was fantastically brilliant, which I found to be quite daunting."

Jo declined to mention just how humbled she felt in Renée's presence. Her circum vitae was enough to set even the most aggressive overachiever on her heels. Jo regretted looking up the details. It was leaving her a little tongue-tied, which hadn't happened to her in years. Often no knowledge at all was a better strategic position than too little.

"But by that time we were in our thirties. I found he had, if not mellowed, grown deeper and richer with time. He really is like a good wine, though a red rather than this white. This is far too light on the tastebuds. I'm the Vouvray to his Burgundy."

"You are at least a Beaujolais or a Bordeaux." Jo spoke before she could stop herself. That this amazing woman would think herself as of so little consequence. Why, that would leave Jo as what, grape juice?

"I had hoped that would get a rise out of you."

Jo blinked. She took another of the decadently buttery escargots to buy herself a moment.

Renée declined to explain, but the tone of the lunch shifted as if she'd passed some test.

"You did a wonderful job on those leases for us. You understood the fine balance we must strike between making money from our more successful lessees yet nurturing our start-ups and struggling entrepreneurs. And be equally fair to all two-hundred plus of our tenants. That really captured our attention."

"Our?" Jo hadn't missed the word choice and rather suspected that Renée was not using the majestic plural.

Renée merely smiled and selected the second-to-last escargot.

Jo return the smile and finished the dish.

Well, that meant that this was indeed a business luncheon. One most likely sanctioned by the board of the PDA, the Preservation and Development Authority responsible for running the Pike Place Market.

When they'd wanted help with the leases, there had been an interview in her own office followed by several meetings in Renée's office. Then Jo had done the job and presented the significant changes before the full board. She'd quite enjoyed the project in retrospect. There had been many interesting facets to consider.

Now, two months later, the basket and the luncheon.

After a brief debate, she decided to forego the Smoked Salmon and Dungeness Crab Salad in favor of the Bouillabaisse.

They were clearly courting her for something. Her hand froze halfway to her glass of wine as the waiter cleared the escargot plate. They wanted her on the board. It was a terrible, double-edged sword.

All PDA board positions were volunteer. It was for the wealthy semi-retirees who cared heart and soul about Seattle, not for a working woman gearing up for a multi-year litigation on the Alaskan

North Slope. Yet serving on the PDA board also carried immense prestige. The position opened every door among the true movers-and-shakers of Seattle. Those connections would make her career.

Was she willing to trade what little free time she had, plus probably a fair bit more, for the opportunity? Not as if that particular question mattered. She clearly didn't know what to do with free time on the rare occasions she did have it. She'd been naïve enough to think that being on a date with Yuri Andreevich was going to be a constructive, or at least pleasant, use of her non-working hours.

Jo Thompson knew she wasn't exactly "owning the jury" when it came to her personal life.

"MAMA!" Angelo had to blink to be sure. But there stood Maria Amelia Avico Parrano at his open kitchen door as if it were the most natural thing in the world. She'd only been to his restaurant twice, once at last year's opening and again last week for Russell's wedding reception.

He rushed over and gave her a hug.

"You don't need to be so gentle!" She hugged him back as fiercely.

He laughed and squeezed her harder until she'd have laughed if he'd left her enough air.

He finally let her go and just looked at her. "You look wonderful." And she did. She'd always been a beautiful woman. He and Russell used to wonder that some man hadn't hounded her into marriage after Angelo's father died while Angelo was still in the womb.

Her black, curling, shoulder-length hair had started to gray, and she'd let it. Her figure was generous, but looked amazing on a woman barely five-foot-four.

"It's retired life. It agrees with me."

"*Una pensionata?!*" His thoughts blanked.

If Graziella hadn't put a hand on his back at that moment, he'd have fallen to the floor.

"Hi, Mrs. Parrano, so glad to have you back in town." Graziella made sure Angelo would remain on his feet, before taking his mother's hands and kissing both cheeks.

"*Bella bambina,*" she patted Graziella's cheek as if she were a twelve-year old girl and not a twenty-eight-year-old master of the front of house at one of Seattle's finest restaurants. Graziella hurried back to her job without appearing to hurry, one of the traits that had made her Angelo's first hire even before he opened the restaurant. The customers always got the impression she was spending ample time with them, even when it was only a moment.

"Retired?" The word choked on its way out.

"Is an old woman allowed to come in?"

That finally got a laugh out of Angelo's constricted throat. He gathered up the suitcase she'd set in the doorway and led her to the side prep table, not presently in use.

"Are you hungry, Mama?"

"Good boy," she patted his cheek. "Just a little pasta and red sauce to get that airplane food out of my tongue." Her accent slid about him like home. Thirty years since she'd come to America to cook for Russell's parents, the Morgans, and she still frequently mangled idioms, which just added to her charm.

He hurried to the line, glad for a moment to collect himself. A quick glance at the order tickets and then down the line showed that they were running smoothly once again, as if last night's debacle had never occurred.

He made two bowls of pasta, sliced a little Biroldo sausage into the sauce, grated some Asiago on top, and carried them back to the table to join her.

"Retired, Mama?"

"Yes." Then, just to make him crazy he was sure, she forked and twirled up some of the linguini and took her time to chew and swallow. She nodded.

"It is good. A little paprika would bring it to life, but it is good."

"But..." Angelo bit his tongue. Paprika wasn't Italian. It was Hungarian or sometimes smoked for Spanish cuisine, but not Italian.

However, he had never won a seasoning argument with Maria Amelia, and he wouldn't now, so he left it be.

"Retired. Yes. My Julia and John, they have retired and are going to travel for a while. They will probably sell the big house unless Russell wants it. They say they will travel until they find where they want to live."

Angelo couldn't imagine the Morgans selling the sprawling mansion from which four generations of the family had run a global shipping empire.

"Wait, they fired you?" Angelo felt it bind in his gut. They may have helped raise him, and Russell might be Angelo's best friend, but they couldn't fire his mother. She'd been their cook for over thirty years. She'd—

"I quit."

Angelo dropped back on his stool and did his best not to look shocked.

"You…" He couldn't even finish the sentence.

"Angelo, sweetheart." She patted his cheek with almost a slap. "You know like I know, there is the point where three becomes the crowd. They were horrified when I give my notice but they were also relieved. It was *perfetto* solution. To make up for relief, they give me part of company, enough that I can do what I want for many, many years. I also make good savings."

Angelo had to look away for a moment and inspect the line. He could see the smooth flow, the pattern of two dozen lunches moving simultaneously through different stages in the kitchen. Manuel had it well under control.

And he could see Julia and John Morgan making sure his mother was taken care of no matter how long she lived. He'd bet they personally drove their cook to the airport for this visit with her son. He brushed at his eyes. They had taken in a single, pregnant Italian country girl with little English, sent her son to college, and treated her like family. He would find some way to repay them. He couldn't imagine how, but he would. He turned back.

"That's good, Mama. That's good." He took a deep breath to regain his composure. "So, now that you can afford to do anything, what are your plans?"

She merely smiled as they each twirled up a forkful of pasta. He bit down on his, agreeing that perhaps his mother was right about the paprika, the sweet, not the hot. Just enough to accent the Biroldo—

"I'm going to live with you," her eyes twinkled as she paused. Then her smile turned ever so slightly wicked. "And help you cook in your ristorante."

CHAPTER 4

*J*o **had blown off** the rest of the afternoon, what was left of it after a three-hour lunch, and gone to the Eastlake Gym. When Renée Linden did a full-on opening argument, Jo had found herself at some loss to offer a clean and cogent rebuttal. And she still didn't know what her plan or intent was, making it all the more confusing. If there were a pending lawsuit on which the Market needed her assistance, why hadn't she simply laid out the bones of the case. Not that Jo would have time to tackle it, but she'd be glad to give them a little advice and hook them up with someone sharp enough to take down whoever was messing with them.

Jo shoved the pin in ten pounds heavier than normal and began working her triceps on the machine. This wasn't her normal workout time. She and Cassidy typically came in with the other early corporates. Hard workouts to get fired up for a guilt-free day because your workout was already under your belt. Perrin never joined them. A true night owl, if she ever went to the gym it would be at midnight.

The afternoon crowd was an odd mix. A lot of mothers getting in a quick half-hour while the kid was at ballet or wherever. There were also a fair number of guys who looked bruiser strong. Like construction workers off work at three who hadn't gotten enough exercise hefting steel girders and giant laminate beams all day.

Jo decided to just keep her head down and do her workout. And hope that she could somehow make sense of what happened at lunch.

"We're retiring," Renée had explained over the entremets of strawberry sorbet with a dark chocolate flake. "Nathaniel and I are going cruising for a while, then we thought we'd winter over in New Zealand. This is our home, but we decided it was time to travel for some reason other than business."

Renée Linden retiring. That would send shockwaves rippling through the Seattle social firmament. Jo still couldn't make sense of that, even by the time she'd worked through biceps and moved on to abs and obliques.

And Nathaniel Linden leaving Boeing management. He was the President of the custom business-jet division, had practically created it. You want your own personal 737 outfitted for entertaining? He was the man. A six-bedroom 747, with an in-flight movie theater that could seat your family and friends each in their own lounge chair before a ten-foot screen with full-surround sound and a garage in the cargo bay to transport your Maserati? He'd make it happen. It was a small, but exceptionally lucrative division.

That had been enough of a shock for Jo, and she'd wager that neither Pike Place Market nor Boeing were the least bit happy about their pending departures.

Jo counted out ten more reps trying not to think, but that wasn't helping.

Her litigator instincts would bet safe money there was still more up the woman's sleeve. She was notorious for never stopping once she'd set her sights on something.

But Jo couldn't quite identify what she'd been after.

That's when Jo's brain had shut down, plain and simple. It was as fatal a mistake in court as it was at a power lunch, but she couldn't get around it. Researching the woman for a year would not have brought her to that lunch prepared for what was fielded at her with Renée's pleasant conversation and a one-two punch of kindness and gentility.

Without actually saying it out loud, Renée had made it clear that they didn't want Jo on the PDA board, which simplified that decision for her. It had been such a relief that she'd ordered the most decadent Soufflé au Grand Marnier she'd ever eaten.

No. The board had its twelve members. But, Renée let slip ever so casually, that she hadn't yet told the board that she'd be resigning as the Executive Director of the Pike Place Market. Because Jo was the first to know other than her husband, she must keep it to herself until she announced it next week.

Jo let the kick bar for working her quads drop back into position with an ear-ringing clang. Half the people in the weight room turned to see if there'd been an accident. She tried to lift it again so that everything appeared to be normal, but couldn't gather enough neurons sending the message to her legs to do so.

Renée had simply wanted "to let Jo be the first to know. As a professional courtesy." Jo had been so dazzled by the lunch and the conversation that she didn't even see it coming until this moment sitting at the exercise machine, her foot hooked behind a bar that was impossible for her to lift.

Renée wasn't merely retiring, she had already chosen her replacement. And, without once stating it in as many words, she'd informed Jo that she was Renée's first and only pick to replace her. She'd simply used the basket and the luncheon to plant the idea in Jo's mind, and then allowed it to have time to build and age like the Royal Oporto Tawny Port they had with the final cheese and pear course.

Jo blew out a breath as if at the end of a brutal workout and not just her third set of reps. The anointed chosen successor to the great Renée Linden and she'd never seen it coming. Never had a chance to react and refuse or, Jo now identified the heart of Renée's finesse, say anything she might regret later such as laughing hysterically in the woman's face. At least not until she'd had time to think about it.

The woman would have made one heck of an attorney and Jo would hate to argue a case against her in court. She wouldn't stand a chance.

ANGELO HAD TRIED EXHAUSTING himself on the step machine, but though his legs burned, his mind was still churning. He went for the elliptical next and set the program to maximum cardio with heavy resistance. The gym was high above Eastlake Avenue, high enough to look over the buildings across the street and allow its patrons to enjoy views of Lake Union and steep Queen Anne Hill if they tired of the television screens while they worked out. High enough that maybe he could get some perspective on what had just happened to his life.

His mama had come to live with him. That was wonderful. Mostly. He had the room. With the success of the restaurant, he'd moved out of the tiny one bedroom and into a two bedroom with a good kitchen right in the heart of Pioneer Square. He'd thought he'd experiment there, but he never did, he always ended up just going to the restaurant at odd hours to test new dishes there. No matter. He could afford it now.

And the last time he'd had a girl up to his apartment... He looked out the window at Lake Union. A cluster of sailboats were skittering across the surface of the lake that made the north boundary of downtown Seattle. He had to think back a ways to remember. Well, okay, so his mother wouldn't be cramping his style there either.

But in his kitchen? No one was as good as his mama in the kitchen. It didn't matter if they actually were, they still weren't. Paprika in the Biroldo sausage? *Sacrilegio!* Then he'd tried it after she left to go to the apartment and take a nap after the flight. It was exactly right, damn it. She'd be fussing with each of his dishes until he didn't recognize them anymore. And worse, they'd probably be better.

At least she'd never know what happened last night. Just last night? He cast his eyes skyward in prayer that she'd never hear how he'd had a total meltdown less than twenty-four hours before.

Sweat poured off him as the elliptical sent him on another hill climb.

Of course, he knew why he'd made such a mess. Too bad there wasn't a thing he could do about it. It was too late. Jo Thompson would take that meal as a personal affront and never speak to him again. He certainly would in her position. He truly hadn't intended to ruin her date with awful food.

God, he hated working out in the afternoon. He should be worrying about dinner prep, instead he was worrying about his mama. When he worked out in the mornings after he'd done the shopping for the restaurant and before lunch prep began, he used to run into Cassidy and Jo on occasion. Casual waves, polite greetings. But the heat that had coursed through his body each time he saw Jo had become too uncomfortable and he'd shifted his workouts to between lunch and dinner service.

Another hill? The machine had it in for him today. He grabbed his towel and wiped off his face and eyes. They stung with the salt from his sweat.

Another mile the machine warned him. And one last high resistance climb. He was dying here. The only way this could possibly be worse…

He focused on a machine two over from him. The woman climbing onto her elliptical was one he'd recognize in a white-out blizzard even if she were wearing a parka and hood. Though that sure wasn't what she was wearing now. A dark maroon sports bra left her shoulders and midriff gloriously bare. It left so little to the imagination that his blood pressure was threatening to pop. Matching running shorts that exposed one of the nicest lengths of leg he'd ever seen. And lemon yellow sneakers like the laugh line on a great joke.

Jo Thompson looked incredible. And she wasn't looking at him. Either hadn't noticed him or, far more likely, was studiously ignoring his existence.

A hundred percent snub.

There were rules in workout gyms. Everyone was in their own space, doing their own thing. You never messed with that. And it was truly bad form to stare at a woman. His own headphones were spilling out The Boss because who else could help you with your Italian mother better than Springsteen. Born to Run? You betcha!

Jo was probably listening to opera. She sure wasn't looking his way. She must have seen him, had purposely left an empty machine between them, and then ignored him to rub in how angry she was about last night's meal ruining her date.

He slowed his pace. The machine began blinking the "Pedal Faster" sign at him. He slowed to a stop. She was staring up at the TV screens set above the wide glass window with the view of the lake. CNN or the James Stewart film. He couldn't tell which she was watching.

He wiped down the machine and headed for the showers.

One glance back showed him a view he'd never forget, the beautiful and brilliant Jo Thompson running away from him at high speed.

CHAPTER 5

"Hey, Angelo."

Jo noticed that he'd parked his Tuscan-yellow restaurant van with dark blue lettering next to her car's passenger door. Glancing over at her he dropped his keys. He leaned down to fetch them, then stood up under the van's mirror. He whacked his head good and hard, then slid nervelessly out of sight.

She sprinted around her car to see if he was still alive.

He sat on the ground beside his dropped gym bag and keys, with his back against the van's door. His head was between his knees and his hands were wrapped around the back of it. A string of Italian that sounded beautiful, but she'd wager was actually some serious invective, streamed out into the air. She'd studied French, which gave her some of the roots, but the sound of the traffic rolling along on Eastlake Ave. muted his words just enough that she couldn't make them out, which was probably just as well.

"Are you okay?" she squatted beside him.

He raised his head enough to inspect his hands.

"No blood." He patted his head gingerly and looked at his hands again. "Feels like there should be though."

"Here, let me look."

Angelo shrugged, winced at the motion, and acquiesced.

Growing up a fisherman's daughter she'd seen enough bumps, bruises, and cuts to last a lifetime. Also enough to make a quick and probably accurate diagnosis.

"No blood. I can't feel a crack. One hell of a bump rising already though." His hair was still damp from the shower and smelled lightly of shampoo.

"Thanks, I knew that."

He sat up and lay his head back against the van door right on his restaurant's logo. "Ow! *Merda!*" He leaned his head back between his knees and reclasped his hands over his head.

Jo wanted to laugh. She knew it wasn't seemly, but it bubbled up inside her anyway. He looked so sad and helpless. She took a deep, pre-jury summation breath, then another and steadied down quickly enough.

She set her gym bag on the ground beside her own car door and sat on it to wait with him until she was sure he was okay. The brutal hour-long workout had done nothing to clear her head of Renée's offer. She'd focused her mind and driven her body until every muscle screamed, but she still didn't know what she was feeling. Even as she waited for Angelo to recover, she could feel her muscles stiffening. She was going to be seriously sore tonight.

Cassidy really needed to get back from her honeymoon. Jo needed a sounding board at the moment and found herself a bit distressed to realize that she really didn't have anyone else.

Angelo sat up more slowly this time, keeping his head well clear of the door.

"How are you feeling?"

He squeezed his eyes closed for a moment in a hard wince, then opened them wide as if trying to make them focus once again.

"Okay, I think." He shrugged. "Mostly like a total klutz." He made a gesture slapping the back of one hand against the other, as if running into a wall. He started to stand.

Jo rested a restraining hand on his arm as he let himself slide the two inches back to the ground.

"Oh! Maybe I'll just sit here for a few more minutes. You should go though. I'm okay. Don't let me keep you here."

"No, that's fine. I want to make sure you're okay."

He nodded his acceptance but didn't say anything more. He closed his eyes and rested his head back very tentatively.

Jo checked to make sure he was still conscious in case he'd actually concussed himself, but his body hadn't gone limp, simply quiet. She'd somehow forgotten how incredibly handsome he was. His short hair, as dark as her own, curled foolishly about his ears compared to her own dead straight fall. His skin glowed with the warmth of a tan from the Italian beaches, though she knew he'd grown up in New York City. Broad shoulders but trim build. And she'd seen how fit he was when they used to run into each other during workouts, though it had been a while.

It was his hands though, presently hanging limply from where his wrists rested on each raised knee, that were his best features. They were slender for a man, but strong from cooking. She'd never actually seen him cook but could easily imagine the exacting confidence and incredible speed they could apply to each task.

"You're speaking to me." Angelo had opened his eyes slit-wide against the sun shining on his face and was studying her.

"No," she worried again about his head perhaps being injured. She hadn't said anything.

"You aren't?" He pointed at her as if there was some question who he meant even though only the two of them sat there.

"I wasn't. Now I am."

"Why not?"

Jo huffed out a breath. "Where did this conversation go astray? I didn't say anything before. Is your hearing okay?"

"My hearing is fine. I'm not hallucinating." He held up two fingers squinted at them as if trying desperately to tell how many really were there. "I thought you weren't speaking to me, as in never again."

"Oh. Why would I do that?"

"Last night's dinner."

Jo blushed. She was pretty sure that it had all been her fault. "Look, I'm really sorry about that."

"What? No, I am. I'm the one who served that food. If you can call it that." Angelo scrubbed his hands over his face. "Thank the great *Patrono* in Heaven that Mama wasn't there. She'd have murdered me."

Jo remembered the charming woman from the wedding. She barely came up to Angelo's shoulder and kept bursting out with how proud she was of him. She couldn't stop talking about how handsome he was, how beautiful his restaurant was, how amazing the food her son had served tasted. And it truly had been amazing. His mother had also clearly read every review and followed every award. Her joy of her son radiated straight from her heart.

Several times Jo had to bite back the envy burning deep in her gut at having a mother like that. A loving parent who cared about how you did, and supported it.

But she was also clearly very Italian. If she knew Angelo had served a meal like last night's…

"Yes, I expect she would have murdered you but good. Thankfully for you, she's three thousand miles away."

All Angelo did was groan and put his head back into his hands.

"Are you okay?"

"No. But that's not your fault."

"Well, last night, I suspect, was." She knew it was. Angelo had been giving her such total puppy-dog eyes at the wedding, it was impossible to miss. Then she'd flaunted Yuri at him without intending to. She might not want to be with the man, but she should be more considerate of his feelings.

"Again, I'm sorry about that."

Angelo raised his head and looked at her. She could see the question clearly and was relieved that he had the decency not to ask. So, she answered it anyway.

"Yuri is a business acquaintance who thought he was more than that. I disabused him of that misconception last night, much to his distress. He should be back in Alaska by now."

"Oh. Good." He slid a hand across his mouth as if to erase the last word. "Uh, I am sorry about the meal."

"That's okay. It made a point of Yuri's shortcomings, a matter I might not have noticed otherwise."

"If you need any assistance in that, you know, getting some guy to show their shortcomings, just bring him by. I'll be glad to ruin another meal for you."

"I'll keep that in mind," she made her tone as dry as possible.

Angelo laughed and she joined in. It felt good. It felt friendly as if they'd each managed to apologize for last night without having to apologize.

He struggled to his feet and she helped him up. He didn't sway much, any more than anyone else who'd rapped their head hard.

"I'm fine. Just need some aspirin. Then I'll be fine."

Jo dug into her gym bag and found her emergency stash and a water bottle.

Angelo took them gratefully.

"Thanks, Jo. And again, I'm sorry about last night."

"Me too. You sure you're okay to drive?"

He nodded and only winced a little at the unwarranted motion. He started to reach for his bag and keys, but she got them before he had to bend over. He'd have a screaming headache by now at the very least.

"Thanks." He had his van's door open.

"Do you want to work out together sometime this weekend?" Now where had that come from? Was she really so needy for company? No, she was simply that desperate for anything familiar in a world that contained something as crazy as Renée's offer.

Angelo looked as surprised as she felt.

"I, uh, usually go for a bike ride on Saturday morning. My sous chef does lunch and we both do dinner. Do you ride?"

"Sure. Loop of the lake?"

"That sounds great."

Jo felt a little manipulative. It was her standard training ride, but it was also a long ride. Yes, she had an ulterior motive, that somewhere along the way they'd be able to discuss Renée's offer to take over the management of Pike Place Market. She needed a sounding board so badly.

But it wasn't just an ulterior motive, it would also be nice to have someone to ride with. Cassidy was a runner and Perrin looked at exercise as a disease contracted by the undeserving as punishment for a wicked former life.

"I'm done shopping for the restaurant by seven."

"Perfect. We can start the ride while the day's still cool. Meet on the trail under the Fremont Bridge at half past?"

With a shared smile and nod they climbed into their cars.

ANGELO BUZZED through the morning shopping.

Or he tried to.

But his mother had insisted on coming along. When he was selecting a long side of swordfish from the iced counter at the Pike Place Market fish vendor, his mother was chatting with Henry.

As he chose only the most perfect avocados and artichokes, she'd found out that Uli had two children and a third one on the way though it wasn't showing yet. At least not that he could politely see.

Maria Amelia greeted the bread baker in passable French, and she stopped them for a cup of espresso and to split a morning baklava at Mister D's Greek Delicacies even though he wasn't really open and serving yet.

Angelo barely tasted it and seared his mouth on the hot coffee.

It was past seven, almost seven thirty by the time he got back to the apartment and changed. Then Russell's cat, Nutcase, still thinking she was kitten-sized, had decided Angelo's hand was an invader from deep space resulting in a long bloody scratch that Angelo had wiped on his bike shorts without thinking, so he'd had to change again and get a Band-Aid.

His mother stopped him in the hallway and he almost exploded with frustration.

"You go have a nice ride. She must be very pretty."

That stopped him cold.

She patted his cheek. "I am only retired. It does not make me blind, *mio figlio.* I hope she is as pretty as that nice girl at the wedding. I see you later at the ristorante." She held the door open and shooed him out with his bike before he could respond.

Angelo had planned to ride the couple miles to meet Jo, now he tossed his bicycle and helmet into the van and sped through the early-morning streets. His nerves may have made him squeeze a couple of red lights on the way.

He found a spot only a few blocks away and almost worked up a sweat sprinting down to where the Burke-Gilman Trail cut under the Fremont Bridge. He was worried that she'd have given up and gone without him, but saw her right away.

He'd thought she looked amazing in workout clothes at the gym. In the warm morning, she wore shorts and a cycling jersey made of the most amazing, brilliant crimson form-fitting Lycra. They covered more, but hid not the least little curve. The dark, wrap-around Oakley shades only served to make her look even more fearsome.

You will speak to her normally. Like a normal person. Angelo admonished himself as he rolled up to where she was stretching her hamstrings with a heel resting on the back of a park bench. A little park was all that separated the paved bike-and-running trail from the Fremont Cut where Lake Union flowed down to the sea.

Already, pleasure boats were working their way along the cut. They were heading for the Chittenden Locks which would let them out onto Puget Sound. He and Jo would be heading the other way. Along north Lake Union, through the University of Washington, and then north beside Lake Washington they'd follow the Burke-Gilman for fifteen miles before turning south.

"Sorry I'm late," Angelo managed against a dry throat. Too glad that he hadn't missed her, which would just give him a new offense to worry about. "My mother…" He cut himself off.

"Is she okay?"

"Sure." She was fine. He was the one going quietly mad.

Jo faced him with those power glasses. "You ready to ride or do you need to warm up a bit?"

"I'm good to go." He'd take his morning shopping at Pike Place Market as his warm up. A slow start and he'd be fine.

Then he looked at her bike and whistled in appreciation. It was an electric-red Rodriguez custom-built road bike with Dura-ace shifters and a lay-down bar. There was no way in hell he was going to keep up with her. The machine was almost as hot as its owner.

"I know. I know. The bike is ridiculous for a rider like me, but it feels amazing. I feel fast just looking at it, even if I'm not. A friend told me it was the best, so Cassidy insisted that's what I should buy. I don't like buying things twice."

After the first mile or so of weaving among the local joggers, they rode clear of the city foot traffic. *Okay, I can do this without making a complete idiot of myself.*

Jo had led the first half mile which had given him a chance to get his legs warmed up and his heart rate under control. Following just a bike length behind Jo was immensely distracting. Her hair flew behind her like a banner from underneath her helmet. Her fine figure was only accentuated by the cycling position and her long legs spun quickly with the evidence of long practice and training. It was enough to make him overheated even without the exercise.

There was the steadiness of a practiced rider about her. Clean strokes, fast spin, and a quiet body position on the long flats of the Burke-Gilman.

At the half-mile mark, she swung to the center of the trail, letting him zip past her on the right side. In his peripheral vision he could see her tuck in close behind him. Now it was his turn to take on the extra work of blocking the wind, letting her rest in the slipstream of his draft. It wasn't a skill for beginners, but she held her position perfectly, her own front tire perhaps a foot behind his rear one. He thought about taking a full mile, but that could look as if he was trying to impress her. He thought of it as being gentlemanly but decided that discretion was the better part of valor and swung aside and let her pass after he'd led a half-mile matching hers.

They rapidly fell into an easy rhythm of alternating lead and draft, spinning along the shore of Lake Washington and its stately homes. The trail, dappled with cool shade and warm sun passed by more easily than it ever had before.

PAST JUANITA PARK, Jo had the lead when they hit the hill. She down-shifted and began the grind up the hill. It was a long slog. At this speed there was no advantage to drafting, this was just about low gears and a lot of spinning. Angelo dropped back a bit and they each focused on their own climb.

She'd woken so sore this morning that she'd almost called Angelo to cancel. Might have, if she'd had his number. She'd arrived only moments before he did, and she half hoped she'd missed him. But now with the miles rolling beneath them, she was glad she'd come. The ride had loosened her muscles and been beautiful so far.

Though, her muscles reminded her as she climbed, the ride was barely half over. A loop around Lake Washington ran forty-five to fifty miles depending on which exact route you took.

And now, for the two miles of the longest climb in the route, she'd just hunker down and think of something else while her legs earned their keep and knocked off the excess calories from yesterday's lunch, and the cheese, salami, and wine dinner she'd fixed from the depths of the Pike Place Market basket.

Her mind had shifted to a place of denial. Even if she had heard the unstated offer correctly and Renée was offering her the position at Pike Place Market, why on Earth would Jo be interested? The last big Alaska case had made her partner in one of the country's elite maritime law firms. That had earned her not only a very nice salary, but also a significant share of the law firm's yearly profits. She wasn't the most junior partner in some thousand-attorney firm, she was the fourth partner in a very elite, very specialized, very highly paid boutique firm. And the North Slope case could easily set her up for many years to come, assuming she won and didn't go off buying jet planes or something equally stupid.

Yes, it would be several years of every waking minute, but she could do that. Her father had just cruised through life, the perfect counterexample. The weather was rough, he stayed in his shack, at least until the bar opened. If he didn't feel like fishing that week, he left the boat tied up. Yes, it had probably extended his existence, but was it worth extending? He was lazy, his wife had left him before Jo's first memory, and his daughter had been gone by sixteen, too young emotionally for college but with the grades and scholarship to get out and not give a damn about the consequences.

Executive Director of Pike Place Market couldn't pay a quarter of what she was making now, or a tenth of what she would make. It wasn't even a reasonable offer. It made no sense.

So clearly, she shifted down another gear as her legs tired, she had misunderstood Renée Linden's unspoken message. Perhaps she was asking Jo to help her select the next Executive Director, maybe head up the search committee which would have good prestige and connections in its own right. Or maybe Renée wanted to make sure she'd be willing to work for the new director on legal issues despite her high profile cases. She'd be glad to, if she had the time. Her offices were at the edge of the Market, she ate most lunches there, and enjoyed doing part of her shopping in the various stalls.

She heard Angelo puffing up beside her. She shifted to the right edge of the shoulder, if he wanted to pass her on a hill climb she had no ego about it. At least not until the moment his wheel edged one inch past even, then she'd upshift and dust his behind if she could find the reserves.

Jo glanced over as he pulled up beside her. She knew she was perspiring, the band inside her helmet was barely holding back the tidal wave of sweat from her eyes.

Angelo looked positively fresh, as if they'd just spent the ten minutes on the flat, or coasting downhill. He'd be very easy to hate in this moment.

"I'll meet you in the park at the foot of the hill. I'll catch up with you."

Before she could even nod, he dropped back and was gone. She twisted her head and saw him turn into the parking lot of a grocery store right before the crest of the hill.

She considered circling back, but then she'd be stopping with the last hundred yards uphill still to go. Screw that. She wasn't going to intimate that she needed a rest in order to beat this hill.

Jo rolled over the highest point of the whole ride and began adding back gears.

She hit the downhill slope going fifteen miles an hour. By mid-descent, she was in a high gear, spinning hard in a full racing tuck, and going fifteen over the twenty-five mile-an-hour speed limit. Praying for no police, she hammered down the hill. Fifteen minutes of grinding work uphill, turned into a three-minute flash down into the heart of Kirkland and straight on into the park.

At nine on a Saturday morning the waterfront park was already busy with professionals and families. The small park jutted out into Lake Washington so that it was surrounded on three sides by water. Early cyclists and joggers packed the park. The shoppers at the boutique shops which wrapped around the bay wouldn't be hitting for another couple of hours.

She rolled out to the very point, past the gazebo, and dropped to the grass.

A quick check on her cycle computer made her do a double-take. They'd chopped fifteen minutes off her best previous time. She wouldn't admit it to Angelo, but she'd driven herself up the climb from Juanita Beach like never before. The cardio settings said that she'd killed off the worst of yesterday's excesses and was making a good dent in whatever ones she'd find for today.

"Chocolate or vanilla?"

She looked up at Angelo as he pulled two supermarket-freezer ice cream cones from the back pocket of his shirt and presented them with a flourish for her consideration. She didn't ask, she just snatched the chocolate one.

He settled beside her as they both peeled the paper wrappers.

When she sank her teeth into it, the cold smacked her overheated body. This wasn't some healthy, demure dish of frozen yogurt. This was a high calorie, fat-turbocharged treat of chocolate and nuts on cheap chocolate ice cream in a really crappy wafer cone, just like all good pre-wrapped freezer cones.

It tasted so fantastically good.

"Oh. My. God!" Her mouth still half full of ice cream. She turned and kissed Angelo right on the lips. "This is wonderful."

It was only as she faced back out over the lake and took a second bite, despite the possible risk of serious brain freeze from eating it too fast, that she realized what she'd done.

Two ways to deal with it. Ignore it or risk a sly look from behind her dark sunglasses to gauge his reaction.

Her brain chose a third. She turned and shot him a chocolate-laced grin, then stuck her tongue out at him.

He laughed and, much to her relief, did the same through vanilla-covered lips.

CHAPTER 6

*A*ngelo's legs were shaking by the time he got back to his condo in Pioneer Square. A hot shower, a high-carb lunch, and then he'd have some chance of surviving Saturday night service. He'd never ridden the Loop of the Lake so fast, or had so much fun doing it. He felt simultaneously exhausted and supercharged.

They'd barely spoken during the three-hour ride, no way to really do it while riding. But it was as if they didn't need to. He never knew what to say to someone so smart and beautiful as Jo Thompson anyway, but doing the ride together had been easy and fun.

In the park they had eaten their cones and laughed about the Thursday night disaster. Who knew he'd ever be able to find the least morsel of humor in the situation, but Jo somehow made the impossible possible.

His mother wasn't at the condo, maybe she was out exploring Seattle. He'd have to remember to take fresh clothes into the bathroom with him. Thankfully his new place had two baths, so they could each have their own. There'd be at last some privacy.

He was halfway through his shower when he remembered where his van was parked. At the Fremont Bridge.

Angelo stuck his head out of shower to check the clock on the bathroom counter.

Great. Just great.

Not only did it mean getting back on his bike, but by the time he got there, if the Seattle Police were operating at their usual level of efficiency, he'd have a parking ticket as well.

FORTY-SEVEN DOLLARS.

Angelo was out the cost of a good bottle of wine and now, as he tried to park behind his restaurant, the one space reserved for his own use had been taken by some useless tourist. Well, he was going to get their behind towed and cost them a serious chunk of change and irritation. Perhaps it would mitigate some of his own.

But it wasn't some tourist. It was his own car, parked in the van's space.

This was Pike Place Market on a Saturday afternoon. There'd be nowhere to park for blocks around that didn't cost at least half as much as his parking ticket. The traffic was suicidal and it took him forever to escape.

He drove down to Pioneer Square and pulled into the secure garage, hauled his bike upstairs, and then set out on his usual walk back up the hill. By the time he was done, it had taken him almost two hours to reach his own restaurant just six blocks from his condo.

Okay, the bike ride had been good. He'd stay focused on that. He had finally found an interest in common with Jo and they'd had a good time. That ranked as a good date. Didn't it?

He'd like to have discussed his mother descending on him. It would be nice to talk it through with her. The thought surprised him a little. He would have liked to hear Jo's opinion. Angelo wagered that it would have been well considered and thoughtful. But the subject hadn't come up and then she'd blanked his brain.

He'd been too surprised to react to the chocolaty kiss, and was glad she'd given him an excuse to not do so by sticking out her tongue at him. If he'd had a moment to think about it, he'd have found some way to screw it up. Instead, he'd laughed at the momentary image of the ever so proper attorney Ms. Thompson sticking her tongue out at a jury if she didn't like their decision.

Angelo walked down the half block of Pike Street that led from First Avenue into the heart of the Market. The uneven brick was as packed with people as the sidewalks. Woe to a tourist stupid enough to attempt to drive on this street. He ignored the fact that he'd fallen into just that trap an hour before while attempting to park his van.

It was warm and sunny. The gelato merchant's success was evident in dozens of people's hands, bright globes of pure, glistening color perched on thin cones stood out among the kaleidoscope of summer attire. Bags held everything from fish and produce to soaps and trinkets. A woman wearing strike-you-dead-with-lust perfume brushed by him, her arm full of dahlias, her hair a bright chop of blond and chartreuse.

Left Hand Books was so crowded that people were visible through the window, doing the very slow shuffle step among the shelves. Henry shot him a friendly salute from the big fish stall right before flinging a twelve-pound salmon through the air toward the cashier for wrapping and sale.

He tossed a couple of dollars to Uli at Frank's Quality Produce and snagged a basket of strawberries to eat as he headed along.

At Mr. D's he gave the rest of the strawberries to Demetrios and his family and turned up Post Alley careful not to look in the Sur La Table display windows. He always heard tourists complaining that they, "really didn't need anything more for the kitchen, but how could they resist" as they staggered out with the overstuffed trademark brown and maroon bags. For a chef, the place was a nightmare. Add on the commercial restaurant and Pike Place Market vendor discounts, and the place was beyond dangerous and often downright lethal.

He was, despite his best efforts, being drawn by the glistening copper Zabaglione pot in the window. His were getting pretty battered with use and some nights having only two caused timing problems.

That's when he noticed the snarl of people up near his restaurant. At first he hoped it was the Perennial Tea Room across Post Alley, but it wasn't. He hustled along and almost got clipped by a car as he crossed Stewart Street.

The day, delightful and warm a moment before, slapped him with a latent heat that had him sweating. People were milling around beneath the discreet Angelo's Tuscan Hearth sign. Another disaster.

He'd apparently dodged the first crisis. No bad reviews had come of the Notorious Thursday Night Fiasco, as Jo had named it. But by the size of this crowd he was too late to recover from whatever was happening this time. They were between services, yet the crowd was massive. Kitchen fire. Or worse.

He resisted the urge to shove his way through the crowd, instead nudging and begging-his-pardon through the claustrophobic horde toward his own door. He'd almost made it inside when he spotted his mother.

She stood with a great smile on her face. Clad in a floppy sunhat, she wore a floaty blue summer dress with a deep cleavage that would have been totally inappropriate on a woman of her age if it didn't look so good on her. A shawl of nearly transparent floral chiffon graced her shoulders. Daisies, she'd always had a soft spot for daisies. Her dark hair flowed to her shoulders and a tray of bruschetta balanced on one of her hands.

His avocados and artichokes.

He slid up beside her and gauged the crowd. They weren't upset. They were smiling. Laughing, chatting, bantering with his mother, and enjoying themselves. They formed a line into the restaurant.

That was it. Service had crashed and was far too slow, and his mother was taking care of entertaining the crowd while they waited.

"Oh, there you are honey. Everyone!" She called out to the crowd and conversations hushed. "This here, he is my son. This food, it is his. Isn't it wonderful?"

A round of applause burst forth that didn't make any sense for people stuck waiting in line. Why would there be a line at two in the afternoon anyway? There were always some patrons in the restaurant even on Saturday afternoons, but never a line out the door between the two main services.

"I think," Maria Amelia leaned close to him and spoke softly, "that perhaps Manuel would like it to have you in his kitchen." She stuffed a bruschetta in his open mouth. "Close your mouth, chew like a good boy, now *tu vai!*"

He went.

EVEN AS ANGELO chewed and went, the flavors began to bloom in his mouth. The lush richness of the avocado, the smooth balance of artichoke heart, a sliver of lemon-cooked swordfish and a chiffonade of fresh basil on toasted, thin-sliced Ciabatta bread was remarkable. It unfolded and unraveled, revealing layer upon layer, leaving him desperate for more.

"Angelo!" Manuel called out as he entered the kitchen. The man practically wept with joy. "Hurry, an apron, three orders of the Cioppino and I will marry you and bear your children."

Angelo grabbed an apron and three bowls. With a rescue operation underway, you didn't ask questions. After five orders of the Cinghiale, braised boar meat over pasta, and a half dozen more of the Stuffed Chicken Picatta al modo di Angelo's, he began being able to see the flow of orders. There were no holdups. In fact, he'd rarely seen the team move food more quickly.

"What's the problem?" He tossed some more pasta with olive oil as a bed for his Braised Venison in Marmora Red Sauce.

"The problem is your mother," Manuel gasped out between commands to the grillardin to refire the duck breast and start another three orders of swordfish.

Angelo really didn't need this. Was his mother going to destroy him?

"She saw the lunch rush fading," Manuel talked between plating orders and yelling for Graziella to put some hustle on it even though she already was. "It was a good one for June, especially on a day when most people want to stay outside in the fine weather instead of sitting in a gourmet restaurant. Next thing I know, she takes a tureen of that chowder we were making for dinner, and a couple dozen spoons out the door. Before I can breathe, the restaurant, she is packed solid. When that ran out, she makes this bruschetta. You tasted it? *Estupendo,* eh? And she is gone out on the street again giving that away too. We've never had a Saturday like this one."

Chowder gone. He needed to start a soup base for dinner service to replace that. He yelled for Marko. The boy came running, wiping the soap suds from his hands. Angelo dug into his wallet and pulled out whatever cash he had.

"Go. Buy green beans, baby ones, none bigger around than a chopstick, more artichokes, fresh parsley, and another thirty pounds of swordfish. Go, don't gawk at me, *tu vai.*" It felt good to order someone else to jump on it.

Marko went at a dead run.

"If they're out of swordfish," Angelo yelled after him, "tell Henry you need twice that in fresh tuna."

"Hope he heard you," Manuel muttered. "Now I need at least a dozen more batches of fresh pasta dough. Go." Angelo knew better than to mess with the flow sliding through and around Manuel's station.

He went.

CHAPTER 7

*J*o *answered the pounding* on her door. Only one person ever pounded on her door, and never like this. She found herself near to running across the charcoal deep-pile carpet of her condo and yanking the door open.

Perrin practically collapsed into her arms. She looked as if she'd been in a battle and lost badly.

"What happened? Are you okay? Should I call the police?"

"Oh," Perrin leaned on her and allowed herself to be led into the apartment. "Thank God you're home. Take off your clothes."

From anyone other than Perrin, Jo would have been offended and made a sharp riposte. But with Perrin things always made sense, eventually.

"You look awful. Can I get you some food or something?" Her slender frame was actually weaving with the effort to remain standing. Her hair was a frantic mess and she wore no makeup, revealing an abnormally sallow complexion. Both were so unusual for Perrin that Jo again checked her friend for cuts and bruises. Perrin was always immaculate in how she presented herself to the world. Outrageous, often, but always perfectly presented and attired.

Perrin braced herself against Jo's cherrywood coat rack almost taking herself and Jo's coats to the floor. "I'll be fine once you try this on." She wiggled a white dress bag she held slung over one shoulder that Jo hadn't noticed.

"When was the last time you slept?"

Perrin waved one of her fine-fingered hands. "I dunno. Cassie's wedding? Maybe a couple nights ago? What day is this? Never mind, don't care." She shoved Jo toward her bedroom. "Now go get naked and try this on. And if you look in the mirror before I tell you, you're dead."

Jo started down the hall toward her bedroom. Perrin followed close behind leaving palm prints in the middle of the glass of more than one of the framed pictures as she stumbled into walls. When Jo reached out to steady her, Perrin simply slapped her hands aside and nudged her along.

Once in the bedroom, Perrin hung the dress bag on the back of the door and collapsed onto the quilted white bedspread. But in seconds she was back on her feet and vibrating with energy as she opened the bag.

"Turn around and get undressed."

Jo moved to close the curtains.

"Forget the curtains. You're like a gazillion stories up in the air. No one can see you unless they have a monster telescope like on top of one of those mountains, and if they do, all they're going to see is how gorgeous you are."

Jo closed the curtains anyway, she had her standards, no matter how much Perrin enjoyed pushing them. Once they were closed, she shed the sweatshirt and pants.

Perrin rolled her eyes. "The woman is home alone and she wears a bra. You're crazy, you know that? Lose it."

Normally Jo would have argued at least for form's sake, but Perrin looked so wound up and simultaneously so fragile, that Jo simply obeyed.

"Damn but it sucks that we're both straight."

Jo refused to blush at Perrin's catty remark.

"Okay, close your eyes."

"You're kidding."

"Jo-o!" Perrin stamped her foot.

Jo closed her eyes and heard the zipper on the bag open the rest of the way. It was hard to resist peeking but she managed by thinking instead of the map of the North Slope continental shelf and the implications of melting ice access to oil and mineral resources.

"Arms out."

She held them out and cool fabric slid over them, the sensual slickness of silk.

"Okay, now up."

She raised her arms and the fabric slid down over her face and shoulders. She'd worn a lot of Perrin's creations over the years. Back in college the results could only occasionally be conferred with a label better than "interesting." But a decade later, "good" was a low standard and "exceptional" had almost become the norm with the occasional "sensational" like Cassidy's wedding dress and the two bridesmaid dresses.

Jo did her best to ignore the way the fabric wrapped around her like a full-body kiss. She hadn't been made so aware of every inch of her skin in a long time.

Perrin began tugging and adjusting, settling the dress into place.

"Can I look yet?"

"Don't you dare!" Perrin's voice was half shout, half mumble as though her mouth was full. Jo would bet it was, at least partly. She'd seen Perrin dozens of times, radiating near-mad intensity during a fitting, with her fingers flying deftly over the fabric, and a bunch of pins clamped in the corner of her mouth.

"Okay," more of a mumble. Then her voice cleared as she stuck the spare pins back into a cushion, or perhaps into Jo's bedspread. She'd best check before lying down tonight. "I'm almost there. I got the idea when I saw that celery green on you last weekend."

Jo typically wore black powersuits, but it had been nice to wear such a pretty dress for the wedding. It had been so pretty that it had made her feel almost confident as a woman.

"There, okay," Perrin turned her slightly and pulled her half a step sideways. "You really should be wearing heels, but you hate them so I designed it so that I can make it work without. I'll do that later, though your legs in heels would be positively amazing. Open your eyes."

Jo did. Perrin had placed her directly in front of the full-length, beveled mirror that covered her closet door. But she didn't recognize the woman reflected there.

Perrin came up beside her, scooped up a handful of Jo's hair and held it up before turning to inspect the result in the mirror.

"I thought your hair should be up, but now I'm not sure." She let it down again and brushed it back off Jo's bare shoulders.

"What's this?" the far away voice was all Jo could manage. The floor-length dress started at her feet like the palest blue sea foam, with a thousand tiny overlaps of fabric. The pattern built and strengthened as it flowed around her hips, somehow accenting their womanly curves while making them appear trim. From there it bloomed upward, wrapping her breasts in the palest-blue waves, as gentle as they were bountiful. A slit did indeed reveal some leg, but ended just above the knee allowing the dress to cling, but allowing the wearer to move about freely and look dazzling as well.

Perrin was rummaging through the jewelry on Jo's dressing table, probably turning it into a hopeless tangle. She returned with the strand of Jo's mother's pearls, the only thing she had from the woman she couldn't remember. Her dad claimed that she'd left them behind by accident, but she doubted that once she learned it had been his wedding gift to her mother. Perrin scoffed after a moment and tossed them carelessly onto the bedspread.

Next the gold chain and dangling orca she'd worn for the date with Yuri.

"Almost." Perrin tossed that on the bed as well.

She finally held a silver chain bearing a sparkling silver filigree medallion with an amethyst-colored backing that Jo had loved and bought, but never found anything to wear it with.

"Oh my God." Jo was finally able to see the breathtaking woman in the mirror. "You made...my wedding dress?"

Perrin's reflection finished fastening the chain then peeked over Jo's shoulder. Her face was pixie bright.

"Am I good, or am I good?"

Jo could only gaze in amazement. "No, you're way better than good."

"Wait until you see the back."

Perrin spun her around and grabbed a hand mirror from the table scattering a couple of necklaces and an earring to the carpet.

It felt as if nothing were there and Jo was worried about having to let Perrin down gently. She wasn't the sort to wear a risqué dress, especially not to a wedding, most certainly not to her own, and Perrin should know that by now.

But when she had the hand mirror aligned with the one behind her, Jo could only shake her head in amazement. The line of the dress followed the line of her hair. With her hair down, there would be constant flashes of bare shoulder and glimpses of skin, but it was somehow, impossibly, demure as well. The conservative shape of the rest of the back balanced the piece perfectly and made her look impossibly enticing.

In profile, well, her chest was too big, but it didn't look like it in this dress. The dress design accented without embellishing.

She turned to hug Perrin, "It's incredible!"

With their arms around each other, they turned to look back in the mirror.

"It's just incredible. I've never looked so beautiful." She rose up on her toes and considered. Maybe she'd wear heels on this one occasion.

Perrin looked simply radiant. "I've also got ideas for Cassie's and my dress to go with it."

That brought Jo back to reality, which was an almost crushing blow. She'd felt giddy, as if she were flying. And had now crash-landed in a dark swamp.

"Uh, Perrin. There's just one problem."

"What? What is it?" she began inspecting the perfect dress for some hidden flaw.

"Perrin," she had to take her friend by her shoulders to stop her and make her to focus on Jo's face.

"What?"

"I'm not getting married."

"Oh," Perrin shrugged that away as being of no consequence. "Is that all? That's not a problem."

Jo stared at her. "Not a problem? You give me the absolutely perfect wedding dress and now I have no reason to wear it? That's a big problem in my book."

"Phft," Perrin waved a hand again and turned them both back to admire the dazzling woman in the mirror. "With a dress like this in your closet? No worries. You'll find someone to fall madly in love with you, just so you get to wear it."

"Years, Perrin. I've still got years of my career before I'm ready. I'm going to be commuting to northern Alaska for at least two years on my next case for goodness sake."

"Never underestimate the power of a really good dress," her friend insisted cheerfully.

As always, it was pointless to argue with Perrin. Jo looked in the mirror again. One thing Perrin had right, it was a really, really good dress.

PERRIN SLEPT through breakfast and lunch. Jo had stuffed her into the shower and then tucked her into bed in the guest room. She'd only allowed herself to sneak in twice to make sure her friend was actually still breathing.

It felt like being back in college, back when Perrin was so wild that she and Cassidy had often taken shifts making sure she'd be okay after her latest escapade. This time, thankfully, it was just exhaustion. Perrin had stayed straight and sober since she and Cassidy did an intervention during junior year, except for the occasional gal's night out, but that was nothing compared to the bouts with alcohol poisoning Perrin had been habitually pursuing.

By late afternoon Jo sat in the living room doing her best to pretend she was interested in the latest Grisham novel. Normally his legal thrillers kept her riveted, she had every one in hardback, a few of them even signed, but not now.

The problem was that everything was in churn. And the dress was not the least of her problems. Last night, after she'd made sure Perrin was finally settled, she had returned to her bedroom and locked the door. She'd carefully brushed out her hair, knowing it was her best feature, and slipped back into the dress. This time she selected a pair of dark-blue Kate Spade heels making her several inches taller.

She'd studied the woman in the mirror carefully. She remained a mystery. Jo could still smell the stench of fish that had permeated the home of her youth. It had seemed to waft down the high school hallways behind her and no matter how she scrubbed in the shower, she'd never been clear of it.

Her early physical development had drawn the boys, but she'd built up a barrier knowing that the smell followed her. She'd heard the whispers of "arrogant" and "stuck up" and each time they had cut out a piece of her soul.

But she simply couldn't stand what someone would think if they really knew, so she did her best to never let the pain show. She trusted no boys and very few girls and had instead dedicated her every waking minute to getting out of Ketchikan High and Ketchikan, Alaska. Valedictorian, straight four-point-oh student, Native American heritage, a cakewalk for scholarships. She'd left and never looked back. When the call came from Debby Rowe for the tenth year reunion, Jo had asked her as a personal favor to please lose Jo's contact information somewhere dark and obscure.

By the time she'd arrived at Vassar at sixteen, she'd built a barrier so high that none could pierce it. Or so she'd thought. Her roommate, Cassidy Knowles, had been the perfect match, both of them quiet, both younger than others, both dying to get away from somewhere.

What would have happened to them if Perrin Williams hadn't entered their lives was anyone's guess.

She and Cassidy had still been gently probing each other as new roommates by comparing favorite high school classes, when a wild girl had stumbled into their room. "I'm Perrin! Right across the hall!" She had hair in five colors and a henna tattoo that ran up one arm and down the other, "and right over my left breast. Wanna see?" she'd cheerfully begun hauling the hem of her blouse out of her skirt's waistband. Despite her awful background, that she'd shared much more reluctantly, she'd consciously chosen to be a positive person, albeit with an often manic intensity.

For reasons Jo had never been able to unravel, the three of them had been inseparable for the four years following that moment.

Without Cassidy and Perrin in her life, would the woman in the mirror, wearing the dress made of pale blue ocean waves and passion, be staring back at her? Probably not.

Without Cassidy's heart and Perrin's deep-seated joy, Jo would have continued on some perfect track and married some New York stockbroker who would never be as smart as she was.

The woman in the mirror didn't look like Jo. She had a confidence that Counselor Thompson only found in the courtroom wearing black powersuits. She didn't recognize the feminine form that stood before her, constantly running her hands over the fine stitching and soft shapes that encircled her form.

Who was this woman?

What decisions would she make that the Counselor would never even consider?

Jo had no idea, but she watched the woman in the mirror for a long time before taking off the dress and putting it away again.

She'd been careful not to look in the mirror before going to bed.

PERRIN STUMBLED out of the guest bedroom in the early evening as the sun headed toward the Olympic Mountains. It filled Jo's apartment with the warm oranges and reds she so loved. She'd decorated with her west-facing view and this time of day in mind, white walls and neutral carpets so that the changing light of outdoors would fill the room.

Perrin had clearly raided Jo's closet with what should be amusing results but were fetching instead. She'd folded over one of Jo's billowing floral skirts and trapped it about her trim waist with a belt leaving the waistband to flop over the belt. The Vassar college t-shirt, rather than being grossly too large, slid off both of her shoulders leaving a broad expanse of bare skin that made her look cute instead of slutty.

Her hair was still dyed as black as Jo's, making her pale skin and blue eyes even more startling. She'd finished it with Jo's mother's pearls and a pair of bright green and red woolen Christmas socks despite the evening's warmth. On Perrin the outfit looked ludicrous and wonderful.

Jo sighed. Once again Perrin had proved that a woman with a thirty-two inch chest could get away with wearing anything and still look charming.

"What day is it?" Perrin collapsed onto the other end of the red leather sofa at perfect ease. Like a cat waking from a long nap in the sun.

"Sunday. You've been asleep for almost twenty hours."

"Good. Guess I needed it. Do you have any food?"

"How about pizza?"

"Yum!"

Jo dialed downstairs. One advantage of living in a condo built on top of prime downtown retail space, there were a dozen restaurants in her building and they all delivered.

Perrin propped her feet up on the glass coffee table and admired Jo's Christmas socks as she wiggled her toes.

"Now, we need to figure out who you're going to wear that dress for."

"Perrin."

"What happened to that banker you were seeing?" Perrin rolled right over Jo's admonishment.

"That ended months ago."

"Too bad. How about Russell's dad? He was really cute, in an older guy sort of way, seriously rich too, but he seemed pretty attached to his wife."

"Have you heard from Cassidy?" Jo shot for a subject change.

"All I've been doing is your dress. I couldn't stop until it was done. Even Cassidy's didn't attack me like that. I just saw this one in my head and I had to do it. Tell me again you think it's amazing." There. That was why she loved Perrin. Beneath all of that bravado and flair and extrovert assuredness, was a woman cautious, uncertain, and impossibly real.

"Beyond amazing, Perrin. You keep outdoing yourself, but this time you really did."

Perrin nodded. Jo could see that she still had trouble accepting she was any good.

"I need to check in with Raquel," Perrin offered her own subject change. "I left the shop to her all week."

Jo didn't really want to pay for a wedding dress without a wedding, but Perrin had invested so much of herself in it that she'd have to. Even without a major designer label, a dress like that was worth thousands. Even worse than figuring out how much to pay, would be figuring out how to pay Perrin without paying her. Perrin didn't care about money, especially didn't want it from friends, which was one of the reasons she and Cassidy had practically forced Raquel upon her. The woman possessed immense business sense. Maybe Jo would just pay Raquel and tell her not to mention it to Perrin.

"Did she send any pictures?"

"Raqu—" Jo started then cut herself off. They were back to the subject of Cassidy. Even with a decade of practice, it was still hard to keep up with Perrin's mercurial subject changes. Jo again wondered, as she had from time to time, if Perrin wasn't the smartest of the three of them. Probably the most screwed up, which was saying something, but astonishingly intelligent in her own way.

Jo pulled out her iPad and tapped for the last three e-mails from Italy. She checked, yes, they'd been copied to Perrin.

Then she held it out.

Instead, Perrin scooted over so that sat shoulder to shoulder.

Jo tapped for the first image. It was an airplane bathroom shot through a partly open door.

Cassidy's caption on the picture was, "So not!"

"Bummer," was all Perrin had to say to that.

CHAPTER 8

"How's the head?"

Angelo looked up from the bench-press machine to see Jo towering over him. Again she wore little enough to reveal exactly how amazing her conditioning was. Cyclists' legs of strong thighs, a workout-flat stomach, and arms with just that womanly hint of muscle that did nothing to mar the illusion of smooth skin but hinted at lurking power beneath.

"Uh, fine." He lowered and released the handles then sat up. That brought his face level with her breasts, dark green sports bra this time. He struggled to his feet.

"Barely a lump any more."

"Sore from the ride?"

"Not particularly." He'd been teased throughout dinner service for hobbling like an old man. "You?"

"Plenty. Clearly we need to do that more often."

That he liked the sound of. "Anytime."

"Well, I should finish my workout and leave you to yours."

Angelo scrambled for some way to keep her close, even for a few moments.

389

"I'm off today, the restaurant is closed Mondays. We could go for another ride."

"This is my work week. I have to be in the office soon." She glanced down at the slightly scary wristwatch, heart monitor, exercise thing she wore. "Actually, I'm done and headed for the showers or my assistant will beat me up for being late. She's fierce."

They shared a smile over that. Angelo remembered the sweaty years working for one chef after another in New York, and several summers in Italy. The former had cared about time, the latter about flavor. However, both had busted his ass enough on both points that he could really appreciate being his own master. And the fact that he drove his staff as hard as his mentors and himself harder was only par for the course.

Angelo eyed the wall clock. It was barely seven-thirty. Right, that's when they'd gone riding too. Jo was clearly a morning person. He was a night owl who'd learned to be awake for two hours every morning to do the restaurant shopping and a workout before sleeping three more hours.

"After work?"

She'd started to turn for the locker room, but turned back and did that appraising thing.

Then she smiled, "Do you run?"

"Sure."

"I'm training for the Hagg Lake triathlon next month in Forest Grove, Oregon. Meet at five o'clock by your restaurant?"

"Sounds great."

Angelo watched her head off, damn that woman could walk. Then he pictured her in a sleek one-piece swimsuit and decided he'd better look into that triathlon himself and see if it was too late to sign up.

HE WAS ALREADY WELL STRETCHED and warmed up as she trotted up to him. Again those legs killed him. She wore a loose black t-shirt and bright, fluorescent orange running shorts. The wrap-around shades and her hair back in a ponytail swinging easily side to side completed the picture. But she had legs of bloody iron.

He fell in easily beside her. They dropped down Stewart Street and, after a little judicious zig-zagging around tourists, they followed Western Ave. toward Broad Street.

"You enter many tri's?" He'd signed up for the Oregon event online. He'd been lucky enough to catch the last day of registration. He'd been relieved that it was a short one, a mile swim, twenty-five mile bike ride, and a ten-K run. There'd also been a shorter sprint tri, but he figured he could, depending on which Jo was doing, more easily choose to drop down to the shorter one than climb up to the higher one on race day.

"No." They jogged in place waiting for a light change where Alaskan Way cut uphill as Broad Street. "This is my first. Figured I'd embarrass myself where no one else would ever see me."

Whoops! Well, he could always just lose the entry fee.

"Let me know if you want some company."

Again those impenetrable glasses inspected him.

"Green," he noted the light and trotted across the street.

They dropped down through Myrtle Edwards Park and turned north along the shore of Elliot Bay. The water was busy with ferries and sailboats, a pair of container ships, and a ridiculously tall cruise ship. The wind off the water tasted of the ocean and the mountains beyond, crisp and fresh on the warm afternoon. The sun beat down on them from high in the west, heating his back.

They ran in silence and Angelo worked on finding his rhythm. He used to run a lot, but this last year had been so crazy with the success of the restaurant that he hadn't been out much. He knew that he'd have to push to be ready in a month, even for just a ten-K.

At Roy Street, Jo turned and cut uphill. A dozen blocks later they were winding through the mansions that covered the western slope of Queen Anne Hill. The narrow twisting streets wound and climbed in a maze-inspired array and he was quickly as lost as the dumbest rat.

"Wow! There's some serious money here," he managed to gasp out. He'd seen enough of that, growing up in Russell's house. These places weren't as big as the East Coast mansions owned by the New York magnates. The Morgan estate sat on a small island in Old Greenwich, Connecticut with only three other homes across the short causeway that separated them from shore. Their house had been a modest one by Old Greenwich standards, and would be a major one here, but not the biggest or best.

Jo drove up the hills at a steady pace, and he had to struggle to keep up without dying on the slopes. At long last, they crested the hill and ran down along Queen Anne Avenue itself. He could feel his legs unknotting, though his lungs didn't recover as she upped the pace.

Either she was in as amazing shape as she looked, or she was trying to run him into the ground. Or maybe both. She ran as if a demon dogged her heels but as if winged Mercury, the Greek messenger god himself, had blessed her feet.

They pummeled down the hill on Fourth Avenue. Only the one street clung to the steep north face of Queen Anne Hill, and it dropped straight down. At the bottom of the descent they crossed the Fremont Bridge and hit the Burke-Gilman Trail where they'd started their bike ride, this time on foot.

"This is like the Oregon terrain."

"I knew it." Jo ground to halt and Angelo doubled back to her. He kept jogging in place though she'd stopped.

"Knew what?"

"You signed up for the Hagg Lake Tri today, didn't you?"

Shit! Well, time to be a man about it. He shrugged a, "Yes."

"Are you stalking me, Angelo? What's really going on here?" She was shaking out her legs. He knew they'd be vibrating with the interrupted run. He stopped running and gestured helplessly as his own legs began to vibrate with the sudden break.

Should he try the truth? What the hell did he have to lose? He'd met her barely a half dozen times and she was all he could think about. Fat lot of good it did him.

"Since the first moment I saw you, I don't see anyone else." Angelo traced his hands through the air as if tracing her face.

Jo loved watching his hands as he spoke, it was so, she searched for the right word. It was so Italian.

"A pretty girl goes by," he waved to indicate a long, lean, blonde running by them on the Burke-Gilman path with a graceful, gazelle-like stride. "I don't even see her."

"But you just did." She had to bite the inside of her cheek to not laugh at him.

"I…" He turned to look, but the runner had already passed out of sight under the bridge. "She…" He smacked a palm against his forehead. He looked so perplexed.

"Let me guess," Jo put on her Counselor Thompson tone as Angelo seemed to find it so daunting. "If you were alone, you would have perhaps jogged up to that woman, greeted her in Italian, pretended you were new in town and only knew a little English. And then…let's see…you'd have asked if she knew a 'great gelato place' somewhere nearby."

"Sure," then he blushed a brilliant red, then shrugged in that eloquent way of his. "Probably."

He hedged, but she wasn't buying it. He was too handsome to not know his power over women.

"Last year, before I met you, no problem. Of course I would. She wore no ring, either." He slapped a hand over his mouth. Then shrugged again and uncovered a boyish smile.

"Okay, so I still notice. But since the first time I see you," he flicked a finger against his own temple. "Nothing. I watch them run by and I don't even think, 'Angelo, you should chase that one.' They just go by and I wonder when is the next time I will see Jo Thompson."

His voice was rising and Jo was having trouble swallowing. No one ever talked about her like that. And the faster he spoke, the more an Italian rhythm slipped in, making his voice even more engaging.

"I just can't win with you, can I? No matter what I do, I just screw it all up. I can't sweep you away with the best food at the most romantic wedding I've ever been to. I can't go running with you with not making myself an *idiota*."

"You can't cook dinner for me, you proved that," she couldn't resist the tease. He was past hearing the tone. It struck home and his dark eyes flashed.

"You come by without some *bastardo*, out-sized, 'I'm so gorgeous' Russian and I'll show you what I can cook." His anger rolled louder still. "Hell! Bring him along and I'll show you both what I can do. I'll cook that...that... whatever he is right under the damn table!" He made as if to hurl down a gauntlet.

He took her breath away. No one had ever seen her as he did. Outside of her legal expertise, all men ever saw was her body, but Angelo hadn't glanced down once in his entire tirade.

And he was so impossibly cute about it. So wound up that she could only think of one thing to stop him as he launched into a description of exactly what he would cook to show that Russian what was what.

She clamped his face in her hands and kissed him, hard.

If he hesitated even a second, she didn't notice it go by. He didn't drag her against him. He didn't clutch or grab. He barely moved.

In an instant he went from raging Italian to leaning ever so gently into the kiss. It floated through her like... She was so good with words, she should be able to attach some words to how she felt as he tipped his head in her hands and deepened the kiss. It floated through her like...a kiss. It sounded stupid inside her head, but it was all she had at the moment.

He slid his hands over hers. Caressing them, then holding them in his, and finally sliding them from his face, then rocking back just enough for their lips to part.

"Breathe, *bella signora*. Before you pass out." His dark eyes sparkled so close.

"I'd better take my own advice." He stepped back, dropping her hands after a final gentle squeeze, and made a show of taking a deep breath that ended on a soft chuckle.

Jo managed to drag in some much needed air and shared his laugh for a moment.

"Okay," his voice was a caress. "I expected that kiss to be strong, like a spicy Sicilian sauce, but..." He whooshed out another breath and scrubbed his hands over his face.

She still couldn't respond. Couldn't quite tell if he was happy or upset. Couldn't quite tell how *she* felt about it either.

"Next time we try that," Angelo grinned at her, "I want to be somewhere we won't injure ourselves when our knees give out."

Jo looked down at the hard pavement of the trail then back up at Angelo.

"Please tell me there will be a next time, Jo. Please tell me there will be."

Jo's wits finally came back to her. She'd just received the best kiss of her life from one of the most handsome men she'd ever met.

"Damn straight there's going to be another chance," she assured both of them.

CHAPTER 9

ngelo and his mother arrived at the airport just before midnight. Cassidy's somewhat frantic e-mail had popped up while Angelo had been out running with Jo. They were on a direct flight home and could Angelo or someone pick them up?

She'd been less than clear about why they were aborting their honeymoon after only a week and Angelo feared the worst. Their first trip to Italy had been a four-alarm relationship disaster, but Russell had assured him that everything that had caused that was resolved. After all, he'd married her rather than setting off to sail alone around the world in anger and misery, which was a good thing. Angelo wondered if he should have hidden Russell's boat.

Mama had insisted on coming with him to the airport even though the plane was arriving near midnight. She'd known Russell as long as Angelo had and was just as worried. They'd driven the car down as the van had no back seats.

Now they waited at the head of the escalator for international arrivals. It was a leftover from the days when you could meet arriving flights at the gate, and no one had ever updated it. International flights landed at the secure southern terminal. After people wended their way through customs, they boarded the underground train to

397

the main terminal and rode up the escalator at the end of the secure zone.

That was all well and good. But the escalator popped out in the middle of baggage claim where a total of three uncomfortable seats had been bolted to a gray wall well off to the side. Other than that, you just had to stand in the busiest and narrowest corridor of the whole airport, among a vast array of baggage claim carousels, and wait.

Angelo sucked at waiting.

He'd settled into pacing down past the first couple baggage claim conveyors and back while his mother settled in one of the three awkward seats. Some installation artist had mounted dozens of pieces of abandoned luggage with a massive iron pipe rammed through their centers. Suspended above the baggage conveyor were skewered leather suitcases, punctured nylon carry-ons, a guitar hardshell case pithed like a giant black beetle, a garment bag bullet-shot through the heart, and many more. Like this was supposed to instill confidence in the airlines? He was halfway down the art piece wondering if any of these was the suitcase that had never followed him back from his last trip to California to teach, when he heard the twin cries of "Mrs. Parrano!"

He spun to see his mother embracing Jo and Perrin. Cassidy's plea for help must have gone to them as well.

Damn! He kept forgetting to tell Jo about his mother's moving in with him, never mind that she was making him insane at the restaurant. Already the three of them were talking so fast he couldn't begin to follow. How in the world did women all talk at once and still hear everything? He'd never understood that.

Jo barely broke the flow as she shot him her hotshot attorney look with one raised eyebrow. Well, the news of his mother's move had just come out, probably the retirement would be only seconds behind it.

He tried a shrug to say, "Okay, you caught me. I screwed up. I'll never do it again. Trust me."

Her laugh informed him that she'd read right through his bullshit of best intentions.

The woman made him crazy. All he'd been able to think about was when he'd get a chance to kiss her again. And more. But she'd gone shy at the end of their run, leaving him quickly when they reached his restaurant. He didn't even know where she lived, though by the direction and that she'd walked rather than jogged away without looking back, he figured it was somewhere downtown.

He'd managed not to follow her, but had broken down and Googled her. All he got back was her law offices two blocks from his restaurant and a daunting list of lawsuits. He didn't even understand what most of them were about, corporate craziness of some breed or other, but he poked through them enough to learn that she never lost a case, at least not that he could tell.

He was lusting after one of the top corporate lawyers in the city, one who could slice and dice a corporation or a government lawsuit before breakfast without breaking a sweat. He usually went for the simplicity of a vapid, no-strings-sex kind of women. Workout girls were a nice bonus, though he'd learned the hard way to never pick up a woman at the gym he used. It made things awkward after the breakups. He'd tried dating other chefs, but between their mutually workaholic schedules and his generally superior cooking skills, those never lasted. Now he was chasing a woman who was probably smarter than most of the people on the planet. He should be running full tilt the other direction.

Then why had her kiss rooted him to the ground? One moment he'd been raging against something he still couldn't quite recall and the next his world had gone quiet. All he'd known were the cool touch of her hands and the burning heat of her lips. He'd always been the one in calm control and he wasn't liking the change.

Jo continued to chat with his mother as if they were long lost friends.

Oh God! His mother hadn't only become friends with his butcher and his seafood supplier. She was also charming the woman he wanted to date. If she did become his girlfriend... Maybe he should just leave quietly, go back to his restaurant, and throw himself on a chef's knife. Then he'd be comfortably dead and the craziness in his head would stop. *Bene!*

Another train must have unloaded downstairs as a fresh flood of passengers flowed up the escalator. That's when he spotted the friendly face. A friendly male face.

"Sanctuary!" He hustled past the three women, through the crowd streaming off the escalator, and over to the elevator where he'd spotted Russell Morgan.

He stopped, put his hands on his hips, and looked down at him.

"And what the hell happened to you?"

he three women enveloped Cassidy and it was left to Angelo to keep a level head and roll his friend's wheelchair to the side, freeing a blockage in the flow of traffic when the next elevator load spilled out. He considered trying to also move the four women, now catching up on news, out of the way, but decided that his long-term survival would be improved if he left them to their own devices.

He rapped his knuckles sharply on Russell's leg cast, noted the slight wince and rapped it once more with a little more force.

"How in the hell did you break that?"

"It was Cassidy's idea."

"Was not." Somehow she'd heard despite the half-dozen paces and stream of tired tourists that separated them. She came over to stand beside her husband's wheelchair. The hand she stroked over his head and down his neck was gentle and told Angelo that at least the relationship hadn't blown up unlike their last trip to Italy.

"Mr. Athlete here decided he just had to try parasailing behind a power boat."

"You said it looked like fun."

"No," Cassidy rested a hand on his shoulder. "I said it looked like stupid fun."

Russell just harrumphed.

Angelo rapped his knuckles on the cast again and would have received a sharp jab in the ribs if he hadn't dodged quickly.

"How long?"

"Damn thing itches. It's already too long."

"Six weeks," Cassidy kissed him on top of the head. "And he's already got three weeks of complaining in during the first forty-eight hours. I can't begin to tell you how much fun this is going to be."

"That does it. I'm never going back to that stupid country."

This time Angelo's mother rapped her knuckles sharply on Russell's cast and he caught his breath sharply.

"You no say that about my country or I no make you my special biscotti."

Russell looked up at her, "Yes, Nana. What are you doing in Seattle?"

"Good boy," she leaned down and kissed him on top of the head just as Cassidy had. "And no making Cassidy crazy. I know you."

She turned to Cassidy, "I warn you. He is even a worse patient than my boy Angelo."

"Baggage." Angelo grabbed the handles to the wheelchair and pushed he and Russell clear of the group. "We definitely need to find baggage."

"And a bar," Russell put in.

"Definitely a bar," Angelo agreed.

———

ANGELO HAD OVERRULED the women's vote to head straight home in a very simple way. He'd settled Russell into his car and gotten behind the driver's wheel. Then he drove them out of SeaTac airport, across Highway 99, and right into the 13 Coins Restaurant parking lot. It was their traditional stop after crazy trips. The place offered twenty-four hour fine dining and alcohol from six in the morning until two the next morning.

He'd dragged Russell here after his ill-fated first trip to Italy with

Cassidy and let him drink himself straight through oblivion and into passed out. Russell had made sure Angelo got good and loose, though stopped him short of plastered, after he'd returned from his first time as a guest instructor at the Culinary Institute of America last fall. Cassidy had kept telling him what fun it was to teach there, and he'd fallen for it like a babe in the woods. He still shivered at the memory of it. The CIA wanted him back this fall, but he had never been one to get up in front of a room full of people. Just let him hide in the kitchen and cook. Besides, he'd need to buy a new suitcase.

The 13 Coins had deep booths with high, dark leather backs and soft lighting. You could crawl into a booth and not be seen for hours. The waitresses were discrete, understood the necessity for speed on drink orders, and always offered to keep track of your flight time if you were outbound to make sure you didn't miss your plane. Even the stools in front of the bar were tall, cozy, and wrapped around you shutting out the rest of the world.

In the middle of the room were low tables and comfortable chairs scattered about like someone's living room. They found a table with room for six plus Russell's extended leg.

"I came down wrong is all."

"Yes. Right on top of a jet skier's head, then got tangled in the controls as it rolled over."

"You thought those looked like fun too."

"Suicidal stupid fun? Yes. Something any rational, thinking human would actually do? Not so much. Don't you hear adjectives?" She turned to face everyone else. "I took a nap on the beach and next thing I know a polite Italian ambulance driver is waking me up. The guy he landed on was the cameraman and his camera is now deep in the Mediterranean Sea, so we, thank God, don't have video of it. Though if we did, I could lord it over him whenever he got out of line." Cassidy was clearly enjoying herself. Quite happy with being right, she did nothing to halt the sharp rap Maria Amelia Avico Parrano landed on Russell's cast each time he whined.

"Are you trying to extend my lifespan or something?" Russell groused at his wife.

Angelo shook his head and whispered to his friend, "Still a crazy thought, you being married."

Russell nodded in agreement and he studied his beer while Cassidy kept going. She was having way too much fun at Russell's expense, which Angelo was trying not to laugh about in his friend's face.

"Hey, you're the one who showed me that I loved you. So if you die before I do, I'm going to have to kill you." Cassidy dipped up a cracker full of the Crab and Artichoke Dip clearly feeling she'd won the point.

Angelo would have to agree that she would have to kill him, so, out of loyalty he kept his mouth shut. All he really wanted to do was run everything by Russell, but he couldn't with his mother and Jo sitting right there. And he wasn't so sure he wanted to talk about Jo with him anyway. He could hear Russell's answer right now without asking.

"She's hot. You should go for her."

Not really helpful. The first part he couldn't argue with. The second part he already knew, it just scared the crap out of him.

Jo sat between his mother on one side and Cassidy and Perrin on the other. They were just far enough away that he couldn't make out their soft conversation.

"What happened to you?"

Angelo turned to face Russell. "What are you talking about?"

Russell rolled his eyes toward Jo.

So much for not bringing it up. "Uh, I hit my head. And we went for a bike ride together." Could he sound more stupid? "And a run." Yep, he could.

Russell studied him over his beer for a while before continuing his thought.

"You know, this whole being married thing is strange. It changes your outlook in some really interesting ways."

"Like what?" Angelo tried not to scoff, but it must have come out that way.

"Like being married to Cassidy makes me think of the other two as my sisters. I always thought they were beautiful and a lot of fun. But now it's more than that."

Angelo sipped his own beer in acknowledgment.

"I love you like a brother, but if you hurt one of them, I'm gonna be hurting you so much worse. Whether or not I'm still in this cast."

Angelo slumped in his chair. Okay, that was even less helpful than he'd expected.

"Angelo didn't tell me you had moved here to Seattle." Jo had gone with ginger ale. She'd needed to be awake in under five hours and headed to the gym before work. She really needed to be home in bed, not chatting with Angelo's mother in some all-night in-crowd airport bar.

"Ah, I was more than right. You are the girl who rides the bicycles. That is good."

Jo eyed her carefully, but the smile was genuine. A quick glance showed Cassidy's attention was with Perrin at the moment which, Jo decided, was a good thing.

"My Angelo's taste. Sometimes it is good, sometimes not so good. I tell him that he should find someone as pretty and nice as you, and now he has."

Jo glanced over at Angelo, slumped in his chair and pretending to ignore Russell. "So you told him to chase me and he does? Doesn't speak much for his initiative."

"No. No." Maria flapped Jo's words away. "He said he was going riding, and I tell him I hope she's as nice as the pretty one at the wedding. The boy, he doesn't say a word yes or no, not that I gave him the chance." Her smile was easy. "It does good to keep that one a little off his balance. He is too sure of himself. Men always are. Cassidy does it to Russell, I've never before seen him so fascinated, as if he is always waiting for the next act of the magic show to see what Cassidy will do next."

"It's true," Cassidy joined the conversation. "Around Russell I get all of these great ideas. It's like our thoughts spark off each other."

"And your bodies, I hope," Perrin leaned in from Cassidy's far side.

"Oh yeah," Cassidy smiled at her. "Seriously."

"Until he earned the cast," Jo noted.

"It ends mid-thigh," Angelo's mother offered a far-too-wise smile.

"It does," Cassidy sighed happily. "Indeed it does. You know, Italian hospital beds aren't all that narrow."

"I knew it!" Perrin flagged the waitress for another cosmopolitan. "Where else?"

"Well, we hadn't gotten to the sailboat yet. But we did stay with my friends at their villa in the Piedmont. In the middle of the vineyard they have a splendid little gazebo and a spread of grass open to the night sky."

Jo heard her sigh echoed by the other two women as well.

"Then there was this powerboat with a small, but well-appointed cabin on Lake Como. Let's just say that we spent a lot of time on the water, but didn't see the lake very much."

"Then the *idiota* broke his leg." Maria pulled Cassidy over across Jo's lap and kissed her cheek in sympathy before letting her go.

"Then the *idiota* broke his leg." Cassidy sipped her wine. "I'd be angrier if he didn't keep apologizing so much. He does feel really awful about ruining the honeymoon."

"Well," Jo thought about all that was going on in her life and felt guilty for saying it from such a selfish place of needing to talk to Cassidy, but it was true anyway. "We're really glad you're back safe. And had some fun."

"We did." Then Cassidy grinned a bit and blushed. She glanced sideways at Perrin who burst out laughing.

It only took Jo and Maria a moment to catch on.

"Of course Russell did need some help getting back and forth to the bathroom on the flight home," Perrin said right on the verge of one of her merry giggles.

"He did," Cassidy acknowledged, her smile deepening. "He did indeed."

Jo spent most of Tuesday inhaling international law. The UNCLOS, United Nations Convention on the Law of the Sea, had been ratified by all parties bordering the Arctic Ocean, except for the United States. As usual with international treaties, even ones the U.S. sponsored, it remained unapproved despite all common sense and decency.

That didn't stop the U.S. from claiming Territorial Waters to twelve miles offshore, the Exclusive Economic Zone to two hundred nautical miles and, in addition, trying to claim continental shelf out to three-hundred-and-fifty miles. They were attempting an undersea land grab much of the way to the North Pole. All of the countries were.

The U.S. government was also claiming some of the same territory as Canada. Oddly enough the border where the Russian claim neighbored Alaskan waters to the west was clear and undisputed. Of course the Russians and Norwegians couldn't agree on anything. And Canada was duking it out with Denmark over a tiny, useless uninhabited island. That made the whole thing a pretty typical international fiasco.

In addition, the melting of the polar ice was opening up the Northwest Passage for shipping for the first time in recorded history. No one could agree which law would take precedence in case of a disaster, like a wreck requiring rescue in the deep Arctic or an oil spill. As the Passage actually existed primarily among Canadian-owned islands and the Alaska seaway, the points of law should be clear, but they weren't. Canada's laws were much stricter than those in UNCLOS and no one could agree on any of it.

Jo had been brought in because, putatively, the fisherman were being chased out of the entire Beaufort Sea even though only a small wedge not much bigger than New Jersey was all that was under contention. Yet the oil companies had been granted six leases for exploration in the disputed region. The yelling had barely begun and because of her success fending off the madness in the last lawsuit, she'd been brought aboard to do so once again.

As to what fisherman was crazy enough to want to fish in the Arctic, she couldn't imagine. Or perhaps she could.

Jo pulled up the legal complaint that had started the whole cascade of suits and countersuits on her screen and scanned the signatories. Earnest J. Thompson had signed. The chance of him ever striking a hundred miles beyond Ketchikan were so minimal as to be laughable. That her father might make the insanely hazardous three-thousand mile voyage simply to fish wasn't even a possibility. But he had signed nonetheless.

It was so ludicrous that she could almost certainly use it against the small fishermen if needed. Probably one signatory in a hundred actually might fish the Arctic Ocean if given the chance. After all, she wasn't being paid to represent the fisherman. Or, it would give her a chance to recuse herself from the case based on conflict of interest that now existed, no matter how marginal.

Jo set that thought aside. First, it was a flimsy excuse to get out, and second she knew that to do so was always tempting in the first month or so of research on a new matter. In the beginning, lawsuits were terribly messy. The larger the lawsuit, the worse the mess. Relevant documentation could be spread across dozens of states or even countries. The pertinent fifty-eight articles of UNCLOS had clearly been drafted by committee, worse, an international multi-lingual committee. Hundreds of pages of brilliantly impenetrable legalese that, once analyzed in the full sight of legal case precedents, probably signified little to nothing.

She closed her eyes and rubbed her forehead. The lack of sleep was starting to tell on her and it was only two o'clock. Three more hours, plus she really should put in four or five more to make up for missing all of Friday afternoon. Her whole body throbbed with the exhausted beating of her heart, as if it were pumping out tired blood with each stroke instead of the freshly oxygenated little red cells she so needed.

"You need a break, boss."

Jo hadn't heard Muriel come in. She didn't bother to open her eyes.

"No, I just need sleep. And maybe one of those big shots of adrenalin they punch into your heart."

"How about another piece of chocolate? I saved some."

"Anything would help." Jo held out a hand without bothering to look. Something cool and solid slid against her palm and she looked up.

A slim tube-style vase of pale-blue blown glass bore a single red rose.

She blinked again, but it remained in her hand. It really was there.

"Let me guess. No note again."

"Not even a 'PPM' one this time," Muriel simply smiled at her. "What am I doing wrong that I'm not getting gift baskets and beautiful red roses?"

"I'll get you one of each for Christmas."

"But then I'll know who it's from. Besides, that's over six months away."

Jo considered if another piece of chocolate with an aspirin chaser would avert the pending headache.

"I'm too tired to guess, just tell me."

Her assistant raised her hands palm out. "I don't know this time. Honest. I even grilled the delivery guy, a nice young boy named Marko. Phone-in order, no idea who sent it. Even gave him a nice tip from your petty cash, and he didn't give. Want me to hound the owner for the name on the credit card? Actually, I can't, I'm not sure what shop he was with. But I could call around."

Jo scowled at the rose. Renée? Not likely. Angelo? She'd left him less than a dozen hours earlier at the bar. He and Russell had been talking about speedboats and parasailing. Apparently, despite Russell's broken leg, his head was dense enough to think it had been a pretty cool experience. That left Yuri and she definitely didn't want to think about that.

She set the rose by her monitor. It was pretty after all and the vase was exquisite in its simplicity. Another Renée bribe she decided.

"That wasn't chocolate."

Muriel pulled out a bar of chocolate she'd tucked in her skirt pocket. She wore a close-fitting white angora sweater and an actual fifties' poodle skirt, except that it was black with pink poodles instead of the other way around. Knowing her assistant's attention to detail, she probably had on bobby socks and two-tone whatever they were called shoes. Jo sat up a bit straighter to see as she reached for the chocolate that Muriel broke off and handed over, but the desk still blocked her view.

Without being asked, Muriel raised a foot for her to see. Black bobby socks topped with pink lace and those white-and-tan shoes.

"Saddle oxfords," Muriel informed her recognizing the blank moment.

Jo nodded. They'd long since stopped trying to figure out how they knew what the other was asking without, well, asking. It wasn't because they'd been working together for five years either. They'd done it since the first day Muriel had showed up, fresh from college with a resume in her hand.

Jo ate the chocolate, dark, candied ginger–chili pepper this time. She wanted to close her eyes and just lay her head on the desk, instead she focused on convincing her body that she'd just eaten some magic, high-energy candy rather than soothing dark cocoa.

"You also have a visitor. Or will in another two minutes."

"Who?" that straightened Jo back up a bit. Yuri had gone back to Alaska, hadn't he? She waved a hand toward her jacket.

Muriel took it from the hanger on the back of the office door and handed it over.

Jo pulled it on and checked the lie of it in Muriel's appraising look and quick nod. She was going to have her power armor in place in case it was Yuri.

A tap on her partly open door and Renée Linden stuck her head in.

"I'm not interrupting, am I? Oh, what a pretty rose. Who sent you that?"

"I THOUGHT you might like to see the shoot for my final ad campaign. They can be quite fun actually." Renée led Jo out of the office and toward the Market. "I still haven't had a chance to talk to the board, their next meeting isn't until tomorrow evening. I hate to impose, but I'd appreciate keeping it between us girls until then."

"Of course," Jo granted easily. What she hadn't found, despite two days of thinking about it, was a gracious way to inform the most influential female power broker on the Seattle scene that Jo's answer was a definitive, "No." Part of the problem was she didn't know if her guess was right, though she had circled back around to it being a job offer.

However, the answer was no even though Renée hadn't technically made the offer, at least not in as many words. Even if she had, Jo wasn't going to take the Executive Directorship, it still made no sense.

Her first intention, of informing Renée of her decision while in her own office and on her own turf, had somehow failed. Perhaps on a stroll through the Market she'd find the right moment to acknowledge Renée's kind and subtle offer to suggest her for the Executive Directorship and to thank her kindly as she turned her down.

"We do a great deal of tourism marketing," Renée was telling her as they walked together down Pike Place and into the heart of the market. "We use websites, airplane magazines, participation in television cooking shows, and the like. I decided that it was time we expand that clientele. The Pike Place Market has long been a destination visit for travelers, but I think there is a high-end that we've been missing."

Jo nodded. It made sense. She'd seen the Market change and shift over the decade she'd been in Seattle. There were still the odd little kiosks at the north end where amateur artists rented six feet of table to display hand-crafted earrings or their latest knit fashions for toddlers. Cute and very good for what it was. But in the heart of the Market there were some true artists selling their wares. Clothing designers, high-end galleries, and antique stores specializing in rare collectibles had joined the food entrepreneurs which were the backbone of the Market's image.

There was no mistaking the photo shoot when they found it at The Glass Shoppe. There were two photographer's assistants adjusting umbrella flashes, one with a couple extra cameras dangling around her neck. A thin, young man sat next to an open makeup case of immense variety. A short rack on wheels waited outside the shop sporting a small but tasteful selection of high-end clothing to be ready when needed.

At the center of the bustling array were a photographer and his model.

Jo gasped. There was no mistaking her. She'd been on enough covers over the last year to be unmistakable.

"Melanie."

Renée simply nodded. "You see, I'm right. Everyone knows her. She's immensely marketable right now. I managed to find her when she was traveling through Seattle, so it was not too hideously expensive to hire her. We only have her for the day, but I think it will definitely be worth it."

Jo had seen her in person once, but she couldn't quite place where. A failing that she could only credit to how Renée was overloading her neural pathways. She absolutely couldn't afford to be out of the office, yet here they were, chatting pleasantly at an advertising shoot that had absolutely nothing to do with her.

They watched as the magnificent, six-foot tall supermodel swept her waist-length blond hair over her shoulder and flirted, using her trademark ever so slight French accent, with the slightly shy vendor in his small shop. The photographer snapped away. Like most of the Market's spaces it was deceptively small but had been used incredibly well to display the blown glass art making it feel much larger.

Blown glass. She glanced around. There, behind one of the photographer's silvery umbrella flashes stood a display of exquisite little bud vases in all the shades of flowers. It only took a moment to note that there wasn't one to match the pale blue vase now holding a rose on Jo's desk.

A delivery boy named Marko, huh? From an unknown flower shop? And a vase purchased right here in the Market. She kept her smile to herself but placed a small wager with herself that Angelo had someone named Marko working in his restaurant. One who wouldn't reveal the sender despite a nice tip because he was protecting his boss and his job.

Neither Yuri nor Renée, Angelo had sent the rose. Well, that was awfully sweet of him. She knew this shop well enough to know that the vase hadn't been cheap either, she owned a couple of this artist's pieces herself.

But she had reconsidered their kiss during the rest of their run and only seen it reemphasized last night at the airport bar. Angelo was nice enough. And he would be too easy to get close to with his smooth accent and stunning looks. But he suffered from a problem similar to Yuri's. First, she wasn't ready to be involved with anyone for a couple more years and second, she wanted someone as serious about their career as she was.

That wasn't quite right, Angelo was serious about his cooking. Maybe even as ambitious in his own way. But her career was a whole different world than a single nice restaurant in Seattle. And his college had been cooking schools, not Vassar. Not University of Washington's School of Law.

He wasn't beneath her, that was too demeaning a thought. But neither was he what she was looking for, even if her body kept reacting as if he were.

"This is the last shoot of the day," Renée interrupted her spiraling thoughts as they watched a clothier offer Melanie a different jacket and a dark scarf that transformed her from casually elegant to delightfully urban.

"We did jewelry, antique cars, the little ones that were toys in the 1930s and '40s. I've been working here for almost two decades and had no idea they commanded such prices. And a number of others. The haute couture shop was to have followed this, but it closed last week. I always thought it was a tad silly myself. Simply too surreal for even an opening night at the opera. At least on this coast."

Jo inspected Renée's outfit and saw another reason the woman might feel that way. She was ruthlessly fit, as was probably only achieved with a personal trainer, and impeccably dressed in a simple maroon dress that shouted to take this woman seriously, without masking that she was a woman. It was an outfit that Jo herself would have selected if she could afford such tailoring. Her dark blond hair had highlights and not a hint of gray, worn just long enough to reach her collar, and held back in a no-nonsense clasp that was simple enough to have come from Bartell Drug Store but perfect enough that it probably came from Nordstrom.

An image was forming in Jo mind's eye. It started with Melanie and filled out slowly like a camera pulling back to reveal the surroundings. An image of this beautiful, shining woman in a dusky, warm Italian kitchen.

"Did you shoot a restaurant?"

Renée shook her head. "We considered Maximilien's, but we frequently feature them in our ads and we wanted these to be different."

"Have you been in Angelo's Tuscan Hearth since they remodeled?"

Renée inspected her intensely for half a heartbeat then smiled radiantly.

Jo wondered at the meaning of those two emotions side by side.

"No, I haven't." Renée's smile didn't diminish, but it felt as if were part of another conversation that was again eluding Jo. "I do keep meaning to go in. Coming back into the city with Nathaniel after we both finally get home from work simply hasn't happened."

She looped a hand through Jo's arm. "That's a brilliant idea. Come."

Jo had intended to go back to work. Had to. But was making little progress in that direction.

o felt a bit like a scout leader as she led the troop down the old bricks of Pike Place and turned up Post Alley. Behind her followed Melanie and Renée talking about how charming the Market was on a summer day. Apparently Melanie had been here only once before and that had been a chill and spitting winter's day. Not a day when the smell of the sea was battled back by fresh flowers, sweet pastries, and rich coffee thick on the Seattle air.

Following them were the photographer, his laden assistants, the makeup guy, clothier, and several others apparently connected to the shoot that she hadn't noticed in the surrounding crowd.

As it was only a block away, they'd decided it was better to show up and ask forgiveness later rather than calling ahead.

She asked the others to wait outside, taking only Renée, Melanie, and the photographer in with her.

"Table for four?" The slender Italian woman greeted them. Jo remembered her as the hostess from last week's meal with Yuri. She'd been terribly gracious about Jo's request to see Angelo. Gracious. Graziella.

"Graziella. I was wondering if Angelo might be available."

The hostess' memory was clearly up to the challenge as well. "Ah, Miss Thompson. Table seven."

They were both careful not to look toward the offending piece of furniture.

"A moment please." And the woman was gone.

Angelo breezed into the room, his apron immaculate, his smile radiant.

"Why hello, Miss Thomp— Melanie!" He rushed forward and greeted the supermodel with a kiss on each cheek and then a profound hug though she towered several inches over him.

"Angelo!" They slid into rapid Italian leaving Jo stupefied.

They laughed together. The kind of laugh that only happened when you were flirting. Angelo was flirting with a supermodel right in front of her. She'd been planning to thank him for the flower if they found a moment alone, but now he was holding hands with a supermodel and they were talking excitedly over one another, just inches apart.

Jo's body flashed hot and then very, very cold. The power suit she'd put on in case her visitor was Yuri, which then looked appropriate beside Renée's perfect, understated attire, now did its job. Jo's clothes wrapped around her like armor. Sensible heels, navy blue slacks with a perfect crease that matched her wide-lapelled jacket. The dress white blouse with the muted-floral bow tie. She'd taken down federal cases in this exact outfit. She could deal with one lousy Italian restaurateur while wearing it.

Clearly the whole shooting plan had passed back and forth and been approved in Italian, as moments later Graziella was escorting in those who had waited outside while Melanie toured the restaurant on Angelo's arm.

Had the man been playing her? Simply wanting someone to amuse himself with while his supermodel lover was flitting about the world on her climb to fame and fortune? Melanie made Jo feel downright dowdy.

ANGELO COULDN'T STOP LAUGHING. Melanie kept going on about how she'd clearly fallen in love with the wrong man, because Angelo was so much more handsome. Then she told a rather racy story of how Zaia, Essence, and Stella Star had been found naked together in a bathroom at the Carlton. He hadn't heard that one about her fellow models, but Melanie told him he must search on it, as the person who found them had indeed had a smartphone that linked video directly to YouTube. It might not have been so bad if the three women hadn't been having a screaming match about sleeping with the same film director.

"You have made it so beautiful," she kept looking around the restaurant and he couldn't stop himself from grinning.

"This was the second try. The first one was pronounced 'butt ugly.'"

"Russell?" Her voice sounded a touch sad as she said his name, so he did his best to gloss over it as if he hadn't noticed the change.

"His words exactly. But he helped me do this."

"That man," she sighed lightly. "He does have an amazing eye. No one has ever made me as beautiful as he did with a camera. Not even Claude, though he is better than most." She flicked a long red finger-nail in the direction of the photographer who was moving about the restaurant checking angles through one lens and then another.

"He still…"

"Angelo, buddy," Russell swung through the kitchen door on crutches. The few mid-afternoon diners startled at Russell's bull-in-china-shop shout. "You gotta save me. I'm bored to dea—"

He came to a halt when he spotted Melanie, all of his bluster gone. As far as Angelo knew, they'd never spoken since that awful day a year ago February.

Melanie had pulled back her hand from Angelo's arm and hunched her shoulders a bit. It didn't look good on her.

Though his heart ached, he didn't know how to help them. Melanie had fallen in love with Russell, who had neither understood nor returned the emotion, though they'd been lovers at the time. Involved. "The Season's Hot Item" according to the tabloids. The flashy heir to the Morganson shipping empire, and the molten super-model. No one but Angelo knew that both their emotions had been caught up as well, that not only the glamour had kept them together as long as they were.

"Hi Russell," Angelo reached deep for some tiny bit of casual. "Melanie's in town for an ad shoot for the Market. They decided to drop in and use my restaurant for one of the ads."

All they did was stare stone-faced at each other and Angelo didn't know what to say. Couldn't figure out how to help them out of their mutual pain and embarrassment.

"It was my idea," Jo came up beside Russell and laid a friendly hand on his arm as if nothing were amiss.

Didn't the woman have any sensitivity in that severe suit of hers?

"You and Angelo did such a beautiful job of redecorating. And your art on the walls. It was irresistible."

"Uh, thanks."

She *was* doing it. By avoiding the subject of their mutual pain entirely, Jo had gotten Russell to relax a half-inch, though his hands still clamped around the crutch handles as if holding on for dear life. But that little bit of easing on his part had in turn removed some of the hunch from Melanie's shoulders. Angelo would have tried step-ping straight into the breach, whereas Jo just circled around it as if it wasn't even there. It was as artful as the muted paintings and crys-talline photographs on his walls.

"I thought over by that table, the one by the central hearth, would look really splendid." Claude had clearly recognized Russell, but his tone clearly said, this is my shoot, that is my choice.

Russell's gaze begrudgingly shifted from Melanie's face to the room about them.

"No."

Claude blinked and suddenly looked like a fish out of water.

Angelo could see Russell swallow hard, then it became a bit too obvious that he wasn't going to look back at Melanie now that he'd looked away, but there was nothing Angelo could do about that.

"No," Russell cleared his throat and tried again. "That's a four-topper. It's the right position, Claude, but for the photograph you'll want a two-person table even though she's the only one seated there. It's an ad. She's waiting. Waiting for the viewer of the ad to come join her." He swung off on his crutches to direct the change.

Melanie turned to Angelo and mouthed a "Thank you" before bending down to lean her cheek against his. He could feel her hands in his squeeze long and hard, then steadier. She stood, her shoulders back and nodded once.

Angelo turned to Jo to thank her as well, but she was no longer beside Melanie.

"None of these clothes are right," Russell was riffling through the rack by the front door.

"It's all I brought," the clothier was complaining.

Jo had moved over beside Russell. Angelo watched her turn that appraising attorney gaze on Melanie and slowly inspect her from shoes to hair. Her eyes didn't track over to Angelo even in the slightest flicker.

She pulled out her phone and dialed.

He moved closer to hear the conversation.

"Perrin? This is Jo, I'm at Angelo's and we have a bit of an emergency. Could you bring over your dress from last Saturday, the one you wore? A pair of heels, not platform, but spike. In," she glanced at Russell, "red."

Russell nodded.

"Fingernail red. Thanks."

"No lipstick. Only a little makeup," Russell told the man who'd set up his kit on a side table. "You shouldn't be able to see it at all."

Then the room kicked into action.

"*I fall for zis...*" *Melanie* pointed an elegant finger negligently at Russell. "Zis fool and you are the one who marries him. How does this happen?"

Cassidy grinned at Jo and squeezed her hand beneath the dinner table. No one knew better than she how many potholes and pitfalls Cassidy had discovered along that particular road.

"Just my punishment, I suppose."

Melanie threw back her head and laughed. Any easy, joyous sound.

Jo marveled at how the tone of the room had changed over the last few hours.

First, it had all been a great rush of preparation. Part of it clearly to distract from the tension in the room.

Then Perrin had roared in from her design store a couple blocks up the hill. Not only with the green bridesmaid dress, but also with about a third of her shop on a long rolling rack, just in case, which added to the mayhem. They'd shot four different outfits, but Jo was pleased that her instincts had been right. Perrin's dress with its long lines and surprising reveals had fit Melanie perfectly with only a few minor adjustments, and had been the star of the shoot. Thankfully they were of a size, even if Melanie was taller. The height had revealed a little more arm and a fair amount more leg while hugging her body perfectly. Melanie still wore it and swore she was never giving it back, much to Perrin's vocal protests and obvious delight.

Russell had coaxed a camera from one of Claude's assistants and, somehow without offending the notoriously irritable photographer, had taken what everyone, including Claude, had agreed were the best shots.

Renée, on discovering Russell's previous ownership of one of the top boutique ad studios in New York, had somehow coaxed him into agreeing to build the ads based on his and Claude's photography. Claude, being a purist, photographer only, had managed to not be offended after only minimal coaxing on Jo's part.

Cassidy had arrived in search of her errant husband and soon they were all gathered around one of Angelo's exquisite meals.

Jo was relieved by that. She worried that she'd become a curse for him. But he produced amazing food in unbelievable quantities despite how shabbily she'd treated him earlier this afternoon. It was Cassidy who'd straightened her out over the appetizers.

"Remember the first time we saw them, that Valentine's Day?"

And now Jo did. She, Cassidy, and Perrin had been out drinking. Celebrating Jo's partnership in her new firm if she remembered correctly. And Cassidy breaking up with the drip she'd been seeing. Melanie and Russell had breezed through the bar on the way to the restaurant. Her back had been toward the entrance and she'd caught just a brief glimpse, no wonder she hadn't been able to place the moment.

"I got the story out of Angelo because Russell wouldn't tell me." Cassidy confided so that the others at the table wouldn't hear. "The three of them were close friends in New York. Can you believe that my husband used to date her but ended up with me? It makes no sense."

Jo thought it made perfect sense, at least as soon as you saw the way Russell looked at Cassidy. She was the center of his world, perhaps even more than he was the center of hers. If that were possible.

Jo had finally registered that it wasn't Angelo who was thrown by Melanie's sudden appearance, it was Russell. And something about it had hit him far deeper than "they used to date." Yet Russell had managed to move past that, even if he wasn't quite back to his usual blusterous self. He might sound it, but to Jo's trained ear the testimony of his bravura didn't quite ring true.

She had also overheard him at one point during a break in the shoot whispering to Melanie. Whispering that he was so sorry.

"I have a suggestion." Jo hugged Cassidy for a moment so that she could whisper in her friend's ear.

"What?"

Angelo hadn't been so much flirting with Melanie as trying to help his friends. And he'd done it so well that it had mostly worked. He was such a good man, it was hard to credit.

"I think," Jo told Cassidy, "that when you take Russell home tonight, you should be especially nice to him. He's a very good man."

Cassidy had smiled and nodded. And she hadn't looked the least bit upset by the burden.

"You are in rare form tonight, my son."

Angelo's mother patted his back as he fussed over the final plating of the desserts.

"I tried. I really tried."

"I quote that short thing to you, 'You no try, you do'."

"Yoda," Angelo supplied.

"Yes, whatever. Finish that and you deliver it. Manuel and me, we finish the dinners. You go be with your friends and with the bicycle lady."

Angelo wiped the edge of a spotless plate and tried to calm his nerves.

Jo was pissed at him about something. He knew that much. When Russell had drifted through the kitchen at one point, he'd asked, but his friend had no idea. He'd tried to offer Angelo a warning scowl of poaching on his honorary sisters, but Angelo was too worried about what he might have done to care.

It was like whenever he was with Jo, she was the most amazing woman he'd ever met. And then the lawyer would appear and he felt like an undereducated slob who couldn't do anything right.

"Go. You fussing like an old woman. I'm an old woman, you are not. So you are not allowed to fuss like one."

"Yes, Mama." He kissed her cheek, then picked up the tray and tried to breeze through the door.

He served the dessert, describing it as he went around the table. Practiced diners like these would absolutely want to know what they were eating.

"This is my mother's Panna Cotta recipe, with a few twists. Atop her Italian cream, I floated Tarocco-blood-orange-infused eighty-five-percent dark cocoa sauce topped with honey-glazed strawberries. Rather than a grappa, I've paired it with espresso. Though I would suggest Marolo Barolo Grappa if you'd prefer that."

Only as he finished serving did he dare look at the people around the table. Russell, with his broken leg propped on a chair, and Claude were busy discussing ad composition at one end. Renée was listening closely, making occasional suggestions. The four other women sat down the table, Melanie and Perrin on one side, Cassidy and Jo on the other.

He looked at Jo last, trying to be careful about gauging her temperature. He took the last Panna Cotta and espresso for himself and hesitated. Jo slid her chair slightly toward Cassidy and pulled her dessert over as well, opening just enough room for him at the end of the table.

He'd take that as a good sign.

He set his dessert in the cleared space and pulled over a chair from the next table as he fielded all of the compliments about the meal and the dessert that rippled up and down the table.

Jo was silent as she took one bite, then another.

He settled enough to try his own. It was the best he'd ever done. Even his mother had not tried to alter what he'd added to her old recipe. She'd simply tasted it then turned away to walk to the sink. At first he'd thought she was going to spit it out.

She'd run a little water over her fingertips then patted them dry on her apron and brushed them lightly over her eyes. If he didn't know better, he'd suspect her of blinking back tears before she turned clear-eyed to tell him how wonderful it was.

"Thank you for the rose. It's beautiful."

Jo wasn't looking at him. It was if she were speaking quietly to her dessert.

"You're welcome." The second word came out on a dry rasp despite the chocolate and cream coating his tongue.

Then she looked at him with those dark, amazing eyes and he almost fell forward. They were so clear that their depth felt infinite, and their gaze cut clear through him until his soul lay bare before them.

She looked back down at her dessert but didn't take another taste.

He waited, barely hearing the buzz of laughter over something that enveloped the rest of the table but left them alone together.

"I have to work late tomorrow." Again that quiet comment in the direction of her dessert.

"How late?" He held his breath not really daring to understand what he thought he understood.

"How late do you have to work?"

Angelo struggled to get his thoughts moving. "On a Wednesday, I can be done by nine."

Jo looked up at him again.

For the length of three breaths she said nothing, merely studying him.

"That sounds good," was all she said and returned to her dessert.

Angelo looked down at his own Panna Cotta, then up the table.

He was pretty sure that someone was asking him a question, but he couldn't hear it over the pounding in his ears.

"*Aaaaaaaaaaaahhhh!*" *Jo wanted to* pound her head on the desk. Not that it would solve anything.

The whole discovery process had been completely screwed up. A dozen filings with the court would be necessary to straighten it out before she could even initiate a serious review of the key case documents. And she should really start writing those now. She'd need at least five interrogatories, and probably more. She already had a deposition list going and it was only the fifth or sixth day she'd been working on the case.

Muriel would know what else she needed to do to fix this mess. Jo hated it when they didn't bring her in right at the start of a case. This one had muddled along for months in the lower courts before anyone realized that it was going to become a major piece of litigation with ramifications easily reaching into the billions. Arctic Ocean mineral rights, oil reserves, fisheries, Northwest Passage navigation... The list was rapidly growing.

Some idiot in Juneau, with no real knowledge of Maritime Law and apparently wholly unaware of the applicability of International Sea Law, had advanced the case to Alaska's Supreme Court. It should have gone straight to Federal. Instead, there were now dozens of interest groups suing and countersuing with no idea that most of their noise was meaningless but would take months of work to sweep aside.

Why had she sent Muriel home? Just because the woman had a date was no excuse. Muriel had remained uncomplainingly until Jo had used up very possible second, including her time to go home and change which was just plain cruel on Jo's part. It was only in a fit of martyrdom that she'd told Muriel to finally go and have fun. What had Jo been thinking when she did that?

Then there was Renée Linden's parting comment last night still churning about in Jo's brain like a nasty little whirlwind wreaking destruction upon any line of reasoning.

Not once in all of yesterday afternoon and evening that they'd been together had Renée mentioned that she was recommending Jo for the position, making it especially hard for Jo to turn down something that hadn't been offered. Nor had Jo found a way to even once intimate that she'd discovered that is what the woman was planning. Because Jo would sound like a fool if she were wrong.

Yet, at the end of the evening, Renée had rested a gentle hand on Jo's forearm and said, "I knew you would be wonderful at this. So many think it is about doing the job. You and I know that it is about finding the right people to do the job." And then she'd disappeared into the dark Seattle evening before Jo could get her verbal-acuity feet back under her and even consider forming an intelligent response.

And then there was Angelo.

Okay. Somewhere in the middle of the night she'd finally understood the ugly emotion that had swamped her at seeing Angelo and the beautiful Melanie together. Jealousy. What did she have to be jealous about? One kiss. Okay, two if you counted the ice cream kiss from the bike ride. Being a guy probably meant that he did, but being a sensible member of the female gender, she definitely didn't.

Yet she did.

Okay, damn it! Two kisses.

They'd shared two kisses totaling something on the order of ten seconds. Perhaps longer. She wasn't so sure about how long that second kiss had lasted. Hard to estimate time when your mind blanked beneath the electric-shock wave of sensation.

But none of it should be enough to justify jealousy.

And then once she'd absolved him from the crime of flirting with Melanie, beyond his being male and Italian and Melanie being drop-dead gorgeous and a close friend, what had she done? She'd invited him out on a date.

What kind of a date started at nine on a weeknight? When she wasn't working, she'd normally be in bed with a good book by nine. That supposedly gripping Grisham novel still sat there untouched. That wasn't like her either.

If she wasn't herself, who was she turning into?

She flashed momentarily on the opening of Alice in Wonderland. The part where Alice can't make sense of her world or remember her multiplication tables and decides she must not be Alice after all, but rather a sad little girl named Mabel and she weeps a pool of tears.

"I must be Mabel."

"Really? I thought you were Jo Thompson. Did I bring these to the wrong office?"

Jo jerked upright in her chair to see Angelo leaning against the doorjamb of her office holding a small white box.

"How long have you been there?"

"Long enough to find your office by your screams. Strange thing to do all alone in the night."

"How did you get in here? And what's in there?"

"One question at a time, counselor." He moved easily across the room to sit in one of the client chairs across from her desk. He looked gorgeous. His faded jeans were tight fitting, not because they were tight, but because he had such good muscle under them. His shirt was unbuttoned only two buttons from the neck, but that was at least one too many as it hinted at his strong chest and raised her temperature in an unseemly fashion. She almost asked him to stand and turn around for a moment just to see that wonderful taper from shoulder to hip, then lectured herself sharply to behave.

They were just getting together for a date, which she was really too busy for anyway. She'd make them some tea in the office kitchen, they'd share whatever treat he'd brought and now set in her In Basket, then she'd send him on his way.

"I got in here because your building guard is Manuel's cousin, Manuel is my sous chef, and we feed her when she finds someone she wants to really impress."

"So you just bribe your way into any building you want?"

"Oh," he sat back and folded his hands behind his head looking perfectly relaxed. "We chefs have our ways. To answer the rest of your question, the outer door to your offices is unlocked and I found your office because it is the only one with the light on. And also, you know, the screams."

Jo fought the heat that rushed to her cheeks and reached for composure.

"The door was unlocked because it's a secure elevator so the last one to leave, tonight being me, actually usually being me, would lock up. But courtesy of Manuel's cousin, her master passcard to the elevator, and your relationship with her…"

"Don't go there," Angelo cut her off. "Won't do you any good. Dora's nineteen, good at her job, and a lesbian. Our relationship is purely caloric."

Jo would give good money to know how he looked so relaxed when she so wasn't.

It was a good thing Dora had been the security guard on duty or Angelo would have had no compunction about turning around and sprinting out the door when faced with the edifice that was the sixteenth floor entrance to Stanley, Tu, Rolfmann, and Thompson. Every single thing about their offices had reeked of intimidation and power.

First, the thick glass doors with the four names in gold leaf, didn't open like doors, with handles. They shot aside with a soft, "whoosh!" like they were from Star Trek. Not some clunky supermarket door either. One moment the things were there blocking him out. The next moment they were gone, and the fittings were so seamless it was hard to tell where they'd gone into the sides of the ebony archway that dared the intruder to pass beneath. He half expected a Stargate vortex to shimmer to life and swallow him whole.

Five feet into the office, they'd magically reappeared behind him like an invisible cage. He'd considered returning to the elevator just to make sure he could escape if needs be, but he knew if he started down that road there'd be no turning back.

The lobby was all dusky blues: the carpet, the leather furniture, the walls. Even when the lighting automatically came up, it was subtle and indirect. The ceiling appeared to be fathomless glass, as if you could look up into it forever and never find yourself. Behind the receptionist's desk, a wall of floor-to-ceiling windows threatened to spill you over a dozen stories down into Elliot Bay. Even at night, it looked precipitous. A bad place for anyone who feared heights.

Offices ranged right and left along the Sound-view face of the building.

The only light had been at the end of the left-hand corridor, which is how he had arrived at Jo's equally intimidating corner office. The walls were dark-smoked glass. The photographs of wilderness sunsets and morning vistas were framed in bright stainless steel which appeared to float off the glass walls like magic in some futuristic art gallery. They offered the only color other than the dark wood of Jo's desk which was covered with a large, ocean-blue map. That was then buried deep in files that appeared to have been deposited in stages like layers of stone. There was no clock, but rather a projection of one from somewhere behind the glass. The clock face, very similar to the giant one looming over Pike Place Market that he could see many stories below through her window, simply shown deep red on the smoky glass.

And in the middle of all the futuristic reek of power had been Jo with her head down in her hands.

That's when he'd found his equilibrium. No matter how high-powered she might be, no matter the trappings around her, she was a woman obviously deeply tired and frustrated.

Somehow, her heartless office made her, by contrast, so much more human. A human Jo Thompson he could deal with. The power-suited Counselor Thompson, name partner of the law firm, that one scared the shit out of him. So, he would just pretend that one wasn't present. He glanced down at a glass coffee table and spotted a copy of something called the ABA Journal and the cover had a picture of Jo and three guys grouped around her but a half-step behind her. They were probably Stanley, Tu, and Rolfmann. Angelo absolutely was going to pretend that he hadn't seen that.

And she looked so distressed that he reset his agenda even as he watched her. Tonight she didn't need an eager lover, he hoped that's what she'd been suggesting. Tonight she looked as if she needed a friend.

"So, what's going on?" He'd just ignore her question about how he looked so relaxed, because if he thought about it, he wouldn't be.

"Everything. Nothing. It's… I'm…" Then she scrubbed her face for a moment and flipped a fistful of hair back over her shoulder. "I'm a mess."

"But such a beautiful mess."

"You're so Italian."

"Sue me," he grinned at her.

"Don't tempt me, Angelo. At this point that might just cheer me up."

"So if you sue me, do I get to see more of you, or less?"

She slipped a bright pink pen behind her left ear which held her hair back on that side, leaving the other side free to spill strand by strand forward over her right shoulder. He had to blink to resist the mesmerizing movement of sliding hair like liquid midnight.

"I'd see you more because of depositions," she tapped a stack of notes, "and discovery," she slapped a tall stack of files then had to grab and re-center them to keep them from falling.

"Sounds good. Let's do it."

"But also much less socially, and never without opposing counsel in attendance to protect your rights."

"Ah, well. Now that doesn't sound so good. Not unless she's very cute."

Jo laughed then scowled at him. He'd ignore that as well.

"So what is all this mess?" He'd had Russell look over his restaurant lease renewal agreement a few weeks ago, because he didn't understand such things. They'd made a few minor tweaks, but Russell had declared the thing really fair, so Angelo had signed. What Jo had ranged across her desk looked utterly meaningless. Overlong pages of paper had numbers running down the left side and strange blocky headings on the first page. The long, yellow legal pad already had a dozen pages folded under and the exposed page was mostly full of tightly spaced notes.

"It was supposed to be the next year of my life, but I'm afraid it's going to be the next five. I really don't want to spend the next five years commuting to Alaska."

"Alaska?" Angelo did his best to hide his distress at the idea of her being so far away. Especially for so long.

"North Slope mineral and oil exploration rights," she patted one pile of files. Then another, "Fishing rights." And a third, "International agreements. And disagreements." A fourth.

"All controlled by international law, superseded by case law, governmental protests, diplomatic letters, and U.N. negotiations." She aimed a finger at various piles.

"U.N.? As in United Nations?" Angelo could feel his cool slipping once again and struggled to find it and pull it over him like the cloak of baked mozzarella on an Eggplant Parmigiana.

"Yes. It's pretty exciting actually. I might get my first chance to argue a case in front of the U.N. Maritime Court."

She couldn't have named anything more impossible. The White House made more sense than the U.N. The U.N. was the place he'd gone on a high school class trip, had a toured lecture while hovered over by a dozen security guards. It wasn't technically in New York. It was in some weird International Zone that wasn't even a part of the United States.

"Whoa! We're talking about that big building on the Eastside midtown Manhattan? The one with the hundred and something flags around it?" He blew out a breath. "That's too unreal. Let's get you back down to Earth." He nudged the white box still sitting in her In Basket.

She glanced at it without reaching across the piles to pick it up.

"If it's more of your Panna Cotta I will charge you with malfeasance and criminal intent regarding the condition of my waistline."

"Mal what? And you have an amazingly attractive waistline."

"Intentional wrongdoing." The waistline comment appeared to fluster her. He'd have to remember that. It was as if she'd shed a little bit more of the lawyer when he said it.

"Oh. No, it's not Panna Cotta." He was starting to like the way she spoke. At first it had put him off, but it was simply a different world than his own. They were both specialists, just very different specialists. The Alaska thing worried him though.

He nudged the box again and she finally gave in.

She took it and peered inside. "What are they?"

"Very decadent."

"I guessed that much. How decadent?"

He smiled when she looked up at him with those dark eyes of hers. "Very."

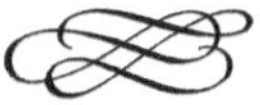

Decadent? Jo really needed something to be decadent right at the moment. Not Alaska, not case law, not Pike Place Market, not even a triathlon. She needed something that was wholly for her. And she knew exactly what it was, but it was so outrageous she didn't want to risk even speaking in case that somehow ruined it.

She closed the little white box and rose without a word. She left some part of herself in that leather office chair. If she'd been less tired, she might have returned to gather it back up, but at the moment she just didn't care. She tapped the control embedded in the desk's surface and the tight-focused overhead desk lamp faded to darkness leaving only the soft glow of the walls and the city lights from the windows. Angelo found her jacket on the back of the door and held it out for her.

Past the lobby and through the doors. She hit the button on her keyring remote. The doors snicked shut and locked, then the lobby lights dimmed to a soft glow. Nineteen stories down to the parking garage and into her BMW Z4 roadster.

Angelo whistled appreciatively, but when he would have spoken, she shook her head. She'd had way too many words today. And yesterday. And the damned day before.

He bowed his acquiescence as if he were a butler in full tails rather than a chef in jeans, a loose button-down shirt, and scuffed sneakers. He held the door for her until she was settled in her seat, then closed it gently. Climbing in beside her, he took the small white box and she fired off the car and flipped the switch to open the convertible top.

She loved this car. It had been a bonus the day she made partner and had her name added to the Stanley, Tu, and Rolfmann letterhead. The stunning magazine ad for the BMW had been her screensaver for six months and the partners had noticed and purchased it for her as a bonus for the big win she'd pulled off on behalf of the fishing corporations last year. She liked working for this firm. She truly did. But she wasn't going to think about them anymore tonight.

The BMW ad had been a hell of an ad, the long-legged blonde in thigh-high red leather boots and a single red rose contrasted with the jet-black car with black leather upholstery. She almost missed a gear shift when she connected that Melanie must have been the model in the ad. Cassidy had found out that Russell had shot and composed it, and Jo now knew that the supermodel had been his favored subject while he was still a professional ad photographer in New York. Was it because they'd been lovers, or because she was so beautiful? Well, it was interesting either way.

The car tires screamed along the coiled ramp leading upward from deep underground, the engine humming as if eager for the open road, and they almost launched onto the city streets. Angelo reached a hand over and slid his fingertips just once along her thigh. Like an electric shock, her pulse rate jumped by a third.

Ten blocks. She could make it ten blocks. Besides, tackling him in the tight confines of the car wasn't terribly practical on well-lit city streets. Not that it wouldn't be interesting to try.

She whirled down into the condo's underground parking and rolled into her spot.

They took hands as they approached the elevator.

Once the elevator passed the lobby floor with no one else getting on, she pushed him against the cool steel wall and threw herself at him.

He was more than up to the challenge. His kiss crushed against hers. His arms, those splendid, chef-strong arms, wrapped her so tightly against his chest that she'd probably have trouble breathing, if she'd cared to.

It was the last concern on her mind.

She nipped his ear, ran a tongue along his neck and bit the base of his throat. This wasn't the Jo she knew and maybe that was a good thing. She could hear Muriel in the background somewhere telling her to drag the man into her lair.

Damn straight!

Jo ran her curled fingers down his chest, her short, practical nails making a slick sound over his linen shirt. She dug them into his pecs and he groaned in her ear.

That groan reached right down inside her. She had the power to make a beautiful man groan with need. Her last concerns about Angelo as a lover dissipated. For tonight she didn't care about past or future, education or ambition. She deepened the kiss until the heat raged over her skin.

The elevator dinged her floor. She grabbed him by the belt at the front of his pants and dragged him into the hall and down to her condo door.

She opened the door, but didn't waste time placing her keys in their little bowl. She tossed them aside and heard them plink off a picture.

"Not one word," she growled as she slammed the door to her lair and shoved Angelo back against it. "Just make me feel. That's all I want. I just want to feel. Don't make me think. Don't let me think."

She dug her hands into his hair and tasted his lips again. She felt the smile and growled. He grunted as she shoved him against the door again driving their hips together hard.

His hands were on her. Rather than clawing her breast, he leaned down to take it in his teeth through blouse and bra.

Jo tried to strip off her jacket, but he stopped her.

In moments she stood with her skirt pooled around her feet, her blouse and bra open, but still dressed in the power jacket.

She shoved his shirt up in her need to feel flesh on flesh.

Trapped by the shirt bunched around his armpits while she rubbed against that beautiful chest, he flexed and clawed at it until he could get it off.

Jo drove his pants down until she could cradle him in her hands.

"God, I just want to feel."

He recovered protection from his pocket as his pants fell to the floor and slid it on even as she nipped at his chest.

They drove against each other with a mutual cry of relief and finished the job right there against the door.

ANGELO WAS BLIND. It was the only explanation. He was blind and his wildest fantasy, that now lay draped against him gasping for each breath, must be in his mind's eye. That dusky skin of Jo's face and arms had driven his dreams wild. He now knew it ran all the way down the length of her body unbroken by tan lines of lighter skin. Her entire body shone lustrous.

Jo lay against his shoulder and all he could think was how much he needed to do that exact same thing again right now, if only his body was ready. Well, even if his wasn't, hers was.

Before she could recover, he lay her back on the charcoal carpet and did something he'd been fantasizing about since the first time he'd seen her. He might be physically spent for the moment, but he was dying to taste her, wondering if she tasted as good as she looked.

She tasted better.

As the dim lights of the city shone into the darkened apartment through the tall windows, he reveled in her body. The side of her breasts had the light salt of a sweaty sheen. The tips themselves throbbed sweetly against his tongue when he scraped them with his teeth. That soft line where hip met leg harkened to the entertaining savory of a fine meal. But when he ran his tongue along her and she arched against his mouth with intense need, he knew he had found the main course and drove her until she cried out and dug her fingers into his shoulders to hold on.

When the last shudder had rippled beneath her flesh and his own need was climbing once again, he scooped her up in his arms and carried her into the bedroom.

It was several maddening, body-aching hours before their mutual needs wound down enough for his head to stop spinning. He'd had entertaining little amuse bouche, one-bite taste, relationships. He'd had women who were a nice appetizer or even a fine meal. Counselor Jo Thompson was a full five-course banquet. Every time he thought he'd sated her, or himself, she had proved him splendidly wrong.

They laughed, they clung, more than once she whimpered and he may well have done the same, but they didn't speak a word.

When at last they collapsed from exhaustion, he fetched her a warm washcloth and a dry towel. When she would have cleaned herself, he did it for her, driving her up again, making himself mad with touching her.

Afterward, when he figured that neither of them could take any more, he fetched the little white box which had somehow survived their frantic entry into the condo.

He tucked Jo in under the quilt and then slid in beside her.

Opening the box, he held one of the dark chocolates out to her mouth.

She took it from his fingers leaving a small nibble on his fingertips.

She fed him the other, he sucked on her fingertips as he took it until she actually moaned. Or perhaps it was because of how he stroked the glorious bounty of her breast beneath the covers.

He tasted the richness of the dark chocolate as it melted in his mouth. When he broke through to the interior, the flavors exploded into his mouth. Layers began with a wash of sweet Courvoisier liqueur and orange zest. At the very last, he bit into the dark fruit and the cherry built into a heady denouement. Then the surprise, the tiny burst of the lemon and carob chocolate chip he'd slipped into the cherry where the pit had been.

"Oh my God," Jo sighed and curled into his arms. "Now that is very, very decadent."

CHAPTER 16

"*Where are you going?*" Jo's voice was warm and slurred with sleep.

Angelo had been trying to leave without waking her, managed pants and socks, but couldn't quite figure out what to do with his torn shirt. Maybe a stapler. He'd torn it himself as the only way to get it off fast enough. Even that idle thought had his body responding.

He came back to the bed and looked down at her. The white quilt was tucked up around her chin and her dark hair spilled over the pale green pillow case. The city lights did little to light the room in the predawn darkness, just enough for him to admire the picture she made. He leaned down to kiss her but she stopped him with a long bare arm that snaked out from beneath the covers and planted in the middle of his chest.

"Trying to slip off in the middle of the night?"

"It's almost five."

"Still. You're one of those men who doesn't want to wake up next to a woman." Her tone had gone accusatory and was heading toward counselor.

He brushed his fingers along her cheek.

"I have to go shopping for the restaurant. The fish monger will be opening shortly and I like having the first pick."

"Oh."

"Oh?" he did his best to hide his smile but it wasn't working. She looked so amazingly good all curled up and warm beneath the covers.

"Oh." Her hand shifted from warding him off to pressed against his bare chest for a moment. Then she pulled her arm back beneath the covers which she used to pull the covers up even tighter beneath her chin.

He settled beside her and brushed the backs of his fingers on her impossibly soft cheek. This time when he leaned in, she allowed the kiss, a soft lingering moment that refired his blood.

"I, uh…" she protested. "I don't know what happened."

"We made wild passionate love all night, how could you forget?" He did his best to sound mortally offended.

"I remember that part." She raised her head from the pillow enough to brush her lips on his. "Trust me, I remember that part. I'm just not sure who you were with. It didn't seem like me."

"Oh, I don't know," Angelo traced the line of her body through the quilt, down over breast, waist, and hip. "I found the contrast, ah, invigorating." At one point last night after he'd gotten her naked, he'd had her put the power jacket back on. Just the power jacket. It was the sexiest thing he'd ever seen, cleavage almost to her belly button, better than sheer cotton or fine lace. It had been a while before he'd allowed her to remove it again.

"Invigorating?" She practically shouted in his face. "Invigorating?"

He brushed down the quilt and attacked her breast with his tongue as he slid his hand down her body.

In moments her arms had wrapped around the back of his head dragging him into that lovely softness deeper and harder than he'd have dared on his own. He didn't let her go until she arched against his hand and cried out when she came, curling against him and holding on as her body let go like an explosion.

He'd never been with a woman who so responded to his every touch. It was as if he unleashed a whole different person from the sophisticated Jo Thompson every time he touched her. He'd also never met a woman who he responded to so deeply. Whatever he'd thought about his physical attraction to Jo Thompson had been a gross underestimate.

"Invigorating?" he tried not to crow in triumph as she giggled at his question. Who would ever have thought that Jo Thompson could giggle?

"Okay. Yes. I'll give you that point."

When she at last relaxed, she tried to drag him back into bed by the remains of his tattered shirt.

He protested that he had to leave. "Mama will be waiting to go to the Market."

"That's a new one." Her voice was little more than a whisper.

It was. He suddenly felt sixteen again, slipping back into the house hoping his mama wouldn't know what he'd been out doing in the night. He really needed to figure out what was going on there.

He glanced at the bedside clock. And he really needed to get going, period. All he wanted to do was crawl back in with Jo, but that simply couldn't happen right now.

"I have to go. I'm sorry."

She nodded and stretched languidly, back on her way to sleep. Rather than jumping on that incredible body, he pulled the covers up around her neck and tucked her in.

"Russell left a windbreaker when he was here right before the wedding," her voice softened toward a sleepy mumble. "It's on the coat rack."

The jacket was too long for Angelo. Russell was enough taller that it almost fit Angelo like a mini dress. But it was better than going through Pike Place Market in a shredded shirt.

He slipped out of the condo and hurried downstairs to begin the ten-block walk to the Market.

ANGELO'S MAMA was already flirting with Henry the fishmonger when he arrived out of breath; he'd jogged much of the way trying to make up time. He didn't want anyone else getting the scoop on him. But Charlene from Maximilien's was already there, he usually beat her to the day's best catch.

Not today, she had some incredible looking mahi-mahi set aside and about thirty pounds of steamers in from Penn Cove.

He couldn't regret the cause for delay, but it wasn't good.

His mother continued to chat with Henry, then she winked at him.

Perfetto! Now his mother was going to tease him about not coming home last night.

He poked through the various proteins and was considering the shark, but wasn't feeling terribly inspired by it. Charlene headed off, giving him a cocky salute obviously pleased with her coup.

"Is she gone?" Maria Amelia appeared at his shoulder and looked down the long tiled corridor of the Market to make sure Charlene wasn't stopping at the produce vendor or the cured meats counter.

"She's gone, Mama."

"Good. She's pretty, Angelo. But not as pretty as your lawyer friend."

She *was* pretty. But she'd never done anything to fire his blood. She was also married to her pastry chef and had been for years. However, even thinking of Jo for a moment turned his thoughts to mush. He had to get moving. Turning back to Henry, he pointed toward the shark, but his mother slapped his hand aside.

She led him around behind the counter and waved a negligent hand. Out of sight at Henry's feet were three huge mesh bags of the most perfect sea scallops still in the shell that he'd ever seen. Beside them, a tub of ice sported some beautiful squid, perfect for side dishes of fried calamari rings.

She patted Henry on the cheek, "He's such a good man. So sweet."

Henry beamed.

His mother might make him crazy, but his menu was really going to shine tonight.

CHAPTER 17

"*ive o'clock at Cutters.*" Jo didn't even greet Cassidy when she answered the phone. Just issued the order.

"Uh. O-kay." Cassidy's voice was hazed with sleep.

Jo looked at the clock floating on the glass wall of her office. It was barely seven. The morning light was bright enough that the overhead lights were faded down to almost nothing. "Oh, sorry. I didn't realize the time."

Cassidy was usually awake by now, but she certainly didn't sound it at the moment.

"S'okay. Russell and I, we were just, sort of, uh, continuing the honeymoon."

Great, now she felt even worse. Unable to sleep after Angelo left, she'd skipped her morning workout and come straight to work. She hadn't even stopped for a bagel and cream cheese or anything else fattening and satisfying. She'd had her usual tasteless power drink and driven to the office. She had to drive to work most days now because she didn't want to be walking home on the city streets after dark, which is when she was typically departing. Even though it would be the longest day of the year soon, she'd wager it would be a long time before she walked home during daylight hours again.

Muriel would be arriving shortly and the next round of case files would follow not long after. She wasn't up to facing this day.

Jo rubbed at her gritty eyes and apologized again for rousing Cassidy from her marriage bed.

"Sounds major," Cassidy's voice was a little more coherent.

"I...," Muriel rolled in on cue and dropped a to-go cup of coffee off on her desk. "Yes, it is." She dragged the words out until Muriel had drifted to her own office across the hall. "But I can't get into it at the moment."

"Okay."

"It's you I need to speak to." She felt crappy for saying it that way, but knew Cassidy would get the message. Jo didn't need Russell or Perrin, it was Cassidy's level-headed thinking she needed at the moment. And, most of all, it was her former roommate's reaction she was worried about.

After only the briefest of pauses, Cassidy replied, her voice fully awake. "See you at five."

Muriel brought in the first stack of the morning and looked for a space to set it on Jo's desk.

"Someone looks as if they had great sex last night."

Jo groaned to herself. That was the problem with working with Muriel for five years, she couldn't hide a single thing from her.

She took the first file of the day and began slogging her way through it.

JO HADN'T SHOWN up at the gym, not that he'd really expected her to, so Angelo had made his workout short. He'd started with lots of energy, but within ten minutes his body was dragging, within twenty it was stopped. Trying to function on two or three hours of sleep wasn't cutting it.

He needed to rethink his need for personal masochism. Of course she had the good sense to sleep while she could. She was a sensible woman. But not as sensible as she wanted you to think.

There was a wild streak hidden deep inside Jo Thompson that had startled, aroused, and fascinated Angelo. Brilliant, beautiful, and lethal. When he'd coaxed her back into that power jacket, and just that power jacket, she'd taken absolute control. It was a role reversal he wasn't used to. He didn't object, but he'd found most women wanted to abandon themselves to his control. Not Counselor Thompson. In that jacket, she'd climbed atop him and used him until his mind blanked and his body ached. Or had his body blanked and his mind ached? Whatever it was, it had been incredible. Out of the jacket, she'd gone soft and gentle, wrapping herself about him to welcome him in. He couldn't imagine ever getting enough of her.

After shopping and the lame excuse for a workout, he'd crawled home and sacked out until it was time to go to the restaurant for lunch service. A shower and shave did little to restore his equilibrium and nothing to erase the self-satisfied smile in the mirror. He practically floated up the six blocks to work.

"I hear she's at it again," Mr. D warned him when he stopped by to share a morning espresso.

Angelo didn't need to ask who, nor did he pause to finish his shot before running up Post Alley behind Mr. D's, dodging cars and slow-moving pedestrians who were plodding up the steep hill, so steep that the sidewalk had bumps built into the concrete to keep you from slipping back downhill.

Once again, a line, thankfully shorter this time, had formed in front of the restaurant. They didn't open for another hour, what was Maria Amelia doing this time?

Angelo slowed in order to appear calm when he arrived, though his heart was pounding far harder than the mere block-and-a-half run justified.

The patrons weren't lined up at the door, they were lined up at the kitchen window. He'd sometimes left it cracked open to let the cooking scents spill out into the alley as an advertisement. Now, someone had installed a small counter that stuck out from the window sill and the window sash itself was slid all of the way up.

He stumbled to a halt at the edge of the crowd and stared.

Inside the window sat his mother. She wore a deep purple dress that clung to her curves and exposed a cleavage worthy of Sophia Loren. Her laugh sparkled out.

A smiling customer left the line and passed Angelo. She bore a tiny cup of espresso and a flaky cornetto, an Italian croissant filled with, he didn't need to lean in close to see, he could smell the sweet Italian sausage and pepper.

There was no posted menu, just a sign that said, "$3" next to a jar. He noticed that most people slipped in a five anyway and left happy. His mother's charm was apparently sufficient for the two-dollar tip. Even at five dollars, it was a bargain. The cornetti were large, flaky, and still steaming. The espresso was dark, rich, and served in an amount a little bigger than an Italian portion but not so big as an American one.

He slipped into the restaurant. There she sat, perched on her stool by the window. Her bare legs casually crossed and exposed by a knee-length skirt that rode just up on her thighs. She wasn't racy, but she was a fair amount too attractive, for even an Italian mother, and especially for his mother. He slipped up across from her and leaned against the window's wall, pretty much out of view of the customers.

"You're not going to make much money that way, Mama," he whispered just loud enough for her to hear in between customers.

"Sweetheart, I am losing you money." She smiled as if that were the goal.

But Angelo knew better. He left Maria Amelia to charm the next early morning patron after taking a cornetto and espresso for himself and leaving an, "I love you, Mama," behind. He strolled over to Manuel as he enjoyed the rich sausage in the almost painfully warm pastry.

"Better gear up, Manuel. We've got another lunch rush coming."

Manuel just smiled at him, took a bite of his own, almost-finished cornetto, and went back to work. Angelo pulled on an apron. He'd spent the night with a woman who presented more mystery and fascination after being with her, rather than less as usually seemed to be the case. His mouth was watering for the next bite of his second breakfast. His mother was actually fitting in at his restaurant. And they were about to get hammered by a massive lunch rush.

It was a very good day.

CHAPTER 18

utters Crabhouse was their go-to bar when they needed to talk. Jo and Perrin had met here on and off for years. Then when Cassidy had returned to Seattle to be with her ailing father and purchased a condo practically next door, it had become a fixture in their lives. Whenever someone had a crisis or a triumph, commiseration and celebration were handed out in equal shares at Cutter's.

The outer bar was lively, as it was one of those places that urban professionals went to see and be seen, which could be very fun. But it also allowed them to slip into the anonymity of the crowd, each clustered in small but very watchful groups, and gain a pleasant level of privacy. Good cocktails, great appetizers, and what Cassidy acknowledged as an acceptable wine cellar certainly helped.

It also sat a block from both Jo's office and Cassidy's condo and only three from Perrin's Glorious Garb in Belltown with her apartment above her store.

Jo scanned the room as she came in the front door, waiting for a couple who didn't quite understand that they had to keep going down a barely labeled side hall to reach the entry to the restaurant. Despite it having good food and some of the best views in Seattle, Jo and her

453

friends rarely went for a meal, opting instead for the more relaxed community of the bar.

Cutter's trademark focaccia scented the air with rosemary and olive oil. Garlic of steamed clams and the bright bite of lemon for oysters wrapped around her and welcomed her in. The bright afternoon light shining in from the long wall of windows facing the Seattle waterfront actually left the bar feeling warm and friendly by contrast.

Jo could feel her shoulders easing even as she spotted Cassidy. Perrin sat close beside her, looking much better than the last time Jo had seen her. Though her hair was now bleach-white rather than the Jo-Thompson-black that it had been.

Cassidy spotted Jo and offered a near invisible shrug. It said, "I know what you said, but tough."

And Cassidy, as usual, was right.

Jo did need to talk to her college roommate, but whatever else might be going on, Perrin was a true friend and would do anything for her.

Cassidy had snagged them three tall stools at a small table by the window. Only about a third of the tables were occupied, leaving a bit of a hush in the bar. But it was barely five o'clock, give it half an hour and the place would be humming.

Cassidy had worn a simple silk blouse and designer jeans with flats, a serious dress down for her. She really was still on her honeymoon, which made Jo feel all the more guilty for dragging her away from it. Perrin wore one of her own designs, again in the pale green of the bridesmaid gowns, but this time as a peasant blouse fallen off one shoulder. The floral skirt showed a long flash of her fine legs and looked great with her simple sandals. Jo had to stare at it for several moments before she recognized it as her own skirt, stolen from her closet, and redesigned to be more updated. She'd liked that skirt, but there was little point complaining about it to Perrin.

Jo searched wildly for some safe topic to start with as she joined them, and landed nowhere near one.

"Did Perrin tell you about the dress she made for me?" Jo needed to cut her tongue out now. She knew it was going to be going straight downhill from this point on.

———

Jo RARELY DRANK, and almost never finished the first drink when she did, but when the second Honey Citrus Martini disappeared and a third one replaced it without her quite figuring out how it happened, she knew she was in trouble. The Dungeness Crab Cakes, Buffalo Wings, and Steamed Manila Clams in a sauce so luscious they were still dipping it up with another round of focaccia, had slid by just as easily over the last hour.

Thankfully, the dress turned out to be the right topic after all. It ended up that Perrin hadn't mentioned it to Cassidy. She wanted to drag them all off to Jo's apartment to see it right away, but she and Cassidy had vetoed that. Then Perrin rescued Jo's poor lead-in by starting on her idea for a line of custom wedding dresses, not designed as dresses, but designed for individuals.

"You'll be the Howard Roarke of fashion." Jo wondered blearily what neuron had remembered that tidbit of information.

"No. First, in case you haven't noticed because they're so small, I actually do have breasts. So I can't be anyone named Howard."

"You do," Jo acknowledged. "They look good on you too. Better than they would on Gary Cooper."

Perrin tipped her head sideways. "You're drunk. You aren't making sense any longer."

"Gary Cooper played Howard Roarke in the movie The Fountainhead." Cassidy took up the gauntlet and tried to carry it down the field or across the polo ground or whatever one did with a gauntlet. "It's about an architect who believes that every design must be unique to the place and the materials."

Perrin stared down at her Cosmo for several long seconds before replying. "But I'm not building buildings. I'm designing wedding dresses. And I'm saying that they need to be unique for each woman. Jo's dress would look stupid on you."

"Because I don't have Jo's amazing breasts."

"Exactly!" Perrin flagged down a waitress with a loud, "Hey cutie!" Which turned a dozen or so heads at their end of the lounge.

She was cute in a brunette, clingy-top clad way though Jo would never have thought of her that way. Let alone shouted it out for the whole bar to hear.

"Is it me," Perrin studied the table, "or did we run out of food?"

"I can fix that," the waitress was unflappable.

"Cool, thanks!" Perrin turned back to Jo. "What was I talking about?"

The waitress didn't even blink before wandering away. Jo wondered what would be coming next.

"Wedding dresses," Jo supplied.

"No. No, that wasn't it." Perrin searched the table again, this time apparently looking for her last topic rather than the next appetizer.

"Jo's breasts?" Cassidy offered as she sipped her wine.

"Bingo!" Perrin nudged Cassidy's arm almost tipping them both off their stools.

"So. What happened from, 'I have no one to wear a wedding dress for' to an hemergency meeting?" Perrin blinked hard then repeated more slowly and clearly. "E-mer-gen-cy meeting. Nope, not that drunk yet. He-emergency meeting. Hey! That must be it."

She nudged Cassidy again but harder. Cassidy was better braced this time.

"Jo got laid. That's the problem." Then she turned to Jo. "Why is that a problem?"

Jo did her best not to groan. Somehow Perrin always found her way back to the topic, even when Jo no longer wanted her to. Over the first two drinks, she'd come to terms with just having to figure it out herself. It would be safer, easier that way. What part of her had thought that Cassidy, being Angelo's best friend's wife, was the proper confessor for Jo's sins?

"Because it was with Angelo."

Jo slapped her hand over her mouth, but she'd said it and now it was out in the world. She should have opened with the job offer that Renée was using to make her crazy. That had to be safer than this. Anything would have been safer.

She gauged her friends' reactions.

Cassidy had gone very quiet. She looked like she did when tasting a new wine. Rolling the idea around on her tongue, letting it build and flow to see how it tasted.

Perrin practically shouted, "Shrimp and crab cocktail!" Her attempt to drunkenly hug the waitress while she still bore the next appetizer almost caused the woman to bobble the plate, but she was good enough to save the moment.

"Cute and smart! Too bad I'm straight. Are you?"

The waitress shook her head no.

"Bummer. Any takers?" Perrin asked Jo and Cassidy. Cassidy rolled her eyes and Jo just shook her head.

"Oh well," Perrin addressed the waitress. "No luck here, sorry about that. Girls, we have to remember to tip her extra nice." The waitress smiled easily and drifted off at a call to the next table. Another reason Jo liked Cutter's, the waitresses could deal with Perrin. Other places she tended to blow them out of the water and they never recovered.

Jo thought that maybe at least on one front, she might have dodged the bullet. Cassidy was still testing the idea and edging up on her opinion.

"Well, I knew he was attracted to you. But that was last year before I started dating Russell."

"You didn't date Russell," Perrin corrected her. She held up a finger and began counting. "First you despised his very existence. Then second, you fell head over heels in love with him. After that, third, you couldn't figure out what to do about it."

"I married him."

"Okay, that's fourth. But it took you long enough."

Jo considered that this might be an opportunity for her to quietly slip away but rather than rising to Perrin's tease, Cassidy turned back to face Jo, trapping her on her stool.

"And now, with no buildup, you, ah…"

"Jumped his bones," Perrin filled in when Cassidy hesitated.

"Well," Jo thought of trying to explain the wedding and the way Angelo looked at her and how uncomfortable that had made her feel. But it had also made her feel feminine. When she thought of herself as a woman, it was the power suit one who came to mind. The lawyer feared far and wide, feared even more because she was a female and had kicked ass every time she'd entered a courtroom since her first mock trial in college. But Angelo kept seeing a different Jo, one she didn't know, and, much to her dismay it was a version of Jo that she was finding she wasn't very comfortable with.

She thought of trying to explain the disastrous meal, his banged head, and how he'd been so cute about it. And their working out together. And… She couldn't wrap her head, never mind her tongue, around how it had happened. Though she'd never behaved in such a fashion with any lover before Angelo, "jumped his bones" was also alarmingly accurate.

"Sort of did that," was the best response she could muster for Perrin. She reached for her martini to slake her dry throat, but it was already half gone and she really needed to slow down. Instead she dipped some crab in the cocktail sauce to buy herself a moment.

"When?"

"Last night!" Perrin answered for her. "That's why we're having the he-mergency meeting today." She pulled one sleeve onto her shoulder causing the other one to fall off.

Perrin leaned in. "Was it good? Yep, that blush nails that part of it."

Jo did her best to use sheer willpower to fight the heat rising in her face, which only made her cheeks burn hotter.

"Did he stay the night?"

This time Jo gulped some of her martini. When she recovered her breath from the scorch of alcohol sliding down her throat and the citrus twang had cleared her head a bit, she nodded.

"He stayed until it was time to go shopping."

"Yes!" Perrin did a fist pump and almost elbowed a passing guy in the crotch. "Damn good sign. And he's so awfully pretty. Is he prettier naked?"

"How do you do that?" Jo's voice had drifted out of her control and it came out half in anger but got snarled up in a laugh on the way out.

"Do what?" Perrin did her best to look all innocent, sitting up extra straight. This caused her blouse to slide off both shoulders making her look even more elfin than she usually did.

"Make me tell you things I never intended to say?"

"You're avoiding the question, counselor. All I want to know is, is Angelo Parrano as pretty naked as you'd expect?" She said it in a voice declarative enough that the women at two nearby tables paused and listened for the answer.

Jo ground her teeth and fought back the urge to scream.

"Yes, curse you. He's fucking gorgeous." That made two of the women at other tables look away. Two others sighed in what sounded like envy before they turned back to their own tables.

"Jo swore," Perrin dropped her jaw in mock horror. "He must look really amazing."

"Look, feel, made me feel… Beyond amazing." Now that she'd started, she couldn't shut up. But he had. There'd been a heat, a need, a yearning, that would have been unnerving if it hadn't been so completely mutual. He'd opened up whole new worlds of sensation that she hadn't known existed. She wasn't a prude, or inexperienced. But Angelo's body had simply been made for her. Every shape, every muscle, every texture had fit her perfectly. And while she'd had good lovers before, she'd never had one who made it so much fun. She'd found ways to tease him to madness, until his breath came in short, hot gasps, and he'd begged her to finish him off or just kill him now.

"It was," her voice sounded soft and dreamy even to herself, "the most incredible sex I've ever had."

"Then why are we having a he-mergency meeting?" Perrin placed an elbow on the table and propped her chin in her hand as if that were the only thing keeping her head off the table.

"Because," Cassidy still spoke in that slow analytic voice of hers. "Because she's afraid I'll be upset."

"Why?"

"Because I'm married to Russell."

Jo nodded, but Perrin simply looked more confused.

"She isn't sleeping with Russell. You are. She is sleeping with Angelo."

"Actually we didn't sleep much." The gin was talking. That was definitely the gin and not Jo Thompson. She really hoped that was true.

"Now she's bragging," Perrin poked at the cocktail sauce with another shrimp.

"She is," Cassidy agreed. Cassidy straightened and only wobbled a little in her chair.

"We'll just all be adult about this. We're all grown and, uh, you know, worldly sorts of people. We'll just make sure that we all end up being friends."

"Or lovers," Perrin never missed.

"Or lovers." Cassidy acknowledged.

"Or married." This time Perrin positively smirked at Jo. "Told you not to underestimate the power of a good dress."

"I'm not marrying Angelo, I'm only sleeping with him."

"Except you said you weren't sleeping with him. Just having lots of sex."

Cassidy held out her hands to stop the conversation. Taking a deep breath, she tried to steer the conversation back to the point.

"We'll just be adult about this."

Jo nodded, thinking about she and Angelo groaning together in the shower until it had echoed off the walls.

"We weren't very adult about it."

Perrin cocked her head to one side, still held up only by her chin on her palm. "You were juvenile about sex?"

"No, more animal."

"Now we're getting somewhere! Cassidy, we need to get Jo drunk far more often. This is way too much fun. Waitress, where did that cute butch gal go? We need another round."

Jo looked down, but her martini was empty. Yup, she really was in trouble now.

CHAPTER 19

"My girlfriend is moving** to Hawaii."

The phrase sent chills up Angelo's back.

First, it struck him as far too reminiscent of Jo's statement about heading to Alaska for much of the next three-to-five years. Second, it was coming from his patissier, Eugene, at the end of another brutal shift. Angelo didn't need him to be distracted when they were so busy they could barely breathe.

They sat around the stainless prep table. Graziella lay with her head on her arms as if someone had shot her. Marlys the grillardin had kicked ass on the grill tonight and now she looked like the kicking had been the other way around. Vic and Valerie who'd done such yeoman service on the fryer and the soups were still upright and Angelo couldn't imagine how. Marko was still finishing the last of the dishes. Angelo would go over there and drag him to the table in a headlock as soon as their late dinner was ready.

Manuel was throwing together a batch of his No-Knife Pasta. He'd shredded fresh tomatoes by tearing them apart with his fingers, then added a liberal sprinkling of torn basil and oregano leaves, some smashed garlic that already spiked the air, and a fistful of Kalamata olives, all sprinkled with red pepper flakes and olive oil. He'd mixed

463

together the last of the day's fresh pasta, mainly fettuccini and penne. And if Angelo had the energy, he'd bless the man because otherwise he would have felt obligated to do it himself.

He wouldn't trade last night with Jo for anything, though eight hours extra sleep sounded awfully good right now.

But exhaustion wasn't the real problem. The real problem was his mother, who he'd finally forced to go home an hour ago. Running Angelo's Tuscan Hearth had evolved into a science. Open at eleven thirty and be three-quarters full for lunch, an afternoon dribble, and two seatings at dinner. Close the doors at eight, finish the second service by nine, done and clean by ten. With the shopping and prep it was only twelve to fourteen hours a day, with everyone getting a couple hours off in the afternoon or perhaps an early leave on a quiet night.

That was about the easiest restaurant job Angelo had ever had, or at least the fewest hours. Add on the two days closed every week and it was downright cushy. It also, he knew, would make his staff insanely loyal by keeping such an easy schedule.

But Maria Amelia Avico Parrano had thrown a hatchet into that the last several days. There was now a line sufficient to fill half the restaurant the very moment they opened the doors, and the tables were packed solid by noon. Afternoon was the staff's time to shift over to dinner prep, cook the staff dinner, often they could even eat together, or run some personal errands. Now they stayed at busy-lunch levels right to the five o'clock start of dinner for theater goers. And when he'd locked the outer doors tonight, he'd still had two parties of six and three of five that hadn't even been seated yet. They'd been more than happy to wait, especially as his mother had served them wine and complimentary hors d'oeuvres while they waited.

His mother was just too pleasantly charming and too incredibly beautiful. She flitted between the cookline and the table service. When Graziella and her two assistant waiters were swamped, his mother showed up on the floor with the black pepper grinder for the patron's salad or the parmesan shaver for their pasta. When Valerie was seasoning the soup, his mother was there to taste and give her an opinion. Angelo himself had agreed with Maria Amelia so many times that he was beginning to sound like a parrot. Even when it was his idea in the first place, her agreement with him somehow instead sounded like his agreement with her. Just trying to figure out how that happened made his head hurt all over again.

Manuel dumped the pasta into a massive colander, flipped the pasta right back into the pot and tossed in all of the ingredients. A couple fistfuls of mozzarella and Asiago then he dropped the pot in the middle of the table.

"Hey Marko!" Angelo didn't have the energy to go and grab the kid. So he'd be both lazy and devious, killing two noodles with one fork. "Bring over some bowls and forks."

"We gotta get some more help on the line." Manuel dropped onto a stool.

"That's not the problem." He took the dishwasher-hot bowl from Marko, which would have singed his fingers if he didn't have a cook's calluses. "Okay that's not the only problem."

He nudged Graziella from her nap. "Food, Grazie."

"You're welcome," she mumbled.

"Not thanking you. Eat, *per favore*." He nudged her again and she came fully awake, shook her head to clear it, and tried to serve herself from the big pot. She almost lost it all to the table.

"Then what is the problem?" Manuel took the bowl from her fumbling hands, filled it, and handed it back before she noticed it was gone. Then he filled another and slid it down the table to Angelo. Angelo skidded his empty one back.

He dug in and took his first real bite of food in over eight hours, perhaps twelve hours since he'd had his mother's cornetto. He couldn't be sure any more.

"Oh, Manuel," the flavors bloomed in his mouth. Simple, fresh, clean. Three spices, perfectly ripe tomatoes, and olives for depth. "Damn, you're good, my friend."

Manuel was a dark Mexican from Oaxaca in the south, squat, broad-shouldered, and quiet.

"Did I ever tell you how I met this guy?" Graziella had been there, with him since before he opened the restaurant, but the others simply shook their heads.

"This guy," Angelo took a mouthful of pasta and then aimed his empty fork at Manuel's chest and spoke around his food a bit. "He shows up at my kitchen door. It was the same day I installed the grill and thought I was finally getting somewhere. He stood silhouetted in the back door of the kitchen."

"'Italian?' is all I say to him." Manuel joined in his own story.

"That was it, one word. When I said it was, he just nodded and walked away. I didn't think anything more of it."

Manuel just grinned at him.

"You were a little spooky," Graziella told him then turned to the others. "Half an hour later he walks back into the kitchen with a couple of shopping bags from the Market. Without a word he pulls out a knife, a beautiful piece of chicken, some sherry, and three other ingredients. He just walked in and started cooking as if he owned the damn place."

"That basil-mustard-lemon chicken poached in sherry was truly spectacular," Angelo told him. "Simpler even than this, nowhere to hide any mistakes. I'd had this whole plan of interviewing and training my sous chef. Had to have at least culinary school and ten years' experience. Manuel took the job that afternoon. A crazy Mexican who cooks Italian."

"Want to try my Chinese?"

"Don't even think it!" Angelo knew he'd be a goner the day Manuel left.

He laughed quietly. "Thanks boss. It's been great. But we need help. Why you say that *no hay problema?*"

Angelo dug into his pasta one more time hoping to find another answer.

It was a problem and Angelo knew it. But it wasn't the only problem. Hiring more people didn't scare him, he had the cash flow to do that. It was the other idea that was worrying him spitless.

They all ate in silence for a minute or two while he tried to collect his thoughts. They were drooping, every last one of them.

"The problem," he went to the walk-in cooler and found himself a beer to balance the heat of the red peppers and tang of the garlic. "The problem."

Shit! He was already in over his head, might as well go the rest of the way. He got back to the table and faced his team, they deserved to know.

"The problem is that we don't have enough seats in this restaurant. Between the amazing cooking and service we've been doing, and what my mother has taught us about marketing ourselves better these last few days, there just aren't enough seats here."

"Well," Valerie looked up at the ceiling. That's where she and Vic lived, right over the restaurant. "I guess we could move."

Manuel was shaking his head. "No! The kitchen, she matches the restaurant. If we go up, we need bigger kitchen. That fix nothing."

"Right. What we need," Angelo knew he was going to hate himself in the morning. "What we need is to open a second restaurant."

The collective groan was exactly the answer he'd expected.

"But my girlfriend is moving to Hawaii," Eugene repeated his news as if it were a protest.

"That'll give youse more time to make fine Italian desserts." Marlys, the grillardin, used her fake Brooklyn mobster accent and slapped her drinking buddy on the back almost making him snort his pasta.

No one quite knew how the two of them got along. Marlys hailed from a good Italian family in Brooklyn. She and Angelo had met when he was working a restaurant in Brooklyn Heights, he'd been the master of the grill then, and she'd been in charge of the fryer. When he'd started the restaurant, she'd been one of his first calls. Her lover had just dumped her and she leapt at the chance to move out of the city.

Eugene, was, well, to put it kindly, a slightly annoying kid from Colorado. But he made exquisite pastries.

Angelo knew they double-dated on several occasions, Eugene and Audrey, Marlys and whatever woman she was seeing at the time. On the cookline they were always talking movies or the latest hot television series that Angelo had never heard of, they were seriously into media. Eugene was also into online gaming, though not in a deep fanatic kind of way, and Marlys kept teasing him about not living in the real world. As if performing detailed analyses of this week's shape-shifting-vampire-British-spy episode placed her on such superior footing.

"No," Eugene planted his fork in his pasta as if for emphasis. "I'm going with her."

That shocked the table to silence. For two years the core team had remained inviolate, except for Marko joining them just six months ago when Ricky had decided to go to college, in astrophysics of all unlikely things. To lose their patissier was unimaginable. There was no position harder to replace. Angelo was the only one who could possibly fill in, but he'd need to work full time at just pastry and he had a restaurant to run.

"Are you, uh," Angelo struggled to find his voice and keep calm. "Are you sure?" It was also hard to imagine the sallow-faced boy in the land of sea and sun. Boy. He was four years younger than Angelo, but he always seemed to be eighteen going on sixteen.

"I was going to tell you today, but service never stopped."

Angelo glanced at Marlys. She looked surprised and worried. Neither of them had missed the way he'd phrased it. Not, "My girlfriend and I are moving to Hawaii," but rather "My girlfriend is moving." Did he know Eugene well enough to point out that maybe she didn't want him to follow her and was being too nice to say so? He remembered Heather at the CIA. She never said, "No, we're done." She simply kept not finding time to be with him. It had taken him a while to learn that while some women said no and weren't listened to by the jerks, there were some women who simply didn't know how to say no.

He opened his mouth and shut it again when Marlys shook her head. He'd leave her to delve into it. In the meantime, he'd start hunting for a new pastry chef, two of them if he was going to open another restaurant. Gods but his head hurt. Maybe he'd be better off if Jo went to Alaska, because whether or not Eugene remained, he wasn't going to have time to breathe, never mind sleep or fall in love.

That shocked him bolt upright.

He never fell in love. He fell in lust. Lust was fun, healthy, and made the passage of time exceedingly pleasant.

That's all he had with Jo. She was beautiful, enticing, and did really wonderful things to his hormone balance.

Counselor Jo Thompson was the one, again, causing him trouble. That woman was interesting, intense, brilliant, and had him near-enough hypnotized. He was definitely under her spell.

He took a bite of the now-tasteless pasta as the others began probing Eugene about what he would be doing in Hawaii, but he couldn't hear their words.

What in hell had Counselor Thompson done to him?

CHAPTER 20

"***Y**ou're a witch!"*

Jo burst out laughing and completely lost her rhythm on the rowing machine. Her legs stretched at full extension, but her hands lost the handle which retracted with a sharp snap. Without the tension of the rower handle, it was hard to sit back up.

Angelo leaned over and placed a warm, solid palm on the center of her back and provided the leverage for her to sit easily upright.

She looked up at him standing beside her, a towel over his shoulder. They'd missed each other for three days in a row. First she hadn't gone to the gym, then he hadn't. She'd drifted by the restaurant on her way through the lunchtime Market, but the long lines told her not to risk disturbing him. At night, all she was doing was working crazy hours, then plummeting into bed.

Now they were together in the Eastlake gym.

She looked up at him and everything that she'd told herself she wasn't feeling burst through her body in a flash of animal heat. She hoped the flush of her workout would hide the flush rising to her cheeks.

"Yes, a proud member of the order of…" she tried to come up with something witty. "The raw need for your body," came to mind but she discarded it. "The order of legalus witchcraftia." It was the best she had off the cuff.

He looked *so* good standing there. His hands casually holding the ends of the towel looped behind his neck. Sweat shone on his chest above the line of the black tank top. His arms were flexing in a way that told her he'd just finished with the weight machines.

"How did you discover my secret membership?" She felt goofy around him. He was looking at her as if he'd devour her right there in the middle of the gym floor. She was lousy at flirting with men, much better at staring them down into silence until they slunk away. But somehow she was flirting with Angelo. She tasted the salt of sweat when she licked her upper lip only afterward realizing that too could be a flirtatious gesture.

"Well," he dropped down to sit sideways on a recumbent-cycle machine next to her rower. "My first suspicion was Cassidy."

"Cassidy?" What did she have to do with the nice flirt they had going?

"Cassidy. When she bewitched a confirmed bachelor like Russell, I knew something was suspicious about you three."

"The three witches of Eastlake?" She reached for her own towel and wiped at her face before draping it around her own shoulders in such a way that it hid most of the exposed skin above her sports bra.

"Something like that. At the wedding Josh Harper described you three as beauty, truth, and joy."

Cassidy was the great beauty of their threesome and Perrin had to be joy. That left her as truth. While accurate, she could wish for a somewhat sexier label.

"But I think he missed the mark."

"Oh?" What was she besides truth? Hard working lawyer, no social life, no personal activities except her solo pursuit of a triathlon simply to provide focus for the one thing she ever did for herself, working out. She found a peace in wearing her body toward exhaustion, and exhilaration in discovering what she could do, but no more.

"Yes," Angelo clearly hadn't been distracted by her reverie. "I think that my problem with you is that you embody all three elements."

Beauty. Truth. Joy. No one had ever called her joyous before. And while she was often labeled beautiful, none of those who did so had been interested by the deep 'truth' that was far more a part of who she was.

"All three?" She could become deeply attached to being seen that way. "Does that make me the head witch?"

"More the goddess template of which all others are but pale copies."

"That does it," she burst out laughing. "That is so over the top, Angelo. How do you come up with these lines?" She pushed to her feet and he did the same bringing them closer together. But even as he shrugged it off with a laugh, his eyes did not change. If it wasn't a line… That possibility was not one she'd ever consider.

She stroked fingertips down his cheek.

"That's sweet, but I am a real woman, Angelo. Flesh and blood. Not worthy of any pedestal."

"I'd argue the point, but I'd rather see you again."

Jo checked her watch. "I have phone conferences to Washington and Alaska this morning and this is Friday and you're open late."

His eyes clouded for a moment with worry, but the look was fleeting.

"We could ride together again tomorrow? I don't want to get in the way of your training."

Damn the man for being so considerate. Yes, she needed to ride, but what she wanted was to feel even half of what Angelo had made her feel their first night together.

"Sure, a ride sounds great." Then the Evil Jo took over, the one with too much lust and sex on her mind. "If you meet me on the other side of the locker rooms, I'll give you my spare key and the code for the elevator. Maybe you can bring your bike over after work tonight, then we can ride in the morning." She'd never been so forward in her life and found that she was holding her breath to see his reaction.

Consciously ordering herself to breathe didn't work, so she held on and waited, hoping he'd answer before she passed out.

He didn't make her wait too long.

"And how in the world am I not supposed to put you on a pedestal? You're bloody glorious."

ngelo risked the front hall light to help him navigate inside the unfamiliar apartment. Bike, helmet, and shoes he left against the wall and crept through the entryway.

The kitchen was immaculate, so immaculate that he wondered if she used it much. A quick peek in the refrigerator revealed the answer of, "not much." Leftover containers roughly equaled number of food products.

The combined dining and living room was almost Spartan except for one wall which was a solid, tight-packed bookshelf. Half law books and half thrillers. He looked closer, most of them legal thrillers. Clearly she was interested in nothing other than law. So what the hell was she doing with him? A woman like her should be with—

Angelo cut himself off. Don't go there. She should be with him, that's who.

The room was female, but in an odd way it wasn't feminine. Or maybe he had that backwards. It was feminine in the perfect taste that had been applied to the selection of furnishings and art. It wasn't female in its lack of what he would typically expect: brightly colored pillows, knick-knacks, or a knit throw over the couch.

Of course his own décor was primarily a wall of cookbooks. So he wasn't one to talk.

The perfect control of her entire world revealed yet another facet of Jo Thompson. Her car was incredible, her apartment exquisite, her personal conditioning exceptional. As a matter of fact, the only thing that didn't fit her was that disaster she called a desk in that terrifyingly powerful office. It had looked as if a bomb had gone off there and he'd bet it was far worse by now. He hadn't seen it in three days but he'd wager it had begun breeding on its own.

He turned off the hall light and slipped into the master bedroom. She'd left a soft blue nightlight on for him. Without it, the heavy curtains would have left the room pitch black. Again, the perfect feminine. Dusky carpet, white walls, white-stained oak furniture, and floor-to-ceiling white curtains. He wondered what lay beyond those. He'd gotten turned around in the building and certainly hadn't bothered to consider the view his first time here. A quick peek revealed a sweeping panorama of Seattle, Puget Sound, and moonlight on the Olympic Mountains. He could get to like this. He let the curtain slip shut.

The room smelled like Jo. Not some strong floral or citrus scent, as far as he knew she didn't wear perfume. But it smelled of her nonetheless. A scent, a flavor that he hadn't been able to erase from his mind since their first ice-creamed kiss. She reminded him of sky and sunlight and, with all apologies to his history teacher, the deep richness he'd always imagined surrounding the Greek Fates, the three women who measured and cut the time of a man's life. Or better yet, Gaia, wasn't she the mother of the Three Fates, or something like that? She really did remind him of a mother goddess. The incredible beauty, the perfect posture as if she were dancer rather than lawyer, the groundedness in who she was. Didn't the woman have any doubts about anything?

In the soft light, he could just make out her hair spread across the white pillow and the deeply embroidered white bed quilt. She lay on her side and the scattered hair hid her face leaving only a dark sheen upon the pillow.

That's when he remembered her in her office, the dark hair spilling over her face, right after she'd screamed in frustration.

No. He had to keep reminding himself. This wasn't Counselor Jo Thompson, not in this room. Here was his lover. That sounded awesomely good. It sent a shiver and a heat washing the length of his body.

Strictly human, he reminded himself. No pedestals allowed, no matter how he wished to place her upon one. He undressed and slipped in beside her appreciating the softness of the flannel sheets and the warmth and scent of Jo Thompson that pervaded the bed.

As gently as he could, he brushed the hair back from her face.

She sighed as he did so.

"Angelo." It was barely a whisper.

"Right here, Jo."

She slid up against him, draping an arm over his ribs and curling to bury her face against his chest. Then, with another sigh, she fell back asleep.

And what was he supposed to do with that? His body thrummed with need. Her face on his chest placed her hair where he could nuzzle it and inhale even more deeply of sky, sun, and Mother Earth. Her hair, long and thick, was also soft and smelled freshly of a light shampoo.

He considered waking her, but didn't have the heart to do so. She must be as exhausted as he felt. Eugene still insisted he was departing at the end of the month. Barely two weeks' notice. Even in a foodie-town like Seattle, there was no way to find a good patissier so quickly. He would put out notices for several positions, hoping to find his way through the current madness as well as begin staffing the new restaurant.

No! He had to stop his whirling mind. He wouldn't bring work into this place. He didn't care what Jo said or didn't, he'd declare this a sanctuary, even if it was one without pedestals. He simply wouldn't tell her that he'd done so. In this place at least, it would only be about the two of them, the overwhelmed Italian and the woman who filled his senses as if she were indeed born of heaven.

Then he thought of something that calmed his nerves.

Even mostly asleep, she'd called him by his name as if he filled her thoughts as much as she did his.

JO WOKE SLOWLY to the smell of coffee and bacon. Coffee! Her body woke faster simply for knowing caffeine would be consumed shortly. She opened one eye and saw the empty pillow beside hers. It was dented. But she'd gone to bed alone and woken alone.

To the smell of coffee her body reminded her. So, she'd apparently been alone at either end, but not in the middle? Had he held her in the night? She thought so, felt as if she had been held, but couldn't be sure.

Unravished. Held or not, her body was distinctly unravished. The man tells her she is beautiful like a goddess and then doesn't touch her. It was enough to make a girl downright irritable.

Coffee. Right, she was always irritable before coffee.

She slid from beneath the covers wearing the extra-large gray t-shirt with the arched maroon "Vassar" fading over her chest.

Angelo stood at the stove cooking, his back mostly toward her. He wore only his jeans riding low enough on his hips to reveal that his underwear probably was still somewhere in her bedroom. His bare back rippled slightly as he tended the bacon. God he was beautiful. She was about to slip up behind him when she noticed the cloth-covered cookie sheet on the counter. It had been set with napkins, silverware, and a large stoneware mug that steamed thickly of caffeine and French roast. An impromptu breakfast tray.

Breakfast in bed! She'd never had that except when she'd made it for herself. Well, she certainly wasn't going to spoil being spoiled for a morning, and scooted back to the bedroom slipping between the covers. Be awake? Feign sleep? Jump him the moment he got through the door and to hell with the consequences? No, that was too high a risk to the precious caffeine.

Jo went for the second option, burying her face in the pillow that smelled of Angelo, how she'd missed that when she woke up was beyond her, and listened to the song of her pulse gaining tempo rapidly.

She ignored the first whispered, "Jo?"

At the second, closer call of her name, she made a show of waking slowly. Then she had an idea, but she'd have to be fast if she wanted to hide the smile.

"Jacob?" She dragged aside a fistful of hair and looked at Angelo confusedly through a curtain of what remained.

He stood balancing the improvised tray and revealed that breathtaking chest of his on full display.

"I was expecting Jacob," she shot for a pout and thought she did pretty well.

"And why were you expecting Jacob?" Rather than looking put-out, Angelo's smile was radiant. Oh well, so the tease hadn't really worked. Or had it?

"Because Jacob would have ravaged me in the night rather than leaving me to sleep."

"Well, I could ravage you right now, but your omelet would be cold. And your coffee."

"Coffee!"

Angelo made a pout in return as he rested the tray at the foot of the bed. "Well, I now know where I rank. Below coffee. And Jacob."

"Well, Jacob is pretty special." Jo sat the rest of the way up in bed. "Now shed those jeans and get back in here under the covers."

He dropped his jeans. His desire, previously revealed merely as a bulge in his trousers, was now very evident.

"Ooo, come to Jo." She reached out.

Angelo took a step back. "You'll spill the coffee."

"No," Jo slid off the edge of the bed careful not to jostle the tray and slid her hand around him. "No, I'll take you right here on the carpet."

"But your breakf—" His breath cut off as she ran both her hands over him. When she slid them up between his legs and grabbed his buttocks then pulled him forward between her breasts, his knees let go and he half eased and half collapsed to the floor.

There, still wearing her t-shirt, Jo straddled atop and settled down over him. They set about ravaging each other.

CHAPTER 22

*J*o lay on *Angelo's* chest and hummed. Her entire body hummed, there was no other word for it. If she were a musician, she'd say she felt like a string vibrating ever so softly and perfectly in tune. What the hell, she'd use the metaphor even if she wasn't a musician, it certainly fit.

Angelo stroked the hum forth by running his hands from her shoulders down over her buttocks and back along her thighs to the knees where she knelt over him. Then returning by the same route.

"Breakfast shouldn't be that much colder." His tone was wry. They had certainly sparked their need off each other and it had burst forth fast and hot.

"That was barely a ravage."

"Consider it a deposit on a ravage."

Jo clung to his glorious shoulders and nuzzled his chest for a moment longer.

"Okay, I'll try to work with that. I should demand a signed and notarized letter of further intent to ravage, but I'll trust you this one time." Jo climbed off him and scooted back onto the bed.

Angelo continued to lie there on the floor looking all handsome and content.

481

"Your omelet is congealing, Master Chef Parrano."

He smiled but didn't move. "Too late for that, Counselor Thompson."

She took a forkful. Barely warm, but still light and fluffy with the nicest hint of oregano.

"Still yummy."

Then Angelo pushed to his feet. "Do you have a pen and paper?"

She pointed at the nightstand. She kept them in the top drawer in case she thought of a good case argument or line of research and didn't want to lose the thought in the middle of the night.

He scrawled on the pad quickly, tore off the page and folded it in half, and handed it to her. Then he bowed formally and joined her cross-legged on the bed.

She opened the note as he took his coffee.

I, Angelo Parrano, being of weak mind but sound body, do hereby intend, promise, swear, vow, affirm, and otherwise commit that I shall hereafter happily ravage one Jo Thompson at every opportunity.

Signed, Angelo Parrano

Addendum: Ravaging also available by special request.

"I don't have a notary handy. I hope that's okay."

She couldn't meet his eyes. She'd hugged the note to her chest without realizing it. She held it out and read it again.

It wasn't the promise to ravage that had set her heart stuttering. It was that he'd done it in her language. She'd received plenty of mash notes over the years, though most of them had been back in Schoenbar Middle School when she'd been among the first of the girls to develop a chest. But even the couple that she'd received as an adult had never so thoroughly acknowledged who she was. They'd always been about her body, not about her. The fact that he'd used the "sound mind" quote from a standard will, probably without intending to evoke death and estate law, only made it more charming.

He offered her a forkful of omelet that she dutifully took and chewed, though she barely tasted it. There was another taste on her tongue. One she didn't know, couldn't identify. No, not a taste. A taste that made her think of Angelo's wonderful skin.

This was as if there was flavor running all through her insides. It was good, but unfamiliar. It was as if it came from the inside rather than the outside, but she still couldn't define it. But she knew how it made her feel. It made her feel desired. It made her feel alive.

She climbed from the bed and carefully tucked the precious note under her alarm clock. Then she shifted the tray to the top of the dresser, and, facing Angelo, stripped the t-shirt off over her head, dropped it behind her, and climbed back into bed.

His eyes were transfixed upon her, the coffee mug frozen halfway to his lips. She'd never had such an effect on a man and it made her feel freer than she could have imagined possible.

She lay back on the pillow atop the covers, "By special request."

He set his coffee on the coaster on the nightstand.

Then he slid over her and whispered in her ear, "By special request."

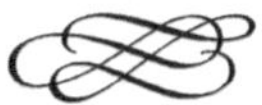

"**M**ama. *We need to* talk."

Angelo and his mother were walking in the sun together, moseying along First Avenue from the apartment up to the restaurant. The Saturday morning traffic was busy with some tourists, some locals, and monstrous city buses jockeying for position like sumo wrestlers amidst a stampede of Chihuahuas. Seattle was always busy during the day. Thankfully, unlike New York, the city did sleep at night. He liked that, felt it added some character that the Big Apple had somehow lost.

Men kept turning to look at them. No. To look at his mother and he didn't like it a bit. She wore her hair loose, with a bright floral scarf over it. The powder blue sweater swept low across her chest and clung in all of the right places. She wore a dark skirt that wrapped tight about her hips and revealed good legs.

He wanted to buy her a trenchcoat.

"Is it about this girl, this Jo? When does she come by? When do I get to sit and share a meal with her?"

"No, it's not about Jo." They'd never made their bike ride. Hell, they'd barely made it through breakfast.

"What I see, my son, is a very happy man. But he confuses me. It also looks as if you slept last night. That is not a nice thing to do to a new girlfriend. You are not supposed to sleep a wink together."

"Mama!" He really couldn't be having this conversation with her. And she agreed with Jo that he should have just ravaged her though she'd been sleeping so sweetly. What the hell did he know anyway, he was just a guy.

"What? I don't get to be glad for my boy? Sex is good for you. You should marry her."

"We are so not having this conversation."

"Why not? You marry her and we can all live happy together."

Angelo caught his shoe on a shifted block in the sidewalk and almost planted his face on Madison Street. The cars were bolting down the steep Seattle hills as if the waterfront shops would float away before they got to visit every one. Or, perhaps more realistically, as if the last available parking spot on the full length of Alaskan Way was about to be filled.

His mother grabbed his arm to keep him on the sidewalk and burst out laughing. It was such a merry sound. He was being sassed by his mother. What was up with that?

"It was the restaurant I wanted to talk about." And he definitely didn't want to talk about Jo or marriage or married life with his mother in the apartment or…

She harrumphed at him as they waited for the red light at Spring Street.

"Okay, so talk."

"You shopped with Manuel this morning, like I asked?"

"Of course I did. I take care of things so that you can not sleep with this Jo, but instead you—"

"Mama!"

She offered an elaborate shrug that only an Italian mother could achieve which told him, "Fine, change the topic if you want but I gave birth to you and cleaned your bottom and you still need someone much smarter than you to take care of you and this topic is not even a little bit done with."

Angelo inspected the blue sky between the towering buildings, searching for patience. William was just unlocking McCormick and Schmick's as they passed by. Angelo waved at him as he put out the "Lunch Specials" sign, a classy chalkboard sign with cheerful yellow chalk. Angelo's Hearth didn't do "specials" but he was considering it. The board did catch the eye.

"Hey, Angelo," they knew each other by name, but not much more. Then he turned to his mother, "Hello, Mrs. Parrano. When are you going to leave your son and come live with me in sin?"

She patted his cheek as if he were a little boy rather than a man her own age, "Just as soon as your wife stops choosing your clothes for you. You are dressed far too nicely to have chosen that yourself." They traded air kisses.

William did look sharp, even if Angelo couldn't quite identify why. He looked at his own comfortable clothes and knew his mother had not been talking to William alone.

Angelo rolled his eyes at her back.

William just winked at him over her shoulder.

Once they'd left William behind, Angelo opened his mouth and then closed it sharply. Had she charmed every male in the whole city while he wasn't watching? If he started down the path of that topic, he'd never find his way to where he wanted to go.

"Mama," he tried again. "I'm going to have a problem at the restaurant and I was hoping you could help me." What on Earth was he doing? Jo. This was Jo's fault. She'd cooked up the idea this morning when they'd finally pulled on handy clothes and then taken their cold breakfast and reheated coffee out onto her umpteenth floor balcony. The egg and bacon flavors had still been good, but retoasting the toast hadn't helped the texture of it. He'd told her about Eugene leaving and the complications his mother was causing the restaurant.

"It's perfect, Angelo," Jo had assured him as she glowed in the morning light and ate cold eggs. "It sounds as if she's doing wonderful things for you, but I would conjecture that retired life is not sitting well with her. I'll bet she's bored. She wants to help you, which is so sweet. I wish I'd had parents, or even one parent like that."

When he'd asked her about that, the subject had changed without his really noticing, at least not until just now.

"My pastry chef, Eugene, is following his girlfriend to Hawaii," he told his mother.

"Is he sure that she wants to be followed?" She didn't even miss a pulse beat before jumping to the question that had taken Angelo some time to arrive at. And that Marlys had been unable to answer when Angelo had gotten her aside.

Angelo gave her a shrug that felt both uncomfortable and made it clear that in the end it was none of his business.

"The problem is, Mama, I need a pastry chef, at least until I can hire another one."

"And what does this have to do with my shopping with Manuel?"

"That's different. Last night I decided that you have made us too successful. So," he took a deep breath because it was still too huge to really comprehend. "I'm going to open another restaurant."

"Just like that?" She stopped in front of a storefront window and posed with her hands on her hips. Not realizing that she'd taken exactly the pose of the anorexic, aqua-clad mannequin in the clothing store window behind her. He started to smile until he saw the fire on her face.

"Just like that you go and decide to open another restaurant and you don't even consult your mother?"

"Ah..."

A business man in smart Saturday attire, but still swinging his briefcase on the way to work, cut right between them without a glance either way.

"Ah. Mama, I'm sorry. I didn't think—"

"No! You no think!" She began ticking points off on her fingers. "You no think about little treats to advertise your food. You no think that Manuel can shop just as good as can you." As her ire rose, her English frayed even more than usual around the edges.

"This Eugene," she flicked her fingers. "You are so worried about losing him. Well, his Panna Cotta is not one-half so good as mine. His Zabaglione is a disgrace. And his Lemon Olive-Oil Cake is so sad that little girl Graziella could make better. You no understand why you, the head chef, the owner, spend so much time at the desserts. Let him go, that boy is why you waste so much time with them. Oh," she continued her rant as more people passed close by eyeing him curiously as to why the beautiful Italian matron was yelling at him.

Angelo stepped across the flow of people through a gap until they at least stood side-by-side without blocking the sidewalk, but her tone did not soften in volume or ire, despite their now standing barely a foot apart.

"Oh, he is a good enough cook. But he has no heart," she thumped the center of his chest hard enough to sting while making her point. "No heart in his chest!" Thumping him again. "And no heart in his food. Let him go. Let him find out how fickle love can be. Let him learn like your father never learn—"

She stopped herself, her expression shifting abruptly to one of deep distress.

"My father what, Mama?"

She looked away down the street, turned back when he rested a hand on her arm. Tears were welling in her eyes.

"Mama?" the sinking in his stomach left a bitter taste in his mouth.

"I should have told you." Her gaze veered away from his. She never did that. Maria Amelia always looked right at you with those wide, dark eyes.

"Told me what?" He had to ask, yet would bet that he didn't want to know. He could see something in her eyes.

"He's still alive, isn't he?"

She nodded then shrugged a "maybe."

Angelo couldn't think of how to react to that. His mother continued before he could react.

"Your father," then a flash of that heat came back into her eyes even as she blinked against the tears, "he had no heart. I tell him I'm pregnant and I never see him again. My family was very Catholic. So, I was sent to America to have my baby, to have you. But my Julia and John, they take me in and I cook for them. They love you like their own son when you are born and I stay. I never hear from your father

489

again. I'm sorry. I should have found a better and sooner way to tell you, but I never could."

Angelo leaned against the cool window so that his knees did not let go. His father hadn't died, he'd left a pregnant single mother.

"You told me he was dead." He'd never felt so lost. Nor had he ever wanted to kill a man before. Leaving his mother? If he ever met the man, he'd murder him.

"He was dead to me." Again that impossible strength and undeniable truth. She had that in common with Jo, an ability to speak from perfect truth. How scared she must have been, but she had come through it and he'd wanted for nothing. His mother had pampered and punished him with equal amounts of Italian passion. And loved him no matter what he'd done.

"Did you love him?" That felt intensely important, as if he might cease to exist if the answer was no.

But his mother nodded and sniffled.

"What was his name?"

At that she smiled softly and brushed a hand down his cheek.

"His name was Angelo."

ANGELO AND MARIA sat in the little coffee shop at the corner and held hands across the table. Little potted palm trees scattered about the shop offered a feeling of privacy, even though their table sat close against the glass with the First Avenue crowds just beyond. The coffee was good enough to justify the price.

"Is he still alive?"

She shrugged again.

"Are you still married to him?"

At that she blushed for a moment and inspected her coffee.

"Mama?"

"I was young. He was so beautiful, you look much like him. He too was a chef. He taught me to cook and he taught me to make love."

"But you weren't married?"

Again the eloquent shrug.

Angelo looked around as if someone else had the answer among the people waiting for coffee or walking the trek from the Market to Pioneer Square. He was a bastard, born out of wedlock. He probed the feeling, like you might a sore tooth, with great care. Every memory of his mother was a fond one, he had not suffered. His mother had seen to that. Fine. He'd often wondered about the man, and now, surprisingly, found that he didn't care about him anymore. It didn't matter that his father was useless, his mother was only all that much more amazing for it.

"I just hate to think of you having been alone all these years, Mama."

"Who said I was alone? Did I say I was alone?"

Again they were abruptly in a territory Angelo really didn't wish to tread. Mothers weren't supposed to have sex and lovers, not even beautiful Italian mothers.

"I was not so foolish as to flaunt my men in front of my teenage son no matter how many empty-headed girls my son flaunted in front of me."

"They weren't empty-head—"

"Feh! The only boy in this whole world with worse taste in women than my son is Russell Morgan."

She held up her hand to stop his protest before he even made it.

"It took a good woman with good sense like our Cassidy to see what was there beneath all of the dirty clothes."

Okay, but it wasn't just Cassidy. "Melanie was good for hi—"

"No!" She stopped him again. "She wasn't."

"But she—"

"Yes. She is nice lady, I know that. But all she did for Russell was stroke his ego. She did no hold his heart even if he so dumb he almost break hers." She placed a hand over her heart in sympathy. "That one, she is so pretty and so lost."

Lost? Melanie was about the least lost person Angelo had ever met. Successful supermodel, her own manager, as sharp a businesswoman as he'd ever met, and still a fun lady. Before he could form a coherent protest, she pinned him again with her dark gaze.

"Who holds your heart, my Angelo?"

How in the world had they looped back around to Jo?

"See," his mother aimed a neatly trimmed nail at his heart. "I see even if you are too *stupido*. So, I ask again, when do I see this girl my son is sleeping with? Sleeping with." She smacked her hand to her chest again as if mortally offended. "I can no believe you are so *stupido*."

"Fine, Mama. You win. Monday. The restaurant is closed Monday. I'll see if she is available Monday." Oh, God. He'd just agreed to "bring Jo home for approval." First, Jo just might kill him for doing that. Second, was it possible he was actually serious about her? Serious enough to bring her home?

He was.

Angelo took a deep breath and tried the thought again. From the first time he'd seen Jo Thompson, his ability to be seriously intrigued by other women had been swept away. Had he even gotten to a second date with anyone since then? Not that he could recall. All he could think of was Jo Thompson. God above! He really was gone on her.

Bring her home for approval? Bring her home for keeps was more what he was feeling. He'd never felt that before. He knew almost nothing about her, but in some ways he knew her better than he knew himself. He could read her moods easily and enjoyed every one of them. She'd gotten all the way under his skin. Russell was right, he was in so much trouble. Who knew it would feel so good when it happened?

"Good," his mother must have read something in his expression that she acknowledged with a very satisfied nod. "I cook a wonderful dinner. You have such a nice kitchen in your condo. You have not such good taste in decorating, but you are smart, the kitchen is good. The location too I like very much. It is such a nice change from the Morgan mansion. So much happens in Pioneer Square. You are such a good boy to let your Mama live there."

As if he'd had a choice. Angelo buried his face in his hands. His head ached. This had started as such a simple conversation. At least Jo had told him it would be simple.

At the warm touch of his mother's hand, he looked up into her eyes.

"Of course, I would love to be your pastry chef. Though you must hire at least two more in the kitchen and another for front of house and do it very fast. They must be good people, I will help you pick them out. You will train them right." She brushed her hands together as if dusting them clear of all of the impossibly complex problems which she now declared resolved.

"Now, tell me about your new restaurant," she took a sip of her coffee.

He eyed her carefully, wondering where the trap lay.

"I thought you were angry I didn't consult you first?"

"Surprise? Yes. Angry? With my Angelo?" A brush of her hand over his hand again. "I am so proud I could die. I'm only angry I did not think of it first. So tell me."

So Angelo did.

CHAPTER 24

*J*o was *just returning* from a half hour swim in the lapless,
jet-current pool on the fifth floor gym of her condo. She
still preferred to work out at the gym on Eastlake. They
had more machines, on-site trainers, and classes whenever she needed
the motivation. But they didn't have a swimming pool, and the condo
had three of the powered tanks where you could swim in place against
a driven current. She wore a light robe over her damp swimsuit and
flipflops as she headed down the hall to her condo. Cassidy and Perrin
were coming back down the hall, clearly not finding her home.

"You're all wet," Perrin observed as they hugged. Today she wore a
simple summer dress that looked shockingly normal when compared
to the other clothes she usually wore.

"I know. I know." Perrin looked down at herself. "It's so…pedes-
trian. But I wanted to remind myself of how it felt. Streetwear rather
than fashionwear. I'm playing with some ideas. We came to see
the dress."

The dress. Jo had managed not to think about the dress. Cassidy
simply smiled at her. No, she wasn't humoring Perrin, she'd come to
see the dress as well.

What the hell. Jo led them back down to her condo.

In the bedroom, Perrin stooped and pulled something from under the edge where the quilt brushed the floor.

"What's this?" Dangling from her finger by its elastic band was a pair of dark red men's briefs, Angelo's underwear that they'd been unable to find as he was leaving. It must have slipped free as she was making the bed before her swim. Thank God she'd done at least that much.

She took it quickly, "Nothing." Though she imagined it felt warm against her palm.

Perrin grinned wickedly even as Jo stuffed it in her robe's pocket.

"Gee," she placed a red-painted nail to her lips and turned to Cassidy. "I wonder if a certain Mr. Parrano is walking the streets of Seattle commando this morning."

Cassidy smiled back at Perrin conspiratorially but winked at Jo, "Oh, I hope so. I really hope so."

Jo fought the desire to stare down at the rug and hide her face behind a fall of hair. Instead, she faced it head on.

"I am pleased to report to this court of inquiry, that he is indeed walking the streets without underwear." She clenched her hand on them in her pocket. Nor would he be getting them back anytime soon. Like a scalper's prize, they were hers now, though she had no idea why she'd want them.

"And is he well sated?" Perrin always wanted details.

"If he isn't, it's not for lack of trying."

She held her pride for a moment longer and then the three of them burst out laughing together.

Then she went into the bathroom to dry her hair before she tried on the dress.

"OH, JO." Cassidy's sigh said it all.

Perrin looked so pleased when Jo had put on the high-heeled shoes. She fussed with the hem a bit.

"I'll change it just a little so that you can wear these down the aisle, but dance in low heels."

"You won't change a single thing on this dress," Cassidy brushed Perrin's hands away. "You don't mess with perfection. Jo can take dance lessons."

Jo didn't know when she'd ever find time for a class, but Cassidy was right. It would be worth learning to dance in these so that she could look this good. She considered the woman in the mirror. This time, rather than the dark of night with closed curtains, the room was flooded with sunlight. The fabric revealed another facet that hadn't been visible before. Its pale blue material was ever so slightly iridescent as if Jo herself was glowing.

If Angelo could only see her now, he'd maybe keel over dead and need that "weak mind and sound body" phrase for his will.

Had she really just had that thought? Had she really just thought of Angelo while wearing a wedding dress?

Of course she had. They'd just spent a whole night and morning together. And true to his promise, he had thoroughly ravaged her leaving her head spinning and her body buzzing. So, of course she was thinking of him. But that's all it meant. She was thinking of him. And she was wearing a wedding dress. It didn't mean the two were related in any way other than a coincidence of timing.

The phone rang. She swished over to the nightstand to pick it up. She'd never swished before in her life.

"Oh. Hi, Angelo."

She glanced back at Cassidy and Perrin who weren't even for a moment considering leaving the room. Perrin grabbed Jo's robe from where it draped on the bed and fished out Angelo's underwear then began waving them at her.

"I found something you lost." Oh, no. She hadn't said that. She really needed to cut her own tongue out. Maybe she'd just kill Perrin as soon as she got off the phone. She turned away to concentrate.

"Oh thanks. I'll have to get those."

"Just like that? Just 'get those'?"

Angelo spluttered for a moment.

"I'm at the restaurant."

"And…" she teased him, knowing she had him trapped. "That's no excuse. What is it worth to get them back?"

"Go, Jo!" Perrin was giggling in the background. Jo closed her eyes to block out her friends. This was a very private conversation and they both were having it in public.

"Well," she could hear dishes clattering over the phone which must be the only reason he hadn't heard Perrin.

His voice went soft.

"I did have this one idea. If we ever have a day off together. There's a very private spot atop a mountain on one of the San Juan Islands that a friend showed me."

"And would this friend have been female?"

"Crap!" she could imagine him flushing red and looking around to try and find a way out of the hole he'd just dug. She let him dangle for several seconds before deciding to rescue him.

"Consider it a date."

"Really? Uh, really? That's wonderful." His voice went smooth for a moment as if someone was passing close by. He dragged out the start of the next sentence until whoever had finally passed out of earshot.

Jo would bet he wasn't fooling a single person on his staff except himself.

"I'll make it worth your while," he finally continued. "After all, I like my underwear."

"I like it better when it's off you."

Perrin cheered again and Jo wanted to slap herself.

"Okay. Whew. That took my breath away."

They appreciated the mutual images of being unclothed together in silence for several moments.

"Was there a reason you called?"

"Oh, yes," Angelo's voice shifted from smooth and warm to practically businesslike, as if he were suddenly afraid of her or something.

"My mother wants you to come to dinner on Monday."

"She what?" Jo's skin flashed cold.

"She's a great cook, as you know, and she wants to make a dinner for you. Get to know you and so on."

Her shock was so deep that all she could mumble was an, "Okay, I guess."

"Wonderful. I'll call later with details. Gotta run. Bye." And he was gone.

Jo set the phone back very slowly and stared out at the view trying to collect her thoughts into some semblance of order.

"So, what's the date? You said, 'Consider it a date.' We heard you. You can't lie to us." Perrin came around in front of her still waving Angelo's underwear. Jo took them, but having no pocket in the dress, simply tossed them back on the bed.

"Oh," Jo tried again to picture a dinner with Mrs. Parrano and failed. "There's a mountain in the San Juans. He wants to make love on top of it."

"Ooo. Starlight. Go at night. There's nothing like making love by starlight."

Jo had never done such a thing, though she'd take it under consideration.

She really should stop trying to avoid Perrin's questions, it never worked anyway.

Cassidy came up beside her and placed a hand around Jo's waist.

"What is it, Jo? There's something else."

Jo could only nod.

Perrin came up on her other side. Jo held onto both of them for support as she stared out the window, unable to see anything.

"He, ah, his mother, Angelo's mother, ah, Mrs. Parrano." Jo had turned into a babbling idiot. She clamped her tongue hard enough between her teeth that she thought she could taste enamel.

"She wants to meet me."

"But that makes no sense," Perrin protested. "You already know her."

"She wants to have me over for dinner. Angelo's mother wants to cook a meal for me."

"Yes!" Perrin pumped a fist in the air. "The power of the dress!

Yes!" She began dancing about the room, the skirt of her sun dress swirling and bouncing.

"Oh, Cassidy," Jo said quietly. It came out frightfully close to a moan.

"It'll be okay," Cassidy tightened her arm around Jo's waist as Perrin danced around them in the tiny circles that Jo's bedroom furniture barely allowed. "It'll be okay."

All Jo could think was that he was a chef and hadn't even known to sugar coat it.

The phone rang again. She almost didn't answer, but Cassidy nudged her.

"Yes, Angelo? What now?"

CHAPTER 25

o kept her hands clenched on the wheel of her rental car.
If she squeezed it any tighter, the wheel might snap. She
already didn't have any blood in her fingers. Ordering
her fingers to relax their death grip didn't ease them in the slightest.
They weren't stupid, they knew they were holding on for dear life.

The car rocked lightly as the ferry from the Ketchikan Airport
lurched through a wave. Ketchikan Airport hadn't fit on the same
shore as the small fishing town backed by steep hills that had called
gold-rushers to their doom or fortune. So, they'd built the airport on
the island on the other side of Tongass Narrows. The airport ferry
only took a few minutes. Would these few minutes be enough to bribe
the ferry captain to turn left and just see how far they could get?
Anchorage? Dutch Harbor? Russia?

The phone call had been just before lunch on Saturday and now Jo
was going to be having dinner in Ketchikan, Alaska. Assuming she
could keep anything down. Her single least favorite place on the
planet. She didn't hold it against the state, the town, or the people in
it. Well, not as much as she held it against one person in particular.

But he was no longer in it and that was the problem.

Earnest Jack Thompson was dead. And it was now up to his only child to deal with whatever mess he'd left behind.

MURIEL HAD a reservation waiting for her by the time Jo landed and called to check in. Jo couldn't remember what Muriel had said about it, so she would just head for her usual retreat up on the hill at the edge of town and hope for the best. She hated to impose on Muriel on a Saturday morning, as they were supposed to be working that afternoon and Sunday. But when she'd received the phone call, her brain had muddled and she'd become wholly incompetent. Any court in the land would have declared her so, including a jury of her friends.

Perrin and Cassidy had removed the wedding dress while she'd stood like a lifeless mannequin. They'd given her clothes and she'd put them on. Now, looking down as she waited for the ferry to carry her across the Tongass Narrows, Jo saw that she wore hiking boots, her Calvin jeans, and an REI rain jacket. Under that, her blue blouse and a dark gray flannel shirt. She didn't even know she still owned a flannel shirt. Well, her friends had dressed her appropriately for this adventure.

Her friends. They'd taken care of her. Packed for her. Muriel had found the flight and Cassidy had delivered Jo's mortal remains to the airport. She'd wrap that support around her and be strong.

Deep breath.

Another.

It was jolted from her by the ferry jarring hard against the dock pilings. The dock pilings in Ketchikan, Alaska.

She was so screwed.

She kicked on the windshield wiper to clear the heavy mist and ducked her head down.

She didn't wave at the deckhand, doing her best not to look at Dave Garvey as she rolled by inches away from his toes. The years had been hard on the former star wide receiver and king of auto shop class. Jo shouldn't be so mean about him, he'd always been decent to her—by never noticing she existed.

This was going to kill her. She was turning back into her fifteen-year old worst self. She was a lawyer of national and soon to be international repute, God damn it.

She sat up straighter and eased her grip on the wheel. Just in time to come face-to-face with the ferry's Captain, Steven Lancaster. He hadn't added the thirty-pound beer gut which now weighed down Dave. He looked great.

"Hey, Jo!" He shouted it loud enough to be heard through the tightly closed windows. Loud enough to be heard throughout the town. Well, it would be out soon enough anyway. The locals weren't that big a community. Her graduating class had been a hundred-and-forty-six strong, and in all likelihood about a hundred-and-forty-five of them still lived in town. Ketchikan was the sort of town that everyone talked about leaving, but no one actually did.

She'd run into this the few times in the past when she'd been forced to fly in here for meetings. She actually scheduled dinners with her father when she was in town only partly as a reason to see him. Mostly it had been to avoid her former schoolmates as much as possible. Her meetings here were typically all-day ones and much livelier after all the fishermen in the crowd had their three-beer lunches. Afterwards, anyone attending who she'd known from her youth, tried to get her to "Go out on the town" with them. That meant a total dive like the Crab Hole or some other hideous bar.

Steve showed no sign of letting her just roll on by, so Jo lowered the window. The air was cool on her face. It smelled of ocean, deep forest, and thirteen feet of rain every year.

"Hi, Steve! How are you doing?" That sounded normal, didn't it?

"Great! Heard about your dad. Sorry." He didn't look too contrite, but then he knew what her home life had been like. "Any chance of seeing you while you're in town? Marta and I eat at the Crab a couple times a week."

"Marta? Marta Benkowitz?"

"Marta Lancaster." He corrected her but his grin of pride showed she'd gotten it right. Steven and Marta? Sure, why not? Steve had always been an easy-going, cheerful guy that everyone liked. Even if he wasn't the smartest guy around, he was one of the nicest. Marta was shy, dark, and pretty enough. She was also one of the few that gave Jo a run for her money on test scores. As close to a friend as Jo ever had in Ketchikan, which wasn't saying much. An odd couple, but Steve's smile showed that it was clearly working for them.

"The Crab? Ah, sure." She was going to have to shoot herself. She'd just agreed to go back to the Crab Hole. Of course, that had been her dad's favorite bar, his second home. She'd have to go there anyway to make sure his bar tab was settled.

A horn blared behind her making Steve look back at the remaining ferry load.

"Mainlander," he scoffed then returned his attention to her. "Just let Gerta know when you're in and we'll come down and join you."

"Gerta."

"Yeah. Ukrainian lady. Barely speaks English. But she showed up one day looking for work and old Fred hired her. Rumor is they're an item but it's hard to tell because Fred never talked all that much anyway and no one can understand her when she does. But the food's almost edible now which is a nice change."

"Okay. Good to see you doing so well." Then she waved and drove off the ferry and into hell.

CHAPTER 26

nable to eat, Jo had merely curled up in her room at the Cape Fox Lodge, hidden under the covers, and prayed for sleep. Somewhere during the third movie of an Adam Sandler marathon, she hated Adam Sandler, slapstick humor, and the world in general, she'd finally fallen asleep for a few fitful hours.

Sunday morning she tried the house, but, though the black and gold letters spelling out "Thompson" still clung tenuously to the mailbox as they always had and the same old fishing gear littered the porch, she couldn't get in. The door was locked, which was unusual. They hadn't been well enough off to have anything worth stealing, so why bother. The obvious spare key under the mat was gone, too. It had probably been used to lock the door.

Jo then went down to find his fishing boat, but didn't remember what slip it was in. Well, she thought she did, but the Eloise wasn't there. Maybe she'd finally sunk, though the dark waters alongside the finger pier hid any evidence if it had sunk at dock. The marina was empty of people, surprising even for a Sunday morning, so she couldn't find anyone to ask. Right. It was June in the salmon fishing capital of the world. The run was on and every fisherman who could crawl onto a trawler, or snag a tourist, would be out on the sea or up in the fjords making a living.

Well, the hook had been baited and it had dragged her back to Alaska. Now it was time to see just how fast she could get unhooked. Since not even the Crab Hole was open at this early hour, she went for a drive through the town, a major mistake.

Two cruise ships had arrived in the night and she could see a third pulling into the Tongass Narrows even now. The population of the town had just doubled for the day. The historic waterfront was already clogged past reason, the few cars stupid enough to brave the lower streets of the town crept their way between pedestrians, even at seven in the morning. By mid-morning the lower streets would be wholly impassable except on foot, and barely then. It took her forever to escape the congestion.

As a result, rather than cruising by some pretty little shops, she was up driving through the back roads. The middle school and high school looked exactly the same, except for another decade of age and moss on the roof. They were okay, her only refuge other than the library. She didn't go there just in case Mrs. Freson was still head librarian. The woman had given her a vision of the outer world. She'd grown up in Seattle, gone to Vassar, and for reasons beyond Jo's imagining, ended up in Ketchikan with four kids in the four grades ahead of Jo.

Mrs. Freson had fed Jo's need to know, her need to escape. Having four kids ahead of Jo, she knew which courses Jo would be taking and what books, both fiction and non, would enhance the relatively mundane teachings aimed at fisherman's and shop owner's kids. They were mostly headed to work at the fish plant or servicing the cruise ships hitting Water Street like gunshot, leaving a wide damage path and never quite enough money in their wakes.

It might be nice to see her. Sit down and visit about how Vassar had changed, about how she was doing in Seattle. Somehow it was too sensible, too rational, too normal.

The last thing Jo wanted was for anything in Ketchikan to start feeling normal.

The second to last thing Jo wanted to do was see Mrs. Freson and burst into wracking sobs that Jo suspected were lurking just below the calm outer surface she was struggling to present. She continued past the library without stopping.

At the far end of town, the fish packing plant where she'd worked part time in the gift shop during the summers was at full roar. She definitely didn't stop there, way too many former classmates and coworkers. Though she couldn't resist slowing down to see if it looked even a little different. "Severely weathered" was the standard paint job of Ketchikan, Alaska, and the packing plant was no different. Some of the cars were newer models, but not enough for it to really look different.

Finally, unable to escape the town, as the road simply ended five miles past either side of Ketchikan, she'd gone back to the lodge, lay down on the bed for a few minutes, and finally gotten much of the sleep she'd missed last night.

***

IT WAS LATE that afternoon by the time she again braced herself to venture out into the Alaskan "sunshine." A bright gray sky offered a near blinding brightness in every direction, backed by just enough moisture in the air to drench your hair if you walked through it, but not enough to justify an umbrella. That was a laugh, she had become a city girl. Umbrellas were useless in Ketchikan, because rain here often rode in on gale-force winds. And she hadn't come equipped with a hood or hat. Even crossing from hotel to rental car had dampened her freshly dried hair.

Driving back through town, only touching the back roads this time, the windshield wipers squeaked and stuttered across a windshield too dry to wipe properly and too speckled to ignore. Once she reached her destination, she parked, but couldn't force herself to get out of the car.

Jo looked up through the rental car's windshield at the spitting sky. She tried to ignore the new car smell that was rapidly mutating to take on the sickening overtones of lichen and moss, no matter that the windows were sealed tight. The tall fir trees were standing stock-still against a uniform bright gray sky. No big blow coming for at least the rest of the day, probably not the one after that either. Other than the light precipitation, this was a perfect fishing day. And she was certainly about to go fishing—for any clue she could find.

Looking back down from the sky, she glared at the bar across the street. The Crab Hole was really too nice a name for the place. It bore a notorious paint job. Fred was a cheap bastard, or maybe he just didn't care, no one could decide for sure and it wasn't a topic he bothered with. Either way, he bought the mis-mixed paints at the paint store for half price. Someone orders five gallons of peach that comes out puce? The Crab Hole's south wall will be puce for the next five years. Half the trim pale-piss yellow, the rest of it pumpkin orange. The only thing that never changed was the large, carved-wood sign. Until you knew what it was, it was hard to make sense of it.

Jo could still remember the heat on her cheeks when at the age of eleven she'd finally figured it out.

A crab hole is what the crab fisherman called a place in the ocean that crabs gathered. Often a dip in the ocean floor, it caused crabs to swarm and cluster. Good crab holes are deeply protected secrets passed down generation to generation within a family. Crabber captains lie to their crews about their actual coordinates to hide the locations. So she'd always thought the Crab Hole was named for a good place to go crabbing.

At eleven years old, Jo's mind had finally matured enough to unravel the aged, weather-softened carvings of the sign. It was a male crab mounted on a female's back. That wasn't so unusual. The Arctic Bar just down the road had a logo of two grizzly bears humping. What was out of place on the Crab Hole sign was the very obvious, once you knew how to see it, human penis that the crab was ramming up the she-crab's backside.

People thought it made the place colorful. Tourists who made it this far down the waterfront always took a picture of themselves with the sign over their shoulder in the background. Only a few, however, had the nerve to venture inside. This was completely a locals' watering hole.

Jo forced herself from the car and tried to forget how many times she'd gone through that door looking for her father. She wished she'd worn gloves, but forced herself to take the door handle shaped like a giant crab claw, a hand-worn electric green at the present time, and go inside.

Almost twenty hours a day of sun here in mid-June Ketchikan, and at four in the afternoon the bar was a place of shadows and smoke. Right, you could smoke in bars in Alaska, she'd forgotten that. New York State and Washington State barely let you smoke in your own home, which was fine with her.

Here, a low cloud of nicotine stained the walls a motley brown. Mixed with the ever constant smell of deep-fry fish and chips and grilled burgers, that were not bought for their "percent lean," it had a palpable nastiness that was bitter on the tongue and nose, stung the eyes, and left her feeling the instant need for another shower.

For "ambiance" the Crab Hole had the KTKN broadcast offering inaudible but constantly murmuring talk radio that no one listened to, but it filled any overlong silences, as if there was a busy background debate going on in the room. The other entertainment was an old Wurlitzer juke box that might have been worth something, but hadn't worked since as far back as Jo could remember. She'd dreamed for hours as a little girl of all of the places it could take her. California Dreaming, Girl from Ipanema, both the Dionne Warwick and the Frank Sinatra versions, she'd even wanted to ride The Last Train to Clarksville, wherever that was. Back then, it took an active interest to make out the faded titles through the layers of grease on the curved glass front. Probably wholly invisible by now.

The whole scene created a miasma so thick that it could have been chopped up and sold for poisoning typical house pests. The atmosphere blurred the backs of the regulars at the bar until they appeared to blend together.

But Jo didn't need to see them clearly to know who they were. Adam, Bernie, Carl, and Dan. God, had nothing in the place changed? She'd been gone a dozen years and all they'd done was get a little wider and Carl's long hair showed a little grayer where it hung down in a severely dated mullet. Dan, the massive Tlingit, so big he must be part Samoan, anchored the row on the fourth stool. The fifth stool at the bar was empty. They always sat in alphabetical order for reasons none of them claimed to remember. The bar would have to find an Eric or Evander to sit on the stool that had belonged to Earnest Jack Thompson as surely as if he'd bought and paid for it.

From the hazy shadows she inspected the rest of the bar. A thousand, maybe ten thousand crab shells had been glued to the wall. No legs, just the shells so close together they were nearly indistinguishable. Not just Dungeness and Alaskan King. Travelers who had braved the Crab Hole went home and sent in new ones from all over the world. Blues, spider crab, stone, rock, South American land crab... She'd learned them all, when bored with sitting at some sticky table doing her homework and sipping a Coke. Floor to ceiling, the shells covered the wall.

The place looked as if some mad painter had blotched the walls with a ragged sponge then covered the whole place in dust to gray out any real sign of shape, color, or semblance to anything natural. Rather than crab shells, the ceiling had been mostly covered with dark blue mussel shells, with some gray clam and white oyster mixed in. That was almost pretty, if a little oppressive as it wasn't a very high ceiling.

There were a dozen or so patrons. The locals were quiet and wore tough working clothes or sensible sweaters for the cool summer day. But there were a few tourists off the cruise ships, the more adventurous ones who were seeking that "authentic Alaskan experience," all marked very clearly by the urban clothes and cruise ship attitude that was practically tattooed on their foreheads.

God, she'd hated that as a kid. Because of her half-Alaskan heritage, she looked native enough for all of the tourists to want a picture of her up against some wall of the Crab Hole as if she were an attraction placed there for their own enjoyment. She'd started charging them a quarter a shot. Her father's sole comment about the whole situation was that she should charge a buck. She tried it and it worked. Almost well enough that she stopped minding as much, though not quite. She spent most of her take at Parnassus Bookstore which left her canning factory gift shop paychecks to go into the college fund savings account.

Behind the counter sat Fred, looking old and craggy exactly as she'd always remembered. Near him, drawing a beer, was the woman Steve had mentioned. Gerta stood about Jo's height. She had short blond hair, a narrow face, and athletic shoulders. Jo wondered if Fred had hired her to continue the alphabetical chain.

Gerta had noted Jo's entrance right away, though her only reaction had been a quick glance of dark eyes. Fred must have noticed Gerta's attention, as his gaze drifted in Jo's direction.

The smile he offered when he recognized her was slow, slow and sad. He was the one who'd called her to tell her that her father was dead.

Jo SAT on her father's stool in the Crab Hole, hoping that no one with initials "H" and "I" showed up while she was here or she might never escape. It was creepy. She'd never sat here before, not even in her dad's lap that she could remember. He hadn't been a lap kind of guy.

Thankfully he also hadn't been a drunk, particularly. Not the way she always thought of them anyway, staggering out of the Seattle clubs at two a.m. as likely to walk into walls as along the sidewalk. Or the burnout alkies begging around Pioneer Square.

Yes, her father had gotten off the boat, gone to his stool at the Crab Hole, and not moved until closing or near enough. But he nursed only a couple beers each night. It was some sort of sad male bonding that caused these five guys to perch every night in front of Fred's bar and talk sports, fishing, weather, and tourists. Which was most of their repertoire, leaving a lot of time for KTKN to drone quietly in the background.

Fred no longer got up to wait the tables. "Too damn much arthritis in my old hip." He'd practically become one of his own patrons anchored to a stool, just on the other side of the bar. Gerta serviced the tables, cooked the fry or grill orders, and tended the bar with a quiet efficiency and actually appeared to be happy with what she was doing.

"Better than nuclear specialist in Ukrainian Army," Gerta had offered in barely recognizable English when she noted Jo's attention. Actually, if Jo hadn't grown up in a town where there were many Russian fishermen, she'd not have understood Gerta at all. And once Jo had unraveled Gerta's words in her head, by which time the woman had moved on, Jo hoped that she hadn't heard them correctly.

Fred had gotten Jo a beer personally, even though she hadn't wanted one. But she was too polite to say so, and knew Fred didn't serve wine, nasty or otherwise. All of them from Adam to Fred were clearly at a loss of what to do with the empty stool, it had probably been filled nearly every night for thirty or more years. Gerta didn't appear to be bothered by much of anything.

"It was fast," Fred told her. "Funny, he wasn't the drunk one. It was the one who hit him that was out of his gourd. Twenty-two year old tourist kid who just totally screwed up his own life. After he hit your dad, he overcorrected and drove into that new antiques place on Madison. Busted up his leg and hip and what the Californian owner claims is about a quarter million worth of the ugliest crap you've ever seen. For a while we didn't know whether or not his old man was going to kill him before the cops let him out of the hospital on bail."

"And," Bernie chimed in, he always liked adding the last line to a story. "Rumor is he was far more pissed about the antiques coming out of his insurance than some manslaughter charge his son might get slapped with."

"Didn't come out right there, Bern." About the only statement Adam ever made was correcting Bernie.

Somehow it was appropriate that drink had been the instrument of death for Earnest Thompson, even if she wasn't going to say so in this bar.

"'Course he had less than six months to live," Carl offered.

"He what?" Jo leaned forward to look around Dan's bulk.

"Liver," Bernie offered without really turning to look at her as if he were still trying to puzzle out what was wrong with his last utterance.

"Prostate, ya' fool," Adam corrected.

Dan, as usual, said nothing. He simply dug into a pocket, set a key on the bar with barely a sound and slid it over to her. The house key. Dan was big, but he was also the youngest at the bar, probably only in his late fifties or early sixties. As such, it had clearly been his task to climb the fifty-six stairs to her father's shack and oversee what needed overseeing.

Jo didn't want the key and all that it implied, but she didn't want to offend Dan either. She nodded to him and stuffed the key in her pocket.

She'd just found out her father had been dying anyway, that he hadn't told her, and she could think of nothing to say. Oh God, she was fitting right in at the bar of the Crab Hole.

"Jo, I knew you come!"

Before she could identify the voice behind her, she was tipped back on the stool and swept into a kiss.

Yuri Andreevich!

One arm around her shoulders held her tipped back and off balance, the other started at her hip but was on her breast in a moment. He drove the kiss at her even as she shoved against his massive chest, to little effect.

He broke the kiss for a moment. "I know you come here when your father die. And now he no longer scare you away from beautiful Alaska and you can stay here for me and we can make many babies together."

He leaned back in and she managed to shove him aside long enough to say, "No!" Her entire system was galvanized with revulsion. She didn't think there was a way to make the Crab Hole worse than it was, but Yuri had found one.

He drove at her again with his whiskey breath and she slapped him as hard as she could, putting every inch of her workout muscles into it.

Yuri's head barely turned. He just smiled. "I knew you missed me. Now we can make love like two Russian wildcats."

Abruptly she was free, so fast that she'd have fallen to the floor without Dan's steadying hand on her back.

"The lady said, 'No'!"

She turned to see which of the alphabet gang had pulled Yuri off. They were all off their stools and moving in, but the fist that connected with Yuri's jaw hard enough to snap his head back belonged to Angelo. Angelo was a head shorter, but with shoulders just as wide as Yuri's. Yuri stumbled back into a crab-shell covered wall with a loud crunch that broke dozens of shells showering tiny flakes of calcium carbonate to the floor.

Angelo didn't give him a moment to recover. Two more hits, gut and chin again. Before Yuri could collapse to the floor, Angelo grabbed him by the hair and the back of his belt. He got him into a stumbling run and ran him at the heavy wooden entry door.

Angelo released him just as he hit. Yuri crashed through the front door, opening it with his head, and tumbled out onto the sidewalk. A short scream came from some tourist he almost bowled over as he collapsed against a car parked at the curb. A little display of local color. Another tourist snapped a photo even as the door swung shut.

Angelo came back to her slowly. The others were gathered around her asking if she was okay. Even Fred had made it out from behind the bar. But that was all a mere background buzz.

"How?" Jo gestured helplessly toward the wall of shattered crab shells.

"I grew up with Russell. He was always getting us into some *rissa*. Scuffle."

"Oh. Uh. What are you doing here?" She didn't know whether to laugh or cry or shout or throw herself at him.

He stopped a foot away, massaging one hand with the other.

"I, uh… You shouldn't be alone when family dies. Cassidy said you had no one else and she couldn't leave Russell, so I came."

"But how?" She really wasn't being very lucid was she. She pointed toward the door Yuri had so recently exited as if that would complete the question she couldn't formulate. It swung open as a couple tourists came in, looking over their shoulders at the man now up on all fours and shaking his head.

Angelo shrugged in that Italian fashion of his. "I came in and saw you at the bar. I didn't want to disturb you." He pointed at a half-finished beer sitting at a small table to the side.

She stepped in until their bodies brushed together. She ran a finger down his cheek.

"Thank you," she barely mouthed it then simply wrapped her arms around his neck and lay her head on his shoulder. Yuri didn't really matter, the alphabet gang would have pulled him off in a moment more, though it wouldn't have been half as satisfying.

But no one had ever dropped everything and come two thousand miles just because she shouldn't be alone. Being in Angelo's arms was the first rational thing that had happened to her since the awful phone call.

"ADAM, Bernie, Carl, Dan, Fred, and Gerta. This is Angelo." Jo couldn't stop holding his hand and Angelo wasn't complaining for a second. Gerta found him another stool somewhere in the back, and Jo had them shoved together so close that they couldn't sit without touching.

Russell had mentioned over Sunday breakfast at Cassidy's condo that Jo's dad had died and she'd gone to Alaska. Without thinking, or even saying goodbye, he'd simply walked out the door and headed to the airport. No luggage, nothing. Just two phone calls. One to Manuel that the restaurant was his for the moment. The other to his mother to help Manuel. Mama had said only one word when she heard why he was already racing to the airport, "Go." Then she'd hung up and he could only hope everything would be okay.

The whole flight north he'd been torn. A summer Sunday, he really should be at the restaurant. He'd abandoned everyone at a moment's notice. On the other side, he couldn't get to Alaska fast enough.

Russell had texted him sometime during the flight and he got the message when he landed. Cassidy had recalled some college story about a bar called the Crab Hole. Who could forget a name like that? Starting there for lack of a better idea, he'd rushed in and come to a halt when he'd seen her at the bar with an untouched beer sitting in front of her. He'd almost gone forward, but he knew this scene from a dozen different bars, though never one this oddly decorated. He recognized the slow conversation of regulars. She knew these people and they knew her.

He'd raised a single finger to the bartender and tipped his hand as if opening a beer tap. She'd brought a pint of whatever she had on draft to the side table he'd chosen. From there he could watch Jo's profile. Only sitting there watching her, did he finally realize that he could have just called her cell phone when he landed. But that didn't matter now, he'd found her anyway.

It was odd to watch. She fit in and she didn't. The conversation, so slow and sporadic as to be almost nonexistent, had continued in its way. They liked her and she them. It was so obvious that she was a part of their world. Yet, though he'd never seen her so dressed down, she still stood out like a tourist. Her clothes were too new, too well coordinated. Her jeans didn't just fit, they clung. Her hair wasn't just clean, it shone.

He'd fallen so far under the spell of watching her that he hadn't seen the big Russian arrive. Yuri had swept Jo into his arms like a long lost lover. Angelo had been frozen in place. It couldn't be. He couldn't have so misread the situation, it just couldn't be. He'd kill himself. The betrayal hit him like a leaden weight that almost brought the half beer in his empty stomach back up as bitter bile.

Then he heard the whispered, "No," and the sharp slap. That was all the motivation he'd needed. She'd begun to struggle in earnest even as he reached her side. It had been a pleasure taking the man down. His hand still stung like hell, though not a chance he'd be admitting it anytime soon.

Gerta had given him an ice pack for which he was immensely grateful. He discretely wiggled his fingers again to make sure they weren't broken. You could cook despite cuts and burns, but a broken hand would be a whole different matter. With one hand in ice and the other clamped onto by Jo, he wasn't able to drink his beer, but that was the only fault he could find with the moment.

he stories slowly unwound around Jo. The stories of her father's friends huddled at the Crab Hole bar revealed a man she knew, yet didn't know.

"He spoke even less than old Dan here. That's why they ended up at the end of the bar. Whereas I never shut up which is how I ended up in the middle." Carl spoke after a long, comfortable pause. In any other company, he'd be the silent one, but he was definitely the talker of this group.

"Adam and Bernie, well, they're the youngsters. I think you were already born by the time they came along."

Twenty-eight years they'd been sitting at this bar and they were still the youngsters. She shared a smile with Angelo.

After another silence, Fred looked at her. "Strange seeing the two of you sittin' so close like that. Earnest and Eloise used to sit that way. Had six stools here for a pretty fair time. She came off one of the cruise ships and just didn't leave. She glowed the way you do, Jo. That's why she named you for the girl in that book Little Women. Said you had that same life in you."

Jo hadn't known that. It had seemed a little obvious, but she liked knowing it for certain. She'd taken Jo March to heart. That incredible strength. When she went into the courtroom, she kept the picture clearly in her head of Jo March taking on the whole world. Though on the inside she'd always felt more like Beth, the quiet, shy one.

"You'd sit in her lap," Fred sipped his beer to drag out the story. "The two of you would just glow. You look so much like her, it's hard to credit. You partly got your daddy's coloring, but everything else you got from your mama."

"Why did she go? Why did she leave us?" Angelo's tight hold on her hand was the only thing that gave her strength to ask the question without her voice breaking. She had a thousand questions for him too, but for the moment all she could do was hold on as tightly as she could and draw stability from his being here beside her. It felt as if she was making some commitment that she wasn't sure she was ready to make, but she'd have to unravel and straighten that out later. Her past was threatening to overwhelm her and for now all she could do was hold on.

The guys at the bar all looked at one another, as if no one wanted to speak first. The bar was quiet. Tourists didn't come to dinner at a place like the Crab Hole and the locals who did wouldn't be along for a while. With so many hours of sunlight in mid-June, dinner happened later and breakfast earlier than in the winter. For now, it was the six of them on one side of the bar, Fred on the other, and Gerta standing behind Fred leaning casually against his back with her arms over his shoulders. Jo had found out she was older than she looked, in her early fifties, and Fred was, she knew, in his seventies. Whatever was going on there, they looked comfortable together. Clearly the bar would someday be hers and she and Fred and the other locals were fine with that.

"She faded," Dan spoke for the first time since asking if Jo was okay while Angelo threw a man half-again his size through the door. His first full sentence since she'd arrived. His deep voice made it a proclamation. The others nodded.

Carl took over. "I liked her, but Dan's right. She faded here. Faded until the light in her went out and she had to leave to go find it again.

Something in old Earnest broke the day she left. But he could no more leave than she could stay."

"She never done divorce him." Again the deep declaration.

"One postcard is all Earnest ever spoke of." Carl inspected his beer then the mussel-shell ceiling as if searching his memory and finding nothing else. "Sent it the day she left. Jes' to let him know she were alive. Maybe said something about goin' to feed kids in Africa or somethin'. Don't quite recall. No return address. Postmarked at Seattle airport."

Jo looked over at Angelo. His mother was so alive, so vital, so present. She'd been and clearly still was such a force in Angelo's life. What would that be like?

Well, that was something she'd never know.

CHAPTER 28

ver Fred's protests, Jo had settled the bar tab, though it wasn't too bad. Her father used to pay it off once the fishing season income started rolling in. Knowing he was dying, he'd sold the Eloise, "Which came as close to killing him as your mother leaving. Then he started into paying his tab monthly, makin' the rest of us look bad." Bernie, of course.

So, that was done. One less thing for her to worry about was all she could think. They'd already cremated him. Tomorrow evening the new owner was going to take them all out on the Eloise and scatter the ashes. She hadn't committed to that, but she hadn't said no either.

She had promised she'd come back through before leaving town. Still holding her hand, Angelo walked with her as she headed up Young Street, then Warren Street to her father's house.

"What day is this?" Jo's brain had already become scrambled by the events of the last two days. "Sunday?"

"Sunday," Angelo confirmed.

"How could you leave the restaurant?"

Angelo laughed and shook his head, "I don't really know, I just had to. I wondered about that on the flight up, but some part of me must

523

have known it would be okay, even if I wasn't thinking very clearly. Manuel can run the restaurant as well as I can. Apparently Graziella has had her eye on someone for front of house help, and she's going to do a trial this afternoon. My mother loved your idea, so she's going to be filling in for Eugene. There is no way I would ever have thought that up. How did you?"

Jo shrugged. She noticed the gesture was very unlike herself, but was one she saw on Angelo all the time. What other influences was she picking up from him?

"It simply made sense. Your mother is charming, a brilliant cook, and you clearly love each other so much that you can barely stand it. So, of course, she'd want to be with you." Now why had she phrased it that way? Of course, his mother would want to help him. But that's not what she'd said. Nor what she'd thought. "Want to be with Angelo." Why did that phrase feel as if she were speaking of someone other than his mother? She pulled her flannel shirt tighter against the back of her neck.

Angelo inspected the sky which had briefly eased from misting to merely humid. With the temperature in the sixties it only dampened the air, rather than being muggy. He looked back down, apparently he hadn't found anything up there to help him find a response to that.

They turned onto the old wooden stairs leading up to Warren Street. They slowly climbed above narrow Hopkins Alley where there were steep banks of scrub and low trees, below ranged the backs of old warehouses wearing their gray paint as if to compete with the gray sky. The stairs creaked and groaned as they climbed them, but by Ketchikan standards this was a major thoroughfare, you could walk two abreast without a problem. Once they broke free of the warehouses they had a clear view over the tops of a light industrial stretch of Water Street and out to Pennock and Gravina Islands defining the Tongass Narrows.

Jo saw a jet lifting off the runway on Gravina, slowly filling the Narrows with its dull roar before turning south for friendlier climes. She'd pay good money to be done and aboard. Now there was the constant thought of her youth. "Get me out of here!" She could feel the shout rooted deep inside. But just as when she was a girl, she kept it bottled deep inside. Kept it there because once again her life had drifted out of her control.

No escape for today at least. All of the businesses she'd need to contact would be closed on a Sunday. Maybe she could escape tomorrow.

She squeezed Angelo's hand again, just so pleased that he was there with her. That anyone was there with her.

Because next came the hard part.

ANGELO LOOKED at the strange houses lining the uphill side of whatever street they were on. His head was still spinning at the foreignness of this place. Sure, it was technically on U.S. soil, but it didn't belong there. Everything was surreal. An airport separated from the town it served by a ferry that didn't stand a chance in rough weather. And this was Alaska. He'd bet that there was a lot of waiting for the waters to be calm enough for the ferry during the winter months, which up here was probably about ten months of the year.

And the Crab Hole…he had to send some of his New York friends there, it was performance art at its finest, and most authentic. No edgy display observed by urban crowds dressed in black. That crab shell art and the patrons had been for-real surreal.

This street reminded him oddly of the Amalfi Coast of Italy. Houses perched on the edge of impossible cliffs. Long, stick-like understructures reaching multiple stories down to the street to support the front of houses who had their backsides planted firmly against the hill. He knew where they were going before Jo even turned toward it, and he really hoped he had it wrong.

Beyond a pickup truck made of equal parts red metal and brown rust, towered a house. A house that had clearly been built before the apocalypse and somehow survived. It perched upon a structure he wouldn't trust to hold up a garden shed. Twenty-foot tall four-by-fours with a couple of two-by-four cross braces looked impossibly spindly, too little to support even the stair rail nailed into the side of them, never mind the house atop.

A long flight of stairs climbed along the sloping hillside straddled by the stickframe understructure. The steps reached the back end of the shack where the house rested its butt against the cliff face. The only entrance was on the right side at the very back end of the house against the cliff.

The one-story structure that perched twenty or thirty feet above them might have once been white. Or perhaps blue. It was hard to tell with all of the peeling paint. He could see the green encroachments of moss or lichen or something else that wasn't supposed to be growing on buildings but had on this one. This is where James Patterson should put his next psychotic murderer. There'd be no question about what had twisted up the villain.

Angelo opened his mouth to ask if she'd actually lived here, but snapped it shut when he saw that her dark skin was almost sheet white and her jaw was clenched so hard he was afraid for her next dentist appointment. He changed tacks.

"Do you really have to go up there?"

Her nod was tight, but affirmative. She was staring up the steps wide-eyed, having stumbled to a halt with her hand barely inches from the rail.

"Okay," he'd be the stable one at the moment, even if merely looking at the place made him want to rent a flamethrower and call it done. "Let me have the key."

He didn't comment on her chilled fingers as she handed it over, merely led the way up the stairs, trusting that she'd follow. It took a few moments, but he began to feel the structure shaking with steps other than his. At the top he kicked aside a spool of rotting fishing line and unlocked the door.

Showing none of the hesitation he felt, he stepped inside, leaving the door wide open, and flicked on a light. Electricity was still working. That was a good start.

They entered at the back, where house met slope. A door straight ahead was tightly closed. A narrow, dark hallway led to the front of the house. Being braver than he felt, Angelo went down the hall hoping the building didn't collapse from under him. Another closed door to the side. Then the main room. The front half of the house, the part perched out in space on spindly legs, was a single room. Kitchen, living, and what euphemistically could be called dining, faced a window hazy with dried salt. The furnishings were old but looked serviceable. The room was clean and neat, nothing much here but a sofa, a couple of chairs, and an old television.

One more door at the far end of the room stood open. The back half of the house, other than the narrow hall to the door, had clearly been divided into three rooms. Two bedrooms, with the bath in the center would be his guess.

How had the miracle of Jo Thompson come from such a past? He turned to look at her. She stood at the threshold to the main room, posed as if perfectly calm and collected. Her hands tucked easily in the front pockets of her rain jacket. And tears running down her face.

"Okay, I'm getting you out of here." Angelo tried to sweep her out of the room and out of her father's house, but Jo held her ground.

"No. I need to do this now before I lose all of my nerve. This isn't hard," she spoke more to herself than Angelo. It had to be easier than the murder scene she'd had to visit and catalog as an intern, an experience that had driven her hard into corporate law where most of the crimes occurred in sterile board rooms.

"What are we looking for?"

She'd think of it as collecting evidence. That's all. Objective. She could be objective.

"A box."

"Any more guidance than that? What's in it?"

"An empty one, or a bag. We're going to make one quick pass and gather any paperwork we can find, checkbooks, stuff like that. One pass, then out."

Bless Angelo. He came back moments later with an old wooden box out of which he'd dumped a pile of broken winch blocks that her father had been meaning to repair since before she left for college.

"Could you do that one?" she indicated her father's room. She simply couldn't go in there.

He was gone in moments. She'd have to remember to thank him later. Thank God her father was a creature of habit and not a pack rat. By the time Angelo came back with the box about a third full, she'd completed her pass on the living room. Checkbooks in the second drawer of the coffee table along with two unpaid, but not yet overdue bills. A quick flip revealed that he'd gotten a hundred thousand for his boat, but medical and other outstanding bills had chewed up about half of that. He'd always lived season to season, and she remembered all too well how hard the bad seasons were. At his death, his savings were probably the highest they'd ever been in his life.

She found his spare truck keys. She'd drop them at the Crab Hole in case anyone wanted the old vehicle. The first drawer of the file cabinet revealed neatly filed bills in the separate hanging folders that she'd set up for him long ago. She pulled the most recent from each folder so that she'd know who to cancel. The other drawer included the truck title, which would go with the keys, and a small life insurance policy in her name. How hard had it been for him to maintain that? It wouldn't have paid for a year of her college or what she now made in a month or two, but she was touched nonetheless.

Finally, she found what she'd really been wanting, his will. The old envelope cracked with age as she opened it. The paper had yellowed, but was otherwise fine. Jo flipped to the back page, signed and witnessed, dated shortly after she was born.

She flipped back and scanned down the first page. Dan was named as the executor if Jo was under eighteen, otherwise Jo was executor. That simplified matters immensely.

Jo made it halfway down the next page before her knees let go and she dropped onto the couch.

Her father's will named both Jo and Eloise Thompson as beneficiaries. Fifty-fifty split if they were both surviving and Jo was over eighteen.

Now she was legally required to find her mother, the woman who had abandoned her before she was three.

CHAPTER 29

"*ogether." Angelo said when* Jo froze at the last room. The door by the entrance must be Jo's bedroom.

He opened the door, turned on the light, and stepped inside. There was a narrow, north-facing window that had been overgrown by moss. A tree in full leaf pressed hard against the cracked glass. The overhead bulb behind a faded papier-mâché shade did little to light the room.

It was perhaps the most depressing place he'd ever been. A desk, a narrow bed, and a closet that stood empty. The walls had posters curling from the damp, of astronauts and the space shuttle. Of the Martian surface and fantastic science fiction spaceships.

"Those were from my 'How far can I really get from Alaska?' phase," Jo stared at them blankly.

"I would say that culturally, you succeeded."

"I don't know," she kept staring at the curling posters. "Ketchikan doesn't look quite so bad as an adult. You couldn't pay me to live here," she threw up her hands, normally so quiet, in a very Italian gesture as if to block the possibility of such a thought. "But there is community. There are good people here. They're just not my people.

When I was a kid, I swore that I would never again set foot on Alaskan soil for as long as I lived."

Angelo eyed her carefully. "Yet your legal practice is mainly Alaskan."

"Don't remind me." She shuddered. And to Angelo's eye, what she'd intended to be mock horror had turned to very real disgust.

This was not the time or place to ask about that particular problem. So, instead, Angelo looked about the room, narrow enough to touch both walls with out-stretched arms and barely twice as long.

"Anything in here you want? If not, I'm getting you out of here."

"Let me go through the desk drawers just in case."

Nothing surfaced, and Angelo was going to shoo her out when he spotted a picture on the wall that didn't seem to fit the others.

"What's that one?" He pointed at the one image. It was small. A postcard of a penguin Photoshopped to be flying above the clouds with a little thought bubble. "Look Ma, I'm an eagle!" You could see the penguin's trajectory was failing and headed for a splashdown in the ocean far below. The "Ma" had been crossed out and replaced with "Jo" in faded pen.

Jo reached out slowly and pulled out the thumbtack holding it to the wall.

She turned it over and held it so that they could read it together.

Dearest Jo, I could find no way to fly in K-kan. By the time I could remember even how to crawl, it was too late for us. Say hi to Dan for me. All the best! Eloise (not the boat)

And a somewhat pathetic smiley face.

It was dated five years ago.

SHE AND ANGELO had a quiet night at the Cape Fox Lodge. They ate a meal at the restaurant, with no seafood involved, as if they'd both been overwhelmed by the Salmon Fishing Capital of the World. Jo had the Russian Chicken and Angelo the Pepper Steak. They split a piece of Chocolate Cheesecake, but had been unable, or unmotivated to finish it.

She slept like the dead, curled against his chest, wrung out to her very core. Somewhere in the middle of the night she'd needed more. He'd woken easily, in that quiet way of his, and been very good to her, kissing away her tears of exhaustion that found their way out even as her body released the spring wound so tightly inside.

In the light of morning, with room service pancakes cooling on the small table, she'd finally faced the task of sorting through the box. Angelo stayed out of the way, pretending to watch a baseball game with the sound turned way down, which she appreciated. When she had it sorted and started on the phone calls, he'd gone for a run. A dozen phone calls later she'd arranged for someone to clean out the house, someone else to sell it in the name of the estate, the land had to be worth something. She cancelled utilities, medical, and car insurance. By the time the first round was done, she had a couple of pages of a hotel pad covered with notes.

She could draft her first motion for probate, except for the conditions of the will that mandated she find a woman twenty-six years gone. She could argue for probate in absentia and probably get it. Even throw her mother's half into a trust in case she ever surfaced. But was it worth the pain and aggravation? She didn't know, couldn't think. So she set it aside for the moment.

Angelo drifted back in just as she started digging into what he'd recovered from her father's room. No letters. No strange postcards from the past. Mostly junk she could just throw out once she'd looked at it. Near the bottom, there was a photo. Her father and a woman she didn't recognize, or at least not completely.

She'd snooped often enough as a child trying to find some evidence of her mother, and found none. Yet here in a cheap wood frame stood a much younger version of her father, his face and hair dark with Tlingit blood. Behind him, the newly painted prow of the Eloise, her name in bold blue lettering on the white hull. Beside him, a pretty woman with her own dark hair almost down to her waist, but fair features, perhaps of the

East Coast, perhaps California. She wore bright yellow fisherman boots, jeans, and a plaid flannel shirt. Though her eyes seemed hidden, hazed in some way that Jo couldn't quite discern, her smile appeared bright.

And she cradled a tiny child in her arms. A child, Jo now knew, who had skin the color of her father's and the features of a mother she'd never met but would recognize in the mirror.

"ONE LAST STOP, then we're gone." It was early in the afternoon and she and Angelo had managed two seats on the evening flight back to Seattle.

Jo pulled up in front of the Crab Hole and cursed when she saw the "Closed for Funeral" sign. She checked her watch and cursed again, there was still plenty of time.

They drove down to the docks, the Eloise still floating in the slip. A small group had clustered on the dock. Jo parked and took the truck title and keys with her, and the postcard.

"Engine's conked," Carl informed her. "Doesn't matter a damn, crematorium screwed up the preserve-the-ashes order, so there's not a damn thing to scatter anyway. Didn't know you could get a cremation with no ashes, but seems you can order it that way. We figured we'd go down to the end of the pier, drink a pint, and piss inta the Narrows."

Jo managed a laugh. It was so fitting that it was sad and funny and touching all at the same time. Her body didn't know what to do with the collision of the conflicting feelings and so she just nodded her head in approval.

She pulled out the title and keys, "Do you need a truck?"

"Aw, shit. Yeah, one of us will take the damn thing. Best thing to do for that beast is drop her off the end of the pier to make a fish reef for divers, like them old battleships."

Jo hugged him. She knew that was as close as any of them would get to saying they'd liked her father and would miss him. He held her lightly when he returned the gesture, patting her back like a child's.

"He was damned proud o' you. Even when we didn't understand what you were doin', he was so proud of you. Missed you as much as Eloise, but was damn fucking proud."

She wondered if he meant Eloise her mother or Eloise the boat after he'd sold her. She decided the politic action was not to inquire.

Then Carl was gone and turned into the wind so that he'd have an excuse to wipe at his eyes.

Each came to hug her goodbye and pat her back. Fred groused about his arthritis and that if anyone else was gonna die before him they'd better be doin' it soon or he wasn't comin' to any of these shit-heads' funerals. Gerta offered Jo a nod. Bernie said something about it being a good thing they didn't have any ashes or old Earnest might get pissed when they pissed on him." Adam just rolled his eyes at Bernie's back and shook her hand.

Angelo, bless him, was hanging with them by the Eloise easing any awkwardness. He gave them someone to speak to besides Earnest's daughter after they'd already said goodbye to her.

When Dan came up to her last of all, the others had moved off a bit to check on the status of the engine repairs and to get a beer. Dan gave her a big, hard hug as if she were his own daughter somehow. Being hugged by Dan was like being enfolded in the arms of a gentle papa bear, someplace warm, soft, and very safe.

He started to turn away, and Jo almost let him go. It was an option. Burn the will and postcard, turn her back, and let the state take it all. She was technically in violation of the laws of probate for doing what executor tasks she'd done so far, by canceling utilities and removing items from the house. She should first have filed the death certificate and will with the state who would then certify her in the role of executor.

However, she was licensed to practice law in Alaska and while this wasn't her area of specialty, she knew the Alaskan laws well enough to know the penalty wouldn't amount to much more than a scowl from the judge, if that. At this point, she could take the wooden crate back and dump it on the living room floor, throw the key in behind it, and walk away clean.

Except it wouldn't feel clean.

Instead, she stopped Dan with a hand on his arm, and pulled the postcard from her coat pocket. His broad, dark face went bright when he saw the writing, then sad before he could possibly have read even the few lines there.

"You were closest to her, weren't you?"

Dan nodded slowly, "In coupla ways." He rubbed a meat cleaver-sized hand across his face. "Earnest sat ta' end. Eloise sat twixt us'n. He wanted her included."

"She stayed in touch."

"Birthdays an' such. Yours and mine. I kep' in touch on hers."

"You know where she is." Jo had figured that must be the message, "Say hi to Dan." Her mother had stayed in touch with Dan, knowing he'd be in touch with Earnest and so could hear how her daughter was faring. Her father had been smart enough to understand that when he'd seen the postcard, but he'd still been hurting enough to not forward the card. There'd been nothing on the card for him. But he hadn't been angry enough to throw it out either. She'd give good money to know if he'd tacked it to the wall when it arrived, almost a spit in Jo's eye of "you'll never see this because you never come home" or had he tacked it up when he found out he was dying, specifically so that Jo would find it.

Dan didn't look away.

In that look, she saw the pain of knowledge. Earnest had sat next to him for the last five years knowing for a fact that Dan was in touch with Earnest's departed wife, the wife he'd remained married to until death did he part. Her father must have mentioned the postcard. She could almost hear the conversation at some moment when only the two of them were there at the bar.

"Got a postcard."

Dan waiting in silence.

"For Jo."

A slow turn and meeting of their gazes.

"From her mother."

A long silence, followed by a slow nod on Dan's part.

A mutual turning away.

Then five more years of sitting side by side with that conversation now hanging between them.

Jo scrubbed at her arms to remove the chill of that on a warm day, knowing full well that's exactly how it had been.

"March," Dan said after such a long pause that Jo almost didn't catch it. "Eloise March." Then he turned, joined the others, and they headed down to the end of the pier to drink together and piss into the Narrows. Angelo hung back, waiting for Jo.

"March" for Jo March, for Little Women and the strong mother, Marmee March, who Eloise must have wished she could be. Everything done in the literary tradition, as Eloise had been part of that tradition before her daughter.

That Dan had said nothing more meant that her mother either couldn't be found, or could be found very easily.

That in turn meant…

In Seattle, by looking in the phone book. All Jo had needed to find her mother all this time was her chosen last name.

CHAPTER 30

"I love you."

Jo was shocked to stillness at the whisper. The jet had just slammed on the power to roar down the Ketchikan airport runway and get her out of this place. She turned to Angelo praying she hadn't really heard it. But he wasn't facing out the window with a first time visitor's curiosity, he was looking right at her.

She shook her head slowly once as the jet's roar peaked and then the plane abruptly rotated its nose off the runway and pointed for the sky.

Angelo nodded.

"You can't."

His face pained. Obviously not the answer he wanted. Well she didn't have that answer. He simply couldn't.

He didn't ease his grip on her hand.

"I can. And I do. And, before you go there, I'm not one of 'those' guys. You're only the third woman I ever told that. The first two were my mother and Cassidy on the day she married Russell."

Jo swallowed hard. It actually hurt to do so, but she couldn't work up any moisture. The dry air brushing across her face from the little overhead vents didn't help at all. The jet continued to roar almost as loudly as her pulse thundered in her ears.

She tried to remove her hand, but Angelo held onto it.

"I love you, Jo Thompson."

"But," this was crazy. "But why?" He'd just seen her at her very worst. Ketchikan had almost killed her. It probably would have if not for his presence.

Angelo's laugh was soft and, thankfully, not bitter.

"Okay, let's ignore the fact that you are easily the most beautiful woman I've ever been with."

She doubted that, looking all gorgeous and Italian the way he did.

"The most fun in bed."

Jo had to admit she'd never had such a good time with a man, not ever.

"And you're far and away the smartest. We can also ignore the fact of how you smell." At that he leaned in, using the fact of her incarceration in the narrow plane seat by the bright "Fasten Seatbelts" sign as they continued the climb out, and inhaled such a long sniff by her ear that she almost giggled.

"I take that back. I can't ignore how you smell. It is a flavor I can never fully understand but could gladly spend a lifetime trying to reproduce. God, you smell so good, Jo."

"I did take a shower. It's called soap."

He didn't deign to answer that with more than an Italian wave of the hand to dismiss her attempted misdirection. It was hard to argue, he smelled amazing to her as well. That's why she kept curling up with her face pressed against the center of his chest. It was like someplace she'd never known, like…she didn't have the word for it.

"What I also can't ignore was watching you with the alphabet gang."

"What about them?" Defensive. She could feel her spine stiffen and her chin rise as she prepared herself for their defense. She was feeling protective of her father's drinking buddies, which was utterly ridiculous, but an undeniable fact as well.

"You were so kind to them."

That knocked her back in her seat.

"They were in so much pain. They aren't sure who they are without your father there. You sat at that bar on his stool and you stood on that dock and told them it would be okay. That came straight from the heart, Jo. Straight from a really amazing heart."

Jo tried to imagine who Angelo was talking about, it wasn't anyone she recognized. All she'd done in Ketchikan was find out that her past hadn't been neatly left behind. Instead it had risen like a specter of evil until her past now blocked every path forward. Like the case she'd managed not to think of for forty-eight hours, the one burying her desk. The case that would bring her back to Alaska.

That was it. There was her defense.

"Angelo, you're really sweet. But you can't love me. Besides, I'll be in Alaska for a lot of the next three to five years." No matter how awful that fact itself sounded.

The plane leveled out and Jo could see the steward starting down the aisle with the drink cart.

"You can't do that."

"My case is in Alaska. North Slope. There is an immense amount of relevant information there, both documentation and individuals who will need interviewing. I'm going to have to be there, and at the capital in Juneau, as well as New York. So you can't love me, because I won't be here."

COULDN'T Jo see the pain it caused her each time she mentioned going back to Alaska, even as the plane was, at this moment, setting her free of the place? Angelo could see it written on her face. If he ignored, no, if he set aside his own pain at the moment, he could see hers as plain as a crack in an eggshell.

It was so hard to think straight around her. He could kick himself for saying he loved her when she was so emotionally strung out. He hadn't meant to. Hadn't known it was there to say until he did. It had been such a surprise he wasn't even sure he'd said it aloud until she turned to face him.

Now, not only had she thrown it back in his face unanswered, Counselor Thompson had turned it into a full-court defense and was now performing courtroom dissection on it.

Gods, who knew that loving someone could hurt this much? *Sì*, it was too soon, too fast. If it felt too fast for him, no matter how true, how must it feel for her? He'd even screwed up falling in love.

Jo had just been through emotional hell. He'd never been someone's lifeline like that before, at least not a woman's. He'd smacked Russell a couple of times during his courtship of Cassidy, or rather his non-courtship of her, but the guy had needed it.

Jo was a wholly different matter. For Russell, it had literally been a smack on the head. He'd wager that Jo wouldn't appreciate that at the moment, even if she needed it.

Having Jo hang onto him as she had these last two days had left him feeling pretty damned powerful. In some ways, punching Yuri had been the least of it no matter how good it felt. Standing beside her in the apartment, sitting with her father's friends at the bar, waiting at their crazy but somehow appropriate funeral so that she could touch each person's heart. They were so good together as a couple, they hadn't even had to talk about it.

Okay. Angelo took a deep breath. Okay. Another breath. Jo's emotions were stirred up and he'd just have to accept that. And his timing sucked, he could admit that too. He'd have to shut up at the moment about how much she filled his heart. It was like heat and ice at the same time flashing through his body in alternating waves with each beat of his heart. But he could keep quiet about that for her sake. For now.

What he couldn't ignore…

"Jo! How can a woman so smart as you even think of going back to Alaska? It tears you up."

"No, Angelo." Jo was gone. Counselor Thompson now sat in the airplane seat beside him. Somehow she'd recovered her hand from his without his even noticing. "I know you want me to stay in Seattle. I like you. We have fun together."

"Fun!" he cut her off. "Fun? I tell you I love you and you tell me we 'have fun' together?" Okay, maybe he couldn't keep his mouth shut. He tried again.

"I'm not talking about me, Jo." He waved away the drink cart lady. When she tried to distract Jo, he waved her off again. "For the moment, I'm not talking about how much I love you and how much you fill my heart."

The drink cart lady now wasn't going anywhere. She made a show of serving the threesome on the other side of the aisle, but had to ask them to repeat what they wanted several times. Well, he was the one who'd decided to confess his love on an airplane, now he'd have to live with that for the rest of his life.

Angelo closed his eyes to concentrate. Jo was so big on words. He had to be careful and choose just the right ones. He opened his eyes and looked at her, really looked. But those dark eyes only showed clear and cool rather than the soft warmth they usually radiated.

"I'm not talking about my heart, Counselor Thompson. I'm talking about yours."

"I think I know my own heart."

"Then how can you go back to Alaska?" It burst out of him. It was so damned obvious that she couldn't go. Not for three to five years. It sounded like a prison sentence. She'd die just as some part of her mother had, though he was smart enough to not use that argument. Even if she didn't end up at the Crab Hole bar, she might as well. Her heart would shrivel and die, like those old men who didn't even know how to say goodbye to a companion who had sat with them every night for decades.

"I can go back to Alaska because that's my job," her voice was rigid. "I'm very good at my job."

"But is your job good at you?"

JO FLAGGED the steward who was only just moving away and asked her for a ginger ale on ice. It gave her an excuse to not look at Angelo. She wished she had a book that she could read, or at least pretend to.

She reached for the in-flight magazine, but there wasn't one in the seat-back pocket before her. There were two of them in front of Angelo, but she wasn't going to reach across or ask for one.

Instead, she took her soft drink and peanuts and stared straight ahead.

Her job was just fine.

She'd won her first class debate in high school. She'd led the Vassar debate team to a statewide victory, even if a little school in Maine had won the regionals. Editor of the Law Review at the University of Washington. Partner at an elite law firm at an unprecedented twenty-seven years old.

Her job was just fine. Though it did feel as if she were protesting perhaps a little bit too much. But really, her job was just fine.

And anyway, Angelo didn't love her. He was a guy. He was a really decent guy for coming to Alaska to be with her, but he was still a guy. He'd just tangled up loyalty and lust with deeper emotions. He didn't love her, he only thought he did.

Jo closed her eyes, leaned her head back against the seat, and let the humming of the engines fill her head, ignoring the pleading look on Angelo's face.

He didn't love her, she assured herself. Especially when her career started taking her places he couldn't follow.

CHAPTER 31

"I got the call."

Russell's voice was loud in the empty restaurant kitchen followed by the clomping of his crutches as he pushed in through the back entry door. Front-of-house service had ended two hours ago, cleanup had finished the hour before, and the restaurant had been Angelo's alone since. He'd shooed his mother out and started working on the menu for the new restaurant.

It needed a different feel, a different flavor. Perhaps northern. The Piedmont region of Italy was in the north, but so was Venice, though he was less of a fan of east Italian flavors. Lombardy was a possibility, everyone had heard of Lake Como now that George Clooney had his villa there.

"What call?" Angelo added a pinch of rosemary to the cream sauce, stirred and tasted it again. It tasted flat. No matter what he did, it—

Russell whacked Angelo's leg with one of his crutches.

"Hey! Ow!"

"What call? Think, man. I'm married to your girlfriend's best friend. You did something to freak out Jo. She cuts off all communication with any of her friends and for some reason I don't pretend to understand, it's now up to me to fix the whole screwed up mess. So,

545

I'm figuring we'll deal with it tomorrow instead of half an hour to midnight tonight. Then the stupid phone rings. Guess who's on the line?"

"The Pope."

Russell hobbled to the cooler and pulled out a couple of beers.

"No, worse than that."

"I don't know. Who?"

Russell slowly eased down onto one of the stools by the prep table with a groan. "Never break your goddamn leg, Angelo, it's a real pain in the ass."

"And the leg."

"And the leg," Russell agreed with him.

"I'll remember that." For lack of any better idea, Angelo opened the beer Russell had set out on the counter and poured some into the sauce. A stir, a taste.

"Well, that takes care of that."

"Awful?"

"Godawful." Angelo turned off the burner, dumped the pot in the big steel sink, and splashed some water into it before sitting on the stool facing Russell. "So who was on the phone worse than the Pope?"

"Maria Amelia Avico Frickin' Parrano."

Angelo swore and knocked back some of his beer. Definitely worse than the Pope.

"So, I'm half undressed for bed and more than halfway to coaxing Cassidy to join me when the call comes in. Then what the hell happens? Next thing I know, I'm dressed, and my loving wife is closing the door on my ass telling me not to bother coming back until I fix it. Hell of a honeymoon."

Okay, he'd felt like shit before, but this was perhaps a new low.

"So," Russell leaned back and folded his hands in his lap. "What the hell did you do to her?"

"I told her I loved her." Damn, he really had to work on not saying that out loud. It took too much out of him.

"No shit?"

"No shit."

"And you do?"

Angelo could only nod. He couldn't even speak. Like his soul had been taken out, run through a blender, then turned into a really crappy cream sauce.

"What did she say?"

Angelo didn't even bother to shrug. To hell with her. Let her go back to goddamn Alaska. He closed his eyes. That thought hurt even worse.

"Oh man," Russell groaned.

Angelo couldn't agree more.

"WHAT THE HELL, JO?"

Jo yelped and dropped her briefcase which thudded onto the deep pile carpet, clipping her foot hard enough that she fell into a leather armchair.

As she'd entered the lobby of Stanley, Tu, Rolfmann, and Thompson from her office, the lights had sensed her motion and turned on. They'd revealed a very tired looking Cassidy Knowles slouched low on a dusky blue leather sofa.

Jo rubbed her foot a moment longer, but nothing appeared broken.

"What are you doing sitting in the dark? Why didn't you come back to my office?" Jo's heartrate was still up. Interestingly, seeing Cassidy, she should be feeling joy at seeing her friend or chagrin at how she'd been avoiding her. Instead she felt a little depressed. Some conspiratorial part of her mind had been waiting for Angelo to come by and visit her. He hadn't even called. Not that she could really blame him.

"I did come back." Cassidy pulled in her feet enough for Jo to sit at the other end of the couch.

Jo recovered her briefcase from the middle of the floor, set it on the coffee table then sat.

"But you were on the phone to some crazy place…"

"The Chairman of the Danish Maritime Authority's Shipping Tribunal."

"Too much stratosphere for me."

"Says the woman trained in wine by Robert Parker."

Cassidy shrugged, "Wine tasting. Creators of international maritime law. We each have our comfort zone and that one sure isn't mine. So, I backed off. You took so long to finish your call that the lights decided I wasn't here and turned off. Didn't see any reason to argue with them."

"It is," Jo checked her watch, "past one a.m."

"What are you doing working this late?"

"Well, it's a big and important case and I—"

"Blah. Blah. Blah." Cassidy made her quacking duck hand sign from college whenever she caught Jo over-defending her position. It had actually been exceptional training for trials, as she now automatically heard Cassidy's quacking noises whenever she was about to say too much. Her main challenge had been to not smile at the image during a serious courtroom moment.

Jo bit the inside of her cheek, then tried again. "It'll be the most important—"

"Wah. Wah. Wah." More quacking duck.

Jo knew from experience of many years that Cassidy could go all night and never repeat a sound. Even when they were drunk, Cassidy somehow kept track.

She knew why Cassidy was here. Jo wanted to confide in her, but it wouldn't work that way. Cassidy was newly married and through those eyes, thought that in order to be happy, everyone else should be as well. Perrin was a total romantic, which meant she was of the same mind, only more so. If she mentioned Angelo's declaration of love, which was still freaking her out, she'd never hear the end of it.

"I was offered a new job." Jo had already decided to not take it, but she didn't need to tell Cassidy that. At least not right away.

"Whacka. Whacka. Whac—Uh, what?" Cassidy blinked.

"Renée Linden is retiring and wants me to take over her job."

Cassidy jerked upright to stare at her. She gestured toward the

Market. "That Renée Linden? The one behind like, I dunno, everything?"

Jo nodded. "That Renée Linden. She's retiring and thinks I should replace her as the Executive Director of the Pike Place Market. She's been courting me for a couple of weeks."

"Weeks?!" Cassidy's voice whooshed out and she dropped back on the couch. "I once managed to hold out for forty-three minutes when she wanted me to serve on a board for the Friends of Emerald City Opera. The other board members actually made me a plaque in honor of my holding out for so long. It ended up being fantastic and fun, but it sure didn't look like it from the outside. Weeks? Really?"

Jo nodded. She'd forgotten about that connection. When Renée retired, that position would probably be opening as well. Except Renée wasn't just a member of Friends of the Opera, she headed that board which placed her on the board of the Opera itself. Jo's head throbbed.

"You're turning her down?"

Jo did her best to remain impassive.

Cassidy squinted her eyes. "You are. Okay, Thompson. That one you're going to have to explain."

"Cass, it's one a.m. and—"

"And you're going to explain this one to me in short, simple, unlawyerly words because it is, as you say, one a.m."

"I'm sure Russell—"

"Is presently with Angelo. He's having some kind of meltdown. His mother got so worried that she called Russell a couple of hours ago."

Jo closed her eyes and counted to ten. It didn't help, so she counted to twenty with no better results.

"Oh shit, Cass. It's all so screwed up." At thirty she rose to her feet.

"I can't do this." Jo picked up her briefcase. She straightened her jacket. Straightened it and tried not to think about how much fun Angelo had made of taking it off her. He'd made her feel so desirable, so important, so…

"I can't do this. I have a phone conference with the undersecretary of the United Nations Division of Oceans and Law of the Sea tomorrow at seven a.m. I…" They were real reasons she couldn't talk about everything that was screwed up with her personal life, aside from the fact that it would take all night and she needed the sleep, but even those felt as if she were making excuses.

"I…" She made it one step toward the door and got stuck again. "I can't do this."

Cassidy came up to hug her, and some preservation instinct had Jo stepping back. She ignored the pain on Cassidy's face.

"I'm sorry. I just can't. You— Renée— Angelo— The will— My mother—" She was stuttering worse than her father's old truck engine which had refused to turn over when she and Angelo had tried it. She finally slapped a hand over her mouth to stop herself.

"I can't, Cass. I just can't," she mumbled through the hand over her mouth.

"You'll call me when you can?"

Jo nodded, blinking hard against the tears.

"I'll be the first?"

Jo nodded again.

"I mean it Thompson. Repeat after me, 'I'll call Cass first.' Right? Say it."

"You first," she mumbled.

"Okay," Cassidy nodded to herself, pulled her sweater straight like Captain Picard readying himself for battle. "Okay. Now, you're coming home with me."

"But—"

"But nothing Thompson. I'm not having you drive. I'm not leaving you alone tonight. I live two blocks away, you're coming with me and that's final."

Jo could only nod and keep her hand in place. There'd never been a friend in the world like Cassidy Knowles.

And God, did she need a friend right now.

Even if she couldn't speak to her.

CHAPTER 32

"*Hi, honey.*" *Jo heard* Russell call out from the living room as Cassidy opened the front door to their condo. "Can you believe that goofball told her that he loved her?"

Cassidy spun to face her as all the blood drained from Jo's brain. Only the power suit kept her from simply fainting to the floor.

"Even worse, Jo clearly lost her mind and told him she didn't care for him."

She braced a hand on the still-open front door as her stomach heaved. She was about to barf the energy bar she'd eaten ten hours earlier all over Cassidy's perfect white carpet.

"He was somewhere between murdered and so mad I'm glad he doesn't own a gun. Once I got him really drunk, he started mumbling that she was killing her soul, but he wouldn't explain that one. I dumped him in the guest bedr—" Led by his long-hair black cat, Russell came around the corner of the hallway on his crutches and stopped dead.

He and Jo stared at each other for an eternity that may have lasted less than five seconds but they were seconds stretched beyond all reckoning.

"Shit! Jo. Hi. I'm… Oh, shit!"

551

Jo turned and ran.

Cassidy called after her, but Jo bolted into the emergency stairwell and almost tumbled down the concrete steps.

When she heard Cassidy's call getting closer, she turned and sprinted up the nearest steps. It was a mistake. She'd meant to go down. She thought she'd be trapped, but it was all that saved her.

Cassidy roared into the stairwell the same moment Jo turned the corner onto the next landing up.

Cassidy went down.

Jo collapsed on the stairs a half flight above where Russell held the door open. Separate but together, they listened to the pounding echoes of Cassidy's downward footsteps and frantic calls.

"Shit!" She heard Russell in such pain she almost went to reassure him. "I'm such an idiot!"

He wasn't the only one.

Jo DIDN'T dare go home, for Cassidy would surely follow her there. And she didn't want to find a hotel room, and be one of those red-eyed weeping women trying to hide some deep unhappiness for everyone to see and whisper about.

She did the only thing she could think of after she heard Cassidy return and tell Russell she was indeed going to check Jo's apartment.

Jo walked down the twenty flights and out into the night. Four blocks into Bell Town, she arrived at Perrin's Glorious Garb. The shop's lights were out, as was the studio light in the back. She went around to the side door and pressed the buzzer that served the six upstairs apartments.

She leaned on the buzzer.

A sleepy and distorted, "Who?" crackled out of the speaker.

"Jo." Her throat was so tight that it ached to create the single word. All she could taste was the salt of her tears that must have started again without her noticing. All she could see was the tiny squawk box.

The door buzzed sharply enough that Jo almost fell backwards off the low stoop, but managed to stop herself by grabbing the door handle.

Perrin met her at the head of the stairs.

One look at Jo's face was apparently all she needed. She led Jo down the narrow hall painted an improbable lime green and through a chartreuse door.

Perrin didn't cross-examine her. Didn't prod or poke. She only asked one question, "Should I call Cassidy?"

Jo could only shake her head before she pitched face first onto Perrin's couch and cried herself to sleep.

CHAPTER 33

*J*o *made it to* the morning phone call. Kept Muriel in the room for it because she knew she wouldn't remember a word of what was said. Afterward, over her protests, Muriel sent her home.

Per her assistant's instructions, which she'd written down and handed to Jo, the first thing she did was take a long, hot bath. Despite doing so, she remained numb to the core. Then she made coffee and ate the large apple muffin with the crunchy crumb topping that she always avoided, which Muriel had made her promise to pick up on her way home.

Now she sat out on the balcony with her unopened John Grisham book in her lap. She glanced down at Muriel's list.

Buy decadent muffin

Go home

Take hot bath, a long one, with bubbles (recommended: get undressed first)

Muriel's voice came through loud and clear.

Make coffee

Get that book you keep talking about not having time to read

Go to balcony (clothing optional)

Jo had pulled on shorts and her Vassar t-shirt which felt impossibly decadent for ten in the morning. Hearing Perrin in the back of her head, she had not put on a bra, which left her feeling unclothed despite being covered.

Eat muffin and drink coffee (you got dressed, didn't you? Knew you would.)

Open book (you're almost there)

Read book

Do not come back to the office today (Would tell you not to think about the office, but that would only make you think about the office, so I shouldn't have written this sentence to begin with, but it's too damn late and I'm not rewriting the list.)

She'd signed it with her cell phone number, a clear invitation if she needed to talk. But Jo didn't. She needed to think. But every time she tried, it all got snarled up in her head.

Her phone rang. That would be Cassidy. By now Perrin would have woken up and called Cassidy to let her know that Jo was alive.

She let it ring.

She couldn't seem to achieve Step 8. Open book. It was simply too much effort. Instead she sat and watched Seattle from on high. Very little street noise reached her twentieth floor condo. Big diesel trucks climbing the steep hills of downtown Seattle, the occasional siren, nothing else reached her from the ground. Instead, there was the distant roar of the jets climbing north out of SeaTac airport. Some headed to Ketchikan, and some just headed the hell away.

Jo knew the latter was a false sanctuary, but it attracted her nonetheless. Wing off to Europe or New Zealand. Change her name and become a beach babe in Costa Rica like they'd always joked about in college, to escape finals week. The three of them breaking hundreds of hearts in some tropical paradise. Probably be a lot less fun than it sounded.

The main sound on her balcony was the gentle breeze brushing past her, kicked into merry swirls by the shape of the building. Below and before her, the city and the Sound glittered under the bright morning sunlight. It had been some time since she'd simply sat and enjoyed.

She tried to think of the last time she'd totally stopped. And couldn't. No run, no swim, no bike ride. No case law, no social outing, no Angelo.

It tore away her breath to even think his name.

God. She sounded pitiful. In that moment, some part of her rose up and decided she was sick of whiny Jo Thompson.

She was not some whiny female.

She just wasn't.

Jo opened her book.

The bookmark was caught by the breeze and threatened to flutter out to sea. By the time she trapped it in the corner of the balcony, she'd lost her place in the book. A sudden urge to throw the whole thing off the balcony ran through her until she had to clamp her hands hard and set the book down carefully on the small steel table beside her half-finished muffin.

Action. She was an action person, and here she was taking none. That's why she was feeling so overwhelmed. She'd take this day off and deal with everything: past, present, and future. And she'd been avoiding the easiest one.

Do that one, then she'd get herself back on track without any problem.

She went inside and picked up her cell phone. A voicemail and a text from Cassidy. She didn't bother to listen to the voicemail. To Cassidy's texted, "You okay?" she replied, "I'm fine now. Will call tonight. Tell Russell he's still fine with me."

She dropped the phone before Cassidy could respond and pulled out the phone book from where it gathered dust in the bottom desk drawer. Somehow doing a simple Internet search was too personal, too close to actual contact. Somehow it felt as if it risked letting the person know you were looking them up, even if it didn't really.

Good old White Pages. "March, Eloise." Just one. Redmond, Washington. She was here. Ten miles across the lake. Jo noted down the address and phone number. Now she just needed to decide whether to have some probate attorney contact her or do it herself. She could file initial probate with the Alaskan court and simply include the contact information, it wasn't as if it was a complex estate with any decisions to be made. The court would send notice and, barring protest by either party, cut everything in half and issue a pair of checks.

Jo pulled the Alaska documents out of her In Basket, they'd left the wooden crate at the Cape Fox Lodge along with most of the trash. Such a pitifully thin stack to define an entire life. She pulled out a couple of empty file folders and organized the information quickly. Closed accounts, open items, estate documents. No death certificate. She drafted a quick note requesting a copy of the death certificate and put it in an envelope to the Ketchikan Coroner's office.

For lack of anything better to do with the postcard, she dropped it in with the will and ignored the slight pinch of filing away the only contact she'd ever received from her mother.

The only thing that didn't fit in any file was the photo. She propped it in the middle of her desk. She wasn't afraid of the past. Bring it on, she told the photo. Nor the future. Bring it on.

Next she started drafting a nice, "Thank you but no thank you," note for Renée. She rapidly filled a whole sheet on a yellow legal pad with phrases and crossouts, reasons and desires. She slashed a big "X" across the whole page, flipped that page over to the back, and glared at the blank sheet now in front of her.

It was a relief as visceral as a cold shower when her phone rang with the tone she'd programmed for the main lobby.

That wouldn't be Cassidy, Perrin, or Angelo. She'd given the elevator code to each of them. She picked up her phone trying to remember if she'd made any recent online orders.

JO HAD BARELY PULLED on decent clothes by the time the elevator whisked Maria Parrano into her apartment.

"What a beautiful picture."

Of course, it was the first thing Angelo's mother had gravitated to in the entire condo.

"You look wonderful, Mrs. Parrano."

"Maria."

"You look wonderful, Maria." And she did. The flowered summer dress and flat, strapped leather sandals made her look both comfortable and elegant. The yellow leather purse was bright and cheerful. She did nothing to hide her age, but it was hard to credit her with a thirty-year old son.

"Is that you?" Maria had picked up the cheap frame as if it were something precious.

"No, it's my mother."

"I meant in her arms."

"Oh, yes. That's me. Only child."

"She looks so sweet."

"Me?"

"Your mother."

Jo finally caught up with the conversation. "I wouldn't know. She left when I was two."

Mrs. Parrano, Maria, lay her fingertips over her lips for a long moment in apology. "I'm sorry. Do you know much about her?"

As she told Maria what little she knew, Jo poured them both a fresh cup of coffee and led them out onto the balcony where her novel remained unopened, her place still lost.

"Redmond is close, isn't it? Really? Have you called her?"

"I don't know if I'm going to."

Maria nodded. "It's hard. When Angelo was in high school I received a note from a friend. My Angelo, his father, had contacted her to find out how I was and how the baby was doing. He didn't even know baby's sex or that I was gone to America. I decide that someone who care so little about me and about my beautiful boy that he waits fifteen years to ask the question, he does not matter. So I tell my friend to tell him nothing. If she ever hear from him again, she does not tell me. There are times I doubt myself, but it was good. It was right."

Jo wished she had that kind of strength, but she'd never had a parent to teach her. She'd learned to put up the façade, to pretend she had strength, so that no one could see through her. Well, none but Cassidy and Perrin.

Yet somehow...

Angelo didn't see through the façade, but neither did he see the façade. He saw her as strong to begin with. As if it actually were a part of who she was.

"I just found out that my mother, Eloise, stayed in constant touch with a mutual friend through all the years. I don't know if Dan asked my father's permission or not, but he liked her and answered her back." Her mother had at least cared more than Angelo's father. That wasn't much in her favor, but it was something.

"She sent me a card, which my father left on my old bedroom wall for me to find." She'd decided that was how it must have been. Her father didn't have any meanness in him. Useless, lazy, disconnected? Yes. Mean, no. She went and fetched the postcard from the file.

Mrs. Parrano read it several times then brushed at the corners of her eyes.

"I wish my Angelo had done so much. She made the choice yours. You could have asked this Dan or tear this up and throw it away. She leave it all up to you. That is a very hard and brave thing to do." She handed back the card carefully. "I hope I have a chance to meet this woman some day."

Jo looked at the card for a long moment and then tucked it into the Grisham novel. She still didn't know if she wanted to meet her mother or not.

Jo HAD CERTAINLY SAT with enough witnesses over the years to know that Maria Parrano was sitting on some topic that was very uncomfortable and struggling to find some way to say it. Jo sighed inwardly. Well, she had decided this was her day scheduled to deal with things. If she remembered correctly, and she'd have to call Muriel later to be sure, she'd be on a flight to New York tomorrow afternoon. So, now was the time.

"Sometimes, Maria, it is easier if you just say it."

Maria sipped her coffee again, but didn't look away. Jo was learning that Angelo had inherited his directness fair and square from his mother. Or was it something ingrained in the Italian genetic code?

"I don't know you, Jo Thompson. I would like to, but I do not."

"Yes, I'm sorry about missing dinner, but my father—"

Maria's hand wave of dismissal was so like Angelo's that Jo had to bite her cheek not to smile.

"What you did was more important and we will eat together soon, you and I. I like to think that we would be friends."

"I would like that too." And Jo was a bit surprised that she wasn't just being polite. Maria Parrano was a very pleasant person to sit with.

"You're sweet," she patted Jo's knee without making it belittling. "But I have come to ask you a favor."

A chill crept up Jo's spine. A deep breath. A nod. She didn't dare speak.

"I know there is something between you and my boy. I know that it is deep and important to both of you, and I don't want to pry. But my Angelo is hurting so much. Can you at least tell me why so that I can help him somehow?"

This wasn't what she'd expected. She'd thought Angelo had sent his mother to plead on his behalf. Instead, the mother had come herself out of love for her son.

"You love him very much, don't you?" At Maria's knowing nod Jo had to look away. It wasn't enough, so she stood up and walked the ten feet to the far end of the narrow balcony and back.

How would her life have been if she'd had a mother like that? Who could guess? If her mother were still in Ketchikan, would Jo have ever left? Would she have been driven to become who she was? Oddly, she could trace nearly every success in her life back to that moment of abandonment. Her motivation to learn, to excel, to be better...

To be better than her own mother? To show her...what?

She sat abruptly.

"What is it, my girl?" Maria's words shifted strangely in her head, combining oddly with her thoughts.

"I suddenly don't know why I do the things I do."

Maria took her hand, and massaged it as if to warm it. Her hands were like her son's, slim, but strong. Calluses where a knife was held, dozens of tiny scars from a lifetime of cooking.

"I cook for thirty years. I raise two boys, as much mother to Russell as Julia was mother to Angelo. Suddenly one day their boy is married and they decide to retire. John and Julia, they suddenly don't know what to do. I worry, but I listen to my heart and I know what to do. I know to go be with my Angelo."

Maria pulled her over and kissed Jo's cheek.

"And you help him see that I can help him. Tell him to let me make pastry. Oh, I think he would have found out the idea himself, but sometimes that boy moves so slow."

"Sometimes he isn't so slow." Her voice felt dreamy and distant. As if it belonged to someone else. Maybe Counselor Thompson had deserted her for the day, leaving only a lost Jo behind.

"Oh?"

"He told me that he loved me." It didn't kill her to say. It didn't even leave a bitter taste. It was simply a fact, a fact too unreal to, well, be real.

"When do he say so?"

Jo cast her mind back until once again she was sitting on that impossible flight.

"Right after my father's funeral, while the plane was taking off." She could feel the shuddering of the jet and taste the dry air pumped into the cabin as she worked her jaws to pop her ears.

"No," Maria breathed it out as little more than an astonished whisper.

Jo could only nod. Here it came, the defense of her boy and why wasn't Jo sensible enough to—

Maria Parrano slapped her hand sharply against her thigh with a loud smack.

"That *idiota*. I can no believe he do that to you. Is my son so *stupido?* He must be. Well, serves him right his heart is all hurt."

Jo could only watch her wide-eyed as her rant continued.

"Men, they are so…" Maria tapped her own temple sharply. "What is the word I want?"

"Dense?"

"Yes," Maria squeezed Jo's hand. "Dense that is good word for my Angelo. You not have enough on your mind, so he must add love just then. Dense. Dense. Dense."

Jo couldn't stop watching the woman in amazement. Jo couldn't have said it better herself. And it felt nice to have Maria on her side. It helped confirm that she hadn't lost her mind simply because she didn't love Angelo back.

"Of course," Maria put her other hand over Jo's. "You are so crazy about him. That is so easy to see, except I bet he can no see that or he not be so miserable. You make him wait Jo. You make him wait until you are good and ready to say you love him. Oh, I do like you. It will be so fun to have you as a daughter. So fun!"

Easy to see? Sure she liked Angelo but—

Now Maria looked directly at her with those dark warm eyes that sparkled with inner light.

"You take your time, Jo Thompson. You are too busy, too many things, they push at you. When you have time. After you decide about your mother and settle all of your father things, then is time to decide you love him. Not before then. Not now."

Then she smiled again so strongly that Jo could feel herself smiling back despite the cry of protest that lurked inside, but couldn't seem to find traction to leap off the tip of her tongue.

"After you do, oh, then you and me, we will have so much fun!"

Jo never did get the note to Renée finished. She had an acceptable first draft, but it wasn't near to sufficient. It wasn't a matter of polishing the language, she simply had to throw it out and start over yet again. And she definitely wasn't going to see Angelo, but she called Cassidy and Perrin for a get-together. The first of them she'd promised, and both she owed.

"Somewhere new. Somewhere different. Not near the Market."

Cassidy picked Vito's and by seven they were tucked side-by-side into a deep, burgundy faux-leather booth with two glasses of a local red that Cassidy recommended. On the other side, Perrin had a rum drink of the unlikely name Janky Panky that had turned out to be a nice mix of sweet and mule kick. They had a Beef Carpaccio and steamed clams with sausage that might give Cutter's a bit of a challenge.

"It's like Angelo's place gone bad." Perrin squinted up at the black wall and acrylic painted Italian waiters barely revealed by the dim candlelight. "Like I keep expecting a mob boss to show up in a '40s zoot suit carrying a violin case." She leaned out of the booth and looked around the restaurant. "But here it would have a violin in it."

The jazz pianist at the grand was far enough away to make it easy to talk, but close enough to reveal that she was good.

Perrin leaned out and looked toward the pianist this time. "Hey, she's cute, too. I like long blondes."

"What is it with you and women?" Cassidy's tease was an old one. Anyone who might look good in one of Perrin's designs elicited the cute comment.

"Oh, I've tumbled a girl or two in my time."

Cassidy almost snorted her wine.

"Didn't stick. I'll take the guys." Perrin winked at Jo when Cassidy glanced down to see if she was wearing any of her wine.

Cass had always had a slightly narrow view of the world, and every now and then Perrin found a way to give it a good sharp poke.

"So," Perrin settled in her seat. "Are you better now?"

Jo nodded, "Much."

"Good. Then let me just say, What the fuck was that?"

Jo could do this. She'd told Mrs. Parrano, Maria, a nearly complete stranger. She could tell her best friends. And, as she'd advised Maria, she'd just say it before she could second guess herself.

"When I was up in Alaska, getting on the plane, Angelo told me that he loved me."

"And that shorted out your brain for what reason?"

Not quite the reaction she'd been expecting. Neither showed shock and amazement.

"Because my father had died seventy-two hours before. And at his funeral, which was five geriatric guys and an ex-Ukrainian Army woman pissing off the end of pier in his honor, I found out my mother lives in Redmond."

"Which Redmond?"

"The one like ten miles that way." Jo pointed over her shoulder. Or was it the other way? Vito's was partly below street level, dark and dive-like. There was no obvious view of Puget Sound to provide direction. She took a breath and just said it again to see if she could.

"Then he tells me that he loves me." It came out, but it still wasn't easy.

Cassidy studied her wine.

Perrin just shrugged, "Okay, minus ten points for timing but about plus five gajillion for having the good sense to fall in love with our Jo. So what's the problem?"

"What did you say?" Cass spoke softly. Right at the heart of the matter. If she hadn't been so involved in food and wine, Jo might have tried to convince her to go for law. She had the right kind of mind, but her palate was world class.

"I'm not ready. I didn't say anything."

"What?" Perrin took up a clam on her small fork and waved it at Jo, dribbling garlic butter–white wine sauce up and down the middle of the table. "Tell me one thing wrong with him other than lousy timing. Wait, does he have good timing in bed?"

"In the bed, in the shower, on the floor. Exceptional timing." She knew how to make Perrin crazy. "He's talking about Russell's sailboat, especially since Russell can't really use it with a broken leg."

Cassidy's grin was easy. "Yes, his sailboat offers many, many possibilities."

Perrin groaned in voyeuristic delight, placed a hand over her heart and panted a few times.

"That was good for me. Was that good for you? So," she waved her clam again and dribbled some more. "Tell me one thing wrong with him." She finally ate the clam.

"I'm not ready."

"Evading the question, Counselor. Naughty, naughty lawyer. Are you in love with him or not?"

Jo tried to answer the question. She really did. She opened her mouth and nothing came out. She closed it then tried again.

"Maria Parrano thinks I am."

Cassidy twisted to look right at her. "You talked to Angelo's mother about Angelo being in love with you?"

"He's not in love with me, he only thinks that he is."

Perrin pointed another clam at Jo, but faced Cassidy. "Is it just me, or is she avoiding every question we put to her?"

"It's not you." Cassidy's voice was grim. Grim enough that maybe she was thinking of changing over to law.

"She trapped me."

"How?"

"She was nice. Okay? Are you happy? She was nice to me. She told me how excited she was that I was going to be her daughter and how much fun we'd have together." Now that she'd started Jo couldn't stop. Her voice kept rising and she couldn't reel it back in.

"What am I supposed to do with that? Tell me one thing I want more in my life than that? I want my mother to be there for me and for us to have fun together. Then my mother's lover offers…" She waved a hand helplessly.

"Your…mother's…lover?" Perrin was grinning. "I thought we were talking about your lover's mother. Or is there something going on between Eloise Thompson and Angelo that we need to know about? Because we all know how Perrin loves salacious tidbits." In the middle of the last sentence Perrin started tipping over into giggles despite her best efforts at a straight face.

Cassidy's cough didn't sound one bit like a cough.

Jo gave up. What could she do? In moments all three of them were howling with laughter.

Jo was sitting on the plane, the country rolling along beneath her. Now she had two missions in New York.

Her primary purpose was a meeting with the Undersecretary of Maritime Law at the United Nations tomorrow morning. It was just a preliminary meeting. Information gathering. It would be six long months of research and planning before she'd be ready for even the first meeting with the lower level representatives of the nations with Arctic claims. Most of that six months would be split equally between Juneau and Barrow. She needed to switch that. Hitting Barrow in mid-winter was not part of her plan. Barrow first, then Juneau. Even if Barrow would make Ketchikan look like paradise.

Jo ignored the sudden knot in her stomach, putting it down to airplane food.

Her secondary task was a last minute "favor" for Renée Linden. Jo really had to hand it to the woman, she was a spectacular strategist. After days without any contact whatsoever, she managed to drop by Jo's office as she was double-checking her briefcase and gathering her coat before leaving for the airport. Again, not enough time for a proper conversation.

But somehow, as a favor to Renée, Jo was now hand-carrying a folder of ad proofs to New York for the supermodel's approval. Not FedEx, not Internet. It was to be a hand carry and a personal meeting.

Melanie, the supermodel, was going to meet her at the airport so that they could go over the proofs together. Something about Russell refusing to release them without her final approval. It made sense if they'd been friends. It sort of made sense.

Actually, it made no sense at all. Apparently Melanie was flying out of JFK shortly after Jo was flying in, so that part worked. But none of the rest of it did. Renée had clearly slipped another fast one by her and the hidden strategy eluded Jo the rest of the way across the country.

* * *

"RUSSELL, HE DOES SUCH BEAUTIFUL WORK." Which sounded even better in Melanie's exquisite voice.

The Palm Bar and Grille at JFK was pleasant with dark wood decor and prompt service. They'd opted to split a Crab Louie Salad, and even though Jo had only had the one glass of wine last night, she opted for a diet Coke as did Melanie.

They had a spread of six different ads that could be based on The Glass Shoppe photo shoot in the Market on the table between them.

"I like this one the best."

Jo had to agree. "You do look incredibly sexy in that one. Good for a Playboy or a GQ placement. But what do you think of this one for Condé Nast?" It was more playful. Rather than the flirty punch that

Melanie delivered so consistently, it had captured her with a smile just being surprised from her lips as she turned to a vase of the deepest red that arced like a tulip petal.

"You are good at this." Melanie tipped her head one way and another. "I have to think about this one some more. I usually go for the sexy, but this is interesting. You are right of course, use this for them. I need to think about other demographics of my market. I won't be the most beautiful one forever."

Not on display, Melanie actually had very little accent or affectation. Her hair was hanked back in a long ponytail. Her skin with minimal makeup was more human. And her accent, rather than suggesting France, hinted ever so slightly at New York. Upper East Side perhaps.

They went through the rest of the ads relatively quickly in between slow bites of crab salad. Then they reached the ads built on the images that had been shot at Angelo's. The difference was immediately obvious.

"Those are all Claude's, aren't they?" Melanie indicated the reject pile.

Jo checked the photo index list and compared the photo numbers. "Every one."

"Russell is so good. I'm glad he picked up the camera again. It is a part of who he is. He had such a talent. I never look so good as when Russell takes the picture."

There was some note in her voice that Jo couldn't help noticing. "You love him very much, don't you?"

Melanie glanced at her then looked away. But she didn't need to say any more.

Jo rested a hand on her arm. "I'm sorry. That was rude of me. I didn't know."

Melanie stared for another long moment at the far end of the bar before turning back to Jo. Then she shrugged those perfect shoulders helplessly.

"At first, I fell for Russell because he is sooo handsome and we look so good together. Then I find that he is worth many, many millions. I liked the sound of that also very much."

Even without the French accent, Melanie had clearly hidden inside its mask so long that it shifted her speech patterns.

"I grew up poor. I really liked the sound of that money. And then I liked Russell. And then…" Again the elegant shrug. "I was not strong enough or challenging enough or something I no understand. He is good with Cassidy, better than he would be with me. We would have had one of those two-year marriages on the front page of the Enquirer with all of the ugly at the end. It is better that we did not."

Jo squeezed Melanie's arm.

They sorted the ads based on Angelo's in an easy accord that required few words.

There was one more folder at the bottom of the box. Melanie opened it while Jo made notes for Renée.

"Oh," Melanie's soft exclamation drew Jo's attention.

It took her several moments to make sense of the images Melanie was spreading out across the table.

She vaguely remembered Russell snapping photos during the meal, just some quick candids. No flash umbrellas, no makeup artists, no clothier.

There were two shots of Melanie and Perrin both looking stunning in Perrin's designer clothes. Russell had done one mockup of each, the first one for Pike Place Market, and the other for Perrin's Glorious Garb. The second one was the killer. They were huddled together as if conspiring to break every heart they came upon. Bare shoulders, a deep, deep V-neck on Perrin, an amazing length of leg from Melanie.

"Oh. Perrin, she must use this one."

"She'd can't afford your rates, Melanie. And she never takes charity, not even from her friends."

"Nonsense. You tell her I have already taken payment for this, I never gave her back the green dress. I like it too much."

Jo's attempts to thank her were lightly brushed aside.

"It is done." To prove her point, she tossed the ad using the two of them for the Market into the reject pile.

"Now, what are these?"

Jo looked down at them and blushed. It was her and Angelo. Jo in her power suit and Angelo in his immaculate charcoal dress shirt sat shoulder to shoulder, sharing Panna Cotta. They had lifted their spoons at the same moment as if they were about to feed each other, though Jo knew they hadn't.

"This one, it sizzles. It makes me feel hot all over." Melanie fanned herself with her hand.

Russell had faded the table under the text. The walls were a soft haze. All that remained in focus were the identical desserts, the identical espresso cups, and the identical expressions.

"No," her mouth was dry and a sip of Coke did nothing to ease the sensation. "We can't use this one."

"Why the hell not?" For just a moment, Melanie's voice took on a Lower West Side grind.

"It's… I don't know. It's just…"

"It is lovely," Melanie insisted, her soft French firmly back in place and a slight blush on her features that Jo tactfully ignored.

She tried to look at it and see the two people on a date, not herself and Angelo, but couldn't manage it.

Melanie picked up a cherry tomato and bit down on it.

"There is a photograph that Russell took of me. He is such an *imbécile* that he does not understand what he took a picture of, until much later. Then he sent me a copy with a very nice apology that cut like a knife in my heart." She reached over to her purse and slipped it out of an inside pocket, then slid it across the table.

Jo had seen Melanie look many ways in many ads. Tantalizing, distant, teasing, voracious, but this was different.

It was a close-up of Melanie's face, her features lit from below by the bright blue of a bubbling hot tub. No bathing suit straps where her perfect shoulders rose just above the water. A vase of red roses the color of Melanie's lips floated nearby. Her eyes were wide and her smile soft.

"It looks like…you're in love." Jo regretted it the moment she said it, but that's how it looked.

"*Oui.*" Melanie agreed sadly. "And so I was, with the *imbécile* behind the camera. He is such a good man."

Then she put one finger on her much-handled photo and slid it across the table next to the ad Russell had made of Jo and Angelo eating dessert together.

Jo's gaze drifted from Melanie's photo to the ad.

She looked at both of her and Angelo's expressions. Now it was easy to see what showed there.

ngelo kept his attention divided between his sauce and the woman auditioning to be the new aboyeur. As the expeditor, she would direct all communications between the tables and the cook line. A single mistake could snarl the entire line and cause a cascading wreckage of service that could take hours to recover from. However, a good expeditor could improve the line's efficiency dramatically.

He'd given Graziella a free hand to at least test an assistant. She'd been working as hostess, head waitress, and expeditor. Far too much for one person in a busy restaurant. She was very social and enjoyed the front of house, so she'd brought in Luisa to try out for aboyeur. Luisa could almost be Graziella's twin. They were both tall, sleek, and dark haired with classic, straight Italian noses gracing their pretty faces. The main difference rapidly became apparent. Graziella always asked and cajoled, even pleaded in a pleasant tone. Luisa got flirtatious, funny, caustic, whatever it took to get what she needed to make everything run smoothly.

Angelo liked her already. If Manuel approved her after today's test, he'd hire her on a two-week trial. She'd just moved back to the States from two years studying in Italy. Rather than spending time in cooking school, she'd worked restaurants in different regions for three months at a time. She knew food well enough, but it appeared that she understood restaurants intimately.

Her Italian, she admitted, had remained fairly miserable. But when Angelo had pretended to totally botch an order to gauge her response, she'd proven her command of at least the invective portion of the language. She could swear better than Russell, and she made it sound much more pleasant. For one thing, Russell's accent sucked.

His mother came over for a taste of the new sauce he was fooling with on the side. She let it roll on her tongue for several long moments.

"That is for the seafood linguini at the new restaurant?"

He nodded.

"So, you decided to go Piedmonte without asking your mother?"

Her tone no longer struck fear into his heart. "Piedmonte and Lombardia. They're close. I still need to work on the name. Angelo's Nord Italiano Hearth or maybe Angelo's North Italian Hearth."

"The second one, your *patroni* are in America. The sauce, it's good."

She turned back to her pastry station where she was making chocolate biscotti for dipping in a thickened vanilla-coffee cream she'd created.

Angelo waited for the other shoe. For the "a little soy sauce would make that nice" or "maybe if you added a bit of elk meat." But she didn't.

"Love you, Mama," he called to her.

"You only love me because I no insult your beautiful sauce," she shot back and they shared a smile.

A smile that froze on his lips when he looked up and saw who stood at the kitchen door. The kitchen volume dropped by half as his staff spotted his reaction and then its cause. They might not know the whole story, but Angelo supposed his own rocketing and crashing emotions had been hard to miss.

"Jo." It wasn't even a whisper, but it was all he could manage. He hadn't seen her since they'd parted in stiff silence at the airport to find their separate cars. It hadn't even been a whole week and yet it felt like a year.

She wore the power suit, but the jacket was open, the floopy bow tie missing, and the blouse open just one button. She looked exhausted from travel and nervous to be in his kitchen. He'd never brought her back here and felt suddenly very self-conscious. She looked so incredible, standing there shifting from one foot to the other. A small, practical, wheeled suitcase rested beside her, her briefcase in her hand.

"I thought you were in New York."

"I was."

"I thought you were supposed to be in meetings all day."

"I cancelled them."

He opened his mouth but closed it with a snap that nipped the end of his tongue painfully when his mother poked his ribs with the handle of a wooden spoon. Before he managed to turn on her, she gave him a shove that almost sent him stumbling into Marlys. His grillardin stepped out of the way and let him pass down the line and around the end of the cook stations until he stood close in front of Jo.

"Here. You'll get run over if you remain there." He took the suitcase and rolled it under the side prep table, its little plastic wheels making loud thumps on the seams between the tiles, so loud they seemed to echo about the kitchen. The table was presently covered with piles of vegetables and iced filets of sole to prep for the dinner service. She slipped her briefcase under the table as well.

"This is out of the way for the moment." A waiter came through the swinging door they'd just cleared, bearing an armload of dirty dishes. Graziella didn't believe in trays and tubs on the floor and Angelo agreed. The waiter delivered them to Marko with an ear-ringing clatter.

Angelo glanced over and saw that Manuel had shifted to cover his position on the line and had turned down the heat under his sauce as well. Good man. Now he had to face Jo.

"I'm sorry to interrupt. You're busy and—"

"Look, I'm the one who's sorry. I shouldn't have blurted it out like that. I wasn't thinking. It just came out."

"Did your mother or Cassidy chew you out about that?"

"No." He glanced toward his mother. "Were they supposed to?" He waved the question away. It meant she'd told his mother and...he turned back to Jo with a shrug.

"They didn't have to. I sort of figured it out slowly on my own." It had taken him most of the last four days, but he wouldn't mention that. He tried to read her expression, but he couldn't make sense of it. Counselor Thompson, he could read her pretty well. And when she was Jo, everything was so obvious on her face that they could have whole conversations without a word. This woman standing before him, he was less sure of.

He wanted to shout out how much he'd missed her, but he couldn't. It would simply kill him.

He'd drifted through the week, shopping, cooking, sleeping, and then doing the same thing again. It was as if someone had dropped him in a vat of gelatin that was slowly setting to solid around him. He kept struggling against it because he didn't know how to stop. Now that she stood in his kitchen, it was as if the gel had never been and he'd come back to life.

"I shouldn't have said it and I wanted to formally apologize." He folded his arms over his chest to keep his hands still. He knew it sounded stiff, but it was the best he could manage.

She waited, shifted again.

What more was he supposed to say? Cast the remaining shards of his broken heart at her feet and watch it be stomped again like a tiny grape?

Jo looked around her, but not as if she was seeing anything. Her hands, those beautiful, elegant, calm hands that could drive his body to such distraction...weren't calm. They were practically fluttering about her lap.

She was nervous. He'd never seen her nervous. Frustrated at work, out of place and confused in Alaska, but never nervous.

"I've been in the air for almost sixteen hours with only three hours on the ground in New York before turning back around. I had really lousy connections coming back, but it was the fastest I could get here."

"Fastest?" He didn't dare to hope, squashed the glimmer of it as well as he could, wrapped his arms tighter across this chest.

She pulled out one of the stools from under the prep table and sat down on it.

Angelo kicked one loose and sat facing her. A glance showed that most of the line was watching them surreptitiously, except for his mother who was making no bones about what she was paying attention to. He was glad the patissier station was at the far end of the cookline. The kitchen had never in two years been so quiet while a meal was in progress.

"I've had sixteen hours to think about something you said. And you were right, Alaska would kill me. Another multi-year lawsuit would do me in, too, even if it made my career. By the end I would be bitter and angry. I don't want to be that."

"That, uh, that sounds good. Does that mean that you'll—" He couldn't finish the sentence, but Jo nodded anyway.

"I called Renée Linden last night just before I got on the return flight. You are now talking to your new managing landlord, the Executive Director of the Pike Place Market. Still sounds crazy when I say it. Well, I'll have some time to get used to it as that will take most of a month to switch over. She's informing the board of her retirement right now. Muriel and I have to go meet them in fifteen minutes but Renée assures me that's just a technicality."

"Oh my God, Jo. That's incredible!" Angelo wanted to shout. He couldn't think straight. He'd now have time to court her. She wouldn't be running out of his life to a place filled with bad memories for her. He wanted to reach for her, but it was too much. He rested his hands firmly on his thighs and clamped them there.

"And you're closed Mondays and Tuesdays still, right?"

"Uh, right." That was a real problem he hadn't been able to solve. Maybe he could shift some of his hours somehow so that he could see more of her. But he hadn't come up with a solution yet.

"New restaurant, too? Same hours?" She was switching over to that Counselor Thompson role that had so captivated him.

"Hadn't thought that far ahead, but, uh, sure. Probably. Why?"

"Good. I only have," she checked her watch, "twelve more minutes and I have a bit of ground to cover."

"Okay. You're in Seattle. You're quitting your job as an attorney. Are you okay with that?"

She reached out and touched his hand for a moment. A contact that rippled up his arm so powerfully it made his breath catch in his chest.

"Bless you, Angelo, for thinking of me and my feelings. It's not something I'm very good at. Actually, the Market's business is so complex now, that being an attorney is a distinct advantage. Apparently it is one of the reasons Renée first considered me. I'll still be practicing law, I will simply be doing it on a more reasonable schedule. Speaking of schedule…"

"I can—"

"Shush! Ten minutes to go."

God, but she simply slayed him when she was in this mode. There'd never been another woman like her.

"The Market has a number of vendors who only work on the weekends. I'll be telling the board that my hours are Wednesday through Sunday. I'll have Monday and Tuesday off as well. I'm not sure what I will do with a career that fits into only five days a week, but that's a different issue."

Angelo couldn't help himself. He leaned forward and wrapped his arms about her in a quick hug. He'd be able to see Jo. They'd share weekends.

Wait! That was if she wanted to keep seeing him. Well, she was here, wasn't she? Talking to him. Had cancelled her meetings back East. He held her a moment longer, reveling in the magical scent that was Jo Thompson, praying he was even partly right about what was happening.

All his anger, all his hurt was sliding toward the floor drain like old dirt in soap suds. And if he was wrong, he'd go right down the drain after them. That cooled down his heart a bit.

He managed to sit back, but felt like an overeager little boy. He kept reaching out a hand to touch her knee, or her hand where it rested on her thigh, just to prove to himself that she was here, real, and so warm.

"Seven minutes. Well, I've spent most of the last seven hours practicing this." He saw her take a deep breath then she whispered to herself, "I can do this."

Clearly, whatever was next came hard. He took one of her hands in both of his.

"You are the strongest woman I've ever met, Executive Director Jo Thompson. You can do anything."

She nodded several times as if slowly building layers of reassurance like a layered torta.

"Melanie told me I could."

"Melanie?"

She waved his question away for another time with a perfect flick of her fingers.

"Would you come with me tomorrow morning after you finish your shopping for the restaurant?"

"Of course—"

Jo held up a hand to cut him off. He couldn't help himself, he kissed her fingertips. She actually caressed his lips and he almost wept with how good it felt.

"I'd like you to come with me to go see my mother."

He couldn't be prouder of her if she were a new restaurant. It was a shock, not what he'd been expecting her to say, but it was still fantastic.

"Yes, of course I will go with you."

Then she took another deep breath, glanced at her watch, then glanced down the now silent cookline toward his mother.

Maria Amelia Avico Parrano nodded some silent answer to whatever Jo's silent question was.

Then Jo turned back and took both of his hands in hers and held them tightly.

"I was thinking… If we like my mother… I was thinking we could invite her…" Another deep breath. "We could invite her to the wedding."

"The wedding?" Angelo's ears were ringing. "Whose wedding?"

"Well, Perrin made me this absolutely killer wedding dress. It would be a waste not to wear it, especially as you claim that you love me."

"I do," Angelo couldn't believe his ears. "Oh Jo, I love you so much I don't know what to do with all the feelings inside me. I'm like a potato in a microwave without enough vent hol—"

She leaned in and kissed him as a roar of applause rang through the kitchen. Pots and pans were banged with ladles, the butts of knives were pounded against cutting boards.

She shifted back just a little, just enough for him to see her lips as there was no chance of hearing her over the cheering.

"I love you."

It was all he needed to know.

WHERE DREAMS ARE OF CHRISTMAS

CHAPTER 1

aria Amelia Avico Parrano sat at the take-out window of her son's restaurant in the heart of Seattle's Pike Place Market. Outside her window, the morning bustle of Post Alley would just be starting. Inside, the kitchen sounds of the busy prep crews of Angelo's Tuscan Hearth were already echoing behind her. Manuel, Angelo's *sous chef,* was pushing his new assistant Nora to see if he could make her panic. Maria smiled to herself, no luck yet.

Luisa and Graziella were rehearsing the new menu items for the daily fresh sheet. "Black sea bass poached in a Piedmonte Roero Arneis, that's a slightly sweet white wine of northern Italy, with a rub of basil…"

Maria let the words drift into the background. Served with a surprise pairing of a young Barbaresco red, it would be an innovative pleasure on the palate. The other noises were starting to sound so familiar, it was if she'd never been anywhere else. Six months she'd been in Seattle since her retirement. Retired at forty-seven, it still made no sense.

But the couple she'd cooked for the last three decades in New York had retired and didn't need a resident chef any more. They had rewarded her most comfortably and now she had a place here at her son's restaurant. And it was time.

She flicked on the heater switch, in moments a warm wash of air blew onto her legs. When she slid up the kitchen window to face the chill first day of December, the cold wasn't bad. Russell, her son's best man at the beautiful fall wedding, had installed another heater over the outside of the window to radiate a wall of warmth down onto the customers and an awning to keep Seattle's December rains at bay.

Russell was such a sweet man, she really didn't need that much protection. She had helped raise both Angelo and Russell, her son and her former employer's boy, so of course they saw her as old and frail. That was their role in life. Youth was supposed to think that way. But she didn't feel that way. Not even a little.

Besides, she had far too much fun selling coffee and pastries at her take-out window to stop merely because of the weather. Already some of her regulars were loitering on the wet brickwork of Post Alley and quickly clustered around the window as soon as she opened it.

"Good morning, Maria." The near chorus was music to her ears.

"Hello Clara, Joseph, and William. I don't see you as much as I do when the weather is nice. Don't you love your Maria any more?" She handed William his cappuccino first to soften the tease. He dropped a five dollar bill in the jar she'd set out. She'd made a decorative tile with "Breakfast $5" worked in lavender against a yellow glaze at one of those paint-it-yourself pottery places. "The price," she would tell people, "she is fixed in stone." Then she gave William a fresh *cornetto*.

"What's in it this morning?" he took a big bite without waiting for an answer. "Oh my god!" He managed to mumble with his mouth full, a smile on his face, and crumbs clustering on the lapels of his sharp lawyer's suit.

"It's a sweet *Prosciutto di San Daniele* with a fresh, tangy *Robiola Bosina* cheese."

By that time Clara had bitten into hers and had her eyes closed, as usual, to relish the tastes. Joseph went for the cappuccino first, still looking more asleep than awake. Other regulars had queued up as they paid and chatted, only moving to the edge of the awning and the radiant heat as others pressed inward.

The milling, happy crowd attracted other Pike Place Market tourists. Inside of five minutes there were more people that she didn't recognize than ones that she did.

Henry came over from the fish market and she refused his money, as she had a hundred times before, but he always offered. Henry always held back the best of the day's catch for Angelo or Manuel each morning, today it was the black sea bass.

"Maria, when are you going to marry me?"

"I could never marry you, Henry. You always smell of fish. I could no marry such a man." He of course knew that was a little joke. His fish were always so fresh and he kept everything so clean. He was a vendor, and a very smart one, not a fisherman.

"I'll give it all up for you." He flashed her one of his smiles.

She was half tempted to at least date him. He was such a nice man, and good looking, even if a bit round in the belly. His graying hair would go silver and make him a very handsome older man. But, though she liked him, there was no spark.

Maria wanted spark. She wanted electricity, lightning bolts. She only hoped that she hadn't waited too long and missed her chance.

She served and chatted with a dozen more tourists after Henry left. Her son had found lightning. And Russell too. The two boys were so cute in married life it was hard to credit that they were men grown, always doting on their wives while trying desperately to appear the strong men they couldn't help being if they tried. Their wives, Jo and Cassidy, were both such exceedingly competent women, they made her feel out of her depth. All she had ever done was cook and raise the two boys.

But she'd felt that spark once in her life. She'd felt it right to the very core of her being. A love for a no-good, useless man who had walked away after taking her virginity and leaving her pregnant with a son. Maria had been forced to come to America to hide the shameful pregnancy of an unmarried Italian Roman Catholic girl. She'd never gone back to Manarola for more than to visit.

She wanted fire. She wanted someone who made her blood burn and her heart race. For an hour, perhaps two, she smiled and teased and enjoyed herself immensely. It had become her contribution to her son's success. He was the great chef, but she knew how to charm the people.

The morning always went too quickly; another dozen *cornetti* and she'd be sold out for the day. She made her usual bet with herself. Today she guessed that nine, perhaps ten of the people she'd served would be back for an Italian lunch when the restaurant opened. Even one additional customer would pay for the minor loss she took on each breakfast she sold.

She served a young Chinese couple who didn't speak a word of English, or Italian either. It didn't matter. She helped them figure out which bill to put in the jar and they left ready to explore the waterfront with their breakfast in hand.

A man drifted to the take-out counter window during a momentary lull.

Maria Amelia recognized him. Lately, he'd often wandered by in the mornings, slowing down but never stopping. He always appeared to want to, but never quite managed.

Her greeting elicited little more than a friendly nod. A shy one. He wore old sneakers with white socks, dark-brown khakis that had started to fray where the hems scuffed along the ground, a red flannel shirt under a faded jeans jacket, and a baseball cap with some computer-looking logo. The whole outfit had clearly been worn several years too long, probably from a Goodwill store. He didn't have a beard, but needed a shave badly. It was long enough she could see it would have a little salt in the pepper if he let it grow.

For all that he was quite the handsomest man she had served that morning. Not the prettiest, so many of the young men were pretty. Those fresh clean faces that thought they knew the world while having seen none of it.

This man had seen much of it. Perhaps too much, perhaps not, but it showed on his solid features and in the soft brown eyes that didn't skitter aside despite his unease, or downward despite her low-cut dress. She wouldn't mind much if they did, after all, why was a woman built the way she was if not to share it a little bit. But she liked that he didn't go there.

He stopped uncertainly several steps from her window, just at the point where she could see the rain dripping off the awning, splashing onto the brim of his hat, and trickling off the brim and into his open jacket.

The man pulled out a wallet, made a back-and-forth motion with his fingers as if searching for money, then shoved it back in his pocket.

As he turned away, Maria called to him.

"Don't go."

He stopped, this time with the drip falling down the back of his neck. When he looked back at her, his nice eyes looked just a little wild. Fear that he couldn't afford to pay even so little for a breakfast.

"Here, it's my last. You should have it." She held out a *cornetto* and cappuccino.

He hesitated, so shy it was almost painful to watch.

"I always save the best for last. So these must be for you."

The man came and took them, careful not to touch her as he did so. His nails needed trimming, but the hands were good ones. He didn't use them for manual labor, but they showed a man who had used them for more than office work his whole life. A few small burns and nicks she recognized as someone who cooked, and wasn't very good at it, which only made her like him all the more.

He almost managed a smile before turning away and hurrying into the rain.

HIS CHEEKS BURNING WITH SHAME, Hogan Stanford hurried down Pike Place Market's Post Alley until he was out of sight of Maria's window. Then he circled around to the antiques place at the corner of Post and Stewart and peeked back toward Angelo's Tuscan Hearth.

It was a gray, drizzling December morning, freezing water was trickling down his back, and he was a complete and total idiot.

He hadn't been able to say a word.

He'd first noticed her from his condo's window which faced Puget Sound. Watching the tourists mob up and down the four short, bricked blocks of Pike Place Market had become one of his favorite pastimes. Even if he didn't like to join the fray, it always seemed so full of life.

And in the midst of it all there had been a flash of color, of sky blue and gold that had glittered in the crowd. That was what had finally drawn him outdoors to wander the streets of the Pike Place Market. On his third outing, he'd spotted her again. It had been a warm day for December and she'd worn her tan camel hair coat open. That day she'd been wearing a red skirt, a vivid orange blouse, and a sunny yellow kerchief over her dark, curling hair, like a flower in bloom. But he had no doubt that it was the same woman. It simply had to be, there couldn't be two women in the world who glowed so brightly.

He'd been so stunned by her beauty that he'd lost track of her when she must've ducked into a store. It took him another week to spot her again, though at least now he had a face to go by. This time she sat in the window at Angelo's Tuscan Hearth Ristorante, framed by the wood-and-brick window frame, like a Botticelli.

Today she'd been dressed in brilliant blues as she served up breakfast and charm in equal portions. She shone like a ray of sunshine in an otherwise dark world on this dreary December day. At least he was pretty sure it was December now.

He peeked again around the brickwork corner and back up Post Alley. She was bantering happily with another customer. Leaning her elbow on the counter and resting her chin on her hand, she looked as if she could happily visit away the whole morning. It was an ability he had never understood. He didn't know whether to be impressed by how natural she was, or be nervous that she would talk everyone to death and be a bore. Yet she never appeared to bore anyone, though he had watched her many times. He decided that she had an uncanny awareness of the mood of each individual she met.

Hogan noted with some chagrin that she served the woman a *cornetto* and a paper cup. The one still warm in his hands hadn't been her last after all. Thinking him homeless, she said it to make him feel less embarrassed. People were never that nice. It had to be an act…but again, it didn't feel like one.

Being stupid, Hogan. It was one of his trademarks, but he just couldn't approach her. Half a dozen times over the few weeks since he'd spotted her, he'd walked by while she was serving, trying to work up the nerve. Finally this morning he'd managed it.

Now she slid her window down. In moments, the soft red glow of the overhead heater faded to black. Finally sold out. He shifted back around the corner and out of sight of the restaurant, then rested his back against the wet brick. The moisture slowly seeped through at his shoulders and butt.

She was so different from the dark and brooding Vera who had totally screwed up his life.

He knew he had to get out and speak to someone. All he'd wanted was one moment in the glow of a woman as bright and cheerful as the one in the restaurant window.

And then he'd looked in his wallet and realized that the smallest bill he was carrying was a hundred.

Then she'd decided he was homeless.

How sad was that?

And he'd let her think it.

Really sad, he answered his own question, knowing it was absolutely true.

CHAPTER 2

*H*ogan *had two places* to be, which was an improvement. For the last six months, he'd only had the one, his condo. His buddies—his buddy, he'd chased off pretty much everyone except Eric by being Mister Gloom for so long, had insisted that he get out. There was only so long you could hole up in a condo at the heart of a city as alive as Seattle.

So, now he either sat watching at his condo's window a dozen stories into the sky above the world of the Pike Place Market. Or he wandered the half mile down to the Lawrence Armed Forces Shelter in Pioneer Square.

He wasn't a vet, but Eric Lawrence didn't hold it against him, though some of the guys had at first. Now that he'd shown up every afternoon for a month they were starting to forgive him for never having served. He'd spent his twenties fighting computer code and corporate politics, a far less lethal environment. He'd loved doing it, but now he was mid-forties, financially set for life, and he was done. Corporate wars had taken the fun out of it.

The guys at the shelter let Hogan work in the kitchen and keep to himself. Mostly.

Richie was in rare form today and clearly his PTSD needed a target. As usual, Hogan was it.

"Hogan, man," all of Richie's diatribes started that way. On days like this he couldn't just chop vegetables and leave Hogan in peace. Each time it was something different. Richie had lost all connection to normal but seemed to keep hunting around looking for it, hoping someday he'd hit it by chance.

"Hogan, man, I can't believe you never even shot anybody."

Today wasn't going to be the day.

"You don't know what you can really do until then."

Hogan, kept his focus on the chowder kettle. It was an exceptional device, absolutely suited to one purpose, making large batches of soup quickly. To make the chowder, it took two large number ten cans of condensed chowder, that came out in a near solid, brownish mass, filled with a thousand bits of white potato, and gray clams. Even the green flecks of parsley were included. Add two gallons of milk and set the timer for twenty minutes. The steam-jacketed kettle heated it through without scorching, as long as he remembered to stir it and scrape the bottom every five minutes. A long handle then let you tip the contents right into the serving inserts for the steam table. He liked the efficiency and single mindedness of it.

A trait it shared with Richie. The man was starting in on the different methods of killing the enemy that he had supposedly experienced. To hear him talk, he had won Desert Storm singlehandedly back in the '90s and been at the shelter ever since. Even Eric didn't know how much of Richie was real and how much came from his primary hobby, collecting war movies. He claimed it was the only thing that kept him calm, the sound of war a constant in the background.

Richie was the most extreme person in the kitchen. There was room for five of them, and not a lot more. Richie and Sam worked at a long steel table. Today they were filleting great tubs of cleaned fish, wielding long curved knives as if they were extensions of their arms. The fish flew into stacks, neat little butterflied pieces just perfect for making the fish and chips for tonight. Standard Friday fare.

His friend Eric was at the dishwasher and his wife Betsy worked battering and breading the fish as fast as the other two men sliced it up. Eric had had an easy tour, but none of the three friends who'd signed up when he did had come home. So, he paid back his missing friends by founding the kitchen.

He'd recruited Hogan just recently. They'd met at a bookstore and both reached for the last copy of the new Clive Cussler book at the same time. That was all the opening Eric needed, ever. When he'd learned Hogan was at loose ends, he'd dragged him down to the shelter, "Until he found something better to do." After a month, Hogan hadn't found anything better. And the work at the shelter was becoming more important to him, helping out, making a difference, even if it was a small one.

Hogan began chopping the heads of lettuce and throwing them in the big tubs of water to stay fresh. Cans of beans, beets, and a half dozen other items would be opened right before service to set up the salad bar. Then a half-dozen chilled onions to slice up thin.

He wished Richie would stop saying, "Hogan, man" so that he could think about Maria. He'd heard someone call her that one day. The fishmonger, in his big voice shouting to her, "Maria, my love. You must run away with me." Her laugh had sparkled and lit the rainy day as if it had struck fire and rainbows.

That was a good metaphor for her. Fire and rainbows, heat and life, vibrant and multi-spectral.

He wondered if she smelled as good as her kitchen.

That's when he noticed the smell in this kitchen. He rushed to the chowder pot. Scorched. The chowder would be fine, but it would take him an extra half hour today to get it clean.

Not that he had anything better to do.

CHAPTER 3

"**M**ama!"

"Angelo!" Her tone, as strident as his, brought him to a halt. "What you got to yell for?"

Her son blushed. A grown man of thirty, newly married, and a successful restaurateur and she could still make him blush. He was so sweet. It made her feel all motherly inside. It also made her feel old, and she didn't like that at all.

"Now," she took him by the hand and led him over to the stainless steel prep table to one side of the kitchen. The tubs of the iced black sea bass filled one end. A big wheel of Parmigiano-Reggiano cheese, dusky inside its thick rind and ready for breakdown, sat on the other.

He dragged against her, but she was firm. The last thing Nora or Manuel needed during their lunch preparations was whatever had upset her son. Then she spotted the newspaper in his hand and she suspected that she knew. She pushed him onto one of the stools and pulled another from under the table for herself. There was the dough for a new puff pastry she was developing that would need tending shortly, but it could wait five, perhaps ten minutes.

"Sit like a good boy. Manuel," she called over to Angelo's head chef, "make a bowl of pasta with some of Nora's nice Bolognese."

"It's not ready yet," he grumbled even as he made two plates and brought them over.

"Yes it is, Manuel. Now stop plaguing the girl and tell her that she is doing fine. She's worried sick that she won't be good enough."

He winked at her and offered the sly grin that so rarely creased his handsome Mexican features. The fact that he was the best Italian chef she'd ever met, after her son of course, was only one of life's little oddities that she so enjoyed.

"Don't you wink at me, young man. You go tell Nora that she is doing wonderful or I tell her that you are sweet on her whether or not you are."

He blanched, "No, I—" Then his tongue tied into a knot just as Graziella breezed into the kitchen with the day's first orders. Now wasn't that interesting.

Manuel wisely retreated, a quick glance showed that her son had missed his chef's reaction to the queen of the front of house. They would make such a beautiful couple. Manuel's dark complexion reflected his Oaxacan heritage and Graziella glowed just as richly with the shade of the Mediterranean. His square features and broad shoulders were in sharp contrast to her slender build. Both had black hair, his short and curled, and hers was a man's dream, often in a thick braid, at other times free and floating along behind her. She was taller, but Manuel didn't appear to mind. Yes, they would make a beautiful couple, though she would worry about that later. At the moment she had to worry about her son and her puff pastry, in that order. And neither would wait long.

"Mama," Angelo laid the paper down beside his pasta bowl. A circle around one of the ads on the personals page. Yes, that was it.

"Why do you read such things," she waved a fork of Nora's pasta Bolognese in the paper's general direction before tasting it. Oh, it was so good. "You are a married boy, you shouldn't be reading the personal ads."

"I didn't."

"Then why are you in here complaining?"

"Mama! Henry read it and asked if that could possibly be my mama? I read the ad and what was I to think?"

She hadn't really counted on Henry the fishmonger reading it. He was a little too pushy about being in love with her and she had decided definitely no. She also hadn't planned on her son reading it. So simple an ad. Too simple maybe.

Very Italian cook, SWF, 47 seeks friend(s).

Person to laugh with, dance with, and dine with.

Believes in friends, family, and herself.

"Of course I told him it wasn't you. Why would my beautiful mama have to advertise for friends, she is already friends with everyone." Angelo squinted down at the ad then looked back up at her. "It isn't you, is it?"

Maria thought about how it felt. Yes, she knew everybody, their names and that of their wives and children. But how could she possibly explain it to someone like her son? His best friend Russell lived only a few blocks away. Angelo had moved from his condo in Pioneer Square to live with his beautiful Jo in her high-rise condo in the heart of Seattle looking down at Lake Union and out at the Olympic mountains.

Where did that leave her? She had been in Seattle six months now. She came in early, as a good Italian *patissier* had to for her pastry to be perfect and her breads to rise. And by mid-afternoon, she was done for the day. She often stayed through dinner, because she had nothing more to do. Going to sit alone in Angelo's condo in Pioneer Square was not satisfying, and she didn't like to sit by herself at movies or plays. Or restaurants for that matter. She liked people, but who in Seattle did she really know? No one except her two boys, Angelo and his everything-but-birth brother, Russell. It was a good soup, but it had no spice.

She refocused on Angelo's questioning gaze. Some questions, she decided were not to be answered. Time to give him something else to worry about and then go fold her puff pastry dough.

"So my boy," she whispered to gently remind him of who he was pointing fingers at as she stood and collected their bowls. "Manuel and Graziella. What do you think? Their children would be so very cute."

HOGAN STANFORD LEFT the Lawrence Armed Forces Shelter kitchen later than usual. Eric Lawrence had decided on the name for two reasons. First, it kept the riff-raff out. It was a clear sign that said, "There are messed up military dudes in here. If you aren't one, stay away."

The other shelters had so appreciated having so many of the street's hardcases have somewhere else to go, that they'd done everything they could in Eric's rough-start first year.

The second benefit had been that the guys, and the one or two really messed up women, understood each other and were better at dealing with each other's oddities. They'd get into arguments between which force was better or which war tougher, but someone always stepped in when things got too heated. They were like an engine, a really screwed up one that really shouldn't still be running, but it seemed to work despite all of its problems.

By the time Hogan had scrubbed the chowder pot, Richie had been in full meltdown-recovery. In some ways that was even worse. He'd cornered Hogan for a half hour to apologize for being a jerk and to spin out yet another personal story, one that sounded suspiciously like a John Wayne plot. Though Hogan now knew better than to point that out.

When all was said and done, he'd practically crawled out the kitchen door and turned up First Avenue to head back up to his place overlooking Pike Place Market. It had been a good shift, he'd helped put food into a lot of tired vets with cold bellies, but he was exhausted. He'd planned on hitting one of the banks to break one of his hundred-dollar bills so that he could buy breakfast tomorrow. He'd pay with a ten, to pay Maria back for her kindness today. Or would that be rude? It didn't matter, it was too late anyway. Between Richie and the chowder pot, they'd made him miss the end of the banking hours. And her window would be closed before the banks opened in the morning.

He hadn't gone ten steps into the cold darkness of a Northwest evening when he practically ran someone down. He mumbled an, "Oh sorry, just distracted I guess," and made to move on when a hand on his coat sleeve stopped him.

He looked up, startled, into the dark eyes of Maria… He didn't even know her last name. They hadn't been this close this morning. Now they stood mere inches apart. Barely up to his chin in height, she looked up at him.

Her eyes weren't just dark, even in the streetlights they were rich brown, like warm chocolate that somehow sparkled, almost the same color as the lock of her hair that poked out around a bright blue scarf. His first impression that her face was worthy of a Botticelli painting was powerfully reinforced. She reminded him of the one he'd seen in Florence. Maria was a darker-skinned Venus, observing an Allegory of Spring. Her heavy coat of good brown leather, hugged her frame. He knew from seeing her in the window these last mornings, that Maria had glorious curves and a trim waist.

He also knew that he was staring at her far beyond what was appropriate for their casual meeting. "Run," he advised her. At least he thought the recommendation loudly. Any woman with the least common sense would know to run away from him, but she remained.

"Did they give you enough to eat?"

"Huh?" That was the best answer he could manage. What was she…

"The shelter. Did they give you enough to eat?"

He glanced over his shoulder. The Lawrence Shelter lay not a dozen paces behind him, she must have seen him exit the kitchen door.

"No. Yes. I…" He never ate there, because he wanted as much food as possible to go to the men. Eric offered him free meals, but he said it was part of his contribution. He'd planned to go home and maybe cook a hamburger or some chicken. Maybe it was an order-out-Chinese night?

"They serve plenty there. Eric does a good job."

Maria nodded. "Too bad you've already eaten. I'd offer you a home-cooked meal. I don't much enjoy eating alone. Well, have a good night."

He turned to say something as she walked away, anything. He found no words.

"And tomorrow," she spoke over her shoulder. "You come back to the window at Angelo's, I'll make sure you have a good breakfast."

Then she was gone.

Hogan could have felt dumber, he just didn't know how.

He stood at the heart of Pioneer Square so long that a chill finally found its way in to shiver up his spine. The small triangular park that was the heart of the square was a busy bustle of yuppies, though he suspected that term rather dated him. They were hipsters now, weren't they?

Bars and cafes were filling up with them whatever they were. The spare trees, barren of their summer foliage, displayed their winter finery; thousands upon thousands of sparkling white lights threaded through their branches and lit the crowds hustling along the sidewalk. It was getting into the Christmas shopping season and the city's cheer showed.

Down the block, the J&M was already packed, one of the liveliest Seattle bars. Two doors down he could already hear the painfully loud rock roaring out the Central, perhaps the loudest bar in Seattle.

He pulled up the collar on his denim jacket and turned to trudge up the hill back to Pike Street. He could practically hear Richie moaning at him in sympathy, "Aw, Hogan man."

HOGAN HAD TO FIX THIS, it was beyond embarrassing.

He hit a cash machine and pulled out a twenty-dollar bill. He timed his arrival at Maria's window to be after the initial morning regulars, but before she'd have run down her supplies. He'd given himself a stern talking to, so he was as ready as he could be.

Except when he arrived at the window Maria wasn't there. A younger, slender Italian beauty sat there instead. He stumbled to a halt, uncertain what to do now.

The young woman spotted him and waved him over.

He staggered forward the few steps out of the chill rain and into the basking warmth of the overhead heater, dry beneath the cheery red-and-white awning.

"You must be the one Maria described. Manuel," she called back over her shoulder to someone deeper inside the kitchen, "he's here." She handed him coffee, but not the trademark *cornetto*.

"Where's…" The woman didn't even let him finish the sentence. Which was good, he didn't know if calling her Maria when he didn't actually know her was being too forward.

"She's off with her son Angelo. They're looking at a new place for his second restaurant." Her accent was light, mostly American with just a hint of the sensuous tones that filled Maria's voice.

Angelo. Angelo's Tuscan Hearth Ristorante. Everyone knew, even he knew, about the sensation Angelo was creating with his fine Italian cuisine. He was smashing barriers with his traditional cooking techniques and innovative flavors. So many chefs were trending in the other direction until it often didn't even look like food. French Gastronomie had become wholly unrecognizable. Angelo had created his art in flavors.

Maria was Angelo's mother. He'd never met the man, but it was hard to picture her as old enough to have a son grown, never mind one who'd had time to become a rising star at a national, possibly even international level. Oddly, he liked the sound of that. He'd felt a little guilty at his own forty-five to be drawn to a younger woman. It was far too cliché for a Microsoft Millionaire, such a common phrase in Seattle parlance that it had become a title, to be chasing a younger woman. But he and Maria were of an age, which he liked.

"Here you go, *signore*." She held out a to-go container. He almost lost it to the pavement. By the weight of it, there must be a full meal in there, sold out the back window of one of Seattle's finest restaurants.

Sold. Right. He fished after the twenty dollar bill he'd taken care to slip in his front pocket.

"No," the young woman held up a hand, palm out. "She specifically said that your money was no good here."

"But I'm not—"

The woman waved him off again. "Maria was very insistent. And you have no idea what a serious set of circumstances that implies if I ignore it."

He prepared to sally forth once again, but a cluster of locals had arrived and began greeting "Graziella" and making a fuss of asking after Maria. Without even being conscious of it, he was shifted backward until he had departed the warmth of both the window and the heater, was past the protection of the awning, and stood once again on the cold wet brick of Post Alley.

He retreated to a quiet spot, back by the same brick corner he had occupied the day before. He leaned there out of the rain and sniffed the Styrofoam container. It smelled glorious!

He opened it and was pleased to find a small plastic fork had been included. That was a good thing, because it smelled so amazing he would have scooped it up with his bare hands. An omelet with smoked salmon and another taste that took him a moment to place, it was so unexpected. Fresh artichoke heart and some tangy cheese, mascarpone. His tongue was too unskilled to even begin to unravel the delicate spicing beyond salt, pepper, and a touch of fresh basil. One of Maria's *cornetto* had also been included, a delicate center of the lightest lemon and basil custard, with a glaze of slivered almonds and browned butter. It cried to be eaten first.

Hogan did his best to appreciate each bite, but knew he was practically inhaling it.

He really did have to fix this silly misunderstanding, but he hadn't had such a good meal in a long time. He enjoyed it immensely, totally unaware of the cold rain from above, or the woman watching him ever so sadly from the nearby doorway before she entered the restaurant with her son.

CHAPTER 4

Maria had hoped for a few interesting responses to her advertisement. She sat quietly while the shells were baking for tonight's Winter Custard Tart. It would be a dark chocolate custard with slivers of dried pear, apple, and apricot partially reconstituted in a spicy mulled cider. She'd come out to the front of house and was using the computer tucked discreetly into Graziella's greeting station.

The soft warmth of the interior design based on Ligurian countryside villas, and the beautiful photos that Russell had taken while honeymooning there to decorate the walls, made it feel like home. She had lived seventeen years in Italy, thirty in New York, and now six months here in Seattle, but this is what felt like home. Somehow she still felt more Italian than American.

The lights were low. The gray day shining weakly through the high windows leant a warmth to the dusky yellows and brick-reds of the décor, and the dark wood and the so-dark-red-they-were-almost-black tablecloths.

She looked down at the computer screen and was stunned to discover that she didn't have a few responses. Her ad had elicited dozens upon dozens of responses. Only momentarily overwhelmed, she quickly came up with a plan. She would treat this like any grocery order, sorting the produce into good enough for the customer, possibly acceptable, and for the trash.

Perhaps give some real produce to one of the homeless shelters, they must always be desperate for supplies. Yes, she must speak to Angelo and Manuel about doing just that with any of their castoffs or unsold product. For one of the secrets of Angelo's Tuscan Hearth was that everything used was fresh that day. Only soups or sauces that needed to stand overnight to mellow and blend were exempt.

That would be good, especially if it helped feed people like the nervous man who had come back to the window this morning. No, not nervous. He hadn't seemed nervous when they met in Pioneer Square last night. Nor was it shyness.

He was tentative, she decided. So painfully tentative. As if he had lost all self-confidence and had found no way yet to make up for the loss.

Whereas the men, and they were almost exclusively men, who had answered her ad could use a large lesson in humility. Well, she would do her part on that front. She simply deleted every one who talked about sex. Not that she didn't want that as well, but it was not where you started a relationship. Especially not a friendship.

"I liked your ad, Ms. Parrano."

Maria jolted only slightly as she looked up at Graziella. She had swept quietly into the front of the restaurant and begun preparing it for the day. Checking supplies of napkins, fresh tablecloths, tall pitchers of ice water. Well, she hadn't expected to fool a woman as sharp as Graziella.

"You know that's Maria to you."

She shrugged, "I know, but I like calling you Ms. Parrano. It just feels more fitting."

"It just feels old," Maria riposted.

Graziella's laugh lit up the room. "I am younger than your son."

"Don't remind me. You are such a beautiful girl."

"Thank you. I like your ad. It is hard. Men only see us as..." she indicated her body with a wave of her hand.

"And you are complaining?"

"No..." Graziella pulled out the menus and began inserting the day's lunch menu. "But I wish they were interested in more."

Maria smiled to herself. She knew what Graziella meant. Then she saw an opportunity.

"Is there perhaps one person in particular you wished was paying more attention to you?"

Graziella's soft blush and averted eyes were all Maria needed to see. That the girl's eyes had traveled toward the kitchen door before looking down only confirmed what she already knew.

She reached out and with a brush on the cheek drew the girl's attention back to her. "Sometimes my dear girl, it is the woman who must act."

"But what if he—" Then she clapped a hand over her mouth as if she was afraid of what she'd suddenly revealed.

Maria pulled her in and kissed her on each cheek despite the hand still firmly clapped over her mouth.

"You are so sweet. First, if he does not fall down at your feet in praise to the Almighty, he does not appreciate you enough. Second, I happen to believe that he will do exactly that. You must merely let him know that it is welcome. He is too busy being careful around his boss and forgetting how to be a man."

"But Angelo—"

"Phhtt!" Maria waved a hand as if shooing a fly. "My son, he is very good at not seeing anything, not even what is right in front of his face. Just ask that charming wife of his. I will fix him if he makes any fuss. Now leave this old woman to her e-mail, you have a lunch to serve."

Graziella's laugh, gorgeous smile, and quick hug left Maria feeling her age. Not old, but no longer young either. In that middle of life like a good wine, she decided. She would have to remind herself of that when she was with such a young woman.

She turned back to the responses to her ad. Both younger men and older soon traced their path into her trash. Why a nineteen-year old was seeking a "hot mama" was not a question she was the least interested in answering. Nor why men in their seventies thought they could possibly keep up with her.

She wanted to do so much. She had never been drawn to the outdoors, but that didn't mean she didn't want to try it. Maria wanted to learn, explore, and be shocked in wonder. Somewhere she had heard the phrase, "to suck the marrow from life." Like a good Osso Buco, braised veal shanks over risotto. That's what she wanted.

Then she reached an e-mail that brought her to a screeching halt.

The Terrible Trio requests the company of

Maria Amelia Avico Parrano.

Tonight, Cutter's Crabhouse, 6 pm.

No sender's name. Nothing about who the "Terrible Trio" might be. And not a hint of how they knew not only that it was her advertisement, but knew her full name as well.

She deleted it. All those responses, and not a one had made it into her "possibly acceptable" list. She closed her e-mail. And the instant she stood and looked about the quiet restaurant, awaiting the start of yet another lunch service, she knew exactly where she would be at six o'clock this evening.

MARIA HAD VACILLATED AND WORRIED. Her plans to leave the restaurant early enough to go home and change were sabotaged by a lunch rush that used up too many dark-chocolate-dipped, cherry biscotti and she had to make more for dinner to go with her homemade hazelnut gelato.

She did consider going to Perrin's Glorious Garb. Her boy had married Jo, a lovely lawyer of Alaskan heritage who had recently taken over as the manager of the Pike Place Market. One of her friends was an amazing clothier named Perrin Williams. Another of her friends had married dear Russell.

Cassidy Knowles also appeared to be the first woman other than herself who had made any success of controlling Russell's restless energy. Maria had channeled Russell and Angelo's energy by teaching them to cook. Cassidy and Jo apparently both applied a liberal dose of common sense, they kept the two men so in love with them that they never knew which way their heads were spinning.

She had left the newlyweds alone as much as possible. They were all young and didn't need her hanging about them. She'd shopped at Perrin's store a few times. While the clothes were so beautiful, they made the clothes the statement. Maria preferred to wear clothes that attracted attention, but let her be the statement.

So, she went through the Market on the way to Cutter's, leaving herself enough time to browse the shops and stalls.

She found a Christmas scarf that completely suited her ideas of taste. It wasn't candy canes and red-cheeked Santas. It was the color of holly and candle flames. As if it were made for La Festa di Santa Lucia. While that wasn't for almost two weeks, Maria liked the way it brought out the red in her dark hair. It made her feel very festive, which is how a woman should feel around the holidays.

She'd planned on arriving early. That way she could be sipping a glass of wine when the self-proclaimed "Terrible Trio" arrived. She was betting with herself that it was Joseph, Clara, and William. They were always there right when she opened her window. And, she was pleased to note, they had the good sense to bring their ever-rotating line of dates to Angelo's for a proper meal when they wanted to impress them. They were fun and pleasant, it would be a nice evening, that she'd be unlikely to repeat.

If it was someone else, well then, she'd just wait and see. She wasn't above pretending her phone buzzed from the restaurant with a "dessert emergency." She'd have to remember that one, it was a funny line.

Maria was actually a little late by the time she arrived, the scarf had been in one of the last places she'd looked. The invitation hadn't said whether they were to meet in the bar or the restaurant.

The restaurant was down a long corridor, walking right through the servers prep station. It would have been strange if not for the spectacular view that lay in wait for the unsuspecting patron.

The bar sprawled to the left as she entered the door. It was filled with the young and the professionals. So much so that she almost felt out of place. Lawyers radiated power with their suits, but most others dressed to be seen. Even the scruffy, and several of the people had that upscale scruffy look that only comes with success in some software business or the like, were young and exceedingly healthy.

Well, Maria Amelia, you can turn tail and run, or you can fling your power scarf over your shoulder and sweep into the room as if you are the one who belongs.

She did the latter and swept in. It was pleasing to see several men turn to watch her passage toward the long wooden bar at the far end of the lounge, despite their dates' glares. In front of the bar stood a line of stools, mostly occupied, but with none of the dedicated drinkers typical in most bars. No, people came here to see and be seen, not to be life-long patrons.

Opposite the bar was a long wall of glass looking south along the Seattle waterfront. Six o'clock was well past dark on a December night and the city glowed. Pike Place Market was a blare of light to the left.

The view sort of tumbled down the high cliff of Western and into the water past the brightly lit piers of restaurants, tourist shops, and the ferry terminal. Beyond the big new Ferris wheel the view went dark, the expanse of Elliot Bay only lit by the occasional ferry across the water looking like a birthday cake bearing far too many candles. The mountain backdrop had disappeared with the darkness, just the faintest orange outline showing the towering snowy mountains.

The view fit Cutter's Bar, filled it with the vibrancy of what was actually quite a quaint city. They were so proud of the industry and busy doings, the largest city in the Northwest, the portal to Alaska, the bicycling capital of the U. S… Their lists went on and on. She had lived thirty years in New York, the city that never slept. Most of Seattle would be closed by eight o'clock. It was young and terribly pleased with itself, like so many of the patrons she could see in the bar.

"Maria, over here."

She turned, and stumbled to a halt. All of her self-contained bravado slipping off her shoulders like a lost shawl at the surprise. She didn't know if she was ready to face this trio.

At one of the small round window tables, tall with equally high stools that put them on display, sat three beautiful young women.

Cassidy Knowles in her trademark black turtleneck, designer slacks, and leather, calf-length boots. To either side, Jo Thompson ever so formal in her charcoal lawyer powersuit, and Perrin in, well, full-on Perrin was probably the only way to describe her.

The woman's shoulder-length hair was white. Not white-blond, but white. Her dress and leggings beneath were black and form-fitting, even black gloves revealing only her fingertips with unpainted nails. It was as if only her hair and face existed and the rest of her was invisible.

It should have looked alien, as if she'd fallen out of a science - fiction movie, or perhaps Goth. Instead, Maria could see, it was making even the male waiters stumble as they passed by. She was far and away the most stunning woman in the room tonight.

Maria sidled up to the table. She actually always felt daunted by her daughter-in-law and her two friends. They were a family and she wasn't. They traced their lineage all the way back to their first day at college. Maria had never graduated from upper secondary, leaving at seventeen, a year early due to her pregnancy. They were so terribly accomplished; all Maria had ever done was give birth to a son and cook.

"You're the Terrible Trio?" In a way they were. They quite unnerved her.

"Guilty," Perrin declared brightly.

"And proud to be," Russell's wife offered.

"No," Angelo's Jo stopped them all with her calm composure and simple declarative.

"No?" the others asked.

"There are four of us now."

"The Fab Four?" Cassidy offered.

"I've got it," Perrin raised her glass in a black-gloved hand for a toast.

There was a brief delay while they found a drink for Maria to toast with. She took the moment to climb onto the stool that placed them nearly elbow to elbow around the table, though it left her feeling as if she were teetering.

"We are hereby the Fearsome Foursome."

"Hear. Hear." The others raised their glasses, so Maria followed suit.

Perrin knocked back the rest of her Cosmopolitan.

Jo and Cassidy sipped their wine.

Maria knocked back the sip of Perrin's Cosmo that had been poured into an empty water glass for her.

She and Perrin slammed their glasses back down on the table and said in unison, "Hear. Hear."

And just that fast, they welcomed Maria into their inner circle. Suddenly she was very glad she'd come.

"BUT HOW DID you know it was me?" Maria sipped at her wine. Cassidy had picked a local white that perfectly complemented the Oven Roasted Dungeness and Rock Crab Dip. The dish was good, not subtle, but good. The wine pairing definitely elevated it.

"Only someone as dense as my Angelo could miss that," Jo shook her head sadly. Her long, straight black hair swirled across her shoulders: the only indicator of her Alaskan heritage other than her perfect dusky skin. That she was such a beauty and had just been ranked as one of Seattle's most influential women only made Maria wonder how her son, who she loved dearly, had been good enough. "Go Angelo," was all she could think.

"Russell is dense enough. He's even worse than Angelo," Cassidy offered with a thoroughly contented sigh.

"Yes, or Russell," Jo conceded. "Only two such men wouldn't know it was you, Maria. The instant Angelo showed me the newspaper, I knew...and I felt awful."

"Why awful?"

"You were so kind to me when Angelo and I were stumbling our way toward each other, then... I shall be kind to myself by just saying, then I dropped you."

Maria reached out and held Jo's hand. "You, my dear girl, are in a terribly demanding new job and you were newly in love and now married. The last thing you need to be worrying about is a foolish old mother-in-law."

Jo's strong hand squeezed back.

"The next time you say that you're old, you'll be wearing a Cosmo," Perrin raised her glass in threat.

"But I am."

"Before you came, we all agreed, you are the woman we want to grow up to be. We've also decided that you are our style guru. If you weren't so totally scary, we'd have thought to do this much sooner."

"Scary? Me?" There was an adjective she'd never have picked in a thousand years.

"You're beautiful."

"You cook like a dream."

"You dress in a way that just pisses me off." Perrin declared with a shake of her white-white hair. "You always look so effortless. Me, I'm...constructed." She waved to indicate her styling and clothes.

"But that is you, my dear," Maria protested. "You are so breathtaking that I fully expect half the men in the room to need neck braces before the night is over."

"Really?" Perrin appeared surprised. As if she didn't know or trust her own startling beauty. She glanced over Maria's shoulder cautiously.

"They will all have sore necks from turning so often to admire you. And many will be wearing their date's drinks before the night is over for staring so often. That I can guarantee." That one of these women could be less than confident shocked her to the very core.

"You know what makes you really scary?" Cassidy's soft voice stopped the back and forth flow of conversation around the table.

Maria shook her head. Realized she was crumpling her napkin in her lap with her nerves and forced herself to stop even if she couldn't relax.

It was Jo who answered. "How in the world did you raise Russell and Angelo without having to murder at least one of them? That is the true miracle."

"Oh, that was easy," she laughed at their aghast expressions. "Best way to a young boy's head is through his stomach. And when they started noticing girls, I started feeding the girls as well. The boys never thought twice about bringing them to my kitchen. Then Mama Maria would quietly scoot the worst ones right back out the door without the boys even noticing."

"Scary smart," Jo confirmed.

"Totally," Cassidy freshened their wine glasses.

"Wish you'd been my mother," Perrin's voice was soft, barely loud enough for Maria to hear. The look on her face wasn't silly or joking as it had been until this moment. It was very real and remarkably sad.

Maria felt herself melt. Without even thinking, she took Perrin's hand, pulled her into a leaning hug, and kissed her atop her shining hair. They sat back up, but Perrin stared down at the white tablecloth.

Maria knew that lack of a mother had been one of the common bonds between these three friends. Cassidy's had died young, Jo's had abandoned her family while Jo was still a toddler, and Perrin's mother had been viciously cruel and abusive and did not deserve the title. Maria had to wipe her eyes at the pain she saw on Perrin's features.

"I could wish that too, dear," she whispered to Perrin. "You are a wonderful woman and anyone who didn't see that… Well, they didn't deserve you."

Perrin looked up at her, staring until she could see that Maria meant it, tears began trickling down her cheeks and Maria wiped them away fighting against her own.

"Hey," Cassidy protested. "What did we just miss? No crying at this table unless we all do. That's the rule."

Maria kept Perrin's hand in her own as she faced the others. She looked at each of these amazing women.

"I loved raising the boys. But I always dreamed of daughters. I just never dreamed of daughters like you three."

"Oh man." Cassidy groaned.

Jo blinked hard then actually sniffled in a terribly un-Jo-like fashion. "Okay, that did it. You are hereafter stuck with us forever."

Perrin looked away, studying the table in silence. But she didn't release her tight hold on Maria's hand.

It had taken a fresh round of appetizers and drinks to clear the mood of the table.

Taylor Shellfish Farms Steamed Manila Clams saw them through several "Russell and Angelo as young boys" stories. A fresh basket of Cutter's trademark focaccia, practically dripping with olive oil and garlic, covered the latest updates on Perrin's love life. She was desperately in and out of love at least once a month. Her heart apparently only had two modes, full-on and full-off.

Maria privately concluded that her own heart had perhaps been set to full-off without her realizing it. Perhaps it was time to change that as well.

When Cassidy ordered another bottle of wine, this time a magnificent Willamette Valley Pinot Blanc, Maria began to worry about quite how much everyone was drinking, including herself.

"Oh no, not to worry," Perrin signaled the waiter for a fresh Cosmo. "It's another rule of the Terrible Trio."

"Fearsome Foursome," Cassidy corrected her absently as she inspected the new wine as only one of the nation's leading food-and-wine critics could.

"Fabulous Fivesome if one of you married types would please, please, please go ahead and get pregnant so I could be an auntie." Perrin was on a roll. And when she was, there was clearly no stopping her.

Jo and Cassidy both blanched white at the thought and raised their hands in surrender.

"The rule is, we're not allowed to get drunk unless we're all together. Ever since college we've had that rule."

"And we've paid for it," Jo's tone was drily funny, suggesting wild escapades.

Maria would guess that those wild times were Perrin's doing. As a matter of fact, she would bet on it. And something about Jo's eyes and a shared glance with Cassidy. Yes, they had made the rule to protect Perrin from herself.

Perrin must not know that about her friends, for she took a totally different reading from Jo's sidelong glance and poked a finger in Cassidy's arm.

"Of course one of us, and I *am* pointing fingers…" As a matter of fact she was forcing Cassidy to lean sideways towards Jo to escape the pressure. "…broke that rule and got horribly smashed in private."

"Those were special circumstances, Perrin." Jo spoke in Cassidy's defense even as she batted away Perrin's hand and helped Cassidy back upright.

"Yeah," Perrin's gaze returned to Maria. She leaned in confidentially and rested her chin on her fist, even though her elbow was nowhere near the table; as if she was so ethereal that she could rest in mid-air.

"Such special circumstances that Russell had to break down the door with his shoulder." Perrin winked and rolled her eyes back toward Cassidy before reaching once more for her drink.

Cassidy and Jo might think they had Perrin bamboozled, but Maria wondered if it might not be the other way around. Perrin knew exactly why the "only get drunk together" rule existed, even if she cooperated with it for the sake of self-preservation, but she wasn't above getting vengeance on Cassidy for underestimating her.

Well, as two could play at that game, she winked back at Perrin before turning to Cassidy.

"So," Maria took a careful sip of her wine and reached for another piece of focaccia. "After Russell broke down the door and you were drunk all by yourself, did he get you naked?"

Perrin almost snorted her Cosmo.

CHAPTER 5

Maria decided she was awake, what she couldn't decide was if it was safe to be. She eyed the alarm clock accusingly, but it hadn't gone off. Not for three more minutes.

She turned it off and sat up tentatively but with only a little twinge. Perhaps, as Cassidy claimed, hangovers were lessened by good vintages and exceptional friends. For whatever reason, other than a small headache that a few aspirin would easily cure, she felt surprisingly good. In some ways she felt better than she had in a long time.

They been such…fun! Russell's mother, Julia Morgan, despite how close they'd been, had been her employer. Julia was the billionaire's wife, Maria was her personal chef. She'd had woman friends, but they had appeared and drifted away just as readily. Maria's entire life had been the Morgan family and raising the boys.

Last night had been a surprise in more ways than one. It hadn't just been a discovery of friends, it had also been a discovery of self. Of how much she'd enjoyed being with other women. Once over the initial surprise, the Terrible Trio had settled in and treated her no differently than they did one another. No layers of respect or distance.

Perrin had dubbed her Mama Maria and Cassidy had jumped right on board with the nickname. Only Jo, ever so reserved Jo, had called her simply Maria. And it hadn't added distance, instead it had somehow been closer, as if she'd truly gained a daughter-in-law.

They had even debated about who to set Maria up with. Perrin had offered several actors, a rock-and-roll guitarist, two different lawyers she'd become bored with, and might well have kept going if Maria hadn't diverted the conversation to who was going to someday capture Perrin's heart.

Maria had now daydreamed past her normal rising time and the baking awaited. Angelo's Pioneer Square condo had little personality, little to hold her here. When she first moved to Seattle, she'd considered fixing it up, imagining how she and Angelo would design it together. Place a large table in the middle of the dining room and always have it surrounded by friends and laughter and good food. Then Angelo had moved into Jo's gorgeous high-rise.

He, of course, in typical Angelo fashion had decorated nothing other than the kitchen. The rest of the rooms were clearly the result of a single run to IKEA. The darkly rich hardwood floor had a few scattered rugs. There were some cheery posters on the walls, but no art and little family.

It didn't feel neglected, it was far too nice a condominium for that. It was comfortable, but it didn't feel like home either. Fixing it up didn't seem important, not when it was just herself. As if it was temporary even though she had no reason to think it was.

There was so little to hold her here. So, she showered, chose a soft-wool red dress and a matching coat that always made her feel as if she were wrapped in a winter fire's warmth, and headed out.

Pioneer Square was still dark and quiet on the cold December morning. Unusually, the sky was clear and she could see the brighter stars and a quarter moon despite the streetlights. A couple of very early risers were shuffling out of the Lawrence Shelter, grabbing a quick smoke huddled together on the sidewalk while waiting for breakfast. She could already smell the characteristic notes on the still air of warming griddles and hot coffee. She hoped the man was still tucked in somewhere warm, she liked picturing the stranger that way.

First Avenue showed only a little of its reputedly seedy past, especially at this hour. The streets were quiet except for the occasional bus. She knew from experience, these were the very first runs of the day. Some mornings she'd step aboard rather than make the eight-block, uphill trek, but today she chose to enjoy the walk. It would also help her work off some of the splendid excesses of last night.

The sidewalk trees were lit with white Christmas lights strung through their branches making them appear coated in crystalline sugar. Shop windows had acquired buntings and garlands. Magic Mouse Toys was, of course, a child's dream of quirky toys. It wasn't New York's mad display at FAO Schwartz at a tenth the size, but it had a sweetness that the other lacked. The gray stone building and its brightly lit windows invited you in, even though the interior would be dark for hours yet.

A coffee shop, not yet open, had filled their window with an entire Santa's village landscape of miniatures, ranging across imaginary coffee-cup icebergs, down bagged-coffee hills.

She enjoyed her walk, a refreshing stroll. The three women, her three self-declared and sworn-for-life daughters, had given her much to think about last night.

There was a change coming.

She didn't know what it might be, but could feel it as surely as a sauce finally coming together. Maria felt that her life, like her cooking, was perhaps best if she let it run intuitively, so she would let it this time as well.

For thirty years her life had been about the stability of the Morgan household. Six months ago with her move to Seattle, it had become about Angelo's restaurant and his courtship of Jo. Maybe this time it would be about her.

She decided that her new friends would approve. If Maria saw change for herself coming, well, she'd welcome it.

HOGAN LOVED the city in the morning, before it was filled with people and crowds. Vera had been a night owl, but he was a morning person, often going for long walks while she still slept. Merely one of the thousand complaints she'd leveled at him.

He had leveled only one at her, infidelity. He only discovered in court the vast extent of her attempts to belittle his manhood, never mind their marriage. The worst part was that it had worked. His lawyer had made sure that she walked away without a single dime of his, and he'd crawled into his condo and disappeared.

Well, he was sick of that. It was time for him to climb back out of his hole. And he knew right where he was going to start. The next time he saw Maria, he'd straighten out all this nonsense of his being homeless and destitute. He might be a lost cause, but he didn't need charity. Not like so many he'd seen. He just needed—

A vision riveted Hogan to the sidewalk by the flower stall at the top of the Market. It was as if his feet had been glued to the brick-work. A woman was walking toward him. She was a vision of fire in the dark, a flame-wrapped wonder with a shock of dark hair that caught red from the streetlights and offered it up as a beacon in the night.

Maria. Before he could react, she had turned down the sidewalk into the Market, a turn that led her away from where he still stood in the shadows.

There would be no better chance than the present. Before he could think of a hundred reasons not to, he called out her name. She turned, and then her face lit with a smile of recognition.

She stopped and waited beneath the bright triple-globe of the antique streetlight that highlighted her like a shop-window ornament.

It took consciously forcing his knees to bend, but he did get his feet moving.

"Good morning, Maria." It didn't come out as too much of a croak, more as if he simply hadn't used his voice yet today. Didn't it?

"Good morning. You know, I don't even know how to call you."

"Hogan," *Dummy would be bloody appropriate as well.* "Hogan Stanford."

"A pleasure, Hogan Stanford." She held out a gloved hand which he shook after too long a hesitation.

He had lost all social graces.

"You couldn't have eaten before leaving the shelter. Aren't their breakfasts any good?"

"I, uh, wouldn't know," he only volunteered afternoons to help with the dinner service.

"Then where do you normally eat?"

He almost turned and pointed up at his condo window. It hung a dozen stories above them and a block to the side. But that felt stupid as if he were too clumsy to speak or explain. He started to form a sentence in his mind.

"You don't. Well, come with me. We'll take care of that." She slipped her hand about his elbow and began to lead him into the Market.

"No, wait, you don't even know me. I could be—" What, a crazed psycho? Even in her most vile epithets, Vera hadn't accused him of that. Hogan Q. Milquetoast had been her nickname for him in the courtroom, which had won her little ground with the judge.

Maria stopped and smiled up at him, as if she knew more about him that he did.

"I'm not poor," he finally blurted out.

"Of course not," Maria agreed amiably. "There are always people worse off than we are. That's kind of you, Hogan Stanford." She made to lead him off again.

The fishmonger, the one always loudly professing his undying love, began opening his shop. Just an easy shout away. He began relaxing on Maria's behalf, not that she needed protection from him.

This was all getting too muddled.

"Maria," he dug in his heels to keep them in place until this was settled.

She turned to face him once again with absolute patience, as if she were dealing with the feeble-minded. Her face wasn't angelic. It was far too filled with life to be so described. It was rich with laugh lines, full lips, and the most expressive eyes on the planet. Sophia Loren could envy such eyes.

"I don't eat at the shelter, because I volunteer there. I help out, I don't want to take their food."

"And you dress…"

He looked down and reassessed his clothes from an outsider's perspective, she'd judged him as broke because his clothes were old and worn. That wasn't it at all. He shrugged, "I dress…comfortably."

Maria covered her mouth with two gloved fingers of her free hand. In moments, he could see the look of consternation turning into a smile.

He smiled in response.

"Well, that's one on me, isn't it?" Her hand remained wrapped in the crook of his elbow. "Well, Mr. Stanford, I said that I was going to make you breakfast and I am. Come along."

Her gentle tug got him in motion.

"And while I'm cooking, you can explain how a man who is not poor, came to be at my window with no money."

Great. Once he explained that he'd only had hundred-dollar bills in his pocket, she'd probably think he was a drug-runner. No, they probably dressed better than he did.

MARIA WAS FIRST into the restaurant. She had always enjoyed this part of the day. The front of the house dark except for a few small sconce lights left on for safety. The kitchen lit only over her workspace, the rest of it filled with soft shadows and the fading reminders of last night's good smells.

She placed Hogan on a nearby stool and started a small pot of coffee.

"Can I help?"

"No, you are my guest. You may sit and tell me about yourself while I recover from my deep embarrassment."

"You don't look embarrassed, you look radiant."

She glanced up in time to see him blush. She was past blushing, but she wasn't past being flattered. She allowed him a moment to recover as she sliced day-old baguette and put it in the toaster. A nice, ripe Roma tomato slice, paper-thin bits of prosciutto, a dusting of minced basil, and a drizzle of olive oil on the toast. It was all ready just as the coffee finished brewing.

He still hadn't spoken, but it hadn't been an uncomfortable silence. She'd rather enjoyed having him watch her cook. Radiant? That was a good word, she liked that one. She set the breakfast between them on a single plate, and two large mugs of coffee. That was one of the American innovations that she liked, the ridiculously oversized coffee mug. What they lacked was any idea of what coffee should taste like. Even Seattle, so famous for its roasts, was typically lacking.

"Wow! That will wake you up," Hogan was staring down into his coffee mug as if it had just attacked him.

"What, you like weak American coffee?"

"No," he ignored her teasing tone. "But I do think that it's a good thing I'm not planning to try and sleep again this week. Have you seen my eyebrows anywhere? I think your coffee knocked them off my forehead." He began inspecting the kitchen floor as if he were indeed searching for them.

She pointed above his eyes.

He reached up and tested that they were still there before releasing a huge sigh of relief.

Maria felt the lifting of her spirits, but masked them with a bite of bruschetta.

He joined her. "Wow, that's perfect. 'The perfect bite' as they say on the cooking shows. But this can't be all you eat."

This time she actually laughed. "This is more than I usually eat. I make this for my guest. Italian breakfast is a biscuit or *cornetto* and strong coffee. It is enough."

"So, your morning window service, that is more properly Italian?"

"If they are plain or filled with a little honey or marmalade, yes. As I make them for Americans?" she shrugged.

Hogan was finding Maria to be very easy to talk with. Casual conversation had always been one of his weakest skills. He could lead a programming team of a hundred individuals and a half-dozen supervisors. What he couldn't do was meet them in the bar after work and not be stilted.

"I arrived at Microsoft just as they were launching their first really stable Windows platform. That was version 3.0a, back in 1989. Summer intern, hotshot geek straight out of the University of Washington."

"Local boy?"

"Yep. Born and raised." He became fascinated with watching her move about the kitchen. It wasn't that she was so beautiful. Okay, it wasn't only that. He liked to think he was above merely prurient fantasies, though Maria's body could convince him otherwise. But he did enjoy watching how she cooked aside from that. There was a confidence, an assuredness as she mixed flour, yeast, butter and a half-dozen other ingredients. No recipe, no second guessing, rarely any measuring cups.

"True locals are pretty rare according to Angelo." Her voice was as rich as her coffee was strong. He liked food metaphors for her, they seemed to fit naturally.

He shook off the fascination with what she was doing and refocused on the conversation. "We are. I always say that Seattle is forty percent California refugees, forty percent East Coast refugees, ten percent from the Midwest, though no one knows why, and ten percent natives, but we're hiding."

Her laugh was musical. It lit the darkened kitchen far more than the spotlight dangling over her station. He scratched his head and wondered how on earth he could possibly make her laugh again. It was a sound he could never tire of hearing.

"And you are in hiding? From what?"

That stopped him. Yes, he certainly was in hiding, but how to explain the darkness inside him to this brilliantly shining woman who stood before him. She'd have no way to understand something so polar opposite to who she was.

"Myself mostly." Far too close to the truth. Couldn't he have just said "Californians" or "lawyers" or "hipsters" or anything else funny? No, he never thought up the punch line until two beats too late. The first beat, when it would have been funny if he'd said it then. The second beat, right after he'd said something far too true.

Back in his old life someone might say, "The system crashes every time I run your code."

He couldn't think to reply, "Have you tried walking it instead?" No, he had to stammer and apologize and promise to work harder. Though he'd become a hell of a good programmer just so he could stop apologizing for his hard work.

"Who was she?" Maria took the dough she'd been preparing and put it in a big standup refrigerator, pulling out another large batch she must have started yesterday.

"My wife."

He saw a brief flash of disappointment across Maria's features. So fleeting that he wondered if even she was aware of it.

"My ex-wife," he corrected.

"And she hurt you so badly?"

What was it with this conversation? Not only was he several steps too exposed, he couldn't appear to catch up with it at all.

"She…" How to describe the impact her vast betrayal had had upon him. Who was he kidding, that it still had upon him.

No. He couldn't face the next sentence. It was too hard.

"Perhaps I should leave you to your cooking. Thank you for—"

Maria aimed a slender rolling pin at his chest across the table.

"No. You can't leave yet. You haven't finished your breakfast."

He looked down. There were still several bruschetta on the plate and his coffee was barely half empty. "If I drink any more of your coffee, I'll need an FAA license for flying through restricted airspace."

Her gentle smile was no less potent than her laugh. "Well," Maria attacked the dough with a dusting of flour and a great deal of energy.

"I wouldn't want to get you in trouble with the FAA. Perhaps you need a lesson in flying under the radar."

"Nowhere low enough to escape Vera's radar." Even to himself he sounded pissed and bitter.

Maria stopped rolling out the dough and studied him for a long moment. Her dark eyes were shadowed by the overhead light. He could feel himself spread as thin as the dough with all his faults clearly visible. Here was where she decided he was too screwed up to bother dealing with and she'd send him on his way.

"There is now a new rule."

"There is?"

"There is," she nodded emphatically to herself. "Yes, it is a good rule. Until I tell you otherwise, Mr. Hogan Stanford, you are not allowed to say that name again or talk about her in any way. Not even to yourself if you can help it."

All he could do was stare at her. "You're serious?"

"You doubt that, you ask my son. Don't mess with Mama Maria. *Proibito!* You will not talk about her, refer to her, what is the word I want, *alludere?*"

"Allude?"

"That simple? Yes, you will not even do that. Not until I decide you are cured of whatever cloud she made over your head."

"She—"

Maria cut him off with a sharp gesture of a single finger to her lips. "I will stop you every time you mention her. Who else do you talk to about her? You must tell them also to stop you."

"Uh, I don't talk to anyone else."

She turned back to her dough, setting a dinner plate rim-down on the dough. With a quick trace of her knife around the edge, she cut a circle. Lifting the plate, she sliced a dozen lines through the dough with the tip of a sharp knife creating long thin triangles that all met at the center.

"No one else?" She didn't look up from her task. It was as if she was giving him a safe space to speak from.

"Not really." He sipped his coffee.

She plopped spoonfuls of a light-yellow custard at the wide ends of the triangles. She rolled them up one by one and the *cornetti* came into being. Placing them on a baking tray, she gave a practiced flick to shape them as crescents. In moments they were lined up, smeared with butter, and adorned with slivered almonds and lemon zest. He could hardly wait to try one. Unbaked, they already looked beautiful.

She maintained her silence until she had completed several trays and slid them into the large ovens ranging along the wall. With a quick swipe, she cleaned off the prep table, then sat on the stool across from him. Taking a bruschetta and her coffee, she finally looked up at him.

It wasn't a look he'd expected. There was no judgment, that he was too much of a loner or what was wrong with him that he didn't have any friends. It was a look of sorrow.

"I talk to everybody." Then she studied the darkness above the worktable lights for a long time before facing him again.

There was just the two of them and the single light. They both sat in the shadows on opposite sides of the table. Mostly what was visible was her hands and her white porcelain cup shining beneath the light.

"But other than three woman I know, I think I too may be as alone."

Hogan couldn't imagine how that could be possible, but he didn't question it either. She was clearly a thoughtful woman. She had noticed what he had not, that he had let his life be defined by his past.

"I'm going to return the favor," he raised his coffee mug as if proposing a toast.

"What favor is that?" Though she raised her mug to share the toast.

"I will agree to not speak about, well, you know who. And you will agree to call on me any time you need someone to really talk to. It doesn't have to be about anything, and it can be at three in the morning."

"A new friend?"

He shrugged, "We all have to start somewhere."

After a long moment, that smile lit her face. Really lit it, her eyes shining from the shadows.

"Have to start somewhere? But where does that mean you are heading?"

Huh! He didn't have an answer to that one. He was still surprised that for the first time in a long time, he was really looking forward to spending time with someone.

"I guess we'll have to find that out along the way."

CHAPTER 6

*H*ogan's *door buzzer snapped* him out of his morose contemplation of the terrible programming on television for the night. He'd been at a loss all day. His attempts to follow Maria's directive not to think about Vera only seemed to have thrown his past into the forefront of his mind. By now it was making him totally crazy. At least he hadn't scorched the chowder pot at the shelter again. Of course, they were having minestrone tonight which didn't burn unless you did something too stupid for even his present state of mind.

He opened the door and almost fell back in shock. There stood Maria Parrano, lovely in a dark blue dress and the same red woolen coat as this morning. Muted with the contrasting blue, she appeared mysterious rather than as a flame under this morning's streetlight. Mysterious was certainly appropriate, as it was a complete mystery as to why she was tolerating him, never mind seeking him out.

"May I come in?" Her voice teased him for his gawking and fumbling, but did it with a kindness.

"Of course." It was only as she entered, that he noticed the two flattened moving boxes under one arm.

"What are those for?"

"Hogan Stanford," she stopped and looked up at him. "There are several things you need to learn for us to be friends. The first is to greet me, the second is to be a gentleman and offer to take my coat."

He fumbled his way through that. She set aside the boxes without explanation.

"Do I get a tour? Or do we remain standing in your entry hall?"

He slapped his forehead with a loud smack. *Get your act together, Stanford.* He took a deep breath to calm himself and then offered her his arm. She took it lightly as he led her in.

THE SHORT HALL opened onto a living room that took Maria's breath away. It wasn't the furnishing, which was nice enough, if a little sparse. It was the view. Hogan's home was far lower than Jo and Angelo's condominium with its magnificent view from high above Seattle. Hogan's view was no less stunning, but it was also intimate in its closeness to the scenery. The ice-capped Olympic Mountains towered in the dark orange of the evening sky. Elliot Bay was spread before them as not even Cutter's Bar had shown it off last night. And, as they came up to the glass, she could see Pike Place Market spread at her feet. It made the world look like it was the inside of a jewel box.

"Why Hogan, this is *fantastico*."

"Uh, thanks. Why are you here?"

She could hear that he hadn't intended it to sound offensive. Maria considered teasing him about it, but decided that a man so unaware of how he was communicating perhaps cared very much about what he was communicating. So, rather than skewering him like a kebab, she answered his question honestly.

"I'm here to help. Why don't you fetch those two boxes while I admire the view a bit more?"

He moved to comply and she turned to inspect the room. The living room had a soft brown leather sofa and matching chair that looked well lived in. That would be his preferred spot. They faced the view more than the television, which she would take as a good sign.

There was a neatness that was surprising for a man so casual about his attire.

The low coffee table sported only the television remotes, a book, and a couple of magazines, *Wired* and *Cook's Illustrated*. Leave it to a computer guy to enjoy the terribly quantitative approach to cooking. She herself had few written recipes, primarily following her instincts and her taste buds.

Another amusing observation that she'd keep to herself were those two magazines. The first was heavily thumbed, a dozen different pages with the corners folded down; clearly topics Hogan wanted to think about and consider more at a later time. *Cook's* was almost pristine. A small crease indicated that it had probably been read, but it didn't inspire.

Beyond the sofa, a long oak table and formal chairs defined a dining space, but looked not just unused, but wholly uninhabited. It should be crowded with friends and family. A jovial gathering place for coming together each week and remembering life's joys in the company of others. Well, it was not her place to suggest such things in another's life, but if she lived here, it would look as well used as Hogan's chair, not like a museum piece.

The space itself was interesting: the view to the front, a long wall of books to the side, a somewhat barren wall backed the dining table, that should be covered with photos of friends and adventures, but perhaps he didn't have any to hang. The doors to the other side wall must lead to kitchen and bedroom.

Hogan returned with the boxes, and Maria fished a roll of packing tape out of her purse. In moments they were assembled.

He was clearly restraining his questions. Perhaps he had learned that she would only answer them as she saw fit. Meant he was smart about people, whether he communicated that graciously or not.

"Now, my friend Mr. Stanford. You are going to go through your apartment. Everything that was a gift from, or reminds you in any bad way about the woman, who you still aren't allowed to speak of, you will hand to me, and I will pack it away."

"Then what?"

"Then we will put these boxes into storage somewhere. Later you may decide if you ever want to open them again. I'm hoping that you have enough good sense that two boxes will be enough. If you have held onto too much, we can get more boxes. You should also feel free to simply throw things out as well." She went back to the coat rack by the front door and retrieved a couple of black plastic garbage bags from her coat pocket. "You don't even have to touch anything. You can just point and tell me box or bag."

Then she began to wonder again about the magazines. She walked over and picked up the issue of *Cook's Illustrated.* Maria held it up as a question.

HOGAN STOOD FROZEN, riveted in place in his own living room by the steady gaze of a woman half-a-head shorter than he was. How had she known? He was interested in cooking, enjoyed the editor's opening story and the science behind what they did.

It hadn't been Vera's magazine, but rather one she kept gifting him year in and year out even though he never cooked anything from it. Yet another little guilt trip he hadn't recognized? Perhaps.

Then he eyed the woman holding the magazine for his decision.

His first instinct was that Maria was trying to be controlling, as Vera had been. Then he winced, knowing he wasn't supposed to be thinking of her, an almost impossible mandate. Contradictory. How do you stop thinking about someone you've been told specifically to be aware of every time you thought about her? A tautological conundrum at best, at worst...bloody impossible.

It was also a depressing shock quite how easily Vera entered his thoughts though the last of the divorce-related tasks was over six months past.

Knowing his first instincts were not to be trusted in anything to do with Vera, he decided that there were two other primary possibilities as to what Maria was up to. First, Maria could be trying to clear any Vera remnants out of his condo to make way for herself. Since she'd thought he was a bum until this morning and he'd not told her how well off he truly was, he thought that unlikely. Second, maybe he should take her statement at face value. Perhaps she was simply that kind.

A feeling ran through him that he was having trouble identifying. A part of him wanted to wrap his arms around her and simply weep.

She didn't wait for him to respond. Reading his expression, she tossed it into the garbage bag. He'd have to remember to cancel the subscription. If he renewed it later, it would be at a later time on his own for his own reasons.

Maria turned once more to await him patiently. Now he had an image of doing something other than weeping on her shoulder.

Not trusting himself to speak, he turned to the bookcase and took down a small brass elephant bookend. It was nice work, but every time he looked at it he could see Vera cooing to the French merchant in Lyons. Bent forward, cleavage very much on show, "her best bargaining position" she always called it. Had she slept with him too? He cast the thought aside and handed the elephant to Maria.

No longer supported, several books fell over. He flopped the first six books on their side and shoved them over as an impromptu bookend.

"What's next?" She returned to stand stalwartly at his elbow.

It was a slow process at first, but one that picked up pace quickly. Box and bag. A lot of bag. A small oil painting in hideous colors that had matched only the hideous price tag. Book gifts he'd never wanted to read to begin with started the "to sell without waiting" box. The runner on the oak table. Knick knacks. Where had all of the knick knacks come from?

Then he started at the front door and began working his way toward the picture windows along the other side of his condo. The office was purely his, no, there was that stupid picture. He was the only one in it, but he could feel her behind the camera. In the bathroom, the toothbrush mug.

How had she insinuated herself so far into his life? Fifteen years of marriage, the last three apparently rife with adultery, was how.

The bedroom, with its view of Queen Anne Hill to the north, was fairly clean. Some old hangers, some ties that he'd never wear again if his life depended on it, and a girlie lamp on the other side of the bed, all pink and fake Victorian.

Each item he identified was whisked from his hands before it could burn his fingers, gone.

He was hardly aware of Maria anymore. She had become an extension of his own thoughts, and a focus for them. With her beside him, he felt strong, able to deal. And with each item they removed, he felt a layer stripped clear. As if Maria were paring him down, peeling off the hard rind to expose…something. The question of what might remain after the last Vera layers were gone was one he wouldn't contemplate at the moment.

Last was the kitchen. The only part of Vera that was here, other than a few more mugs he could hardly bear to handle, was the espresso machine. A good one. It had been a Christmas gift, in a good year. He used it every day.

He turned to Maria and she must have seen the confusion on his face.

"Was it a good memory?"

He could only nod, a tightness in his throat had cut off any words. He'd lost so much. He'd lost his image of a happy family and a happy home. Worse, he'd lost any hope of a happy version of himself. But the espresso machine was from before that time. Vera had given the machine to him when they couldn't afford it, by scraping together an entire year's worth of a dollar per day stuffed into a jar. He'd bought her a used DVD set of some British comedy she'd liked, and she'd given him one of the best home espresso machines made.

What was he supposed to do with that? So much gone. This too?

He slumped back against one of the cabinets and slid down to sit on the floor. Tired. It had been too much, like a knife driven into his guts. It might hurt like hell, but to remove it would hurt even worse.

Maria settled to the floor beside him. It was jarring. He thought of her as so beautiful and such a lady. Yet, other than her dress forcing her to sit with her legs folded neatly to one side, she was probably younger than he was. She said she'd had Angelo when she was young. That meant before twenty. He was newly married at thirty. Maybe she was a year or so older than he was, though that was wholly impossible to credit. She looked and acted so much younger than he felt. Either way, he was sitting on the floor but it still felt strange to see her do so.

She bumped a shoulder against his. As if she were simply offering support. Which is exactly what she'd been doing for, he glanced at the kitchen clock, for almost two hours.

"I'm such a goddamn mess."

"You are."

He laughed, "At least you could not agree with me so readily." He could smell her, without even turning to face her. Warm and spice. Like a winter cider but fresh, so fresh. Like mint or apples on the air.

"I hate to tell you this, Hogan, but you're human. So, you're a mess." Her tone was completely matter of fact.

"But," he didn't know how to express it. "But you're so perfect."

"If you think that, Mr. Hogan Stanford, then perhaps it is time I was going."

"No! You can't. I need to figure this out first." He scrambled around in his brain for some way to not admit out loud what an utterly ridiculous pedestal he had her on. Of course she was human, he just hadn't thought it through until this moment. But he knew absolutely that he didn't want her to leave.

"It's a disguise right?" He turned to her and they were face-to-face only inches apart. The closeness did nothing to change his opinion of her. Her dusky complexion, her thoughtful dark eyes, her outrageously thick hair were all as real as they'd been when she sat in her window like a painted Venus.

"What's a disguise?" Her voice was a little more than a whisper.

"Your perfection. You certainly had me fooled. Here I was thinking you were the perfect woman, which is, as you've pointed out, of course totally impossible. So, I figure you're an alien in disguise. Am I right?"

She eyed him suspiciously, but couldn't fight back the smile that tugged at those full lips.

No longer able to think while this close to her, he leaned in and kissed her.

MARIA KNEW she should be shocked. She was, but not in a bad way. She'd been watching Hogan carefully as she helped him clear the apartment of the unwanted portion of his past. He was decisive. Not bull in a china shop like Russell or driven like Angelo into high-energy flurries that left her and everyone else around him, except apparently Jo, utterly exhausted. Hogan was steady, made decisions quickly with little fuss.

Maria would have said his movements were elegant, but that wasn't quite right. What they were was immensely efficient. Never carry one thing when you could carry three. No returning to clean up what was left behind as pieces were removed, but rather fixing the space immediately. She'd have purged the place, then gone back and tried to figure out what to do with the mess she'd left behind. Hogan's condo looked as well organized as the moment she'd come in; no sign, except in the mounds covering the dining table, that there was substantially less of it.

What shocked her about Hogan's kiss was how good it felt, how natural. She barely knew the man.

For that matter, she barely knew the woman who slid a hand up to tickle her fingers through his hair. Not even with her boyfriend Angelo, the one who had seduced and left her before she was seventeen and for whom her son had been named, had she been so forward. And the men she'd chosen since coming to America, she'd chosen carefully and rarely.

Hogan eased back without pulling away.

"Don't you dare say you're sorry," she whispered, her voice surprisingly husky.

"I'm not, trust me." His voice was in little better condition. Then he kissed her on the forehead. "Surprised, yes. At both of us. But sorry, not one little bit."

"Oh," Maria was a little surprised at both of them as well. She waved a hand toward where they were sitting. "You appear to have swept my feet out from under me."

"That too appears to be mutual. Hell of a place for a first kiss."

"Yes. Years from now we'll be able to say, 'Well, we always had the kitchen floor'."

He laughed, a warm, deep sound that welcomed her in.

"You know," he kissed her forehead once more slowly. "You're doing a lousy job of ruining your disguise of being perfect."

"I'll have to work on that." But she wasn't going to work at it too hard. Not with how good it felt to be leaning up against him.

"*And what then?" Perrin* leaned in close and eager.

Maria wasn't quite sure why she'd called Perrin for lunch. It was Monday and the restaurant was closed. She also hadn't expected Jo and Cassidy to show up as well, though she should have. They were so close that you couldn't call one without calling all three. Perrin's shop was nearby, Cassidy's office was in her home just a few blocks from the Market, and Jo was the Market's Managing Director, even if it was technically her day off as well.

The four of them sat upstairs at Lowell's Restaurant in the Market, a small table close against the windows facing the Sound. She and Perrin were splitting a Chicken Apple Salad, Jo and Cassidy a Grilled Vegetable Panzanella, a Tuscan rustic bread salad.

"He made me an espresso."

Perrin's eyes practically crossed in her confusion, or perhaps disappointment. "You didn't push him down on the floor and use his body until you couldn't stay conscious any longer?"

Maria could hear Cassidy and Jo trying to leap in and cover for her. But they didn't understand yet that Maria needed no protecting, especially not from Perrin.

"I thought about it, but not yet."

Perrin didn't look away, as if Maria's sex life was the most interesting thing on the planet.

"But I knew a part of him wanted me to. So, I left him something to think about."

"Ooo, Jo was right. You are scary smart." Perrin looked impressed. Impressed and thoughtful. She might do well with a little more thinking before she gave away her heart next time.

"So, espresso?" Cassidy went for the subject change.

"Yes, he had this beautiful machine that his wife had given him. He loved the machine, he just hated her connection to it. So I had him make me a decaf espresso which we drank with a delivered Chinese dinner."

"So…" Perrin leaned back in, clearly still eager for more details. "You connected it to you."

Maria guessed that she had, though that wasn't her intent. Then she considered what else had happened last night.

She'd enjoyed herself. Immensely.

Hogan had been both interested in her and interesting himself. They had talked late into the evening. He had tried to call a cab for her, she'd insisted on walking, wanted the fresh air to clear her head. He had insisted on walking with her, her hand comfortable in the crook of his arm as they strolled along.

At the front door to her building Hogan had proven two things. One, that he was an absolute gentleman; she'd had to be the one to kiss him. And second, that first kiss hadn't been a fluke at all. He was very gentle, but he was also very thoughtful. She could practically hear his brain working on how to improve the kiss moment by moment. Maria had let him, simply enjoying the experience. She'd hoped for electricity and had actually found the lightning she'd asked for. Maria Parrano had gone to bed alone, but very content with the world.

"Better he connects with me than that awful woman. I don't know what she did to him, but it must have been horrid."

"Damaged goods," Perrin nodded sagely. "They can be so much fun to fix up."

Maria nodded to let Perrin have the round, but it wasn't what she was thinking.

Hogan Stanford wasn't damaged, but she'd wager he wasn't often understood. Probably not even by himself, perhaps especially not. He was absolutely forthright. What he said, he was. His words fit him. If he disagreed with someone, he'd say it, often so bluntly that it sounded offensive, but it wasn't. Because when he agreed, he was just as blunt and to the point. Other than his occasionally quirky sense of humor, he was exactly as he appeared to be.

Jo and Cassidy had turned to a discussion of the latest bizarre-husband behavior that their new spouses were exhibiting.

Maria interrupted, "To quote Julia Morgan when talking about Angelo and Russell: They're perfect. Because they are perfectly themselves."

"That, Maria, is absolute truth," Jo agreed. The two girls continued comparing notes over their salad.

"Perfect." Just like Hogan, she thought to herself. Perfectly himself.

"What was that?" Only Perrin had overheard Maria's whisper to herself.

"That's what Hogan said I was."

Perrin studied her for a long moment, and then wrapped Maria in one of her open-hearted hugs and kissed Maria on the cheek.

"Of course you are. If he didn't see that in you, he wouldn't deserve you."

Maria held onto her for an extra moment. Now she knew exactly why she'd called Perrin.

HOGAN MET HER, as promised, right after he was finished with volunteering at the shelter.

Maria had offered to make him dinner, but he'd insisted that he had that covered and she should dress warmly. She waited for him outside the shelter, not minding the cold air, though she had worn slacks and a bright knit vest under her coat. Seattle's damp chill was still not as penetrating as the deep cold of New York City winters.

"You're here!" Hogan came up beside her, his face still bright from the kitchen's heat.

"You thought I wouldn't be?"

He kissed her quickly, though not the least perfunctorily, taking the initiative this time, which she liked. He lingered long enough to heat her blood like a schoolgirl's and then began leading her down Yesler Way toward the waterfront.

"I thought that I had made it all up and you couldn't possibly be real. Do you have any idea what it was like to wake up in my apartment without all of Ver—herself's detritus in it?"

He gave her an effusive hug whirling her around three times until her own head was spinning and she actually needed his arm to stabilize herself.

"You're a miracle!" He practically shouted it to the sky. "I dealt with everything last night. After you left, I took out all of the garbage, dropped the books off here at the shelter, and that last box of questionable stuff is down in my basement storage locker. I'm free!" He shot his arms above his head for a moment as if scoring a goal.

His transformation was startling. As if someone had taken away the Hogan Stanford that she was just starting to know and replaced him. He continued to guide her along the evening-lit streets, his left hand clasped warmly over where her own was tucked in his right elbow, she allowed herself to bask in his new-found energy.

Nor was she immune to the compliment of his constant glances in her direction. No woman could be.

"There's something terribly touristy, that any self-respecting local boy could never admit to wanting to do. But taking his girl on a date, that's a good enough excuse, isn't it?"

'His girl?' Maria could barely catch her breath. He made her feel absolutely giddy. "What happened to the Hogan Stanford I met only yesterday?"

"Only yesterday? Wow! That can't be right." He stopped for a moment to blink at her like a surprised owl caught unexpectedly in a searchlight. "Yesterday? And I just kissed you like..." He trailed off uncertainly.

She thought about repeating her warning to not say he was sorry. She didn't want to be with a man who was sorry that he'd kissed her and made her feel so wonderful and desirable. Instead, she pulled him down to her and kissed him long and hard. He barely hesitated, wrapping her tight against him as they stood in the middle of a busy Seattle sidewalk.

They were quiet when they started walking again. It was as if they'd both gone too far and yet neither had gone far enough. She finally had to speak, to say something.

"You're right. Yesterday can't be right. If we met just yesterday then I would be a wanton hussy and you a hustler."

"I dunno. A hustler?" He nodded to himself. "Never been accused of that, but it sounds kind of cool, doesn't it?"

"I have no desire to be a hussy."

"Couldn't if you tried," was his immediate response. "Too much of the lady in you."

They continued until they crossed beneath the towering Seattle Viaduct. Two tiers, each three lanes wide, of highway that dominated the Seattle Waterfront. He had to speak up for her to hear him over the traffic noise.

"I don't know if I'll recognize Seattle when this comes down next year. My dad talked about this being built when he was kid. That would have been the fifties I guess."

The change to the Seattle skyline would be dramatic. It was presently dark and dingy beneath the towering roadway. But old factories were being replaced with boutique stores in anticipation. The change was happening slowly, but it was coming. Soon they would all be exposed to the sunlight and the waterfront would bloom.

They crossed Alaskan Way and reached the broad sidewalk that ran in front of the piers, stretching off down the entire Seattle waterfront. Just two nights ago she had said to the other members of the Fearsome Foursome that she was open to change. Suddenly, everywhere she turned, change appeared to be confronting her.

"So, Mr. Whatever-you-have-done-with-Hogan, what is this terribly touristy thing?"

Like a conjuring magician, he waved his hand to the left. They stepped clear of the cheerfully jostling crowd at the outdoor counter of the Crab Pot Seafood Bar, busy despite the cold.

There, rising above the end of the old wooden pier soared Seattle's newest wonder. The Seattle Great Wheel towered seventeen stories above the waterfront. The massive Ferris wheel, sporting thousands of white lights and dozens of gently swaying gondolas, commanded the waterfront.

Maria looked up at Hogan, who had paused to await her reaction.

"You're right. It is terribly touristy. So, Mr. Stanford, if we get a gondola alone, what kind of a good time are you planning to show 'your girl'?"

That got the expected blush and made her feel rather better. As if he'd just confirmed that the real Hogan Stanford hadn't gone anywhere at all.

* * *

THEY DID INDEED GET their own gondola, not much of a crowd appeared on a Monday evening in early December. Three times around the Great Wheel, just the two of them. Maria knew exactly how horrified Perrin would be that they didn't make some use of their unexpected privacy, but the view out the window was too spectacular.

They sat side-by-side on the padded bench seat, comfortably holding hands. First, they climbed toward the city. It revealed itself in layers, first Alaskan Way running along the waterfront, then the double-deck of the Viaduct, until it too lay far below. Finally the city itself, its soaring skyscrapers like torches lighting the night sky, striving ever upward.

"It's such a young city," Maria gazed out at the shining skyscrapers. So many of them clearly born just in that last decade or so.

"Are you implying that we aren't?"

"I'm still young," Maria laughed. "There is too much life still ahead of me for me to feel otherwise. How about you?"

He kissed her on the temple then turned back to the view. "You make me feel as foolish as when I was twenty. It's quite an odd feeling. Had you asked me a week ago, I might have told you just how ancient I was feeling. But from the moment I saw you a dozen stories below, I began to understand that I was alive for the first time in far too long."

As they reached the apex of the Ferris wheel, Maria tried not to feel uncomfortable. First, just how long had he been spying on her before she'd noticed him hovering beyond her take-out window? He was sounding a bit like a stalker.

Second, she was no one's savior. She was no great heroine. And the man who saw her that way was due for a future let-down of immense proportion. Did she want to be around for that? For the chaos of his emotions? The fall was a long way down. The pity was that she really liked him and didn't want to have to put up barriers between them.

Perhaps detecting her thoughts, Hogan leaned his shoulder gently against hers increasing their connection.

She considered pulling back, but was stopped by his soft voice, barely louder than the sighing of the wind around the gondola car and the gentle creak of its bearings.

"I'm not crazy, Maria. It is not because of you that I realized this, at least not really you."

"You're making even less sense than usual, Hogan."

She could see his silhouette nodding in the dark as they started down. The wheel reached well out over the water of Elliot Bay, a vast darkness below lit only occasionally by ferries and other small boats.

"I know. I'm good at that, aren't I?" He made it sound as if he were a little boy fishing for a compliment.

Maria laughed dutifully, but didn't feel it.

"What I saw from my high window that drew me out into the world again was a woman walking through the Market, I didn't know anything about her. She could have been eighteen or eighty. All I knew was that in a city of grays and blacks and REI jackets, she stood out. She wore a sky blue wool coat down to her calves and the brightest gold hat I've ever seen. I spent a week walking the Market, looking to once more find that flash of color. To find the woman who would dress so brightly and uniquely."

He pointed out a shining ferry leaving dock from just a few piers down. It sparkled on the dark water. Maria knew they shared the same thought of it being pretty enough to point out, but not wanting to interrupt the conversation. Such simple communication between them. Perhaps he wasn't really all that strange.

"That whole week I spent looking and hoping, simply wanting to see how alive someone like that must appear up close. Knowing there was little or no chance of finding her, still I searched. What I realized was that I was searching for something more important. I'd lost a piece of myself somewhere. Lost it so badly that I had to wander about pretending I could find it somewhere other than within myself."

Maria liked this story. Could feel his absolute involvement in it. This wasn't some tale a man told to a woman he was interested in. This wasn't a stalker who had followed her, he was a man looking for himself. He was working it out even as they swung down closer and closer to departing ferry.

"I don't know who it was that I saw from my high window. There's no way for me to tell, but I like to think that it was you."

Maria kept her lips tightly pressed together. The coat and hat he had described were indeed hanging in her closet, though she'd never thought of them as anything special.

"By the time I spotted you in your Botticelli window—"

"My what?" She turned to study him as they swung through the lights at the bottom of the wheel's arc and started their second journey around the wheel.

"That's how you look. Didn't you know? Right down to the simple golden frame around your window at Angelo's. I thought it was famil- iar, so looked it up online. It's almost a perfect match for the one around Botticelli's *Allegory of Spring* hanging in Florence."

She was going to kill Russell. Maria had just thought it was pretty wood trim. But of course Mr. World-famous-photographer Russell, who had such an amazing eye for art and composition, would have known exactly what he was doing when he had so kindly offered to set her up with a way to sell breakfast treats and gain new customers for Angelo's restaurant. She'd have to check the outside wall to make sure there was no little "description of the image" plaque bolted up as if she were hanging in a museum.

"Anyway, at that moment, I didn't care if I found that lady or not. For what I saw before me was a woman who clearly understood that life was a gift. It's something I lost sight of, maybe long ago."

They climbed once more into the city's night sky. But Hogan wasn't watching it. He was staring out the window as if desperately searching for some earlier version of himself.

"Maybe that's what Vera took out of me. Sorry, I know I'm not supposed to mention her."

"I give you dispensation this one time," she kept her voice gentle, not wanting him to stop.

He nodded his acknowledgement but his attention was still far away. "I'm not sure though. Maybe it was partly the job. Or a combination of things, some good, some bad. I had to see someone who reveled in the light, reveled in life itself to remind me of what was so important. You do that. It is so rare, so special, how could you not draw me like a beacon."

Now he turned to face her, so close she could see his eyes clearly despite the dim lighting of the waterfront falling behind them as they again swung downward.

"From now on I want to surround myself with people who think being alive is a gift. It has essential importance. I now see that Eric, the man who founded the shelter I volunteer at, has that. You have that. All I can hope to do is find some of that joy in myself and share that as well."

Maria tried to still her pounding heart. Tried to keep her reaction inside her, hidden, to how wonderful a man sat beside her.

She didn't remember the third turn of the Great Wheel at all. Her knees were weak and her lips ever so pleasantly sore as Hogan led her off the Ferris wheel and took her to dinner.

CHAPTER 8

"Are you okay, Mama?"

Maria blinked hard then looked down at what she'd been cooking. The ginger jam that she'd been simmering had scorched. A *bagnomaria* of chocolate had overheated and separated, which was exactly what the double boiler was supposed to prevent. She hadn't done that since she was a little girl standing on a kitchen chair to help her grandmother cook.

"Fine. I'm fine." She began cleaning up the mess. A glance at the clock said that she still had time if she stayed focused. Which would be much easier if she weren't so preoccupied by memories of how Hogan had made her body feel on that third time around the Ferris wheel. Men had fondled her breasts, but Hogan had worshipped them with his hands. He'd scooped her into his lap and run his lips down her neck and his hands over her body until—

"Mama?"

Angelo stood close beside her. A worried look on his face. She patted his cheek and insisted she was fine. He eyed her carefully before slowly rejoining Manuel on the cook line. They were experimenting on a dish for the new restaurant.

Angelo's Tuscan Hearth, which actually leaned more toward

Ligurian fare, was primarily seafood. Liguria lay north of Tuscany, a thin slice of the coast, but it was lesser known. So, Angelo and Russell had named it for the more popular Tuscany. The new restaurant, Angelo's Piedmont Hearth, was a concession to the American clientele rather than the Italian "Piemonte." It would have a whole new menu, based on the stronger-bodied wines of the mountains and the meatier fare of the region.

Maria began scouring the pots quickly. By the time she'd turned back to the cook line, Graziella was there laying out fresh ginger, sugar, and chocolate.

"I know that look, Ms. Parrano."

"What look?" Maria did her best to sound innocent and knew she failed miserably.

"The same look that I saw in the mirror this morning."

Maria inspected her and now saw it blooming out of her. How had Maria missed it, the girl was radiant. A glance at the cook line showed Manuel was very focused on his cooking. How was it that Graziella looked radiant, Manuel was totally in control, and she was an absolute distracted mess with the attention span of a parakeet?

Graziella must have noticed her attention and her scowl. "He fouled the sauce twice before Angelo came in. This is his third try."

Maria laughed and felt much better.

"He is treating you well?"

The young woman's smile and sigh was confirmation enough.

"When do we meet the man putting that smile on your face?"

Maria focused on coarse-chopping the chocolate while Graziella rebuilt the honey-based sugar syrup for the jam.

"Oh, I know him already, don't I? Your special customer. The one Manuel cooked breakfast for. Your charity case?" She turned it into a question of surprise.

"Hogan Stanford is many things, but it turns out that a charity case is not among them. At least not the way I thought he was."

"Who is Hogan Stanford?" Russell snapped a photo with that fancy camera of his.

"Where did you come from?" Maria hadn't heard him come in and didn't know why he was aiming his camera at her. He shifted to the side for a different angle and she threatened him with the chocolate-coated wooden spoon she'd been using to stir with. He took the picture, of course, though he did back off a step.

"I came from New York. But you know that. Not getting forgetful in your dotage, are you Ms. Parrano?"

"Just because you turned out so tall and handsome and I can no longer lay you over my knee, don't think that my spoon is any slower." She had used it frequently to whack him on the knuckles when he and Angelo were young and constantly trying to snatch bits from her cooking pot before they were served.

Graziella stirred the forming syrup to make sure that it heated evenly and didn't foam, "Can I have a demonstration? It sounds like a useful skill."

"I am here by invitation, Maria," Russell insisted. He backed off another step, just in case she decided to carry out her threat, and ran into a dish rack with a large clatter.

"We thought that to advertise the new restaurant, we should introduce the people behind the swinging doors. 'From our kitchen to your table' kind of feel. Make it personal. I wanted to start with two amazingly beautiful women, you know, sex appeal and all that." He gave a knowing leer that looked quite comical because they all knew how besotted he was by Cassidy.

Maria had to admit that it was a good idea and didn't mind the compliment even though it was just so much *fesserie*. And while she didn't like having her picture taken unawares, she knew Russell would make her look so pretty that she wouldn't recognize herself. And with young and glowing Graziella beside her, Maria expected it would come out very well indeed.

"So, who is Hogan Stanford?" He snapped a picture of her protest, but it didn't save his knuckles from a quick rap.

HOGAN WAS IMPRESSED with himself when he visited Maria's window.

He didn't hesitate, or avoid, or have to walk around the block three times. He simply queued up with the others, and other than a brief flash of a smile shared with Maria, he became just another customer waiting his turn. Someone was moving around snapping photos with a very high-end camera. Publicity photos maybe. Hogan almost felt as if he'd look like he fit into the scene.

The December morning was clear and cold, at least for Seattle, upper-thirties. Maria had selected a sweater of soft gray. It was all vertically ribbed, emphasizing the trimness of her waist and her exceptionally fine full-figure. Who was he kidding with that? Fine full-figure indeed. As if he were a priggish poet given to abundant alliteration.

Her magnificent breasts. He could feel his cheeks warm even as he thought the words, but to call them less wouldn't be appropriate either. Not for the man who had just last night so appreciated their texture, the way they fit the curve of his palm, how they had responded to his attentions aboard the gondola. They were not over-large, but were rather emphasized by that slender waist he could practically wrap his two hands fully around.

He allowed his attention to drift. Her neck, the clean lines of her well-defined Italian chin, and lips that he knew were so soft and opened with a soft sigh when…

"Hogan?"

He had progressed to the front of the line without noticing. That is, without noticing anything except how she looked.

"You look incredible."

"Your Botticelli?"

He rapped his knuckles lightly against the gilded window frame in answer.

"Have you had breakfast yet?"

When he shook his head, she set out a coffee and a *cornetto*. He made a show of carefully counting out five one-dollar bills, she'd teased him mercilessly about only having hundreds in his wallet.

"Are you free this evening?" It felt so normal, asking his girl out.

"Come to my condo after you are done at the shelter, I'll make you a nice dinner. Now shoo. You're blocking other customers."

He glanced behind, and there were several people behind him.

"And you too are so pretty that you're distracting me terribly," she said more softly.

He turned back startled. "Did I hear that right?"

She made shooing motions. When he moved off, she called him back to take his breakfast. Okay, maybe he didn't fit in completely. But the coffee was warm in his hands and Maria's smile was warm as well.

He moved off down Post Alley and turned downslope toward the park to enjoy the morning sunshine as he ate his breakfast. It overlooked Elliot Bay, which was an amazing sight on a sunny morning. He'd also be able to see the Ferris wheel and think about—

"Hogan Stanford?" The voice sounded buddy-buddy. A moment later someone clamped a hand over Hogan's shoulder. Hard. He looked over and up. It was the photographer from outside the restaurant, and he was a big man: tall, broad-

shouldered, cliché-handsome. His camera was still clamped in his other hand.

"Uh, yes?"

"So, Hogan. Tell me how you've been doing, buddy?"

Hogan tried to wrench his shoulder free. Managed it on the second try without dislocating anything or losing his *cornetto*. This guy looked easy-going, but his grip had been anything but.

"Uh fine. Would you care to tell me who the hell you are?" The man's confrontational approach had taken Hogan back to one too many corporate meetings. He could feel his spine stiffen and his professional assuredness slip over him like an extra winter cloak.

"Maybe," the photographer looked at him as if there was no maybe about it. "We can work out a trade on that one."

They descended the steep half-block to Pike Place. They crossed the street together into the park at the north end of the Pike Place Market as if seeking a suitable site for the confrontation.

It was still too early for the homeless who worked the park once the tourists came out, so the area was mostly empty. A small ring of grass trapped behind a low concrete wall and a wide walking area. Without Hogan quite being sure how, they ended up side by side, leaning on the steel rail that overlooked the viaduct roaring with morning rush hour traffic and the bay beyond. Sure enough, there was the Ferris wheel off to his left. But to his right...

"So," Hogan faced the big man. "Time to answer the question, or do I call over that friendly policeman?" He nodded to the man enjoying coffee and a cheese Danish a dozen feet farther along the rail.

The big guy glanced over his shoulder. "Rent-a-cop, night security. Won't help you a bit, but you don't need protection from me. At least not yet."

"Oh. And why is that?" He did his best to sound disdainful, impressing even himself.

"I..." the guy rubbed a hand over his face. And in the process almost erased the big bruiser expression from his face. He actually looked fairly pleasant as he continued. "Damn! I'm screwing this up, but I gotta ask. Are you the Hogan Stanford who is putting that expression on Maria Amelia Avico Parrano's face?"

"What expression?" So, this was about Maria somehow. Was she part of some mafia organization?

"The goofy one."

Hogan inspected the photographer again. He didn't look like some mob enforcer. He looked like someone you'd see on the cover of *GQ*. A goofy expression?

"I can only hope it's me." Hogan admitted. He really liked the idea that he wasn't the only one feeling totally ridiculous every time thoughts of last night came to mind, which was constantly.

"Aw shit."

"What? And who are you?"

"Russell. I'm Russell Morgan. Maria is kind of like my mother, except I have a mother too. That sounds stupid."

Russell and Angelo. Maria had talked over dinner last night about raising the two boys.

"Where's your *consigliere?*"

"Who? Oh, Angelo. Fretting over some new venison morel-mushroom sauce. Okay, maybe I came across a little heavy. But nobody has ever made Maria mess up in the kitchen, ever. Nor put that smile on her face. Angelo didn't see it. I probably wouldn't have without my camera. It shows things." He did something with the controls on the back, flicked through the images, and then held it up for Hogan to see.

Just moments ago: Maria sitting in the window, serving the person ahead of Hogan. The shot was mostly from behind Hogan, his own face was hidden, he was more of a soft blur in the foreground giving the impression of a longer line than there'd actually been at the moment. Then Russell selected the next photo.

Hogan was now at the window, still from behind. And Maria's face had lit up with that brilliant smile of hers. The one that made him think of sunny days and laughing women.

"Oh." It was all he could think to say. He hadn't seen the change, he'd been too busy being happy to see her, even if just for that moment. That he had been the one to cause that change utterly floored him. He tried to think of something more intelligent to say, but failed completely.

"So, why are you after her?" Russell turned the camera back off and slung it over his shoulder.

"Are you always this crass?"

Russell grimaced then shrugged. "Yeah, I guess. Ask my wife, she'd probably say I'm being a jerk, but I..."

He trailed off and Hogan decided to help him. "You're just being protective."

Russell nodded.

"Well, I'm glad that she has people to protect her. Though she doesn't strike me as someone who needs much protection."

Russell rubbed a hand over his knuckles as if they hurt. "You don't know the half of it."

THEY SPENT a pleasant hour looking out at the bay and getting to know each other. He was getting to like Russell, who clearly adored Maria. He'd made his own success and walked away to discover himself. And in the process he'd fallen in love.

It was something they had in common. Neither of them had to ever work again, but they weren't built that way. They had to do something. Hogan had lost that, but was slowly rediscovering it at the shelter.

Maria was right, Russell was a good boy. Twenty years Hogan's junior and madly in love with his wife. Hogan didn't know squat about wines, but even he had heard of Cassidy Knowles. A food-and-wine critic who had dropped out to create a wine cooperative of the vineyards of Washington State. She wasn't aiming her sights at keeping Washington as one of the nation's top three wine regions, along with Oregon. She aimed to make it better than Napa.

A particularly fine sloop cruised along the waterfront. That got them onto one of Hogan's favorite subjects, sailboats.

"You're a sailor? Shit! How am I supposed to despise you if you're a sailor?" Russell's protest was vehement enough to turn heads of the first tourists of the morning, also leaning against the cold metal rail to watch the world go by.

"Life is tough, isn't it?"

"Got a boat?"

"Did," Vera had hated sailing, so he'd finally let it go. Maybe it was time to look for a new boat. "Just a little cruiser, a Tartan 34. Miss her on days like this. Clear, good breeze."

Russell was just nodding in sympathy. A non-sailor would make some remark about a thirty-four foot boat not being small. A beginner would be impressed by the Tartan, she'd been a very classy boat. But someone who sailed bigger boats would simply understand. You could go deep sea in a thirty-four if you didn't mind getting slapped around a bit. But what she was made for was just knocking around places like the Mediterranean and Puget Sound, maybe up the Inside Passage to Alaska, something he'd always meant to do, but hadn't.

"You?"

"Yeah. Honey of a boat out at Shilshole Marina. She's a one-of-a-kind fifty-footer. Full keel, just ten-foot-six on the beam."

"Fast." Hogan remarked. A proof that he knew his boats, a compliment to Russell for choosing a boat that was about the sailing more than the comfort, and no comment on the length that showed he knew more than simply the numbers about boats. Whatever her condition, the speed would be the most notable factor in a craft that size.

Russell's phone beeped. He answered.

"Yeah, down at the park rail." He glanced over at Hogan. "How's your coffee?"

Hogan shook it to show that it was long gone empty, then he chucked it in a nearby can.

Russell spoke once more into the phone, "Bring an extra." Then he hung up.

They continued talking about boats they had each admired.

"Hey, Angelo. Give me my coffee."

Hogan turned to face the new arrival. This would be Maria's son and he was very interested in meeting him.

Where Russell was several inches taller than Hogan, Angelo was a couple inches shorter, though almost as broad-shouldered. He wore a white chef's coat open at the throat, apparently glad for the cold air after the kitchen's heat. He had those dark Italian good looks that made all women swoon. He was the male version of his mother's intense beauty. No doubting their relationship. He wondered if there was any of the father in Angelo other than his build. Looking at the two men together, Hogan wondered how Maria had survived raising them.

"Angelo, Hogan. Hogan, Angelo."

They shook hands then Angelo handed over a fresh coffee.

"Where's my *cornetto?*" Russell demanded.

"Dude, Mama sold out half an hour ago. You gotta be quicker than that."

"Shit!" Russell cursed.

Hogan decided to salt the wound. "It was crazy good. Some ginger-chocolate-strawberry mix that shouldn't have worked but was amazing."

Russell groaned and knocked back a big swallow of coffee then was gasping out great clouds of steam into the chill air as he cursed, then sipped again more cautiously.

"So, you like my mama's cooking? I like you already, Hogan."

Russell glanced at Hogan then shot him a wicked grin before facing Angelo. "He likes a lot more than her cooking, buddy boy."

"Huh? What?"

Russell rolled his eyes at Angelo's denseness. "Your mama's got a new boyfriend, one Hogan Stanford."

Hogan wanted to be pissed at Russell for making the news a total bomb drop, but couldn't quite work it out. First, he'd pretty much deserved that for ribbing Russell about the *cornetto*. And it was going to have to come out at some point, he'd just have preferred that it was Maria dealing with it rather than him. Assuming the relationship even went anywhere. Hoping it did.

Angelo turned slowly, like a bull getting ready to charge, until he faced Hogan square on.

"What was that?"

"Yep!" Russell cheerfully overran anything Hogan might have said. "Pretty far along, too, is my guess looking at both of them. Don't punch him, Angelo. Can't be hurting those famous hands of yours."

"Punch him? I'm going to rip him limb from bloody limb."

"If you do," Hogan figured he better say something quick. "You'll end up dropping your coffee. Your mother makes pretty good coffee. It would be a real pity to waste it."

Angelo blinked, now like a bull faced with a red cape held by a rodeo clown that he had no idea what to do with.

Russell snorted out a laugh. "I know. Lot to take in, isn't it? She's hot stuff, Angelo, we've known that since before we grew our first mustaches trying to piss her off. It was only a matter of time before some damn male on the planet wised up to what a dish she is."

Hogan could appreciate what Russell was doing. Having precipitated the whole upset for his own amusement, he was now redirecting Angelo's attention away from Hogan. While he appreciated it, he would fight his own battles.

"She's an amazing woman, Mr. Parrano. She loves you very much you know."

Russell nodded, "She does, Angelo, though the lord alone knows why."

"You too actually, Russell." His observation didn't slow the man down a bit.

"Makes her judgment pretty suspect, don't you think? What about it, Hogan? You gonna trust a lady who loves the two of us like sons? Gotta be something wrong with her."

Angelo chucked his coffee aside, hauled back, and unleashed a huge punch.

Hogan flinched even though it was Russell's arm that took the brunt of the blow. Russell barely rocked back on his heels when it landed.

Instead Russell laughed. Then, after making a smooth hand-off of his coffee cup to Hogan, he wrapped Angelo into a headlock and began rapping his knuckles on Angelo's head, pretty hard.

"Hello! Hello in there!" Russell was practically shouting in Angelo's ear, then he winked at Hogan. "Just think, Angelo. Maybe they've already had sex."

Hogan shook his head in denial and Russell rolled his eyes sadly, as if marking Hogan a fool.

Angelo struggled briefly once more before giving up. He mumbled, "Aw shit!" somewhere in the vicinity of Russell's ribcage then finally relaxed.

Hogan felt sorry for him. Russell let him up. He reached for his coffee, but Hogan handed it to Angelo.

"Hey!" Russell protested.

Angelo merely sneered at him and drank from the cup. "Best man wins."

"That would be me then," Hogan said.

Both men turned to look at him speculatively.

"First, of the three of us," he knew he was risking danger with this one. "I'm the only one who hasn't been beaten on this morning."

"That we can fix," Angelo offered, but there wasn't much heat behind it.

"Second, I figure I'm safe because I can't see either of you explaining to Maria that you beat me up on our very first meeting."

"Damn, Angelo," Russell stole back his coffee. "This guy's smart. We're gonna have to be sneaky."

"Third," now he had both of their attentions. "I win because I'm the one who has a date tonight with Maria Amelia Avico Parrano."

Russell grinned, "Got us there, my short Italian friend, doesn't he?"

Angelo groaned.

"*Hogan?" Maria looked aghast* at the three men entering the restaurant's back door. She'd dreaded this moment, having no idea how she was going to tell Angelo about her boyfriend. Or whatever she was going to call Hogan.

She started to feel relief that it had occurred without her, but decided they wouldn't be laughing together if the two boys knew. Maybe Hogan had somehow identified and befriended them both to make it easier. She had no idea what was going on.

"Maria!" Hogan called out happily. Dropping a to-go cup into the garbage, he walked up to her. No, he swaggered, looking immensely male and pleased with himself. Just steps before he reached her station he winked at her broadly.

Then he kissed her. Not a little kiss, but one that shifted her from bewildered to melting. She could feel his smile turn just a little wicked.

"I told you, Angelo, and I told you," she became vaguely aware of Russell's teasing tone over the buzzing in her ears. "Parents have sex too. Lucky for us or we'd never have been born."

Angelo whimpered quietly.

She pushed Hogan aside and saw that they had quite the audience.

Russell had an arm draped over her son's shoulders, perhaps holding him from charging at Hogan, perhaps merely keeping him upright. Graziella stood by the kitchen door and looked even more melty than she had this morning. Manuel, the *sous chef,* and Nora beside him, were grinning at their boss' complete confusion.

A couple of the other line cooks were applauding. Marko, the young dishwasher, was the only one apparently sharing Angelo's state of shock. She was becoming a second mother to the teen and apparently Ms. Parrano with a boyfriend was more than he could imagine.

Russell shook Angelo in a friendly fashion. "Maybe parents only have really bad sex, leaving all the good sex for us young studs." Russell winked in Hogan's direction.

Hogan had slid a hand around her waist, and appeared far too pleased with himself.

Maria grabbed a wooden spoon and whacked Hogan on top of the head.

"Hey! What? Ow!"

"You! You get out of my kitchen. You already mess up my food once this morning. Out! Out! Before you make me mess up even more." She chased him to the back door.

Then just before he ducked through to escape, she stopped him with a hand on his jacket. Two could play at this game.

She pulled his head down into a kiss and let herself flow against him. He felt so good, it was impossible. But it was so very real at the same time.

Then she scooted him out the door with a soft, "Shoo!" and a slap of her wooden spoon on his backside for good measure.

Maria turned back, and squared her shoulders to face whatever the consequences were.

Angelo came up and took both her hands. He squeezed them hard and looked her right in the eye.

"Does he make you happy, Mama?"

She shrugged. Happy was such a small word for how Hogan Stanford made her feel. "Yes, Angelo. He does so far."

He didn't speak, but merely wrapped her in a fierce hug. Over his shoulder she could see Russell grinning at them.

Maria tried not to cry, but she'd raised two such good boys that she couldn't help herself.

"Tonight, I am cooking you a special dinner."

Maria's apartment had been overflowing with wondrous smells when he arrived.

Once she'd buzzed him through the locked door, it could have been a different world though he was just two blocks from the shelter. Seattle was like that. It was a small enough city that shelters backed onto art galleries and condos towered above seedy bars which were just two doors down from a good French restaurant in one direction and a narrow *Pho* noodle shop in the other.

Her condo was on the seventh floor, well above the vibrant mix of the Pioneer Square evening. Even in the night he could see that she had a decent view over the viaduct to the Sound. When that came down in a year or so, it would be magnificent. The contractor had done a good job on the sound insulation, you couldn't hear the roadway much at all.

The furnishings were not fancy or complex, IKEA mostly. "They were Angelo's," Maria explained. The kitchen, however, was magnificent.

A red sauce was simmering gently on the back burner and filled the apartment with layers of olfactory wonders. It was a heady blend of tomato and spice and possibility.

They shared a glass of Barolo as he regaled her with tales of meeting Russell and Angelo. She set him to making tiny prosciutto bruschetta dressed with olive oil and fresh mozzarella. She formed meatballs with practiced, delicate gestures, and slid them into the sauce to cook.

He fed her a bruschetta and she kissed his fingers. He held a glass of wine for her to sip as she worked on the salad. A drop of wine caught at the corner of her lips and he kissed it away.

Her eyes were so dark when they looked up at him. Worlds were revealed there. Worlds of desire, and of hope.

Without a word, he moved to the stove and turned off the burner.

She washed her hands and was toweling them dry when he drove his fingers into her hair and kissed her. That soft sigh as her lips parted against his absolutely slayed him.

He went to lead her to the bedroom, though he didn't know which door to head for.

She undid the knot on her apron, and pulled it off over her head.

For the brief moment that gesture forced their lips apart, she whispered, "We'll always have the kitchen floor."

He lay her down on the smooth, polished oak. And then feasted upon her.

SPAGHETTI AND ITALIAN MEATBALLS, while sitting naked on the kitchen floor. Spumoni ice cream sandwiches in a hot shower, dripping cherry, pistachio, and chocolate flavors faster than they could eat them. They eventually had made love in the bed as well before collapsing into sleep.

Hogan rarely slept more than five hours. He awoke seven hours later when Maria's alarm went off. Thankfully, being a wise woman, she'd set it a little earlier than she really needed.

CHAPTER 10

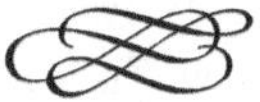

Hogan hated missing Maria's breakfasts, but shifting his schedule at the shelter was worth it. Eric let him move to morning and lunch prep, with Monday and Tuesdays off so that his schedule matched Maria's. With the quality of the additional foodstuffs that arrived from Angelo's restaurant, only a day or two old, he could have asked for anything and Eric would have given it to him.

The shelter was being more fun as well. Richie was as weird as ever, but Hogan stopped being his primary target. He now shared that particular gift more equally with the other kitchen volunteers. Eric teased about making Hogan an honorary KP-private, after all, only on Army Kitchen Patrol did anyone have to peel so many potatoes.

Hogan knew the place hadn't changed, so it must be him. He supposed it made sense, because he certainly didn't recognize the Hogan Stanford of mere weeks ago whose favorite place was sitting quietly at his living room window. It was as if the Seattle he'd grown up in and always loved had come back to life for him.

Maria knew surprisingly little of Seattle, having only lived here for six months and spending most of that in her son's restaurant. And she certainly hadn't been here for a Christmas, so he led her to every ridiculous touristy thing to do. Seattle at Christmas was a wonderful city, even if there was a lack of snow except for one fine-dusted evening.

They stood in the cold rain for half an hour to ride on the Christmas carousel that was set up on the Westlake Center mall each winter. Two grownups and hundreds of little kids with harried-looking parents in tow. The carousel was a spectacle of lights and joy. He rode a carved blue charger, and Maria beside him on a splendid lavender mare. They both giggled like they were six again.

He took her on quiet drives through neighborhoods known for their Christmas lights. He saved the "Garden d'Lights" show at the Bellevue Botanical Garden for an especially clear night with a half moon shining high in the sky. They had nearly frozen on the cold, clear night, but the stars had sparkled and the lights had glittered off her hair until he was quite assured that she was magical, no matter how often she denied it.

She had tickled Santa's beard at Macy's in the window below what every Seattleite worth his salt still called the Bon Star. It was a great white star that had shown down Third Avenue every December for decades despite the store's name change.

They rode the ferry from the Seattle waterfront over to Bainbridge Island. He took her to the Streamliner Diner, a 1950s classic of chrome, Formica, and leatherette bench seats. Their return trip through the mid-winter darkness had shown the glorious display of the Seattle skyline from the twin sports stadiums in the south to the Space Needle that still commanded the northern end of downtown.

There was one special thing that Hogan wanted to share with her, but for that he'd need a little help.

"Maria!" She turned from studying the dark waters of Elliot Bay at the call. Cassidy, Jo, and Perrin were trooping down the pier toward her. Hugs and surprise were shared all around.

"What are you all doing here?"

"We were hoping you knew. Russell was being awfully mysterious."

Maria shook her head, "Hogan too. He just said to meet him here."

"Hogan!" Perrin practically crowed with delight. "I told you that's why we hadn't seen her in so long. It's not that she decided we were too much trouble. So tell me. Tell me! Is he really wonderful? Was your first time on the Ferris wheel?"

The Seattle Great Wheel shone just a few piers to the south of where they stood.

"No, it wasn't on the Ferris wheel."

"So…" Perrin drew it out so dramatically that the other girls giggled, despite being overly serious women turning thirty. Perrin tipped her head ever so slightly saying that this would be a great opportunity to tease the others.

"The kitchen floor at my condo."

"Yes!" Perrin did a fist pump and danced a bit about the pier. Her white hair shining where it peeked out beneath a crazy knit hat. It was gray and covered with a line of what looked like tiny blue British police boxes.

Maria shared a moment of shock with Jo and Cassidy about what Perrin had just gotten her to admit, then they burst out laughing in unison.

"Don't worry, Maria," Jo gave her a hug. "Neither of us know how Perrin does it, but if it's about boys, don't ever think you can hide it with Perrin around."

Perrin switched over to an energetic shimmy that might have been a start of a conga line. Maria grabbed her waist and soon they were all dancing about the pier in the reflected city lights.

"Oh, look at that!" Perrin stumbled to a halt and they piled up behind her like a train wreck.

Just a few hundred feet off the end of the pier, a sailboat had turned toward them. Its rigging was festooned with brightly colored Christmas lights. Blues, golds, reds, and greens traced the line of the mast and where the sails would be if they weren't furled. The lights also swooped along the low, sleek lines of the hull and traced each window. A spiral of purple lights even wound around the tiller where several dark figures moved about the cockpit.

"It's beautiful!" Maria felt there was something familiar about the boat. She almost had it when Cassidy cried out.

"Hey! That's our boat!"

Russell's voice floated back to them over the water. "It is, my love."

In moments the boat slid up at a landing beside the pier. The four women scrambled aboard, Hogan meeting them at the rail to offer a hand, and in moments, Russell was motoring out into Elliott Bay once more.

Cassidy hurried to the stern and leapt into Russell's arms. Had he been a lesser man, they'd have tumbled backward off the stern and into the cold waters below.

Angelo popped his head up from below. "Who wants hot cider?"

Jo and Perrin went back to give a hand.

Hogan straightened from re-securing the lifeline, he'd dropped a section of it for them to climb aboard.

Maria pulled his face down to hers and kissed him. "An evening sail! What a pleasant surprise."

He rubbed his hands very possessively from her shoulders to her hips and back. Any chills she'd felt waiting on the dock he banished as if they'd never been.

"Cut it out, you two," Russell called. "You'll just make Angelo nervous."

"And me sooo totally envious!" Perrin walked up to them carrying two steel cups with snap lids. She handed one to each and then hugged them both fiercely.

"Hi Hogan. I'm Perrin. And if I ever find out you don't appreciate Mama Maria enough, you're going overboard, winter or not. We clear?"

"Yes, ma'am." Hogan glanced at Maria for guidance as Perrin made the threat sound completely serious. Maria left him to flounder. Like everyone else, he'd have to figure out on his own how to deal with Perrin.

"So," she winked at Maria before turning back to Hogan. "Kitchen floor, huh? Way to go you two." She gave him a friendly punch on the arm and headed back to the cockpit.

"Uh…" was all Hogan managed.

"I know," Maria empathized. "She does that to you."

"Is she married?"

"No, and don't get any ideas."

"Huh? No, I didn't mean that. I was just wondering if we should observe a moment of silence on the behalf of whatever unsuspecting male she ultimately sets her sights on."

Maria kissed his cheek. "He'll be damned lucky, whoever he is."

"Like me," Hogan hugged her tightly, then she led him back to the cockpit to meet her other friends.

"OH LOOK AT THAT ONE!" It was probably the tenth time Perrin had said that this evening. "It's so sweet!"

Hogan was very tempted to dismiss her as flighty, maybe even empty-headed. The others were careful of her. Perhaps careful *with* her would be more accurate. Protective, maybe overprotective. Except Maria. Perrin was the one Maria was most often beside, which told him that there was far more to the waif-like girl than appeared on the surface. Though it was clear that the three girls worshipped "Mama Maria" almost as much as Angelo and Russell did, it was Perrin who had threatened him. There was something special about her relationship with Maria.

Perrin was pointing off to starboard at the latest boat to join the Christmas Boat Parade. Every year, the boat parade would visit the various waterside communities from Tacoma to Seattle and all around Lake Washington and Lake Union. The lead boat was a tour boat and hosted a different choir each night. Tonight a gospel choir was belting out the carols, not really needing the speaker system. Their music carried clearly over the quiet waters.

The newest arrival at the tail of the boat parade wasn't much to look at. It was a couple on a small boat with a single strand of blue lights. He'd always found blue lights to be a little sad.

"They're so cute. Like a puppy dog just so happy to be here that they don't care how they look."

Hogan had looked at the same boat and seen someone who simply hadn't tried very hard. He liked Perrin's interpretation much better. Maybe he was starting to understand what Maria saw in her.

He turned from the boat and found that he was somehow seated hip to hip with Perrin in the cozy cockpit. By the bright Christmas lights that he'd spent an afternoon helping Russell put in place, he could see Perrin's soft blue eyes very clearly. In that instant he finally understood; he was facing a deeply insightful intelligence masked behind a hyperactive smokescreen. He'd faced corporate executives who couldn't rouse such a focused and intent look.

"Single, divorced, or widowed?"

"Uh, divorced."

"Why?"

"I can't say."

"Can't or won't? Why? Is she famous, or an international spy?" Definitely still a layer of flighty there.

"No," Hogan shook his head. "I'm just not allowed to."

Perrin squinted at him for a long moment, then glanced over his shoulder and back.

"Mama Maria swore you to secrecy?"

Hogan opened his mouth to answer.

"No," she corrected herself. "She said it was bad for you to talk about your ex- or even think about her." Perrin didn't make it a question.

"How did you just do that?"

"What?"

"Answer a complex question correctly without a single fact."

She hit him with that flashing smile and a girlish grin. The flighty chick was back. "Magic."

He laughed, but stopped her from turning away with a light touch on her arm. "No, really."

Perrin sobered and inspected him carefully, then nodded to herself as if deciding something about him.

"Maria said you'd been hurt, but she chose you. That means you're an amazing man because I know that she is scary smart about people. That's means you told her something, but now you can't tell me anything. So, she's trying to help you erase the past." Again that simple shrug, making her conclusion obvious. "I want to grow up to be just like her."

He took both her hands in his, figuring it was probably the only way to keep her focus on him. Then he kissed her on the cheek.

She blinked at him in confusion.

"You're on the right track. You're scary smart, Perrin."

———

"WHAT DID YOU DO TO HER?" Maria held Hogan's hand as they returned up the Pike Street Hill Climb to reach his condo. The Market was mostly closed, so they took the outside stairs at the south edge of the Market to enjoy the night. It was a long steady climb that slowly revealed the waterfront each time they stopped at a landing to look back at the way they'd come.

The boat parade had broken up. A few boats lingered, but most were headed back toward their berths. The girls had gone back with the two boys to return the boat to Shilshole Marina a few miles to the north. Not enough seats in the carpool for all of them to stay together, Hogan and Maria had been dropped back at the pier to walk the few blocks up the hill.

"What did I do to whom? Oh Perrin. Didn't do anything. I like her."

Maria watched Hogan, trying to read those thoughts he kept mostly to himself. You would think after raising Angelo and Russell, she'd be used to reticent men. Of course, Angelo's father had been anything but reticent, he had talked at length about dreams, plans, and the future. None of which had happened. The moment she was pregnant, he was gone. Perhaps reticent was a good thing. Hogan spoke, but mainly when he had something to say.

He deserved some peace tonight, he had survived the gauntlet. He'd impossibly befriended Angelo and Russell, clearly tonight they were as thick as thieves and comfortable together. He'd also won Cassidy and Jo's probationary approval, not an easy task. She'd seen them double-teaming him several times on the boat. They were subtle, handing off questions mixed in idle conversation. Of course, she'd expect no less from two such successful women.

It was Perrin who surprised her. The evening had begun with Perrin threatening Hogan. Not long after, Maria had seen the two speak for just a few moments. Maria would have paid several secret recipes to overhear that conversation, but couldn't figure out how to do it. And it was over so abruptly she'd never had a chance to move closer.

Then Perrin had come over, hugged her, and whispered in her ear. "I'm going to start designing your wedding dress. You'll look incredible." She'd given one of her shrug-off laughs and gone after more mulled cider, leaving Maria in such a state of shock she couldn't speak even when Angelo asked if she was okay.

Wedding dress? She'd seen the dresses that Perrin had designed for Cassidy and Jo's weddings and they were stunning. They were getting press for Perrin's Glorious Garb and Russell had designed a beautiful ad using them. But there was no chance that Maria was ready for a wedding dress. They'd only known each other for... That couldn't be right.

"Hogan, what date did you first come to my window?"

"December first. Why?"

She didn't say anything. It was too little time.

"Oh. December 14th. Our two-week anniversary. And I didn't get you a present. Bad Hogan. Bad Hogan." As if that were his new first name.

"A present?" Her voice was a choked squeak that had nothing to do with reaching the top step and broad landing at the head of the long climb.

"Well, either I owe you a present, or you're busy thinking what I'm thinking."

"And what's that?" she was almost afraid to ask.

He turned her to face him. The moon still shone in the sky above, the brighter stars showing despite the streetlights. Of the whole waterfront, only the Ferris wheel still towered above them, lit red and green in celebration of the season and the boat parade.

"I'm thinking how impossible it is that I've fallen in love in a mere fourteen days."

She heard the word come from his lips.

She knew that it reached her ears, because she heard it.

But it stalled somewhere before it reached her brain.

"Love?"

He nodded, almost sadly. Then he pulled her in and kissed her on the forehead. "I know. We had such a beautiful friendship going on here. Real pain in butt for me to go off and fall in love with you, isn't it? Throws in all sorts of complications. But true nonetheless."

"Complications?" She could barely understand what he was saying. Why did her brain choose that word to whisper? She should be saying — No, she shouldn't! Absolutely not! She was positively not ready to be saying that.

"Yes. Now Angelo is going to have to figure out whether or not he really is going to kill me. Russell I think I can play the fellow-sailor card to buy my safety. Actually, he'd probably just sit back while cheering on both sides whichever way it goes. Jo and Cassidy will definitely escalate from tonight's efforts to a full Spanish Inquisition. Torture with soft pillows, comfy chairs, the whole nine yards of Monty Python. They're very cute when they think they're being subtle."

"And Perrin?"

Hogan pulled her into his arms and wrapped her tight and safe against him. He blocked any chances of shakes or terrors that she expected to be feeling. He nuzzled her hair briefly before whispering his response.

"Perrin. My best guess is that she'll be your maid of honor, holding the shotgun to my back if necessary."

Maria didn't know which way to turn. She couldn't call the girls. Each of their biases were clear. She certainly couldn't sit down with her son, and even less so with Russell. She wanted to call Julia Morgan, but she and her husband were somewhere in Australia, at least according to their last postcard. With her husband's retirement, the two of them had become world travelers.

It was ridiculous. She knew everyone in Pike Place Market, and had no one to talk to. Except Hogan. But he was the last person she was going to be talking to about Hogan.

He'd been very patient and kind with her all week. Not demanding that she respond. Not insisting on the words. She couldn't imagine how it must hurt him. She wanted to say them, but each time she tried, they caught in her heart, bound there as if by chains.

She had loved and lost. It had gotten her a wonderful son and a wonderful life, but that early pain was still wound tightly deep in her breast.

At a loss, Maria finally went by Perrin's store. Her shop was nestled in the ground floor of an old brick building on Second Avenue just a few blocks north of the Market. Hogan told her that this whole area of Bell Town had totally transformed over the last decade. It had been the rundown edge of Seattle's downtown. Now it was the newest.

Tall condos had invaded only in a few places. But the old brick facades were cleaned up and in good shape, filled with dozens of small entrepreneurs in every city block. Boutiques, both tiny and larger like Perrin's, were packed in among food vendors, tiny restaurants, dance clubs, bars, offices of creative design companies... It was an almost dizzying collection of youthful energy.

She ducked through the glass door of Perrin's Glorious Garb, a tinkling bell announcing her arrival. Maria always loved coming here, and not just for the amazing clothing. Perrin had taken over an old 1950s diner and turned it into a generous menu of bold options. The place had a light, cheerful feel that was a pleasure all in itself.

In one red leather booth, all of the tables had been removed to reveal the outfits, sat a trio of women mannequins clad in form-fitting attire. But it wasn't just some clingy fabric, not if Perrin designed it. The blouses and skirts had sculpted collars that made them appear far more provocative than they actually were if you managed to focus on the minimal amount of skin exposed. They were also in powerful colors that would draw an entire room's attention on whichever woman wore these.

She considered how the second one might look on her for a moment. No. Not quite her style. Perrin was right, these were constructed rather than the softer looks that Maria preferred.

In another booth lounged a pair of bridesmaids with their feet propped comfortably on the opposite bench seat, revealing Perrin's magnificent skill at draping and her understanding of a woman's body. They were in a shocking rainbow of color, broad stripes swirling about the mannequin forms. It should have been ugly, even grotesque, yet Maria could almost see herself standing beside three women so clad.

A clerk and a couple women were chatting comfortably in front of a triple mirror, one blond and slender, the other Jamaican dark and bountifully curved. They were both trying on business suits, though that was perhaps the only phrase that connected the two garments.

Wholly different designs and fabrics, but they bore the same clear punch of power. Not "I am a woman in a man's world," but rather "I am Woman! Watch out!"

"Maria!" Perrin came out of the back room and rushed over to give her a big hug. She still had her stark white hair, and her face was still unadorned, but she wore an emerald green blouse and skirt that looked like a flapper's dress, if it had been made for a futuristic science fiction movie out of slick fabrics. She looked incredibly sexy and glamorous. She also looked as if she belonged to a far superior race and had just been beamed down to the Planet Earth.

"Come! Come!" Perrin dragged her through the doors into the back room. It had been the kitchen and was now set up with stylish raincoats on spatula-wielding mannequins, racks of colorful umbrellas dangled from above rather than copper pots and pans, and shoe-lined pantry shelves. She dragged Maria on through an open walk-in freezer lined with shelves of accessories and into her design space through a swinging door installed through the rear of the steel-clad cubical space.

"Go back there. Get naked." Perrin practically shoved her behind a classic Victorian changing screen that blocked off a corner. Its top was draped with half-a-dozen garments tossed negligently over.

"But—" Her attempt to protest was ignored. Maria had her coat off and was halfway to undoing her blouse before she came to her senses. "No. Wait. I came to talk to you."

"That's fine," Perrin came around the corner of the screen and finished the job of removing Maria's blouse. "But I can't talk until I see this on you. No peeking."

Giving in, Maria finished undressing down to her underwear.

"I have your measurements from that dress I made for you a few months ago. So this should be close. You have such a great figure."

Perrin's running monologue made it impossible for Maria to interrupt, or even get her balance. In moments, she was standing with eyes closed as Perrin slipped a dress over Maria's head.

"At first I figured since this would be your first time, I should go all out."

"All out on what?" But Perrin ignored her question.

"Then I thought about you being such a classic beauty that I wanted to showcase that, so I decided simple and elegant. Keep your eyes closed, I just need to do some pinning here. It is the woman we want to really show off."

Maria bore up as well as she could, her head spinning wildly. It made it difficult to keep her balance and more than once Perrin had to steady her.

She had her suspicions as to what the dress was. Then was pretty sure she was right. Perrin had said she'd make a wedding dress for Maria. Well, she wasn't ready for it, but she knew better than to try and stop Perrin when she was on a roll.

"Is this what you did for Jo and Cassidy?"

"You mean accost them in a dark alley and force an amazing dress over their heads with no warning at all?" Perrin mumbled around a mouthful of pins.

"Yes!" Maria felt terribly lightheaded as Perrin made subtle changes that made the dress shift and cling to her skin.

"Uh. Guess so. Never thought about it much. Cassidy not so much. She was the first of us to fall in love, I wasn't really ready for that. It was a real 'Duh!' moment for all of us when it finally happened. Jo?"

Perrin tugged on something that threatened to cut Maria in two, but then eased back off before she had a chance to complain.

"Absolutely. I mugged her outright. If you ever want to see your daughter-in-law all soft and gooey, it was the day I put her wedding dress on her. She wasn't even dating Angelo yet, though they were sweet on each other for months, but they hadn't even figured that out yet. I told her to never underestimate the power of a great dress. It seems that was enough."

Maria opened her eyes in surprise. Perrin was inspecting the dress' bodice critically. When she went to glance down, Perrin put a hand under her chin to stop her.

"Not yet."

Maria focused on watching Perrin's face as she worked. Critical consideration. An inordinate amount of talent focused on the problem of just what to do with Maria's chest.

Perrin tugged a little. "Oh, I know! No peeking!" And she was gone. She returned moments later with a gold chain and a piece of the sheerest fabric Maria had ever seen.

"I better be wearing more than that."

"Yes, you better, or not a single man in the whole place would be able to speak, including the minister. Now be quiet."

Maria stood and was quiet. She closed her eyes again, to resist the urge to peek, and enjoyed the slightly pampered feeling of Perrin bustling about her. So, Perrin had known that Jo should be in love, even before she was. Or knew that she was long before Jo knew it. Or... Maria sighed. This was all getting much too deep for her.

Perrin was like her son in that way. Angelo was a deep chef. His growing success was his combination of an exceptional palate, that she liked to think came from her, and an intense intellectual focus that was all his own. He built layers, depths, whole oceans of flavors that rose and melded into a satisfying whole without either disappointing or overwhelming.

Perrin did the same thing in fabric and clothing design. Deep design.

Maria wasn't deep, she just liked to cook. She liked flavors. Liked the juxtaposition of the unexpected with the tasty. So much of what she did was by intuition and testing, rather than figuring it out beforehand.

Perhaps that was the problem? Hogan had figured out that he was in love with her. And she'd been trying to figure it out as well. It wasn't how she cooked. Maybe it wasn't how she fell in love.

"Okay. Keep your eyes closed until we get to a mirror." Perrin's hands were steadying as she guided Maria forward.

She barely noticed as Perrin slipped high heels on her feet. Sandals.

"You can open them now," Perrin finished positioning her then stepped aside.

Maria opened her eyes.

She almost turned around to see who the mirror was reflecting before she realized that she'd been transformed. Her hair, always worn loose to her shoulders, was swirled atop her head. A simple gold chain adorned her neck. Then the dress…

The dress.

"Oh my god, Perrin."

It was the simplest of dresses. It was "the little black dress" that every woman had in their wardrobe. But there the similarities ended. Every curve, every seam traced a line of Maria's body. Curves enhanced, waist trimmed. A forty-seven year old body that looked twenty-five. But it didn't just look younger. It was a twenty-five year old's shape but with maturity, elegance, even a sophistication that Maria had always known she lacked. The skirt pleated, ever so slightly emphasizing without enhancing womanly hips, as if celebrating the son she had birthed. It swirled just shy of her knees stating, "This woman still has great legs and the confidence to show them." The strapped-leather sandals were merely the capstone on that statement.

"But how…" She turned to view her profile. Maria hadn't looked this good since before she'd gotten pregnant, if then.

She turned the other way. No clearer how the magic had been done.

"You have such great lines, I just emphasized them," Perrin moved in and they looked at her reflection together. "Your neck is your great feature. So, the black dress draws all attention to your beautiful skin. Rather than a plunging neckline, being slightly more covered up will slay Hogan and leave him desperate to see more."

Perrin held up the bit of sheer fabric. She'd done something to it. She slid it over Maria's wrist like a corsage. For some reason that bit of an accent worked, setting off the dark dress, making it clearly a celebration.

"And watch what happens when he finally slides the ring on." Perrin took a thin strip of gold ribbon and wrapped it around Maria's finger.

It caught the glimmer of the golden necklace and stood out ten times more than it would any other way. A black dress that not only showed off the bride within and acknowledged the woman, but also highlighted and celebrated the sanctity of the marriage vows and the purpose of the wedding.

"We'll dress Hogan in a white tux and tails. He'll fight it, but it will be perfect. When you dance in his arms, it will be beyond perfect."

Maria pulled Perrin into her arms.

"You're right. It will be."

Her instincts had known exactly what they were doing when they'd led her to Perrin's shop. The answer was there all the time, she just had to see it herself in the smile worn by the woman in the mirror.

CHAPTER 12

*H*ogan had been bemused by the instruction. So far, he'd been the one to set their plans, showing Maria a new Seattle, the one beyond her normal haunts of Pike Place Market and Pioneer Square. He'd been thinking to take her for drinks and dinner at the Space Needle; the food was good, but the view was spectacular. Or maybe up to the St. James Cathedral for a performance of Handel's *Messiah*. It wasn't St. Patty's in New York, but it was still pretty spectacular.

This time, she'd sent him a simple text. "Waterfront Park. Seven p.m."

So, here he sat on a park bench staring across the water at the site of their first date, the Seattle Great Wheel. Tonight it was lit like a red and green pinwheel, a giant swirling disk against the night sky.

It had been a week since he'd told Maria he loved her. It had simply been true, so he'd said it. Really not one of his smoother moves. For the hundredth time since, he wanted to kick himself, but it wouldn't make it any less true.

Since his declaration, she had been her usual, amazing self. Mostly. He would occasionally catch her watching him thoughtfully. As if he were a loose cannon that might go off without warning.

Actually, that wasn't fair. That was simply what he'd felt like. The most Maria showed was that perhaps she was a little quieter and more thoughtful than usual. But she was still the best companion he'd ever been with.

They talked, he'd never talked so much in all his life, and had a great time doing it. He was a corporate software engineer, she was an exotic, Italian chef. She was a great beauty and he was, well, Hogan Stanford.

And they'd made love. Since he'd been stupid enough to just blurt his feelings out like that, they had made amazing love. What had started as good sex, had become wholly incredible. Tender, gentle, sweet one moment, wildly passionate the next. Such fierce mood swings that it set them both to giggling and other times close to tears. Whatever they might each think or feel, their bodies were very happy together. He ached with need for her no matter how often they sated it. She claimed to be suffering from the same problem.

He would be patient. Honestly he would. Maybe with time, he could get over being such a doofus. Maybe.

"What are you thinking so deeply?" Maria stood only a few feet in front of him. She looked radiant.

"Thinking of you, what else? You have taken over my brainpan. Wiped out my gray matter and filled it with endless, vibrant tapes of a woman who smiles back at me for reasons impossible to fathom."

Then she did just that. Smiled at him, soft and close. An intimate sharing.

When he continued to stare at her, she swirled slightly side to side as if showing off her coat. Her coat! Sky blue, long wool. And a hat more golden than the sun.

He sat bolt upright in shock.

"You! It was you that I saw from my window. All of it was you from the very start."

She nodded, "I almost fell down when you told me about that. You fell in love with me from a dozen stories above without even knowing who I was."

"I did. That's because I'm a smart guy. Either that or insanely lucky." She'd said love. It was the first time she'd acknowledged that he loved her as if it were simply a fact. Which it was. He felt a ray of hope, but quashed it hard. *Always rushing things, Hogan. Just stay relaxed.* He told himself that often, and unsuccessfully.

In answer, she merely held out her gloved hand and tugged him to his feet. Hand in hand she led him south along the sidewalk, turning in at the Great Wheel. To his surprise she walked right by the ticket line, as if she merely wanted a closer look.

He offered to get them tickets, she just shook her head and led him forward.

At the loading gate, she produced a pair of tickets from her coat pocket.

The man signaled there'd be just a short wait. Though several gondolas were loaded ahead of them, they were still standing out in the cold. Not that he minded. Holding Maria's hand in his, smelling the soft scent of her upon the air, he'd be content to stand for hours and watch the bright lights of the Wheel and the Seattle waterfront.

"Here we go." She led him aboard the gondola. But it was different from the other one they'd been in a few weeks ago. It was trimmed in black instead of white. Rather than a long bench seat on either side, there were four armchairs. They looked deep and comfortable. It was also warm; this gondola had a heater. Christmas carols were playing softly in the background. He'd known there was a single VIP gondola on the Wheel, but had never given it further thought.

Maria pushed him gently into the seat opposite hers, so they faced each other knee to knee. With a friendly nod, the attendant locked them in and they were off.

How was he supposed to admire the view with Maria sitting directly opposite him? She opened her coat and set it aside. She wore one of his favorite red dresses and a thin gold chain.

"I haven't seen that before." He traced a finger lightly along the warm metal and cool skin. "It makes your neck look amazing."

She nodded at the compliment, but still didn't speak. Her smile was full of secrets, ones that he had learned she wouldn't be revealing until she was good and ready. Sometimes he could pester the answer out of her, but not when she smiled like that.

Then they swung out over the dock and he looked down in surprise. The floor was made of glass. He could see the steady stream of people in holiday attire, wandering along the pier. So many couples and families.

If he was ever going to have a regret, it would be that he hadn't had children. He and Vera hadn't wanted any, though it had taken him over a decade for him to realize that too was information. He and Maria had met too late in life and now there would be no children. Of course the thought of having a hormonal teenager running around the place when he hit sixty destroyed the image.

He looked again out of the gondola. It was like they were in a glass bubble floating above the city.

Maria handed him a bottle of champagne. It had been opened and capped. She held out a pair of wide-bottomed mugs. She didn't need to explain, flutes on a moving gondola were just asking for a spill.

So, they sipped champagne and watched the city as they rose into the sky. At the very top, Maria broke her long silence.

"This was for you, Hogan. For how you made me feel when you said that you loved me. Like a bubble floating above the city. Not knowing if I was safe, or about to float away. It should have been terrifying, but it wasn't. I wanted you to know that."

For a moment, he thought this was a speech about how it was over. But before the fear could even begin to form, she leaned forward and kissed him in a way that wiped that doubt aside. Deep, tender, lingering. By the time they parted, they had returned most of the way to the bottom.

"Twice more around," Maria said as they swung through the loading station.

As they rose once more, she began talking. She told him of her first passion, of her love for her son, of her being abruptly out of a job when the senior Morgans had retired six months ago.

"There is another thing I want you to know, Hogan. They set me up very well in thanks for my years of service. Very well. I want you to know that because it is important that you understand, I'm not interested in you for your money. I'm at least as comfortable as you are."

Hogan hadn't even connected that. Vera had certainly cared a great deal about the wealth and status, just not enough about him to remain true to her vows. As with any corporate executive, he certainly hadn't helped matters by working so many hours, but neither had he cheated. He'd never even thought about that with Maria. He should have, but he hadn't. And now he didn't need to.

She freshened their glasses as the vista of Seattle and Elliot Bay once again lay far below them.

"There is one other thing you need to know about me, Hogan."

He tipped his mug toward her indicating he was listening.

"I love you so very much that I don't know what to do with all of the emotion inside me."

She took the mug before it could slip from his nerveless fingers.

"Yes, took me by surprise too." She brushed her fingers along the chain at her throat.

"Really? You love me?" His voice, little more than a croak, reflected strangely off the gondola's windows.

"Really. Now, if I know you, Hogan, this would be a good time for you to pull that ring out of your pocket."

He almost asked how she knew, he'd only purchased it this morning. But then thought better of it.

Instead he recalled Perrin's words about Maria, "Scary smart."

Hogan did it right. He knelt upon the sky, the clear glass at the bottom of a gondola a hundred-and-seventy-five feet in the air, and asked her properly.

When he slid the gold band around her finger, it was the happiest he'd ever been in his life.

The third time around the Great Wheel, not a word was spoken, and three of the four seats remained empty.

CHAPTER 13

The air in Hogan's condo seemed to shimmer it was so filled with energy and amazing scents. Maria was proud of Manuel and Angelo, they'd really outdone themselves. The food had poured forth from Hogan's kitchen in such abundance that it was impossible to credit even if the prep work had been done in the nearby closed restaurant. They'd served family style, a dozen heaped dishes arriving on great platters all at once.

The centerpiece was a trio of traditional Christmas *panettone* loaves, tall, cylindrical and baked to a crunchy dark brown. Inside they'd be a soft yellow bread filled with candied orange and raisins.

There was a massive tureen of Natalini, macaroni and meatballs in a capon broth soup and a huge dish of sausage-filled Ravioli alla Genovese buried in Nora's Ligurian basil pesto. Henry had sent over a whole side of halibut to show he wasn't hurt at Maria falling in love with someone else and the boys had roasted it with fennel and baby potatoes. A chicken Marsala, a rack of lamb with an apple compote… the bounty spread far down the table and to Maria, every bit of it smelled like home. After a prayer of thanks and blessing, everyone simply dug in, drank, laughed, and made merry.

Maria and Hogan had decorated the Christmas tree in the living

689

room together last night. It glowed and reflected off the night-dark windows. They'd also brought some of the family portraits from the Pioneer Square condo, the first but not the last to hang on the long wall behind the dining table.

The massive oak table, lit with a dozen candles, was covered with a festive cloth purchased for the occasion. Maria and Hogan sat at the table's head. Everyone was crowded together elbow to elbow. Christmas garlands and long streamers of red and green ribbons were laced among them. And a single streamer of white, black, and gold had been threaded through them all. For so they had been dressed for their marriage; the color of gold the single accent to reflect the bond of their promise to each other.

They had seen no reason to wait. They weren't twenty after all. The ceremony had been small, attended only by their closest friends who even now sat about them. Hogan had managed to arrange for them to wed at St. James cathedral, an intimate afternoon ceremony of as much beauty and simplicity as her wedding dress.

Perrin sat to Maria's right. She squeezed the girl's hand as she held her ring close beside her necklace to indicate how perfect it had been. Neither of them risked speaking, because they'd just start crying all over again.

"They're happy for you," Hogan's whisper tickled her ear.

"Shouldn't they be?"

"No, it's not that. They're genuinely happy for you. Even your son congratulated me and gave me a manly hug right down to a thump on the back that might have dislocated a few vertebrae."

Maria looked about the table. Saw Russell once again wielding his camera, picking his own wife out as she, Perrin, and Jo giggled over something together. Manuel and Graziella sat so close together that it was likely there'd be another wedding celebration soon. The rest of the restaurant staff squabbled and ate and teased down the length of the table. She'd have to get Russell to give her copies for the dining room wall.

"We should do this often," Maria murmured to Hogan.

At his nod, she grabbed up her knife and clanged it on a glass, calling all of them to attention, quieting the gathering.

"My husband and I—" she whooshed out a breath. "Wow! Is that a surprising thing to say out loud."

Jo and Cassidy joined in her laugh and nodded knowingly.

"We," she took the safer road. "We don't want this to be a one-time event. Therefore, as the restaurant is closed Mondays and Tuesdays, you are all invited for dinner every Tuesday evening. Hogan has—"

"We have," Hogan corrected her.

She leaned over to kiss his cheek. He turned enough to make it a far more serious kiss that elicited a round of applause and several catcalls. When she managed to get her breath back, she turned once more to face the gathering.

"My husband and I," it wasn't any easier to say the second time. "Have this great dining table. Every Tuesday it will be where we all are having dinner. You don't need to call, you just need to come whenever you can."

This time the applause didn't have the catcalls. She looked at Angelo. He placed both hands over his heart and then held them out open-palmed to her. A gesture she'd forgotten from his childhood. She silently returned her heart to him, as the table started debating next week's menu.

"You're my family." She could barely mouth the words, managed them only loud enough for the three girls to hear. True to the rules, the four of them were all crying together.

MUCH LATER, after more food, tears, a quick cleanup, and many goodbye hugs, Maria was at last alone with Hogan.

They stood close beside the shining Christmas tree, the only light in the room, and looked out his...their condo window. The quiet Seattle waterfront stretched before them. Off to the left, barely in view, the very highest gondola of the now still Seattle Great Wheel glittered like a star shining in the night.

Hogan held her close from behind. His voice tickled as he whispered in her ear. "Love you, wife." Then he chuckled. "You're right, that is wonderfully surprising to say. I'll have to say it more often."

"I promise I'll never tire hearing it, my husband." Maria lay back against him and slid her arms over his where they encircled her waist.

"They're your children, you know. They all call you 'Mama Maria,' every one of them."

Maria sniffled and nodded, unable to do more.

"I guess that makes them my kids as well," Hogan laughed in surprise at his own words.

She looked up in time to see that slow smile, that she so loved, light up his face.

He took her hand and raised it to kiss her on the ring as if anchoring it in place forever.

"A Christmas table surrounded by *our* family. Who could ask for more?"

ABOUT THE AUTHOR

M.L. Buchman started the first of, what is now over 50 novels and as many short stories, while flying from South Korea to ride his bicycle across the Australian Outback. Part of a solo around the world trip that ultimately launched his writing career.

All three of his military romantic suspense series—The Night Stalkers, Firehawks, and Delta Force—have had a title named "Top 10 Romance of the Year" by the American Library Association's *Booklist*. NPR and Barnes & Noble have named other titles "Top 5 Romance of the Year." In 2016 he was a finalist for Romance Writers of America prestigious RITA award. He also writes: contemporary romance, thrillers, and fantasy.

Past lives include: years as a project manager, rebuilding and single-handing a fifty-foot sailboat, both flying and jumping out of airplanes, and he has designed and built two houses. He is now making his living as a full-time writer on the Oregon Coast with his beloved wife and is constantly amazed at what you can do with a degree in Geophysics. You may keep up with his writing and receive a free starter e-library by subscribing to his newsletter at: www.mlbuchman.com

Join the conversation:
www.mlbuchman.com

Other works by M. L. Buchman: